In the dark city of Haven, where everything's for sale, city-guard cops Hawk & Fisher cannot be bought. A husband-and-wife team with fast blades and even faster mouths, who dare to cleanse Haven's corrupted soul. Together, they are the perfect crimebusters . . . with a touch of magic.

The war against crime is forever.

GUARDS OF HAVEN
The Adventures
of Hawk & Fisher

And don't miss the first three *Adventures of Hawk & Fisher* in

Swords of Haven

GUARDS OF HAVEN
The Adventures
of Hawk & Fisher

Wolf in the Fold

Guard Against Dishonor

The Bones of Haven

Simon R. Green

A ROC BOOK

ROC
Published by New American Library, a division of
Penguin Putnam Inc., 375 Hudson Street,
New York, New York 10014, U.S.A.
Penguin Books Ltd, 27 Wrights Lane,
London W8 5TZ, England
Penguin Books Australia Ltd, Ringwood,
Victoria, Australia
Penguin Books Canada Ltd, 10 Alcorn Avenue,
Toronto, Ontario, Canada M4V 3B2
Penguin Books (N.Z.) Ltd, 182–190 Wairau Road,
Auckland 10, New Zealand

Penguin Books Ltd, Registered Offices:
Harmondsworth, Middlesex, England

Published by Roc, an imprint of New American Library, a division of
Penguin Putnam Inc.
These novels were first published separately in Ace paperback editions by
The Berkley Publishing Group.

First Roc Printing, November 1999
10 9 8 7 6 5 4 3 2 1

Wolf in the Fold copyright © Simon R. Green, 1991
Guard Against Dishonor copyright © Simon R. Green, 1991
The Bones of Haven copyright © Simon R. Green, 1992

Cover art by Jon Sullivan

 REGISTERED TRADEMARK—MARCA REGISTRADA

Printed in the United States of America

BOOKS ARE AVAILABLE AT QUANTITY DISCOUNTS WHEN USED TO PROMOTE PROD-
UCTS OR SERVICES. FOR INFORMATION PLEASE WRITE TO PREMIUM MARKETING DIVI-
SION, PENGUIN PUTNAM INC., 375 HUDSON STREET, NEW YORK, NEW YORK 10014.

Wolf in the Fold

1

A Head Start

When you are tired of life, come to Haven. And someone will kill you.

The city port of Haven was a bad place to be after dark. It wasn't much better during the day. If there was a viler, more corrupt and crime-ridden city in the whole of the Low Kingdoms, its existence must have been kept secret to avoid depressing the general populace. If Haven hadn't been settled squarely on the main trade routes, and made itself such a vital part of the Low Kingdoms' economy, it would undoubtedly have been forcibly evacuated and burnt to the ground long ago, like any other plague spot. As it was, the city thrived and prospered, brimming with crime, intrigue, and general decadence.

It also made a lot of money from tourism.

Such a dangerous city needed dangerous men and women to keep it under something like control. So from Devil's Hook to the Street of Gods, from the Docks to High Tory, the city Guard patrolled the streets of Haven with cold steel always to hand, and did the best they could under impossible conditions. Apart from the murderers, muggers, rapists, and everyday scum, they were also up against organized crime, institutionalized brutality and rogue sorcerers; not to mention rampant corruption within their own ranks. They did the best they could, and for the most part learned to be content with little victories.

They should have been the best of the best: men and women with iron nerves, high morals, and implacable wills. Unstoppable heroes, ready to take on any odds to overthrow injustice. But given the low pay, appalling working conditions and high mortality rate, the Guard settled for what it could get. Most were out-of-work mercenaries, marking time until the next war, but there was always a ripe mixture of thugs, idealists, and drifters, all with their own reasons for joining a losing side. Revenge was a common motive. Haven was a breeding ground for victims.

The Guard squadroom was a large, cheerless office at the rear of Guard Headquarters. It was windowless, like the rest of the building. Windows made the place too vulnerable to assault. The Headquarters made do with narrow archery slits and ever-burning oil lamps. The walls and ceilings were covered with grime from the lamps and open fireplaces, but no one gave a damn. It fitted the general mood of the place. Half the squadroom had been taken up by oaken filing cabinets, spilling over from the cramped Records Division. At any hour of the day or night, it was a safe bet you'd find somebody desperately searching for the one piece of paper that might help them crack a case. There was a lot of useful information in the files. If you could find it. They hadn't been properly organized in over seventeen years, when most of the original files were lost in a fire-bombing.

Rumour had it that if ever the files were successfully reorganized, there'd just be another fire-bombing. So no one bothered.

And three times a day, regular as the most expensive clockwork, the squadroom filled with Guard Captains waiting for the day's briefing before going out on their shift. It was now almost ten o'clock of the evening, and twenty-eight men and women were waiting impatiently for the Guard Commander to make his appearance and give them the bad news. They knew the news would be bad. It always was.

Hawk and Fisher, husband and wife and Captains in the Guard for more than five years, stood together at the back of the room, enjoying the warmth of the fire and trying not to think about the cold streets outside. Hawk was tall, dark, and no longer handsome. The series of old scars that marred the right side of his face gave him a bitter, sinister look, heightened by the black silk patch over his right eye. He was lean and wiry rather than muscular, and building a stomach, but even standing still the man looked dangerous. Anyone who survived five years as a Captain had to be practically unkillable, but even those who didn't know his reputation tended to give him plenty of room. There was something about Hawk, something cold and unyielding, that gave even the hardest bravo cause to think twice.

He wore the standard furs and black cloak of the Guard's winter uniform with little style and less grace. Even on a good day Hawk tended to look as though he'd got dressed in the dark. In a hurry. He wore his dark hair at shoulder length, swept back from his forehead and tied at the nape with a silver clasp. He'd only just turned thirty, but already there were streaks of grey in his hair. On his right hip Hawk carried a short-handled axe instead of a sword. He was very good with an axe. He'd had lots of practice.

Isobel Fisher leant companionably against him, putting an edge on a throwing knife with a whetstone. She was tall, easily six feet in height, and her long blond hair fell to her waist in a single thick plait, weighted at the tip with a polished steel ball. She was heading into her late twenties, and handsome rather than beautiful. There was a rawboned harshness to her face that suggested strength and stubbornness, only slightly softened by her deep blue eyes and generous mouth. Sometime in the past, something had scoured all the human weaknesses out of her, and it showed. She wore a sword on her hip in a battered scabbard, and her prowess with that blade was already legendary in a city used to legends.

A steady murmur of conversation rose and fell around Hawk and Fisher as the Guard Captains brought each other up to date on the latest gossip and exchanged ritual complaints about the lousy coffee and the necessity of working the graveyard shift. As in most cities, the night brought out the worst in Haven. But the graveyard shift paid the best, and there were always those who needed the extra money. As winter approached and the trade routes shut down one by one, choked by snow and ice and bitter storms, prices in the markets rose accordingly. Which was why every winter Hawk and Fisher, and others like them, worked from ten at night to six the next morning. And complained about it a lot.

Hawk leant back against the wall, his arms folded and his chin resting on his chest. He was never at his best at the beginning of a shift, and the recent change in schedules had just made him worse. Hawk hated having his sleeping routine changed. Fisher nudged him with her elbow, and his head came up an inch. He looked quickly round the squadroom, satisfied himself the Commander wasn't there yet, and let his chin sink back onto his chest. His eye closed. Fisher sighed, and looked away. She just hoped he wouldn't start snoring again. She checked the edge on her knife, and plucked a hair from Hawk's head to test it. He didn't react.

The door flew open and Commander Dubois stalked in, clutching a thick sheaf of papers. The Guard Captains quieted down and came to some sort of attention. Fisher put away her knife and whetstone and elbowed Hawk sharply. He straightened up with a grunt, and fixed his bleary eye on Dubois as the Commander glared out over the squadroom. Dubois was short and stocky and bald as an egg. He'd been a Commander for twenty-three years and it hadn't improved his disposition one bit. He'd been a hell of a thief-taker in his day, but he'd taken one chance too many, and half a dozen thugs took it in turn to stamp on his legs till they broke. The doctors said he'd never walk again. They didn't know Dubois. These days he spent most of his time overseeing operations, fighting the Council for a higher budget, and training new recruits. After three weeks of his slave-driving and caustic wit most recruits looked forward to hitting the streets of Haven as the lesser of two evils. It was truly said among the Guard that if you could survive Dubois, you could survive anything.

"All right; pay attention!" Dubois looked sternly about him. "First the good news: The Council's approved the money for overtime payments, starting immediately. Now the bad news: You're going to earn it. Early this morning there was a riot in the Devil's Hook. Fifty-seven dead, twenty-three injured. Two of the dead were Guards. Constables Campbell and Grzeshkowiak. Funeral's on Thursday. Those wishing to attend, line up your replacements by Tuesday latest. It's your responsibility to make sure you're covered.

"More bad news. The Dock-Workers Guild is threatening to resume their strike unless the Dock owners agree to spend more money on safe working conditions. Which means we can expect more riots. I've doubled the number of Constables in and around the Docks, but keep your eyes open. Riots have a way of spreading. And as if we didn't have enough to worry about, last night someone broke into the main catacombs on Morrison Street and removed seventy-two bodies. Could be ghouls, black magicians, or some nut cult from the Street of Gods. Either way, it's trouble. A lot of important people were buried in the catacombs, and their families are frothing at the mouth. I want those bodies back, preferably reasonably intact. Keep your ears to the ground. If you hear anything, I want to know about it.

Now for the general reports. Captains Gibson and Doughty: Word is there's a haunted house on Blakeney Street. Check it out. If it is haunted, don't try to be heroes. Just clear the area and send for an exorcist. Captains Briars and Lee: We've had several reports of some kind of beast prowling the streets in East Gate. Only sightings so far, no attacks, but pick up silver daggers from the Armoury before you leave, just in case. Captains Fawkes and apOwen: You still haven't found that rapist yet. We've had four victims already and that's four too many. I don't care how you do it, but nail the bastard. And if someone's been shielding him, nail them too. This has top priority until I tell you otherwise.

"Captains Hawk and Fisher: Nice to have you back with us after your little holiday with the God Squad. May I remind you that in this department we prefer to bring in our perpetrators alive, whenever possible. We all know your fondness for cold steel as an answer to most problems, but try not to be so impulsive this time out. Just for me.

"Finally, we have three new rewards." He smiled humourlessly as the Captains quickly produced notepads and pencils. Rewards were one of the few legitimate perks of the job, but Dubois was of the old school and didn't approve. Rewards smelt too much like bribes to him, and distracted his men from the cases that really needed solving. He read out the reward particulars, deliberately speaking quickly to make it harder to write down the details. It didn't bother Fisher. She was a fast writer. A low rumble at her side broke her concentration, and she elbowed Hawk viciously. He snapped awake and put on his best, interested expression.

"One last item," said Dubois. "All suppressor stones are recalled, as of now. We've been having a lot of problems with them just recently. I know they've proved very useful so far in protecting us from magical attacks, but we've had a lot of reports of stones malfunctioning or otherwise proving unreliable. There's even been two cases where the damn things exploded. One Guard lost his hand. The stone blew it right off his arm. So, *all* stones are to be returned to the Armoury, as soon as possible, for checking. No exceptions. Don't make me come looking for you."

He broke off as a Constable hurried in with a sheet of paper. He passed it to Dubois, who read it quickly and then questioned the Constable in a low voice. The Captains stirred uneasily. Finally Dubois dismissed the Constable and turned back to them.

"It appears we have a spy on the loose in Haven. Nothing unusual there, but this particular spy has got his hands on some extremely sensitive material. The Council is in a panic. They want him caught, and they want him yesterday. So get out there and lean on your informants. Someone must know something. The city Gates have all been sealed, so he's not going anywhere.

"Unfortunately, the Council hasn't given us much information to go on. We know the spy's code name: Fenris. We also have a vague description: tall and thin with blond hair. Apart from that, you're on your own. Finding this Fenris now has top priority over all other cases until we've got him, or until the Council tells us otherwise. All right, end of briefing. Get out of here. And someone wake up Hawk."

There was general laughter as the Captains dispersed, and Fisher dragged Hawk towards the door, Hawk protesting innocently that he'd heard every word. He broke off as they left the squadroom, and Fisher headed for the Armoury.

"Isobel, where are you going?"

"The Armoury. To hand in the suppressor stone."

"Forget it," said Hawk. "I'm not giving that up. It's the only protection we've got against hostile magic."

Fisher looked at him. "You heard Dubois; the damned things are dangerous. I'm not having my hand blown off, just so you can feel a bit more secure."

"All right then, I'll carry it."

"No you won't. I don't trust you with gadgets."

"Well, one of us has to have it. Or the next rogue magician we run into is going to hand us our heads. Probably literally."

Fisher sighed, and nodded reluctantly. "All right, but we only use the thing in emergencies. Agreed?"

"Agreed."

They strode unhurriedly through the narrow Headquarters corridors and out onto the crowded street. Just a few weeks ago there'd been snow and slush everywhere, but the city's weather wizards had finally got their act together and deflected the worst of the weather away from Haven, sending it out over the ocean. This wasn't making them too popular with passing merchant ships, but no one in Haven cared what they thought.

Not that the weather wizards had done anything more than buy Haven a few extra weeks, a month at most. Once the real winter storms started there was nothing anyone could do but nail up the shutters, stoke up the fire, and pray for spring. But for the moment the sky was clear, and the chilly air was no worse than an average autumn day. Hawk turned up his nose at the bracing air and pulled his cloak tightly around him. He didn't like cloaks as a rule, they got in the way during fights, but he liked the cold even less. The weather in the Low Kingdoms was generally colder and harsher than in his homeland in the North, and it was during fall and winter that he missed the Forest Kingdom most of all. He smiled sourly as he looked out over the slumped buildings and grubby streets. He was a long way from home.

"You're thinking about the Forest again, aren't you?" said Fisher.

"Yeah."

"Don't. We can't go back."

"We might. Some day."

Fisher looked at him. "Sure," she said finally. "Some day."

They strode down the packed street, the crowd giving way before them. There were a lot of people about for the time of night, but with winter so close, everyone was desperate to get as much done as they could before the storms descended and the streets became impassable. Hawk and Fisher smiled and nodded to familiar faces, and slowly made their way into the Northside, their beat and one of the worst areas in Haven. You could buy or sell anything there; every dirty little trade, every shape and form of evil and corruption grew and flourished in the dark and grimy streets of the Northside. Hawk and Fisher, who had worked the area for over five years, had grown blasé and hardened despite themselves. Yet every day the Northside came up with new things to shock them. They tried hard not to let it get to them.

They made a tour of all the usual dives, looking for word on the spy Fenris, but to a man everyone they talked to swore blind they'd never even heard of the fellow. Hawk and Fisher took turns smashing up furniture and glaring up close at those they questioned, but not even their reputations could scare up any information. Which meant that either the spy had gone to ground so thoroughly that no one knew where he was, or his masters were paying out a small fortune in bribes to keep people's mouths shut. Probably the former. There was always someone in the Northside who'd talk.

They left the Inn of the Black Freighter till last. It was a semirespectable tavern and restaurant right on the outer edge of the Northside; the kind of place where you paid through the nose for out-of-season delicacies, and the waiter sneered at you if your accent slipped. It was also a clearing house for information, gossip, and rumour, all for sale on a sliding scale that started at expensive and rose quickly to extortionate. Hawk and Fisher looked in from time to time to pick up the latest information, and never paid a penny. Instead, they let their informants live and promised not to set fire to the building on the way out.

They stood outside the Black Freighter a moment, listening to the sounds of conversation and laughter carry softly on the night air. It seemed there was a good crowd in tonight. They pushed open the door and strolled in, smiling graciously about them. The headwaiter started towards them, his hand positioned just right for a surreptitious bribe for a good table, and then he stopped dead, his face falling as he saw who it was. A sudden silence fell across the tavern, and a sea of sullen faces glared at Hawk and Fisher from the dimly lit tables. As in most restaurants, the lighting was kept to a minimum. Officially, this was to provide an intimate, romantic atmosphere. Hawk thought it was because if the customers could see what they were eating, they wouldn't pay for it. But then he was no romantic, as Fisher would be the first to agree.

The quiet was complete, save for the crackling of the fire at the end of the room, and the atmosphere was so tense you could have struck a match off it. Hawk and Fisher headed for the bar, which boasted richly polished chrome and veneer and all the latest fashionable spirits and liqueurs, lined up in neat, orderly rows. A large mirror covered most of the wall behind the bar, surrounded by rococo scrollwork of gold and silver.

Hawk and Fisher leaned on the bar and smiled companionably at the bartender, Howard, who looked as though he would have very much liked to turn and run, but didn't dare. He swallowed once, gave the bartop a quick polish it didn't need, and smiled fixedly at the two Guards. He might have been handsome in his heyday, but twenty years of more than good living had buried those good looks under too much weight, and his smile was weak now, from having been too many things to too many people. He had a wife and a mistress who fought loudly in public, and many other signs of success, but though he now owned the Inn where he'd once been nothing more than a lowly waiter, he still liked to spend most of his time behind the bar, keeping an eye on things. None of his staff was going to sneak up on him, the way he had on the previous owner. Hawk shifted his weight slightly, and the bartender jumped in spite of himself. Hawk smiled.

"Good crowd in tonight, Howard. How's business?"

"Fine! Just fine," said Howard quickly. "Couldn't be better. Can I get you a drink? Or a table? Or . . . Oh hell, Hawk, you're not going to bust up the place again, are you? I only just finished redecorating from the last time you were here, and those mirrors are expensive. And you know the insurance people won't pay out if you're involved. They class you and Fisher along with storm damage, rogue magic, and Acts of Gods."

"No need to be so worried, Howard," said Fisher. "Anyone would think you had something to hide."

"Look, I just run the place. No one tells me anything. You know that."

"We're looking for someone," said Hawk. "Fenris. It's a spy's code name. You ever heard it before?"

"No," said the bartender quickly. "Never. If I had, I'd tell you, word of honour. I don't have any truck with spies. I'm a patriotic man, always have been, loyal as the day is long. . . ."

"Pack it in," said Fisher. "We believe you, though thousands wouldn't. Who's in tonight that might know something?"

Howard hesitated, and Hawk frowned at him. The bartender swallowed hard. "There's Fast Tommy, the Little Lord, and Razor Eddie. It's just possible they might have heard a thing or two. . . ."

Hawk nodded, and turned away from the bar to stare out over the restaurant. People had started eating again, but the place was still silent as the tomb, save for the odd clatter of cutlery on plates. It didn't take him long to spot the three faces Howard had named. They were all quite well known, in their way. Hawk and Fisher had met them before; in their line of business, it was inevitable.

"Thank you, Howard," said Hawk. "You've been a great help. Now, tell that bouncer of yours, who thinks he's hidden behind the pillar to our left, that if he doesn't put down that throwing knife and step into plain sight, Isobel and I are going to cut him off at the knees."

Howard made a quick gesture, and the bouncer stepped reluctantly into view, his hands conspicuously empty. "Sorry," said the bartender. "He's new."

"He'd better learn fast," said Fisher. "Or he's never going to be old."

They turned their backs on Howard and the bouncer, and threaded their way through the packed tables. Glaring faces and hostile eyes followed the two Captains as they headed for Fast Tommy's table. As usual, Tommy was dressed in the height of last month's fashion, had enough heavy rings on his fingers to double as knuckle-dusters, and was accompanied by a gorgeous young blonde half falling out of her dress. Tommy glared at Hawk and Fisher as they pulled up chairs opposite him, but made no objections. He undoubtedly had a bodyguard or two somewhere nearby but had enough sense not to call them. Hawk and Fisher might have taken that as an affront, and then he'd have had to find some new bodyguards. No one messed with Hawk and Fisher. It was quicker and a lot safer just to tell them what they wanted to know, and hope they'd go away and bother someone else.

Fast Tommy was a gambling man. He got his name as a lightning calculator, though some uncharitable souls suggested it had more to do with his love life. He was a short, squarish, dark-haired man in his early forties, with a gambler's easy smile and unreadable eyes. He nodded politely to Hawk and Fisher.

"My dear Captains, so good to see you again. May I purchase you wine, or cigars? Perhaps a little hot chocolate; very warming in the inclement weather . . ."

"Tell us about the spy, Tommy," said Hawk.

"I'm afraid the name Fenris is unknown to me, Captain, but I can of course inquire of my associates. . . ."

"You're holding out on us, Tommy," said Fisher reproachfully. "You know how it upsets us when you do that."

"Upon my sweet mother's grave . . ."

"Your mother is alive and well and still paying interest on the last loan you made her," said Hawk.

Fisher looked thoughtfully at the gambler's blond companion. "Little old for you, isn't she, Tommy? She must be all of seventeen. Maybe we should check our records, make sure she isn't some underage runaway."

The young blonde smiled sweetly at Fisher, and lifted her wineglass so she could show off the heavy gold bracelet at her wrist.

"She's sixteen," said Tommy quickly. "I've seen the birth certificate." He swallowed hard, and smiled determinedly at the two Guards. "Believe me, my dear friends, I know nothing of this Fenris person. . . ."

"But you can find out," said Hawk. "Leave word at Guard Headquarters, when you know something."

"Of course, Captain, of course . . ."

Fisher leaned forward. "If we find out later that you've been holding something back from us . . ."

"Do I look suicidal?" said Fast Tommy.

Hawk and Fisher got to their feet, and made their way through the tangle of tables to join the Little Lord in her private booth at the back. No one knew the Little Lord's real name, but then, nobody cared that much. Aliases were as common as fleas in the Northside, and a damn sight easier to live with. The Lord was a tall, handsome woman in her mid-thirties who always dressed as a man. She had close-cropped dark hair, a thin slash of a mouth, and dark piercing eyes. She dressed smartly but formally, in that old male style that never really goes out of fashion, and affected an upper class accent that was only occasionally successful. She always had money, though no one knew where it came from. Truth be told, most people weren't sure they wanted to know. She peered short-sightedly at Hawk and Fisher as they sat down opposite her, and screwed a monocle into her left eye.

"As I live and breathe, Captain Hawk and Captain Fisher. Damned fine to see you again. Care to join me in a glass of bubbly?"

Hawk eyed the half bottle of pink champagne in the nearby ice bucket, and shuddered briefly. "Not right now, thank you. What can you tell us about the spy Fenris?"

"Not a damned thing, old boy. Don't really move in those circles, you know."

"You're looking very smart," said Fisher. "Those diamond cuff links are new, aren't they?"

"Present from me dear auntie. The old girl and I were up at Lord Bruford's the other day, meeting that new Councillor chappie. Adamant, I think his name was. . . ."

"Never mind the social calendar," said Fisher. "A set of matched diamonds disappeared mysteriously during a Society bash last week. You wouldn't know anything about that, I suppose?"

"Not a thing, m'dear. Shocked to hear it, of course."

"Of course," said Hawk. "Are you sure you haven't heard something about Fenris, my Lord? After all, someone such as yourself, moving in your circles, would be bound to hear something; perhaps spoken in confidence in an unguarded moment?"

The Little Lord raised an elegant eyebrow, and her monocle fell out. She caught it deftly before it hit the tabletop, and screwed it back in place. "My dear chap, surely you're not asking me to peach on a friend? Just ain't done, you know."

"Those diamond cuff links are looking more and more

familiar," said Fisher. "Perhaps the three of us should take a little walk down to Headquarters, so we can compare them with the artist's rendering of the missing items. . . ."

"I assure you, Captain, I haven't heard a thing about your beastly spy! But of course I'd be only too happy to keep my eyes and ears alert for any morsel of gossip that might float my way."

"That's the spirit," said Hawk. "Noblesse oblige, right? And by the way, I've met Councillor Adamant, and I know for a fact he's never bloody heard of you."

He and Fisher left the spluttering Lord in her booth, and made their way through the last of the tables to their final port of call, a single table at the rear of the tavern, half hidden in shadows. Razor Eddie wasn't fond of even dim light. Hawk and Fisher borrowed chairs from nearby tables, and sat down facing him. Razor Eddie was a slight, hunched figure wrapped in a tattered grey cloak apparently held together only by accumulated filth and grease. Even across a table the smell was appalling. He was said to be so dirty, plague rats wouldn't go near him in case they caught something. He was painfully thin, with a hollowed face and fever-bright eyes. At first glance he looked like just another down and out, but you only had to be in the man's presence a few moments to know there was something special about him. Special . . . and not a little disturbing.

Razor Eddie got his name in a street fight over territory between two neighbouring gangs. He was fourteen at the time, a slick and vicious killer, and already more than a little crazy. He spent the next few years working for anyone who'd have him, just for the action. And then, at the age of seventeen, he visited the Street of Gods and got religion in a big way. He turned his back on his violent past and walked the streets of the Northside, preaching love and understanding. A few people laughed at him, and threw things. Later, they were found dead, under mysterious circumstances. They weren't the last. After a while people learned to leave Razor Eddie strictly alone. He walked through the most dangerous areas in Haven, spreading his message, and came out unscathed. Once, a gang of ten bravos went into the Devil's Hook after him. No one ever saw them again. Razor Eddie had no fixed abode or territory; he slept in doorways and wandered where he would. Neither heat nor cold affected him, and he always seemed to have a little money, even in the hardest of times.

He knew a lot of things, about a lot of people—if you could persuade him to talk. Most couldn't, but he'd taken a shine to Hawk and Fisher. Probably because unlike most other people, they weren't frightened of him. Hawk leant back in his chair and smiled easily at the hunched figure opposite him.

"Hello, Eddie. How's life treating you?"

"Mustn't grumble, Captain," said Razor Eddie. His voice was low and calm and very reasonable, but his eyes shone with a wild light. "There's always someone worse off than yourself. I've been waiting for you. You'll find the spy Fenris in the house with three gables on Leech Street. He uses it as a drop for passing information. You'll know Fenris by his bright green cravat. It's a signal for his contact."

"You're not normally this forthcoming, Eddie," said Fisher, frowning. "What's so special about this Fenris?"

"Unless someone stops him, two great houses will go down in flames. Blood will run in gutters and the screams will never end. There are wolves running loose among the flock, and they will bring us all down."

Hawk and Fisher looked at each other briefly, and when they looked back, Razor Eddie's chair was empty. They looked quickly about them, but there was no sign of him anywhere in the tavern.

"I hate it when he does that," said Fisher. "Well, what do you think? Is it worth a trip to Leech Street?"

Hawk scowled. "Anyone else, I'd take it with a pinch of salt. But Eddie's different. He knows things. And if he thinks we're all in danger because of this Fenris . . ."

"Yeah," said Fisher. "Worrying, that."

"It's the best lead we've got."

"It's the only lead we've got."

"Exactly."

Fisher shook her head. "Let's go check it out."

They grinned at each other, got up, and made their way back through the crowded tables. The restaurant was still utterly silent, their every move followed by hostile eyes. They got to the door, and Hawk paused and looked back. He smiled, and bowed courteously to the sea of unfriendly faces. Fisher blew the room a kiss, and then the two Guards disappeared into the night.

Leech Street was bold and brassy and more than a little shop-soiled. Brightly painted whores gathered together on street corners like so many raucous birds of paradise, or leaned out of first-floor windows in revealing underwear, watching the world go by with knowing mascarad eyes. Street traders hawked jewelry so freshly stolen the true owners hadn't even realized it was gone yet, and hole-in-the-wall taverns provided cheap shots of spirits so rough they all but seethed in the bottle. The air was full of chatter and laughter and the harsh banter of the strip-show barkers. Here and there, gaudily dressed pimps leant casually in open doorways, ostentatiously cleaning their fingernails with the point of a knife, alert for the first sign of trouble. Prospective clients, trying to appear anonymous, thronged one end of the street to the other, eyeing the various merchandise and working up their courage to the sticking point.

Hawk, watching the bustling scene from the concealing shadows of an alley mouth, yawned widely. He and Fisher had been in position for almost an hour waiting for Fenris to show up, and what little tawdry glamour the street possessed had long since worn thin. When you got past the noise and the bright colors, Leech Street seemed more sad and sleazy than anything else, with everyone trying desperately to pretend they were something other than what they really were. Hawk derived some amusement from the attempts of most of the would-be customers to give the impression they just happened to be passing through, but the street itself held no attractions for him. He'd seen the official figures on violence and robbery in this area, not to mention venereal disease. In some establishments, the crabs were reputed to be so big they jumped out on dithering passersby and dragged them bodily inside.

Bored, Hawk leant gingerly back against the grimy alley wall and kicked at an empty bottle on the ground. It rolled slowly away, hesitated, and then rolled back again. After a fruitless hour standing watch, this was almost exciting. Hawk sighed deeply. He hated doing stakeouts. He didn't have the patience for it. Fisher, on the other hand, actually seemed to enjoy it these days. She'd taken to watching the

passersby and making up little histories about who they
were and where they were going. Her stories were invari-
able more interesting than the case they were working on,
but now, after a solid hour of listening to them, Hawk
found their charm wearing a bit thin. Fisher chattered on,
blithely unknowing, while Hawk's scowl deepened. His
stomach rumbled loudly, reminding him of missed meals.
Fisher broke off suddenly, and Hawk quickly looked round,
worried she'd noticed his inattention, but her gaze was fixed
on something down the street.

"I think we've finally struck gold, Hawk. Green cravat
at three o'clock."

Hawk followed her gaze, and his interest stirred. "Think
he's our man?"

"Would you wear a cravat like that if you didn't have
to?"

Hawk smiled. She had a point. The cravat was so bright
and virulent a green it practically glowed. The suspect
looked casually about him, ignoring the birdlike calls of the
whores. He fit the description, what there was of it. He was
definitely tall, easily six foot three or four, and decidedly
lean. His clothes, apart from the cravat, were tastefully
bland, with nothing about them to identify the kind of man
who wore them. For a moment his gaze fell upon the alley
from which Hawk was watching. Hawk damped down an
impulse to shrink further back into the shadows; the movement would only draw attention to him. The spy's gaze
moved on, and Hawk breathed a little more easily.

"All right," said Fisher. "Let's get him."

"Hold your horses," said Hawk. "We want whoever he's
here to meet as well, not just him. Let's give him a minute,
and see what happens."

One of the bolder whores advanced aggressively towards
the spy. He smiled at her and said something that made
her laugh, and she turned away. *He can't just stand around
much longer,* thought Hawk. *That would be bound to attract
attention. So what the hell's he waiting for?* Even as the
thought crossed Hawk's mind, the spy turned suddenly and
walked over to a building on the opposite side of the street.
He produced a key, unlocked the door and slipped quickly
inside, pulling the door shut behind him. Hawk counted ten
slowly to himself and then stepped out of the alley, Fisher

at his side. The house the spy had gone into looked just like all the others on the street.

"I'll take the front," said Hawk. "You cover the back, in case he tries to make a run for it."

"How come I always have to cover the back?" said Fisher. "I always end up in someone's back yard, trying to fight my way through three weeks' accumulated garbage."

"All right. You take the front and I'll cover the back."

"Oh, no; it's too late now. You should have thought of it without me having to tell you."

Hawk gave her an exasperated look, but she was already heading for the narrow alley at the side of the building. Sometimes you just couldn't talk to Fisher. Hawk turned his attention back to the house's front door as it loomed up before him. A faded sign hanging above the door gave the name of the place as MISTRESS LUCY'S ESTABLISHMENT. The sign boasted a portrait of the lady herself, which suggested she'd looked pretty faded even when the sign was new. Hawk casually tried the handle. It turned easily in his grasp, but the door wouldn't open. Locked. Surprise, surprise. Maybe he should have let Fisher have the front door after all. She was a lot better at picking locks than he.

On the other hand . . . When in doubt, be direct.

He knocked politely on the door, and waited. There was a pause and then the door swung open, and a hand shot out and fastened on his arm. Hawk jumped in spite of himself, and his hand started towards his axe before he realized the person before him was very definitely not the spy Fenris. Instead, Hawk found himself facing a large, heavyset woman wrapped in gaudy robes, with a wild frizz of dark curly hair and so much makeup it was almost impossible to make out her features. Her smile was a wide scarlet gash and her eyes were bright and piercing. Her shoulders were as wide as a docker's, and she had arms to match. The hand on his arm closed fiercely, and he winced.

"I'm glad you're here," said the woman earnestly. "We've been waiting for you."

Hawk looked at her blankly. "You have?"

"Of course. But we must hurry. The spirits are restless tonight."

Hawk wondered if things might become a little clearer

if he went away and came back again later. Like maybe next year.

"Spirits," he said, carefully.

The woman looked at him sharply. "You are here for the sitting, aren't you?"

"I don't think so," said Hawk.

The woman let go of his arm as though he'd just made an indecent proposal, drew herself up to her full five-foot-nine, and fixed him with a steely glare. "Do I understand that you are not Jonathan DeQuincey, husband of the late and much lamented Dorothy DeQuincey?"

"Yes," said Hawk. That much he was sure of.

"Then if you have not come to see me in my capacity as Madam Zara, Spirit Guide and Pathway to the Great Beyond, why are you here?"

"You mean you're a spiritualist?" said Hawk, the light slowly dawning. "A medium?"

"Not just *a* medium, young man; the foremost practitioner of the Art in all Haven."

"Then why are you based here, instead of on the Street of Gods?" asked Hawk innocently.

Madam Zara sniffed haughtily. "Certain closed minds on the Council refuse to accept spiritualists as genuine wonderworkers. They dare to accuse us of being fakes and frauds. We, of course, know different. It's all part of a conspiracy by the established religions to prevent us taking our rightful place on the Street of Gods. Now, what do you want? I can't stand around here chatting with you; the Great Beyond calls . . . and I have customers waiting."

"I'm looking for the gentleman who just came in here," said Hawk. "Tall, thin, wears a green cravat. I have a message for him."

"Oh, him." Madam Zara turned up her nose regally. "Upstairs, second on the left. And you can tell the young 'gentleman' his rent's due."

She turned her back on Hawk in a swirl of billowing robes, and marched off down the narrow hall. Hawk stepped inside and shut the door quietly behind him. By the time he turned back, Madam Zara had disappeared, presumably to rejoin her clients, and the hall was empty. A single lamp shed a dirty yellow glow over a row of coats and cloaks on the left-hand wall and a tattily carpeted stairway that led up to the next floor. Hawk took a small wooden wedge from his pocket and jammed it firmly under the front door. That should slow Fenris down if he made a run for it. Hawk carried lots of useful things in his pockets. He believed in being prepared.

He drew his axe. The odds were that the spy Fenris was alone with his contact. He wouldn't want to risk unnecessary witnesses. So, two-to-one odds. Hawk grinned, and hefted his axe. No problem. Things were looking up. If he and Fisher could bring in both the spy and his contact alive and ready for questioning, then maybe he and Fisher could finally get transferred out of the Northside permanently. . . .

He padded silently forward, and made his way slowly up the stairs. With any luck, even if the spy had heard him at the door, he'd just assume Hawk was another of Madam Zara's clients. Which should give Hawk the advantage of surprise if it came to a fight. Hawk firmly believed in making use of every possible advantage when it came to a fight. He ascended the stairs slowly, checking each step first to see if it was likely to creak. He had a lot of experience when it came to sneaking around houses, and he knew how far a sudden sound could carry on the quiet.

He reached the landing without incident and padded silently over to the second door on the left. Light shone around the doorframe. He put his ear to the wood, and smiled as he heard a voice raised loudly in argument. He stepped back, hefted his axe once, and braced himself to kick in the door. At which point the door swung open, revealing the spy Fenris standing in the doorway with a startled expression. For a moment he and Hawk just stood there, staring at each other, and then Hawk launched himself at the spy. Fenris fell back, shock and alarm fighting for control of his features. Hawk glanced quickly round the room, and his gaze fell on the spy's contact—a grey, anonymous man with an icily calm face.

"Stand where you are, both of you!" barked Hawk. "You're under arrest. Throw down your weapons!"

The contact drew his sword and advanced on Hawk. The spy fumbled for a throwing knife. *Oh hell,* thought Hawk tiredly. *Just once, why can't they do the sensible thing and give up without a fight?* He decided he'd better take out the contact first; he looked to be the more dangerous of the two. Once the contact had been subdued, Fenris would likely give himself up without a struggle. Hawk closed in on the contact; the man's face was utterly bland and forgettable, but his eyes were cold and deadly calm. Hawk began to have a very bad feeling about him. He pushed the thought aside and launched his attack. The grey man brushed aside Hawk's axe effortlessly, and Hawk had to retreat rapidly to avoid being transfixed by the contact's follow-through.

The grey man moved quickly after him, cutting and thrusting with awesome skill, and it was all Hawk could do to hold him off. Fenris' contact was an expert swordsman. Hawk's heart sank. When all was said and done, an axe was not designed as a defensive weapon. Hawk usually won his fights by launching an all-out attack and not letting up until his opponent was beaten. As it was, only frantic footwork and some inspired use of the axe was keeping him alive. Hawk had been an excellent swordsman in his younger days, before he lost his eye, but even then he would have been hard pressed to beat the grey man. He was fast, brilliant, and disturbingly methodical. Unless Hawk could come up with something in a hurry, he was a dead man, and both he and the grey man knew it. Out of the corner of his eye, Hawk could see Fenris circling around them with a throwing knife in his hand, looking for an opening. That settled it. When in doubt, fight dirty.

He struck at the grey man's head with his axe, forcing him to raise his sword to parry the blow, and while the two blades were engaged, Hawk pivoted neatly on one foot and kicked the grey man squarely in the groin. The man's face paled and his sword arm wavered. Hawk brought his axe across in a sudden, savage blow that sliced through the man's throat. Blood spurted thickly as the grey man collapsed. Hawk spun quickly to face Fenris. He might have lost the contact, but he was damned if he'd lose the spy as well. Fenris aimed and threw his knife in a single fluid movement. Hawk threw himself to one side, and the knife shot past his shoulder but pinned his cloak firmly to the wall. Hawk scrabbled frantically at the cloak's clasp as Fenris turned and bolted out the door. Some days, nothing goes right.

The clasp finally came undone, and he jerked free, leaving the cloak hanging pinned to the wall behind him. He charged out of the room and onto the landing. He'd come back for the cloak later. He peered over the banister and caught a glimpse of Fenris standing at the foot of the stairs, looking frantically about him. Hawk clattered down the stairs, cursing quietly to himself. He hated chases. He was built for stamina, not speed, and he was already out of breath from the exertions of the fight. Still, Fenris wouldn't get that far. The wedge under the front door should see to that.

In the darkened parlour, the seance was well under way. A mysterious pool of light illuminated a small circular table, throwing sinister shadows on the faces of the six people gathered hopefully around it. Darkness pressed close about the circle of light, hiding the pokey little parlour and giving the six participants a feeling of being adrift in eternity. The air was heavy with the scent of sandalwood, and over all there was an atmosphere of unease and anticipation. Madam Zara rocked back and forth on her chair, as though all around her spirits were jostling for possession of her voice, desperate to pass on messages of hope and comfort to those they had left behind. Madam Zara's head lolled limply on her neck, but her eyes kept a careful if unobtrusive watch on her clients.

It was just her regulars this week. The Holbrooks, a middle-aged couple wanting to contact their dead son. David and Mercy Peyton, still hopeful their dear departed grandfather would reveal to them where he'd hidden the family fortune. And old Mrs. Tyrell, timidly grateful for any fleeting contact with her dead cat, Marmalade. The two couples were easy enough; all they needed were general platitudes on the one hand and vague hints on the other, but having to make cat noises was downright demeaning. If trade hadn't dropped off so much recently she'd have drawn the line at pets, but times were hard, and Madam Zara had to make do with what she could get.

She let her eyes roll back in her head, and produced her best sepulchral moan. She was rather proud of her moan. It had something of the mystic and the eternal in it, and was guaranteed to make even the most skeptical client sit up and take notice. She took a firm grip on the hands of

Graeme Holbrook and David Peyton on either side of her, and let a delicate shudder run down her arms into her hands.

"The spirits are with us," she said softly. "They are near us in everything we do, separated from us by only the thinnest of veils. They wish always to make contact with us, and all we have to do is listen. . . . Hush. I feel a disturbance in the ether. A spirit draws near. Speak with my voice, dear departed one. Have you a message for someone here?"

The atmosphere grew taut and strained as Madam Zara threw in a few more moans and shivers, and then pressed her foot firmly onto the lever hidden in the floorboards. A block of wood thudded hollowly against the underside of the table, making the clients jump. She hit the lever a few more times, producing more mysterious knockings, and then concentrated on getting the right intonations for the Peyton grandfather's voice. People didn't appreciate what mediums had to go through for their money. She could have been a legitimate actress, if only she'd had the breaks.

"The spirit is drawing closer. I can feel a presence in the room. It's almost here. . . ."

The door flew open and the tall thin gentleman from upstairs charged in, glared wildly about him, and then headed for the window. The Holbrooks screamed, and Mercy Peyton fell backwards off her chair. Madam Zara looked confusedly about her, completely thrown. Another figure burst in through the open door, his clothes soaked with blood, fresh gore dripping from the axe in his hand. The Holbrooks screamed even louder and clutched each other tightly, convinced that the Grim Reaper himself had come to claim them for meddling in his affairs. The gentleman from upstairs threw open the window and slung a leg over the windowsill. The second figure charged forward, overturning the table. He grabbed at the young gentleman's shoulder, and just missed as he dropped into the alleyway outside. The second figure cursed horribly and clambered out the window in hot pursuit. The Holbrooks were still clutching each other and whimpering, Mercy Peyton was having hysterics, loudly, and David Peyton was thoughtfully examining the block of wood on the underside of the overturned table. Madam Zara searched frantically for something to say that would retrieve the situation. And just at that moment a large orange cat jumped in through the window from the alley outside and looked around to see what all the fuss was about. Mrs. Tyrell snatched him up and hugged him to her with tears of joy in her eyes.

"Marmalade! You've come back to me!"

Madam Zara mentally washed her hands of the whole situation.

Out in the alley, Hawk found Fisher picking herself up out of a pile of garbage. He started forward to help, and then hesitated as the smell hit him. Fisher glared at him.

"Next time, you're going to watch the back door."

She headed quickly for the main street, brushing herself off as she went. Hawk hurried after her.

"Did you see Fenris?"

"Of course I saw him! Who do you think knocked me into the garbage? And whatever you're about to say, I don't want to hear it. How was I to know he'd come flying out of a window? Now, let's move it. He can't be more than a few minutes ahead of us."

They pounded down the alley and out into Leech Street. Fenris was halfway down the street and running well. Hawk and Fisher charged after him. The crowds turned to watch. Some laughed, a few cheered, and the rest yelled insults and placed bets. A few up ahead took in Fisher's black cloak and moved to block the street. Guards weren't much respected in Leech Street. Hawk glared at them.

"We're Hawk and Fisher, city Guard. Get the hell out of the way!"

The crowd parted suddenly before them, falling back on all sides to give them plenty of room. Fenris glanced back over his shoulder and redoubled his efforts. Fisher nodded approvingly at the more respectful crowd.

"I think they've heard of us, Hawk."

"Shut up and keep running."

Fenris darted down a side alley, and Hawk and Fisher plunged in after him. Hawk was already breathing hard. Fenris led them through a twisting maze of narrow streets and back alleys, changing direction and doubling back whenever he could. Hawk and Fisher stuck doggedly with him, breath burning in their lungs and sweat running down their heaving sides. Fenris ran through a street market,

overturning stalls as he went, to try and slow them down.
Hawk just ploughed right through the wreckage, with
Fisher close behind. Furious stallholders shook their fists
and called down curses on the heads of pursued and pursuers alike.

Hawk's scowl deepened as he ran. Fenris was leading
them deep into the rotten heart of the Northside, but Hawk
was damned if he could figure out exactly where the man
was headed. He must have some destination in mind, some
bolt-hole he could hide in, or a friend who'd protect him.
Hawk smiled nastily. He didn't care if the spy ended up in
the Hall of Justice, protected by all twelve Judges and the
King himself; Fenris was going to gaol, preferably in chains.
It had become a matter of honour. Not to mention revenge.
Hawk hated chases.

And then Fenris rounded a corner at full speed, and
darted up an exterior stairway on a large squat building of
stained and patterned stone. Hawk started after him, but
Fisher grabbed him by the arm and brought them both to
a sudden halt. Fenris disappeared through a door into the
building. Hawk turned on Fisher.

"Before you say anything, Hawk. Look where we are."

Hawk glared around him, and then grimaced, his anger
draining quickly away. Fenris had brought them to Magus
Court, home to all the lowlife magicians and sorcerers in
Haven. The place looked deserted for the moment, but that
could change in a second. On the whole, Guards tended to
walk very quietly in and around Magus Court and not draw
attention to themselves. Certainly, no one ever tried to
make arrests there without massive support from the
Guard, and, if necessary, the army. Otherwise they'd have
been safer playing brass instruments in a cave full of hiber-
nating bears.

"That's not all," said Fisher. "Look whose house he's
holed up in."

Hawk looked, and groaned. "Grimm," he said disgustedly. "All the magic-users Fenris could have known, and it
had to be the sorcerer Grimm."

He and Fisher leant against the wall at the bottom of the
exterior stairway and grabbed a few minutes' rest while
they tried to work out what the hell to do next. Hawk and
Fisher knew Grimm, and he knew them. They'd crossed

swords before, metaphorically speaking, but Hawk and Fisher had never been able to pin anything on him. People were too scared to talk.

Grimm was a medium-level sorcerer with unpleasant personal habits who specialized in shape changing. He could do anything from a face-lift to a full body transformation, depending on the needs, and wealth, of his client. He had no scruples; he'd do anything, to anyone. Criminals found his services very useful, either for themselves, to change an appearance that had grown too well-known, or for taking revenge on their enemies. The Guard had found one up-and-coming crime boss wandering the streets in the early hours of the morning, leaving a bloody trail behind him. It took them some time to identify him. He'd been flayed, every inch of skin removed from head to toe, but he was still alive, and screaming. He took a long time to die in the main city hospital, and he only stopped screaming when his voice gave out.

It figured Fenris would know someone like Grimm. All the spy had to do was acquire a new face and build and he could disappear into the crowds right under Hawk's and Fisher's noses. On the other hand, they couldn't just go barging in after him. Grimm was a sorcerer and took his privacy very seriously. Officially, any Guard could enter any premises in Haven, providing they could demonstrate good cause in the Courts afterwards. In practice, it all depended on whose home you were talking about. Having a Court declare you posthumously correct wasn't much of a comfort, and sorcerers tended to throw spells first and think afterwards. Constant industrial espionage among magic-users had produced a general paranoia and split-second reflexes.

"What do you think?" said Hawk finally.

"I think we should think about this very carefully," said Fisher. "I have no desire to spend the rest of my life as a combination of several small, unpleasant, and very smelly animals. Shapechange sorcerers are renowned for having a very warped sense of humour. I say we stay put and call for backup."

"By the time anyone gets here, Fenris will have his new face and we'll have lost him."

Fisher scowled. "Given the alternatives, I say let him go.

It's not as if he was a murderer or something. Hell, Haven's full of spies. What's one more or less going to make any difference?"

"No," said Hawk firmly. "We can't let him go. It would be bad for our reputation. People would think we'd got soft, and take advantage."

Fisher shook her head. "There has to be an easier way to make a living. All right, let's go in after him. No point in sneaking around. Grimm's bound to have the place covered with security spells to warn of intruders. So, crash straight in and trust to the suppressor stone to protect us. Right?"

"Sounds good to me," said Hawk. "Let's do it."

He handed Fisher the suppressor stone, and she muttered the activating phrase. The stone glowed fiercely in her hand like a miniature star. They started up the exterior stairway, Hawk in the lead, axe at the ready. The stairs creaked loudly. *Great,* thought Hawk, *Just great.* They hurried up the steps to the door at the top of the stairway. Hawk listened carefully, his ear pressed against the wood, but he couldn't hear anything. He tried the door handle and it turned stiffly in his grasp. He eased the door open an inch, and then stepped back. He glanced at Fisher for reassurance, and found she was doing the same to him. He smiled briefly. They both counted to three under their breath, kicked the door in and burst into the room beyond, weapons at the ready.

The sorcerer Grimm was escorting a robed and hooded figure to a door at the far end of the room. He spun round and glared at the intruders, and then pushed the hooded figure towards the far door. The Guards started forward, but the figure was out the door and gone before they got anywhere near him. Which left them facing the sorcerer. Grimm was a huge, broad-chested man dressed in sorcerer's black, with a thick beard and an impressive mane of jet-black hair. He was smiling unpleasantly, like a vulture about to feed on a dead man's eyes.

"You're under arrest, in the name of the Guard!" said Hawk resolutely, and then flung himself to one side as Grimm snatched a ball of fire out of thin air and threw it at him. The fireball hit a chair and incinerated it. Fisher threw a knife while the sorcerer was distracted, and it sank deep into Grimm's arm. He cursed briefly, pulled the knife out, and threw it aside. Hawk and Fisher charged across the room towards him. The sorcerer drew himself up and spoke a Word of Power. The suppressor stone flared up, cancelling out his magic. Hawk and Fisher hit the sorcerer together, throwing him to the floor. There was a short, confused struggle, and then Fisher clubbed him unconscious with the hilt of her sword. Grimm went limp, and Hawk and Fisher rolled off him. They sat together, backs against the wall, and waited for their breathing to get back to normal.

"Well, at least we've got something to show for the chase," said Hawk.

"Yeah," said Fisher. "Pity about Fenris, though. We were that close to getting him. . . ."

"Forget it," said Hawk. "He's long gone by now, with a new face and build, the crafty bastard. We'll have to start over from scratch."

"Right. Our superiors are not going to be pleased with us."

They sat in silence for a while.

"There isn't a reward on Grimm, by any chance, is there?" said Hawk hopefully.

"No chance. There's never been any real evidence against him. Still, he's dropped himself right in it this time. Aiding and abetting a fugitive, resisting arrest, assaulting the Guard . . ."

"Right," said Hawk. "Once he wakes up, he's going to have some very leading questions to answer."

"Assuming he hasn't got concussion, and lost his memory."

Hawk groaned. "Don't. It would be just our luck if we had accidentally scrambled his brains. Come on, let's have a look round the place while we're here. Maybe we'll get lucky and find a clue or something."

They moved cautiously round Grimm's quarters, being very careful not to touch anything without checking it out first. Magic-users were often fond of setting booby traps for the unwary. Hawk's usual method of searching the premises was to trash the place until it looked like a hurricane had hit it, but this room already looked as if someone had beaten him to it. Grimm was one of those people who lived in a permanent mess and liked it that way. His quarters took up the whole of the first floor—a single long room littered with junk and debris of every description.

There were racks of chemicals, glass vials and tubing, pewter mugs and mixing bowls, all scattered over two huge tables. Together with papers and books and what appeared to be the remains of at least three different meals. Hawk tossed aside a discarded shirt and grimaced as he discovered a dead cat, dissected into its component parts and neatly pinned to a display board. Beneath the cat were detailed instructions on how to put the animal back together again. Either Grimm had a really nasty sense of humour, or . . . Hawk decided very firmly that he wasn't going to think about that.

The bed looked as though Grimm had left it exactly as he'd crawled out of it. Fisher peered underneath, just in case, but there was nothing there except dust and a chamber pot. A combination desk and writing table looked more interesting. She eased the drawers open one by one with the tip of her sword, and smiled as she came across a thick sheaf of papers. She ran the suppressor stone over the desk, and then carefully removed the papers, watching all the time in case there was a mechanical booby trap as well. She leafed quickly through the papers, scowling as she tried to make out Grimm's scratchy handwriting.

Hawk looked into a recessed alcove, and his breath caught in his throat. A dozen different faces lined the wall; skins so skillfully taken and mounted they seemed almost alive. Hawk fought down his disgust and looked them over carefully. They were all unique, no two even remotely alike. Presumably they were models for the faces Grimm could give his customers. He'd better get a Guard sketch artist in to make copies. Fenris might be wearing one of these faces. He moved closer and studied them thoughtfully. Whatever else you could say about Grimm, he knew his stuff. The faces were incredibly lifelike. He reached out a hand to touch one, and then snatched his hand back as the face opened its eyes and looked at him. A grimace of pain moved slowly across the flat features, and the mouth stretched in a soundless scream. The other faces stirred, eyes opening across the wall to fix Hawk with the same unblinking look of agonized despair. Hawk's stomach

urched as he realized they were all still alive, pinned up
and endlessly suffering.

Whatever happened, Hawk swore he'd see Grimm brought
to justice for this, at least.

"Isobel, get over here, fast."

Fisher ran quickly to join him, sword in hand, and stared
numbly at the writhing faces on the wall. "My God, Hawk.
What kind of bastard . . . We've got to do something. We
can't leave them like this."

"No, we can't. Try the suppressor stone. Maybe it'll can-
cel out the magic that's keeping them alive."

Fisher nodded, and ran the stone slowly over the staring
faces. One by one the eyes closed and did not open again.
The life went out of the faces, and soon they were nothing
more than empty masks, pinned to a wall. At rest, at last.
Fisher touched a few of them tentatively, but they didn't
respond. The skin was soft, but already cooling. Just to be
sure, Hawk had her run the suppressor stone over the dissected cat as well.

They took turns examining the papers Fisher had found
in Grimm's desk. They seemed to be records of services
Grimm had provided in the past, but no names were ever
mentioned, only initials. It was mostly cosmetic sorcery,
though some of the more bizarre requests made Hawk
blink. There was no accounting for taste. But interesting
though the documents were, there was nothing in them to
tie Grimm in with the spy Fenris. Or at least, nothing Hawk
could recognize. He threw the papers back onto the desk,
and looked frustratedly around him.

"We're not going to find anything here. He's too careful,
too meticulous. Probably keeps the important information
locked up in his head."

"So let the Guard sorcerers get it out of him," said Fisher.
"Let them earn their money for a change."

There was a low groan from behind them, and they
looked quickly round. At the other end of the room the
sorcerer Grimm was rising unsteadily to his feet. He shook
his head once to clear it, and then his gaze fell on Hawk
and Fisher and his face darkened. He smiled slowly, removed his robe and threw it to one side. Ropes of muscle
bulged suddenly across his bare chest and shoulders, pushing out the taut skin. Hawk and Fisher watched transfixed

as the sorcerer changed. His body stretched and swelled impossible muscles crawling over an inhumanly magnified frame. His face trembled, the features shifting grotesquely as his inner rage expressed itself in distorted flesh and bone. His eyes became featureless black pools, and sharp jagged teeth distorted the shape of his mouth. Grimm padded slowly forward, his crooked hands growing razored claws.

"I think we may have a problem here," said Hawk, taking a firm hold on his axe.

"You always did have a gift for understatement," said Fisher. "What the hell's happening to him?"

"From the look of it, I'd say the sorcerer wasn't averse to sampling his own wares. He's got to the stage where he can shapechange at will."

"You know, this strikes me as a good time to get the hell out of here and yell for reinforcements."

"We can't. He's between us and the nearest door. We're going to have to stop him ourselves."

"Oh, great. How?"

"I'm thinking!"

Grimm lurched forward, his jaws snapping shut like a steel trap. There was no longer anything human in his face. Hawk and Fisher quickly separated, to attack him from different sides, and each of the sorcerer's eyes crawled to different positions on his head so that he could watch both Guards at once. Hawk darted in and cut at Grimm with his axe. The heavy steel head sheared through the sorcerer's waist and out again, but no blood flew. The wound closed immediately, the unnatural flesh flowing seamlessly back together again. Fisher cut at Grimm from the other side, to no better effect. The sorcerer reached for Hawk with a gnarled, clawed hand. Hawk quickly retreated, but the hand just kept coming after him as the arm stretched to an impossible length.

"The stone!" yelled Hawk, backing frantically away. "Try the suppressor stone on him!"

"I've already tried that! It doesn't seem to affect him!"

"Well, keep trying!" Hawk threw himself to one side and the clawing hand dug deep furrows in the wall behind him. He darted behind the writing desk. Grimm demolished it with one blow of a spiked arm. Hawk looked quickly round the room, checking for possible escape routes. Fisher clutched the suppressor stone in her hand, muttering the activating phrase over and over again. The stone suddenly flared with light, bright and dazzling, burning her hand with sudden heat. Fisher threw the stone straight at the sorcerer's misshapen face. He snatched it out of midair and looked at it curiously. The stone exploded, ripping the sorcerer's head from his body and shattering every window in the room.

For a long moment there was silence, broken only by soft settling sounds as debris from the explosion pattered to the floor. Hawk and Fisher got slowly to their feet, brushing dust from their clothes. Where the hideous creature had been, lay a headless human body. Hawk shook his head gingerly, trying to shift the ringing in his ears. Fisher put an arm round his shoulders, and they leaned companionably together for a moment.

"We didn't do too well with this one, did we, Hawk?"

"You could say that. Fenris has escaped, with a new face and body. The one man who could have helped us find him is now dead. And on top of all that, we've lost our suppressor stone. Some days you just shouldn't get out of bed."

"Well," said Fisher, "at least this time they can't blame us for being impulsive." Hawk looked at her. Fisher gestured at Grimm's body. "After all, he's the one who lost his head."

2

Fenris Gone to Ground

The cleanup squad finally made its appearance, with a meat wagon not far behind. Two Guard Constables chalked a rough outline round the headless body, and made laborious notes about the state of the corpse. The forensic sorcerer waited impatiently for them to finish, already in a foul mood at being dragged from his bed so early in the morning. Hawk and Fisher leant against a wall together, drinking the late sorcerer's wine and trying to put together some kind of report that wouldn't get them both busted down to Constable, or beyond.

The two Constables unhurriedly compared notes, and then got out of the way so that the forensic sorcerer could do his stuff. He glared venomously at them, then knelt down by the body and rolled up his sleeves. Hawk and Fisher looked at each other and unanimously decided this might be a good time to get some fresh air. On-the-spot autopsies tended to be thorough, but messy. Hawk drained the last of the wine from the bottle he and Fisher had been passing back and forth, and his lips thinned away from the dregs. It had been a piss-poor vintage, but the sourness suited his mood. No matter what kind of report he and Fisher eventually handed in, he had no doubt they were both in real trouble.

They left Grimm's quarters and clattered down the exterior stairway to the street below. The meat wagon's horses tossed their heads and snorted loudly, their breath steaming on the chill air. Hawk looked away. Reminders of his own mortality made him uncomfortable. Strange lights flared in the windows above as the forensic sorcerer set about dismantling Grimm's remaining wards and shields, and defusing any booby traps that hadn't yet been triggered. Fisher hugged herself as a cold wind swept by.

"I can't help thinking we're missing something, Hawk. We know why Fenris came here; to get a new face. But how did Grimm get involved with Fenris in the first place? He had a nice little racket going here. Judging by the records we found, he was already making more money than he knew what to do with. So why risk it all, by dealing with a traitor? He didn't need the money, and there's nothing in his file to suggest he was at all political."

"Maybe he just liked the excitement, the intrigue," said Hawk. "He wouldn't be the first fool to be seduced by dreams of making history, of playing with the real shakers and movers. Or maybe he just had some kind of grudge against the Council, and saw this as his chance for revenge. I've known stranger motives. Doesn't make much difference now, anyway. The man is dead, and our case died with him. Odds are we'll never find out what it was all about."

The low, steady clamour of a brass bell filled both their heads as the Guard communications sorcerer made contact. Hawk shook his head gingerly as the deep ringing sound faded away. "I think I preferred it when he used the gong. That bloody bell goes right through me." He broke off as the bell gave way to the rasping voice of the communications sorcerer.

Captains Hawk and Fisher are to report to Commander Dubois at Guard Headquarters immediately. This instruction has top priority. All other orders are rescinded.

Hawk and Fisher waited a moment to see if there was any more, and then looked at each other. "Didn't take long for the news to reach our superiors, did it?" said Hawk.

Fisher shrugged. "Haven loves bad news. And you can bet there were people lining up for the chance to drop us in it. We've always been too honest to be popular."

"What the hell," said Hawk. "We've weathered worse storms than this."

"Right," said Fisher. "Just keep our heads down, and it'll all blow over."

"You really believe that?"

"No. How about you?"

"No. Even so, Dubois had better not shout at me," said Hawk firmly. "I'm not in the mood to be shouted at. In fact, if he raises his voice to me I think I'll hit him somewhere low and painful."

"How is that going to help us?"

"It couldn't hurt."

"True."

Hawk and Fisher had barely walked through the front door at Guard Headquarters when a Constable appeared, seemingly from nowhere, and insisted on escorting them straight to Dubois' office. Other Guards avoided Hawk's and Fisher's eyes as they made their way through the Headquarters building. Word had got around and no one wanted to risk guilt by association. Hawk smiled humourlessly, and let his hand drift down to the axe at his side. He glanced across at Fisher, and saw that her hand was already resting on the pommel of her sword.

The Constable brought them to Dubois' office and knocked briskly on the door. There was barely a pause before the Commander's voice summoned them in. The Constable opened the door, and stood back for Hawk and Fisher to enter. Hawk strolled casually in, Fisher at his side. The door shut behind them. Hawk listened carefully, but didn't hear any sound of the Constable departing. Now, that was interesting. It meant that the man was still there. Presumably on guard to keep people out . . . or in. Hawk smiled inwardly as he and Fisher bowed formally to Commander Dubois. If he and Fisher decided it was in their best interests to leave in a hurry, it would take a lot more than one Guard Constable to stop them.

Dubois glared at Hawk and Fisher from behind his desk and sniffed disgustedly. "Gods, you're a mess. I've seen beggars in the Devil's Hook who looked more presentable than you two do right now. You're a disgrace to your uniform."

Hawk looked down at himself, and had to admit the Commander had a point. His clothes were badly torn and soaked with blood from the various fights he'd got involved in that evening. A quick glance at Fisher revealed she hadn't fared any better. Her furs were stained and matted from the garbage she'd fallen in outside Madam Zara's. And what with all the exertions of the evening, the fact was they both smelled pretty bad. Hawk had a sudden intense desire to stand downwind of himself. He looked back at Dubois, and put on his best innocent face. Dubois glared at him even harder. The complete lack of hair on his head somehow made his scowl all the more impressive.

"And you've lost your cloak again, Hawk! What happened this time? Someone sneak up behind you and steal it while you weren't looking? Where the hell is your cloak?"

Hawk had to stop and think, so Fisher quickly answered for him. "It's pinned to a wall in a spiritualist's house."

Dubois winced. "I'm not even going to ask you what you were doing at a spiritualist's. I don't think my nerves could stand it. Do you realize, Hawk, you go through more new cloaks in a year than most Guards use up in a lifetime's service to the city? Do you know how much those cloaks cost?"

"Yes," said Hawk. "Because you always deduct the cost from my wages."

"Damn right!" said Dubois. "You're not screwing up my budget for the year. Perhaps you would also like to explain why you failed to turn in your suppressor stone to the Armoury, as ordered."

"Would that help to get us off the hook?" said Hawk.

"Not in the least."

"Then I don't think I'll bother."

Fisher butted in quickly as Dubois' face darkened. "Be fair; it saved both our arses tonight. If the stone hadn't blown up in Grimm's face when it did, we might both have been killed."

"I could live with that," said Dubois.

He picked up a sheet of paper from his desk and frowned at it. Hawk studied the Commander's bowed head thoughtfully. Something was going on. Dubois should be tearing strips off them for letting Fenris get away, not carping about their appearance, or niggling over lost cloaks and the illegal use of a suppressor stone. Dubois had never made any secret of the fact that he didn't approve of Hawk and Fisher's methods, and was usually only too happy to find something about their work he could criticize. The Fenris debacle should have been just what he needed to bust them down to Constable, or worse. Instead, he hadn't even mentioned the spy. If he hadn't known better, Hawk would have sworn Dubois was trying to avoid telling them something unpleasant.

Hawk's mind raced furiously. Maybe the Council had

found out about Fenris getting away, and had decided to blame everything on the two Guards. It wouldn't be too hard for the Council to make out a case of treason against them. They could claim the Guards had deliberately let the spy escape, and then killed Grimm to cover their tracks. Hawk forced himself to calm down. It needn't be that bad. It could be that Dubois just had some really nasty job lined up for them, as penance for failing to bring in Fenris. Now, that was much more likely. Hawk began to relax a little. Whatever it was, he and Fisher could handle it. After five years working the Northside they could handle anything.

Dubois carefully put down the piece of paper, tapped it with his fingers a few times, and then looked up at Hawk and Fisher. "For once in your lives, you've struck it lucky. We know where Fenris is. The Council circle of sorcerers knew that Grimm was somehow involved with the traitors, and kept an unobtrusive watch on him. So when Fenris did a runner with his new face, they were able to follow him magically, all the way to his new hiding place."

"Wait a minute," said Fisher. "If we know where he is, why can't we just walk right in and grab him?"

"Unfortunately, it's not that simple."

"Somehow I didn't think it would be," said Hawk.

Dubois sniffed. "Fenris has gone to ground at Tower MacNeil, just outside the city wall. That much the sorcerers are certain of. But it seems our man has some sorcerous protection of his own, presumably supplied by his superiors. Our people couldn't get close enough to see what his new face looks like."

"No problem," said Hawk. "We burst in there, arrest everyone, and sort out which is Fenris later."

"I thought you'd come up with something like that," said Dubois. "Don't even think about it. The MacNeils are one of the oldest and most respected Families in Haven. We don't dare touch them. If it should turn out one of the MacNeils was the traitor, it would be a major scandal. We have very explicit orders to avoid any such thing. And that, Gods help us, is where you come in."

"All right," said Fisher. "I'll bite. Why us?"

"Well, thanks to you and your partner's incompetence, what description we did have of Fenris is now obsolete. But at least you two have met the man in person. There's always the chance you'll recognize some mannerism or habit that'll give him away. So you are going in there after him, suitably disguised. Your job is to identify Fenris, and get him out of the Tower without anyone else catching on. It's not much of a plan, so the fact that we're going ahead with it will give you some idea of how desperate we are. Any questions so far?"

"Yeah," said Hawk. "What kind of place is Tower Mac-Neil?"

"Home to the MacNeils for fourteen generations. Protected by old sorcery and one of Haven's finest security firms. The head of the Family, Duncan MacNeil, died last month. Which means, luckily for us, that things are in something of a turmoil at the moment. Duncan's son Jamie is to be the new head of the Family, the MacNeil, as he's called. And, as is customary, all living members of the Family will be gathering at Tower MacNeil to pay their respects to the new head, and jockey for positions of influence and power. Nothing like a Family funeral to bring out the vultures. Fenris will presumably be trying to pass himself off as one of the more remote cousins. This is how we're going to get you in."

Hawk and Fisher looked at each other.

"Wait a minute," said Hawk. "You mean we're going to be masquerading as Quality?"

"Got it in one," said Dubois. "What's the matter? Don't you think you can do it?"

"That's not the point," said Fisher. "The last I heard, passing yourself off as Quality was still punishable by death. Is that being waived in our case?"

"No," said Dubois. "Whatever the outcome, officially you were never there. If you do get caught, we'll disclaim all knowledge of you. This is a very delicate situation."

Hawk thought for a moment. "Is this a volunteer situation?"

"Yes," said Dubois. "I volunteered you. Given the alternatives, I wouldn't argue if I were you."

Fisher looked at him steadily. "We don't like being pressured, Dubois. We don't like it at all."

Dubois fought down an urge to shrink back in his chair as a sudden chill ran through him. Without moving a muscle, Hawk and Fisher had suddenly become dangerous. An air of menace and imminent violence filled the tiny office, as though a slumbering wolf had suddenly awakened and shown its teeth. Dubois paled slightly, but didn't flinch.

"Renegade Guards tend to have very short life spans," he said evenly. "If anything was to happen to me, you wouldn't even make it to the city gates."

Hawk smiled. "You might be right, Dubois. But I wouldn't count on it if I were you. We've faced worse odds in the past. We'll do your dirty work for you, this time. I think we owe it to the Council, for letting Fenris get away from us. But if you ever try to pressure us like this again, Dubois, I'll kill you. Believe it."

Dubois met Hawk's cold stare for a moment, and then looked away. When he looked back, Hawk and Fisher were just Guards again. The air of violence was gone, as though it had never been. For the first time, Dubois understood how they'd gained their reputation. He got to his feet and cleared his throat carefully. He didn't want to sound nervous or uncertain. "Let's go. We've got just under two hours to turn the pair of you into regular young flowers of the aristocracy and deliver you to Tower MacNeil."

"No problem," said Hawk. "We can be as aristocratic as the next man, if pushed."

"Right," said Fisher, with an impeccable upper-class accent. "All we have to do is act arrogant and obnoxious at all times, and remember not to blow our noses on our sleeves without crooking our little fingers. What could go wrong?"

Dubois swallowed hard, but said nothing. There were times when mere words seemed inadequate.

He hustled them out of his office and through the bustling corridors to an anonymous file room safely out of everyone's way. He ushered them in, and then locked the door behind them. A Guard medical sorcerer rose quickly to his feet, nodded stiffly to the two Guards and looked enquiringly at Dubois. The Commander nodded, and the sorcerer shrugged. He was a dark and intense-looking man in his early forties, with a professional smile and large, powerful hands. He was overdressed in a dark, formal way, as though he were about to attend a funeral. Hawk looked at him suspiciously. He didn't trust Haven doctors. They seemed to believe in suppositories for everything, from warts to deafness. He started to turn to Dubois, but Fisher beat him to it.

"What's the doctor doing here? We're not sick."

"This is Wulfgang. You can trust him completely."

"Why?" said Hawk. "You got something on him too?"

"Wulfgang specializes in shapechange magic, in a minor way," said Dubois. "Since you both have something of a reputation in Haven, we can't have you walking into Tower MacNeil with your own faces, can we? Wulfgang will give you new faces, which won't be recognized."

Hawk scowled at the sorcerer. "I'm not feeling too fond of flesh-sculptors right now. What's wrong with a good old-fashioned illusion spell?"

Dubois sighed impatiently. "Tower MacNeil, like most Quality households, has security spells to show up such things. The Families take their security very seriously. The shapechange won't register because the spell will have finished its work long before you get there. After you return, with your mission successfully completed, we'll give you your own faces back."

"And if we don't succeed?" said Hawk.

Dubois smiled coldly. "You screw up in Tower MacNeil, Hawk, and you won't be coming back. Now, stop holding things up, and let the sorcerer get to work on you. We're running out of time."

Hawk and Fisher looked at each other, and then sat down on the chairs Wulfgang indicated. The sorcerer smiled reassuringly and ran his hands through a series of practised gestures, muttering under his breath as he did so. A gradual feeling of pressure filled the room, and Hawk's skin crawled as static moved in his hair. The pressure peaked uncomfortably, and then vanished as the sorcerer made a final, decisive gesture. Hawk waited a moment, and then looked down at his hands. They still looked the same to him. He looked across at Fisher, and she looked the same too. He looked back at the sorcerer Wulfgang, who was staring dumbfounded at the two Guards.

"Why isn't anything happening?" demanded Dubois.

"I don't know!" snapped Wulfgang. "I can't understand it; the spell just seemed to slide off them." A sudden thought struck him, and he glared at Hawk. "Are you still carrying your suppressor stone?"

"No, he isn't," said Dubois. "And don't ask what happened to it. That's confidential."

Wulfgang frowned thoughtfully. "There's nothing wrong with the spell, they're not shielded, so what . . . ? Wait a minute. Have you two ever been exposed to Wild Magic?"

"What's that got to do with anything?" said Dubois.

"There's a big difference between the High Magic that most sorcerers use, and the much rarer Wild Magic," said Wulfgang patiently. "High Magic manipulates aspects of the real world; Wild Magic changes reality itself. So if your people have been exposed to Wild Magic . . ."

"We have," said Hawk. "We were up North when the Blue Moon rose."

Dubois and Wulfgang stared at the two Guards almost respectfully. "You were there, during the long night?" said Dubois.

"We were there," said Fisher. "And no, we don't want to talk about it."

"That's why my spell won't work on them," said Wulfgang. "If they were exposed to the Blue Moon's influence, it'll take more than a simple shapechange spell to affect them. I'm sorry, Commander. There's nothing I can do."

Dubois sighed. "I might have known you two were going to be trouble. All right. Thank you, Wulfgang. That will be all. The wardrobe mistress should have arrived by now; perhaps you'd be good enough to ask her to step in here on your way out. And Wulfgang, remember: This meeting never took place. You were never here."

"Of course," said the sorcerer. He bowed politely to Hawk and Fisher, and waited patiently for Dubois to unlock the door so he could leave. Dubois locked the door again after he'd gone.

"While we're waiting," said Hawk, "there's a few things I'd like to get clear. In particular, why Fenris chose Tower MacNeil as his hiding place. Surely among so many Quality he'd be bound to give himself away sooner or later."

Dubois pursed his lips. "We have reason to believe Fenris may be of the Quality," he said carefully. "So he'd have no problem passing himself off as a distant MacNeil cousin."

"Why the hell would one of the Quality want to act as a spy?" said Hawk. "Most spies work strictly for cash, or occasionally political gain. If there's one thing the Quality aren't short of, it's money, and most of them don't give a damn about politics. So what happened to turn Fenris into an agent for a foreign power?"

"If we knew that, we'd know who he was," said Dubois.

"Can you at least tell us something about the information he's stolen?" said Fisher. "That might help when it comes to identifying him."

"I can't tell you anything," said Dubois flatly. "That's being handled on a strictly need-to-know basis. Even I haven't been told. But it must be pretty damned important to have got everyone running round in circles like this. You wouldn't believe the pressure that's been coming down from Above. Let me put it this way: Under no circumstances is the spy Fenris to be allowed to escape from Tower MacNeil. If he tries, you're to stop him, whatever it takes."

"You mean kill him?" said Fisher.

"Whatever it takes," said Dubois.

Hawk smiled sourly. "In other words, it's up to us whether or not we kill a member of the Quality. But if anything goes wrong afterwards, everyone will swear blind we were never given any such order. Right?"

"Got it in one," said Dubois. "You have a natural gift for politics, Hawk."

They sat in silence for a while, each thinking their own separate thoughts. There was a knock at the door. Dubois went over and quietly asked who it was. On getting a satisfactory answer, he unlocked the door. But he still stood well back as it opened, one hand resting on his sword till he saw the newcomer was alone. The wardrobe mistress bustled in, in a hurry as usual. Mistress Melanie was tall and scrawny, with a sharp-boned face and a wild frizz of dark curly hair barely restrained by a leather headband. She was one of those people who had so much nervous energy she made everyone else feel tired just looking at her.

"Are they ready?" she said sharply to Dubois, not even bothering to look at Hawk and Fisher.

Dubois nodded briskly. "The shapechange didn't take.

We'll have to rely on standard disguise techniques. Do what you can with them."

Mistress Melanie made a short tutting sound and glared at the two Guards. "As if we weren't already running behind schedule. All right. Follow me and don't dawdle."

And with that, she disappeared back out the door while her words were still ringing on the air. Hawk and Fisher hurried after her.

A short footrace later, they ended up in the wardrobe department. Hawk had never been there before and looked around with interest. Hundreds of costumes hung in neat rows on wire hangers—everything from the latest Quality fashions to a filthy ragpicker's outfit. A great deal of the Guard's work had to be done undercover; inevitable in a city like Haven, where no one shared confidences unless they had to and absolutely no one spoke to the authorities. Unless there was money in it. Half the Guard's annual budget went to information-gathering, a fact which never failed to infuriate the more penny-pinching members of the Council.

Mistress Melanie sat Hawk and Fisher down in front of the makeup mirrors and studied them thoughtfully. "Yes," she said finally, drawing out the word till it sounded more like *no,* "The scars are going to be a problem, but a good coat of makeup should cover them. No one'll be able to tell, even at close quarters, but don't let anyone kiss you."

"I hadn't planned on it," said Hawk.

Mistress Melanie sniffed. "We're going to have to do something about that eye, of course. A patch is out of the question." She looked hard at Hawk's single eye for a moment, then opened a small lacquered box and rummaged around inside it, finally producing a single glass eye. "Try this."

"No," said Hawk flatly. "Forget it. I hate the damned things."

"I can assure you, you'll find it a perfect match," said Mistress Melanie frostily.

"I said no!"

"Be reasonable, Hawk," said Fisher. "You can't wear your patch. Any member of the Quality who suffered that kind of injury would have it put right at once with a shapechange spell. And since you can't do that, you'll have to use the glass eye. It won't be for long."

Hawk growled something indistinct, and accepted the glass eye with bad grace. He scowled at it for a moment, then took off his patch, put it to one side, and gingerly eased the glass eye into the empty socket. He blinked experimentally a few times, and then glared into the mirror. "Hate wearing a glass eye," he growled. "Makes my face ache."

Fisher looked over his shoulder into the mirror. "She's right, Hawk; they're a perfect match. No one will be able to tell it isn't real."

Hawk sniffed loudly, unimpressed. Mistress Melanie produced a set of clothes for each of them, and thrust them unceremoniously into Hawk and Fisher's arms. "Try these for size. They're based on the statistics in your official records, but I've had to make some allowances. From the look of you, you've both put on some weight since then. Come on, get a move on; I've got to know if I have to make more alterations, and we've still got your makeup to do."

Hawk looked at her and raised an eyebrow meaningfully. Mistress Melanie's mouth twitched. "I'll wait outside while you change. Call me if you have any problems."

She left, closing the door firmly behind her. Hawk took his first good look at his new clothes, and his heart sank. The latest male fashion for the Quality still consisted of tightly cut trousers, a padded jerkin with a chin-high collar, and knee-length leather boots. Plus some rather utilitarian long underwear. The jerkin and trousers were both navy blue with gold thread trim. The military look was *in* this Season. He looked across at Fisher, and smiled as he saw she was even less enchanted with her new clothes. There was a long flowing gown of lilac blue with frothy lace trim, a great deal of frilly underwear, a formidable-looking corset, and a pair of fashionable shoes that looked hideously uncomfortable. Fisher picked up the corset with a thumb and forefinger and held it out at arm's length, studying it dubiously.

"Look on the bright side," said Hawk. "At least there isn't a bustle."

"Do we really have to do this, Hawk?" said Fisher.

"Well, we could fight our way out of here, and make a run for it."

"Don't tempt me." Fisher sighed heavily, and began stripping off her furs. "The things I do in the line of duty . . ."

It took them the best part of half an hour to climb into their new clothes. There were endless buttons and hooks and eyes, and they all had to be done up in just the right order. Hawk could only just get into the trousers. Even with Mistress Melanie's allowances for his somewhat expanded waistline, it was a very tight fit. Fisher had even more trouble with the corset. Hawk ended up having to put a knee in the middle of her back while he pulled the cords tight. Fisher's language became increasingly awful, until finally she was forced to give up from lack of breath. Finally, the ordeal was over, and they stood together before a full-length mirror, judging the effect.

Despite everything, Hawk had to admit they looked the part. Before them in the mirror stood a gentleman and young lady of the Quality, dressed impeccably in the latest finery. Hawk looked splendid and striking, though the scars on his face still gave him a sinister air, and Fisher looked absolutely stunning. The corset had given her a magnificent hourglass figure, and the long gown made her look even taller. She winked at Hawk coquettishly over her paper fan, and they both laughed.

"Been a long time since we looked this good," said Hawk finally.

"A long time," said Fisher.

Mistress Melanie knocked loudly, and swept in without waiting for an answer. She looked them both up and down, and nodded curtly. "You'll do. Now let's see what we can achieve with a little makeup."

Another half hour passed before the wardrobe mistress allowed Hawk and Fisher to look into a mirror again, and what they saw kept them silent for a long moment. Their skin was now fashionably pale instead of their usual tan. Fisher's face had been expertly made up with rouge and eye shadow, taking the edge off the harsh lines, and softening the aggressive chin. Her long blond hair had been piled up on top of her head in a complicated design. Hawk's face had changed completely; with the patch gone and the scars hidden under makeup he looked ten years younger, and somehow more at peace with himself and the world. Fisher looked at him and smiled tenderly.

"I often wondered what you looked like, before the scars."

"Well?" said Hawk awkwardly. "What do you think?"

"I think you look very handsome, my love. But then, I always did."

Hawk leant forward to kiss her, and Mistress Melanie yelled at him. "No touching till the makeup's set! I don't want to have to fix her face all over again!"

Hawk and Fisher shared a wry smile. There was a loud knocking at the door.

"Are you two decent?" called Commander Dubois from outside.

"Near as we ever get," said Hawk loudly, and nodded for Mistress Melanie to let the Commander in. Hawk and Fisher struck carefully aristocratic poses and stared haughtily at Dubois as he came in. He walked slowly over to them, and looked from one to the other and back again.

"I'm . . . impressed," he said finally. "You might just bring this off after all. I wish we had time to give you a full briefing on how to behave, all the little tricks of etiquette and the like, but we're way behind schedule as it is."

"Don't worry," said Hawk. "We know which fork to use, and which way to pass the port. We've been around."

"Right," said Fisher. "You'd be surprised."

"Yeah, well," said Dubois. "We've worked out a rough background for you. You're going to be remote country cousins of the MacNeils; a brother and sister from the wilds of Lower Markham. That's way out on the Eastern border, so no one should be able to trip you up on local details. Make up anything you like; they won't know the difference. But keep it simple. You don't want to end up contradicting each other. Also, they'll expect a certain amount of gaucherie and unfamiliarity with the latest styles, so that should help excuse any foul-ups you do make. Now then, you're going to have to get used to your new names. Captain Fisher can use her given name of Isobel. That's quite a fashionable name at the moment. But we don't seem to have a given name on the files for you, Captain Hawk."

"There isn't one. I'm just Hawk."

"You only have the one name?"

"I've had others. But I'm just Hawk now."

"Be that as it may," said Dubois, in the tone of someone determined not to ask questions he's sure he wouldn't like the answers to. "As far as you're concerned, from now on you're Richard MacNeil. Got it?"

"Richard . . ." said Hawk. "Yeah, I can live with that."

"I'm so pleased," said Dubois. "One last thing: Leave your axe here. We'll supply you with a standard duelling sword. And Captain Fisher will have to go unarmed, of course. No young lady of the Quality would wear a sword. It simply isn't done."

Hawk and Fisher looked at each other.

"No axe."

"No sword."

"Tight trousers."

"And a bloody corset."

They looked hard at Dubois. "We want a bonus," said Hawk flatly.

"In cash," said Fisher.

"In our hands, before we go."

"I can arrange that," said Dubois.

Hawk looked at Fisher. "They must really be desperate."

"Maybe we should hit them for overtime while we're at it," said Fisher.

"Don't push your luck," said Dubois.

3

Ghosts and Memories

Haven was an old city, but the dark and brooding cliffs that overlooked it were older still. Huge and forbidding, they rose out of the restless sea like grim, watchful guardians, protecting Haven on three sides from the raging storms that swept in off the sea. The waves pounded endlessly at the jagged spurs of rock, throwing spray high into the wind even on the calmest of days. Tower MacNeil stood firm and unyielding on an outcropping of dark basalt that jutted from the cliff face like a clenched fist against the encroaching sea.

The Tower was tall and elegant, built entirely from the local white stone, with its distinctive pearly sheen. Its lines were clean and functional, the wide glass windows its only concession to comfort and luxury. It stood five stories tall, surmounted by open crenellated battlements. Down the centuries, Tower MacNeil had defied both time and the elements, as well as countless enemy attacks. Often scarred, and as often restored, it had never once fallen to its adversaries. Brilliant engineering and subtle sorceries maintained the Tower, as it maintained and protected the Family who dwelt within.

But like the cliffs on which it stood, and the dark city it overlooked, Tower MacNeil had its grim and bloody secrets. Within the Tower, something had stirred; something strange and awful, free of its chains at last.

Hawk trudged up the single narrow path, his cloak pulled tightly about him, his head bowed against the gusting wind. This high up on the cliffs the wind blew hard and bitter cold. The wild grasses seemed permanently flattened by the weather, and nothing else grew about him for as far as he could see. Hawk wasn't surprised, given the force of the winds. Anything that dared thrust its head above the ground was probably ripped out by the roots for its impertinence. He raised his head slightly, and scowled as he saw Fisher waiting for him some way ahead, standing on the edge of the cliff and looking out to sea. He took a few deep breaths, fighting to get his breathing back to normal before he joined her. The long steep trail had winded him, but he didn't want her to know that. She'd only make pointed comments about his being out of condition and put him on another diet. Hawk hated diets. Why did everything that was good for you have to taste so bloody bland?

He crossed over to stand beside Fisher on the cliff edge, careful to keep a respectful distance between him and the crumbling stone brink. The wind tugged at his hair and drew tears from his eyes. Fisher nodded at him happily, and indicated the view with a sweeping wave of her arm. Hawk had to admit it was pretty breathtaking. Far below, waves pounded the rocks with unrelenting fury, falling reluctantly back in streams of froth and spume. The choppy sea stretched away to the horizon in endless shades of blue and green and grey, empty of sails for once. Winter was closing in, and ships now were few and far between. The steely blue sky was clear of clouds for the moment, thanks to the city weather wizards, and gulls hung on the air like drifting shadows, tossed here and there by the gusting wind. Their mournful keening was all that broke the morning quiet, save for the distant crash of breakers down below.

"Listen to the sea and the gulls," said Fisher. "So wild, so free. We really should get out here more often, Hawk."

"Maybe we will, come the summer. And you'd better call me Richard from now on, even when there's no one around. We don't want to get caught out on something that simple."

"Sure. Why did we have to be brother and sister? Why couldn't we be husband and wife?"

"Beats me. Maybe we're supposed to get information out of people by romancing them."

Fisher wrinkled her nose. "Not really our style, that."

"True."

"I never get tired of looking at the sea. I never even saw the ocean before we left the North."

"I like the view too, Isobel, but we can't stay here. We have a job to do, and time is pressing."

"I know. It's just that we never seem to have any time to ourselves these days."

"When did we ever?"

"True. Let's go."

They turned away from the cliff edge and made their way back through the grass to the narrow stony trail. The Tower loomed ahead of them, straight and uncompromising against the skyline, silent and enigmatic. Its height made it look deceptively slim until you got close enough to realize just how huge the Tower really was. Hawk thought for a moment on how backbreaking it must have been, hauling building stone up the cliffs to this spot, and then decided firmly that he wasn't going to think about it anymore. Just trying to visualize the logistics was enough to make his head ache. He realized Fisher was staring at the Tower too, and deliberately quickened his step.

"Come on, Isobel," he said briskly. "There's no telling how long Fenris will stay put in the Tower. If he decides to leave before we can get there to stop him, Dubois will have our heads. Probably literally."

"I don't know why Fenris didn't just keep running," said Fisher, picking up the pace. "I would have. What made him think he'd be safe here?"

"The longer he stayed in the open, the more likely it was he'd be spotted," said Hawk. "And the Tower's a good place to go to ground. It's within easy reach of the city but out of everyone's thoughts. I wouldn't have thought to look for him here. If it hadn't been for the Council's sorcerers, he'd have probably got away with it. And let's face it. If worst came to worst, and for some reason the MacNeils decided not to hand him over, we'd have one hell of a job getting him out of the Tower. You'd need an army and every sorcerer in the city to breach those walls, by all accounts. No, my guess is Fenris is probably biding his time in there, looking over his shoulder a lot and waiting for one of his own people to contact him with a safe route out to the Low Kingdoms. Assuming someone hasn't already done so."

"I still haven't figured out what we're going to do once we're inside the Tower," said Fisher. "I mean, we've no idea what he looks like now. He could be anybody. He could be passing himself off as an out-of-town MacNeil cousin, like us, or a friend of one, or a newly hired servant, or . . . Hell, I don't know. The man's a spy, after all; he's used to pretending to be someone he isn't. How are we going to trip up someone like that? This case is a mess, and we've barely even started yet. Do you think we're going to be able to recognize him?"

"Not a hope," said Hawk. "If I had to fight him again I might recognize his style, but I'm damned if I'm going to go round challenging everyone to a duel. Especially without my axe. Have you seen this stupid sword they've given me? One good parry and it'll snap in half. I'd be better off sneaking up behind my opponent and clubbing him to death with the hilt."

"So what are we going to do?"

"Same as usual, lass. Ask lots of questions, keep our eyes open, and hopefully make enough of a nuisance of ourselves that the killer will do something stupid to try and shut us up."

"Great," said Fisher. "I just love being a target."

They both fell silent as they finally drew near the Tower MacNeil. The large, squarish front door was a different shade of white from the surrounding stonework, and Hawk felt a sudden, unsettling thrill go through him as he realized the door had been carved from a single huge slab of polished ivory. He tried to visualize the size of the whale that could donate such a bone, and quickly decided he'd rather not know. He tugged briskly at the bell pull, and then he and Fisher took turns using the black iron boot-scraper. They were Quality now, and had to keep up appearances.

The door swung smoothly open on well-oiled counterweights, revealing a medium-height, heavyset man in his mid-forties, wearing the slightly outdated formal wear that was the accepted hallmark of the Haven butler. He had dark, lifeless hair, a flat immobile face that might have been carved from stone, and a general air of gloomy efficiency for which the long black frock coat was the perfect finishing touch. He bowed formally to Hawk and Fisher, each bow nicely calculated to the inch to show respect for his betters whilst reminding them that as butler of the household he

was a force to be reckoned with in his own right. It was a
masterful performance. Hawk felt like applauding.

"I am Richard MacNeil of Lower Markham," he said
gravely. "This is my sister, Isobel. We've come to pay our
respects to the new head of the Family."

"Of course, sir and madam. I am Greaves, butler of
Tower MacNeil. Please come in."

He stood back to allow them to enter. He seemed faintly
disapproving, possibly because they came from a backwater
like Lower Markham, but most likely because butlers always seemed faintly disapproving. Hawk suspected it was
part of the job description. He strolled into the hallway as
though he owned the place, with Isobel on his arm, smiling
demurely. The smile didn't suit her, but Hawk admired the
effort that had gone into it. Greaves closed the door behind them, and Hawk's ears pricked up as he heard the
sound of heavy bolts being thrown home. It could be that
the Tower MacNeil household was routinely security-
minded . . . or it could be that right now they had reason
to be. He took off his cloak, and found the butler already
there waiting to receive it. Fisher handed Greaves her
cloak, and raised a painted eyebrow enquiringly.

"Are you the only staff here, Greaves? Surely it's not a
butler's place to take the cloaks from guests. Don't you
have any maids under you?"

Greaves's expression didn't alter in the least as he arranged the cloaks neatly on the wall by the door. "Alas,
madam, I'm afraid Tower MacNeil is extremely short
staffed at present. Normally we have a staff of twenty-two,
but everyone else left some time ago."

Hawk looked at him sharply. "And why is that?"

"It's not really my place to say, sir. If you and the young
lady would care to follow me, I'll take you to the MacNeil
himself. I'm sure he will be happy to answer any questions
you may have."

He turned his back on them, politely but firmly, and
started off down the hall. Hawk and Fisher exchanged a
look behind his back, shrugged pretty much in unison, and
followed him. They'd only been in the place a few moments
and already they were up to their ears in questions. What
the hell could have happened here to drive all the servants
out? And since it had happened recently, could it have

something to do with Fenris' arrival? The butler worried
Hawk as well. The man was being far too calm and pleasant. Most butlers were worse snobs than their masters and
would have had coronaries at the mere mention of their
doing maids' work. And yet Greaves seemed to be implying
he was doing all the servants' work at Tower MacNeil.
What kind of hold could keep him at his duty, despite
the humiliation?

Hawk shrugged inwardly. Perhaps Greaves was just angling for a larger than usual gratuity when Hawk left. In
which case, he was going to be disappointed. Wardrobe
might have provided Hawk with aristocratic clothes, but
they'd absolutely declined to fill the purse on his belt. He'd
had to do that, with his bonus money, and he was damned
if he was going to part with one penny more than he absolutely had to.

The butler led Hawk and Fisher down a stylishly appointed passage and ushered them into a large and spacious
drawing room. Early morning light streamed through the
immaculately polished windows, reflecting brightly from the
pure white of the stonework, illuminating the room like a
vision of paradise. The whole ceiling was covered with a
single delightful piece of art depicting nymphs and shep-
herds at play. In a romantic and extremely tasteful way, of
course. Everywhere there were luxurious chairs and
couches, fine displays of wines and spirits, silver trays bearing all kinds of cold food, and every other comfort the mind
could imagine. Hawk did his best to look unimpressed.

Standing with his back to the roaring fire was a tall, well-
built young man with broad shoulders and a barrel chest.
He couldn't have been more than twenty, and his unruly
mop of tawny hair made him look even younger. Neverthe-
less, there was a dignity and strength in his stance, and a
composure in his face, that was quietly impressive. Hawk
didn't need Greaves to tell him this was their host, Jamie
MacNeil. The MacNeil, as he now was. He was dressed all
in black, being still in mourning for his father, but the
clothes were of the finest cut and impeccably fashionable.
He stepped forward as the butler introduced them, and
greeted his two cousins warmly, kissing Isobel's hand with
style, and shaking Hawk's hand in a grip that was firm
without being overbearing. He gestured for the butler to

leave them, and Greaves bowed and backed out, closing the door after him. Jamie led Hawk and Fisher over to the drinks cabinet and politely enquired as to their pleasure. He seemed genuinely pleased to see them, and yet somehow preoccupied, as though part of his attention was always somewhere else.

"So good of you to come," he said graciously. "Did you have a good journey?"

"Bearable," said Hawk, accepting his drink with a nod. "We left our belongings in Haven, ghastly place, and came straight here. Though I gather from your butler that we may have arrived at a bad time . . . he said something about all the servants leaving?"

Jamie MacNeil smiled easily, but Hawk could see the effort it took. "Just a minor domestic crisis, but I'm afraid we're all going to have to rough it for the moment. Please accept my apologies, and bear with us. Do feel free to stay for as long as you wish; there are plenty of spare bedrooms, and Haven's inns are notoriously unsafe."

"That's very kind of you," said Hawk.

"Not at all, not at all. I'll just let Greaves know, and he'll prepare rooms for you and your sister."

He reached for the bell pull by the fireplace, but had barely taken hold of it when the door swung open and Greaves entered. Hawk blinked bemusedly at such a quick response, and then smiled slightly as Greaves stepped to one side and two ladies of the Quality swept in, not even deigning to notice the butler's bow. Jamie smiled at them both, a genuine smile full of warmth and affection, and more than a little concern. Hawk sipped his wine thoughtfully as Jamie spoke quietly to the butler. He was beginning to get a bad feeling about Tower MacNeil. Something was going on here; something he was beginning to suspect had nothing to do with the spy Fenris. He took a healthy gulp of his wine, careful to keep his little finger crooked. On the other hand, he could just be getting paranoid. If Jamie MacNeil knew about the spy, then getting rid of a bunch of gossiping servants was a sensible precaution. But according to Greaves, the servants had left some time ago, long before Fenris could have arrived. . . . Hawk quickly put the thought to one side for later consideration as Jamie dismissed the butler and turned to him and Fisher.

"Dear cousins, allow me to present my sister Holly, and my aunt, Katrina Dorimant."

Hawk bowed and the women curtsied, Fisher with more efficiency than grace. Holly MacNeil was a blazing redhead in her late twenties, almost as tall as her brother, but as slightly built as he was broad. Hawk's first thought was that the poor lass could do with a good meal or two. Her pale face was gaunt and strained, though still attractive, her large green eyes giving her an innocent, vulnerable look, like a young fawn suddenly confronted with a pack of wolves. Whatever was going on at Tower MacNeil, it was clear she knew about it too. Like her brother, Holly Mac-Neil was formally but stylishly dressed in black, which against the paleness of her skin only served to emphasize her frailty. She offered Hawk a trembling hand, and he had to steady it with his own before he could kiss it. He gave her hand a reassuring squeeze before releasing it, and thought he glimpsed a quick smile. Holly and Fisher embraced each other briefly. There was no warmth in it, and Holly held the contact only as long as convention demanded.

Jamie's aunt, Katrina Dorimant, was a roguishly attractive woman in her mid-forties, with a broad grin and flashing eyes. She wore a long, wine-red gown, and enough jewellery to finance a minor war or two. She was average height, with a tight, compact body and a brisk, captivating manner. She smiled widely at Hawk as he kissed her hand, and her eyes lingered on him for a long moment before she turned to embrace Fisher. Once again the embrace was over almost as soon as it had begun, and the two women exchanged a cool, appraising look before dismissing each other with averted eyes. Hawk hid a smile. Fisher had better keep her guard up. Katrina looked like a scrapper.

"Welcome to Tower MacNeil!" said Katrina brightly. "I'm so glad you're here. We need some new blood to stir things up. The place has been awfully gloomy just lately, though I can't think why. Dear Duncan never approved of sour faces when he was alive, and he certainly wouldn't have expected us to wander around sobbing and beating our breasts just because he's dead."

"You never did believe in tears or regrets, did you, Aunt?" said Holly flatly.

"Certainly not. They make your eyes puffy and give you wrinkles."

"Are you here for the reading of the will?" asked Fisher politely.

"Actually, no, my dear. I'm currently separated from my husband, bad cess to the man, and dear Jamie has been kind enough to allow me to stay here until the divorce is finalized."

"I had in mind a few weeks, Auntie," said Jamie good-naturedly. "In actual fact, you've been here five months now."

"Don't exaggerate, dear. It's four and a bit."

"Are we the only guests?" said Hawk. "I can't believe we're the only Family come to pay our respects to the MacNeil."

"There are other guests," said Jamie. "They're upstairs in their rooms at present, but they'll be joining us for a late breakfast soon. We keep very relaxed hours here, especially since the servants left. But it must be said there aren't nearly as many Family here as one might have wished for."

"Why not?" asked Fisher bluntly.

The three MacNeils exchanged a quick glance. "I take it you've never heard of the MacNeil Curse," said Jamie slowly. "Not really surprising, I suppose, buried as you are in the depths of Lower Markham. It's not something we're proud of, and we don't care to discuss it with outsiders. But since you are both Family, and you've come all this way to be here . . . The Curse is the reason why so few have come to pay their respects, even with the reading of the will to tempt them. It's why the servants ran away, and why the Quality no longer accept invitations to Tower MacNeil. Please, be seated, all of you, and I'll tell you of the secret Shame of the MacNeils, and how it has come back to haunt us. I think it's time for the truth."

Everyone found themselves chairs, and drew them up in a semicircle facing the fireplace. Jamie stayed where he was, with his back to the fire, standing almost to attention, with his hands clasped behind his back, so the others wouldn't see them shaking. When he finally spoke, his voice was low and even and very controlled.

"Most people have heard something about the Curse of the MacNeils. That there is a monster which haunts us, and has done for generations. There have been many songs about it, and even one or two plays. Romantic fictions, all of them. We don't object; they help conceal the reality behind the myth. There is a Secret in our Family, handed down from father to eldest son alone, from generation to generation.

"Long ago, in the days before proper records were kept, a child was born to the MacNeils, to the head of the Family at that time. That child was the eldest son, destined to continue the Family bloodline. Unfortunately, he was also horribly deformed. He should have been killed at birth, but the MacNeil was a kind and tender-hearted man. The creature was, after all, his son. Perhaps a cure could be found. The MacNeil all but bankrupted the Family trying to find it, paying for doctors and sorcerers and healers of all kinds, but no cure was ever found.

"The creature became increasingly violent, and eventually had to be put away, for everyone's safety. The MacNeil took full responsibility for his awful son, and none of the Family or servants ever saw it again. Finally, some years later, the creature died, and everyone heaved a sigh of relief. The normal second son became the eldest son, the bloodline continued through him, and everything returned to normal.

"That is not the Secret. The songs and the romances and the plays are based loosely on what I have just told you, and from those distorted stories come the vague rumours that most people mean when they refer to the Curse of the MacNeils. The Secret, handed down from father to eldest son, is very simple. The creature did not die.

"The MacNeil had finally despaired of his monstrous son, and decided it should die, to free the Family of its burden. He gave the creature poison to drink, and walled up its room. He and the second son did the job themselves, rather than risk bringing in workmen or servants who might have talked. And all the time they laboured with bricks and mortar, they could hear the creature pacing restlessly back and forth in its cell. The poison did not kill it. Time and again the MacNeil and his son returned to listen at the wall they'd built, but though the creature had no access to food or water, still it lived. They could hear it moving about in its cell, and sometimes scratching at the walls.

"Years passed. The MacNeil died, and later so did his son, but the creature lived on. No one ever knew of its existence save the head of the Family and the eldest son, the Secret passing from generation to generation to generation when the son reached his majority. And so it went, down all the many years.

"Only this time, something went wrong. My father passed on the Secret to his eldest son, my brother William. But William died just three weeks ago, in a riding accident, and then my father was killed in a border clash, before he could pass on the details of the Secret to me. I was able to piece together what I've just told you from studying his papers after his death, but that's as far as his notes go. Presumably there are other papers somewhere, prepared in case of an emergency, but I've been unable to find them,. No doubt Dad would have got around to telling me where they were, just in case . . . but who would ever have thought he'd die so suddenly. . . ."

Jamie stopped abruptly as his voice broke. Holly rose quickly from her seat and moved forward to hug her brother's arm protectively.

"Is that why the servants left?" said Hawk. "Because the Secret got out?"

Jamie shook his head. "Not long after Dad died, the servants began seeing things. A dark figure, padding through the corridors late at night, or in the early hours of the morning. It always disappeared when challenged. I had the Tower searched from top to bottom by my security people, but they never found anyone. Then, things started to be broken. Vases, glasses, crockery. A chair was found smashed to pieces. Noises were heard at night; something that might have been screams, or laughter. My people began to leave, despite all I could offer them in the way of money or reassurances.

"Even my security people wouldn't stay. They all thought it was the ghost of my father, come back to haunt the Tower. Only I knew better. After all these years, the creature had finally got out. Obviously some part of the Secret dealt with how to keep it confined, and since I didn't know what to do . . . So far, it hasn't been able to leave Tower MacNeil; the Tower's protective wards see to that."

"Why haven't you called in the city Guard?" asked Fisher. "Maybe their experts could find the creature. . . ."

"No!" said Jamie sharply. "This is Family business, and it has to stay within the Family. If the Secret ever gets out, the whole world will know the MacNeil Family is based on a lie. That all of us are descended from a *second* son. The Quality would declare that we had betrayed our bloodline and inheritance, and the MacNeils would be disgraced. Already there are rumours. That's why so few Family have come to declare their fealty to me."

"Apart from us, who else knows the Secret?" said Hawk.

"Just Greaves, my immediate Family, and my other guests, so far."

"This . . . creature," said Fisher slowly. "Has it tried to hurt anyone?"

"Not so far," said Jamie. "But it is getting more destructive. Why? Do you want to leave?"

Hawk smiled slightly. "I don't think so. Isobel and I don't scare easily."

Katrina stirred in her chair. "I can't believe Duncan kept the Secret so long. I had no idea . . . You're quite right, of course, Jamie. The Secret must never get out. We would be ostracised in High Society. Now then, the creature undoubtedly hides by day in the room that used to be its cell. Are you still unable to locate it?"

"I'm afraid so." Jamie's brow furrowed, and he ran a hand through his hair. "The Tower is riddled with secret passages and sliding panels. I know some of them, and Dad's papers revealed a few more, but I still haven't been able to find where the creature is hiding. Presumably the room's location was part of the Secret."

"This is crazy," said Fisher. "If this creature was walled up for centuries, what kept it alive? Everything feeds on something. . . ."

"I don't know," said Jamie. "But whatever the creature is, it's definitely not human. Maybe it hasn't died because it can't . . ."

For a long moment, nobody said anything. The crackling of the fire seemed very loud in the quiet.

"All this started because your father died unexpectedly," said Hawk finally. "Just how did he die?"

Katrina looked at him sharply. "You don't know?"

"Word often gets garbled when it has to travel long distances," said Fisher smoothly. "We want to make sure we've got it right."

"I was just wondering," said Hawk carefully, "if perhaps there had been something unusual about your father's death . . . something that might give us a clue as to how the creature got out of its cell, after centuries of confinement. I mean, its room was supposed to have been bricked up. So, how did it finally get out?"

"I see." Jamie nodded respectfully. "I hadn't thought of that. But no, there was nothing suspicious about my father's death. He was killed in a skirmish with Outremer troops up in the Northern borderlands. He shouldn't really have been there, an officer of his rank. But there had been rumours of new troop movements, and he wanted to see for himself. Dad was like that. Never really trusted anyone's opinion but his own. Anyway, he was in the wrong place at the wrong time, and he and his whole column were wiped out. Just another borderland skirmish. There's been a number of them just recently. Men are dying up there every day, just because our King and the Outremer Monarch can't agree on exactly where the bloody border is. Good men dying for a line on a map . . . I'm sorry. But it's hard not to be bitter sometimes. Dad was a good soldier. He deserved a better end than this. But I don't see how it could have had anything to do with the creature's escape."

"Did anything unusual happen here at the Tower, before the servants started seeing and hearing things?" said Fisher . . .

Jamie thought for a moment. "I don't think so. I remember we were a bit short-staffed for a while about then. A lot of the servants had been going down with colds, but you expect that at this time of the year. A day off, and they were back at work again."

"There's really nothing to worry about," said Katrina firmly. "You'll be quite safe here, I assure you. There's no indication the creature's ever tried to hurt anyone. That is right, isn't it, Jamie?"

"Yes, it is. But I felt it only fair you should all know what the situation is. You see, before the will can be read, the Tower has to be isolated behind protective wards for twenty-four hours. That's traditional."

"You mean, once the wards are up, no one can leave the Tower for a full day?" said Hawk. "No matter what happens here?"

He and Fisher exchanged a quick glance.

"That's right," said Jamie. "But trust me, nothing's going to happen. If the creature had meant any harm, it would have acted by now. All those years of imprisonment must have knocked the fight out of it."

"I'm sure you're right," said Fisher. "But you couldn't have known that, at the beginning. In fact, it must have been pretty scary, especially when the servants started leaving, rather than face whatever it was. So why did you stay? Wouldn't it have been safer to evacuate the Tower?"

"This is my home," said Jamie. "Home to my Family for generations. I won't be driven out of it."

There was an uncomfortable pause.

"Well," said Katrina brightly, "if all else fails, we can always call on the Guardian!"

"Who?" said Hawk.

There was another, longer pause as the MacNeils looked at him strangely. Hawk silently cursed. He knew he should have insisted on a full briefing. Nothing was more likely to trip him and Fisher up than not recognizing some Family in-joke or reference, and this was clearly one of them. Still, the harm was done now. All he could do was try and face it down. He stared innocently back at Jamie and Katrina, and noticed for the first time that Holly wasn't paying any attention to the conversation. Instead, her eyes were far away, as though she were lost in some world of her own. Then Katrina started speaking, and Hawk quickly switched his attention back to her.

"You must have heard of the MacNeil Guardian," said Katrina, speaking slowly and carefully, as though to a rather backward small child. "Perhaps you know him by a different name. The Guardian is one of our more pleasant and comforting Family legends. One of our more remote ancestors is supposed to haunt the Tower, duty bound to protect his descendants from harm. Apparently it's a penance for some bloody crime he later came to regret but was unable to put right while he lived. The legend doesn't say exactly what his crime might have been."

"That's often the way with legends," said Hawk. "You're right, of course. I recognize it now. Has anyone seen this ghost in recent times?"

"No one's seen him for centuries," said Jamie. "Though there have been any number of times when the Family could have used his help. So I'm afraid it is just a legend, after all."

"I believe in him," said Holly suddenly. "I pray every night he'll come to save me. But he never does."

Everyone looked at her strangely for a moment. For the first time, there had been real passion in her voice, and something that might have been despair. Jamie looked at her worriedly, but said nothing, and Holly quickly subsided into silence again. Katrina cleared her throat loudly.

"That's supposed to be a portrait of the Guardian," she said brightly, indicating a dark and gloomy portrait directly over the fireplace. "Painted not long before his death. It's certainly old enough, so who knows?"

They all looked at the portrait. The pigments had darkened gradually over the years, but the image was still clear. The portrait showed a grim, unsmiling middle-aged man, posed uncomfortably in a large upholstered chair. He was dressed in battered leather armour, and his face was lined and weathered. He looked as though he would have been more at home riding a horse into combat than sitting for an official Family portrait. There was an air of strength and wildness about him, and his great mane of white hair and sharp, beaked nose reminded Hawk uncannily of a bird of prey, trained to duty but never tamed. Hawk had no trouble at all seeing him as a man who would do bloody crimes in the heat of passion.

Everyone jumped slightly as the door behind them swung suddenly open and the butler Greaves entered. He stepped to one side, and formally announced the arrival of Marc and Alistair MacNeil. The two men entered together, though with enough space between them to suggest they were neither comfortable nor happy in each other's company. They both bowed briefly to Jamie MacNeil.

Marc was tall and slender, with a broad, bland face and a cool, unhappy smile. He looked to be in his late twenties,

if you ignored his prematurely thinning hair, and he wore
the latest fashion poorly, as though indifferent to the effect
it was supposed to achieve. He looked like the kind of
man who attaches himself to groups at parties, in the hope
someone will talk to him. His handshake was harsh and
perfunctory, and his lips lingered almost obnoxiously over
Fisher's hand. Jamie introduced him as another distant
cousin, from Upper Markham.

"That makes him almost a neighbour of yours," said
Jamie, smiling happily at Hawk and Fisher. "I'm sure you'll
have lots in common to talk about."

"Oh good," said Hawk.

Marc sniffed. "I rather doubt it. No one worth knowing
ever came out of *Lower* Markham."

There was an icy silence. Hawk's hand fell to his belt
before remembering he didn't have his axe anymore. Fisher
quickly dropped a restraining hand on his arm. Marc smiled
stiffly, almost as though daring Hawk to take offense at
such an obvious truth.

"That's enough!" said Jamie sharply. "There will be no
duels in the Tower while I'm the MacNeil. Now apolo-
gize, Marc."

"Of course," said Marc. "I'm sorry."

His tone made the apology sound like another insult.
Hawk's scowl deepened. Fisher tightened her grip on his
arm. Hawk bowed stiffly, and turned his back on Marc to
greet Alistair MacNeil. Marc sniffed again, and turned
away to help himself to a drink from one of the wine decanters set out on the sideboard. Fisher breathed a silent
sigh of relief, let go of Hawk's arm, and took a long drink
from her glass.

Alistair shook Hawk's hand firmly, and kissed Fisher's
hand with old-fashioned style. He smiled at them both, an
open, friendly smile that did much to dispel the cool atmosphere left by Marc's comments. "Good of you to make
such a long journey; it can't have been easy, getting here
from Lower Markham at this time of year."

"We felt we ought to be here," said Fisher. "Did you
have far to come?"

"Quite a way. I'm another of those cousins the Family
doesn't like to admit to knowing. I was brought up here in
the Tower, but the Family packed me off to the Red

Marches when I was a young man. Got a parlour maid into trouble and couldn't pay my gambling debts. Nothing too outrageous, but someone thought I needed to be made an example of, so off I went. Can't say I regret it. I could have come back long ago, but never saw the point. Lovely area, the Red Marches. Marvelous scenery, good hunting, and always a chance for some action on the borders. That's how I heard about Duncan's death. Beastly bad luck, by all accounts. So, I decided it was time to come back and pay my respects to the new MacNeil. Good of you to put me up, Jamie. I couldn't stick Haven. Place has gone to the dogs. Not at all how I remember it."

Hawk studied the man unobtrusively while he spoke. Alistair MacNeil was tall and muscular, though obviously well into his fifties. His stomach was intimidatingly flat, his back poker straight, and if Alistair was carrying a few extra pounds anywhere, Hawk was damned if he could spot them. His clothes were undeniably old-fashioned but exquisitely cut, and Alistair wore them with unconscious style. His iron-grey hair was cropped close to his head, military fashion, but he had the same beaked nose and piercing eyes as the man in the portrait. Alistair caught Hawk glancing from him to the portrait over the fire, and chuckled dryly.

"There is a resemblance, isn't there? You're not the first to spot it. Doesn't look such a bad type to me. Probably just too much energy and not enough wars to keep him occupied."

"Don't glorify the man," said Marc, staring up at the portrait, a large drink in his hand. "A soldier in those days was just a paid killer, nothing more. All his masters had to do was point him in the right direction and turn him loose. Probably killed women and children too if they got in his way."

"They were hard times," said Alistair coldly. "The Low Kingdoms faced threats on all sides. The minstrels like to sing of honour and glory, but there's damn all glory for the quick or the dead on a battlefield. There's just the blood and the flies, and the knowledge it will all have to be done again tomorrow. You should try a spell in the army yourself, Marc. You might learn a few things."

"If you say so," said Marc. He turned his back on Alistair, and stared coldly at Jamie. "May I enquire how much longer we have to wait before the reading of the will? The sooner this tedious ritual is over and done with, the better. The Tower is undoubtedly charming, for its age, but I have business to attend to in Haven."

"We'll get to the will soon enough," said Jamie evenly. "There are two more guests to join us, and then breakfast will be served. I think we'll all feel better for a good meal before getting down to business."

"I'm not hungry," said Marc.

"You speak for yourself," said Hawk.

The door opened, and a faded-looking jester hurried in, unannounced by the butler. At least Hawk assumed the man was a jester. He couldn't see any other reason for wearing an outfit like that, short of an extremely convincing death threat. Personally speaking, Hawk would rather have taken his chances with the death threat. The newcomer was a rotund little man, brimming with eager nervous energy. His bright eyes flashed indiscriminately in every direction, much like his smile, and his quick bow to Jamie MacNeil was little more than a familiar nod. The newcomer was well into his sixties, and looked it, but his costume looked to be even older. It had clearly started out life as a bright and gaudy coat of many colors, but over the many years the colors had faded, stitches had burst, and a whole mess of new patches, clearly more functional than decorative, had been added. And then, finally, Hawk saw the guitar in the man's hand, and his heart sank. Jamie smiled briefly at the man, and then turned to his guests.

"My friends, this is my minstrel, Robbie Brennan. Been with this Family for almost thirty years, haven't you, Robbie? I have to leave for a moment, so play something for my guests; some tale of my father's exploits, in his memory."

Brennan nodded cheerfully, tried a few quick dissonant chords, and launched into an uptempo ballad. He sang three songs altogether, each of them highly romanticized tales of Duncan MacNeil's past. They were all cut from the same cloth, full of great adventures and daring escapes, but though they couldn't seem to decide whether Duncan had been a saint or a warrior, a mighty lover or a devoted family man, they all had one thing in common: All three songs were irredeemably awful. They were badly written, played with no style and too much feeling, and Brennan's voice was all over the place. He had the kind of singing voice that made you long for the sound of fingernails scraping down a blackboard, and an extremely irritating habit of shifting his voice up or down an octave when he couldn't reach the right note.

Hawk's hands closed into fists halfway through the first song. By the second, Fisher had to physically restrain him by clinging determinedly but unobtrusively to his arm. Hawk didn't care much for minstrels at the best of times, which this definitely wasn't, and he had a particular loathing for this kind of smug, cleaned-up hero worship. He usually tended to express this unhappiness by throwing the offending minstrel through the nearest window. Fisher, feeling strongly that this might not go down too well with Jamie MacNeil, clung firmly to Hawk's sword arm with both hands.

Brennan finally ground to a halt in a series of crashing chords and bowed more or less gracefully to his stunned audience. There was scattered applause, possibly out of relief that the performance was over. Hawk was grinding his teeth behind a fixed smile.

"Clap him, dammit," said Fisher, out of the corner of her mouth.

"Forget it," growled Hawk. "If we encourage him, he might do an encore. And I swear if I hear one more hey-nonny-no out of him, I'm going to ram his fingers up his nose till they stick out his ears."

Katrina got the minstrel a drink, and the two of them stood chatting together. Jamie came back into the room and went over to join Hawk and Fisher. He checked to make sure Brennan wasn't watching, and then shook his head ruefully.

"He's not very good, is he? Sorry to put you through that, but it's expected of me that I have my own minstrel. Family tradition and all that. Robbie was my father's minstrel, and I seem to have inherited him. He hasn't improved over the years. Dad had cloth ears, but liked to sing, even though he couldn't carry a tune in a bucket. Robbie suited him very well. Besides, when all is said and done, he and Dad fought back to back on a dozen major campaigns, when they were both a lot younger. Least I can do is give

Robbie a safe berth at the end of his days. I just wish I could convince him to retire. . . ."

He looked round as the door opened yet again, and the butler Greaves ushered in two more guests. Hawk looked too, and his stomach lurched as though one of his feet had just slipped over the edge of a precipice. He knew one of the men in the doorway, and worse still, that man knew Captain Hawk. Jamie moved quickly over to greet the new arrivals, grinning broadly. Hawk struck his best aristocratic pose, and smiled determinedly. It seemed he was about to find out just how good his disguise really was.

Lord Arthur Sinclair smiled graciously at Jamie and strolled amiably forward into the drawing room, wineglass in hand, blinking vaguely about him. He was short, barely five foot tall, and sufficiently overweight so that he looked even shorter. He had a round, guileless face and smiled a lot at nothing in particular, but his uncertain blue eyes gave him a lost, confused look. He was in his mid-thirties, with thinning yellow hair and the beginnings of a truly impressive set of jowls. He was also a drunk.

He had no talents and no abilities, and thanks to his Family, little or no self-esteem. He spent most of his time at parties, while the more conservative members of High Society murmured darkly that he'd no doubt come to a bad end. To the surprise of everyone, not least himself, he'd inherited all his Family's wealth, and for want of anything better to do had spent the last few years trying to drink himself to death. All in all, he was making a pretty good job of it; the first and only time he'd made a success of anything. He dabbled occasionally in politics, just for the fun of it, and had briefly been a member of the infamous Hellfire Club. Which was where Hawk had met him, while working on a case. Hawk tried not to feel too worried. Sinclair had been pretty drunk when they met. But then, he usually was. . . .

Fisher, meanwhile, had been keeping an eye on the other new arrival. Jamie had introduced him to the room at large as David Brook, an old friend. Like most people in Haven, Fisher had heard of the Brook Family; they had a long tradition of high achievement in the army and the diplomatic corps. To excel in one or the other was not unusual, but to excel in both was almost unheard of. Particularly in

Haven, where diplomacy was usually just another way of sneaking up on an encmy when he wasn't looking. But, that was the Brooks for you; brave and intelligent. A deadly combination.

David himself was a brisk, heavyset man of slightly less than average height, well into his late twenties, and dressed impeccably if somewhat gaudily in the very latest fashion. He clapped Jamie companionably on the shoulder, and strode forward to shake hands with the bemused Hawk. He lingered acceptably over Fisher's hand as he kissed it, and Fisher's smile widened approvingly, almost in spite of herself. David Brook was devilishly handsome, in a dark, swarthy way. And he knew it.

He excused himself with polished regret, and moved quickly over to join Holly. She smiled shakily at him with open relief, and for the first time that morning, some of the fear seemed to go out of her. She and David smiled and murmured together with the ease of long affection, their heads so close as to be almost touching. Lord Sinclair shook Hawk's hand and kissed Fisher's, smiling vaguely all the while, and then wandered over to join David and Holly, blinking owlishly as he waited to be noticed. They broke apart reluctantly, and Holly smiled at Sinclair with the kind of resigned affection usually reserved for puppies that are cute and lovable but only barely housebroken.

Jamie returned to top up Hawk's glass, and he nodded gratefully. Jamie noticed Hawk's interest in Holly's admirers, and he raised an eyebrow. "Do you know David or Arthur?"

"No," said Hawk quickly. "But I have heard of Lord Arthur. I understand he likes his drink. . . ."

Jamie snorted. "That's like saying a fish likes swimming. But you don't want to believe everything you hear. Arthur's a decent enough sort, when you get to know him. He and David have always been close. And Holly and David have been practically engaged since they were ten. Childhood sweethearts, and all that. And I'll say this for Arthur; he stuck by us when all our other so-called friends ran for cover."

"He wouldn't be the first to find courage in a bottle," said Marc, appearing as usual seemingly out of nowhere. "Probably too drunk and too foolish to be scared."

"You think so?" said Jamie. His voice was polite, but his eyes were hard.

Marc sniffed. "I know his sort."

"No," said Jamie. "You don't know him at all. Now, if you'll excuse me, I have to consult with Greaves about breakfast."

He smiled at Hawk and Fisher, nodded briefly to Marc, and left. Hawk didn't blame him. Marc's voice had the kind of insensitive arrogance that would have had a saint's hands curling into fists. Fisher fixed Marc with a thoughtful stare.

"You don't approve of Lord Arthur?"

"He's weak. I despise weakness. You have to be strong in this world or it'll grind you under."

"We can't all be strong," said Fisher.

Marc smiled coldly. "You don't have to be. You're beautiful. There will always be someone ready to be strong for you."

He turned away, ignoring Hawk's glare, and went to stare out the wide window at the morning sunlight.

"Take it easy," said Fisher amusedly to Hawk. "We're supposed to be brother and sister, remember?"

"So I'm a very protective brother. Watch yourself with that one, Isobel. I don't trust him."

"I don't trust any of them, but I take your point. Don't worry; I know how to handle his sort."

Hawk looked at her quickly. "We're Quality now; if there's to be any rough stuff, I'll take care of it. You concentrate on being demure and ladylike." Fisher raised an eyebrow, and Hawk had to smile. "Or at least as close as you can get."

Fisher gestured surreptitiously, and Hawk fell silent as Katrina Dorimant came over to join them. She nodded briefly to Fisher and then unleashed the full force of her smile on Hawk. It was a warm, intimate smile, suffused with promise, backed up by dark and unsettlingly direct eyes. Hawk smiled uncomfortably back, unconsciously standing a little taller and sucking in his gut. If Isobel hadn't been there he might have just relaxed and enjoyed it, but as it was . . . He glanced at Isobel and was relieved to find she was smiling, apparently amused at his discomfort. Hawk decided he'd better play this very carefully. On the one hand, he couldn't afford to antagonize his host's

Aunt, but on the other hand, if Isobel stopped finding this funny long enough to get jealous . . . Hawk winced inwardly.

"I'm so glad you're here, Richard," said Katrina smoothly.

"Really?" said Hawk, his voice nowhere near as even as he would have liked.

"Oh yes," said Katrina. "I was starting to think I'd have to spend this weekend all alone. I do so hate to be alone."

"There are other guests here," Fisher pointed out.

Katrina shrugged, without taking her eyes off Hawk. "Alistair's too old, Arthur's too fat, David only has eyes for Holly, and Marc gives me the creeps. I don't like the way he looks at me. I'd begun to despair, until you arrived, Richard."

"I understand you're . . . separated from your husband," said Hawk, out of a feeling he ought to be contributing something to the conversation.

"That's right. My husband's Graham Dorimant, a sort of somebody in local politics. We're going to be divorced as soon as I can get the goods on him."

Hawk felt a strong inclination to turn and beat his head against the nearest wall. Was this case going to be nothing but one complication after another? Not only did he have to worry about Arthur Sinclair recognizing him, but now the woman who was making eyes at him turned out to be the estranged wife of someone else who knew him. Hawk and Fisher had met Graham Dorimant on a previous case, not all that long ago. If by some chance Graham had discussed that case with Katrina . . . A sudden thought sobered Hawk like a rush of cold water. Hawk and Fisher had made a great impression on Graham Dorimant. It could be that he'd described the two Guards he'd met fully enough for Katrina to recognize them even through their disguises. And if she had, what better way to distract them than by making a play for Hawk? But that assumed she had a reason for distracting them, which meant . . .

The door opened, and Greaves entered to announce that breakfast would be served shortly in the dining room. As everyone present moved towards the door, Katrina quickly latched onto Hawk's arm.

"It is good of you to escort me into breakfast, Richard. You will sit with me, won't you?"

"I ought really to sit with my sister," said Hawk, knowing how feeble it sounded even as he said it.

"Oh, don't mind me," said Fisher promptly. "You enjoy yourself, Richard."

Hawk gave her a hard look.

"Breakfast won't be much, I'm afraid," said Katrina chummily as they moved out into the corridor. "Cook left two days ago, along with what was left of the kitchen staff. But Greaves and Robbie Brennan have been managing between them until the new staff arrive."

Hawk looked at her sharply. "I thought you couldn't get servants to stay here, because of the sightings?"

Katrina laughed. "This is Haven, Richard. Money can buy anything here. They won't be top-notch staff, of course, but they'll do. Until we can sort this mess out. Now, what was I saying? Oh yes; breakfast. Cold collation, I'm afraid, but I suppose I shouldn't complain. It's very good for the figure, and I have been putting on a little weight recently."

She glanced coquettishly at Hawk, obviously expecting some chivalrous denial. He was still trying to come up with an answer that was both polite and noncommittal when they reached the dining room, at the end of the long, twisting corridor. The room was grand in design, if not in scale, most of it taken up by the single great table, which looked as though it could easily seat thirty, and another dozen or so if everyone was feeling chummy. A magnificent white tablecloth lay half hidden under the glistening silver service and three blazing candelabra.

Everyone took seats at one end of the table with a minimum of fuss, and Hawk ended up with Katrina on one side and Fisher on the other. Arthur Sinclair was sitting opposite him, and Hawk's heart missed a beat as that gentleman suddenly leaned forward and addressed him.

"Tell me . . . Richard?"

"Yes."

"Yes, Richard . . . something I've been meaning to ask you. Why is your hair black and your sister's yellow?"

"Mother was frightened by an albatross," said Hawk solemnly.

Lord Arthur blinked at him, nodded, and returned his

attention to his wineglass. Hawk looked at the setting in front of him and panicked briefly as he found he didn't even recognize some of the more sophisticated cutlery. *Start at the outside and work inwards,* he told himself firmly, reaching for the outer knife and fork. *It's got prongs on it; it's got to be a fork.* . . . Greaves and Robbie Brennan appeared through the swinging service door, carrying trays of cold meats and artfully arranged raw vegetables.

"When you're ready, Greaves, do you think you could do something about the fire?" said Jamie. "It seems rather cold in here today."

"Of course, sir." Greaves gestured for Brennan to put his trays down on the table and see to the fire. Brennan gave him a look, but did as he was bid.

For a while, there was only the occasional murmur of conversation as everyone heaped their plates and then set about the serious business of breakfast. Hawk in particular tucked into his food with gusto, but Marc, sitting opposite Fisher, seemed to be just toying with his. Hawk assumed he was one of those people who couldn't face a heavy meal first thing in the morning. Meanwhile, the minstrel had called on Greaves to help him get the fire going. Hawk smiled slightly. The butler obviously didn't care at all for being involved in such a menial task. He gave Brennan a hard look, and then reached gingerly up into the chimney to tug at some obstruction. Whatever it was, it didn't want to budge, and Greaves had to try again, harder. And then he and Brennan jumped back from the fireplace with cries of shock and horror as a body fell down out of the chimney and crashed into the grate. It was a man, entirely naked and stained with soot, and very obviously dead. The whole of his face had been burned away by the fire.

4

Wolf in the Fold

For a long moment nobody stirred, and then there was a general scramble round the table as people surged to their feet. Greaves backed away from the body, unable to take his eyes off it, until he bumped into the edge of the table behind him. Brennan stayed where he was, rooted to the spot. Hawk pushed past them both and knelt down beside the dead man. Jamie and Alistair crowded in behind him, peering over his shoulder but apparently unwilling to get any closer than that to the body. Fisher leaned gingerly into the fireplace and peered up the chimney, just in case it held any more nasty surprises. Everyone else huddled together at the far end of the table, torn between edging closer for a better look and making a mad dash for the door. Holly's face was bone white, and she clung desperately to Katrina for support. Katrina patted her niece's hands in an absent-minded, comforting way while she craned her neck to see what was happening. David and Arthur had both moved to put themselves between the ladies and the dead man, as much out of gallantry as anything. Marc stood beside them, gazing with fascination at the dead man.

Hawk did his best to ignore Jamie and Alistair breathing down his neck, and looked the dead man over carefully, starting at what was left of the head and working his way slowly down the body. There were a number of cuts and scrapes, presumably from being wedged up the chimney, but no sign of any death wound. He turned his attention back to the burned face, and winced despite himself. The eyes and nose were gone, and the teeth grinned horribly through a mask of charred flesh and bone. There was no hair left, and the ears were nothing more than blackened nubs. Hawk breathed shallowly through his mouth, trying to avoid the smell. He'd seen many dead men in his time, often in worse condition than this, but there was something disturbingly cold and calculating in the manner of this man's death. He touched the man's shoulder gently with his fingertips. The flesh was cold to the touch, already showing the purplish bruises caused by blood sinking to the lowest part of the body. The dead man had been in the chimney for some time. Maybe overnight. Hawk tried the neck, but it didn't seem to be broken. He worked the dead man's arm gently, and it bent easily at the elbow, indicating rigor mortis either hadn't set in yet or had been and gone. Hawk frowned. That was probably a clue as to how long the man had been dead, but he didn't understand such things. He'd never needed to. That was what forensic sorcerers were for. He looked round sharply as Jamie MacNeil crouched down beside him. Alistair leaned in closer, one hand resting supportively on Jamie's shoulder.

"How did he die, do you think?" said Jamie steadily.

"Hard to tell," said Hawk. "There's no actual death wound that I can see, just the damage to the face."

"Nasty way to go," said Alistair. "I once knew a tribe of savages who killed their prisoners this way; hung them over an open fire till their brains boiled. Nasty."

"I don't think that's what happened here," said Hawk slowly. "Look at the back of the head." He gingerly lifted the burned head off the floor so they could see. "The face has been totally destroyed, but the back of the head is barely touched. I think someone pushed this poor bastard's face into the fire and held it there till he died."

"Gods!" Jamie looked suddenly as though he might vomit, and turned his head away, eyes squeezed shut.

"There's no sign of any struggle here, as far as I can see," said Fisher, her voice coming hollowly from inside the chimney. She ducked her head back out, and beat soot from her hair and shoulders. "Looks to me like he was already dead when the killer stuffed him up the chimney."

She started towards the group round the body, but Alistair moved quickly to block her way. "That's quite close enough, my dear. Please return to the others. This is no sight for a young lady such as yourself."

Fisher was about to ask sarcastically whether he was referring to the dead man's injuries or his nakedness, when she caught Hawk glaring at her. At which point she remembered she was supposed to be a sheltered young flower of the Quality, not a hardened city Guard, and she went reluctantly back to join the others. She put a comforting arm round Holly's shaking shoulders and listened carefully to what was being said about the dead man.

"Any idea who this is? Or rather, was?" said Hawk to Jamie.

The MacNeil looked back at the body. His face was very pale, but his gaze was steady and his mouth was firm. "Whoever he is, he shouldn't be here. The last of the servants left two days ago, and the only guests I know of are all in this room."

"Maybe one of the servants came back," said Alistair.

"Not without Greaves knowing, and he would have told me." Jamie shook his head slowly. "None of this makes any sense. No one could have got in past the Tower's wards without setting off all kinds of alarms. It's impossible. And who would want to kill a man here, and like . . . that? It's insane!"

Alistair gripped Jamie's shoulder firmly. "Easy, lad. Don't go to pieces on us now. You're the MacNeil, and the others will be looking to you for guidance. We have a murderer loose in the Tower somewhere, and we have to find him. Before he strikes again."

"He's right," said Hawk. "This is a very nasty business, Jamie. You'd better call in the Guard."

"No!" said Alistair sharply. "This is a Family matter. We don't bring outsiders into Family business."

Hawk got to his feet and stared at Alistair. "What century are you living in? You can't keep the Guard out of something like this! This is murder we're talking about, not who put some chambermaid up the stick. Our best bet is to get the hell out of here, send for the Guard, and then block off all the exits till they get here. Let them find the killer; they're experts."

"I'm afraid it's not that simple," said Jamie, rising to his feet. "I've already raised the final wards. I did it just now, so that we could get on with the reading of the will. I never thought . . . The wards can't be lowered for another twenty-four hours. That's the way they're designed. I'm sorry; there's nothing I can do. None of us can leave the Tower."

David Brook stepped forward, staring disbelievingly at Jamie. "Are you saying that we're all trapped in here with a killer? That whatever happens, there's no way out?"

"Yes," said Jamie. "I'm afraid so." He stopped abruptly and looked at Hawk, who was frowning down at the body. "What is it, Richard?"

"I was just wondering why the killer took the time to strip the body naked. Presumably the killer didn't want us to be able to identify the victim. Which suggests that at least one of us would have recognized him. That explains the burned face, as well."

There was a short pause, broken by Fisher. "Something else to think about. That body had been wedged quite a way up the chimney, going by the traces I found. Whoever the killer is, he must be pretty strong. It can't have been easy, stuffing a limp dead body feet first up a chimney."

Holly moaned quietly, and several of the others looked quite disturbed by Fisher's remark.

"The man must have been mad," said David. "Madmen are supposed to be incredibly strong, aren't they?"

Alistair cleared his throat meaningfully. "Thank you for sharing your thoughts with us, Isobel, but I really feel you and the other ladies should withdraw. This is not a subject suitable for your tender ears."

"No!" said Hawk quickly. "I don't want anyone going off on their own. Unless they like the idea of being an easy target. Until we know what the hell's going on here, we'd do better to stick together. There's safety in numbers."

Jamie looked at him strangely. "You sound almost as though you've had experience with this sort of thing before, Richard."

Being called Richard brought Hawk up short, as he remembered who he was supposed to be. He shrugged, thinking quickly. "There was a murder at one of the inns Isobel and I stayed at on our way here. I did a lot of thinking about it afterwards, and all the sensible things I should have done. But you're the MacNeil, Jamie, and this is your home. You're in charge. I wasn't trying to usurp your authority."

"Don't be daft," said Jamie. "This is all new to me. If you've got any ideas on what we ought to be doing, speak out."

"Well, to start with I think we should get back to the drawing room. I don't think we ought to move the body, and we can't hope to discuss this mess sensibly while it's lying right there in front of us."

"Are you saying we should just leave the body here?" said Robbie Brennan.

"Why not?" said Alistair. "It's not going anywhere."

"At least cover him," said Katrina unsteadily. "Give the poor man some dignity."

"And just what are we supposed to cover him with?" asked Marc. "I'm afraid I didn't think to bring a shroud with me to breakfast."

"Maybe someone could fetch a cloak from the main hall," said David.

"No!" said Holly quickly. "You heard Richard; it's not safe for anyone to go off on their own."

"We can't just leave the man like this!" said Katrina shrilly, with a stubbornness that bordered on hysteria. "He's got to be covered decently!"

Fisher grabbed one end of the magnificent white tablecloth and gave it a good hard jerk. Food, china, cutlery, and flowers went flying in all directions. The candelabra collapsed, and rivers of spilled wine cascaded over the sides of the table as she kept pulling. The last of the tablecloth finally came free, and Fisher draped it roughly over the dead man. Jamie stared speechlessly at the mess she'd made, and then looked at her. She smiled back at him.

"Can we get the hell out of here now?" she said pointedly. "This place makes me nervous. Besides, I need a good stiff drink, and the good brandies are back in the drawing room."

Hawk fought to keep the smile off his lips. He should have known Fisher wouldn't be able to keep up the demure young lady pose for long. He supposed he should be grateful that at least she hadn't hit anyone yet. He coughed loudly to draw everyone's attention back to him.

"If we're going to move, let's move. If nothing else, I think we'll be safer in the drawing room. It's a lot easier to defend than this place. There are too many doors here for my liking."

Alistair nodded approvingly. "Good thinking, lad. The

drawing room's only got one door, and we can barricade that if necessary."

Katrina's hand rose unsteadily to her mouth, and her eyes widened. "You mean the murderer might try and attack us?"

"It's possible," said Hawk. "We don't know what we're dealing with yet."

"I think you're all worrying needlessly," said Marc. "This is one man we're talking about, not an army. If worst comes to worst, there are more than enough of us here to overpower him."

"It might not be that simple," said Jamie slowly. "There's only one man who could have done something like this. The freak. He's got out, after all these years, and he wants revenge. Revenge on the Family that walled him up alive."

Silence fell across the dining room as they all looked at each other, the tension almost crackling on the air. Hawk silently cursed the young MacNeil. He'd already worked out that the freak was most likely the murderer, but he'd wanted the others safely back in the drawing room before he told them. The last thing he needed was a panic here. He tried his cough again, and everyone's eyes shot to him.

"There'll be time to discuss all this later," he said firmly. "Right now, I want everyone concentrating on getting back to the drawing room safely."

"What gives you the right to give everyone orders?" said Marc. "Why should we listen to you?"

"Because he's talking sense," said Jamie. "All right, Richard, let's take a look out in the corridor and make sure it's clear."

The two of them moved over to the main door, eased it open a crack, then took turns peering out down the corridor. Nothing moved in the clear morning light, and the few shadows were comfortingly small. Jamie looked at Hawk.

"How do you want to do this, Richard?"

Hawk frowned. "First thing, all the men draw their swords. Just in case. I'll go first, then you and Alistair. The women will come after us, with the rest of the men bringing up the rear." He looked back at the others and gave them his best reassuring smile. "There's no reason for anyone to be worried. We're just taking sensible precautions, that's all."

None of them looked particularly convinced. Hawk sighed, and gave up on the smile. He'd always done better with a glare than a smile. He looked at Jamie for help, and the MacNeil quickly got everyone moving with a brisk mixture of tact and authority. Hawk nodded approvingly. Jamie had the right touch; that particular mixture of arrogance and charm that was the hallmark of the aristocracy. Hawk led them out into the corridor, and headed back to the drawing room at a carefully unhurried pace. It wouldn't do to take it too quickly; most of them were so rattled they'd break into a run first chance they got. And that would be a real recipe for disaster. Once they were all just running wildly, the freak could pick any one of them off without being noticed. So Hawk strode along at a casual pace, carefully checking each turn of the corridor as he came to it. Luckily he had a good head for direction. Unlike Isobel. She could get lost going to the jakes in a strange inn, and had done, before now.

The corridor seemed subtly different than it had the last time he'd walked it. The light grew dimmer as they left the windows behind them, and came to depend more and more on the wall lamps. The shadows grew darker and larger, and it was easy to imagine something cruel and menacing waiting patiently in the darkness for them to pass. Every door was a potential threat, every turn in the corridor a potential trap. The quiet seemed increasingly sinister, broken only by the soft scuffing and shuffling of their feet on the polished floor. Hawk hefted the light duelling sword in his hand, and wished more than ever for his axe.

He scowled furiously as he tried to figure out what to do next. The last time he and Fisher had been trapped in an isolated house with a group of guests and a killer on the loose, things had gone terribly wrong. He and Fisher had put a stop to the killings eventually, but not before too many innocent people had died. Hawk's frown deepened. He was damned if he'd let that happen again. He tensed and lifted his sword as someone came up alongside him, but it was only Alistair.

"Hold your water, lad, it's just me. Wanted to congratulate you on how you're handling things. You've had military experience, haven't you?"

"Actually, no," said Hawk. "I know it's not really my place to be taking charge and giving orders, but everyone else seemed too shaken, and there were things that needed to be done. We weren't safe in the dining room."

"You'll get no arguments from me on that, lad. I haven't felt easy in the Tower since I arrived. Place feels . . . secretive. But . . . do you really think the freak is that dangerous? He's only one man."

Hawk scowled unhappily. "I don't know. He's a mystery, and I don't like mysteries. When you get right down to it, the freak is most dangerous because he doesn't fit any normal pattern. Most murders involve people who know each other, people who kill either for business reasons or in the heat of passion. But we're dealing with someone who's spent centuries in solitary confinement, building his madness year by year and honing his hate to a cutting edge. He could do anything, for any reason; which means we haven't a hope in hell of out-thinking him. All we can do is stack the odds in our favour as much as we can."

"Very sensible," said Alistair. He looked thoughtfully at Hawk. "No offence, Richard, but you do seem to know an uncommon lot about murders and murderers. Mind telling me how you came by that knowledge?"

"Of course not," said Hawk, thinking quickly. "There's not much to do in Lower Markham, so I read a lot. Crime fascinates me. Especially murders. So that's what I read about. Mostly."

Alistair made no comment, just nodded and dropped back to rejoin Jamie. Hawk sighed. It wasn't the best answer he could have come up with, but then, thinking on his feet had never been what he did best. Except when he was fighting. But he was going to have to be more careful. He had to think like a Guard if he was going to solve this case, but he couldn't afford to act like one. If Jamie was to find out he'd revealed his Family's darkest Secret to an outsider, and a city Guard at that . . .

There was a collective sigh of relief as they hurried down the last stretch of corridor and reached the drawing room without incident. Hawk was first in, and quickly checked the room was secure. He then ushered the others in, and checked the door for bolts. There weren't any, so he wedged a chair up against the door and settled for that. Some of the tension went out of him, and he let out a long, weary sigh. In a situation like this, looking out for yourself was tiring enough, without having to worry about a bunch of civilians, half of whom were jumping at their own damn shadows.

They were already splitting up into smaller groups, turning to those they trusted most for comfort and support. Jamie and Alistair were talking urgently together, with a fair amount of arm waving from both of them. David Brook and Lord Arthur were trying to help Katrina soothe Holly, who was still trembling pitifully. Marc stood with them, holding a drink for Holly, his face as calm and composed as ever. Hawk studied him a moment, frowning thoughtfully. Of them all, Marc had coped best with the situation. He might well prove a useful ally if things started getting out of control. Whatever else you could say about Marc, the man had guts. Hawk looked away, and his gaze settled on Brennan and Greaves. They were standing patiently together not far from Jamie and Alistair, waiting for orders. Fisher came over to join Hawk with a snifter of brandy in each hand. Hawk accepted his gratefully.

"Well?" said Fisher. "How do you read this? What the hell's going on here?"

Hawk shrugged. "You got me. What little evidence there is points in half a dozen different directions at once. I did some thinking on the way here, and I've managed to narrow it down to three main possibilities. First, and most obvious, is that the freak really has got loose, and has graduated from breaking up the furniture to killing people. That doesn't explain who the dead stranger is, though, or why the freak chose him as his first victim, rather than one of us.

"Second choice, equally obvious: This is all something to do with the spy Fenris. Perhaps the dead man was to be Fenris' contact, and someone killed him to prevent that contact taking place. Or, the dead man could be Fenris, killed by his contact for screwing up his mission. That would explain why the man's face was burned away, so that we wouldn't be able to tell who Fenris really was."

"And finally, there's choice number three: Someone in

this room is a murderer, and killed that man for personal reasons that have nothing to do with Fenris or the freak."

"Great," said Fisher. "Just what we needed. As if this case wasn't complicated enough, we now have a murder mystery on our hands. Great. Bloody marvelous. All right, what do we do? Reveal who we are and take charge?"

"Are you crazy?" said Hawk. "The penalty for impersonating Quality is death by dismemberment, remember? Besides, we don't dare risk our cover until we've got some kind of lead on which of these people is Fenris. Our orders were to prevent Fenris escaping, *no matter what.* We're going to have to do what sleuthing we can undercover, and keep our ideas to ourselves."

"That shouldn't be too difficult," said Fisher. "I haven't got two ideas to rub together."

"Then you haven't been paying attention. We already know Alistair isn't being honest about where he comes from."

"We do?" Fisher looked at him sternly. "You're showing off again, *Richard.* All right, what did I miss this time?"

Hawk couldn't keep all the smile off his lips. "According to Alistair, he comes from the Red Marches. He grew almost lyrical about the marvelous countryside, and the good hunting to be found there. But we passed through the Red Marches on our way to Haven, seven years ago. They've been flooded for the past eighty years. Most of the land is under water now. There's some good fishing here and there, but no hunting. He also talked about getting involved in fighting down on the border, but thanks to the floods, it's been peaceful down there for years. It's the most secure border in the Low Kingdoms these days. But Alistair didn't know that. Interesting, eh?"

"Very," said Fisher. "But why didn't any of the others pick up on it?"

Hawk shrugged. "The Red Marches are pretty remote, and about as far from High Society as you can get. It's probably just a name to most people here. Which is probably what Alistair was counting on."

"I'll tell you who else we ought to keep an eye on," said Fisher, "and that's Katrina. She's still married to Graham Dorimant, who was heavily involved in the local political scene. Since they're separated now, and not at all amicably, it's just possible she might have got involved in outsider politics as a way of getting back at her husband. She could be Fenris' contact. She's been here at the Tower for some time; that could explain why Fenris went to ground here."

"But if he's already met his contact, why hasn't he left?"

"Perhaps he's waiting for her to arrange a safe route out."

"Hold your horses," said Hawk suddenly. "There's another possibility, and one we should have spotted sooner. What if the dead man had been Fenris' contact, and had threatened to abandon Fenris to the authorities, rather than risk any more of the outsider network being discovered? Fenris must know he's facing a death penalty, even if he is Quality. He could have killed his contact to protect himself, and then hidden the body while he tried to figure out what to do next."

"Right," said Fisher. "But he left it too late, and Jamie put the wards up. We've got to identify him before tomorrow, Hawk, or he'll do a runner the moment the wards go down."

"Isobel, will you please call me Richard! Walls have ears, you know, especially in a situation like this."

"Sorry. But if Fenris is our killer, it means we can stop wasting time looking for some imaginary murderous freak. I mean, what proof have we the creature ever existed, apart from Jamie's story?"

Hawk shrugged. "We've seen stranger things in our time."

On the other side of the room, Jamie looked at Alistair almost pleadingly. "We can talk about Richard and Isobel later, Alistair. I've more important things to worry about. What am I going to do about the killing? I'm the MacNeil, the head of the Family; they'll all be looking to me for reassurance and answers I haven't got, and I don't know what to do!"

"To start with, calm down," said Alistair sharply. "Getting hysterical won't help. Let's look at this logically. Now that we know the freak's a killer, what matters most is tracking it down before it strikes again. Which means we have to find the hidden cell. We'll search the Tower from top to bottom, checking each room as we go for hidden panels and secret passages. If the freak got out of his room, there must be a way in. We can split into two groups to save time. I'll take one group, you lead the other. Right?"

"Yes. Right." Jamie breathed deeply twice, and pinched the bridge of his nose hard. It seemed to help. The panic that had all but paralysed him was dropping swiftly away, now that he had a definite goal to focus on. He smiled quickly at Alistair and looked around him. "There's no point in taking everyone with us. The women will be safer here, out of harm's way."

"We'd better leave Lord Arthur behind as well." Alistair's voice was mild, but his gaze was unyielding. "I think he means well, but you can't trust a drunk in a crisis. What about David Brook? Good man?"

"The best," said Jamie. "Good with a sword, level-headed, and doesn't scare easily. Always knows the right thing to do in a tricky situation. I'd trust him with my life. We'll take Greaves, too. He's another steady one; utterly dependable. As for Robbie Brennan . . . he's a stout enough man, and damned good with a sword in his younger days, from what Dad used to say. But that was a long time ago."

"Once a soldier, always a soldier," said Alistair. "The old instincts will still be there, just needing the right moment to bring them out again."

"If you say so. What about Marc?"

Alistair frowned. "He's a cool one, I'll give him that, but I don't know if I'd trust him to guard my back. Still, he doesn't look the type to fold under pressure. And that just leaves Richard. And you know how I feel about him. . . ."

"He seems a solid enough sort," said Jamie. "Somewhat gauche and a bit of a bumpkin, but this is his first trip to the big city, after all. And he was the one who got us all organized when everyone else fell apart at the sight of the body."

"Exactly," said Alistair. "I've seen a good many dead men in my time, but even so, what was left of that poor bastard's face stopped me in my tracks. It didn't throw Richard, though. He was right there, examining the body and cracking out orders. It's not natural, Jamie. And when I asked him about it, do you know what he said? He said murders fascinate him, so he spends all his time reading about them. Never trust a man who reads, Jamie; it gives him ideas. The wrong sort of ideas."

"Maybe. But right now he seems to be the only one of us who knows what he's doing. He goes with us. If only so we can keep a close eye on him."

"I don't trust him," said Alistair. "He's hiding something."

"Everyone has something to hide," said Jamie. "All that matters right now is finding the freak before he kills again. This is my home. Whatever happened through the years, I always felt safe and secure here. The freak's taken that away from me, and I want it back. I want my home back."

Alistair dropped a heavy hand on Jamie's shoulder. "Buck up, lad. We'll find the freak and kill him, and then things'll get back to normal again. You'll see."

Greaves looked disapprovingly at Robbie Brennan as the minstrel helped himself to a second large snifter of brandy. "Look at the state of you. I don't know which makes your hands shake the more, the fear or the drink. The young master will have need of us soon, and he'll be none too pleased if he finds you the worse for drink. Get a hold of yourself, man!"

"Go to hell," said Brennan flatly. "You're a cold fish, Greaves, and always have been. I've never seen an honest emotion cross that cold face of yours in all the years I've known you. It's always been 'yes sir, no sir, can I wipe your arse now, sir?' I've been with this Family for forty years, long before you came along, but I've always been my own man."

Greaves looked at him unflinchingly. "Is this leading anywhere?"

"When I was a man-at-arms in the Broken Flats campaign, I saw more dead men than you could imagine in your worst nightmare. I saw them cut down and ripped apart and piled up in huge heaps under the midday sun, and I never got used to it. Which is why I came out of that campaign sane when a lot of men didn't. Duncan would have understood. It's enough to be strong when you have to be. He never expected a man to be always unmoved and unfeeling, like you. So, right now we've got a freak running loose in the Tower, out for revenge on all of us, but I bet at the end of the day I'll still be standing and you'll be crawling on your knees. Because I know when to bend with the wind, and you don't.''

"You always did have a way with words," said Greaves. "But then, that's all you've got left now, isn't it? Your soldier days were a long time ago. Look at you, shaking and quivering in every nerve, with your snout buried in your glass. And Mister Duncan was always so proud of you, and saying what a fine warrior you were on the battlefield. What would he say if he could see you now?''

"Duncan would have understood." Brennan drained his glass and straightened up a little. "I'll do my bit. You worry about yourself.''

"It's not myself that fills my thoughts, Robbie Brennan. And what worries I have are not for you. It's the young master, the MacNeil himself, that we should be concerned about. He had no choice but to reveal the great Secret to all those . . . people, but it must not pass beyond these walls. If it were to get out, the MacNeil would be ruined. It's up to us to make sure that doesn't happen.''

Brennan frowned. "Just what are you suggesting, Greaves?''

"What I am suggesting, Robbie Brennan, minstrel and sometime friend to the MacNeil Family, is that we make sure only those we can trust leave this Tower alive.''

"If Jamie knew what you're saying . . .''

"He is not to know. It is our job to protect this Family, and do what must be done for its safety. The MacNeil is too young to understand.''

They looked at each other for a long moment, until Brennan finally nodded and put down his empty glass.

Holly accepted a snifter of brandy from Lord Arthur, and nodded her thanks. Her hands were steadying, and some color was finally coming back into her cheeks. She smiled briefly around her, and then lowered her head again. "I'm sorry. I'm not usually like this. It's the shock.''

"It's all right," said Arthur. "We understand.''

"There's no need to hover over her like that, Arthur," said David Brook testily. "Give the poor girl room to breathe.''

Arthur nodded quickly, and stepped back a pace. Holly gripped his hand firmly, and reached out to take David's hand too.

"Please, don't argue. I'm feeling better now. Let's get out of here. We can stay with friends, in the city."

"We can't leave just now, pet," said Katrina soothingly. "You heard your brother; the wards are up. We can't leave the Tower till tomorrow morning. But we're perfectly safe here. Nothing can get to us."

"It'll be all right, Holly," said Arthur. "I won't let anyone hurt you."

David shot him an exasperated look, and turned back to Holly. "We'll look after you, darling. It's obvious who the killer is. It's that damned freak Jamie told us about earlier. All we have to do is track him down."

"No! That's too dangerous. He might kill you!" Holly gripped his hand hard, as though to physically restrain him from leaving. David smiled and patted her hand comfortingly.

"There's nothing to worry about. The freak doesn't stand a chance against all of us. Isn't that right, Arthur? Marc?"

Arthur smiled, and nodded vigorously. Marc turned and looked at them directly for the first time. "We don't know for sure that the freak is the killer. We have no hard evidence, one way or the other. The killer could be anyone. Perhaps even one of us."

There was a long pause as that sank in, and then one by one the others began looking round the room, their gaze lingering on some faces longer than others.

"After all," said Marc, "what do we really know about each other? Even the most ordinary person can do terrible things, under the right conditions. People you've known for years can become strangers in a moment, transfigured by a single insight or a hidden motive. Who is there you can really trust, when you come right down to it? Some days you can't even trust yourself."

"You have to trust someone," said Arthur. "And better a friend than a stranger. Take yourself, for instance. We don't know a single thing about you, except for what you've chosen to tell us. You could have all kinds of secrets, for all we know."

"Oh, honestly, Arthur," said Katrina crushingly. "If Marc did have something to hide, he wouldn't have brought up the subject in the first place, would he? You'll have to excuse Arthur, Marc; his mouth tends to say things before his brain can catch up. Anyway, I think you're barking up the wrong tree, dear. I've known Jamie and David and Arthur for years, and they don't have a malicious bone in their bodies."

"But Alistair, though; that's different. He claims to be just a distant cousin, but he seems to know an awful lot about Family history. He knows things even I didn't know."

"I wish the Guardian were here," said Holly. "I prayed for him to come."

"Yes dear, we know," said Katrina. "But you shouldn't take Family myths so seriously. Most of them are just legends and fireside tales that have grown in the telling."

"The freak turned out to be real," said Holly stubbornly. "So why not the Guardian too?"

"Personally, I have to say I've got a few doubts about Richard," said David thoughtfully. "He seems awfully full of himself, for a minor cousin from Lower Markham. I didn't even know the Family had branches in that part of the world. What about you, Marc? You ever run across either Richard or Isobel before?"

"Never," said Marc flatly. "Their arrival here was a complete surprise to me."

"Now, don't you dare start picking on Richard," said Katrina. "Just because he comes from Lower Markham. We've always known that some parts of the Family have . . . gone down in the world. And remember, he's one of the few people to stick by us, even after he found out about the Secret."

"Yes," said David. "Interesting, that. Why should he and his sister be so loyal? Why come all this way, with winter so close?"

"Presumably, he expects Duncan to make it worth his while in the will," said Arthur.

"Could be," said David. "But that might not be his only motive."

"What other motive could he have?" said Katrina.

"Why don't we ask him?" suggested Marc.

"Yes," said David. "Why don't we?"

But just then Jamie strode forward into the middle of the room and called for everyone's attention, and all conversation died quickly away.

"My friends, I regret to say it, but we can't simply barricade ourselves in here and wait for the wards to go down tomorrow morning. We have a duty and an obligation to find the freak and put an end to its miserable existence."

"But no one's been able to find the bricked-up room for centuries," objected Katrina.

"I've been thinking about the problem," said Jamie, "And I've come up with an idea. Based on certain comments and internal evidence in the notes my father left, I'm pretty sure the freak's cell has some kind of window. Presumably not very large, but enough to allow light to enter. So, I propose we make a tour of the Tower, floor by floor, opening every window and hanging out a marker of some kind, until we've covered them all. Then we go outside and take a look. Whichever window remains unmarked has to be the freak's cell. Shouldn't be too difficult to find the room, with that to point the way."

"It might just work," said Hawk. "It's simple and straightforward. I like it."

"Wait just a minute," said Fisher. "Did you say go *outside* the Tower? I thought we were all trapped in here by the wards?"

"The wards do not become operative until some ten feet beyond the Tower," said Jamie patiently. "And no, I don't know why. The wards themselves were designed hundreds of years ago; I just raise and lower them, as and when needed. Now, if there are no more questions, I think we should make a start."

"Obviously we can't all go," said Alistair. "The women will have to stay here, and someone will have to remain with them, to protect them."

"Right," said Hawk. "And the smaller the search party, the better. No point in risking anyone we don't have to. The freak could be out there anywhere, just waiting for a chance at us. This has to be volunteers only, and people who can look after themselves in a fight. I'll go, for one. Who's with me?"

"You do like to take charge, don't you, Richard?" said Jamie.

"Sorry," said Hawk. "I'm just . . . eager to make a start. But of course you're in charge. You're the MacNeil."

"That's right," said Jamie. "I am. So I'll decide who goes and who stays. Since you're so eager, Richard, you can be part of the group, along with Alistair and myself. How about you, Arthur? Are you any good with a sword?"

"Not really," said Lord Arthur. "Sorry, Jamie, I'm not really up to heroics. But I'll do my best to protect the ladies while you're gone."

"I'd better stay too," said David Brook. "There ought to be one person here who knows one end of his sword from the other."

"I'll go with you, Jamie," said Marc. "I'm fairly proficient with a sword, and I hate being cooped up."

"Mister Brennan and I will be happy to accompany you, sir," said Greaves, stepping forward with the minstrel. Jamie smiled, but shook his head.

"No offense, but I think we'll make better time without you."

"As you wish," said Brennan flatly.

"Don't sulk, Robbie. It doesn't become you. I'd take you if I could, but speed is of the essence, and I think you'll be more useful here. In the meantime, barricade the door behind us once we've gone. Make it sturdy enough to keep the freak out but not so heavy you can't dismantle it fast if we need to get back in here in a hurry. Well, no point in hanging about, is there? We might as well go. Unless there's anything you want to add, Richard?"

"I don't think so, Jamie," said Hawk courteously. "You've covered everything I can think of."

"Then let's go," said Alistair. "We've got a lot of ground to cover."

There was a quick murmur of goodbyes. Jamie took Holly in his arms, and she hugged him hard for a moment before pushing him resolutely away. Hawk pulled the chair away from the door, listened a moment, and then carefully eased the door open. A quick glance up and down the corridor revealed nothing but familiar furniture and the occasional shadow. Everything was still and silent. He stepped out into the corridor, sword in hand, followed by Jamie and Alistair and Marc. The door closed quickly behind them, and there was the sound of furniture being piled against it.

Hawk looked at Jamie for orders, and Jamie hesitated a long moment before nodding to the left. They set off down the corridor, alert for any sudden sound or movement. Despite all that had taken place it was still early in the day, and the corridor was bathed in bright golden sunlight. From out an open window Hawk could hear gulls keening and the distant crash of waves on the rocks far below. Jamie moved over to the window and draped one of the curtains so that it hung out over the windowsill. They continued on down the corridor, swords at the ready, keeping a careful eye on every door they passed. The quiet grew heavy and oppressive, and Hawk's skin prickled uneasily. He hadn't liked breaking up the group, but he could see Jamie was determined to have his way, so he'd gone along with it. But he still didn't feel right about it.

The last time he'd been in a situation like this had been in the sorcerer Gaunt's house. People had insisted on going off on their own, despite everything Hawk and Fisher did to stop them. Most of them had died horribly. He was damned if he'd let that happen again. But there were limits to what he could do in Tower MacNeil; Jamie wasn't about to let him take control of the situation, no matter what. Richard was a minor cousin from Lower Markham, and should accordingly know his place and keep his mouth shut. Hawk smiled sourly. He'd never been very good at that.

He hefted his sword unhappily as they walked along. With only the one eye left, Hawk's depth perception was shot to hell, and his swordsmanship was only a shadow of what it had once been. It didn't affect him so much with the axe. An axe has many qualities and virtues all its own, but subtlety isn't one of them. With an axe, as long as you can see your opponent, you can usually hit him. And a man who's been hit with an axe does not grit his teeth and fight back, as sometimes happens with a sword wound. A man hit solidly by an axe tends rather more to being thrown to the ground with the impact, bleeding copiously and screaming for his mother. Admittedly an axe isn't much use as a defensive weapon, but Hawk never had believed in fighting defensively. He was much more comfortable with an all-out attack, backed up by dirty tricks. Hawk looked disgustedly at the narrow duelling sword in his hand. If it came to a fight, he'd probably be better off throwing the damn thing like a spear.

He scowled, and then winced as a stab of pain flared up around his glass eye. The damn things always made his face

ache after a while. The last doctor he'd seen had told him
the pain was all in his mind, to which Hawk had angrily
retorted that it was all in the eye socket, and what was the
doctor going to do about it? The doctor had recommended
a change to a less stressful occupation, and presented Hawk
with an inflated bill, which Hawk refused to pay.

The tour of the ground floor was accomplished without
incident. The windows had all been marked, and there was
no sign of the freak anywhere. The large rooms, designed
for entertaining were easy to search, and the open, well-lit
corridors offered few hiding places. Jamie led the group
up the curving stairs to the first floor, which was mainly
bedchambers and bathrooms. Everything was still and
quiet, the only sound their own echoing footsteps. Hawk
felt like a child sneaking through his parents' quarters while
they were out.

The endless quiet and occasional false alarms began to
gnaw at Hawk's nerves, but he just shrugged it off and kept
going. He had to set a good example to the others, who
were all starting to show signs of strain. Jamie was getting
jumpy, and showed an increasing tendency to check things
twice or even three times before he was satisfied. Alistair's
scowl was deepening, and he'd taken to hefting his sword
impatiently, as though anxious for a confrontation. And
Marc had withdrawn so far into himself he seemed to be
walking alone through the empty corridors.

The rooms were lavishly appointed, and would have interested Hawk greatly under different circumstances, but as
it was, each gorgeously finished room blended one into another as the tour continued. The first floor passed in a blur
of empty rooms and silent, deserted corridors, and they
made their way up the stairs to the second floor. Hawk
began to wonder if they'd underestimated the freak. They'd
all been talking about him as though he were nothing more
than an animal, all instinct and ferocity, but that was wrong.
The freak was a man, and cunning enough to hide his dead
victim in such a way that the body wasn't found till hours
after the murder. The more Hawk thought about that, the
less he liked it. It was more than possible they were doing
exactly what the freak wanted: wasting time trying to find
his lair while he planned ways of attacking them . . . or
those they'd left behind. . . .

The second floor consisted of servants' quarters; clean and fairly comfortable but essentially nondescript. The only exceptions were Greaves's and Brennan's rooms. The butler's room had a bleak simplicity that suggested he spent as little time there as possible. Everything was neatly lined up and squared off as though for inspection, and Hawk knew without having to be told that woe would betide any maid who moved anything an inch out of place while dusting. Brennan's quarters, on the other hand, were littered with a lifetime's collection of keepsakes and souvenirs, most of them military in nature. There were daggers and swords mounted on the walls, and trinkets and mementoes brought back from a dozen campaigns. Hawk looked them over briefly, and frowned as he realized how dated they were. It was as though Brennan's life had come to an abrupt halt when he came to the Tower; that there was nothing from his new life worth the keeping. . . .

The third floor was storage; endless storerooms packed with the accumulated clutter of generations of MacNeils. Few of the rooms had any windows beyond the narrowest arrow-slits, but Jamie marked them as best he could, and they moved on.

They tramped wearily up the final set of stairs and stepped out onto the open battlements. Hawk took a deep breath as the cold wind hit him, blowing away the cobwebs of fatigue from his mind. The view was magnificent, from the dark labyrinthine sprawl of Haven to the great jagged cliffs that surrounded it, to the vast expanse of the open sea. Gulls hung on the sky far above them, keening on the rising wind like lost souls banned from heaven or hell. Hawk felt he could stand there forever, just drinking in the view.

Alistair stared about him with obvious nostalgia, while Jamie was predictably blasé, having seen it all before. Marc on the other hand, looked once at the sea and the cliffs, and turned away, apparently uninterested. And then he looked out over Haven, and couldn't tear his gaze away. Hawk shrugged inwardly. No accounting for taste.

Finally Jamie led them back down through the Tower to the ground floor. There was still no sign of the freak anywhere, and Hawk could sense they were all beginning to relax a little. The general feeling seemed to be that the

freak would have attacked them by now if he was going
o. Hawk distrusted the feeling. The freak was up to some-
hing, he was sure of it; something so obvious Hawk
couldn't see it for looking. It was as though the freak didn't
care whether they found his lair or not . . . which would
seem to suggest he'd found a better place to hide. Hawk
scowled ferociously and chewed at his lower lip as Jamie
ed them through the entrance hall and out the main door.

The gusting wind caught Hawk's attention again, and he
looked around him. Even after the unobscured view from
the battlements, he'd still been half expecting to see some
shimmering mystical barrier cutting the Tower off from the
rest of the world, but everything seemed perfectly normal.
The cliff edge stretched away before him, and the wind
ruffled the long grass on either side of the trail that led
back down to Haven. A sudden thought struck him. He
only had Jamie's word for it that the wards were actually
there. If by some chance Jamie himself was the spy's contact, what better way to draw attention away from himself
and Fenris than by concocting the story of the murderous
freak? Or could Jamie be Fenris? Either way, it would explain why the spy had headed straight for Tower MacNeil.

But, on the other hand, if the freak was real and the
wards were real, that would have thrown the spy completely off balance. Being trapped in the Tower by the
wards would have been the last thing he'd expected. He'd
have to be getting pretty desperate by now. And desperate
men make mistakes. Hawk pursed his lips thoughtfully. So,
it all came down to whether the wards were actually there.
Either way, the answer to that question would tell him
something important. Unless Fenris had let the freak out
for some reason. . . . Hawk decided he wasn't going to
think about it anymore for a while. It was all getting too
complicated. All that mattered for the moment was checking whether the wards were actually there. He walked casually forward. He hadn't made half a dozen steps before
Jamie called urgently after him, and came running up behind him to grab him by the arm.

"Don't go near the wards, Richard, it isn't safe." He bent
down, picked up a clump of grass and threw it forward. It
flew a few feet and then flared up suddenly, burning soundlessly with a brilliant, eye-searing flame. Within seconds

there were only a few particles of ash, which were carrie
away on the wind. Jamie wiped his hands on a handke
chief, then tucked it neatly away in his sleeve. "Sorry abo
that, Richard. I should have warned you."

"That's all right," said Hawk steadily. "I wasn
thinking."

They both turned away from the wards and joined th
others in circling round the Tower, searching for an empt
window. Curtains and clothing and other markers flappe
fitfully at the many windows and arrow slits. An excite
shout went up as Jamie spotted an unmarked window, onl
to quickly fall away as Alistair and Hawk pointed out tw
more. The four men stood quietly together a moment, look
ing at the Tower and each other.

"Three?" said Jamie. "How the hell can there be thre
windows?"

"Presumably there are two more hidden rooms," sai
Marc.

"And with our luck, two more freaks," said Hawk.

Jamie winced. "Please, Richard. Don't say that. Not eve
as a joke. Things are bad enough without tempting fat
No; whatever those rooms are, they can't have anything t
do with the freak, or Dad would have mentioned them i
his notes."

"Not necessarily," said Alistair.

"We're wasting time," said Marc. "The quickest way t
find out why there are two more hidden rooms is to go an
take a look."

"He's right," said Hawk. "We have to know what's i
those rooms. One of them's got to have the answers w
need."

"Very well, let's go," said Jamie, staring up at the win
dows. "All three rooms are on the third floor. The
shouldn't be too difficult to find."

He led the way back into the Tower and up the stairs
moving at a fast walk that threatened frequently to brea
into a run but somehow never quite did. Hawk admire
Jamie's self-control. It was only the MacNeil's example tha
kept him from taking the steps two at a time at a dead run
They were getting close to the answers now; he could fee
it in his water. He was still cautious enough to keep
watchful eye on his surroundings, but nothing moved in th

shadows and the only sound on the quiet was their own hurried footsteps and harsh breathing. Hawk kept a firm grip on his sword hilt. It was all too easy. Somehow, in some way Hawk didn't understand, the freak was leading them around by the nose. They had to be doing exactly what he wanted, or he'd have attacked them by now. It was the only explanation that made sense.

They burst out onto the third floor, breathing heavily from the stairs, and Jamie strode briskly down the corridor, counting off doorways as he went. He stopped before a featureless stretch of wall, and waited impatiently for the others to catch up. Hawk studied the brickwork dubiously. It looked no different from any other stretch of wall. He looked at Jamie.

"Are you sure this is the right place?"

"Of course I'm sure! I grew up here; I know every floor and every room of Tower MacNeil like the back of my own hand. For example . . ." He walked back a dozen paces, and pressed a piece of stone scrollwork. There was a faint grinding noise, and a section of wall swung slowly open on concealed hinges, revealing a dark, narrow passage. "It's one of the old secret stairways; ends up in the library. One of the more useful shortcuts built into the Tower." He pushed the section of wall shut with a grunt, and it locked silently back into position, with nothing to show it had ever opened.

"Very impressive," said Hawk as Jamie came back to join them. "I'll remember it if I'm in a hurry. In the meantime, if there is a room behind this wall, how do we get in? Break the wall down?"

"That may not be necessary," said Alistair. "Look closely. This particular stretch of brickwork seems more modern than the rest."

They all looked. Hawk was damned if he could see any difference, but didn't say so.

"Look for a hidden catch or lever," said Alistair. "Something that doesn't quite fit, or that seems somehow out of place."

They pressed in close to the wall, running their fingertips across the bricks and mortar, and staring intently at every crack and crevice. In the end, Jamie was the one who found the lever. It was disguised as one of the lamp brackets, and

Jamie had noticed it was a slightly different design than the ones on either side of it. He gave it a good hard tug, and it tilted out of the wall. There was a hesitant rumbling of hidden machinery, and then a section of the wall swung open. Jamie stepped forward to look inside and Hawk moved quickly in beside him, sword at the ready.

The room was small and featureless, lit only by daylight filtering through a narrow slit window. It was completely empty. Hawk scowled and lowered his sword as Marc and Alistair crowded in behind him.

"Why go to all the trouble of setting up a concealed room and then not use it? That's crazy."

"Not really," said Jamie, taking a few steps into the room. "This was probably meant for use as a last-ditch bolt-hole, in times of trouble or unrest. There was a time, not that many Kings ago, when the MacNeils weren't too popular at Court. They made the mistake of telling the King the truth instead of what he wanted to hear, and had the impertinence to stick up for their friends, even when those friends had fallen out of favour. The MacNeils always did have more loyalty than sense. Anyway, this was probably intended as a hiding place for guests the MacNeils weren't supposed to be talking to, or maybe as a refuge for women and children if the Tower was ever put under siege. We MacNeils haven't survived this long without learning a few tricks along the way."

"Damn right," growled Alistair. "Never trust in the gratitude of Kings or politicians. They all have bloody short memories when they feel like it."

Hawk nodded politely, disguising his interest. He hadn't known the MacNeils had a history of bad relations with the Court. That might explain why Fenris had gone to ground at Tower MacNeil in the first place.

"This is all very interesting," said Marc, in a tone that implied it wasn't, at all. "But do you think we could please get a move on? We have two more rooms to find, and the less time we spend on our own up here, the better."

"The lad's right," said Alistair. "We've left the women alone too long as it is."

"They're protected," said Jamie. "They'll be all right till we get back."

Alistair sniffed. "Some protection; a dandy, a drunk,

and two old men. There's no telling what might have happened while we've been gallivanting about up here."

"Then let's stop wasting time arguing and look for the other two rooms," said Hawk, cutting in quickly to head off the row before it got out of hand. "Jamie, is there a tool cupboard, or something like that up here?"

"Of course," said Jamie stiffly. "Why?"

"Well, it just occurred to me that we might not be able to find the hidden mechanisms for the other two rooms, and we might have to get into them the hard way—with sledgehammers and crowbars."

"Good thinking," said Alistair, nodding approvingly. "Well, Jamie?"

"This way," said the MacNeil. He stepped out of the room and started off down the corridor. "Leave the door open," he said over his shoulder. "We might need to find the room again in a hurry."

They found the tool cupboard easily enough, but sorting through the contents took some time. Jamie had never actually looked into it before—that was what servants were for—and he found the contents fascinating, discovering all kinds of things he didn't know he had. He rummaged away happily, while everyone else helped themselves to what they wanted. Alistair and Marc both chose crowbars, hefting them with obvious unfamiliarity, while Hawk went straight for a short-handled sledgehammer with a large flat head. He liked the feel and weight of it. It reminded him of his axe. He swung it easily a few times, and stuck it through his belt. Everyone then had to wait while Jamie searched for a hammer just like Hawk's. He swung it a few times, raised an eyebrow at the weight, and then led the way back down the corridor to the next hidden room.

The hallway grew darker as they moved along. The Tower's architects had seen no reason to waste expensive glass windows on a storage level used mainly by servants, and had mostly made do with arrow slits. There were lamp brackets on the walls at regular intervals, but with all the servants gone, none of the lamps was lit. The group moved from one pool of light to another, plunged occasionally into gloom as clouds passed before the sun, cutting off the daylight. Hawk peered watchfully about him, his free hand resting on the hammer head.

The second stretch of brickwork Jamie indicated looked just as innocuous as the first. Hawk tried all the lamp brackets in the vicinity, but nothing happened. A thorough search of the bricks and mortar failed to turn up any other hidden catches or levers, so they did it the hard way. Hawk and Jamie rolled up their sleeves, Jamie clumsily following Hawk's example, and then they set to work with their sledgehammers on what looked like the weakest spot. The old brickwork gave way surprisingly easily, and they soon opened up a hole big enough for Alistair and Marc to work on with their crowbars while Hawk and Jamie took a rest. When the hole looked big enough, everyone stepped back to let Jamie peer into the gloom beyond.

"Well?" said Mark. "What's in there?"

"Looks like a . . . writing desk," said Jamie. "There are papers on it. I've got to get in there. We'll have to widen the hole some more."

He stepped back, and between them the group knocked and levered away bricks until the hole was big enough for Jamie to squeeze through. Hawk clambered through after him, and then quickly turned to stop Marc and Alistair following him.

"You'd better stay where you are; this looks like a really bad place to be cornered in. Watch the corridor. We'll yell out if we find anything interesting."

Alistair sniffed and turned away, his back radiating disapproval. Marc just nodded and turned away. Hawk moved over to join Jamie, who was leaning over the desk, shuffling through a sheaf of papers and squinting at them in the meager light from the slit window. There was a lamp on the desk. Hawk picked it up and shook it, and heard oil gurgle. He raised an eyebrow. Someone had been in the room recently. Which meant there was a way in that they'd missed. He shrugged and lit the lamp, holding it over the papers. The crabbed handwriting was difficult to read, even with the additional light, but Hawk was able to make out enough of it to give him goose flesh. The author had to be the freak's father. Jamie swore softly as he struggled with the handwriting.

"These are old, Richard, really old. I need to study them. This bit here seems to have been written directly after the freak was walled up and left to die; something about its . . .

unnatural appetites. There are hints here about what the freak actually is, and how to deal with it; all the things Dad never got around to telling me. Richard, we've struck gold!"

"Don't get too excited yet," said Hawk, keeping his voice low. "Here's something else for you to think about: Someone was in here before us, not long ago."

Jamie looked at him sharply. "How can you tell?"

"There was fresh oil in this lamp. What worries me is how he got in."

"Presumably there's a secret mechanism here somewhere, and we missed it."

"Maybe. And maybe there isn't, and our visitor used magic."

They looked at each other for a long moment. "What are you saying?" said Jamie finally.

"I'm not sure. But if there is a secret magic-user here in Tower MacNeil, that could complicate the hell out of things."

Jamie frowned. "Dad was the magic-user in this Family; I never had much of a gift for it myself. He could have been here while he was putting together his notes for me."

"That's a possibility," said Hawk. "But we can't bank on it. Let's keep this to ourselves for the time being. If there is a secret magic-user among us, we don't want to spook him. Or her."

Jamie started to say something, then stopped as Alistair leaned in through the hole in the wall. "What are you two muttering about?"

"Nothing," said Hawk. "We've just found some old papers, that's all. We'll check them out downstairs."

"Right," said Jamie. He went quickly through the desk drawers, and gathered up a few more papers. He rolled them all up and stuffed them inside his shirt. "Let's go. We've still got to find the third room."

They found it sooner than they expected. They rounded a curve in the corridor, and stopped dead in their tracks as they saw a great hole in the wall and debris scattered across the floor. Jagged half-bricks jutted from the sides of the hole like broken teeth, and the wall itself bowed slightly outwards into the corridor, as though there'd been an explosion in the room beyond.

"That's not possible," said Jamie. "We passed this way less than half an hour ago, and there was no trace of this then!"

"It's here now," said Hawk. He knelt down among the rubble and examined it closely in the light of the lamp he'd brought with him from the last room. "This happened some time ago. There's a layer of dust here that hasn't been disturbed. But you're right, Jamie; we did come this way before. You can see our footprints in the dust over there. Strange. There isn't this much dust anywhere else on this floor."

"What does that mean?" said Jamie.

Hawk shrugged. "Beats me. Maybe the servants just didn't feel like dusting this particular bit of corridor for some reason." He got to his feet, and moved over to inspect the broken wall. "This is interesting, too. Look at the way the bricks splay outwards. They must have been hit from the other side, from inside the room. The freak did this himself, presumably with his bare hands."

"Gods save us," said Jamie. "What kind of monster is it?"

Alistair moved over to study the hole, scowling thoughtfully. "Nothing human could have done this. The wall was stout and heavy, built to last." He peered through the hole at the room beyond, and his voice changed. "Richard, bring that lamp over here, would you?"

Hawk did so, and the others crowded round so they could all see into the hidden room. Scattered across the floor of the tiny cell were hundreds of small bones. Among them were the bodies of several small creatures, rats and mice and other things too decayed and corrupt to identify. The room stank of age and decay, like a freshly opened tomb.

"Well, now we know what he ate," said Jamie, his voice too steady to be natural.

"It doesn't explain how they got into a bricked-up room," said Hawk. "Besides, some of the less decayed bodies look practically untouched."

He stepped back from the hole to get some fresh air, and the others gladly took this as an excuse to do the same. They looked at each other for a while, at a loss for words.

Hawk nudged a brick on the floor with his foot, and the sudden grating sound seemed very loud.

"Perhaps there's something in the papers that will explain this," said Jamie finally. "I'll check them when we get downstairs."

"There's only one explanation," said Alistair. "Magic. Some kind of illusion. The hole in the wall was there all the time, and we walked right past it without seeing it. Hell, we must have been practically stumbling over the rubble."

"So what happened to the illusion?" said Hawk. "Why are we able to see the hole now?"

"Perhaps we're being allowed to see it," said Marc. "Perhaps the freak doesn't need to hide it from us any longer."

They all looked at him. "You mean the freak knows we're here, and what we're doing?" said Jamie.

"Haven't you felt you were being watched?" said Marc. "Haven't you had that feeling right from the start?"

"The freak must be a magic-user of some kind," said Alistair. "He set up the illusion after he broke out; first so that the servants wouldn't see the hole, and then so that we wouldn't . . . until he wanted us to. Now he's hiding behind another illusion, dogging us from one floor to another and laughing at us all the while."

"Oh great," said Hawk. "Not only is he inhumanly strong and a killer, but he can mess with our minds as well."

They stood quietly for a while, staring into the creature's cell, because it was easier than looking at each other and admitting they didn't know what to do next. Marc finally broke the silence, his voice soft and reflective.

"Think what he must have endured, shut up in that tiny cell for years on end. No way to measure time, save by the passing of day into night and night into day. No sound save his own voice, no company save his own thoughts. And all the years passing, one into another . . . Did he ever understand why he'd been shut away and left to die, except as a punishment for being . . . different? Perhaps in the end that's what kept him alive so long; a slow-burning fuse of hatred, waiting for a chance at revenge.

"Don't start feeling sorry for the creature," said Alistair. "He's already killed one man. And he would undoubtedly kill you, given the chance."

"We don't know the freak is the murderer," said Marc. "There's no evidence, no proof; nothing to tie him directly to the killing. For all we know, one of us may be the murderer, for reasons of his own."

Hawk studied him thoughtfully but said nothing.

"We can discuss this better downstairs," said Jamie, with just enough of an edge to his voice to make it clear that this was an order and not a suggestion. "It's obvious the freak isn't using his cell anymore, so there's no point in hanging around here. We've been gone a long time. The others will be worried about us."

He turned his back on the gaping hole in the wall, and started off down the corridor, followed by the others. They made their way silently back down the staircase, and all the way down Hawk thought of the dead rats in the freak's cell. He'd studied the fresher bodies very carefully, and as far as he could see, none of them had any signs of a death wound. Just like the dead man in the chimney.

In the drawing room, after the search party left, those left behind at first busied themselves stacking furniture against the door, but that didn't take long. The atmosphere became tense and strained. No one felt much like talking. Holly sat with her back pressed against the wall, her face pale and bloodless. Her hands were clasped tightly together in her lap, and she jumped at every sudden noise or movement. Katrina had given up trying to get through to her, and sat elegantly on her chair, sipping unhurriedly at her wine and thinking her own thoughts. Greaves and Brennan stood self-consciously on guard by the barricade. Brennan had an old short sword he'd taken from a plaque on the wall, while Greaves was holding a heavy iron poker from the fireplace. The butler's cold features could have been carved in stone, as usual, while Brennan looked somehow larger and more imposing, as though having a sword in his hand had awakened memories of the man he used to be. David Brook and Lord Arthur sat close by Holly, trying to comfort her with their presence. And Fisher stood with her back to the fireplace, watching them all unobtrusively, and wishing desperately for a sword.

She wasn't sure she believed in the freak, but that didn't mean there was no danger. In her opinion there were enough human killers around without having to turn to the supernatural to explain a sudden violent death. It was much more likely the killing had something to do with the spy Fenris. She shifted her weight from one foot to the other, and hoped Hawk wouldn't be long. She always thought more clearly when she had Hawk to discuss things with.

Lord Arthur got up and helped himself to another drink. David glared at him. "Don't you think you've had enough, Arthur? You're no use to us drunk."

Arthur smiled. "I'm no use to anyone, drunk or sober, Davey. You should know that. Besides, to a seasoned drinker such as myself, getting drunk isn't nearly so simple as it once was. As my system grows increasingly pickled, alcohol has less and less effect on it. I suppose eventually I shall reach a stage where alcohol has no effect on me whatsoever, but I hope and pray I shall have departed this sad vale of tears long before then. But whatever you do, Davey, don't have me cremated. There's so much booze in my body it would probably burn for a fortnight."

"Don't talk that way," said Holly. "It's depressing."

"I'm sorry," said Arthur immediately. "How are you feeling now, Holly?"

"Better, I think." She smiled at him tremulously. "Do you think I could have a sip of your drink?"

"Of course," said Arthur, and handed her his glass. "Approach it carefully; it's rather potent."

Holly took a cautious sip, and then swallowed hard. She pulled a face and thrust the glass back at him. "And you drink that stuff for fun? You're tougher than you look, Arthur."

"Why, thank you, my dear. It's nice to be appreciated."

They shared a smile. David stirred impatiently. "Don't encourage him, Holly. We might need his sword yet."

"If we ever reach the stage where everything depends on me and my poor skill with a sword, then we will be in serious trouble," said Arthur calmly. "I have all the fighting skills of a depressed rabbit. I never was much of a warrior; I always believed in seeing the other fellow's point of view. Preferably over a glass of something. No, Davey; if trouble occurs, I have every confidence that you will defend us nobly. You're the swordsman here."

"That's right," said Holly. "You always had to be the

hero, David, even when we were young. I'd be the captive Princess, and you'd be the valiant hero on his milk-white charger, come to rescue me. I always needed saving back then for some reason or another."

"I remember," said Arthur. "I always had to be Davey's squire, even though I was the eldest. I didn't mind. My father was furious when he found out, though. *You're a viscount!* he used to thunder. *The son of a Lord! Try to act like one!* I always was a disappointment to Dad." He shrugged, and taking a healthy sip from his drink, looked directly at Holly. "They were good days, then. When we were young, and the world was so simple."

"You're getting maudlin, Arthur," said David warningly. He turned to Holly and smiled reassuringly. "There's really nothing to worry about, Holly. I'll protect you, just as I always have."

"And I'll do my bit, however small," said Arthur. "I would defend you with my life, Holly."

Holly smiled genuinely for the first time, and reached out to clasp each of them by the hand. "I feel so safe with you two here. My guardians."

"They've been gone too long," said Katrina suddenly. "It shouldn't take this long to check a few windows. Do you suppose something's happened to them?"

"It's too early to start panicking," said Fisher. "They haven't been gone an hour yet."

"Is that all?" said Holly. "It seems longer."

"It's the waiting," said Fisher. "Time always drags when you're waiting for something to happen."

"It still seems too long," said Katrina stubbornly. "I'm sure Jamie didn't intend for us to be left alone this long. Something's happened, I'm sure of it. I think someone ought to go after them and make sure everything's all right."

"Don't look at me," said Arthur. "I may be drunk, but I'm not crazy."

"Damn right," said Fisher. "No one is to go off on their own. It isn't safe."

"Who the hell do you think you are, giving everyone orders?" said Katrina angrily. "Hold your tongue, and remember your place. David, if Arthur hasn't the courage to go, I'm sure you'll . . ."

"Not this time, Katrina," said David firmly. "For once, I find myself in agreement with Arthur. If the freak is roaming about out there, a man on his own would make a perfect target. And no, you can't send one of the servants, either."

"Thank you, sir," said Greaves. Brennan grinned.

Katrina slumped back in her chair and pouted. "So; we just sit here and wait for them to come back, do we? What if they never come back?"

"They'll be back," said Fisher.

Holly looked at her. "How can we be so sure?"

Fisher smiled. "I have faith in my brother. We've been through a lot together."

"Yes," said Katrina darkly. "I'll just bet you have."

Fisher looked at her with a slightly raised eyebrow, and Katrina decided to go back to pouting.

The trip down through the Tower seemed to take forever. The stairs fell away endlessly before them, curling round and round the inner wall. Hawk's thighs ached from the strain, and his back ached from the tension of constantly waiting for an attack. They were at their most vulnerable on the stairs, and the freak must know it. He'd never get a better chance at them. But landing corners came and went without an ambush, and doors passed unopened. Hawk's scowl deepened. He almost wished the freak would attack and get it over with. But they reached the ground floor without incident, and Jamie led the way back to the drawing room.

Hawk brought up the rear, sword at the ready, his gaze still darting from shadow to shadow. He was beginning to wish he hadn't left the sledgehammer up on the third floor. Alistair and Marc moved close together, also with swords at the ready, almost treading on Jamie's heels. Hawk didn't blame them. It was always when you were nearly back to safety that your adrenalin really began to pump. It was only then, when you stopped thinking about your mission and started thinking about being able to relax and take it easy again that you realized how much you had to lose if something were to go wrong at the last moment. He hung back a little, giving himself room to move, and swept the surrounding corridor with a steady, professional gaze. It wasn't likely the freak would make a move now, after turning down so many other, better opportunities, but Hawk wasn't about to drop his guard just because safety was so near at hand.

Jamie reached the drawing room door, banged on it with his fist, and called out his name. Marc and Alistair moved in close behind him, staring almost hungrily at the door as they listened to the barricade being dismantled. Hawk stood with his back to the door, watching the corridor. He looked left and right at random, careful not to give any attacker a pattern he could anticipate and elude. There was a movement to his right, and he looked sharply round to find Alistair beside him, looking slightly sheepish.

"Must be getting old," said Alistair gruffly. "Forgetting to watch my back, just because I'm nearly home. You'd make a good soldier, lad. You've got the right instincts. You sure you've never had any training?"

Hawk cast about for a convincing answer, but was saved by the sound of the drawing room door opening. Jamie hurried in, followed by Marc and Alistair. Hawk took one last look round the empty corridor, then backed unhurriedly into the drawing room. He kicked the door shut and pushed a heavy piece of furniture up against it. And then, finally, he put away his sword and allowed himself to relax a little.

Holly and Katrina were taking turns hugging the breath out of Jamie, while David and Lord Arthur clapped Marc and Alistair on the shoulder and pumped them for details about what they'd found out. Greaves and Robbie Brennan nodded politely to Hawk as he put down his lamp, congratulated him on his safe return, and set about rebuilding the barricade. Fisher came over to Hawk and offered him a brandy, which he accepted gratefully.

"Any sign of the freak?" she asked quietly.

"We found his lair, but he was long gone. Jamie's got some documents that should fill us in on what the freak actually is. Apart from that, it was pretty much a wasted journey. One bit of bad news: There's a good chance the freak is a magic-user. We ran into a pretty good illusion spell up around his lair."

Fisher pursed her lips thoughtfully. "That's all we

needed. Did you come across anything that might tie in with Fenris?"

"Not a damn thing. I'm beginning to wonder if we might have been sent on a wild-goose chase. I haven't come across anything to suggest Fenris was ever here."

"The circle of sorcerers said they tracked the spy right to Tower MacNeil."

Hawk sniffed. "I wouldn't trust that lot to cast my horoscope."

Fisher smiled. "Are you going to tell Commander Dubois that, or shall I?"

At that point, Jamie launched into an excited, only slightly exaggerated account of their journey. Fisher listened skeptically while Hawk enjoyed his brandy. He might not know much about vintages, but he knew enough not to waste a chance at a good brandy. It wasn't often he could afford the good stuff on a Guard's wages. Jamie finally wound up his report, and spread out the papers he'd found on one of the larger tables so that everyone could take a look at them. With perseverance, and a little discreet elbowing, Hawk and Fisher made sure they got places in front of everyone else.

The pages were faded and cracked, and written in several different hands, running from the time of the freak's birth to well after his incarceration. One writer was definitely the freak's father. The others could have been anyone, from members of the Family to some of the MacNeils' security people. The story that finally emerged from the assembled pages was more than a little unsettling.

The Family could have lived with the physical abnormalities exhibited by the freak at birth. Occasional unfortunates were inevitable when the Quality became as inbred as it had in Haven. It wasn't until the child grew older that they discovered just how inhuman he really was. The freak didn't need food or drink; he drained the life force out of anyone and anything that came within arm's reach of him. At first, no one understood what was happening. When those close to the child felt ill and listless, they just put it down to a bug that was going around. Then someone gave the freak a puppy for his sixth birthday, and the Family watched in horror as he drained the life right out of it. The freak laughed delightedly and clapped his hands again and again, glowing with health and vitality, while the puppy lay shrivelled and still on the carpet.

After that, the freak was kept in isolation. Poultry and small animals were provided to satisfy his "unnatural appetites," but no one save his mother and father ever saw him again. And they were always careful to visit him only after he'd just been fed. The father spent years searching for a cure, almost bankrupting the Family in the process. And then the mother went to visit her son one day, and never came back. By the time the household realized she was missing, it was far too late. His father found him squatting beside her body, singing in her voice. The MacNeil almost fainted with shock when the monstrous child addressed him in his dead wife's voice. It seemed he didn't just suck the life out of people; he took their memories as well. The freak actually thought he was his own mother. For a time . . .

The MacNeil finally did what his Family had been begging him to do for years. He had a secret room constructed on the third floor, and walled up the freak inside it. Since the boy was only ten years old, the MacNeil gave him poison to drink first. It didn't work. The freak lived on, draining the strength out of anyone who passed by his room. The MacNeil was at his wits' end. Since he'd already told everyone the freak was dead, and established his second son as heir, he didn't dare go outside the Family for help. So he did the only thing he could. He evacuated the Tower, and left it empty long enough to weaken the freak. He hoped the freak would die, but it didn't. He could hear it screaming. Eventually, he went back inside and made a small opening in the wall. And fed his son a rat. He slowly taught the freak to drain only food that was offered, and not the person who fed him. It took a long time, but the MacNeil was patient. And when the freak had finally learned, he let his Family back into Tower MacNeil.

They couldn't leave the Tower permanently. People were already asking questions. And they couldn't kill the freak. His magic had grown as he got older, tapping into people's minds until they were afraid to antagonize him. As long as he was fed regularly he remained quiet, and the Family learned to live with it.

Years passed. One by one, everyone who knew about

the freak died, until it became a Family Secret, handed down from father to eldest son. Feed the freak what he wanted, and he would remain quiet. And so it went, down the many years. The freak lived on, in his cell. Until finally Duncan MacNeil grew careless, and never got around to telling his new eldest son. He died in battle, and the supply of living food stopped. And the freak woke up hungry.

"The rest of it seems fairly obvious," said Hawk. "He drained the servants to begin with, as they passed unknowing by the hidden room. Remember the colds they kept getting? Then he broke out, and drained all the life out of someone."

"The dead man in the chimney," said Jamie. "But why did he burn the victim's face?"

"I think I know," said Hawk. "But you're not going to like it. Remember, when he drained his mother, he acquired her voice and memories. Even thought he was her, for a time. I think he took one of your guests, Jamie, destroyed the victim's face so it couldn't be recognized, and then took his place. Only the memories were so strong, after so many years' abstinence, the freak forgot who he was and thought he was the person he'd killed. That's why we haven't been attacked; because one of us is the freak, and doesn't know it."

For a long moment they just stood there and looked at him.

"That's ridiculous!" said David. "How could he not know what he is?"

Hawk shrugged. "All those years alone must have driven him crazy. Maybe his own personality had become so fragile . . ."

"Wait a minute," said Alistair. "What about the illusion on the cell wall? The freak kept that up for a while, and then dropped it when he realized it wasn't needed anymore. How could the freak do that if he doesn't remember who he is?"

"Maybe he remembers sometimes, when he has to, to protect himself," said Hawk. "How should I know? I'm not an expert on freaks or madness!"

"You're accusing one of us of being the freak?" said Katrina shrilly. "That's crazy! Jamie, tell him it's crazy!"

"Be quiet, Auntie," said Jamie. She looked at him reproachfully, but his face was stern and uncompromising. At that moment he looked every inch the MacNeil, head of the Family, and Katrina subsided, limiting herself to a couple of bad-tempered sniffs. Jamie looked hard at Hawk. "If one of us is a murderer, and truly doesn't know it, how can we tell who it is?"

"Perhaps there's something in the documents," said David. "Something we missed."

"No," said Alistair flatly. "Young Richard has summed up the papers' contents very thoroughly. He didn't miss a thing."

"We've got to do something," said Katrina stubbornly. "That . . . creature could be leeching the life out of us even as we speak."

"Has anybody felt ill recently?" said Marc. "Does anyone feel tired or listless?"

They all looked at each other, but nobody said anything. Hawk frowned as he tried to judge how he felt. After the hectic events of the past night and early morning he'd have been surprised if he hadn't felt a little frayed around the edges, but he couldn't say he felt unusually tired. He cocked an eyebrow at Fisher, and she shook her head slightly.

"We have to find the freak," said Jamie. "Find him and kill him. He's too dangerous to be allowed to live."

"Right," said David. "If we don't find him before he feeds again, he could be the only living thing left in this Tower when the wards go down tomorrow morning."

Holly paled suddenly, and turned away. Arthur looked hard at David. "Steady on, old chap. You're frightening the girls."

"Shut up, Arthur," said Jamie. "This is serious."

"Are you sure we can kill the freak?" said Marc. "He's not human. Perhaps he can't be killed by ordinary methods."

Alistair nodded thoughtfully. "You mean like silver for a werewolf, and a wooden stake for a vampire?"

"Perhaps the reason why they didn't kill him is because they couldn't," said Marc slowly. "If that is the case, the wisest thing for us to do would be to lock ourselves up in our rooms, barricade the doors, and wait it out till morning. As soon as the wards go down, we could make a run for it."

"And leave the freak free to turn on the city?" said Jamie. "Hundreds of people could die before he was finally hunted down and destroyed. The Secret of the MacNeils would become the Shame of the MacNeils. I can't allow that. The freak is our responsibility. It's a Family problem. And we have to deal with it."

"Besides," said Hawk quickly, "splitting up is a bad idea. There's safety in numbers."

"So you keep saying," said David. "What's the matter, Richard? Can't you cope without someone to hold your hand?"

"That's enough, David!" said Jamie sharply. "Richard's done very well by us so far. Now listen to me, all of you. There's still one source of information we haven't consulted, and that's my father's will. There may be something in the will that can help us, so Greaves and I will set up the right conditions for the reading. It may take a little time, and I think we could all use a break to freshen up, so I suggest you all repair to your rooms and compose yourselves until we're ready down here. But, just to be on the safe side, I think it might be wise if no one was to be left on their own. So choose a partner and stick with them at all times. Happy now, Richard?"

"Not really," said Hawk. "But it's better than nothing. I'll look after my sister."

"Of course," said Jamie. "Aunt Katrina, if you'd be so kind as to look after Holly . . ."

There was a brief rumble of conversation as the others sorted themselves out. David and Arthur paired up together, leaving Marc and Alistair to form the final pair. Neither of them looked too happy about it, but they both made diplomatic noises. Brennan realized he was left on his own, and quickly volunteered to help set up the reading of the will.

There was a pause after that as everyone waited for everyone else to make the first move. Jamie broke the mood by nodding curtly to Greaves and Brennan to help him dismantle the barricade at the door. It was soon done, and everyone set off up the stairs to the bedrooms on the next floor, eyeing each other suspiciously when they thought no one was looking. Hawk still wasn't happy about the group splitting up, but Jamie was the authority here, not him; he couldn't push the matter too hard without arousing suspicions. Besides, he could use the opportunity to talk with Isobel in private. He always did his best thinking when he could discuss things with Isobel. And he had a strong feeling he was going to need all the help he could get on this case.

5

Plans and Secrets

Hawk and Fisher watched closely as the others disappeared into their rooms on the second floor, and made careful mental notes as to who was staying where. You never knew when information like that might come in handy. Jamie escorted Hawk and Fisher to their room, and even opened the door for them. Hawk thought about offering him a tip, but decided Jamie wouldn't see the joke. Jamie made the usual polite remarks about hoping they'd be comfortable, and Hawk made the usual polite remarks in reply. Then they all smiled at each other, and Jamie went back down the corridor. Hawk immediately closed the door, locked it, and put his back against it. His chin dropped forward onto his chest, and he let out a long slow sigh of relief. Fisher made vague grunts of agreement from where she lay stretched out full length on the bed, indifferent to the damage it was doing to her dress.

"I never knew behaving respectably could be such hard work," said Hawk finally. "I've done so much smiling it feels like I went to sleep with a coat hanger in my mouth. I don't know if I can keep this up till tomorrow morning."

"I don't know what you're complaining about," said Fisher unsympathetically. "At least you don't have to be sociable and cope with a corset at the same time. My waist isn't on speaking terms with the rest of me." She sat up slowly and carefully, levered off her fashionable shoes, and wriggled her toes gratefully. "I don't know how women can bear to wear those things. My feet are killing me."

Hawk threw himself into the nearest chair, slumped back, and stretched out his legs before him. It felt good to be able to relax, even if only for a while. The chair was almost sinfully comfortable, and Hawk closed his eyes the better to appreciate it. Some moments were just too precious to be interrupted. But it didn't last. There were too many more important things clamouring for his attention. He opened his eyes reluctantly, and glanced round the room Jamie had given them; just on the off chance he'd spot something that would let him ignore his problems for a while, till he felt better able to deal with them. The room looked back, determined not to be helpful.

It was fairly luxurious as far as Quality standards went; and Quality standards went pretty far. There were thick rugs on the floor, an assortment of classically elegant furniture, and a bed with a mattress deep enough to swim in. Paintings of famous military scenes covered the walls (military art was *in* that Season), and half a dozen small nude statuettes smiled and posed tastefully on alabaster pedestals. And over by the window, half hidden by drapes heavy enough to block out the harshest sunlight, stood the room's own private liquor cabinet. Hawk smiled. Now, that was what he called civilized. He started to lever himself up out of his chair, but Fisher intercepted his gaze, and shook her head firmly.

"You've had enough for one day, Hawk. Let's try and concentrate on the matter at hand. Namely, what the hell is going on here? Every time I think I've got it worked out, something else happens that throws it all back up in the air again."

"It's not really as confusing as it seems," said Hawk, settling back in his chair. "It just looks that way because we don't have all the facts yet. Or if we do, we haven't got them arranged in the right order. What's really complicating the hell out of things is that we're dealing with two separate cases here. On the one hand we have an escaped killer freak, disguised as one of us by an illusion, while on the other hand we have our missing spy Fenris, disguised as one of us by a shapechange. We can't sort the two cases out because they keep interfering with each other, and we can't tell which evidence belongs to which case."

"Could that be deliberate?" said Fisher, thoughtfully massaging her left foot and staring off into the distance. "Maybe Fenris recognized us despite our disguises, and let the freak loose himself, as a way of throwing us off his trail."

"I don't think so," said Hawk slowly. "The way we look

now, our own creditors wouldn't know us. And from the mess the freak made of his cell wall, I don't think he needed any help in getting out. But certainly Fenris could be using the situation to keep the waters muddy. I would, in his shoes."

"He might know who we are, regardless of our disguises," said Fisher. "There could be a leak at Headquarters. Hell, half the force is on the take these days, one way or another."

"True. But how many people actually know about us? Commander Dubois, Mistress Melanie, and that sorcerer doctor, Wulfgang. That's all."

"That's enough," said Fisher flatly. "Whatever information Fenris has, it must be bloody important to have panicked the Council so badly. And if it's that important, it must be worth a lot of money to the right people."

Hawk thought about it. "All right. There's a chance Fenris knows who we really are. Which means we can't trust anyone here."

Fisher smiled. "What's new about that?"

Hawk scowled. "I can't believe we've been here all this time and we're still no nearer identifying Fenris. Look: We know Fenris went to the sorcerer Grimm for an emergency shapechange. That means the body he's got now isn't his usual one. Which means we can eliminate all the people here who can prove they've had the same form for more than twenty-four hours."

Fisher looked at him. "That's brilliant, Hawk. Why didn't we think of that before?"

"Well, we have been rather preoccupied."

"Right," said Fisher. "So, that cuts out Jamie, Katrina, and Holly. And the two servants, Greaves and Brennan."

"And Lord Arthur," said Hawk. "I've met him before. And since Arthur and Jamie have both known David for some time, that just leaves Alistair and Marc." Hawk nodded slowly to himself. "And we've already established Alistair is lying about where he comes from; he didn't know the Red Marches are flooded these days."

"Yes," said Fisher, in a voice that indicated she was about to get picky. "But he does seem to know a hell of a lot about MacNeil Family history. How would our spy know things like that?"

"He could if he was a friend of the MacNeils in his true form. According to Jamie, his Family have a long history of bad feelings with the Court. Which would explain why Fenris made a beeline for Tower MacNeil in the first place. But, on the other hand . . ."

"We shouldn't dismiss Marc out of hand. Do we have any actual evidence against him?"

"Nothing so far. He's a quiet sort; hasn't much to say for himself at the best of times. Doesn't seem to care much for us, but we can't drag him off in chains just for that." Hawk frowned. "But . . . in all the time we've been here, Marc hasn't volunteered one thing about his past; not a single damned thing about who or what he was before he came to Tower MacNeil. Interesting, that."

Fisher shook her head. "Just because he hasn't opened up to us doesn't mean he hasn't talked to the others."

"True. So, for the time being I think we'll concentrate our attention on Alistair, as far as finding the spy is concerned. Tracking down the freak is going to be rather more difficult."

"Why? Once again it has to be someone not well known by the others. The freak might have taken on someone else's memories, but he's still stuck with his own face. So, we're back to Marc and Alistair again. And if Alistair is Fenris, then Marc has to be the freak. Right?"

Hawk shook his head regretfully. "Nice try, Isobel. Unfortunately, it's not that simple."

Fisher groaned. "Somehow I just knew you were going to say that. All right, what have I missed this time?"

"You're forgetting the illusion spell the freak cast to cover up the hole in the wall on the third floor. It's quite possible the freak is still messing with our minds, to make us see someone else's face, instead of his own. Which means he could be anyone. Male or female. And with complete access to that person's memories, there's no way anyone's going to trip him up with an unexpected question."

"Oh great," said Fisher. "So where does that leave us?"

"Wait. It gets worse. It seems to me the freak may be interfering with our minds in other, *subtler* ways as well. Jamie seemed quite determined to split up the group, despite everything I've said, and everyone else just went along with it. Which is rather unusual, considering this bunch can't normally agree on anything without several minutes worth of arguments, insults, and recriminations. Perhaps the freak influenced everyone to accept Jamie's idea, in order to make us easier targets."

Fisher looked at him thoughtfully, still holding her bare foot absently in her hand. "It's possible, I suppose. But how could we tell, one way or the other? And besides, if they're all being influenced, why aren't we? If the freak was controlling the way we think, then this idea wouldn't have occurred to us at all. Would it?"

"That's a good question," said Hawk. "Wish I had a good answer."

"Hell," said Fisher. "I'd settle for a bad one."

Holly sat unhappily in her chair by the fire while Katrina Dorimant studied her makeup in the dressing-table mirror. *Looking good,* thought Katrina contentedly. *Don't look a day over twenty-five. Not bad for an old broad past forty. Graham never did appreciate me, rot his socks.* She smiled. Graham might not have, but there were those who had. Sometimes in Graham's own bed. He never was very observant. She pouted at her reflection. It was all his fault anyway. If he hadn't spent all his spare time and money on his silly politics, instead of lavishing it on her, they might still be together.

She'd told him right from the start; she was prepared to put up with a lot of things from him, but coming second wasn't one of them. She expected all his attention all the time. She wasn't unreasonable; she realized he had commitments. She just wanted him to be there when she needed him. What was so unreasonable about that? Things had been different when they first met. He'd been all over her then, bright and witty and attentive, always ready with a smile or a compliment or an out-of-season flower. When he finally worked up the nerve to ask her to marry him, long after she'd decided to accept, he'd promised her faithfully that she'd always come first with him. Graham was always very big with promises. She should have remembered that promises were a politician's stock in trade.

He'd been so *funny,* then. She missed his sense of humour more than anything. He could always make her laugh, no matter how dark the day.

Still, she hadn't done so badly for herself since she left him. She ran up the bills and he paid them, just as always. And why not? That was what men were for. Among other things. She smiled. Richard MacNeil was an unexpected bonus. Tall, dark, handsome, and wonderfully innocent in the ways of the world. He all but blushed every time she looked at him. She pulled the front of her dress down another inch to show off more cleavage, and considered the effect in the mirror. No, better not. She wanted to attract Richard's attention, not give him a coronary. Besides, it would undoubtably scandalize Jamie, and she couldn't afford to get on his wrong side at the moment. Dear Jamie; so young and already so prudish. Never even had a girlfriend, as far as she knew. She'd have to do something about that, once this nonsense was over and done with. In the meantime she'd do better to concentrate on Richard. He needed . . . encouraging. She produced a small silver makeup case from inside her sleeve, opened it, and pawed thoughtfully through the contents.

"Aunt Katrina, what are you doing?"

Katrina glanced round at Holly. "Ah, you've decided to come out of your snit at last. I thought you were going to sulk all day because Jamie paired you off with me instead of your precious David."

"I was not sulking!"

"Of course not, dear; you were just thinking very hard, and that's what made you frown. Now be a pet, and don't interrupt while Auntie fixes her face."

Katrina removed a tiny black patch from the makeup case, balanced it on the tip of her finger, and pressed it firmly onto the right side of her face, just above the jaw. It was very slightly but quite definitely heart-shaped. Katrina turned her face back and forth, studying the effect in the mirror.

"Aunt, what is that?"

"It's a beauty spot, dear. They're all the rage. And I do wish you'd call me Katrina, especially when we're in company. 'Aunt' makes me feel positively ancient."

"A beauty spot," said Holly, doubtfully. "What's the point of it?"

"The point is to attract a young man's interest. Beauty spots are supposedly there to cover some minor flaw or defect; this intrigues the young gentleman as to what that flaw might be, and how he might get a look at it. Personally, I just think they look pretty."

Holly thought about it for a moment, and then shook her head. "Not really my style."

"Yes, well, at your age you don't need such artifices. Gods, I'd kill for a complexion like yours. Still, at least you're taking an interest in things again. How are you feeling now, Holly dear?"

"Better, I suppose. I'm sorry I went all to pieces downstairs, but it all just got too much for me. I've not been sleeping well recently. I'm sure I could cope a lot better if I wasn't so tired all the time."

Katrina sighed, and put away her makeup case. She turned to look at Holly sternly. "Have you been taking that potion the doctor prescribed?"

"Yes. It doesn't help. It doesn't stop me dreaming. That's why I don't sleep; I'm afraid to. It's always the same dream. I'm lying in bed, in the dark, unable to move, and there's something in the room with me. I can't see it, but I know it's there. It comes slowly closer, creeping towards the foot of my bed. I can hear its heavy footsteps, and its harsh breathing. And I know it wants to do something to me; something horrible. I know I'm dreaming, and I try to wake myself up, but I can't. It starts to heave itself up onto the end of my bed. I can feel the mattress sink down around my feet, feel the creature's horrid weight on my legs. I try to scream, but I can't make a sound; and that's when I finally wake up. Only each night, the creature seems to get a little further before I can wake myself up. That's why I'm so afraid to sleep, because I know that one night I'm not going to wake up in time."

"You poor dear!" Katrina got up and moved quickly over to kneel beside Holly. "Why didn't you tell the doctor all this?"

"I did. He said it wasn't that unusual a dream for a girl my age, and advised Jamie to get me married off as soon as possible. I wasn't supposed to hear that, but I was listening outside the door. Jamie said he'd think about it. But my dream is real. I know it. That's why I began praying for the Family Guardian to come and save me. He's my only hope now."

Katrina's eyes narrowed. "Men! Now don't you worry, Holly, as soon as this nonsense is over I'll see Jamie gets you the best doctors and specialists in Haven. They'll find out what's really wrong with you, and what to do about it. In the meantime, you need something to take your mind off things. Come with me, dear. Come on!"

She took Holly firmly by the arm and dragged her over to the dressing table. Ignoring Holly's protests, Katrina sat her down before the mirror and retrieved her makeup case from her sleeve. She took hold of Holly's chin and turned her face back and forth, frowning thoughtfully as she studied the girl's pale and tired features in the mirror.

"Don't you worry about a thing, dear. Auntie is going to remake your face from top to bottom. You won't know yourself when I'm finished. Then you can walk into the will-reading with your head held high, and knock them all dead. David isn't going to believe his eyes the next time he sees you!"

"But Katrina, I don't wear makeup. . . . Jamie doesn't allow it. . . ."

"Oh hush, dear, and let Auntie work. You think about David, not Jamie. I'll take care of him."

Marc and Alistair sat stiffly in chairs on opposite sides of the room, carefully not looking at each other. They'd taken turns freshening up in the adjoining bathroom, and now they were waiting to be called downstairs for the reading of the will. In all the time they'd been alone together they hadn't exchanged a dozen words. Alistair crossed and uncrossed his legs, and drummed his fingers on the arm of his chair. He glanced briefly at the liquor cabinet, and looked away. That wasn't what he was here for. His Family needed his help, and he wouldn't let them down. He looked round the room Jamie had given him. There'd been quite a few changes in the decor since he was last here. He didn't like them. Too bright and gaudy, by half. But, fashions change, and he had been away a hell of a long time. . . .

He looked over at Marc, who was sitting perfectly still, staring at nothing, his face as inscrutable as ever. Was this what the Family had come to, a cold fish like him? The MacNeil blood must be running pretty damned thin these days. The man looked more like a funeral director than a young blade of the Quality. Alistair stirred impatiently. He found Marc's continued silence intensely irritating. There were things he needed to say, things he needed to discuss with someone, important things; and who had Jamie paired him off with? An undertaker who'd taken a vow of silence, with all the open emotions of a garden statue.

Alistair settled back in his chair and put a curb on his impatience. He shouldn't be too hard on the lad. After all, Marc was all alone and a long way from home. He was probably just shy and ill at ease. He could be waiting for Alistair to make the first move. Alistair ran through half a dozen possible openings, designed to lead the conversation round to what he wanted to talk about, but faced with Marc's cold visage they all seemed either fatuous or foolish.

All right, then; to hell with being polite. Be direct.

He leaned forward in his chair and fixed Marc with his gaze. "You've been doing a lot of thinking, young Marc. Who do you think the freak is?"

Marc met the older man's gaze unflinchingly. "I don't know, cousin. It could be any of us. If Richard is right, and the creature truly no longer remembers what it is, then I suppose it could even be you or I, and we wouldn't know. It's a frightening thought; the possibility that you might not be who you think you are, but actually someone else entirely. And yet I'm not sure that I agree with Richard. In order to pass as one of us, the freak must be maintaining a fairly complex illusion spell. How could he do that, and not be aware of what he is?"

"I don't know," said Alistair. "But the mind's a funny thing. Maybe part of him remembers; just enough to protect him without breaking the hold his new memories have on him. But even so, we're still dealing with someone who's spent most of his life going crazy in solitary confinement. Even with his new memories to lean on, he's bound to find himself in situations he can't cope with. And that's when his true nature can't help but reveal itself."

Marc looked at him thoughtfully. "I take it you're about to suggest someone you think has been acting out of character."

"Exactly," said Alistair. "I don't like the way Richard's been acting. He's from a very minor branch of the Family, lives in the middle of nowhere, and by his own account has

spent most of his life with his nose in a book. But ever
since we found the body, he's been taking charge, snapping
out orders and generally behaving more like a hardened
soldier or a Guard. It's as though he's confused the memories of who he's supposed to be with those of the people
he read about. And out of all of us, he's always seemed
the least scared. Perhaps because deep down he knows he's
got nothing to worry about."

"You may have something there," said Marc slowly.
"I've been watching Richard, too. He was very quick on
picking up the freak's story from the papers Jamie found,
wasn't he? Have you told anyone else of your suspicions?"

"Only Jamie. He won't listen to me."

"We need evidence. All we have at the moment are suspicions. We can't condemn a man purely on doubts and
theories."

"We'll get evidence," said Alistair. "All we have to do
is watch him. Sooner or later he'll give himself away, and
then I'll kill him with my bare hands."

David paced impatiently up and down, glaring at nothing
and everything, while Arthur freshened his glass with a bottle from the room's liquor cabinet. He'd dragged the cabinet over to the bed, and was now seated with his back
against the headboard and his legs stretched elegantly out
before him. He watched David indulgently for a while, and
then coughed politely. David shot him a glance without
slowing his pacing. Arthur smiled at him.

"Do slow down a little, Davey. You're wearing a path
in the rugs and making me positively dizzy. Jamie will call
us when it's time."

David dropped reluctantly into the nearest chair, stirred
uncomfortably, and then shifted forward until he was sitting
right on the edge of the chair. "Arthur, how can you be so
calm after everything that's happened? Has the booze finally given up on rotting your liver and decided to go after
your brain now? One of us is a murderer, an insane monster just waiting for his chance to kill again. And we're
trapped in the Tower with him!"

Arthur thought about that for a moment. "Does it really
matter that he's an *insane* monster? I mean, a sane one
would be just as bad, surely?"

David looked at him disgustedly. "I should have known better than to expect any sense out of you. For once in your life, Arthur, try to concentrate on what's happening around you! Holly's in danger here. Doesn't that mean anything to you?"

"Yes, it does. You know that. I'll do anything I can to protect her and keep her safe. But right now she's safe in her room behind a locked door. Just like us. What else can we do now except wait for Jamie's call?"

"I don't know!" David shook his head slowly and relaxed a little. "I'm sorry, Arthur. I shouldn't take it out on you. I'm just . . . scared, that's all. Scared that something bad's going to happen to Holly, and I won't be there to stop it. I've always been her protector, even more than Jamie; standing between her and the bad old world. Taking all the knocks and bruises so she wouldn't have to. I'd die for her, Arthur. But all I can do now is sit on my backside and wait for something to go wrong. I just feel so bloody helpless!"

"We all do, Davey. Save your strength. Save it for when it's needed."

David sighed heavily. "I never was very good at waiting. I've always needed to be doing something, anything."

"Our time will come. In the meantime, why not have a drink?"

David looked at him sternly. "That's your answer to everything, isn't it? Get smashed out of your mind till the world stops bothering you. Don't you know that stuff's killing you?"

"Sure," said Arthur. "But what makes you think I give a damn? Nobody else does, so why should I buck the trend? It's not enough just to live, Davey; there has to be some purpose in it, some reason to get out of bed in the morning. And I never found one.

"For a while I tried to be the kind of man my Family wanted, but after they all died I lost interest. There didn't seem any point in it once they were gone. I had all the money I'd ever need, and the estate practically runs itself. So, mostly I just settled for having a good time. Believe me, Davey, you'd be surprised how deadly dull having a good time can be after a while. One party blurs into another, the days drag on, and sometimes you think the night is never going to end. I can't seem to get interested in anything anymore. Nothing really matters to me. Except you and Holly. You're important to me, Davey. You do know that, don't you?"

"Of course," said David. "We've always been friends, the three of us. Always will be."

"Friends," said Arthur. "Yes." He took a long drink from his glass.

"You need a woman in your life," said David. "Surely at all those parties there must have been someone, some woman who made your heart beat faster. . . ."

"There was one woman I loved. But I never told her."

"Why not?"

"Because I cared for her too much to ruin her life by becoming a part of it. I've messed up my own life quite thoroughly. I'm damned if I'll drag her down with me. Besides, she already has someone, someone who'll make her much happier than I ever could."

David shook his head. "Arthur, you mustn't think so badly of yourself."

"Why not? Everyone else does. Even you."

"That's different. I'm your friend. All your friends worry about you."

"Friends," said Arthur, sipping at his drink. "I used to think I had a lot of friends. After all, there's no one so popular as a drunk with money. But I had to make out my will the other week. Instructions from the Family lawyer. So there I was, sitting at my desk in my study, and I found there was hardly anyone I wanted to leave anything to. I know lots of people, but the only time I ever see them are at parties. Not one of them ever called at my house during the day to say hello, or ask how I was, or just to chat for a while over a glass of something. In the end, I found there were only three people in my life who I thought might regret my passing. You, Holly, and Louis Hightower. That's it. And be honest now. How many of you would even bother to come to my funeral if it was raining?"

"There is nothing so boring as a maudlin drunk," said David firmly. "If you're just going to feel sorry for yourself . . ."

"It's a dirty job," said Arthur. "But someone has to do it."

"Oh, stop it! Of course you have other friends. What about Jamie?"

"He's your friend, not mine. He just puts up with me because of you and Holly."

"Look, if you're so determined to kill yourself, why are you dragging it out? Do the honourable thing and put yourself out of your misery! Oh hell . . . I'm sorry, Arthur. You'd think I'd know better by now than to argue with you while you're drunk. Just . . . snap out of it. You've got a lot to live for. There's a lot more to life than drink."

"I don't care for drugs," said Arthur. "I'm a traditionalist at heart."

"You're just trying to annoy me, aren't you? Look, you can't kill yourself. Think how upset Holly would be. Now let's change the subject. Gods, you can be depressing at times, Arthur. You're not the only one with problems, you know. I have problems too, but you don't see me crying into my wine over them."

Arthur looked at him steadily. "You've never had problems. You've always been handsome and popular. Your Family bend over backwards to indulge you. Women have been chasing you ever since your voice dropped. You have so many friends your parties often spill over into a second house. What problems do you have, Davey? Not being able to choose which shirt to wear next?"

David looked at him for a long moment. "You know your trouble, Arthur? You're so wrapped up in your precious self-pity you can't see beyond the end of your own nose. Haven't you ever wondered why I spend so much time with you and Holly and Jamie, instead of running off to join the army and see the world, like the rest of our contemporaries?"

Arthur frowned. "That's right. Your Family's famous for its strong tradition of military service, isn't it? Practically obligatory, from what I've heard. I suppose I just assumed you had more sense than the rest of your Family. All right, tell me. Why aren't you in the army?"

"Because the army wouldn't have me. I spent two years cramming with my tutors to get me past the Military Academy entrance exams, two years working my guts out, and I still didn't pass. I didn't even come close. Whatever it takes to be an officer, I don't have it. There was nothing my Family could do. There were all kinds of strings they could have pulled on my behalf, once I got into the Academy, but not even their influence could persuade the Academy to accept such a spectacular failure as me.

"They couldn't even get me into the diplomatic corps, where most of our Family's second-raters end up.

"My father threatened to disown me. Most of my Family aren't talking to me, and those that are never miss an opportunity to remind me how badly I let them all down. And as for my friends, practically everyone I grew up with is in the army now, scattered across the Low Kingdoms, defending our borders. Some of them have already died doing it. And every time I find a familiar name in the death lists I think *That could have been me. That should have been me.* We've more in common than you think, Arthur."

Arthur looked at him unflinchingly. "I'm sorry, Davey. You're right, I should have known, but I just never thought about it. You see, you're the only man I ever envied. Because you've got the only thing I ever wanted. You have Holly."

There was a long pause as they looked at each other. To his credit, David didn't look away. "So it is her. We often wondered, but you never said anything. Holly and I love each other, Arthur. We always have. We're going to be married soon. I wish . . . things could have been different. We used to be so close, the three of us."

"We were children then. Children grow up."

There was a sudden knocking at the door. The two men jumped to their feet as the door burst open and Jamie hurried in.

"What is it?" asked David, as Jamie shut the door behind him. "What's happened?"

"Relax," said Jamie. "There's no emergency. I just needed someone to talk to. I don't know what to do. At the moment I'm pinning all my hopes on Dad's will, that there'll be something in it that can help us, but it's a slim hope at best. I'm not up to this. In the past, whenever there was a problem, I could always turn to Dad. He always knew what to do. Now there's just me, and everything's going wrong."

"Oh hell," said David. "Another one."

"Ignore him," said Arthur quickly. "You mustn't blame

yourself, Jamie. You're doing everything you can. We understand how hard it is. It's not easy, learning how to stand on your own feet. Some people never do learn. But you're doing fine so far. Isn't he, Davey?"

"Damn right," said David. "You found your father's papers, didn't you? Without them, we might never have found out what kind of monster we were dealing with."

"I can't help feeling Dad would have done things differently," said Jamie. "He was the great warrior, after all; the great hero. Everyone said so, even the King. I was so proud of him . . . even though I never got to see much of him. He was away with the army a lot, especially after Mother died when I was young. But he was spending more time at the Tower just recently, and we were really getting to know each other. And then he had to go and die in that stupid little clash on the border. I couldn't believe it when I heard. How could he have been so *stupid?* He didn't have to go up there in person, not someone of his rank. He must have known it wasn't safe up there! But he went anyway, because he couldn't bear to miss out on the action. And he got himself killed, leaving Holly and me alone. And on top of all that, he hadn't even bothered to tell me the Secret, as he should have!"

He was close to tears, his face bright red with anger and frustration. Arthur took him by the arm, and gently but firmly made him sit down on the nearest chair. "It's all right to be angry, Jamie," he said softly. "I was angry at my Family when they all died so suddenly, going off and leaving me all alone. But it wasn't your father's fault. He didn't mean to leave you. He just made a mistake, that's all; a simple mistake in judgment."

"Right," said David, sitting on the arm of the chair. "Everyone makes mistakes, Jamie. Even a great hero like your dad."

"The whole border situation is a mess right now," said Arthur. "Practically everyone I know has lost somebody to one border clash or another. If Outremer doesn't back down soon, we could find ourselves in a full-fledged war."

"It won't come to that," said David. "No one wants a war, at least no one that matters, and no one really cares about the borders. It's just politics, that's all. The diplomats will sort it out. Eventually."

"We're getting away from the point," said Arthur. "Which is, all you can ever do is give it your best shot, and hope that's enough. That's all your father would expect of you, Jamie. That's all any of us expect of you. You're doing fine. Don't let anyone tell you otherwise. Right, Davey?"

"Sure," said David. "We'll find the freak and kill him, and no one will ever have to know about it."

"Right," said Arthur. "Care for a drink, Jamie?"

Greaves looked round the library and nodded approvingly. Everything was where it should be, ready for the reading of the will. Duncan would have been proud to see all his wishes carried out to the letter. The chairs had been set up in a semicircle facing Duncan's favourite desk. The wax-sealed will had been placed neatly in the middle of the desktop, ready to be opened. All it lacked now was the man himself.

Greaves' breath suddenly caught in his chest, and he looked away. He'd known the master was dead for some time now, but somehow the reading of the will confirmed it, made it real. Duncan would never again come striding through that door, to warm his hands at the fire and roar for cigars and his best brandy. Once the will was read, Duncan would become just a memory, a portrait on the wall; and young Jamie would be the new MacNeil in fact as well as name. Greaves sighed. He'd serve Jamie faithfully, just as Mister Duncan had ordered, but it wouldn't be the same. Mister Duncan had been a great man, and Greaves would miss him.

He felt suddenly tired, and sat down on one of the chairs, something he would never have done if anyone else had been present. But it was all right; there was no one to see him. Robbie Brennan was off on an errand, and Mister Jamie and the guests were all safely occupied upstairs. Greaves leaned back in the chair and looked slowly around him. The library had always been his favourite room. Many an evening he had served Mister Duncan and his guests as they sat in the library, telling and retelling marvelous tales of their younger, soldiering days. And Greaves had moved from chair to chair, handing out glasses of mulled wine and dispensing cigars, inventing extra tasks so that he could stay a little longer and listen, too.

The butler scowled, pursing his lips tightly together. It was all gone now. No more evening stories. No more fine parties of great people for him to look after. And the MacNeil himself dead and lost on a battlefield too far away even to imagine, let alone visit. There had been little warmth in Greaves's life as a butler, only orders and duties and the comfort of knowing his place and keeping to it. But Greaves had always thought of himself as someone who might have been Duncan MacNeil's friend if things had been different. And now the man was dead, and Greaves would never be able to tell him that.

The door opened and Greaves was quickly back on his feet, but it was only Robbie Brennan, carrying the extra candelabrum Greaves had sent him for. Greaves pointed silently to where he wanted it, and Brennan lowered it carefully into place. He straightened up and glared at Greaves.

"That has to be it. We've moved everything in here that isn't actually nailed down."

"The MacNeil was very particular in his wishes," said Greaves calmly. "Everything had to be just so. But we are finished now."

"Good," said Brennan. "I think I've done my back in, shifting that desk. I'd better go and tell Jamie his guests can come down now."

"Just a minute . . . Robbie. I want to talk to you."

Brennan looked at the butler in surprise as Greaves sat down again and gestured for Brennan to pull up a chair facing him. He did so, and looked at Greaves curiously.

"Robbie, tell me about Duncan," said Greaves quietly. "Tell me about the Duncan you knew, in your younger days."

"Why?" said Brennan.

"Because I want to know. Because I miss him."

Brennan shrugged uncomfortably. "You've heard all the songs, but you can forget them. Songs are for entertainment, not history. I first met Duncan forty-four years ago, almost to the month. He was a young officer, the ink still wet on his commission. I was a mercenary out of Shadowrock, serving with Murdoch's Marauders. An impressive name for a bunch of killers, half of them running from the law under names their mothers wouldn't have recognized.

"Duncan and I first saw action together at Cormorran's

Bridge. The way the official histories tell it, it was a tactical defeat for the other side. I was there, and it was a bloody massacre. We lost five hundred men in the first half hour, and the river ran red with blood and offal. Murdoch's Marauders were wiped out; only a handful of us survived. The main army was broken and scattered, heading for the horizon with enemy troops snapping at their heels. There were bodies everywhere, blood and guts lying steaming in the mud. The flies came down in great black clouds, covering the dead and the dying like moving blankets. Duncan and I ended up fighting back to back in the shallows. We would have run, but there was nowhere to run to. We were surrounded, and the enemy weren't interested in taking prisoners. So, we made our stand, and vowed to take as many of them with us as we could. No one was more surprised than us when the enemy finally retreated rather than face approaching army reinforcements, and we were both still alive. We were a mess, but we were alive.

"We stuck together after that; we knew a hint from the Gods when we saw one. We worked well together, and slowly became friends as well as allies. The army sent us here and there, and we saw a lot of action in the kinds of places minstrels like to call colorful. Arse-ends of the world, most of them. We fought in twenty-three different Campaigns down the years, and not one of them for a cause that was worth so much blood and dying. Still, we got to see some of the world. Had some good times together. Even had a few adventures that had nothing to do with the army; but none of them the kind of thing you'd want to make a song about.

"Ah hell, Greaves. What can I tell you that you don't already know? Duncan was a good soldier and a better friend. He had a bit of a temper, but he was always sorry afterwards, and his word was good, unlike quite a few I could mention. He brought me here to the Tower, when my soldiering days were over, and made me a part of his Family in all but name. That's my old sword, hanging on the wall there. And you tell me you'll miss him? I miss Duncan with every breath I take. When I wake up in the morning, the first thing I remember is that he's dead. It's like there's a hole in my life that he used to fill, and now it's cold and empty. I should have been there, Greaves. I

should have been there with him. Maybe I could have
done . . . something. He never did watch his back enough.
But I wasn't there, because we both thought I was too old.
So he died alone, among strangers, and I'll spend the rest
of my life wondering if I could have saved him if I'd
been there.

"What do you want me to say, Greaves? That he liked
you? He did, as far as I know. Wait until after the will; I'll
read his eulogy then. I wrote it myself years ago; just needs
a little updating. I'll say all the right things, make all the
proper comments, sing his praises and not mention any of
the things he'd rather were forgotten. Things that might
shock young Jamie and his friends. I'll polish up his memory one last time, and we can all say goodbye. You have
to learn to say goodbye, Greaves. It's the first real lesson
every soldier learns."

Brennan finally ran down, and the old library was quiet
again. Greaves nodded slowly. "Thank you, Robbie. There
were many things Mister Duncan could not bring himself
to tell me about his past, perhaps because he thought they
might distress me. But I wanted to know them anyway.
Because they were a part of him. But he is not really gone
from us, you know. He has left behind the young master,
Jamie. There is a lot of his father in him."

"I suppose so," said Brennan. "Sure, he's a good kid. Is
there anything else, or can I call the others down now?"

"We have to protect Mister Jamie!" said Greaves
fiercely. "He is the MacNeil now. I think I know who our
killer is. He masquerades as Quality, but he does not have
the true stamp of the aristocracy about him. Never mind
who; I am not certain enough yet to point the finger. But
when the time comes, he must die. And Mister Jamie may
not be able to do the deed. He's young, and largely un-
tested. If he should balk, we must do the task for him.
The Secret must not get out. Or we betray Duncan's name
and memory."

Hawk hurried down the corridor to the bathroom, clutching
at the right side of his face with his hand. He banged on
the bathroom door with his fist, waited a moment to see if
anyone would answer, and then pushed open the door and
hurried in. He slammed the door behind him with his foot,

and made for the washbasin. He splashed some water into the bowl, and then reached up and carefully eased the glass eye out of his aching eye socket. He leaned against the wall as the pain slowly receded, letting his breathing get back to normal, and then he dropped the eye into the basin. It stared up at him reproachfully, as though someone had told it about the problem being all in Hawk's mind. He turned his back on it, and massaged the right side of his face. He was already feeling a lot better. When this case was over he was going to have to have a stiff talk with himself as to which part of his mind was in charge.

He turned back and studied himself in the wall mirror. With his right eyelid closed to hide the empty socket, he looked somehow furtive. Not to mention half-witted. If someone came up to him on the street looking like that, he'd arrest the man on general principles. He glared down at the offending glass eye. The pain was almost gone now, but he had no doubt it would start creeping back as soon as he replaced the eye. As if he didn't have enough to worry about. The case was complicated enough when he took it on, but now things were definitely getting out of hand. Not only was he nowhere near identifying the spy Fenris, he also had to find a magic-using killer freak before it killed everyone in the Tower; whilst, at the same time, keeping the increasingly paranoid others from figuring out that Richard and Isobel MacNeil weren't all they were supposed to be. Hawk sighed, heavily, and fished the glass eye out of the water.

He held it up to the mirror, and then practically had a coronary as he saw the door start to swing open behind him. He crammed the glass eye into his socket, checked quickly that he'd got it the right way round and pointing in the right direction, and then turned smiling falsely to face Katrina Dorimant. She had a hand to her mouth, and was blushing prettily.

"I'm so sorry, Richard, but you forgot to lock the door. I'll wait outside."

"No, it's all right," said Hawk quickly. "I'm finished. You can come in. I'm . . . just leaving."

"There's no hurry," said Katrina, walking slowly towards him. "No need to rush off on my account. I only came in to freshen up. Besides, I've been looking for a chance to get you on your own."

"Oh yes?" said Hawk, in a voice that wasn't as steady as it might have been. He started to back away, and immediately bumped into the wash stand behind him. "What did you want to see me about?"

"No need to be bashful, Richard dear. We don't need to play games, surely; not at our age. We're of an age where we can say what we mean, and pursue those things we desire without hiding behind false modesty. You're a very attractive man, Richard."

She stopped immediately in front of him, so close her bosom pressed lightly against his chest as she breathed. Her upturned face brought her mouth dangerously close to his, and he could feel her warm breath on his lips. Hawk swallowed hard.

"You are a married woman," he said hoarsely, clutching at straws.

"Oh, don't bother about Graham. No one else does. We'll just have to be discreet, that's all. I've seen you watching me, Richard, when you thought no one was looking. Watching me, wanting me, desiring me. I can feel the passion rising within you. Why try and deny it? My heart is beating faster just at the closeness of you. Feel it!"

She grabbed his right hand and held it firmly to her breast. Her skin seemed impossibly soft and warm under his hand, and her perfume filled his head. He thought about calling for help, and then quickly decided against it. If Isobel was to find them like this, she'd kill both of them. Or laugh herself sick. Hawk wasn't sure which would be worse. He tried to surreptitiously pull his hand free, but she had a grip like a beartrap.

"Don't fight it, Richard," murmured Katrina, practically breathing the words into his mouth. Her eyes were dark and dangerous. "You do find me attractive, don't you?"

"Uh . . . yes. Sure. It's just . . ."

"Just what?"

"This is hardly the right place for a romantic assignation," said Hawk, improvising wildly. "Someone might come in."

"We could lock the door."

"They'd get suspicious! Besides, Jamie will be calling us

down for the reading of the will soon, and we wouldn't want to be interrupted, now would we?"

"The will. Yes, of course." She let go of his hand and stepped back, frowning thoughtfully. "You're right, my dear; this isn't the right time. But don't worry, Richard. I'll sort something out. Just leave everything to me. And the next time we meet, things will be very different, I promise you. See you later, my darling."

She kissed the tip of her index finger, pressed it to his lips, and then turned and left the bathroom, carefully closing the door behind her. Hawk swallowed hard and slumped back against the washstand. Just when he thought the case couldn't get any more complicated . . . The bathroom door burst open, and Hawk almost screamed. Fisher looked at him.

"What the hell are you so jumpy about?"

"Nothing. Nothing at all. What is it?"

"Jamie's just called us down for the reading of the will. Are you all right? You look a bit flushed."

6

A Dead Man, Talking

The library had been designed for quiet contemplation, or perhaps the occasional late-night reminiscences of a few old friends. Cosy and comfortable, a refuge from the hurly-burly of the world. Now that it was crammed from wall to wall with several chattering MacNeils and their friends, the room seemed small and cluttered and not a little cramped. Hawk and Fisher were the last to arrive, and hung back by the door to look the place over before plunging in. Fisher was interested in who was talking to whom, and what that implied. Hawk wanted to know where Katrina was, so he could be sure to avoid her, and how many exits there were to the room. He always liked to know where the doors were, in case he had to leave in a hurry. You picked up habits like that, living in Haven. He was relieved to note there was only the one door. It simplified things. He turned his attention to the gathering.

David, Holly, and Arthur were standing with their backs to the fireplace, toasting each other with cups of steaming punch. They were smiling and laughing as though they didn't have a care in the world. As though they'd forgotten all about the dead man and the disguised freak. Hawk sniffed, and shrugged inwardly. The Quality were well known for ignoring things they didn't want to think about. Behind them, Greaves was down on his knees, encouraging the crackling fire with vigorous use of a poker. He had his coat off and his sleeves rolled up, and looked thoroughly disgusted with the whole business. Presumably in the past he'd had underlings he could call on to deal with such menial tasks.

Over by the desk, Marc had backed Katrina into a corner and was apparently addressing her about something earnest and worthy and incredibly dull. Certainly Katrina's desper-

ation was becoming clearer by the minute as she smiled
mechanically and looked past Marc for something she could
use as an excuse to escape him. Hawk looked quickly away
before she could lock eyes with him, and watched thoughtfully as Alistair took a book from one of the shelves and
flipped slowly through it. Jamie and Brennan were arguing
quietly about something just behind him, and Alistair was
going to great pains to make it clear he wasn't listening.
Hawk nudged Fisher's elbow, and the two of them moved
over to join Alistair. Hawk had a strong feeling Alistair
was keeping something back, apart from the matter of the
Red Marches, and this seemed as good a time as any to
find out what. Alistair looked up as they approached, and
nodded amiably.

"Something interesting?" said Fisher, glancing at the
book Alistair was holding.

"Not really, my dear. Just old Family history." He
snapped the book shut and replaced it on the shelf. "You're
looking very fresh, Isobel. The short rest seems to have
agreed with you. In fact, you look quite splendid. Tell me,
is there a young man in your life yet?"

"Oh, yes," said Fisher. "Can't seem to get rid of him.
What about you, Alistair? Do you have any Family of your
own, back in the Red Marches?"

"No. They all died some time ago. I've been on my own
ever since. But I still come, when the Family calls. As we
all do." He looked round the crowded room, and scowled
disapprovingly. "Though in my day we came for the sake
of the Family, not ourselves. Look at them; gathered together like so many vultures, waiting to see who can snatch
the biggest titbits from the dear departed." He stopped,
looked at Hawk, and cocked an eyebrow. "No offence intended, Richard."

"Of course," said Hawk calmly. "Personally, Isobel and
I will be grateful for whatever largesse Duncan may leave
us, but that's not why we're here. We just wanted to meet
Jamie and get reacquainted with the Family. We've been
out of touch too long."

"A long way to come, just for that. Lower Markham's
pretty remote, after all. In fact, I wasn't even aware the
Family tree had any branches in that area. Tell me, what
branch of the Family are you descended from?"

There was an awkward pause, as Hawk chose and discarded a dozen names, and hoped desperately Fisher would bail him out. It quickly became clear that she was as thrown as he was. Hawk smiled easily at Alistair, and fought to keep his voice calm and even. "I believe we're descended from Josiah MacNeil, on our father's side."

Alistair frowned. "Josiah? I was just looking at the Family tree in that book, but I don't seem to recall . . ."

"Wrong side of the blanket," said Fisher quickly. "That's why he left Haven in the first place. You know how these things are. . . ."

"Oh, I see. Yes, of course. Happens in the best of Families. . . ." Alistair smiled, just a little coldly and nodded to them both. "If you'll excuse me . . ."

He moved away to join Katrina and Marc. Katrina looked openly relieved at being rescued from Marc's monologue. Hawk and Fisher looked at each other, and smiled grimly.

"That was close," said Fisher.

"Right," said Hawk. "If it had been any closer, it would have been behind us. We should have spent more time working out a background on the way here. It's always the niggling little questions that catch you out."

"We can worry about that later. Right now, the day's dragging on and we're no nearer working out which of this bunch is the freak and which is the spy. What are we going to do?"

"Mingle, and keep our eyes and ears open. What else can we do? We can't just drag them off and interrogate them one by one. Unfortunately. We'll just have to keep digging away, and hope somebody lets something slip."

"It's possible, I suppose," said Fisher, looking unobtrusively around her. "They're scared, all of them. Some of them are hiding it better than others, but you can feel it on the air. If the atmosphere were any tenser, they'd be choking on it. As it is, they're all smiling too much and laughing too loudly; making a pretence of enjoying themselves so they won't have to think about what's been happening."

"I don't blame them," said Hawk. "One of them is a murderer, and they could be talking to him right now and not know it. Even worse; they might be him and not know it."

Fisher shivered quickly. "That's spooky."

"Damn right."

"Let's split up, and see if we can get a few helpful answers to some carefully phrased questions. I'll try Alistair again, since he has such an eye for a pretty face. You try Holly and her two swains."

She was already off and moving before Hawk could raise his objections. Lord Arthur might not have recognized him so far, but Hawk had a strong suspicion he shouldn't press his luck. Drunks sometimes had a way of seeing things that other people missed, especially things they weren't supposed to spot. Hawk shrugged, and moved over to join the group by the fireplace. Greaves had given up on the fire and had gone over to try and mediate between Jamie and Brennan, but David and Holly greeted Hawk warmly, and Arthur presented him with a cup of the steaming punch. Hawk blew on it cautiously, and took a careful sip. It tasted hot and spicy, and then blazed down his throat to explode in his stomach.

"Hell's teeth," said Hawk respectfully, when he got his voice back. "No wonder you're all looking so cheerful. This stuff is strong enough to bring a smile to a dead man's lips."

"Thank you," said Holly, blushing. "It's an old Family recipe I found in a cookbook. I thought it might be fun to try it out."

"If your ancestors drank this stuff on a regular basis they must have had insides like old boots," said David, and Holly giggled.

"I don't know what you're all making such a fuss about," said Arthur, draining his cup in easy swallows. Hawk stared at him openly, half convinced that smoke was going to come pouring out of his ears. Arthur just smiled his usual vague smile and held out his cup to Holly for a refill.

"I think you've had enough for the moment, Arthur," said Holly firmly. "You mustn't be greedy."

Arthur nodded and looked at David. "I hope you're not going to let her boss you around like this, Davey."

"Damn right I'm not," said David. "I'm my own man, always have been. I go my own way, come what may."

"You always were stubborn," said Holly, leaning against

David as he put an arm around her waist. "But so am I, when I want to be. You needn't think you're going to have everything your own way, David Brook."

"We'll discuss this later," said David, and whispered something in her ear that made her giggle again. Arthur looked resignedly at Hawk, and though he'd been drinking steadily ever since Hawk first saw him, he seemed just as calm and sober as ever. Interesting, that.

Holly, on the other hand, looked quite perky. Hawk thought at first that she was flushed from the heat, but then realized it was expertly applied cheek rouge. At some point during her brief absence Holly had subtly remade her face with a liberal use of makeup. She looked ten years older, much more sophisticated, and altogether more fashionable. Though perhaps not as pretty or as pleasant, if truth be told.

"Well?" said Holly, grinning. "What do you think?"

"Sorry," said Hawk, "I didn't realize I was staring. You look very splendid. Do I perhaps detect Katrina's hand in this transformation?"

"Got it in one," said Holly. "I couldn't believe it was me, the first time I looked in the mirror."

"You look marvelous," said David.

"Very striking," said Arthur.

"Jamie hates it," said Holly, the corners of her mouth turning down. "He still thinks I'm ten years old. He wanted to send me back to my room to wash it all off, but as Robbie is busily pointing out, the will is to be read soon, and they can't have that without me. Jamie's in a frightful temper. Serves him right for being so pompous."

"Well," said Arthur, after a slight pause, "only a few moments now to the reading of the will and the great share-out. I take it you're hoping for a suitable windfall, Richard?"

"Arthur!" said Holly, shocked, but David just chuckled.

"Since Arthur and I won't be getting anything out of the will, it allows us to be a little more direct," he said impishly. "Even in the face of sudden death and supernatural freaks, the MacNeils can still find time to argue over money."

"Oh quite," said Arthur. "Still, some of us don't have to worry about inheriting money; not when they can marry it instead."

David looked at Arthur sharply, as though unsure whether to react to the barb or not, and then smiled and laughed and hugged Holly to him. "That's right, Holly. I'm just an unscrupulous fortune hunter after your inheritance! Probably strangle you on our wedding night and flee the country on a coal-black horse! Isn't that what the villains always do in those romances you read?"

"It seems Arthur isn't the only one who's had too much punch," said Holly sternly, though a smile tugged at her lips. "Don't worry, Richard, they're always like this. And I'm sure you'll find Father has left you a generous reward for making such a long journey here."

"Oh, I expect there'll be a little something," said Hawk. "But that really isn't why we came. Isobel and I are both comfortably well off. Mostly because there's not a lot to spend money on in the wilds of Lower Markham."

"I sometimes wish that was the case in Haven," said David wryly. "There are all kinds of expensive temptations here. Right, Arthur?"

"You should know, Davey. I think between us we've managed to lose money in every card game, gambling den, and race course in Haven. I tell you, Richard, not only is Davey the world's worst card player, but some days he just can't wait to find a horse that's going to lose so that he can put some money on it."

David glared at him. "This from a man who once bet the deed to his house that he could drink one glass of every potable an inn had to offer!"

Arthur raised a sardonic eyebrow. "I won the bet, didn't I?"

"That's not the point!"

"Boys! That's enough!" Holly looked apologetically at Hawk. "Maybe the punch was a bad idea after all. They're not normally this rowdy."

"You're right," said David. "It's only money, after all. Take our minds off it, Holly, with some juicy titbit of gossip." He grinned at Hawk. "Holly's always up on the latest gossip."

Holly scowled. "I used to be, until all the servants left. You'd be surprised what servants hear. For instance, have you heard about Jacqueline Fraser? Her husband came home unexpectedly and found her in bed with the head groom! Apparently it wasn't just the horses he'd been giving a good rubdown. Anyway, he threw her out without a penny! She had to go begging to her own Family for support. What made me think of that was . . . well, I can't help worrying if something similar might happen to Katrina. I mean, I haven't heard anything definite yet, and Graham's always been very good about paying her bills so far, but he could change his mind tomorrow, and then where would she be?"

"Still here, sponging off Jamie, I should think," said David briskly. "At least she and Jacqueline both have a Family to back them up. I sometimes think my Family would stand by and watch me go under without a single qualm. Tightfisted bunch, the lot of them. Still, bad luck about poor Jackie. I hadn't heard about that. Her husband never did have a sense of humour. You know, it never ceases to amaze me how much there is going on in High Society these days. There ought to be a news-sheet that concerns itself with nothing but gossip and rumour; just so that we could keep up with everything. Maybe I'll start one myself. There might be money in it."

"Really, Davey," said Arthur, feigning shock. "You'll be talking about going into trade next. I had no idea your debts were so worrying. I'm afraid you'll have to give up your disgraceful gambling habits if you're going to support Holly in the manner to which she's accustomed."

"I think we'll manage, thank you," said David frostily.

"Of course we will," said Holly. "Stop teasing him, Arthur."

"Sorry," said Arthur immediately.

On the other side of the room, Katrina chattered blithely on, unaware of how glazed her audience's eyes were getting. Fisher smiled determinedly, Alistair nodded politely while staring into his cup of punch, and Marc's thoughts were obviously elsewhere. Fisher didn't blame him. She'd never known anyone who could talk so much and say so little. Even Katrina's gossip was boring. And then Fisher's ears pricked up as she finally caught something interesting.

"Wait a minute," she broke in, not even trying to be polite about it. "Are you saying Duncan may not have any money to leave? At all?"

"Of course I'm not saying that," said Katrina, her eyes

flashing angrily, as much at being interrupted as anything else. "My brother was a very wealthy man. It's been generations since our Family had to concern itself with money. It's just that Duncan was always very careful with money while he was alive, and I don't see why that should have changed just because he's dead. So anyone who came here expecting to get rich off Duncan's death is probably in for a very nasty shock."

She managed to look disparagingly at all three of them while not looking at any of them in particular. Alistair smiled coldly.

"The fact that you too are hoping for a decent-sized legacy has nothing to do with your opinion, of course."

Katrina stared calmly back at him. "I don't know what you're talking about."

"Don't you? From what I've gathered of the way you treated your husband, it's a wonder he's supported you as long as he has. Your only hope for independence is whatever your dear departed brother may have bequeathed you. Seems to me we may not be the only ones in for a shock."

For a moment Katrina glared at him openly, her face hardening into ugly lines, and then she recovered herself and smiled sweetly at Alistair. "I think I know my own brother better than some reprobate banished by the Family so long ago that most of us can't even remember it."

Fisher's ears pricked up again. She'd assumed Alistair and Katrina had at least known each other in the days before Alistair was exiled, but now apparently Katrina was saying she'd never heard of him before he turned up at the Tower. Which was another small piece of evidence that Alistair might not be who he was supposed to be. . . .

"The money doesn't matter," said Marc suddenly. "What matters is finding the killer among us, before his hunger gets the better of him again. Or has everyone forgotten about that?"

"No," said Alistair patiently. "Not all of us. But it has to be said there's nothing like the imminent distribution of large amounts of money to distract the attention. Let them get it out of their systems, and they'll be ready to concentrate on more important matters again. In the meantime, at least this way we can keep an eye on each other. Ah, it appears Jamie is finally ready to start."

A sudden silence fell across the library as everyone turned to watch Jamie take his place behind the desk. He looked down at the folded and sealed will, reached out as though to touch it, and then drew back his hand. He looked out at his attentive audience and smiled briefly.

"I'm sorry to have kept you waiting so long. Holly, Katrina, and Robbie . . . please sit in these chairs at the front. Then we can start."

The three he'd named moved uncertainly forward, glancing at each other as Jamie courteously but firmly settled them into three specific chairs immediately before the desk. He selected another at the front for himself, and then indicated that everyone else was allowed to sit where they wanted. Hawk chose an end seat near the door, only just beating Fisher to it. She sat next to him, apparently relaxed and at ease, but her hand kept drifting back to where she normally wore her sword. Hawk didn't blame her. Will readings were notorious for bringing out the worst in people even under ordinary circumstances. With the freak manipulating their thoughts and feelings, anything could happen.

Jamie moved back to stand stiffly behind the desk, waiting patiently until everyone was settled and quiet. Then he leaned forward and broke the wax seal on the will, and spoke a Word of Unbinding. A subtle, barely felt tension in the room suddenly broke and was gone, replaced by the sense of an almost tangible presence hovering by the desk. Jamie moved quickly out of the way and took his place on the other side of the desk, in the chair he'd set aside for himself. He'd barely taken his seat when the air behind the desk suddenly rippled and flowed, and a large stern figure was sitting where Jamie had stood. Hawk didn't need to be told that this was Duncan MacNeil.

Duncan was a broad, imposing man with a barrel chest, harsh but not unpleasant features, and close-cropped red hair and beard. He was in his late fifties and looked as though he'd spent most of his life in the wilds on one campaign or another. He wore the latest fashion with an uncomfortable air, as though he would rather have been wearing the trail clothes and chain mail of a soldier on the road. His gaze was direct and uncompromising, and Hawk could tell Duncan would have been a hard man to cross.

The late MacNeil looked out over the assembled group and smiled slightly.

"If you're listening to me now, then I've been dead for some time. I'm not really here. This is just an illusion, a moment in time recorded by magic, so I can tell you my wishes after I'm gone." He paused, stirred uncomfortably, and glanced at the chair where Jamie was sitting. "You know, this was hard enough the first time, when I made out my will for your brother William. I thought it would be easier this time, but it isn't. Poor Billy. He wanted so much to follow in my footsteps, but he was never cut out to be a soldier.

"Well, Jamie, you're the MacNeil now. I want you to know that whatever happens, I was always proud of you. I should have told you that before, but somehow I never got round to it. We always think we've got all the time in the world for all the things we want to do and should do, but time has a nasty habit of running out on you just when you need it most. I should have made out this will before. Don't know why I didn't. Perhaps Billy's death made me too aware of my own mortality . . . I don't know. Fact is, there are a lot of other things I've been putting off, but I'll take care of them when I get back from the border. Sorry, I'm wandering. Let's get on with it."

He looked down and read from the will in his hands.

"Be it known; I leave my entire estate to my son Jamie, with the exception of certain bequests I shall describe shortly. He shall be the MacNeil in my place, and speak for the Family in all things. Look after your sister, Jamie. See she wants for nothing and marries well. She's your responsibility now."

The dead man looked at the chair where Holly was sitting. "To my daughter Holly, I leave her mother's jewels. She always meant for you to have them. I wish I could have spent more time with you, my dear. You grew up to be a very beautiful young lady, a lot like your mother. Look after your brother. See that he has good advice when he needs it, and when you've got him alone nag him unmercifully till he marries. The Tower always seems a happier place with a pack of kids running loose in it."

"Is that it?" said David angrily. "Jamie gets the estate, and all you get is some old jewellery?"

"Hush, David," said Holly. "Not now."

David slumped back in his chair and folded his arms angrily, while Duncan MacNeil looked at Katrina and smiled wryly.

"To you, sister dear, I leave ten thousand ducats. That's all. Enough to give you some independence till your divorce comes through, but not enough that you can afford to put it off too long. Knowing you, you'll drag the process out as long as you can just to get back at Graham, and I won't have that. I always liked Graham. More than I liked you, if truth be told, and it might as well be, now I'm dead. We never warmed to each other, did we, Kat? Too late now. I don't know whether to feel sad about that, or relieved. Divorce Graham, and make a new start with someone else. Assuming you can find someone else who'll put up with you."

He turned to Robbie Brennan, and his smile softened. "Robbie, old friend, you get twenty thousand ducats. It's my hope you'll stay at the Tower and be as good a friend to Jamie as you were to me, but if you feel you have to leave, the money should help you on your way. We had some good times together, you and I. I'd have left you a damn sight more than twenty thousand, but knowing you, you wouldn't have taken it. Money always did make you nervous. The Gods know I've tried to give you wealth and position time and again over the years, and you've run a mile from all of them. But I wish you'd take my sword, at least. You know you always admired it, and it's no use to me now. Whatever you do, Robbie, be happy."

"They never did find his sword," said Robbie softly. "It was lost, somewhere on the battlefield."

Duncan looked out over the chairs before him, and Hawk felt a chill run through him as the sightless eyes passed over him. Duncan cleared his throat, and looked back at the will before him. "To my butler Greaves, who has always served me faithfully, five thousand ducats. And to every member of the Family who has come to the Tower to pay homage to the new MacNeil, five thousand ducats.

"That's it. I've said my piece. May the Gods preserve and protect you from all harm."

The air shimmered and he was gone; the last sight of Duncan MacNeil of Tower MacNeil. There was a long silence. Hawk glanced at Greaves, to see how he'd taken being lumped in with the visiting relatives rather than being singled out for reward as he'd obviously expected. The butler was leaning forward on his chair, and tugging at his collar as though he couldn't breathe. His face was pale and sweaty, and he looked sick. He lurched to his feet suddenly, clawing at his throat. Alistair rose quickly from his seat to hold and support him, while everyone else scrambled to their feet. The butler grabbed at Alistair, fighting for air, his eyes bulging from his face. Hawk moved in quickly beside Alistair as Greaves suddenly collapsed, and they lowered him to the floor. His skin was icy cold to the touch, and he was trembling violently.

"What is it?" said Jamie, his voice cutting through the general babble. "What's happening? Is he ill?"

"I don't know," said Hawk, yanking open the butler's collar. "Looks more like he's been poisoned."

"No," said Marc suddenly. "That's not it. Look at him. Isn't it obvious what's happening? The freak's grown hungry again! He's draining the life out of that man while we just stand around and watch!" He glared about him as everyone but Hawk and Alistair backed away from the trembling figure on the floor. "Leave him alone, you bastard! Leave him alone!"

"Somebody do something!" said Holly shrilly. "Don't just let him die!"

Greaves grabbed weakly at Hawk's arm and tried to say something, and then his breathing stopped and the life went out of him. Hawk searched for a pulse in the man's neck, but there was nothing there. He closed Greaves's staring eyes and then looked up at the others and shook his head slowly. Holly was sobbing quietly, her head pressed against David's chest as he held her tightly. Arthur patted her shoulder comfortingly, his face pale but angry. Katrina sat down suddenly, her face turned away from the dead man. Robbie Brennan was staring intently from one face to another, as though looking for the mark of the killer in their eyes. Hawk got slowly to his feet, and Alistair stood up with him, the man's face cold and determined.

"This has gone on long enough," he said roughly, his words clipped short by barely controlled rage. "I'm damned if I'll lose anyone else to the freak. I've kept my peace till now because I wanted to be sure before I made any accusations, but I can't keep quiet any longer. If I'd spoken out before, maybe Greaves would still be alive."

David gently pushed Holly away from him, and his hand dropped to his sword belt. "Are you saying you think you know who the imposter is?"

"Out with it," said Jamie sharply. "If you've any evidence against one of us, I want to hear it."

"Greaves knew who the freak was," said Brennan. "He told me earlier that someone here wasn't the aristocrat they pretended to be. He didn't give me a name, though."

"And that's why he died," said Alistair. "The freak wanted him dead before he could identify our imposter. But I'll give you a name: Richard MacNeil."

There was a flurry of shocked gasps and curses as everyone backed quickly away from Hawk, except for Fisher who stayed at his side, and Alistair, who stood facing him. Hawk stood very still, careful to keep his face composed and his voice even.

"I'm not the freak, Alistair. There's no evidence against me, and you know it."

"Get away from him, Isobel," said Alistair.

"You're all crazy!" said Fisher. "He isn't the freak!"

"You can't be sure," said Katrina. "Even the freak himself doesn't know who he is."

"Get away from him, Isobel," said Alistair.

"In case you've all forgotten," said Hawk tightly, "may I remind you that the man we found in the chimney had been dead for some time, long before Isobel and I got here."

"We don't know when he died for sure," said Robbie Brennan. "You're not a doctor. Whatever else you are."

"Besides," said David, "the freak could have killed the real Richard soon after he got here and taken his place, so as to throw us off the track after the first murder."

"There's too many *ifs* and *maybes*," said Jamie. "We need evidence."

"All right," said Alistair. "You want evidence? How about this: He's lied to us constantly, from the first time we met him. He said he was from Lower Markham, but none of us ever knew we had any Family there. Marc's from Upper Markham, and he'd never heard of him. Rich-

ard claimed to be descended from Josiah MacNeil, but I
never heard of a MacNeil with a name like that. And according to the Family History I checked right here in the
library, no one else has ever heard of him either. Richard
makes out he's some quiet, book-reading type, but he acts
more like a soldier or a brigand. Presumably from the
memories of someone he's drained. But whatever else he
is, he's not true Quality. He doesn't know his place."

"And he was right there beside Greaves when he collapsed," said Brennan excitedly. "Greaves grabbed at Richard when he knew he was dying, and tried to say his name!
We all saw it!"

"This is ridiculous!" said Fisher quickly. "Everything
Richard has said is true! I ought to know!"

"You can't be sure of anything," said Alistair. "It's obvious he's been clouding your mind right from the start.
That's why you've been acting a little oddly yourself. Now
please, Isobel, stand away from him. We have to deal with
the freak before he kills again, and we don't want you
getting hurt."

Hawk backed away, looking quickly around him as Alistair drew his sword. Jamie and David were already reaching
for theirs. Hawk drew his own sword, but without his axe
he didn't like the odds at all. He glanced at Fisher, who
raised an eyebrow slightly and glanced at the door. Hawk
nodded briefly, grabbed the nearest chairs and overturned
them between him and the others, then turned and ran for
the door with Fisher close behind him. There was a roar
of outrage as Alistair led the others after them, kicking the
chairs out of the way. Hawk charged out into the corridor,
waited a second for Fisher to get clear and then slammed
the door in Alistair's face. He held the door handle tight,
pulled a wooden wedge from his pocket, and jammed it
under the door. He'd brought the wedge in case he needed
to ensure his privacy, but it was proving its worth now. He
ran down the corridor to the stairway and started up it
without slowing, taking the steps two at a time. Fisher ran
beside him, holding up her skirts to run more easily.

"Where are we going?" she demanded.

"Damned if I know," said Hawk. "I just want to put
some space between us and them. We've got to find somewhere we can hide out for a while and do some hard think-

ing. Our only hope is to prove my innocence by revealing the real freak."

"Not forgetting the spy we came here to find," said Fisher.

Hawk scowled. "I hate this case. We should have held out for a bigger bonus."

"Right," said Fisher.

They both shut up and saved their breath for the stairs.

7

DEATH OF A LONELY MAN

For a time there was nothing but chaos and bedlam in the library as everyone shouted at everyone else. Alistair finally got the floor by shouting the loudest and glaring down anyone who tried to object. He stared grimly about him as the noise gradually subsided and a sullen silence fell across the room. Jamie and David had their swords in their hands, and looked dangerously eager to use them. Arthur was clumsily trying to comfort Holly, who was clearly only putting up with him to keep him calm. Katrina had retreated to the fireplace, and was glaring suspiciously out at the room, gripping the heavy iron poker with both hands. Robbie Brennan had thrown aside his short-sword and taken down his old claymore from its plaque on the wall, hefting the great length of blade with professional skill. Marc was still kneeling beside the fallen butler, apparently unable to believe the man was really dead. Alistair looked unhurriedly about him.

"There's no need to get yourselves in such a panic; it'll take us a while to get the door open, but the freak can't get out of the Tower. The wards are still in place, remember? He's still here somewhere, hiding with the girl. If he hasn't killed her already. Finding him isn't going to be easy; the Gods know there are enough bolt-holes and hiding places he could crawl into. But wherever he's gone to ground, we can't just go chasing after him. The cornered rat is always the most dangerous. And knowing Richard, I wouldn't put it past him to have set up some very nasty booby traps for us to walk into. So, we'll go after him, but we'll do it in a sensible, professional way, checking each floor room by room and watching our backs at all times. Anyone have any problems with that?"

Marc rose slowly to his feet. "We have to kill him. That's all that matters."

Holly sat down suddenly, her hands folded in her lap like a child's. "I can't believe that all this time Richard was the freak. I liked him."

"So did I," said Alistair. "But I didn't let that blind me to his constant lying and evasions. Richard is the freak, Holly; don't doubt it for a minute."

"Of course he's the freak," said Jamie impatiently. "He ran when we challenged him, didn't he? If he wasn't guilty, why did he run?"

"But then why did Isobel go with him?" said Holly. "She swore he wasn't the freak."

"He'd probably been messing with her mind for so long she no longer knew what was true and what wasn't," said Brennan.

"Then why did Richard take her with him?" insisted Holly.

"Food," said Alistair. "He's woken up and remembered who he is, and he's hungry."

"If we're to have any chance of saving her, we've got to get moving," said Jamie.

"Of course," said Alistair. "But we're not all going. Too large a group would just slow us down, and I don't want anyone with us who can't look after themselves in a crisis. The two ladies will stay here, of course, so someone will have to stay with them, to protect them. Any volunteers?"

Holly looked immediately at David, but he shook his head. "I've got to go with them. They're going to need my sword. Arthur will stay with you, won't you, Arthur?"

"Of course," said Arthur. "I'll keep you safe, Holly. I know how to use a sword. I'll die before I'd let anyone hurt you."

Holly didn't even look at him; her gaze was fixed accusingly on David. Marc cleared his throat.

"I'll stay. I'm not much good with a sword, but given time I think I can build a bloody good barricade against that door."

Alistair nodded to him curtly. "I take it the rest of you are with me?"

"Damn right," said Brennan. He was standing straighter than usual, and he held himself with a brisk, professional manner that made him look twenty years younger. "The freak has to pay for Greaves's death. Greaves wasn't the easiest of people to get along with, but he was still a good man, for all that. We were never friends, but I would have trusted him with my life and my honour. He didn't deserve to die like that. I'm going to find the freak and cut him into bloody pieces."

"We won't find him by standing around here talking about it!" said Jamie. "The freak's caused my Family enough heartbreak. It's time to put an end to him. We're going, Alistair; right now."

Alistair bowed slightly. "You are the MacNeil. Just give me a moment to force the door open, and we'll be on our way."

Jamie hefted his sword. "I want him dead, Alistair. No mercy and no quarter. I want him dead."

Hawk and Fisher finally staggered to a halt somewhere on the third floor and leaned against a wall, heads bowed, fighting for breath. Fisher wiped the sweat from her face with her sleeve, and looked back the way they'd come. The corridor was quiet and deserted, the shadows undisturbed. She looked down at her bare feet, and winced. She'd kicked off her fashionable shoes some time back, so that she could run faster, and the cold from the bare stone floor had nipped unmercifully at her feet. Hawk reached up and took out his glass eye, sighed with relief, and dropped the eye into his pocket. The ache in his face immediately began to subside. All in the bloody mind. . . . He looked down at the duelling sword in his hand, sheathed it and sniffed disdainfully.

"If I'd had my axe, I'd never have run. I'd have stood my ground and chopped them all up like firewood. I mean, running from odds like that. . . . If this ever gets out, we'll never live it down."

Fisher shook her head slowly. "We can't fight them, Hawk; they're just innocent bystanders. They don't understand what's going on here."

"I'm not so sure I do anymore," said Hawk. "This case has got completely out of hand. Look, there's no point in going any further. The only place above this is the battlements, and there's not enough room to manoeuvre up there. We're safe enough here, for the time being. It'll take the others a while before they can get this far, so let's use that time to get some hard thinking done. We ought to be able to figure out who the freak is by now."

Fisher looked at him. "And what makes you think they're going to listen to us? More than likely they'll cut us down on sight."

"We'll just have to make them listen."

"In that case, I want a sword. I can be much more convincing with a sword in my hand."

Hawk looked at her, amused. "I thought we weren't supposed to hurt them because they were just innocent bystanders?"

"I just meant we shouldn't kill them. Apart from that, anything goes. No one chases me up three flights of cold stone stairs in my bare feet and gets away with it."

Jamie and David made their way slowly along the first floor, carefully checking each room as they came to it. It hadn't taken them long to work out an efficient system. They'd stop and listen carefully at the door, while Alistair and Brennan kept a watchful eye on the corridor. Then David would ease the door open, Jamie would kick it in, and they'd both charge into the room, swords at the ready. Once they were sure the room was empty, they'd turn the place upside down, just in case there were any secret hiding places Jamie didn't know about. Then out into the corridor, and do the same with the next room. Over and over again. The long run of empty rooms was starting to take its toll on their nerves, but Jamie and David stuck at it. Having to just stand and watch helplessly as the freak drained the life out of Greaves had hardened their hearts till there was no room in either of them for anything but revenge.

Jamie still had trouble believing Greaves was dead. The man had been with the MacNeils for more than twenty years; to Jamie it seemed as though he'd always been there. He'd often played with Jamie when he was a child, and been his confidant and advisor when no one else could be bothered to listen. He'd never been a warm man—there had always been something distant about him—but he was always there when Jamie needed him. And now he was gone; dead and gone, like all the others, and there was no one left to tell him what to do for the best. He was the MacNeil now, and the Family depended on him. His Family and his friends. He was damned if he'd let them down.

Alistair kept a careful watch on the empty corridor as Jamie and David ransacked another room. The girl Isobel worried him. Why should she insist on sticking by her brother when it must have been obvious to her that he was the freak, and her real brother was dead? Surely the freak couldn't be controlling her that completely. . . . No, if he had that kind of control, that kind of power, he wouldn't have run from them in the first place. Could it be that Isobel had seen something in Richard that proved he was still who he claimed to be . . . ? Alistair scowled. Richard had to be the freak; it was the only explanation that made sense after all the lies he'd caught the man in. Isobel just didn't want to believe her brother was dead. Alistair sighed, and hefted his sword thoughtfully. He'd have to be careful she didn't get hurt when they finally cornered the freak and killed him.

He glanced at Brennan, who was studying the darker shadows and alcoves with professional thoroughness. The man looked solid and reliable and somehow more alive than he'd ever seemed before. It was as though the man he'd once been had woken up and taken over from the second-rate minstrel he'd become. Alistair felt a hell of a lot safer with this new Brennan to guard his back. Jamie and David meant well, but they had no real experience with blood and pain and sudden death. That was why he let them check out the rooms. Wherever the freak had gone to ground, it wouldn't be in any of the rooms. He was too clever for that. No; far more likely he'd be using one of the old secret passages or hidden bolt holes, waiting for a chance to jump out on his unsuspecting pursuers and pick them off one at a time while they were busy searching empty rooms. . . .

Alistair took a deep breath, and let it out slowly. And swore to himself that when the moment finally came, no trace of compassion would stay his hand.

Hawk and Fisher sat side by side on the cold stone floor with their backs to the wall, as far away from the stairs as they could get. They'd been arguing for what seemed like hours, and they were still no nearer agreeing on anything. There were just too many theories and too few facts. They were after two men, not one, and anything that fit one case inevitably didn't fit with the other. They finally fell silent, staring up and down the gloomy, curving corridor. They didn't dare light any lamps for fear of giving away their position, and the shadows all around seemed dark and menacing and not a little mocking.

"There has to be an answer here somewhere," said Hawk wearily. "But I'm damned if I can see it."

"Keep looking," said Fisher. "We're running out of time. They'll be here soon. There must be something we're missing, something so obvious we're looking right past it."

"All right," said Hawk, "Let's try turning the problem on its head. Assume that all our assumptions so far are wrong. Where does that take us?"

"Right back where we started," said Fisher. "We can't just throw everything out, Hawk."

"Why not? Our assumptions aren't getting us anywhere. Start at the very beginning. We've been assuming the spy Fenris went to the sorcerer Grimm for a complete shapechange, so that no one would be able to recognize him. Which meant that anyone who could prove they'd had the same appearance for the past twenty-four hours could be ruled out as a suspect. But . . . what if the spy had *already* been to Grimm for a shapechange earlier on, and had just gone back there to get his old shape back?"

Fisher looked at him. "How the hell did we miss something that obvious?"

"Trying to do two jobs at once. This is the first real chance we've had to sit down and think things through since we got here."

"That's true. But if Fenris didn't change his appearance, then that throws everything wide open again. He could be anyone. That shapechange was the only way we had of separating Fenris out from the pack."

Hawk grinned. "There's one other way. Dubois told us the spy is a member of the Quality. And like I said at the time, why would one of the Quality want to be a spy? The usual incentives are politics and money, but most Quality don't give a damn about politics and already have more money than they can hope to spend in one lifetime. But one of our merry band here at Tower MacNeil has money problems coming out of his ears. He's admitted he has huge gambling debts, and even more damning, he actually talked about starting a business venture, a gossip paper, on the grounds it might make him money. What respectable member of the Quality would dirty his hands with vulgar trade unless he was desperate to pay off his debts?"

"David . . ." said Fisher. "David Brook. You're right Hawk; it fits!"

"He couldn't go to his Family or friends for the money without admitting he'd made a fool of himself, and his pride wouldn't allow him to do that. The moneylenders would want security he didn't have; he doesn't actually own anything solid until he inherits his estate on his father's death He was hoping to marry money through Holly, but according to Duncan's will, all she gets is some jewellery and whatever allowance Jamie feels like granting her."

"Right! That's why he got so upset on her behalf at the will reading!"

"Right. Holly was his last chance. He must have known he couldn't depend on her, and that's why he took to spying. With so many of his Family in the army and the diplomatic corps, he had opportunities to get at all sorts of information. He's our spy, Isobel. No doubt about it."

"Wait just a minute," said Fisher. "That's all very well but it doesn't help us one damn bit with our current problem, which is how to identify the freak before the others get here. If we can't point a convincing finger at someone else, they'll kill us. Or we'll have to kill them. And if we end up having to kill a bunch of Quality, even in self-defence, that's the end of us in Haven. All the Families in the city would declare vendetta against us, and the Guard would withdraw our immunity rather than openly confront the Quality."

"All right," said Hawk. "Don't panic. I'm working on it I still think it's Alistair. He lied to us about the Red Marches, and he was very quick to condemn me as the freak. Perhaps he thought he could turn suspicion away from himself by accusing me."

"He was pretty eager, wasn't he?" said Fisher. "And it's interesting that no one seems to actually remember him being banished from Tower MacNeil in the first place. He had to have been a contemporary of Duncan's, so how is it Katrina had never even heard of him?"

"Because Alistair doesn't exist," said Hawk. "He's just a mask the freak created to hide behind. Well, at least now we should be able to sow a few doubts; assuming we get a chance to speak our piece."

He broke off suddenly and looked towards the stairs. They both tensed as they heard quiet, furtive footsteps slowly drawing nearer. They rose quickly to their feet, throwing off their tiredness with practiced ease. They'd be tired later, when they had the time. Fisher's hand dropped to her side where her sword should have been, and she cursed briefly.

"We never did get round to finding me a sword." She reached out and took an oil lamp from its niche in the corridor wall. She shook it and listened to the oil gurgle, unscrewed the lamp into its two parts, and spilled the oil in a wide sweep across the floor. She then threw away the lamp, took a box of matches from her pocket, and held them concealed in her hand.

"Good thinking," said Hawk. "I've always admired your essentially sneaky and devious nature."

"You say the nicest things," said Fisher.

The footsteps grew louder. Hawk drew his sword, and he and Fisher stood side by side. Jamie and David appeared round the curve of the corridor, and came to a sudden halt as they saw their prey waiting patiently for them. Alistair and Brennan moved quickly in beside Jamie and David. Hawk fixed Jamie with his best authoritative gaze.

"Listen to me, Jamie; I'm not the freak, but I know who is."

"Kill him," said Jamie. "Shut his lying mouth."

The four of them started forward, swords raised. Hawk cursed, but held his ground. "Listen to me, dammit! I can prove what I'm saying!" Jamie broke into a run, David only a step behind him. Hawk looked at Fisher. "All right; do it."

Fisher struck a match. It flared up on the first try, and she dropped it into the oil. It caught in a second, and flames leapt up to block off the corridor. Hawk and Fisher backed away from the searing heat, and then tensed as a dark figure came hurtling through the flames. It was Alistair.

He stood before them, smoke rising from his smouldering clothes, his mouth stretched in a cold and deadly grin. He stepped forward, sword at the ready, and Hawk went to meet him. Sparks flew in the narrow corridor as steel rang on steel, and Hawk knew right away that he was in serious trouble. Alistair was a superior swordsman, and Hawk wasn't, anymore. With his axe in his hand he could probably still have given a good account of himself, but as it was it was all he could do to defend himself. He backed slowly down the corridor, using every trick he knew to buy himself some breathing space, but Alistair knew them all, and their counters. He began to press home his attack, his death's-head grin never once faltering. And then Fisher stepped out of the shadows to Alistair's left, and kicked him expertly behind the knee. He collapsed and fell forward as pain exploded in his leg. Hawk and Fisher turned and ran down the corridor.

Alistair slowly forced himself back onto one knee, paused for breath, and then got to his feet, favouring his aching leg. He'd underestimated Isobel. He wouldn't do that again. He looked back, and saw the others gingerly making their way round the edges of the dying flames. He gestured impatiently for them to join him, and started down the corridor after his prey, ignoring the pain in his leg.

Farther down the corridor, Hawk stopped suddenly and Fisher almost ran into him. "What is it, Hawk? Problem?"

"More like a stroke of luck," said Hawk. "I remember this bit of corridor. There's a secret passage here . . . somewhere. Jamie showed it to me earlier on." He pressed hard against a particular piece of stone moulding, and a section of the wall swung soundlessly open. Hawk grinned.

"Grab a lamp, Isobel. With any luck, it'll be ages before the others can be sure we're no longer on this floor."

Fisher took a lamp from the wall and lit it, and the two of them plunged into the narrow tunnel. The section of wall closed silently behind them.

In the library, Holly sat staring disconsolately into the fire. The quiet crackling of the flames was the only sound in the room. Arthur had tried to keep her spirits up with his usual dry humour and amusing anecdotes, but he soon stopped when he realized she wasn't listening. She couldn't seem to concentrate on anything but the thought that David was in danger and there was nothing she could do to help him.

She still couldn't believe how easily Richard had taken her in. Taken them all in. She should have sensed something was wrong about him . . . but she hadn't. Instead, she'd actually found him rather likeable, in an unpolished kind of way. The thought depressed her, and she looked listlessly round the room, searching for something her eyes could settle on that wouldn't require her to think or feel anything in particular. Arthur was sitting next to her, his eyelids drooping, a glass of something as always in his hand. He looked half asleep; either the drink or the strain was getting to him. Sitting next to him, Katrina glared blindly straight ahead, lost in thought, the heavy iron poker still clutched firmly in both hands. Her knuckles showed white from the fierceness of her grip. And Marc was sitting comfortably in his chair, a little away from the rest of them, staring thoughtfully at nothing. He seemed perfectly relaxed and at ease, and Holly looked at him enviously. Sometimes it seemed to her that she'd never feel relaxed again.

The flames leapt up suddenly as a log shifted in the fire, and Arthur studied it out of one eye for a moment, before letting it half close again. In a way, he almost wished he'd gone with the others. At least then he would have been doing something, instead of just waiting and worrying, not knowing what was happening. Maybe it was all over by now, and they'd found Richard and killed him, and everything could get back to normal again. Or maybe Richard had killed them all, picking them off one at a time from hiding, and was now on his way back down the stairs, to finish the job and silence everyone who could identify him. Arthur stirred unhappily, but kept his features relaxed and his eyes half closed. He didn't want Holly to see he was worried. She looked scared enough as it was.

His hand dropped self-consciously to the sword at his side. He'd had the same training all young Quality men went through as a matter of course, but truth be told he'd never drawn the blade in anger in his life. He'd never given much of a damn about his honour; certainly not enough to risk his life in a duel over it. Besides, he'd never been much of a swordsman, and he might have got hurt. But it wasn't just his life that was at stake now. There was Holly to think of. She was depending on him and Marc to defend her if things went wrong. Arthur's mouth tightened. Probably Marc would turn out to be an expert with a sword, and he wouldn't be needed. That was how things usually went. No one had ever needed Arthur in his life. But if worst came to worst, and there was only him left between Holly and the freak, he hoped he'd find the courage to do the right thing, for once in his life.

He looked across at Marc, and frowned slightly. He couldn't say he'd never warmed to the man. He seemed pleasant enough, in a dull, earnest kind of way, but basically Marc had all the character of a block of wood. He had no interests or opinions of his own, and absolutely no sense of humour. It wasn't often that Arthur found someone he could feel superior to, and he rather enjoyed the novelty, but there was something about Marc he didn't care for. He was too quiet, too bland, too self-effacing. It just wasn't natural for a man to be that polite. And then Marc raised his head and looked at Holly, and Arthur felt a sudden chill go through him. Marc looked different somehow. He looked . . . Arthur sat up straight suddenly as the thought hit him. Marc looked hungry.

Marc turned his head to look at Arthur, and smiled pleasantly.

"Something wrong, Arthur?"

Arthur tried to clear his throat, but his mouth was very dry. "I don't know."

"You look as though you've seen a ghost. Or something worse. What do you think, Arthur? Have you seen something worse?"

"Maybe. Maybe I have."

Katrina looked at them both, frowning. "What are you two talking about?"

"We're talking about me," said Marc. "It's a fascinating subject, really." He rose lithely to his feet and stood with his back to the fire, smiling easily at them all. "Tell me, Arthur, when did you first begin to suspect?"

"I'm not sure," said Arthur numbly. "Maybe earlier on, when I noticed you never ate anything that was offered to you, and although you always had a glass of wine in your hand, you never drank from it. Drunks notice that kind of thing. And you were always too self-controlled, too unaffected by the things that were happening here."

"Ah yes," said Marc. "Emotions. I never could get the hang of them. Unless you count hunger as an emotion. I'm always hungry."

"No," said Holly, her eyes widening as she shrank back in her chair. "It can't be. You can't be . . ."

"I'm afraid so," said Marc. "And they've all gone off and left the three of you alone with me. We're quite safe in here. No one can get to us; I've seen to that. Or did you never consider that a barricade will serve just as well to keep people in, as well as out?"

Katrina glared at him, holding her poker before her. "You come near me, and I'll kill you, you . . . freak!"

"Such a harsh word," said Marc. "But unfortunately for you, perfectly accurate. I'm afraid I've waited as long as I can, and I really don't care to wait any longer. The others will be busy killing each other by now, so we shouldn't be interrupted."

"You don't have to do this," said Holly. "We wouldn't tell anyone about you. Honest."

"Oh, I think you would," said Marc. "If you had the chance. But I'm afraid I can't afford to leave any witnesses. So I'll take care of you three first, and then I'll go upstairs and introduce myself to whatever survivors there may be. I couldn't do that before; I wasn't strong enough. And the memories got in the way. But now Greaves is mine, the memories are under control, and after I've drained the life and strength out of you as well . . . When the wards go down tomorrow morning, I shall leave this Tower and go down into the city, and I will feed and feed and feed, and never be hungry again.

"I think I'll start with you, Holly. I've always admired you. Like a rose without a thorn; so pretty, so vulnerable. That's why I came to you in the night, while you slept, and took a little life from you, to keep myself going. Your memories drifted through my mind like petals on a breeze, sweet but unsatisfying. Did you dream of me, perhaps? I'd like to think you did. I dreamed of someone like you for years. And now you're mine."

He started towards Holly, and Arthur scrambled to his

feet. He drew his sword and put himself between her and the freak, hoping he looked more impressive than he felt.

"Get away from her, you bastard. I won't let you hurt her."

The freak just stood there, smiling. "Very nicely said, Arthur. Now put away your sword and sit down. I'll get round to you, when I'm ready."

"I mean it!"

"I'm sure you do. But there's nothing you can do to stop me. As long as I'm within arm's reach of someone, I can drain the life right out of them. Besides, it's obvious from the way you're holding your sword that you don't really know how to use it. Marc knew about things like that, and now, so do I. I wonder what I'll know when I've emptied your head, Arthur. How to mix cocktails, perhaps?"

"Stay back," said Arthur. His voice sounded shaky, even to him, but at least his sword hand was steady. He'd often dreamed of standing between Holly and some unidentified villain, being the hero of the moment, but now the time had come and he'd never felt so scared in his life. But he wouldn't back down. Holly needed him. The thought steadied him, and he stepped smartly forward, his sword shooting out in a textbook lunge. Marc sidestepped elegantly, and dropped a hand on Arthur's outstretched arm. The sword fell to the floor as his hand went numb. A wave of shuddering cold swept through him as the strength went out of him and into Marc. He fell limply forward, his face striking hard against the floor, but he couldn't feel it. He tried to get to his feet again, and couldn't move. He would have been frightened, but his thoughts were growing too dim even for that. And then Marc's hand was suddenly jerked away from his arm, and his thoughts began to clear.

Marc fell back a step as Katrina swung the iron poker with both hands again. The first blow had connected strongly enough with Marc's head to send him staggering sideways, but there was no sign of any wound. *Of course not,* thought Katrina crazily. *He's not really there. That's just an illusion of Marc. Behind the illusion, he's probably bleeding like a stuck pig.* The thought comforted her as she swung the poker again, putting all her strength into it.

Marc's hand shot out at the last moment and intercepted the poker, absorbing its momentum with hardly a jolt, though Katrina's hand went numb from the impact. Marc smiled at her, and her eyes rolled up in her head as he sucked the strength out of her. She collapsed in a heap, and Marc let the poker drop to the floor beside her. He turned to face Holly again, and then stopped as Arthur grabbed him by the ankle. Marc tried to pull free, and couldn't.

Arthur's fingers whitened as he put all his remaining strength into his grip. Holly needed him. Nothing else mattered. Marc bent down and picked up the poker he'd dropped. Arthur knew what was going to happen, but didn't have the strength to turn his head away. He couldn't even shut his eyes. Marc struck down hard with the poker, and Arthur's vision disappeared behind a sudden rush of blood. He still wouldn't let go. Holly needed him. Marc hit him again, and again.

Holly burst out of her chair and threw herself at Marc, screaming and flailing at him with her fists. Marc stumbled backwards and almost fell, but he quickly regained his balance and grabbed one of her waving arms. She fell to her knees as the strength went out of her, and he smiled down at her.

"Don't be so impatient, Holly. I'll be with you in a moment." He bent down and struck repeatedly at Arthur's hand with the poker. The sound of bones breaking and splintering was horribly loud on the quiet. Marc pulled his foot free, threw aside the poker, and turned back to look at Holly. "There; that didn't take too long, did it? Now I'm free to give you my full attention."

He smiled slowly. "You know, Holly, you're all I ever dreamed of, down all the years, locked away in stone and silence. I watched the light come and go through the narrow slit of window, and listened to the gulls screaming, and felt the slow turning of the seasons . . . and dreamed about what I'd do when I finally got out. At first I dreamed of blood and pain and sweet revenge, and then I dreamed of the world beyond the Tower, and all the terrible things I would do there, and then I dreamed of women, and all the warmth and kindness and beauty I've always longed for, and never known except in dreams."

"But the years passed, and the dreams got mixed up with each other, until I really don't know what I want anymore.

I want you, Holly; you're all I ever dreamed of. So I'm going to hurt you and drain you and hurt you some more and maybe finally I'll hurt you till you die of it, because I want you so much it hurts. Come to me, Holly. No need to be afraid. After all, I'm just one of the Family."

Holly jerked her arm free from his grip and scrambled to her feet, backing away across the room as he came unhurriedly after her. She looked desperately around for help, but Katrina was lying unconscious on the floor, and Arthur was only moving feebly, despite the desperation on his bloody face. Holly wanted to cry, for them and for herself, but there wasn't time. She kept backing away, and Marc kept coming after her, still smiling. She wanted to scream for help, to Jamie or David or one of the others, but she knew they were too far away to hear her. There was no one to help her. So she'd just have to do it herself.

You're a MacNeil. Act like one.

She chanted that silently to herself, like a prayer or a penance, as her gaze swept the room, searching for something she could use as a weapon. Maybe a brand from the fire; she could set his clothes alight. Except that the fireplace was on the other side of the room now, and he stood between it and her. There were heavy paperweights on the desk, but even as she looked at them, Marc intercepted her gaze and moved to block her way to the desk. She thought about making a dash for the door, but one glance was enough to convince her that she'd never be able to dismantle the barricade before Marc got to her. She smiled humourlessly. She'd felt so safe behind that barricade. . . . Think, dammit, think! She passed by an oil lamp on the wall, and without hesitating snatched it from its niche and threw it at Marc with all her strength. She just had time for a brief fantasy of his being consumed by blazing oil, and then Marc's hand shot up and snatched the lamp effortlessly out of midair. He put it gently down on a nearby chair, and smiled condescendingly.

"Your problem, Holly, is that you keep thinking I'm human. And I'm not. Not really. Why don't I show you what I look like? What I really look like. Would you like that?"

Holly tried to say something, but her throat had clamped shut, and she couldn't make a sound. She'd somehow ended up by the desk, and her desperate gaze fell upon a slim silver letter opener. She looked quickly away again in case Marc had noticed, but his gaze seemed fixed on her. For the first time, he'd stopped smiling. Something stirred in her mind, like suddenly becoming aware of a background noise that had just stopped. Marc seemed to ripple and flow, like something far away seen through a heat haze, and then Marc was gone and the freak stood before her.

Her first thought was *That's not so bad.* She'd been expecting something hideous, some awful misshapen thing, with fangs and claws and bulging eyes, but instead he looked surprisingly ordinary. He was average height but very thin and bony, wrapped in clothes that were too big for him. Marc's clothes. Holly supposed that wearing them made the illusion easier to maintain. Or perhaps it just made the freak feel more like an ordinary man. His left arm and leg were severely twisted, and his left shoulder was clearly lower than the other, but none of it was enough to mark him as a freak. And then she looked at his face, and didn't know whether to laugh or scream. It was a normal enough face, surrounded by long greasy hair and a stringy beard, and flecked with blood from a recent scalp wound, but sometime in the past, the mouth had been sewn together. The heavy black stitches had sunk deep into the lips, compressing them into a thin white line. Holly wondered who'd done it; presumably the father, before walling the freak up in his cell. *And why not?* she thought crazily. *He doesn't need a mouth, after all.*

"How do you speak?" she said shrilly.

The mouth twitched in something that might have been meant as a smile. "It's all part of the illusion, my dear. You hear what I want you to hear. But this has gone on long enough, I think. It's time."

He started towards her, his laughter sounding in her mind. She snatched up the letter opener from the desk and thrust it between his ribs. He grunted once, a dark hungry sound like a pig at its trough, and grabbed both her arms, ignoring the blood coursing down his side. Holly tried to struggle, but all the strength went out of her at his touch. She couldn't even scream as the freak's thin white mouth slowly widened into a grin, the heavy stitches tearing through his lips.

And then a section of the library wall swung open, and Hawk and Fisher plunged out into the room. The freak spun round, throwing Holly to one side. Hawk hesitated just long enough to take in the situation, and then cut at the freak with his sword. The freak raised his arm at the last moment, and the blade cut into his arm instead of his throat. Hawk danced back out of range as the freak reached for him, blood dripping unheeded from his arm. Fisher circled round to try and get behind him. Holly struggled to get to her feet. Hawk stepped in to cut at the freak again, and fell to his knees as every muscle in his body turned to mush. He shook his head sickly, managing somehow to still hang on to his sword, though he no longer had the strength to lift it. The freak reached down and took Hawk's face in his hand. The fingers tightened, and Hawk's cheekbones shifted and creaked under the rising pressure. Fisher snatched a burning brand from the fire and thrust it at the freak's back. The strength went out of her fingers as she came within range, and the burning brand fell from her grasp onto the rug before the fireplace. Flames leapt up as the rug caught fire.

Holly threw herself at the freak, the sudden weight catching him by surprise and knocking him away from Hawk. The freak landed on his back on the burning rug, and flames leapt up around him as his clothes caught fire. He surged to his feet again, throwing Holly to one side, and lurched back and forth, beating ineffectually at his burning clothes with his hands. There was a silent puff of blue flames as his hair ignited. Hawk and Fisher had got some of their strength back, and were on their feet again. Hawk still had his sword, and Fisher snatched up a heavy footstool to use as a club. Holly rose to her feet, ignoring her smouldering clothes, and looked around for something to use as a weapon. The freak turned his back on them and made for the door. He tore apart the barricade, throwing aside the bulky furniture with inhuman strength, and pulled open the door. He staggered out into the corridor, and Hawk and Fisher went after him.

The flames were leaping high now, and his skin was beginning to blacken, but still he never made a sound. He glanced back at his pursuers, made for the stairs, and then stopped as he looked up and saw Jamie leading his party down the stairs towards him. The freak looked back and forth, his mutilated mouth twisted in a snarl, and then his power leapt out, driven beyond its usual limits by hate and desperation. One by one those on the stairs slumped to the ground, their eyes slowly closing as the last bit of strength drained from them, until only Alistair remained on his feet. He advanced slowly down the stairs, his face eerily lit by the flames that still leapt around the freak.

"It's no use, boy," he said softly, so that only the freak would hear. "Your power can't affect me. I'm no more human than you are."

They stood face to face for a moment, staring at each other, and then Alistair's sword shot out and buried itself in the freak's chest. He collapsed silently to the floor, twitched a few times and lay still, curled around his death wound. The leaping flames tugged at his clothes, but did not stir him. Alistair pulled out the sword, and then carefully and methodically cut off the freak's head, just in case. One by one, the others rose unsteadily to their feet as strength flowed slowly back into them. Alistair sheathed his sword, and went over to Hawk.

"It seems I owe you an apology. I was so sure you were the freak. But then, I'm only human."

Back in the library, the room became a bedlam as everyone talked at once, explaining and apologizing and generally relaxing. Holly fussed around Arthur, wrapping his broken hand in a cloth and trying to clean the blood from his face with a handkerchief soaked in wine. David kept squeezing Arthur's shoulder, and telling him incoherently how well he'd done. But finally Jamie confronted Hawk, and everyone else shut up so they could listen.

"I think you owe us some answers," said Jamie. "All right, we were wrong about you being the freak. I'm sorry, but you have been behaving very suspiciously. Who are you, really, and what are you doing here? And what the hell happened to your eye?"

"I can't tell you who I am," said Hawk flatly. "But I can tell you why I'm here. Isobel and I came here looking for someone."

"Who?"

Hawk turned and looked at David. "Do you want to tell them, or shall I?"

David shrugged, and met the MacNeil's gaze unflinchingly. "Sorry, Jamie, but I'm afraid I've rather let the side down. I'm a spy. I stumbled across a piece of information I knew Outremer would pay a hell of a lot for, and the temptation was just too great. I needed the money, you see. I owe a hell of a lot, what with one thing and another, much more than you ever knew about, and some of my creditors were becoming very insistent. There was even talk of debtors' prison. My Family had already made it clear they wouldn't be responsible for my debts anymore, and without their backing the moneylenders wouldn't even see me.

"It wasn't difficult, making contact with Outremer. You'd be surprised how many agents they have here in the city. But in the end it all went wrong, and I ended up running for my life. So I came here, to hide out while I waited for my contact to show up. I had to come anyway, to see what Holly was going to get from the will. I was banking on her inheriting a fortune, to get me out of the hole I'd dug for myself. She'd have loaned me what I needed. Hell, you'd have given it to me outright, wouldn't you, Holly? You never could deny me anything."

"Why the hell didn't you ask me for the money?" said Jamie hotly. "I wouldn't have let you go under, for the sake of a miserable few thousand ducats."

"I couldn't ask you, or any of my friends," said David. "I didn't want you to know what a fool I'd made of myself. I have my pride. It's all I've got left now. I won't give it up. I won't stand trial, either. Arthur, look after Holly."

He turned and ran out the door, and into the corridor. Hawk and Fisher went after him. Hawk paused at the door to order everyone else to stay put in the library, and then he and Fisher charged down the corridor and up the stairs in pursuit of David Brook. They were both tired after their struggle with the freak, and David soon outdistanced them. They pressed on, following the sound of his feet on the stairs. They passed the second floor and the third, and still David led them on.

"Where the hell does he think he's going?" panted

Fisher. "There's nowhere left now but the battlements, and once he's there, we've got him cornered."

"Not necessarily," said Hawk. "There's still one way down, if he wants to take it."

They finally burst out into the morning air, and found David sitting on the edge of the far parapet wall, waiting for them. Fisher started forward, but Hawk put a restraining hand on her arm. The sunlight was almost painfully bright after the gloom of the third floor, and Hawk stood quietly a moment, letting his eye adjust. David sat patiently, his legs dangling over the long drop. He was smiling slightly.

"Come away from the edge," said Hawk finally. "It's dangerous."

"Look at the view," said David. "Isn't it marvelous? It feels like you can see forever."

"Is that why you dragged us all the way up here?" said Fisher. "To admire the view?"

David shrugged, and smiled. "I won't ask you how I gave myself away. It doesn't matter. I was pretty much an amateur at the spying game, anyway. But I would like to know who you really are."

"Hawk and Fisher, Captains in the city Guard," said Hawk. "We're the ones who chased you through half of Haven last night."

David raised an eyebrow. "I'm impressed. I've heard some of the stories they tell about you two. Are they true?"

"Some of them," said Hawk.

"What did you do with the sorcerer Grimm?"

"We killed him," said Fisher.

"Good," said David. "The city probably smells better now he's gone. I wouldn't have dealt with him at all if my contact hadn't insisted."

"Who was your contact?" said Hawk.

David shrugged. "It was always someone different. They didn't trust me enough to let me see anyone important."

"What about the information?" said Fisher. "What was so important that so many people had to risk their lives because of it?"

David stared out across the sea. "The Monarch of Outremer is coming here, to Haven, to meet with our King and hammer out a Peace Treaty to put an end to the border clashes, before they start really getting out of hand. But there are those on both sides who would profit greatly from a war, people who don't want the peace talks to succeed. Knowing the exact date and time and place of those talks was therefore of very great value to those with an interest in sabotaging them. And I knew. I just happened to be in the wrong place at the wrong time, and nosy enough to look at a sheet of paper left lying carelessly on a desk. And that's how it all started. As simply as that."

"Come away from the edge," said Hawk. "You might fall."

"I'm not going back," said David. "If I were put on trial, it would disgrace my Family's name. I can't do that. I've been enough of a disappointment to them as it is. Besides, my friends would be found guilty by association, just for knowing me. And Holly would be hounded, ostracized, because she was close to me. I can't have that. I think Holly could be happy with Arthur. Don't you?"

"Yes," said Hawk. "He cares for her."

"Good," said David, and pushed himself out and away from the wall. He didn't scream, all the way down to the rocks at the bottom of the cliffs.

8

Saying Goodbye

The wards finally went down at ten o'clock the next morning. A subtle vibration came and went on the air, and the solid weight of Tower MacNeil seemed to settle itself more comfortably, and as suddenly and simply as that, it was over. Hawk ceremoniously opened the front door, and he and Fisher stepped out into the brisk morning air. It was a fine sunny morning, with only the cold nip of the wind to remind them of how close winter was. Gulls rode the wind on outstretched wings, crying and keening, and from far below came the endless crash of waves on the rocks.

Only Jamie and Robbie Brennan were there to say goodbye, and Hawk and Fisher were just as happy that way. It had been an uncomfortable time for all of them, waiting for the wards to go down. Hawk and Fisher might have saved the day, but their very presence was a reminder of things the MacNeils were eager to forget. The four of them stood together a moment, two within the Tower and two without, none of them sure what to say for the best. In the end, Jamie coughed awkwardly, and they all looked at him expectantly.

"You've done my Family a great service," he said firmly. "The freak is finally at rest, and the MacNeils are free of their Curse, if not their Shame. I wish you'd let me reward you in some way. Just saying thanks doesn't seem nearly enough."

"Thanks are all we want," said Hawk. "We're just grateful you haven't insisted on knowing who we really are."

"I have a strong feeling I should," said Jamie, trying not to stare at Hawk's closed right eye, "But I'm equally sure I wouldn't like the answer. You'd probably only lie, anyway."

Hawk and Fisher grinned, and said nothing.

"I'm afraid we're all the send-off you're going to get," said Brennan. "The others have all managed to be very busy just at the moment. Holly and Lord Arthur are comforting each other, as best they can. For the moment they both miss David too much to think of anything else, but I wouldn't be surprised if they ended up staying together. I think they'd be good for each other. Who knows? Maybe she'll even stop him drinking."

Hawk smiled. "It's possible, I suppose. Stranger things have happened."

"Aunt Katrina is upstairs packing," said Jamie. "I told her she was still welcome to stay as long as she wished, but it would appear she can't wait to leave. She says she doesn't feel safe here anymore. I can understand that. I've lived all my life in the Tower, and I don't feel the same about it now. It's as though an old and trusted friend had suddenly revealed a dark and violent side to his nature, something you'd never even suspected before. I'll probably get over it, but I don't think I'll ever really trust the Tower again."

"Where's she going?" said Hawk.

Jamie shrugged. "Back to the city. I don't think she herself knows where she's going yet."

"Maybe she'll go back to her husband," said Fisher.

"I hope not," said Brennan. "For his sake. I wouldn't wish Katrina on my worst enemy. At least not unless I was in a really nasty mood."

"What about Alistair?" said Hawk. "He spent most of yesterday evening trying to avoid us."

"He's around somewhere," said Jamie. "Hiding his face. I think he still feels guilty about accusing you of being the freak. No doubt he'll turn up again, once you're safely gone."

There was another pause as they ran out of polite, unimportant things to say.

"I'm sorry about David," said Hawk finally. "He wasn't a bad sort. We would have taken him alive, if we could."

"I know that," said Jamie. "I've no doubt it happened just the way you described. David was many things, but he was never a coward. He knew there was only one thing he could do to protect his Family, and he did it. I don't know what I'm going to tell them. Some of the truth is bound to come out, eventually. I can't even bring his body home to them. The tides have already taken it out to sea. I still feel guilty about him, you know. I was his friend. I should have realized something was wrong. If I had, maybe I could have found a way to help him, before he got mixed up with the wrong people. . . ."

"Stop that," said Brennan firmly. "If David had wanted you to know, he would have told you. He had enough opportunities. But his pride wouldn't let him. Or perhaps he just didn't want to drag his friends down with him. Whatever happened is his responsibility, no one else's. You're the MacNeil now, Jamie. You must learn not to worry about things that can't be changed."

Jamie nodded slowly, but still looked unconvinced. Hawk decided this might be a good time to change the subject, and cleared his throat loudly. "What about you, Robbie? What are you going to do with yourself, now that Duncan's left you such a sizeable windfall?"

Robbie grinned. "Damned if I know, to be honest. But I might just do a little travelling. It's a long time since I was out in the world. There's bound to have been a lot of changes, and I think I'd like to see some of them while I still can. Not that I haven't been happy here, Jamie, but it's not the same with Duncan gone. I'll look back from time to time, see how you're getting on; sing you any new songs I've picked up."

"Yes, of course," said Jamie. "That would be nice."

Brennan laughed. "You're not fooling anyone, Jamie. You never did appreciate my singing."

"It's an acquired taste," said Jamie solemnly. "And I've only been listening to you for about twenty years."

They all smiled genuinely, and Hawk put out his hand to Jamie. The MacNeil shook it firmly. There was a quick burst of handshaking all round, and Hawk led Fisher away, before the goodbyes could become awkward again. They set off down the trail that led to the city, and didn't look back.

"Well," said Hawk finally, "how did you like being one of the Quality, Isobel?"

Fisher snorted. "The food was good and the wines were splendid, but the company sucked and I hate their idea of fashion. The corset pinches me every time I breathe, having my hair piled up like this makes my head ache, and these shoes are killing me."

Hawk smiled. "Just be grateful we didn't have to mix with a dozen or more Families in High Society."

"I am grateful," said Fisher. "Believe me."

"I don't think we did too badly. We didn't hit anyone."

Fisher shook her head. "You don't have the right attitude for High Society, Hawk."

"Hark who's talking."

They laughed quietly together, and made their way back down towards Haven.

Alistair stood alone in the drawing room, looking up at the portrait of the Family Guardian hanging over the fireplace. The room was very quiet, the only sound the soft crackling of the fire. He knew he didn't have much time before the others would come looking for him, but still he hesitated, torn with indecision. It was such a long time since he'd last walked the corridors of the Tower. He hadn't realized he'd miss it so much.

He looked round the drawing room, deliberately not hurrying himself, taking in all the details. They'd made a lot of changes since his day. He didn't care for most of them, but then, fashions change. He walked slowly round the room, smelling the flowers and admiring the paintings and tapestries, and letting his fingers drift over the polished surfaces of the furniture. He couldn't stay. It was his home, but he couldn't stay. He didn't belong here anymore. The young girl Holly had begged for him to come, and so he had, but he wasn't needed anymore. The freak was dead at last, finally at peace.

He turned back to face the portrait again. It was time to go, before the others realized he wasn't really Alistair Mac-Neil after all. He wanted so much to stay, to walk in the real world, to see the sun rise and fall and feel the wind on his face . . . but he still had his penance to fulfill. The penance he'd taken on so many years ago, for the terrible things he'd done to his son, the freak.

The MacNeil Family Guardian held his head high and disappeared back into the portrait hanging over the fireplace, waiting to be called again, in time of need.

Whenever they might need him.

Guard Against Dishonor

1

Chacal

There are bad cities, there are worse cities; and then there's Haven.

By popular acclaim the vilest and most corrupt city in the Low Kingdoms, Haven in midwinter gleams purest white under falls of frozen snow, and its towers shine with frost and ice like pillars of crystal. But only from a distance. The snow on the ground is a dirty grey from the unceasing factory smoke, and grey-faced people trudge wearily through the snow-choked streets.

Seen up close, Haven is an ugly city, in more ways than one. Even in the early morning, when the killing cold grips the streets like a clenched fist, there is still no peace for the city. There are still deals to be made, conspiracies to be entered into, and blood to be spilled. Death is a way of life in Haven, and sudden violence the pulse of its narrow streets.

And only the city Guard, stretched to breaking point at the best of times, stands between the city and open, bloody chaos.

Hawk and Fisher, husband and wife and Captains in the city Guard, strode briskly down the crowded street towards Guard Headquarters, their prisoner scurrying along between them. Winter had finally come to Haven, despite everything the city weather wizards could do, and the bitter air was several degrees below freezing. The street was ankle-deep in snow and slush, and thick icicles hung from every building. Roofs groaned under the weight of a week's accumulated snow, and the iron-grey sky promised more blizzards to come. But still people packed the street from end to end; men, women, and children jostling each other impatiently as they hurried to and from work. No one jostled Hawk and Fisher, of course. It wouldn't have been wise.

It was eight o'clock in the morning, but so dark that street lamps still burned at every corner, their amber glare doing little to dispel the gloom. Hawk hated the winter, and not just because the recent flu epidemic had hit the Guard badly and he and Fisher were working a double shift for the third day running. Winter meant hard times in Haven, and hardest of all for the poor and destitute. In every street, in every part of the city, there were bodies lying stiff and cold, caught out in the freezing night because they had nowhere else to go. They ended up in sheltered doorways, or huddled together under tarpaulins in back alleyways, sharing their meager warmth as best they could. Every day the garbage squad made their rounds and hauled the bodies away, but there were always more. Hawk found a young girl once, curled in a tight little ball over a street grating. She couldn't have been more than five or six years old, and her staring eyes had frozen solid in her head. Hawk hated the winter, and sometimes he hated Haven too.

Captain Hawk was tall, dark-haired, and no longer handsome. A series of old scars ran down the right side of his face, and a black silk patch covered his right eye. He told lots of stories about how he got the scars, most of them contradictory. His thick furs and official black cloak made him look impressively bulky, but underneath his winter uniform he was lean and wiry rather than muscular, and building a stomach. He wore his shoulder-length hair loose, mostly to keep his ears warm, and kept it out of his vision with a plain leather headband. He'd only just turned thirty, but already there were streaks of grey in his hair. At first glance he seemed like just another bravo, a sword-for-hire already past his prime, but few people ever stopped at a first glance. There was something about Hawk, something cold and unyielding that gave even the most belligerent hardcase pause to think twice. On his right hip, Hawk carried a short-handled axe instead of a sword. He was very good with an axe. He'd had lots of practice.

Captain Isobel Fisher walked confidently at his side, echoing her partner's stance and pace with the naturalness of long companionship. She was tall, easily six feet in height, and her long blond hair fell to her waist in a single thick plait, weighted at the tip with a polished steel ball. She wore a battered and almost shapeless fur hat, pulled down low to protect her ears from the bitter cold. There was a rawboned harshness to her face, barely softened by her deep blue eyes and generous mouth. She was handsome rather than pretty, her gaze was cool and direct, and she didn't smile much. Sometime, somewhere in the past, something had scoured all the human weaknesses out of her, and it showed. She wore the same furs and cloak as Hawk, though with rather more grace and style. She wore a sword on her hip, and her skill with it was legendary, in a city not easily impressed by legends.

Hawk and Fisher, feared and respected by one and all as the toughest and most honest Guards in Haven. They had a lot of enemies, both inside and outside the Guard.

Their prisoner was a short, scrawny, harmless-looking man, wrapped in a long fur coat, topped off with a pair of fluffy earmuffs. His thinning black hair was plastered to his head with rather more grease than necessary, and he had a permanent scowl. Benny the Weasel was not a happy man.

"You're making a terrible mistake," he repeated for the tenth time, in what he imagined was an ingratiating tone. "Let's be reasonable about this."

"Sorry," said Hawk, without looking round. "I'm only reasonable at weekends. And Fisher doesn't believe in being reasonable. Says it's bad for her image."

"Right," said Fisher, glaring horribly at a nun who hadn't got out of her way fast enough.

"This is all a misunderstanding," said Benny doggedly. "I am a legitimate businessman."

Hawk snorted derisively. "Benny, you are a small-time villain who makes most of his money running a nasty little protection racket, advising local shopkeepers of all the awful things that might happen to them or their premises if they don't keep up the payments. Only this time you were dumb enough to do it in person, in front of Fisher and me. What's the matter, both your leg-breakers down with the flu?"

Benny sniffed. "You can't get good help these days. Look, I am an important figure in the community. I know my rights. I pay my taxes. Technically, you work for me."

"Then you should be pleased to be getting such value for your money," said Fisher. "We witnessed a crime and arrested the criminal on the spot. What more do you want?"

"You won't get away with this!" said Benny desperately. "I have friends. I have influence. You won't be able to make this charge stick. I'll be out on the streets again before you can blink!"

Hawk looked at him. "You know, Benny, you're starting to get on my nerves. Now, be a good fellow and shut your face or I'll have Fisher take you into the nearest dark alley and reason with you for a while."

Benny glanced at Fisher, and then looked quickly away when he discovered she was smiling at him. He'd heard about Fisher's idea of reasoning with people. If she did it where they lived, it tended to play hell with the furniture. Benny had second thoughts, and they walked the rest of the way in silence.

Guard Headquarters loomed up before them, a massive squat stone building with heavy oaken doors and arrow-slit windows. It had the look of a place constantly under siege, which wasn't far off the mark. Riots, hexes, and fire-bombings were a part of everyday life for the Headquarters, but no one had ever closed it down for more than a few hours. It had its own sorcerers, and everyone in the building went armed at all times, from the clerks to the Commanders. It took a lot to disrupt the Headquarters' even running, though last year's rash of possessions had come close.

The main doors were always open, but everyone knew that could change in a second if danger threatened. A long-established spell on the doors saw to that, and tough luck if anyone got in the way. A steady stream of people bustled in and out of the building as Hawk and Fisher approached with their prisoner. There was the usual mixture of Constables and the people helping them with their enquiries, along with anxious relatives searching for the recently arrested, and backstreet lawyers touting for business. And of course there were always those who'd come to the Guard for help, all with the same thinly disguised look of fear and desperation. Most people only went to the Guard when they'd tried everything else. The law was harsh and brutal, and weighted heavily in favour of the rich and powerful. There were Guards who were sympathetic, and would do what they could for those in real need, but for the most part the poor had no reason to trust the Guard. Like everything else in Haven, justice was for sale. Everyone had their price. Everyone except Hawk and Fisher.

Benny thought fleetingly of making a run for it, then noticed that Fisher's hand was resting casually on the pommel of her sword, and quickly thought better of it. He sighed heavily, and accompanied Hawk and Fisher through the main doors and into the crowded lobby of Guard Headquarters. The wide, low-ceilinged room was packed from wall to wall, and the noise was deafening. Mothers and grandmothers sat in little groups against the walls, chatting and gossiping and keeping a watchful eye on their children as they scampered back and forth, getting in everyone's way. None of them had any real business at Headquarters, but the Guard let them stay. It was the only place in that area where small children could play safely. Besides which, the Guard Constables had found they could pick up a lot of useful information by casually listening in on the women's gossip.

Over by the booking desk in the centre of the lobby, a seething mob of people screamed and shouted and pleaded, together with much shedding of tears and beating of breasts, but the three desk Sergeants took it in their stride. They'd heard it all before. They nodded more or less sympathetically to worried relatives, glared at the lawyers, and got on with booking the various criminals as the Constables brought them forward, as though the utter bedlam around them was of absolutely no interest.

Hawk and Fisher made their way through the shifting mass of bodies by sheer determination and liberal use of their elbows. Hawk hammered on the desk with his fist until he got a Sergeant's attention, and then handed Benny over into his keeping. The Sergeant fixed him with a malicious grin.

"Well, well, what have we here? It's not often you grace us with your loathsome company, Benny. What did you do to upset Hawk and Fisher?"

"Nothing! I was just minding my own business . . ."

"Your business is illegal, Benny, and if you were stupid

enough to do it in front of those two, you deserve everything that happens to you." He struck the large brass bell
beside him, the sharp sound cutting cleanly through the
surrounding babble, and a Constable came over to the desk
and led Benny away. Hawk and Fisher watched them go,
Benny the Weasel still loudly protesting his innocence.

"We won't be able to hold him, you know," said the
desk Sergeant.

Fisher looked at him sharply. "Why the hell not? We'll
both give evidence against him."

"It'll never come to trial," said the Sergeant. "Benny has
friends, hard though that is to believe. The word will come
down, and we'll have to let him go."

Fisher scowled. "Sometimes I wonder why we bother
making arrests at all. These days, it seems practically every
villain and thug we meet has connections with someone
higher up. Or the judge gets bribed. Or the jury gets
intimidated."

"That's Haven for you," said the Sergeant. "Hey, don't
look at me. I just work here."

Fisher growled something indistinct, and allowed Hawk
to pull her away from the desk. They elbowed their way
back through the crowd, glaring down any objections, and
found a place by the huge open fireplace to warm their
hands and take a seat for a moment. They nodded amiably
to the half-dozen Constables already there. None of them
actually had any business that required their presence at
Headquarters, but none of them were that keen to give up
the nice warm lobby for the freezing cold outside. Hawk
turned around and lifted his cloak to warm his backside at
the fire. He smiled happily and looked out over the lobby.

A small group of whores, looking bright and gaudy and
not a little chilly in their working finery, were waiting patiently to be booked, fined, and released so that they could
get back to work as quickly as possible. Some politician or
newspaper editor must have had a sudden attack of principles, or been leaned on by some pressure group, and declared loudly that Something Should Be Done about the
rising tide of vice in Our Fair City. So the Guard made a
big show of arresting whoever happened to be around at
the time, the pimps paid the fines out of their petty cash,
and business went on as usual. Hawk shrugged. It was none

of his business. He nodded to a few familiar faces, and then tensed as one of the girls was viciously backhanded by her pimp. Hawk strode quickly over to them and dropped a heavy hand on the pimp's shoulder. The pimp spun round, knocking the hand away, and then froze as he realised who it was. He was young and muscular, with a ratty-looking moustache, dressed to the nines and proud of it. He studied Hawk warily.

"What do you want, Captain? I'm clean."

"You wouldn't be clean if you washed every day with sulphuric acid. You are a pimp, Sebastian, the lowest of the low, and I know you of old. I thought I warned you about maltreating your girls."

"Me? Hurt my girls?" said Sebastian, looking around him as though to invite the world to witness his harassment. "I love my girls like sisters! Who sees they always have nice clothes to wear, and looks after all their needs? They're like family to me, all my girls. They just need a little firm guidance from time to time, that's all."

"Your associate and business partner, that nasty little thug Bates, is currently awaiting trial for 'firmly guiding' one of your girls by slashing her face with a razor," said Hawk. "I know you, Sebastian; I know you and all your nasty little ways. And if I discover you've been firmly guiding any of your girls again, I shall be annoyed with you. You do remember what happened when I got annoyed with Bates, don't you?"

The pimp nodded reluctantly. "He's making good progress. He should be out of hospital soon."

"Really? I must be losing my touch. Keep your hands off the girls, Sebastian. Or I'll tie your fingers in knots."

Sebastian smiled and nodded as though it hurt him, and disappeared into the crowd. Hawk watched him go, nodded politely to the whores, who ignored him, and made his way back to the fire. Fisher was down on her knees, playing with a few children too young to be afraid of a Guard's uniform. Hawk watched for a while, smiling gently. Isobel was good with kids. They'd talked about having children of their own more than once, but somehow it never seemed to be the right time.

The crowd suddenly erupted in shouts and screams, and backed quickly away as a prisoner who'd broken away from his escort lashed about him with a knife he'd somehow kept hidden. He grabbed for one of the children by Fisher, obviously intending to use the child as a hostage. Fisher glanced round and back-elbowed him viciously in the groin. She rose unhurriedly to her feet as the prisoner hunched forward over his pain, then rabbit-punched him. He collapsed and lay still. Fisher kicked the knife away from his hand and went back to playing with the children. Two Constables dragged the unconscious prisoner away.

Hawk decided regretfully that they'd killed about as much time as they could get away with, and they ought really to get back to the job. They were barely halfway through their second shift. He tried concentrating on all the overtime they were racking up, but it didn't help. His feet were numb, his forehead still ached from the cold, and his back was killing him. Hawk hated the winter. He collected Fisher, waved goodbye to the kids and their unresponsive mothers, and strode resignedly out into the waiting cold. And the first thing he saw was Benny the Weasel shivering in a borrowed cloak as he tried unsuccessfully to hail a sedan chair. Hawk and Fisher looked at each other, and strolled casually over to join him. Benny saw them coming, and clearly thought about making a run for it, before better sense took over. He drew himself up to his full five foot six and tried to brazen it out.

"Benny," said Hawk reproachfully, "what do you think you're doing out here?"

"They let me go," said Benny quickly, his eyes darting from Hawk to Fisher and back again. "All the charges have been dropped. That's official. Told you I had friends."

Hawk and Fisher stepped forward, took an elbow each, and carried Benny kicking and protesting into the nearest back alley. As soon as they put him down, he tried to bolt, but Hawk snagged him easily and slammed him against the wall, just hard enough to rattle his eyes and put a temporary stop to any complaints. Hawk brought his face close to Benny's, and fixed him with his single cold eye.

"No one walks when we bring the charges, Benny. Not ever. I don't care what kind of friends you've got, you are guilty as hell and you're going to stand trial."

"They won't accept your evidence," said Benny desperately. "The judge will let me off. You'll see."

Hawk sighed. "You're not getting the message, Benny. If we let you walk, all the other scum will start thinking they can get away with things. And we can't have that, can we? So you are going to walk back into Headquarters, make a full confession, and plead guilty. Because if you don't, Fisher and I will take turns thinking up horrible things to do to you."

"They won't convict me on just a confession."

"Then you'd better be sure to provide plenty of corroborative evidence. Hadn't you?"

Benny looked at Hawk's implacable face and then glanced at Fisher. She had a nasty-looking skinning knife in her hand, and was calmly paring her nails with it. Benny studied the knife with fascinated eyes and swallowed hard. Right then, all the awful stories he'd heard about Hawk and Fisher seemed a lot more believable than they had before. Hawk coughed politely to get his attention, and Benny almost screamed.

"Benny . . ."

"I think I'd like to confess, please, Captain Hawk."

"You do realise you don't have to?"

"I want to."

"Legally, you're not bound to do so . . ."

"Please, let me confess! I want to! Honestly!"

"Good man," said Hawk, standing back from him. "It's always refreshing to meet a citizen who believes in honesty and justice. Now, get in there and start talking while we're still in a good mood."

Benny ran out of the alleyway and back into Guard Headquarters. Fisher smiled and put away her knife. The two Guards left the alley and made their way unhurriedly down the street, heading back to their beat in the Northside.

The Northside was the rotten heart of Haven, where all that was bad in the city came to the surface, like scum on poisoned wine. Crime and corruption and casual evil permeated the Northside, where every taste and trade was catered to. Various gangs of drug dealers fought running battles over lucrative territories, ruthlessly cutting down any innocent bystanders who got in the way. Spies plotted treason behind shuttered windows, and many doors opened only to the correct whispered password. Sweatshops and crowded slum tenements huddled together under broken street lamps, and the smoke from local factories hung permanently on the air, clawing at the throats of those who breathed it. Some said the Northside was as much a state of mind as an area, but states of mind don't usually smell that bad.

Hawk and Fisher strolled through the narrow streets, nodding to familiar faces in the bustling crowd. Speed was a way of life in the Northside; there were deals to be made, slights to be avenged, and you never knew who might be coming up behind you. Hawk and Fisher rarely let themselves be hurried. You could miss things that way, and Hawk and Fisher always liked to know what was going on around them. They'd had the Northside as their beat for five years now, on and off, but despite their best efforts, little had changed in that time. For every villain they put away, the Northside produced two more to take his place, and the soul-grinding poverty that was at the root of most crimes never changed from one year to the next. In their most honest moments, Hawk and Fisher knew that all they'd really done was to drive the worst crimes underground, or into other areas. Things tended to be peaceful as long as they were around, but they couldn't be everywhere at once. Occasionally one or the other would talk about quitting, but they never did. They wouldn't give up. It wasn't in their natures. They took each day as it came, and helped those they could. Even little victories were better than none.

The stone-and-timber buildings huddled together as though for warmth, their upper stories leaning out over the streets till their eaves almost touched. Piles of garbage thrust up through the snow and slush, and Hawk and Fisher had to be careful where they put their feet. The garbage collectors came once a month, and then only with an armed guard. The beggars who normally lived off the garbage had been driven from the streets by the cold, but there were still many who braved the bitter weather for their own reasons. Business went on in the Northside, no matter what the weather. Business, and other things.

In the light of a flickering brazier, an angel from the Street of Gods was throwing dice with half a dozen gargoyles. A fast-talking salesman was hawking bracelets plated with something that looked like gold. A large Saint Bernard with a patchy dye job was trying to bum a light for its cigar. Two overlarge rats with human hands were stealing the boots off a dead man. And two nuns were beating up a mugger. Just another day in the Northside.

A sudden burst of pleasant flute music filled Hawk's and Fisher's heads as the Guard communications sorcerer made contact. They stopped to listen and find out what the bad news was. It had to be bad news. It always was. Anything else could have waited till they got back to Headquarters. The flute music broke off abruptly, and was replaced by the dry, acid voice of the communications sorcerer.

Attention all Guards in the North sector. There's a riot in The Crossed Pikes tavern at Salt Lane. There are a large number of dead and injured, including at least two Constables. Approach the situation with extreme caution. There is evidence of chacal use by the rioters.

Hawk and Fisher ran down the street, fighting the snow and slush that dragged at their boots. Salt Lane was four streets away, and a lot could happen in the time it would take them to get there. From the sound of it, too much had happened already. Hawk scowled as he ran. Riots were bad enough without drugs complicating the issue.

Chacal was something new on the streets. Relatively cheap, and easy enough to produce by anyone with a working knowledge of alchemy and access to a bathtub, the drug brought out the animal side of man's nature. It heightened all the senses while turning off the higher functions of the mind, leaving the user little more than a wild animal, free to wallow in the moment and indulge any whim or gratify any desire, free from reason or remorse or any stab of conscience. The drug boosted the users' strength and speed and ferocity, making them almost unstoppable. It also burned out their nervous systems in time, leaving them paralysed or mad or dead from a dozen different causes. But life wasn't worth much in the Northside anyway, and there were all too many who were willing to swap a hopeless future for the savage joys of the present.

Hawk and Fisher charged round the last corner into Salt Lane and then skidded to a halt. A large crowd had already gathered, packing the narrow street from side to side. The two Guards bulled their way through without bothering to be diplomatic about it, and quickly found themselves at the front of the crowd, facing The Crossed Pikes tavern from a safe distance. The tavern looked peaceful enough, apart from its shattered windows, but a Guard Constable was sitting on a nearby doorstep, pressing a bloody handkerchief to a nasty looking scalp wound. Blood covered half his face. He looked up dazedly as Hawk and Fisher approached him, and tried to get to his feet. Hawk waved for him to stay seated.

"What happened here?"

The Constable blinked and licked his dry lips. "My partner and I were the first here after the alarm went out. There was fighting and screaming inside the tavern, but we couldn't see anything. The crowd told us there were two Constables already in there, so my partner went in to check things out while I watched the crowd. I waited and waited, but he never came back. After a while it all went quiet, so I decided I'd just take a quick look through the door. I'd barely got my foot over the doorstep when something hit me. I couldn't see for blood in my eyes, so I got out of there quick. I'll try again in a minute, when I've got my breath back. My partner's still in there."

Hawk clapped him on the shoulder reassuringly. "You take a rest. Fisher and I'll have a look. If any more Guards come, keep them out here till we've had a chance to evaluate the situation. Are you sure it's chacal-users in there?"

The Constable shrugged. "That's what the crowd said. But there's no way to be sure. As far as I can tell, anyone who was in the tavern when the trouble started is still in there."

Hawk squeezed the Constable's shoulder comfortingly, and then he and Fisher moved off a way to discuss the matter.

"What do you think?" said Hawk.

"I think we should be very careful how we handle this. I don't like the sound of it at all. Three Guards missing, another injured and so spooked he can't bear to go near the place, and an unknown number of rioters who might just be out of their minds on chacal. The odds stink. How come we never get the easy assignments?"

"There aren't any easy assignments in Haven. We've got

to go in, Isobel. There could be innocent people trapped in there, unable to get out."

"It's not very likely, Hawk."

"No, it's not. But we have to check."

Fisher nodded unhappily. "All right; let's do it, before we get a rush of brains to the head and realise what a dumb idea this is. What's the plan?"

"Well, there's no point in trying to sneak in. If there are chacal-users in there, they'll be able to see, hear, and smell us coming long before we even get a glimpse of them. I say we burst in through the door, weapons at the ready, and hit anything that moves."

"Planning never was your strong suit, was it, Hawk?"

"Have you got a better idea?"

"Unfortunately, no."

Hawk grinned. "Then let's do it. Don't look so worried, lass. We've faced worse odds before."

He drew his axe and Fisher drew her sword, and they moved cautiously over to the tavern's main entrance. The door was standing ajar, with only darkness showing beyond. Bright splashes of blood marked the polished wood, below a series of gouges that looked unnervingly like claw marks. Hawk listened carefully, but everything seemed still and quiet. He put his boot against the door and pushed it wide open. The two Captains braced themselves, but nothing happened. Hawk hefted his axe thoughtfully, and glanced at Fisher. She nodded, and they darted through the doorway together. Once inside they moved quickly apart to stand on either side of the door, so they wouldn't be silhouetted against the light, and waited silently for their eyes to adjust to the gloom.

Hawk held his axe out before him, and strained his ears against the silence. A fire was burning fitfully at the far end of the tavern, and some light fell past the shuttered windows. The tavern slowly took form out of the gloom, and Hawk was able to make out chairs and tables overturned and scattered across the floor, as though a sudden storm had swept through the long room, carrying all before it. Dark shapes lay still and silent among the broken furniture, and Hawk didn't need to see them clearly to know they were bodies. He counted fourteen that he was sure of. There was no sign of their killers.

Hawk moved slowly forward, axe at the ready. Broken glass crunched under his boots. Fisher appeared silently out of the gloom to move at his side. He stopped by a wall lamp, and working slowly and carefully, he took out his box of matches and lit it, while Fisher stood guard. It wasn't easy lighting the lamp with one hand, but he wouldn't put his axe down. The sudden light pushed back the darkness, and for the first time Hawk and Fisher were able to see the full extent of the devastation. There was blood everywhere, splashed across the walls and furniture and pooled on the floor. Most of the bodies had been mutilated or disfigured. Some had been torn apart. Loops of purple intestine hung limply from a lamp bracket, and a severed hand beckoned from a barbecue grill by the fire. Most of the bodies had been gutted, ripped open from throat to groin. Whoever or whatever had done it hadn't bothered to use a blade. Fisher swore softly, and her knuckles showed white on her sword hilt. Hawk put the lamp back in its niche, and the two of them moved slowly forward. The tavern was still and silent, full of the stench of blood and death.

They went from body to body, methodically checking for signs of life, but there were none. They found the three Guards who'd gone in to face what they thought was a simple riot. The only way to identify them was by their Constable's scarlet cloak and tunic. Their heads were missing. There was no sign anywhere of their attackers. Hawk wondered briefly if they might have made their escape during the confusion, but he didn't think so. Every instinct he had was screaming at him that the killers were still there, watching, and waiting for their chance. He could almost feel the weight of their gaze on his back.

The tavern's bar had been wrecked. There wasn't an intact bottle or glass left on the shelves, and the floor was covered with a thick carpet of broken glass. Hawk drew Fisher's attention to the bartop. The thick slab of polished mahogany was crisscrossed with long, curving scars that made Hawk think again about claws. He looked at Fisher, who nodded slowly.

"Are you thinking what I'm thinking, Hawk?"

"Could be. We've been working on the assumption this was the work of chacal-users, but more and more this is starting to look like something else entirely. I don't see how anything human could have caused injuries like those, or claw marks like these. I think we've got a werewolf here, Isobel.''

Fisher reached down and pulled a silver dagger from inside her boot, and held it loosely in her left hand. Just in case. She moved behind the bar, and then signalled quickly for Hawk to come and join her. He did so, and the two of them stood looking down at the bartender, lying wedged half under the bar. His throat had been torn out, and there were bite marks on his arms where he'd lifted them to defend himself.

"Werewolf," said Fisher.

"Maybe," said Hawk. "I don't know. The bite marks look wrong. A wolf's muzzle would leave a larger, narrower bite. . . ."

Something growled nearby. Hawk and Fisher moved quickly out from behind the bar to give themselves room to fight. They glared about them, but nothing moved in the shadowy, blood-spattered room. The growl came again, louder this time, and then a heavy weight hit Hawk from above and behind, throwing him to the floor. Glass crunched loudly beneath him as he rolled back and forth, trying desperately to tear himself free from the creature that clung to his back, pinning his arms to his sides with its legs and reaching for his throat with clawed hands. He tucked his head in, chin pressed to his chest, and then nearly panicked as he felt teeth gnawing at the back of his head. He got his feet underneath him, glanced quickly about to get his bearings, and then slammed himself back against the heavy wooden bar behind him. The creature's grip loosened as the breath was knocked out of it, and Hawk pulled free. He threw himself to one side, and Fisher stepped forward in a full extended lunge, pinning the creature to the bar with her sword.

For a moment, no one moved. Hawk and Fisher stared incredulously at the blood-soaked man transfixed by Fisher's sword. His clothing hung in rags, and he held his hands like claws. Blood soaked his hands and forearms like crimson gloves, and there was more blood spattered thickly over his livid white flesh. His eyes were wide and staring. He snarled silently at the two Guards, showing his bloody teeth, but he was still just a man. And then he lunged forward, forcing himself along the impaling blade, his bloody hands reaching for Fisher's throat. She held her ground, watching in fascination as the jagged-nailed hands grew steadily nearer. Part of her wondered crazily what had happened to wreck his nails like that.

Hawk lurched to his feet, lifting his axe. The killer lunged forward again, blood spilling down his gut from where Fisher's sword pierced him, snarling and growling like a wild animal. And then Fisher lifted her hand with the silver dagger in it, and cut his throat. Blood sprayed across her arm, and she watched warily as the light went out of his eyes and he slumped forward, dead at last. She pulled out her sword and he fell limply to the floor and lay still. Hawk came over to stand beside her.

"He must have been up in the rafters," he said finally. "All this time, just watching us, and waiting."

Fisher looked up at the ceiling. "There's no one else up there. But I can't believe one man did all this, drug or no drug."

Hawk looked down at the dead user. "Maybe we shouldn't have killed him after all. There are a lot of questions we could have asked him."

"He didn't exactly give us a choice," said Fisher dryly. "Besides, he wouldn't have been allowed to talk. We'd have had to keep him in gaol till he came down, and by then word would have reached his suppliers. They'd either have sprung him or killed him to keep his mouth shut."

Hawk scowled. "It has to be said Headquarters' security isn't worth spit these days. Particularly when it comes to drug arrests. You know, it wasn't this bad when we first joined the Guard."

"Yes it was," said Fisher. "We just weren't experienced enough to recognise the signs. There's a lot of money in drugs, and where there's a lot of money there's a line of Guards with their hands out."

"This day started out depressing," said Hawk, "and it's not getting any better. Let's get the hell out of here and file our report. If one chacal-user can do this much damage on a rampage, then this city is in for some interesting times."

A low growl trembled on the air behind them. Hawk and Fisher spun round, weapons at the ready. The tavern looked just as still and quiet as before. None of the bodies had moved. The growl came again, but this time low and subdued, sounding almost more like a groan. Hawk glared in the direction of the sound, and his gaze came to rest on an overturned table leaning against a wall. It was a big table, with room for one, maybe two, people behind it. Hawk silently indicated the table to Fisher, and they moved slowly forward. There were no more growls or groans, but as he drew nearer, Hawk thought he could hear something dripping. Something . . . feeding.

They reached the table in a matter of moments, moving silently through the gloom. Hawk put away his axe and grabbed the rim of the table with both hands, while Fisher stood ready with her sword. They counted to three silently together, and then Hawk braced himself and pulled the heavy table away from the wall with one swift movement. Fisher moved quickly forward to stand between him and whatever was waiting, and then both she and Hawk stood very still as the table revealed its secret.

The second chacal-user was a young woman, maybe seventeen or eighteen. Her face was bone-white, with dark, staring eyes, and her hands and forearms were slick with other people's blood. She held her hands like claws, but made no move to attack Hawk or Fisher. Someone, presumably the other user, had ripped open her stomach. It was a wide, hideous wound that should have killed her immediately, but the chacal was keeping her alive. She lay propped against the wall in a widening pool of her own blood, and as Hawk and Fisher watched she dipped a hand into the ragged wound in her gut, pulled out a bloody morsel, and ate it.

Oh, dear God, she's been feeding on herself. . . .

Hawk moved forward, and put a gentle restraining hand on the girl's arm. "Don't. Please don't."

"Get away from her, Hawk. She's still dangerous. We don't know how many people she's killed here."

"Get a doctor," said Hawk, without looking round.

"Hawk . . ."

"Get a doctor!"

Fisher nodded, and hurried over to the main door. Hawk put the girl's hand in her lap, and brushed her long, stringy hair from her face. The user looked at him for the first time.

"Something went wrong," she said slowly, her voice barely rising above a murmur. Hawk had to lean close to understand her. Her breath smelled of blood and something worse. Her dead white skin was beaded with sweat. "This wasn't supposed to happen. They said it would make us feel like Gods. I'm cold."

"I've sent for a doctor," said Hawk. "Take it easy. Save your strength."

"They lied to us. . . ."

"Can you tell me what happened?" said Hawk. "You said something went wrong. What went wrong?"

"It was a new drug. Supposed to be the best. Like chacal, only stronger. We were going to be like Gods. We were packing it up at the factory, ready to ship it out. Leon took some, for a lark. We tried it here, just a little. And then everything went bad."

"Tell me about the factory," said Hawk. "Where is it?"

The girl's hand drifted towards her wound again. Hawk stopped it, and put it back in her lap. She looked at him. "I'm cold."

Hawk took off his cloak and wrapped it around her. She was shivering violently, and sweat ran down her face in rivulets. There was no color left in her face. Even her lips were white. Her breathing grew increasingly shallow, and when she spoke Hawk had to concentrate hard to make out the words.

"Morgan's place. The Blue Dolphin. In the Hook."

"All right, lass, take it easy. That's all I need. We'll get the bastards. You rest now. The doctor will be here soon."

"Would you hold my hand? Please?"

"Sure." Hawk took off one of his gloves and held her left hand, squeezing it comfortingly. Warm blood spilled down his wrist. "All right?"

"Hold it up where I can see it. I can't feel it."

Hawk started to lift her hand up before her face, but she'd stopped breathing. He was still holding her hand when Fisher finally came back with the Guard doctor.

"I didn't even find out her name," said Hawk, pulling his cloak around his shoulders. Guard Constables and Captains summoned to the scene by the communications sorcerer spilled around Hawk and Fisher as they moved in and out of The Crossed Pikes tavern. They were carrying out the dead and lining them up in neat rows on the snow, ready for the meat wagon when it arrived. The Guard doctor hovered over them like an anxious relative, making notes on cause of death, for when the forensic sorcerer arrived. A large crowd had gathered, but were being kept back by two Constables. Hawk knelt down suddenly, and started roughly cleaning the blood from his hand with a handful of snow. Fisher put a hand on his shoulder and squeezed it comfortingly.

"You did all you could, Hawk."

"I know that."

"She killed at least a dozen people in there. Probably more."

"I know that too." He got to his feet and pulled his glove back on. "Before she died, she told me where they're making the stuff she took. It's Robbie Morgan's place, down in the Devil's Hook."

Fisher looked at him sharply. "Standard procedure would be to contact Headquarters and tell them the factory's location. Since you haven't done that, I assume there's a good reason why not?"

"I want these bastards, Isobel. I want them bad. It's a new drug, you see; they haven't released it yet. Can you imagine what the Northside will be like once this super-chacal hits the streets? We've got to stop it now. While we can."

"So let the Drug Squad handle it. That's what they're paid for."

"Oh no; I'm not risking this one going wrong. You can guarantee some Guard would tip Morgan off, in return for a sweetener. The Drug Squad would get there just a little too late and find nothing but an empty warehouse. That's happened too many times just recently. So I think we'll do this one ourselves."

"Us? You mean, just you and me?"

"Isobel, please; I haven't gone completely crazy. Morgan's probably got a small army of security people protecting the Blue Dolphin. But we've got a small army ourselves, right here. There's a dozen Constables, five Captains, and even a sorceress. We'll leave a few people here to mind the store, and take the rest."

"On whose authority?"

"Mine. If we bring this off, no one's going to ask any questions."

"And if we don't?"

Hawk looked at her steadily. "This is important to me, Isobel. She died right in front of me, scared and hurting, and there wasn't a damn thing I could do to help her. Just this once, we've got a chance to make a difference. A real difference. Let's do it."

"All right. Let's do it. But how are we going to get the others to go along on an unofficial raid?"

Hawk smiled. "Easy. We won't tell them it's unofficial."

Fisher grinned back at him. "I like the way you think, Hawk."

They finally ended up with an impromptu task force of ten Constables, two more Captains, and the sorceress Mistique; all blithely unaware that they were about to break every rule in the book. Which was probably for the best. That way, if anything did go wrong, Hawk and Fisher could take all the blame on themselves. Besides, no one with the brains they were born with would have volunteered if they'd known the truth. At which point Hawk decided very firmly that he wasn't going to think about the situation anymore. It was depressing him too much. All that mattered was shutting down the drug factory, and Morgan as well, if possible.

Hawk had heard about Morgan. Most people in Haven had, one way or another. He'd made enough money down the years from drugs, prostitution, and murder to buy himself respectability. He was seen in all the best places, belonged to all the right clubs, and these days was officially regarded as above suspicion. In fact, he still had a dirty finger in every pie in Haven, though no one had ever been able to prove anything. But Hawk and Fisher knew, like every other Guard. They had to deal every day with the violence and suffering his businesses caused. Hawk frowned thoughtfully. It wasn't like Morgan to get so personally involved in a scheme like this, having the super-chacal packed and distributed from one of his own warehouses. And it also wasn't like him to get involved with such a dangerous drug. The more traditional drugs brought less publicity, were just as addictive, and therefore just as profitable. Hawk shrugged mentally. Every villain makes a mistake sooner or later, and Morgan had made a bad one.

Hawk and Fisher led their people through the Northside at a quick march, heading for the Devil's Hook. They made an impressive spectacle, and the crowds drew back to let them pass. It was almost like a parade, but nobody cheered. The law wasn't popular in the Northside. Hawk looked back at his people, and smiled to himself. They might just bring this off after all. The Constables were some of the toughest Guards in Haven. They had to be, or they wouldn't have been working the Northside. And he knew both the Captains, by reputation, if not personally.

Captain Andrew Doughty was a medium-height, stocky man in his late forties; a career Guard, with all the courage, cunning, and native caution that implied. He was blond-haired, blue-eyed, and glacially handsome, and his job was his life. He had a good enough reputation with his sword that he didn't have to keep proving it, but he liked to anyway, given the chance. He'd had a lot of partners in his time, but worked best alone. Mostly because he didn't trust anyone but himself.

Captain Howard Burns was a tall, lean man in his late thirties, with an unruly mop of dark hair and a thick spade beard. He was an expert in personal and company security, and worked mostly in the Westside, overseeing the transfer of money or valuables from one location to another. He took his work very seriously, and had several official commendations for bravery. He had no sense of humour at all, but then, no one's perfect. Especially not in Haven.

Hawk had worked with both of them in his time, and was glad he had someone apart from Fisher to watch his back this time. They were both good men, men he could depend on. The only real wild card in the pack was the sorceress Mistique. She was new to the Guard, and still looking for a chance to show what she could do. Mistique was a tall, slender, fluttering woman in her early thirties, dressed in sorcerer's black, carefully cut in the latest fashion to show lots of bare flesh. If the cold bothered her at all, she didn't show it. She had a long, horsey face, and a friendly, toothy grin that made her look ten years younger.

She had a husky, upper-class accent and wouldn't answer questions about her background. She also had a thick mass of long black curly hair she had to keep sweeping back out of her eyes. All together, she wasn't exactly the most organized person Hawk had ever met, but she was supposed to be bloody good at what she did, and he'd settle for that. Morgan's warehouse would undoubtedly be crawling with defensive magic and booby traps. The only real problem with Mistique was that she hardly ever seemed to stop talking. And she wore literally dozens of beads and bangles and bracelets that clattered loudly as she walked. Hawk made a mental note not to include her in any plans that involved sneaking up on the enemy.

And then they came to the Devil's Hook, and Mistique's chatter stumbled to a halt. Even casual conversation died away quickly as Hawk led his people into the Hook. It was a bad place to be, and they all knew it. The Devil's Hook was the single poorest, most decayed, and most dangerous area in Haven. A square mile of slums and alleyways backing onto the main Docks, the Hook held more crime, corruption, and open misery than most people could bear to think about. The squalid tenement buildings were crammed with sweatshops that paid starvation wages for work on goods that often fetched high prices in the better parts of the city. Child labour was common, as was malnutrition and disease. No one ventured into the stinking streets alone or unarmed. The Guard patrolled the Hook very loosely rather than risk open warfare with the gangs who ran it. The gangs weren't as powerful as they once were, thanks to some sterling work by the sorcerer Gaunt, but after he left Haven the bad times soon returned as new gangs established themselves and fought for territory. Nobody was surprised. No one made any complaints. The Hook was where you ended up when you had nowhere else to go but a pauper's grave.

All in all, the perfect spot for a new drug factory.

The Blue Dolphin was a squalid little lock-up warehouse, on one end of a rotting tenement. Chemicals from nearby factories had stained and pitted the stonework, and all the windows were boarded up. It was cheaper than shutters. The street was deserted, but Hawk could feel the pressure of watching eyes. He brought his people to a halt outside the warehouse, and quickly set up a defensive perimeter. The last thing they needed was a gang attack while they were occupied with the drug factory. Fisher moved in close beside him.

"Are you sure this is the right place, Hawk? If Morgan's got a packing and distribution setup here, he's going to need a lot more room than this pokey little warehouse."

"This is the place," said Hawk, hoping he sounded more convinced than he felt. When all was said and done, all he had to go on was the dying words of a girl already out of her mind on chacal. He pushed the thought to one side. He'd believed her then; he had to believe her now. Or she had died for nothing.

"There are mystic wards all over the place," said Mistique. Hawk jumped slightly. He hadn't heard her come up behind him. The sorceress smiled briefly, and then turned her attention back to the warehouse. "I can't quite make out what kind of wards, though. Given the circumstances, I think we ought to tread carefully, just in case."

Hawk nodded, and gestured to two of the Constables. They moved forward and cautiously tried the warehouse door. It was locked, which surprised no one. One Constable kicked the door. His clothes burst into flames that leapt up around him in seconds. He screamed shrilly and staggered back, beating at his blazing clothes with his hands. The other Constable quickly pulled him down and rolled him back and forth in the snow to smother the flames. Hawk scowled. He hadn't expected to hit a magic defence this quickly. He made sure the injured Constable would be all right, and then turned to the sorceress.

"Get us in there, Mistique. I don't care how you do it, but do it fast. They know we're here now."

The sorceress nodded eagerly, her earrings jangling accompaniment. She stared thoughtfully at the door, and wisps of fog began to appear around her, circling and twisting on the still air. The misty grey strands grew thicker, undulating disturbingly as they drifted away from the sorceress towards the warehouse door. The mists looked almost alive, and purposeful. They curled around the door, seeping past the edges and sinking into the wood itself. Mistique made a sudden, sharp gesture and the door exploded. Fragments and splinters of rotting wood rained down on the Guards as they shielded themselves with their cloaks. Where the door had been, there was now nothing but an impenetrable darkness.

Mistique turned to look at Hawk. Strands of fog still swirled around her, like ethereal serpents with no beginning or end. "Fast enough for you, darling?"

"Very impressive," said Hawk courteously, trying hard not to sound too impressed. "Can you tell us anything about what's beyond the doorway?"

"That's the bad news, I'm afraid," said Mistique. "The darkness is a dimensional gateway, leading to a small pocket dimension, the inside of which is a damn sight bigger than that lock-up. I've knocked out the protective wards so we can get in there, but I've absolutely no idea of what might be waiting for us. Sorry to be such a drag, but whoever designed this beastly setup was jolly good at his job."

"All right," said Hawk. "We'll just have to take it as it comes. Brace yourselves, people; we're going in. I want Morgan alive, and preferably intact so we can ask him questions. Anyone else is fair game. I'd prefer prisoners to corpses, but don't put yourselves at risk. We don't know what kind of odds we'll be facing. Try not to wreck the place too much; you never know what might turn out to be useful evidence. Right. Let's do it."

He hefted his axe and walked forward, Fisher and Mistique on either side of him. From behind came a brief whisper of steel on leather as the Guards drew their weapons and started after him. Hawk gritted his teeth and plunged into the darkness. There was a sharp moment of intense heat, and then he burst through into Morgan's factory. His first sight of the place was almost enough to stop him in his tracks, but he forced himself to keep going to make room for the others coming behind. Morgan's warehouse was an insane mixture of planes and angles and inverted stairways that could not have existed in anything but a pocket universe.

There was no up or down, in any way that made any sense. People walked on one side of a surface or another, or on both, and gravity seemed merely a matter of opinion. Simple wooden stairways connected the various level planes, twisting and turning around each other like mating snakes, and walls became floors became ceilings, depending on which way you approached them. Hawk shook off his disorientation and concentrated on the force of armed men rushing towards him from a dozen different directions. He didn't have to count them to know his own small group was vastly outnumbered.

"Mistique!" he yelled quickly. "Take out the stairways. Bring this place down around their ears!"

"I'm afraid we have a slight problem, dear," said the sorcerer, staring off into the distance. "Morgan has his own sorceress here, and I'm rather tied up at the moment keeping him from killing us all."

"Can you take him?"

"Probably, if you stop interrupting. And if you can keep those nasty-looking men-at-arms away from me."

Hawk yelled instructions to his people, and the Constables moved forward to form a barrier between Mistique and the approaching men-at-arms, while Captain Doughty and Captain Burns stayed at her side as bodyguards. Fisher looked at Hawk.

"And what are we going to do?"

"Find Morgan," said Hawk grimly. "I'm not taking any chances on his getting away. Mistique, when you're ready, don't wait for orders from me. Just trash the place."

Mistique nodded, absorbed in her sorcerous battle. Thick strands of fog twisted around her like dogs straining at the leash. Hawk started down the nearest stairway, with Fisher close behind him. They hadn't gone far when Hawk heard the first clash of steel as his people met the men-at-arms. He didn't look back.

In what might have been the centre of the mad tangle of planes and stairways was a more-or-less open area with a lot of excited movement. It seemed as good a place as any to start looking. The stairs turned and twisted under Hawk, and he quickly learned to keep his gaze on his feet and ignore what was going on around him. A man-at-arms in full chain mail came running up the stairs, waving his sword with more confidence than style. Hawk cut him down with a single blow, and hurled his body over the side of the stairway. The dead man fell in half a dozen different directions before disappearing from sight in the maze of stairways.

More men-at-arms came charging towards Hawk, six men in the lead, with a lot more on the way. Bad odds, on a rickety wooden staircase. He looked quickly about him, and grinned as he spotted a large flat plane not too far away. It stood at right angles to him, but then, so did the two men on it, frantically packing paper parcels into two large crates on a wide table. He looked back at Fisher, and pointed at the plane. She raised an eyebrow, and then nodded sharply. They clambered up onto the narrow wooden banister, which creaked dangerously under their weight, and leapt out into space towards the right-angled plane. Gravity changed suddenly as they left the stairs, and slammed them down hard on the bare wooden plane.

Hawk and Fisher hit the floor rolling, and were quickly up on their feet again. The two men packing were already gone. Hawk hefted one of the small paper parcels, and then looked at the size of the packing case. That crate could hold an awful lot of drugs . . . if it was drugs. A horrible thought struck him, and he opened the packet and sniffed cautiously at the grey powder inside. He relaxed slightly and blew his nose hard. It was chacal. The sharp acidic smell was quite distinctive. Fisher yelled a warning, and he threw the packet aside and looked up. A man-at-arms leaned out from an upside-down stairway overhead and cut at Hawk with his sword. Hawk parried with his axe, but couldn't reach high enough to attack the man. He backed away, and the swordsman moved along the stairway after him. There was a strange, dreamlike quality to the fight, with both men upside-down to the other, but Hawk knew better than to let the strangeness distract him. If he couldn't figure out a way to get at his opponent, he was a dead man. An axe wasn't made for defence. He bumped into the table, and an idea struck him. He grabbed the open packet and threw the chacal powder into the other man's face. The man-at-arms screamed, and dropped his sword to claw at his eyes with both hands.

"Hawk!"

He spun round to find Fisher standing at the edge of the plane, fighting off three of the five men-at-arms who'd jumped down off the banister after the Guards. Two already lay dead at her feet. Hawk sprinted over to join her, ducked under the first man's sword, and swung his axe in a vicious sideways arc. The heavy steel axehead punched through the man's chain mail and buried itself in his rib cage. Bones broke and splintered, and the impact drove the man-at-arms to his knees, coughing blood. Hawk yanked the axe free and booted the man off the edge of the plane. The dying man fell upwards out of sight.

Fisher had already cut down another of her opponents, and now stood toe to toe with the last remaining adversary. Steel rang on steel and sparks flew as the blades met, hammering together and dancing apart in a lightning duel of strength and skill. Hawk started forward to help her, and then stopped as he saw more men-at-arms running down a winding stairway to join the fight. Fisher saw them too, and quickly kneed her opponent in the groin.

"Get the hell out of here, Hawk. Find Morgan. I'll hold them off." She cut her opponent's throat, and sidestepped neatly to avoid the jetting blood. "Move it, Hawk!"

Hawk nodded abruptly, and turned and ran down the other stairway, heading once again for what had looked like the centre of operations. From behind him came the clash of sword on sword as Fisher met the first of the new onslaught, but he didn't look back. He didn't dare. He pressed on through the maze, passing from stairway to plane to stairway and cutting down anyone who tried to get in his way. All around him Morgan's people were running back and forth, looking for orders or weapons or just heading for the exit. Morgan wouldn't have gone, though. This was his place, his territory, and he'd trust in his men and his sorcerer to protect him. A sudden piercing scream caught Hawk's attention, and he looked up and round in time to see a man dressed in sorcerer's black stagger drunkenly across a plane at right angles to Hawk's stairway. Streamers of thick milky fog burst out of his mouth and eyes and ears. His head swelled impossibly and then exploded in a spreading cloud of crimson mist. The body crumpled to the floor as the last echo of the sorcerer's dying cry faded slowly away.

Hawk grinned. So much for Morgan's sorcerer. He was close to the centre now; he could feel it. There were drugs and people and men-at-arms everywhere, and there, straight ahead, he saw a familiar face in an earth-brown cloak and hood. Morgan. Hawk ran forward, cutting his way through two swordsmen foolish enough to try and stop him. Their blood splashed across his face and hands, but he didn't pause to wipe it off. He couldn't let Morgan escape. He couldn't.

Hold my hand. Hold it up where I can see it. . . .

Morgan looked once at the bloodstained Guard rushing towards him, and then continued stuffing papers into a leather pouch. Three men-at-arms moved forward to stand between Hawk and Morgan. Hawk hit them at a dead run, swinging his axe double-handed. He never felt the wounds he took, and when it was all over, he stepped across their dead bodies to advance slowly on the drug baron.

Seen up close, Morgan didn't look like much. Average height and build, with a bland face, perhaps a little too full to be handsome. A mild gaze and a civilised smile. He didn't look like the kind of man who'd made his fortune through the death and suffering of others. But then, they never did. Hawk moved slowly forward. Blood ran thickly down from a wound in his left thigh, and squelched inside his boot. There was more blood, soaking his arms and sides, some of it his. Even so, Morgan had enough sense not to try and run. He knew he wouldn't make it. They stood facing each other, while from all around came shouts and screams and the sounds of fighting.

"Who are you?" said Morgan finally. "Why are you doing this?"

"I'm every bad dream you ever had," said Hawk. "I'm a Guard who can't be bought."

Morgan shook his head slowly, as a father chides a son who has made an understandable mistake. "Everyone has his price, Captain. If not you, then certainly someone among your superiors. I'll never come to trial. I know too much, about too many people. And I really do have friends in high places. Quite often, I helped put them there. So I'm afraid all this blood and destruction has been for nothing. You won't be able to make a case against me."

Hawk grinned. "You're the second person who's told me that today. He was wrong, too. You're going to hang, Morgan. I'll come and watch."

There was a muffled sound from behind a drapery to their right. Morgan glanced at it, and then looked quickly away. For the first time, he seemed a little uneasy. Hawk moved slowly over to the curtain, unconsciously favouring his wounded leg.

"What's behind here, Morgan?"

"Experimental animals. We had to test the drug, to establish the correct dosage. Nothing that would interest you."

Hawk swept the cloth to one side, and froze for a moment. Inside a crude, steel-barred cage lay a pile of dead young men and women, tangled together. Some were barely teenagers. The bodies were torn and mutilated, and it was clear most of them had died tearing at each other and themselves. One man's hand was buried to the wrist in another's ripped-open stomach. A young girl had torn out her own eyes. There was blood everywhere, but not enough to hide the characteristic colorless white skin of chacal use. Hawk turned back to Morgan, who hadn't moved an inch.

"Where did you get them?" said Hawk.

Morgan shrugged. "Runaways, debtors' prisons, even a few volunteers. There are always some ready to risk their lives for a new thrill."

"You know what this new drug does," said Hawk. "So why are you getting involved with it? There isn't enough bribe money in the world to make the Guard overlook the slaughter this shit will cause. Even the other drug barons would turn against you over something like this."

"I won't be here when it breaks," said Morgan. "There's a lot of money in this. Millions of ducats. More than enough to leave Haven and set up a new and very comfortable life somewhere else. You could have a life like that, Captain. There's enough money for everyone. Just name your price, and I guarantee you I can meet it."

"Really?" said Hawk. He stepped forward suddenly, grabbed a handful of Morgan's robe and dragged him over to the steel cage. "You want to know my price, Morgan? Bring them back to life. Bring those poor bastards back! Go on; give just one of them his life back and I'll let you go, here and now."

"You're being ridiculous, Captain," said Morgan evenly. "And very foolish."

"You're under arrest," said Hawk. "Tell your people to lay down their weapons and surrender."

"Or?"

Hawk grinned. "Believe me, Morgan, you don't want to know."

"I'll have to speak to my sorcerer first."

"Don't bother; he's dead."

Morgan looked at him blankly, and then open terror rushed across his face. "We've got to get out of here! If he's dead, this whole place could collapse at any moment. It's only his magic that kept it stable!"

Hawk swore briefly. He knew real fear when he saw it. "Tell your men to surrender. Do it!"

Morgan started shouting orders, and all over the maze of planes and stairways the fighting came to a halt. Hawk yelled orders to his men, and the Guards began herding Morgan's people towards the dimensional portal. Hawk dragged Morgan along himself, never once releasing his grip on the drug baron's robe. The stairway began to sway and tremble under his feet. A nearby plane cracked across from end to end. Streams of dust fell from somewhere high above. There were creaks and groanings all around, and the wooden handrail turned to rot and mush under Hawk's hand. Morgan began pleading with him to go faster. Mistique appeared out of nowhere in a clattering of beads and bracelets and ran beside them as they hurried towards the portal.

"So, you did get the little rat after all. Well done, darling."

"I wish you wouldn't call me that in front of the men," said Hawk. "Can you use your magic to hold this place together long enough for us all to get out?"

"I'm doing my best, darling, but it's not really my field. We should all make it. If we're lucky."

They reached the portal to find it bottlenecked by the last of Morgan's people. The drug baron screamed at them to get out of the way, but Hawk held him back. Guards encouraged the slow movers on their way with harsh language and the occasional kick up the backside. The remaining stairways broke apart and collapsed in a roar of cracking timber. The planes spun and twisted in midair, fraying at the edges. Loose magic snapped on the air like disturbed static. The last of Morgan's people went through, and Hawk and Morgan and Mistique followed the Guards out.

The cold of the street hit Hawk like a blow, and his

vision clouded briefly as pain and fatigue caught up with him. He shook his head and pushed the tiredness back. He didn't have time for it now. He handed Morgan over to two Constables, along with dire threats of what he'd do to them if Morgan escaped, and looked round for familiar faces. Fisher appeared out of nowhere, safe and more or less sound. They compared wounds for a moment, and then hugged each other carefully. Captain Burns came over to join them as they broke apart. He looked bloodied and battered and just a little dazed.

"How many did we lose?" said Hawk.

Burns scowled. "Five Constables, and Captain Doughty. Could have been worse, I suppose. Though I won't tell Doughty's widow that. Did you get Morgan?"

"Yeah," said Fisher. "Hawk got him."

And then there was a great crashing roar, and the whole tenement behind them collapsed amid screams of rending stone and timber, and the death cries of the hundreds of people trapped within. Flying fragments of stone and wood tore through the air like shrapnel, and then a thick cloud of smoke billowed out to fill the street from end to end.

2

GOING DOWN

Hawk pulled and tugged at a stubborn piece of rubble, and bit by bit it slid aside. The stone's sharp edges tore at his gloves and the flesh beneath, but he hardly felt the pain through the bitter cold and the creeping numbness of utter exhaustion. He'd lost track of how long he and the others had been digging through the wreckage, searching for survivors. It seemed ages since the collapsing pocket dimension had pulled the whole tenement building down with it, but the air was still thick with dust that choked the throat and irritated the eye. There were still occasional screams or moans or pleas for help from people trapped deep within the huge pile of broken stone and timber, which stretched across the narrow street and lapped up against the opposite building.

Hawk supposed he should be grateful that only the one building had come down, but he was too numb to feel much of anything now. He looked slowly about him as he stopped for a brief rest. The adjoining buildings were slumped and stooped, with jagged cracks in their walls, yet somehow holding together. The Guard had evacuated them, just in case, and their occupants had willingly joined the dig for survivors. Even in the Devil's Hook, people could sometimes be touched by tragedy.

There was no telling how many might still be trapped under the debris. Slum landlords didn't keep records on how many desperate people they squeezed into each dingy little room. The Guard were trying to keep a count, but most of the dead they dug out were too disfigured to be easily identified, and sometimes all that could be found of the bodies were scattered bits and pieces. The rescuers worked on, fired now and then from their exhaustion by the sudden appearance of a living soul, pulled raw and bloodied from the darkness under the rubble. Guards and prisoners worked side by side, along with people from the Hook, all animosities forgotten in the driving need to save as many as they could.

Not that everyone had proved so openhearted. Morgan had flatly refused to lift so much as a finger to help. Hawk was already half out of his mind with concern for the injured, and knew he couldn't spare even one Constable to watch over the drug baron. So he just punched Morgan out, manacled the unconscious man to a nearby railing and left him there. No one objected, not even his own people. A few of them even cheered. Hawk smiled briefly at the memory, and returned to work.

They had no real tools to work with, so they attacked the broken bricks and stone and wood with their bare hands, forming human chains to transfer the larger pieces. They worked with frantic speed, spurred on by the screams and sobbing of those trapped below, but soon found it was better to work slowly and carefully rather than risk the debris collapsing in on itself, if a vital support was unwittingly removed. Most of the bodies were women and children, crushed and broken by the horrid weight. Crammed together in one room sweatshops and factories, they never stood a chance. But some survived, sheltered by protecting slabs of masonry, and they were reason enough to keep on digging.

And all the time he worked, Hawk was haunted by a simple, inescapable thought; it was all his fault. If he hadn't led the raid on Morgan's factory, the pocket dimension wouldn't have collapsed, taking the tenement with it, and all those people, all those women and children, would still be alive.

Eventually the fire brigade arrived, encouraged by the presence of so many Guards. Normally they wouldn't have entered the Devil's Hook without an armed escort and a written guarantee of hazard pay. They quickly took over the running of the operation, and things began to go more smoothly. They set about propping up the adjoining buildings, and dealt efficiently with the many water leaks. Doctors and nurses arrived from a nearby charity hospital, and began sorting out the real emergencies from the merely badly injured. Fisher took the opportunity to drag Hawk over to a doctor, and insisted he have his wounds treated. He didn't have the strength to argue.

More volunteers turned up to help, followed by a small army of looters. Hawk waited for the doctor to finish the healing spell, and then rose to his feet, feeling stiff but a damn sight more lively. He walked over to confront the looters, Fisher at his side. The first few took one look at what was coming towards them, went very pale, and skidded to a halt. Word passed quickly back, and most of the would-be looters decided immediately that they were needed somewhere else, very urgently. The ones who couldn't move or think that fast found themselves volunteered to help dig through the rubble for survivors.

The work continued, interrupted increasingly rarely by a sudden shout as someone thought they heard a cry for help. Everyone would stop where they were, ears straining against the quiet as they tried to locate the faint sound. Sometimes there was nothing but the quiet, and work would slowly resume, but sometimes the cry would come again, and then everyone would work together, sweating and straining against the stubborn stone and wood until the survivors could be gently lifted free. There were hundreds of dead in the rubble, and only a few dozen living, but each new life snatched from the crushing stone gave the exhausted volunteers new will to carry on. Nurses moved among the workers with cups of hot soup and mulled ale, and an encouraging word for those who looked as though they needed it. And still more volunteers came to help, drawn from the surrounding area by the scale of the tragedy.

More Guards arrived, expecting riots, chaos, and mass looting, and were shocked to find so many people from the Hook working together to help others. Fisher set some of them to blocking off the street, to keep out sightseers and ghouls who'd just get in the way, and put the rest to work digging in the ruins, so that those who'd been working the longest could get some rest. Some of the Guard Constables weren't too keen on dirtying their hands with manual labour, but one cold glare from Hawk was enough to convince them to shut up and get on with it.

It was at this point that the local gang leader, Hammer, arrived, along with twenty or so of his most impressive-looking bullies, and insisted on talking to the man in charge. Hawk went over to meet him, secretly glad of an excuse for a break—and a little guilty at feeling that way. So he wasn't in the best of moods when the gang leader delivered his ultimatum. Hammer was a medium-height, well-padded man in his early twenties. He dressed well, if rather flashily, and had the kind of face that fell naturally into a sneer.

"What the hell do you think you're doing here?" he said flatly. "This is my territory, and no one works here without paying me. No one. So either pay up, right here, where everyone can see it, or I'll be forced to order my people to shut you down. Nothing happens in my territory without my permission."

Hawk looked at him. "There are injured people here who need our help. Some of them will die without it."

"That's your problem."

Hawk nodded, and kneed Hammer in the groin. All the color went out of the gang leader's face, and he dropped to his knees, his hands buried between his thighs.

"You're under arrest," said Hawk. He looked hard at the shocked bullies. "The rest of you, get over there and start digging, or I'll personally cut you all off at the knees."

The bullies looked at him, looked at their fallen leader, and decided he just might mean it. They shrugged more or less in unison, and moved over to work in the ruins. The local people raised a brief cheer for Hawk, surprising him and them, and then they all got back to work. The gang leader was left lying huddled in a ball, handcuffed by his ankle to a railing.

The hours dragged on, and the search turned up fewer and fewer survivors. The fire brigade's engineers set up supports for the adjoining buildings; nothing elaborate, but enough to keep them secure until the builders could be called in. People began to drift away, too exhausted or dispirited to continue. Hawk sent most of his Guards back to Headquarters with Morgan and his people, the crates of chacal now carefully labelled and numbered, and the gang leader Hammer, under Captain Burns's direction. But Hawk stayed on, and Fisher stayed with him. Hawk didn't know whether he stayed because he felt he was still needed or because he was punishing himself, but he knew he couldn't leave until he was sure there was no one still alive under the wreckage. Someone cried out they'd heard something, and once again everything came to a halt as the diggers listened, holding their breath, trying to hear a faint cry for help over the beating of their own hearts. One of the men yelled, and everyone converged on a dark, narrow shaft that fell away into the depths of the ruins. One of the diggers dropped a small stone down the shaft. They all listened hard, but no one heard it hit bottom.

"Sounded like a child," said the man who first raised the alarm. "Pretty quiet. Must be trapped at the bottom of the shaft somewhere."

"We daren't try to widen the hole," said Fisher. "This whole area is touchy as hell. One wrong move, and the shaft could collapse in on itself."

"We can't just leave the child there," said a woman dully, kneeling at the edge of the shaft. "Someone could go down on a rope, and fetch it up."

"Not someone," said Hawk. "Me. Get me a length of rope and a lantern."

He started stripping off his cloak and furs. Fisher moved in close beside him. "You don't have to do this, Hawk."

"Yes I do."

"You couldn't have known this would happen."

"I should have thought, instead of just barging straight in."

"That shaft isn't stable. It could collapse at any time."

"I know that. Keep an eye on my furs and my axe, would you? This is Haven, after all."

He stood by the shaft in his shirt and trousers, looking down into the darkness, and shivered suddenly, not entirely from the cold. He didn't like dark, enclosed places, particularly underground, and the whole situation reminded him uncomfortably of a bad experience he'd once had down a mine. He didn't have to go down the shaft. There were any number of others ready to volunteer. But if he didn't do it, he'd always believe he should have.

Someone came back with a length of rope, and Fisher fastened one end round his waist. Someone else tied the other end to a sturdy outcropping of broken stone, and Hawk and Fisher took turns tugging on the rope to make sure it was secure. One of the men gave him a lantern, and he held it out over the shaft. The pale golden light didn't penetrate far into the darkness. He listened, but couldn't hear anything. The hole itself was about three feet in diameter and looked distinctly unsafe. Hawk shrugged. It wouldn't get any safer, no matter how long he waited. He sat down on the edge, very slowly and very carefully, swung his legs over the side, and then lowered himself into the darkness, bracing his back and his knees against the sides of the shaft. He took a deep breath and let it out, and then inch by inch he made his way down into the darkness, the lantern resting uncomfortably on his chest.

Jagged edges of stone and wood cut at him viciously as he descended, and the circle of daylight overhead grew smaller and smaller. He moved slowly down in his pool of light, stopping now and again to call out to the child below, but there was never any reply. He pressed on, cursing the narrow confines around him as they bowed in and out, and soon came to the bottom of the shaft. He held up the lantern and looked around him. Rough spikes of broken wood and stone protruded from every side, and a dozen openings led off into the honeycomb of wreckage. Most were too small or too obviously unsafe for him to try, but one aperture led into a narrow tunnel barely two feet high. Hawk called out to the child, but there was only the silence and his own harsh breathing. He looked back up the main shaft, but all he could see was darkness. He was on his own. He looked again at the narrow tunnel, cursed again briefly, and got down on his hands and knees.

The rope played out behind him as he wriggled his way through the tunnel darkness in his narrow pool of light, stopping now and then to manoeuvre past outcroppings from the tunnel walls. The child had to be around here somewhere. He couldn't have come all this way for nothing. He thought briefly about the sheer weight of wreckage pressing from above, and his skin went cold. The roof of the tunnel bulged down ahead of him, and he had to lie on his back and force himself past the obstruction an inch at a time, pulling the lantern behind. The unyielding stone pressed against his chest like a giant hand trying to crush the breath out of him. He breathed out, emptying his lungs, and slowly squeezed past.

In the end, he found the child by bumping into her. He'd

just got past the obstruction when his head hit something soft and yielding. His first thought was that he'd run into some kind of animal down in the dark with him, and his imagination conjured up all kinds of unpleasantness before he got it back under control. He squirmed over onto his stomach, wishing briefly that he'd brought his axe, and then stopped as he saw her, lying still and silent on the tunnel floor. She looked to be about five or six years old, covered in dirt and blood, but still breathing strongly. Hawk spoke to her, but she didn't respond, even when he tapped her sharply on the shoulder. He pulled himself along beside her, and saw for the first time that one of her legs was pinned between two great slabs of stone, holding her firmly just below the ankle.

Hawk put his lantern down and pushed cautiously at the slabs, but they wouldn't budge. He took hold of the girl's shoulders and pulled until his arms ached, but she didn't budge either. The stones weren't going to give her up that easily. Hawk let go of her, and tried to think. The air was full of dust, and he coughed hard to try and clear it from his throat. The side of his face grew uncomfortably warm from having the lantern so close, and he moved it a bit further away. Shadows leapt alarmingly in the cramped tunnel and then were still again. He scowled, and worried his lower lip between his teeth. He had to get the child out of there. The tunnel could collapse at any time, bringing tons of stone and timber crashing down on her. And him too, for that matter. But there was no way he could persuade the stone slabs to give up their hold on her foot. He had no tools to work with, and even if he had, there wasn't enough room to apply any leverage. No, there was only one way to get the child out. Tears stung his eyes as the horror of it clenched at his gut, but he knew he had to do it. He didn't have any choice in the matter.

He squirmed and wriggled as best he could in the confined space, and finally managed to draw the knife from his boot and slide his leather belt out of his trousers. There was a good edge on the blade. It would do the job. He took a close look at the stone slabs where they held the child's foot, checking if there was room enough to work, but he already knew the answer. There was room. He was just putting it off. He looped his belt around the girl's leg, close up against the stone, and pulled it tight, until flesh bulged thickly up on either side of it. Hawk hefted the knife, and then brushed the little girl's hair gently with his free hand.

"Don't wake up, lass. I'll be as quick as I can."

He placed the edge of the knife against her leg, as close to the stones as he could get it, and began sawing.

There was a lot more blood than he'd expected, and he had to tighten the belt twice more before he could stem most of the flow. When he was finished, he tore off one of his sleeves and wrapped it tightly round the stump. His arms and face were splashed with blood, and he was breathing in great gulps, as though he'd just run a race. He turned over on his back again, grabbed his lantern, and began inching his way back down the tunnel, dragging the unconscious girl along behind him. He didn't know how long he'd spent in the narrow tunnel, but it felt like forever.

The tunnel roof soon rose enough to let him get to his hands and knees again, and he crawled along through the darkness, hugging the child to his chest. He suddenly found himself at the base of the main shaft, and stopped for a moment to get his breath. He ached in every muscle, and he'd torn his hands and knees to ribbons. But he couldn't let himself rest. The little girl needed expert medical help, and she was running out of time. He held the girl tightly to his chest with one arm and slowly began to climb back up the shaft, with only his legs and his back to support his weight and that of the child.

It didn't take long before the pain in his tired muscles became excruciating, but he wouldn't stop. The girl was depending on him. Foot by foot he fought his way up the shaft, grunting and snarling with the effort, his gaze fixed on the gradually widening circle of light above him. He finally drew near the surface, and eager hands reached down to take the child and help Hawk the rest of the way. He clambered laboriously out and lay stretched out on the rubble, squinting at the bright daylight and drawing in deep lungfuls of the comparatively clean air. Fisher swore softly at the state of his hands and knees, helped him sit up, and wrapped his cloak around him. Someone brought him a cup of lukewarm soup, and he sipped at it gratefully.

"The child," he said thickly. "What have they done with her?"

"A doctor's looking at her now," said Fisher. "And as soon as you've finished that soup we're going to get one to take a look at you, as well. God, you're a mess, Hawk. Was it bad down there?"

"Bad enough."

Eventually he got to his feet again, and Fisher found him a doctor who could work the right healing spells. The wounds closed up easily enough, but there was nothing the doctor could do for physical and emotional exhaustion. Hawk and Fisher looked around them. The dead and injured had been laid out in neat rows on the snow, the dying and the recovering lying side by side. A large pile of unidentified body parts had been tactfully hidden under a blood-spattered tarpaulin. Hawk shook his head numbly.

"All this, to catch one drug baron and his people. Tomorrow there'll be a dozen just like him fighting to take his place, and it will all have to be done again."

"Stop that," said Fisher sharply. "None of this is your fault. It's Morgan's fault, for having set up a pocket dimension here in the first place. And if we hadn't acted to stop the super-chacal being distributed, there's no telling how many thousands might have died across the city."

Hawk didn't answer. He looked slowly about him, taking in the situation. Engineers and sorcerers had got together to stabilize the surrounding buildings, and people were being allowed back into them again. That should please the slum landlords. Even they couldn't charge rent on a pile of rubble. Firemen were moving among the wreckage, shoring up the few broken walls and inner structures that hadn't collapsed completely. A few people were still sifting through the rubble, but the general air of urgency was gone. Much of the real work had been done now, and most people had accepted that there probably weren't going to be any more survivors. The volunteers had gone home, exhausted, and Hawk felt he might as well do the same. There was nothing left for him to do, he was out on his feet, and it had to be well past the end of his double shift. He was just turning to Fisher to tell her it was time to go, when there was the sound of gentle flute music, and the dry, acid voice of the communications sorcerer filled his head.

Captains Hawk and Fisher, return to Guard Headquarters immediately. This order supersedes all other directives.

Hawk looked at Fisher. "Typical. Bloody typical. What the hell do they want now?"

"Beats me," said Fisher. "Maybe they want to congratulate us for finally nabbing Morgan. There are a lot of people at Headquarters who'll fight for the chance to ask him some very pointed questions."

Hawk sniffed. "With our luck, they'll probably screw it up in the Courts, and he'll plea-bargain his way out with a fine and a suspended sentence."

"Relax," said Fisher. "We got him dead to rights this time. What can possibly go wrong?"

"What do you mean, you let him go?" screamed Hawk. He lunged across the desk at Commander Glen, and Fisher had to use all her strength to hold him back. The Commander pushed his chair back well out of reach, and glared at them both.

"Control yourself, Captain! That's an order!"

"Stuff your order! Do you know how many people died so we could get that bastard?"

He finally realised he couldn't break free from Fisher without hurting her, and stopped struggling. He took a deep breath and nodded curtly to Fisher. She let go of him and stepped back a pace, still watching him warily. Hawk fixed Commander Glen with a cold, implacable glare. "Talk to me, Glen. Convince me there's some reason behind this madness. Or I swear I'll do something one of us will regret."

Commander Glen sniffed, and met Hawk's gaze unflinchingly. Glen was a tallish, blocky man in his late forties, with a permanent scowl and a military-style haircut that looked as though it had been shaped with a pudding bowl. He had large, bony hands and a mouth like a knife-cut. He'd spent twenty years in the Guard, and amassed a reputation for thief-taking unequalled in the Guard. He'd been day Commander for seven years, and ran his people like his own private army, demanding and getting complete obedience. Ordinarily, he didn't have to deal much with Hawk and Fisher, which suited all of them.

Glen pushed his chair forward, and leaned his elbows on

the desk. "You want me to explain myself, Captain Hawk? Very well. Thanks to your going after Morgan without waiting for orders or a backup, we now find ourselves faced with major loss of life and destruction of property within the Devil's Hook. We still don't know exactly how many died because of your actions, but the current total is four hundred and six. The Hook's still in shock at the moment, but when they finally realise what's happened, and that the Guard was responsible, we're going to be facing riots it'll take half the Guard to put down! On top of that, there's the cost of rebuilding and repairs, which is going to run into thousands of ducats. The landlord of the tenement is suing the Guard for that money, and he'll probably win. And finally, you assaulted a gang leader in front of his own people. Does the word *vendetta* mean anything to you, Captain Hawk?"

"I don't give a damn about any of that," said Hawk, his voice carefully controlled. "What I did was justified by the circumstances. Morgan was preparing to distribute a drug that would have killed thousands of people and torn Haven apart. Now, explain to me, please, why this man was allowed to go free."

"There was no evidence against him," said Glen flatly.

"No evidence? What about the super-chacal?" said Fisher. "There were crates of the damn stuff; I helped number and label them."

"I never saw any drugs," said Glen. "Neither has anyone else. And none of the prisoners had any drugs in their possession when they were searched here. None of them had even heard of this super-chacal you keep mentioning. And thanks to your efforts, we don't even have any proof the pocket dimension ever existed. That leaves only your word and that of your men. And that's not good enough, against someone like Morgan. He's a man of standing in the business community, and a pillar of society. He also has a great many friends in high places. People with influence. He hadn't been in Headquarters ten minutes before pressure began coming down from Above. Without real evidence, we didn't have a case. So I let him go, along with all of his people. I might add that Morgan is strongly considering suing us for false arrest, and you in particular

or assault. I can't believe you were stupid enough to hit
him in front of witnesses."

For a while, none of them said anything. It was very
quiet in Glen's office, the only sound the murmur of people
going back and forth about their business in the corridors
outside.

"There were crates of the drug," said Hawk finally. "If
they've disappeared, it can only mean they vanished on
their way here, or they were removed by people working
inside Headquarters. Either way, we're talking about corrupt Guards. I demand an official investigation."

"You can demand anything you want; you won't get it."

"I want to talk to my men, the Constables who were
with me on the raid."

"I'm afraid that's not possible. They've already been detailed to other duties. Haven't you got the picture yet, Captain? As far as our superiors are concerned, this whole
incident is a major embarrassment, and they want it forgotten as soon as possible. You've got some very important
people mad at you. At both of you. They're looking for
scapegoats, and you're tailor-made to fill the bill."

"Let me see if I've got this straight," said Hawk, his
voice dangerously calm. "Morgan has walked. So have all
his people. And several tons of the most dangerous drug
Haven has ever seen have gone missing. Have I missed
anything?"

"Yes," said Glen. "I've been instructed to suspend both
of you, indefinitely, while a number of official charges
against you are investigated. Charges such as reckless en-
dangering of life and property, disobeying orders, assaulting
citizens without provocation, brutality, and possible collu-
sion in a vendetta against a faultless pillar of society. That
last was Morgan, in case you were wondering."

Hawk grabbed Glen's desk with both hands and threw it
to one side. Papers flew on the air like startled birds as he
grabbed two handfuls of Glen's uniform, picked him up,
and slammed him against the nearest wall. He thrust his
face close to the Commander's, until they were staring into
each other's eyes.

"No one's suspending me, you son of a bitch! Those
drugs are still out there, waiting to be distributed! They

have to be found and seized, and I can't do that with both hands tied behind my back! Do you understand me?"

Glen looked over Hawk's shoulder at Fisher, standing by the overturned desk. "Call your partner off, Fisher."

She shrugged, and folded her arms. "This time, I think I agree with him. If I were you, I'd agree with him too. Hawk can get very upset when he thinks people are conspiring against him."

The door burst open behind them and two Constables rushed in with drawn swords, alarmed at the sounds of violence from the Commander's office. Fisher drew her sword and quickly moved to stand between them and Hawk and Glen. Hawk slowly put Glen down, but kept a tight hold on him.

"Tell them to leave, Glen. This is private."

"Not anymore," said Glen. "Not after your foul-up this morning. You can't fight your way out of this one, Hawk. Not even you and Fisher can take on the entire Guard."

Hawk grinned suddenly. "Don't bet your life on it, Glen. We've faced worse odds in our time. Now, tell those over-eager friends of yours to leave, and we'll . . . discuss the situation."

He let go of Glen, and stepped back a pace, his right hand resting casually on the axe at his side. The Commander nodded, and gestured for the two Constables to leave. They looked at each other, shrugged, put away their swords and left, not quite slamming the door behind them. Glen looked at Hawk.

"You've upset them."

"Oh dear," said Hawk. "What a pity. I'm not going on suspension, Glen. I've got too much to do."

"Right," said Fisher.

"Help me pick up my desk," said Glen, "and we'll talk about it."

Hawk did so, while Fisher leaned against the wall, still holding her sword. Glen picked up his chair, and sat down behind his desk again. He glanced briefly at the papers scattered over the floor, then fixed his attention on Hawk and Fisher.

"All right, no suspension. But I'll have to find somewhere to put you so you're out of sight until things calm down again."

"Sounds sensible," said Fisher. "What did you have in mind?"

"I can't have you working together; word would be bound to get out. But as it happens, I've got two jobs to fill that should suit the pair of you nicely. As you know, even though officially you shouldn't, Peace Talks are taking place in Haven at the moment, to try and put an end to the border clashes between the Low Kingdoms and our traditional enemy Outremer, before they get out of hand. The Talks themselves seem to be going well enough, but there are a number of political and business interests on both sides who would like very much to see them fail. Captain David ap Owen is currently in charge of security, but he's been under a lot of pressure and could use some assistance. Think you could handle that, Captain Fisher?"

"Sounds fair enough to me," said Fisher, glancing at Hawk. "What level of security are we talking about?"

"Absolute minimum. Officially, the Talks aren't happening here at all. We can't use troops to guard the delegates; that would be too conspicuous, so there'll just be yourself, Captain ap Owen, and a dozen Constables in plainclothes. We can't use any magical protection, either. Same reason; it would just attract attention. So if anything happens, you're on your own. By the time you could get word to us it would all be over, one way or the other. You'll have to cope with what you've got."

"Do the delegates know that?" said Hawk.

"They suggested it. They're expendable, and they know it. Well, Captain Fisher, is the assignment to your liking?"

"Sounds like fun," said Fisher.

Glen looked at her for a moment, and then turned to Hawk. "I need someone to find the drugs that went missing. Surprisingly enough, I had worked out for myself how dangerous this super-chacal could be. I want to know how the stuff disappeared, and where it is now. And if you should find a way to incriminate Morgan in the process, I wouldn't be at all displeased. Find yourself another partner, someone you can trust, but keep your head down, and stay out of the public eye. If anything goes wrong, I'll swear blind you were acting on your own, and it's all nothing to do with me. I can't afford to have Morgan's friends as enemies. You'll report directly to me, and no one else. Is that acceptable, Captain Hawk?"

"Sounds good to me," said Hawk. "Why didn't you tell us this earlier?"

"You didn't exactly give me a chance. You were more interested in feeling aggrieved and wrecking my office."

Fisher smiled. "Next time, talk faster."

"Besides," said Hawk comfortingly, "it wasn't much of an office anyway."

Glen looked at him.

Hawk was working on his second beer when Captain Burns found him. The Cloudy Morning was a semiofficial off-duty tavern for the Guard, a traditional place for winding down at the end of a long shift. It was fairly basic as taverns go, with no frills and few comforts, but the beer was good and reasonably cheap, and the Guards needed a place where they could talk freely without having to worry about who might be listening. The place was run by an ex-Guard, and the general public were politely encouraged to drink elsewhere, unless they were Guard groupies. There were such, though not many Guards encouraged them. They tended to get obsessive.

The place was crowded, as usual at the end of a shift, and Captain Burns had to squeeze his way through the press of bodies to reach the bar. Several Guards called out to him, and clapped him on the shoulder as he passed, but he just smiled and kept going. Hawk's message had sounded fairly urgent. He finally reached the bar, grabbed a seat as it became vacant, and sat down beside Hawk. For a moment Hawk didn't look up, staring into his beer. Then he took a long swallow, and gestured for the bartender to bring Burns a beer.

"I'm surprised you're still on the loose," said Burns. "The smart money was betting you'd be arrested the moment you set foot in Headquarters. You've upset some really powerful people this time, Hawk."

"There was some talk of suspension," said Hawk. "But I talked the Commander out of it."

Burns smiled. "Yeah, I heard. Did you really bounce him off the walls of his own office?"

Hawk looked at him innocently. "Would I do such a thing to a superior officer?"

Burns nodded to the bartender as his drink arrived, and sipped it appreciatively. "So what's happening with you and Fisher? All forgiven?"

"Hardly. We've been split up, and told to keep our heads down. But I've got a case to work on, and I'm looking for a new partner."

For a moment, Burns didn't get it, and then he looked sharply at Hawk. "You mean me? We hardly know each other."

"I've seen you fight, and I thought you might like a chance to get back at the bastards who killed your partner. Besides, Morgan isn't going to stop with Fisher and me. Eventually, he's going to go after everyone who helped destroy his factory. He takes setbacks personally. If you don't go after him now, while he's vulnerable, you can bet that sooner or later he's going to be coming after you."

"You've got a point there," said Burns. "But you've got a real nerve, you know that? You got me into this mess, and now I'm supposed to help save your neck."

"Are you in or not?"

"Of course I'm in. I don't really have any choice, do I? And you're right about one thing, at least. I'd worked with Doughty on and off for nearly eight years. He was a good partner. Never had much to say for himself, but the best damned swordsman I ever saw. I always felt safer with him to guard my back. I didn't see who killed him at the factory. Everything was happening too fast. But even if I didn't see whose hand held the sword, I know who was responsible for his death."

"Morgan."

"Right. I'm with you, Hawk. But it's not going to be easy. Morgan has influential friends. The kind of people it's dangerous to cross."

"Everyone keeps telling me that," said Hawk calmly. "It's not going to stop me. I can be dangerous too, when I put my mind to it. But I shouldn't worry about his precious friends too much. If we bring Morgan down hard enough, his friends will desert him like rats leaving a sinking ship rather than risk being brought down with him."

Burns shook his head amusedly. "You almost make it sound easy. All right, what do we do first?"

"Well, to begin with we could do with another drink. We've got some hard thinking to do."

Burns chose his words carefully. "Not for me, thanks. I think better on a clear head."

"You're probably right," said Hawk. "But it has to be said, there's something about Haven that drives a man to drink." He looked at his empty glass, then pushed it regretfully away. "You know, when I first joined the Guard, I really thought I could make a difference. I was going to be a force for justice, and put all the bad guys behind bars, where they belonged. It didn't work out that way. Crime and corruption are a way of life for most people here. Some days I think the only way to clean up Haven would be to burn it down and start over again."

Burns shrugged. "I've lived here all my life, but from what I've heard, Haven isn't really that different from any other city. We're just more honest about it here. You mustn't let it get to you, Hawk. You can't expect to undo centuries of corruption overnight. Real change always takes time. In the meantime, we do our best to hold things together, and every now and again we get a chance to put away a piece of slime like Morgan. Settle for that."

They sat for a while in silence, each thinking his own thoughts.

"Where did you come from originally?" said Burns.

"Up north. There were family problems over my marriage to Isobel, so we struck out on our own. Travelled around a lot, and finally ended up here. It seemed a good idea at the time."

"There are worse places than Haven."

"Name two." Hawk looked thoughtfully into his empty glass. "It was my fault, you know. If I hadn't gone barging in, without checking the situation properly, I might have found a way to shut down Morgan's factory without destroying everything. And all those men and women and children would be alive now."

"Maybe," said Burns. "But I doubt it. Morgan was ready to ship those drugs out. If we'd burst in even an hour later, we'd probably have found nothing but an empty warehouse. But either way, it doesn't make any difference. You did what you thought was right at the time. That's all any of us can do. Beyond a certain point, worrying about past mistakes just becomes self-pity and self-indulgence."

Hawk looked at him, and smiled. "Maybe. Let's talk about Morgan, the bastard. The first thing we have to do is figure out where the super-chacal disappeared to, and then try and link it directly to Morgan in a way he can't shrug off. Which means asking pointed questions and making a nuisance of ourselves until people tell us what we want to know."

"Just once," said Burns, "wouldn't you like to try it the easy way? Morgan is going to have to shift the super-chacal in a hurry, so that he can't be caught with it in his possession. Which means using established channels of distribution. And there aren't that many people in Haven who can handle a deal that size. All we have to do is discover which distributor has suddenly become very busy, and we'll have our first lead."

"But that's only part of it," said Hawk. "We also need to know which Guards took money from Morgan to look the other way while the drugs went missing."

"If you say so," said Burns. "But Hawk, we're going to do this professionally, right? Getting personally involved in a case is always a bad idea. It stops you thinking clearly. In Haven, you win some and you lose some. That's just the way it is."

Hawk looked at him. "I don't believe in losing."

3

Talking Peace and War

Fisher strode scowling through the well-ordered streets of Low Tory, and wished Hawk was with her. She didn't like leaving him alone in his present mood. He'd taken the deaths in the Hook personally, and right now he was mad enough and depressed enough to do something stupid. Usually it was the other way round, with Hawk keeping her from doing something dumb, but there were times when he needed her to see the right path clearly. He needed her now, and she couldn't be with him. Commander Glen had made it very clear that their splitting up was a condition of their continuing to work. Still, they'd had time to discuss who Hawk should choose as his new partner, and Captain Burns seemed solid enough. She wondered what her own new partner would be like. Probably turn out to be some ex-mercenary with more muscle than brain, and even less ethics. There were a lot like that in the Guard.

She looked unobtrusively about her as she strode along, trying to get the feel of the new area. She hadn't worked Low Tory before, but by all accounts it was an upwardly mobile, middle-class area, full of merchant families so long established they were city aristocracy in all but blood and breeding. They were indecently rich, had a finger in every political pie, and, as a class, showed all the ethical restraint of a shark in a feeding frenzy. Having reached the pinnacle of their profession, their ambition turned in the only direction left to them, and they set their sights on the Quality. Even in Haven, the poorest aristocrat could still look down his nose at the richest trader. So, in recent times certain wealthy merchant families had been negotiating marriage contracts with the more impoverished Quality Families, quite openly offering to pay off a Family's debts in return for marriage into the Quality. The results were rarely happy, with the nouveau Quality snubbed and openly mocked by High Society, but the practice persisted.

As a result, Low Tory had flourished in the past few years, tearing down the faded and crumbling houses of the lesser Quality and replacing them with grand new mansions that rivalled and occasionally even surpassed the old Family Halls and Granges of High Tory. The streets were wide and open and bordered with neat, orderly rows of specially imported trees. New walls had been replaced with newer walls carefully constructed to appear old and weathered. Everything had to look right. Unlike most of Haven, the streets were calm and quiet and practically deserted. Regular patrols by private guards and men-at-arms saw to that. Only those with approved business in the area were allowed to tarry in Low Tory. To Fisher, more used to the bustling crowds of the Northside, the streets appeared almost eerily deserted.

The recent snow had been shovelled aside into tidy piles at the street kerbs, but here and there small bands of workmen still struggled with the more stubborn drifts. Servants attired in finery more costly than that worn by some lower-class merchants hurried along, looking neither left nor right, bearing messages and business documents and an almost palpable sense of their own self-importance. Private guards patrolled in pairs, looking faintly embarrassed by their overelaborate uniforms. None of them looked particularly pleased to see Fisher. She ignored them all, and concentrated on the directions she'd been given. They'd seemed simple enough back at Guard Headquarters, but Fisher had a positive genius for getting lost, and today seemed no different. Still, after a certain amount of backtracking she'd finally found the right street, so all she had to do now was locate the right house.

It occurred to her that this street was actually surprisingly busy, by Low Tory standards. There were half a dozen workmen lackadaisically shovelling snow, and as many servants strolling unhurriedly up and down the street. A hot-chestnut seller was tending his brazier, but showed remarkably little interest in drumming up trade. Two men were bent over an open sewer grating, but seemed to be spending as much time watching the street as anything else. Fisher had to smile. Try as they might, some Guards just couldn't get the hang of plainclothes work. It wasn't enough to look the part; you had to act it as well. Still, it showed she was in the right place.

None of the plainclothes people made any move to approach her, for which Fisher was grateful. She wasn't in the mood to explain what she was doing there without Hawk. She finally reached her destination, and stopped at the main gate to study the surroundings with an experienced eye. It was a plain, pleasantly unornamented house, standing a way back from the street in its own grounds. The high stone wall surrounding the snow-covered lawns was topped with iron spikes and broken glass. Fairly impressive, but the tall iron gates were unlocked and unguarded. She'd have to speak to someone about that.

She pushed the gates open and walked into the grounds. A few yards away stood a life-sized figure of a warrior, carved from pale marble in the classically idealized style popular in the last century. It carried a sword and shield, and was minutely detailed, even down to bulging veins on the muscular arms. Fisher looked away. She didn't care for such statues. They'd always given her the creeps as a child.

As she passed the marble warrior, there was a low, grating sound as the statue slowly turned its head and looked at her. Fisher jumped back, her hand dropping to her sword. She stayed where she was, her heart beating painfully fast, but the statue made no further move. Fisher edged closer, a foot at a time, and reached out to poke it with a hesitant fingertip. It felt hard and unyielding, the way marble should. Fisher took a deep breath and backed away, still keeping a careful eye on the statue. The thing must be part of the house's security system. They might have warned her. . . . She turned her back on the marble figure and continued on her way. Behind her she again heard a low grating sound as the statue turned its head to follow her progress. Fisher wouldn't let herself look back, but walked a little faster, despite herself. Up ahead, scattered across the grounds, were three more statues, staring off in different directions.

Snow crunched loudly under Fisher's boots as she approached the house. Now that she'd had a chance to get used to the idea, she approved of the statues. Simple but effective security, and completely unobtrusive until activated by an intruder. She couldn't help wondering what other surprises Captain ap Owen might have set up in the grounds. The thought had only just crossed her mind when a huge dog suddenly appeared out of nowhere right in front of her. She stumbled to a halt, and the great hound thrust its head forward, sniffed at her suspiciously, and then vanished into thin air. Fisher opened her mouth to say something, and a second, different dog appeared out of nowhere just to her left. It was even bigger than the first, its head on a level with her belt. It sniffed at her, wagged its tail, then snapped out of existence. Fisher realised her mouth was still hanging open, and shut it. Guard dogs. Of course. Entirely logical. She walked on, and tried to get her breathing to go back to normal.

She finally came to a halt before the massive front door, beat on it smartly with her fist, and made a quick use of the iron boot-scraper. *And if anything else appears, I'm going to hit it first, and ask questions afterwards.* The door opened almost immediately, confirming that they'd been watching her.

The man in footman's uniform looked convincing enough, and even had the barely civil bow and haughty expression down right, but there was no getting away from the fact that he was simply far too muscular for a gentleman's servant. He stood back politely as she entered the brightly lit hall, then shut the door firmly behind her. The sound of a key turning in the lock was quickly followed by the sound of four separate bolts sliding home. Fisher smiled, and relaxed a little. Maybe they did know what they were doing here, after all. She handed the footman her cloak, waited patiently while he figured out where to hang it up, and then allowed him to lead her down the hall and into the study, where Captain David ap Owen was waiting for her.

The study was too large to be really cosy, but had all the comforts money could buy. Captain ap Owen sat behind a large, ornate desk, talking quietly to someone who looked as though he might be a real footman. Ap Owen glanced at Fisher as she came in, but finished giving his instructions before waving both footmen away. He got up from behind the desk and came forward to greet Fisher with an outstretched hand. His handshake was firm, but hurried, and he sat down on the edge of the desk to take a good look at her. Fisher stared back just as openly.

Captain ap Owen was in his mid-thirties, and a little less than average height, which meant he had to tilt his head back to meet her gaze. It didn't seem to bother him as much as it did some people. His build was stocky rather than muscular, and his uniform had a sloppy, lived-in look. Fisher approved of that. In her experience, Guards who worried too much about their appearence tended not to worry enough about getting the job done right. Ap Owen had flaming red hair and bright green eyes, along with a broad rash of freckles across his nose and cheekbones which made him look deceptively youthful and open. His apparently relaxed stance was undermined by an unwavering slight frown and occasional sudden, jerky movements. Even sitting still, he gave the impression of a man constantly on edge, just waiting for an attack so he could leap into action.

"Take a seat, Captain Fisher," he said finally. "Glad to have you with us. I've heard a lot about you."

"It's all true," said Fisher easily. She dragged a chair over to the desk, ignoring what that did to the carpet, and slumped gracelessly into it. The chair was a rickety antique, but more comfortable than it appeared. She looked sharply at ap Owen. "I take it you've heard the latest news about me?"

"Of course," said ap Owen. "If it hadn't been for your recent . . . troubles, I'd never have got you on my team. Make no mistake, Captain, everyone here, including you and me and the six delegates, are all considered expendable. If these Talks work out successfully, fine; if not, no one's going to miss us. They'll just start over, with new delegates and new Talks. The odds are we're all going to be killed before the Talks are over. There are a lot of people out there who want us dead, for various political and business reasons, and I haven't been allowed enough men to ward off a determined attack by a group of lightly armed nuns. Had to be that way. The whole idea of this operation is to be unobtrusive and hopefully overlooked. Personally, I think it's a dumb idea, given the number of spies and loose mouths in this city, but no one asked my opinion. The point is that if things go wrong and our cover is blown, we are supposed to defend these Talks with our lives, and we probably will. Even though they and we are completely replaceable."

"I see you're the kind of leader who believes in a good pep talk," said Fisher. "Are you normally this optimistic?"

Captain ap Owen grinned briefly. "I like my people to know what they're getting into. Ideally, this should have been a volunteers-only operation, but since we couldn't tell them what they'd be volunteering for, there didn't seem much point. How much did they tell you about our situation here?"

"Not much. Just that it was minimum security, with essentially no backup."

"You got that right, but it's not quite as bad as it sounds. The Talks aren't actually taking place in the house itself, the building's far too vulnerable. Instead, a Guard sorcerer has set up a pocket dimension, linked to the house. It's been so thoroughly warded, a sorcerer could walk through this place from top to bottom and never know the dimensional gateway was here. Clever, eh?"

"Very," said Fisher carefully. "But pocket dimensions aren't exactly stable, are they? If you know about my current problems, then you can understand that I'm a bit bloody wary about going into another pocket dimension."

"Don't worry about it; once the dimension's been established, it's perfectly secure. The only reason Morgan's fell apart is because he designed it that way, with booby traps in case he was discovered. He didn't want any evidence surviving to incriminate him."

Fisher looked at him blankly. "You mean it wasn't Hawk's fault after all? Then why didn't Commander Glen tell us that? He must have known . . . Damn, I've got to talk to Hawk!"

She jumped to her feet, but ap Owen didn't budge. "Sit down, Captain Fisher. You're not going anywhere. No one here is allowed to leave these premises until the Talks are over. It's a matter of security. You must see that."

"You can't stop me leaving."

"No, I probably couldn't. But if you did leave, Glen would undoubtedly have you declared a rogue, and put out an order for your arrest. And how is that going to help Hawk?"

Fisher glared at ap Owen, then nodded reluctantly and sank back into her chair. "That's why Glen sent me here, so Hawk would be left alone with his guilt. He's always easiest to manipulate when he's feeling guilty. Glen wants Hawk to go on believing it was his fault, so he'll be properly motivated to go after Morgan. Damn him!"

There was an uncomfortable silence. When Fisher finally spoke again, her voice was calm and cold and very deadly. "When this is all over, there's going to be an accounting between me and Commander bloody Glen."

"Assuming we get out of this alive," said ap Owen.

Fisher glanced at him sharply. "You're a real cheerful sort, you know that?"

"Just being realistic. Let me fill you in on the six delegates taking part in the Talks. They're a pretty rum bunch themselves, particularly the Outremer delegates. They were mad as hell when they arrived. Apparently it took them the best part of five weeks to get here through the winter weather, and that was before the worst of the storms hit. I don't see why they couldn't have just teleported in."

"Teleports don't work that way," said Fisher. "It's hard enough to shift one person over a short distance. There isn't a sorcerer alive with the kind of magic it would take to teleport three people from one country to another. There are lots of nasty ways for a teleport to go wrong. Get the decimal point in the wrong place and you could end up appearing a hundred feet above your destination. Or under it."

"I didn't realise you were such an expert," said ap Owen dryly.

Fisher shrugged. "I've had some experience with travelling that way."

"Actually, the weather is something of a blessing. The storms are keeping Outremer's more disruptive elements from getting here. Let's just hope the storms continue till the Talks are over."

"Maybe someone should have a word with the city weather wizards."

"No, low profile, remember? Nothing that would attract attention."

"True. All right, tell me about the delegates. Who's representing the Low Kingdoms? Anyone I might have heard of?"

"Maybe. Lord Regis is heading the home team. This is his house we're in. Mid-forties, old Haven Family, good reputation, with an impressive background in the army and the diplomatic corps. Can't say I warm to him myself. Smiles too much, and takes too long to shake your hand. Likes to clap you on the shoulder while looking you right in the eye. Hail-fellow-well-met type. He gets on my nerves something fierce, but he goes down well enough with the other delegates.

"Then there's Jonathon Rook, representing the Merchants Association. Early forties, and better padded than the average sofa. He likes his food, does Jonathon. Sharp as a tack when it comes to business, but he does love a title. Practically milorded Regis to death this morning, while we were waiting for the Outremer delegates to show up. Word is he's angling for a Family marriage for his eldest, more fool he.

"And finally, there's Major Patrik Comber. You've probably heard of him. Led his battalion into Death's Hollow to rescue a company of his men who'd been cut off by Outremer troops. Took on better than five-to-one odds, and kicked their arses something cruel. Won all sorts of medals, and a swift promotion. He also sacrificed a lot of good men in the process, but the minstrels don't usually mention that."

Fisher grinned. "I can see you're going to be a real barrel of laughs on this job. How about the Outremer delegates? Do you like them any better?"

"Not much. The leader is Lord Nightingale. Pleasant enough sort, but I don't think I'll turn my back on him. He's got cold eyes. Then there's William Gardener for the merchants, and Major Guy de Tournay. Can't tell you much about them. Gardener likes his drink and talks too loudly, while de Tournay's hardly opened his mouth to me since he got here."

Fisher frowned thoughtfully. "Interesting that both sides have put forward a lord. The Quality aren't normally considered expendable. Particularly not someone as noticeable as Lord Regis. And from what I've heard, Major Comber's something of a popular hero at the moment. The Powers That Be must be taking these Talks pretty seriously."

"Seems likely. Both sides have been losing a lot of men and equipment in the border skirmishes, and it's getting expensive. You know how the Powers That Be hate to lose money. Of course, they hate to lose face even more, which is why it's taken till now to set the Talks up."

"All right. Fill me in on what security measures you've set up here. If we're not allowed to call attention to ourselves, it cuts our options down to practically nothing, doesn't it?"

"You've got that right," said ap Owen grimly. "For all the good we'd be in a real crisis, we might as well not be here. I take it you spotted the plainclothes people outside? I'd be surprised if you hadn't; everyone else knows who and what they are. Luckily, they're just out there for show. My real undercover operatives have been here for days, establishing their characters and getting to know the area. We didn't just choose this place on a whim, you know. Both the grounds and the surrounding streets are wide open, with nowhere to hide. The way we've got things set up, no one can get within a hundred yards of this house without being spotted a dozen times. And since we haven't a hope in hell of beating off an armed assault, at the first whisper of an attack, or even an intended attack, the plan is for all of us to retreat into the pocket dimension and seal it off.

"In theory, we should then be perfectly safe. No one can get at us without the proper co-ordinates, known only to a top few people, so all we have to do is sit tight and wait until reinforcements arrive, and the emergency is over. Of course, there's always the very real possibility that the delegates themselves will seal off the dimension at the first whiff of trouble, leaving us out here to fight off the attackers. In which case, we get to earn our money the hard way. Got it?"

Fisher nodded glumly. In other words, it was another damned watching brief. Lots of sitting around doing nothing, waiting for something to happen and hoping it wouldn't. It was at times like these that Fisher seriously considered the simple pleasures of a desk job, and the security to be found in lots of nice safe paperwork. Of course, she'd be bored out of her mind in a week . . . Ah well, if nothing else, she should be able to catch up on her sleep here. Working two shifts in a row had drained most of her strength, and helping Hawk drag survivors out of the tenement rubble had all but finished her off. She felt as if she could go to sleep right there in her chair, She caught herself slumping forward, and quickly sat up straight. Almost without realising it, her eyes had been closing, and she'd actually come close to nodding off. That would have made a great first impression on Captain ap Owen. She glanced quickly at him to see if he'd noticed anything, but he was apparently absorbed in leafing through the papers on his desk.

"Tell me about the Talks themselves," she said, to show she was still with it. "Are they making any progress?"

"Beats me. I'm just the hired help round here; no one tells me anything. I'm not even allowed into the pocket dimension unless one of them calls for me, and though the delegates take an occasional break out here, none of them are much for small talk. As far as I can discover, their brief is to agree on a border frontier both sides can live with, and put an end to all those squabbles over which ragged old piece of map takes precedence. Both the Low Kingdoms and Outremer are going to end up losing some territory, so both sides are throwing in lucrative trade deals as sweeteners to help the medicine go down. Whatever happens, you can bet a lot of people living near the border will wake up one morning to find that overnight they've become citizens of a different country. Poor bastards. Probably end up paying two sets of taxes."

Fisher frowned. "Those special trade deals are going to put a lot of noses out of joint in the business community. Nothing like a little preferential treatment to stir up bad feelings."

"Right," said ap Owen. "And let's not forget, there's a hell of a lot of money to be made out of a war, if you've got the right kind of contacts with the military."

"Any more bad news you'd like to share with me?"

"You mean apart from political extremists, religious fanatics, and terrorists-for-hire?"

"Forget I asked. Do you think it'll come to a war, if the Talks fail?"

"I don't know . . . Countries have gone to war over a lot less in the past. The Low Kingdoms have traditionally preferred action to talk, and Outremer can be touchy as hell where its honour is concerned. I wouldn't be surprised if a war did break out, but then it must be said I have something of a vested interest in war. I've always made most of my living as a mercenary. I only ended up as a Guard because I'd spent too long between jobs and the money had run out. Ironic, really, that I should end up protecting Talks whose purpose is to keep me and my kind out of work. You ever been caught up in a war, Captain Fisher?"

"Just once," said Fisher. "Several years back. It's funny, you know; at the time I would have given everything I owned to be somewhere else, somewhere safe. But now, looking back, it seems to me I've never felt so alive as I did then. We were fighting for great stakes, and everything I did mattered; everything I did was important. But I wouldn't go through it again for all the money in the Low Kingdoms' Treasury. I saw too many good people die, saw too many people I cared for hurt and maimed."

"Did you win?"

"Yes and no." Fisher smiled tiredly. "I suppose that's true of any war. Our side won in the end, but the Land was devastated by the fighting. It'll take generations to recover. I suppose you've seen a lot of war, as a mercenary?"

Ap Owen shrugged. "More than I care to remember. One war is much like another, and the campaigns all tend to blur into each other after a while. Endless marching, rotten food, and lousy weather. Waiting for orders that never come, in some godforsaken spot in the middle of nowhere. And every now and again, just often enough to keep your nerves ragged, there'll be a sudden burst of action. You get used to the blood and the flies and seeing your comrades die, and there's always the looting to look forward to afterwards. I could have been a rich man a dozen times over, if I could have kept away from the cards and the dice and the tavern whores. I started out fighting for a cause, but that didn't last long. First thing you learn as a mercenary is that both sides believe they're right.

"So why have I spent most of my adult life fighting for strangers? Because I'm good at it. And because, just as you said, you never feel more alive than when you've just cheated death. In its way, that feeling's more addictive than any drug you'll find on the streets." He broke off, and smiled at Fisher. "You're a good listener, Fisher, you know that?"

Before she could say anything, a ring on ap Owen's finger pulsed with a sudden silver light, and he rose quickly to his feet. "That's the delegates' signal; they're going to take another break. Just stay back out of the way, for the time being. I'll introduce you if I get a chance, but don't expect any great show of interest. We're just hired help as far as they're concerned."

Two footmen entered the study in response to some un-heard summons, carrying silver trays laden with assorted delicacies of the kind Fisher hadn't seen in the markets for weeks. Whoever was funding these Talks obviously didn't believe in doing things by halves. The footmen put down their trays on the main table, by the cut-glass wine decant-ers, then withdrew without saying a word. Fisher decided they were probably real footmen, if only because of their supercilious expressions.

Ap Owen stood before his desk, staring at the far wall. Fisher followed his gaze, but couldn't see anything of inter-est. She started to ask something, and then shut up as a door appeared out of nowhere, hanging unsupported on the air a few inches above the floor. It was plain, unvar-nished wood, without pattern or trimmings, but its very presence was subtly disturbing. A mounting chill emanated from it, like a cold wind blowing into the room. Fisher's hand dropped to her sword, and she had to fight to keep from drawing it as the door swung slowly open.

The delegates appeared through the doorway, chatting quietly together, and headed for the food and wine without so much as a glance at ap Owen and Fisher. The door shut silently, and disappeared. Fisher took her hand away from her sword. Ap Owen moved in beside her and quietly iden-tified each delegate by name. Fisher looked them over care-fully without being too obvious about it.

Lord Regis of Haven was of average height and weight, and in pretty good shape for a man in his early fifties. He had dark, flashing eyes and a quick smile buried in a neatly trimmed beard. He used his hands a lot as he talked, and nodded frequently while he listened. Lord Nightingale of Outremer was twenty years younger, six inches taller, and muscular in a broad, solid way that suggested he lifted weights on a regular basis. Which was a little unusual. As far as most of the Quality were concerned, strenuous exercise was something best left to the lower classes. The Quality only exerted themselves in duelling or seducing. Usually both, as one often led to the other. Nightingale, on the other hand, looked as though he could have picked up Regis with one hand, and torn him apart with the other. If Regis was aware of this, it didn't seem to bother him.

The two traders, Rook and Gardener, were talking together quite amicably, smiling and laughing as they rummaged through the out-of-season delicacies on the trays. Fisher's stomach rumbled, but she made herself pay attention to the two merchants. William Gardener of Outremer was in his early forties, with thinning hair and a droopy moustache. He was skinny as a rake, but wore clothes of the very latest cut with casual elegance. Jonathon Rook was the same age, and dressed just as well, but had the kind of figure politely referred to as stout. His hands were weighed down with jewelled rings, and he paid little or no attention to the expensive food with which he was stuffing his face. Fisher moved in a little closer to listen in on their conversation. They both studiously ignored her, which suited her fine. It soon became clear that both merchants thought they had a lot to lose in the event of a war, and were pressing for peace at practically any cost. It was also clear they were finding it an uphill struggle.

Major Comber and Major de Tournay stood a little way off from the others, talking quietly and only picking at their food. They were both in their late thirties, with short-cropped hair and grim faces. They'd swapped their uniforms for civilian clothes, and Fisher was hard put to tell which of them looked the most uncomfortable. They both glared at her when she got too close, so she didn't get to overhear what they were saying. She sensed, however, that neither one was too pleased with the way the Talks were going, from which she deduced that neither side had gained the upper hand yet.

They all finally put down their plates and turned away from the table. Captain ap Owen coughed loudly, and then again, louder still, and having got their attention, introduced Fisher to each of them. Fisher bowed formally, and got a series of perfunctory nods in reply. Lord Regis smiled at her coldly.

"Good to have you with us, Captain. Your reputation precedes you."

"You don't want to believe everything you hear," said Fisher easily. "Only the bad bits."

Regis smiled politely. "Is your partner, Captain Hawk, not here with you?"

"He's working on a case of his own at the moment, and can't leave it, I'm afraid. But not to worry, my lord. You're safe in our hands."

"I'm sure we shall be."

"I trust you'll pardon my interruption," said Lord Nightingale, looking only at Lord Regis, "but we are rather short of time. Perhaps you could continue this conversation later . . ."

"Of course," said Regis.

He nodded politely to Fisher and ap Owen, and turned to face the far wall. The door reappeared, and swung silently open. Fisher shivered suddenly. She tried to see what lay beyond the door, but there was only an impenetrable darkness. The delegates filed through, and the door swung shut behind them and vanished. Fisher sank back into her chair and stretched out her legs. This was going to be a long, hard job, she could tell. She looked thoughtfully at the food left on the table, but didn't have the energy to get up and go after it. She hoped Hawk was taking it easy, wherever he was, but doubted it. Without her to keep an eye on him, there was no telling what he'd get up to.

4

A Matter of Trust

Hawk led Captain Burns into the rotten heart of the North-side. The streets grew steadily narrower, choked with filthy snow and slush, and bustling crowds that made way for the two Guards without ever looking at them directly. Even so, they made slow progress, and Hawk had to fight to control his impatience. The pressure seemed to be bearing down on him from every side now, but he knew his only hope of dealing with it was to stay calm and controlled. His enemies would be delighted to see him striking out blindly in all directions and missing the real targets. Besides, he didn't want to spook Burns. And yet behind his grim, impassive face, Hawk's thoughts danced restlessly from one problem to another, searching for answers that eluded him. The super-chacal was out there somewhere, poised to sweep across the city in a tidal wave of blood and death. Morgan was out there too, hidden somewhere safe and plotting the deaths of everyone who knew the truth about his new drug. Not to mention Hammer, the gang leader from the Devil's Hook, and his threatened vendetta.

And also back at the Hook, the little girl Hawk had rescued from underneath the wreckage was lying in a hospital bed, still in a coma. The doctors didn't know whether she'd ever regain consciousness.

On top of all that, the Guard wanted his scalp for screwing up, and they'd taken Isobel away from him. Some days you just couldn't get a break. Hawk realised Burns was speaking to him, and looked round sharply.

"I'm sorry. What?"

"I said," Burns repeated patiently, "is it always this bad here? I'd heard stories, of course, but this place is disgusting."

Hawk looked around at the squalid buildings and the

ragged people, and the overriding sense of violence and despair that rose from them like an almost palpable mist. After five years working the Northside he'd grown inured to most of the misery and suffering, for the sake of his sanity, but it still disturbed him enough to appreciate how bad it must seem to an outsider. Haven was a dark city wherever you looked, but the Northside was dark enough to stamp out the light in anyone's soul eventually. Hawk realised Burns was still looking at him for an answer, and he shrugged harshly.

"It's quiet today, if anything. The snow and the cold are keeping most people off the streets, even the beggars, and those who are out and about aren't hanging around long enough to start any trouble. But you can bet that somewhere, someone is starting a fight, or stabbing someone in the back for no good reason. There's all sorts of crime here, everything you'd expect in an area as poor as this, but the violence never ends. To a Northsider, everyone is an enemy, out to steal what little he has, and most of the time he's right. There's little love or comfort here, Burns, and even less hope. And the only thing the Northsiders hate more than each other is an outsider. Like us."

"How do you cope with working here?" said Burns. "I'd go crazy in a week."

Hawk shrugged. "I've seen worse. All you can do is try and make a difference for the best, where you can. What brought you here from the Westside?"

"Doughty and I were filling in for some Guards who were down with the flu. When I heard they were sending us here, I seriously thought about calling in sick myself, but of course it was too late by then. Doughty didn't mind. There wasn't much that bothered him."

"I'm sorry about your partner," said Hawk.

"Yeah. He had a wife, you know. Separated three years back, but . . . Someone will have told her by now. I should have done it myself, but she never liked me anyway."

They walked in silence for a while, not looking at each other.

"So, what's the plan?" said Burns finally. "Are we headed anywhere in particular?"

"I thought we'd start off with Short Tom," said Hawk. "Has a nice little distribution setup, down on Carlisle

Street. He'll move anything for anyone, as long as the money's right. Not one of the biggest, but certainly one of the longest established. I doubt he's handling the super-chacal himself, but he'll probably have a damned good idea who might be."

"Will he talk to us? Do you have a good relationship with him?"

Hawk looked at Burns. "This is the Northside, no one here talks to the Guard willingly. We're the enemy, the ones who enforce the laws that keep them in their place. The poverty here's so bad, most people will do anything to escape it. They don't care who they rob or who they hurt. All they care about is making that one big score that will finally get them out of the Northside. You can't reason with people like that. Short Tom will talk to me because he knows what will happen to him if he doesn't."

Burns stared straight ahead of him, his face expressionless. "I don't approve of strong-arm tactics. I put on this uniform to help people, not oppress them."

"You've spent too long in the Westside, Burns. They still like to pretend they're living in a civilised city over there. Here in the Northside, they'd quite happily cut you down for the loose change in your pockets, or a chance at your boots. The only thing that keeps them off my back is the certain knowledge that I'll kill them if they even think of raising a hand against me. I have to be obviously more dangerous than they are at all times, or I'd be a dead man. Look . . . I used to think the same as you, once. There are good people here, same as there are good people everywhere, and I do my best to help and protect them. Even if it means bending or ignoring the rules to do so. But when you get right down to it, my job is to enforce the law. Whatever it takes."

"Being a Guard doesn't give us the right to beat up someone just because we think they might have information that might help us. There are procedures, proper ways of doing things."

Hawk sighed. "I know. I've read the Manual too. But the procedures take time, and for all I know, the super-chacal's already seeping out onto the streets. I could threaten to arrest Short Tom, maybe even drag him down to Headquarters and throw him in a cell to think things over. But I couldn't hold him for long, and he knows it. I don't have the time to be a nice guy about this, and to be blunt, I don't have the inclination. My way works, and I'll settle for that. I've never laid a finger on an innocent man, or killed a man who didn't deserve it."

"How can you be sure? How can you be sure you haven't killed an innocent man by accident? The dead can't defend themselves from other people's accusations. We're Captains in the Guard, Hawk—not judge, jury, and executioner."

"I go by what works," said Hawk flatly. "When the people in the Northside start playing by the rules, so will I. Look, there are just four Captains and a dozen Constables to cover the whole Northside. We can't be everywhere at once, so we have to let our reputations go ahead of us. It's a big area, Burns, and rotten to the core. All we can ever hope to do is keep the lid on. Now, I don't care if you approve of how I do my job or not; just watch my back and don't interfere. The only thing that matters now is stopping Morgan and his stinking drug."

Burns nodded slowly. "Of course, finding the super-chacal would go a long way towards reinstating you in the Guard, wouldn't it?"

Hawk looked at him coldly. "If you think that's the only reason I'm doing this, then you don't know me at all."

"Sorry. You're right, of course. Hawk, can I ask you something . . . personal?"

"I don't know. Maybe. What?"

"What happened to your eye?"

"Oh, that. I pawned it."

Short Tom's place was a two-storey glorified lean-to, adjoining a battered old warehouse on Carlisle Street. The street itself was blocked from one end to the other by an open-air market and the tightly packed crowd it had drawn. The tattered, gaudy stalls crowded up against each other, and the vendors behind them filled the air with their aggressive patter. Most of them were bundled up to their ears in thick winter furs, but it didn't seem to be slowing them down any. Some of them were all but jumping up and down on the spot in their attempt to explain just how magnificent and amazingly affordable their goods were. Hawk glanced at a few stalls, but wasn't impressed. Still, with Haven's

Docks closed by the winter storms, goods of all kinds were getting scarce, and even rubbish like this was starting to look good. The smell was pretty bad, particularly around the food stalls, and Burns pulled one face after another as he and Hawk made their way slowly through the crowd. Even their Guards' uniforms couldn't make them any room in such a crush.

Short Tom's lean-to loomed up before them, looking more and more unsafe the closer they got. It looked like it had been thrown together on the cheap by a builder in a hurry, trying to stay one step ahead of his reputation. The walls weren't straight, the wood was stained and warped, and the door and window frames were lopsided. It was a mess, even by Northside standards. Still, it was no doubt cheap to rent, and for a man in Short Tom's line of business, that was all that really mattered.

Two large bravos in heavy sheepskin coats stood before the main door, arms folded, glaring impartially about them. Hawk walked up to the one on the left, and punched him out. The second bravo yelped in disbelief and started to unfold his arms. Hawk kicked him in the knee, waited for him to bend forward, and then knocked him out with the butt of his axe. No one in the milling crowd paid any attention. It was none of their business. Burns looked at Hawk.

"Was that really necessary?"

"Yes," said Hawk. "They wouldn't have let us in without a fight, and if I'd given them a chance to draw their swords, someone would have got seriously hurt. Most probably them, but you never know. Now follow me, watch my back, and let me do all the talking. And try to at least look mean."

He stepped over the unconscious bravos, pushed open the door and stepped through, followed closely by Burns. Inside, all was surprisingly neat and tidy, with clerks sitting behind two rows of desks, shuffling pieces of paper and making careful entries in two sets of ledgers. One of the clerks shouted for them to shut the bloody door and keep the bloody cold out, and Burns quickly did so. Hawk glanced at him, and shook his head. Far too long in the Westside. He looked back at the clerks, who had finally realised who the newcomers were. One clerk opened his mouth to shout a warning.

"Don't," said Hawk.

The clerk looked at the axe in Hawk's hand, thought about it, and shut his mouth.

"Good boy," said Hawk. He looked about him, and the clerks shrank down behind their desks. Hawk smiled coldly. "My partner and I are going upstairs to have a nice little chat with Short Tom. Just carry on as normal. And by the way, if anyone was to come up after us and interrupt our little chat, I will be most upset. Is that clear?"

The clerks nodded quickly, and did their best to look as though the idea had never entered their heads. Hawk and Burns strolled casually between the desks and up the stairway at the back of the room. Burns watched the clerks' faces out of the corner of his eye. They'd all recognised Hawk by now, and there was real terror in their faces, and not a little awe. Burns frowned thoughtfully. He'd heard stories about Hawk—everyone had—but he'd never really believed them. Until now.

They found Short Tom in his office, right at the top of the stairs. It was a nice little place, neat and tidy and almost cosy, with thick rugs on the floor, comfortable furniture, and attractive watercolor landscapes on the walls. Short Tom looked up as they entered, and his face fell. Not surprisingly, given his name, he was a dwarf, with stubby arms and legs and a large head. He wore the very latest fashion, and it was a credit to his tailor that he didn't look any more ridiculous than anybody else. He was sitting at a normal-sized desk, on a custom-made chair, and he pushed it back slightly as he reached for a desk drawer.

"I wouldn't," said Hawk. "I really wouldn't."

Short Tom nodded glumly, and took his hand away from the drawer. "Captain Hawk. How nice to see you again. Absolutely marvelous. What do you want?"

"Just a little chat," said Hawk. "I've got a problem I thought you might be able to help me with."

"I'm clean," said Short Tom immediately. "One hundred per cent. I'm entirely legitimate these days."

"Of course you are," said Hawk. "In which case, you won't mind my bringing in the tax inspectors to go through all your invoices, will you?"

Short Tom sighed heavily. "What can I do for you, Captain?"

"Morgan's got a small mountain of drugs on his hands that he has to move in a hurry."

"He hasn't contacted me. I swear he hasn't."

"I know he hasn't. You're not big enough for this. But you can give me some names. With a deal this urgent, there's bound to have been talk already."

"I've heard about your run-in with Morgan," said Short Tom carefully, "and I can't afford to get involved. I'm just a small-time operator, dealing in whatever odds and ends the big boys can't be bothered with. As long as I know my place, no one bothers me. If I start talking out of turn, Morgan will send some of his heavies round to shut me up permanently. You'll have to find your help somewhere else."

"Thousands of people could die if we don't stop this drug hitting the street."

"That's not my problem."

Hawk raised his axe above his head and brought it sweeping down in one swift, savage movement. The axe-head buried itself in Short Tom's desk, splitting the polished desktop apart. Hawk yanked the axe free and struck the desk again, putting all his strength into it. The desk caved in, sheared almost in two. Splinters flew on the air, and papers fluttered to the floor like wounded birds. Short Tom sat very still, looking down at the wreckage of his desk. He raised his eyes and looked at Hawk, standing before him with his axe at the ready.

"On the other hand," said Short Tom very politely, "I've always believed in co-operating with the forces of law and order whenever possible."

He came up with four names and addresses, all of which Hawk recognised. He nodded his thanks, and left. Burns hurried after him, having almost missed his cue. His last glimpse was of Short Tom staring glumly at what was left of his desk. Burns followed Hawk down the stairs and back through the rows of clerks, all of whom were careful to keep their eyes glued to their work as the Guards passed. Hawk and Burns stepped out into the street again, and Burns winced as the bitter cold hit him hard after the comfortable warmth of the offices. He stubbed his toe on something, and looked down to find the two bravos who'd guarded the front door still lying where they'd fallen. Only now they were stark-naked, having been stripped of every-thing they owned. Their flesh was a rather pleasant pale blue, set against the dirty grey of the snow. Hawk chuckled.

"That's the Northside for you."

"We can't just leave them like this," protested Burns. "They'll freeze to death."

"Yeah, I know. Give me a hand and we'll dump them back in the offices. Short Tom will take care of them. But let this be a lesson to you, Burns. Never give a Northsider an opening, or he'll steal you blind. And the odds are there's not one person in this crowd who would have lifted a finger to help these two bravos. They'd have just left them there to freeze. In the Northside, people learn from an early age not to care for anyone but themselves."

"Is that where you learned it?" said Burns.

Hawk looked at him, and Burns had to fight down an urge to look away from the glare of the single cold eye. When Hawk finally spoke, his voice was calm and unhurried.

"I think we're going to get on a lot better if you stop acting like a character from a religious pamphlet. I don't know how you've managed to survive this long in Haven; I can only assume they've had a hot flush of civilisation in the Westside since I was last there.

"Look, Burns, let's get this clear once and for all. I'm only as hard as I need to be to get the job done. I take no pleasure in violence, but I don't shrink from it either, if I decide it's necessary. I didn't see you holding back when we were fighting for our lives in Morgan's factory."

"That was different!"

"No, it wasn't. We're fighting a war here in the North-side, against some of the most evil and corrupt sons of bitches this city has produced, and we're losing. For every villain we put away, there are ten more queuing up to take his place. The only satisfaction we get out of this job is knowing that things would be even worse without us. Now, am I going to have any more problems with you?"

"No," said Burns. "You've made yourself very clear."

"Good. Now help me get these two bravos inside before they freeze their nuts off."

It didn't take long to discover that none of the distributors knew anything about Morgan's super-chacal. The word

from every one of them was that Morgan had gone to
ground after his release from custody, and no one had
heard anything about him since. Hawk gave them all his
best, menacing glare, but they stuck to their story, so in
the end Hawk decided he believed them. Hawk and Burns
stood together in the street outside the last distributor's
warehouse, and looked at each other thoughtfully.

"Maybe Morgan's set up his own distribution network,"
said Burns.

"No," said Hawk. "If he had, I'd have heard about it."

"You didn't know about the super-chacal."

"That was different."

"How?"

"The drug could be produced and guarded by relatively
few people, hidden away in the pocket dimension. A new
distribution system would need a lot of people, and someone would have been bound to talk. No, Morgan has to be
using an established distributor. Maybe someone who
doesn't normally move drugs, but has the right kind of
contacts."

"Maybe." Burns pulled his cloak tightly about him, and
stamped his feet in the snow. "So, what's our next step?"

"We go and talk with the one man who might know
what Morgan is up to; the man who knows everything
that's going on in the Northside, because nothing happens here without his approval. The big man himself:
Saint Christophe."

Burns looked at him sharply. "Wait a minute, Hawk,
even I've heard of Saint Christophe. He takes a cut from
every crime committed in Haven. Word is he has a dozen
judges in his pocket, and as many Councillors. Not to mention a personal army of four hundred men, and a private
mansion better protected than Guard Headquarters. We
don't stand a chance of getting in to see him, and even if
we did somehow manage it, he'd probably just have us
killed on sight. Slowly and very horribly."

"Calm down," said Hawk, amused. "We're not going
anywhere near his house."

"Thank all the Gods for that."

"I've got a better idea."

Burns looked at him suspiciously. "If it involves bursting
in on him where he works and smashing up his desk, you

are on your own. Saint Christophe is the only person in the Northside with an even worse reputation than you."

"Have you finished?" said Hawk.

"Depends," said Burns darkly. "Tell me your idea."

"Every day, at the same time, Saint Christophe has a bath and sauna at a private little place not far from here. It's pretty well guarded, but there's a way to get in that not many people know about. I did the owner a favour once."

"And at what time of day does Saint Christophe visit this bathhouse?" said Burns.

"About now."

Burns nodded glumly. "I thought so. You've had this in mind all along, haven't you?"

Hawk grinned. "Stick with me, Burns. I know what I'm doing."

Burns just looked at him.

The private baths turned out to be a discreet little place tucked away on a side street in a surprisingly quiet and upmarket area right on the edge of the Northside. It stayed quiet and upmarket because the Northside's more successful villains used the area for their own rest and relaxation, and everyone else had the sense to stay out of their way. Everyone except Hawk.

He walked breezily down an alleyway and slipped into the baths through a door marked "Staff Only." Burns hurried in after him and shut the door quickly behind them, his heart beating uncomfortably fast. Hawk looked around once to get his bearings, then set off confidently through a maze of corridors that Burns wouldn't have tackled without a map and a compass. Every now and again they encountered a member of the staff, but Hawk just nodded to each attendant briskly, as though he had every right to be there, and the attendant just nodded back and continued on his way. Burns grew increasingly nervous, and felt a growing need to find a privy.

"Are you sure you know where you're going?" he whispered harshly.

"You must learn to trust me, Burns," said Hawk airily. "The owner himself showed me this route. We'll find Saint Christophe in cubicle seventeen, just down this corridor here. Assuming he hasn't changed his routine."

"And if he has?"

"Then we'll just walk up and down the corridor, slamming doors open, till we find him."

Burns realised with a sinking heart that Hawk wasn't joking. He thought about the number of major villains who were probably relaxing all unknowing behind the other doors, and swallowed hard. He started to plot an emergency escape route back through the corridors, realised he was hopelessly lost, and felt even worse.

Cubicle seventeen looked like all the others, a plain wooden door with a gold filigree number. Hawk put his ear against the door and listened for a moment, then stood back and loosened the axe at his side. Then he kicked the door open, strolled casually into the steam-filled sauna and leaned against the door, holding it open. Burns stood in the doorway, keeping one eye on the corridor, in case some of the staff happened along. The steam quickly cleared as the temperature dropped, revealing Saint Christophe sitting at the back of the room, surrounded by twelve muscular female bodyguards wearing nothing but sword belts.

The bodyguards surged to their feet, grabbing for their swords as they recognised the Guards' uniforms. Hawk just leaned against the door, and nodded casually to Saint Christophe. Burns wanted desperately to draw his sword, but had enough sense to know it wouldn't help him much if he did. His only hope was to brazen it out and hope Hawk knew what he was doing. He squared his shoulders and lifted his chin, and gave the bodyguards his best intimidating glare. If it bothered them at all, they did a great job of hiding it. And then Saint Christophe stirred on his wooden bench, and everybody's attention went to him. He gestured briefly to his bodyguards, and they all immediately put away their swords and sat down again, ignoring the two Guards. Burns blinked. He couldn't have been more surprised if they'd all started speaking in tongues.

Saint Christophe was a big man, in more ways than one. Though no longer personally involved in any particular racket, every other villain in the city payed him homage, not to mention tribute. He funded a great many operations, and planned many more, but never took a single risk himself. He ran his organization with brutal efficiency and was reputed to be one of the richest men in Haven, if not the

Low Kingdoms. He had a partner, once. No one knew what happened to him. It wasn't considered prudent to ask.

The man himself was over six feet tall, and was reputed to weigh three hundred and fifty pounds. Sitting down, he looked almost as wide as he was tall, a mountain of gleaming white flesh running with perspiration. Rumor had it there was a surprising ammount of muscle under all the fat, and Burns believed it. Even sitting still, Saint Christophe exuded an air of overwhelming menace—partly from his imposing bulk, and partly from his unwavering, lizardlike gaze. His face was blank and almost childlike, his features stretched smooth like a baby's by his fat, an impression heightened by his thin, wispy hair. He moved slightly, and the wooden bench groaned under his weight. His bodyguards were already beginning to shiver from the dropping temperature, but he didn't seem to notice it. His gaze was fixed entirely on Hawk, ignoring Burns, for which Burns was very grateful. When Saint Christophe finally spoke, his voice was deep and cultured.

"Well, Captain Hawk. An unexpected pleasure. It's not often you come to see me."

"I have a problem," said Hawk.

"Yes, I know. You have a talent for annoying important people, Captain, but this time you have surpassed yourself. The Guard wants you suspended, a gang from the Devil's Hook has declared vendetta against you, and Morgan wants your head on a platter. You've had a busy morning."

"It's not over yet. I need to know how Morgan is going to distribute his new drug."

"And so you came to me for help. How touching. Why should I help you, Captain Hawk? It would make much more sense to have you killed, here and now. After all, you've caused me much distress in the past. You've shut down my operations, arrested and killed my men, and cost me a great deal of money. I really don't know why I didn't order your death long ago."

Hawk grinned. "Because you couldn't be one hundred percent sure they'd do the job. And you know that if they didn't kill me, I'd kill them, and then I'd come after you. And all the bodyguards in Haven couldn't keep you alive if I wanted your head."

Saint Christophe nodded slowly, his face impassive. "You

always were a vindictive man, Captain. But one day you'll push me too far, and then we'll see how good you really are with that axe. In the meantime, my offer to you still stands. Leave the Guard, and work for me. Be my man. I could make you rich and powerful beyond your wildest dreams."

"I'm my own man," said Hawk. "And there isn't enough money in Haven to make me work for you. You deal in other people's suffering, and the blood won't wash off your money, no matter how many times you launder it through legitimate businesses."

"Anyone would think you didn't like me," said Saint Christophe. "Why should I help you, Captain? You spurn my friendship, throw my more-than-generous offers back in my face, and insult me in front of my people. What is it to me if Morgan is pushing a new drug? If it wasn't him, it would be somebody else. The market's appetite is always bigger than we can satisfy."

"This drug is different," said Hawk flatly. "It turns its users into maddened, unstoppable killers. A few hours after the drug hits the streets, there'll be hundreds of homicidal maniacs running loose in the city. The death toll could easily run into thousands. You can't sell your precious services to dead people, Christophe. You need me to stop Morgan because he threatens your markets. All of them. It's as simple as that."

"Perhaps." Saint Christophe leaned forward slightly, and his wooden bench groaned loudly. His bodyguards tensed for a moment, and then relaxed. "This is important to you, isn't it, Captain?"

"Of course. It's my job."

"No, this is more than just your job; it's become personal to you. One should never get personally involved in business, Captain; it distorts a man's judgment and makes him . . . vulnerable. Let us make a deal, you and I. You want something from me, and I want something from you. I will agree to shut down all distribution networks in Haven for forty-eight hours. More then enough time for you to find Morgan and put a stop to his plans. In return . . . you will leave the Guard and work for me. A simple exchange, Captain Hawk. Take it or leave it."

"No deal," said Hawk.

"Think about it, Captain. Think of the thousands who'll die if you don't find Morgan in time. And you won't, without my help. You really don't have a choice."

"Wrong. You're the one who doesn't have a choice." Hawk fixed Saint Christophe with his cold glare, and the bodyguards stirred restlessly. "The Guard still has some of the super-chacal we confiscated from Morgan's factory. Whoever made the drug disappear from Headquarters missed one batch. So either you co-operate, and tell me what I need to know, or I'll see that when the drug finally gets loose, you'll personally get a good strong dose. If Haven's going to be torn apart because of you, I'll see you go down with it."

"You wouldn't do that," said Saint Christophe.

"Try me," said Hawk.

For a long moment, nobody spoke. The atmosphere in the sauna grew dangerously tense. Burns glanced from Hawk to Saint Christophe and back again, but neither of them looked to be giving way. He let his hand drift a little closer to his sword. All it would take was one sign from Saint Christophe, and the twelve bodyguards would attack. Hawk might actually be able to handle six-to-one odds with that bloody axe of his, but Burns had no false illusions about his own fighting skills. Maybe, if he was quick enough, he could jump back and slam the door in their faces, slow them down enough for him to make a run for it. That would mean abandoning Hawk . . .

"Very well," said Saint Christophe. "I agree. I will see to it that the distribution networks are shut down for twenty-four hours."

"You said forty-eight," said Hawk.

"That was a different deal. You have twenty-four hours, Captain. I suggest you make good use of them, since regretfully I have no idea as to where Morgan might be at present. He seems to have disappeared into a hole and pulled it in after him. But Captain, when this is over, you will answer to me for your threats and defiance. Please close the door on your way out."

Hawk turned and left without speaking. Burns hurried after him, shut the cubicle door firmly, and then ran after his partner as he strode off down the corridor.

"I don't believe what I just saw," said Burns in amazement. "You faced down Saint Christophe without even drawing your axe, and got him to agree to help the Guard. That's like standing in the harbour and watching the tides go out backwards."

Hawk shrugged. "It was in his interests to help, and he knew it."

"Where did you find the extra batch of super-chacal? I thought it had all disappeared."

"It did. I was bluffing." Burns looked at him speechlessly. Hawk grinned. "There's more to surviving in the Northside than knowing how to use an axe."

Hawk was never sure how he knew when he was being followed, but over the years he'd learned to trust his instincts. He glanced at Burns, but he was apparently lost in his own thoughts and hadn't noticed anything. Hawk slowed his pace a little, and found various convincing reasons to look innocently around him. He frowned as he spotted not one tail but several, moving casually through the crowd after him and Burns. Whoever they were, they must be pretty good to have got so close without his noticing them before. His frown deepened as he realised the tails were gradually moving so as to surround him and Burns. It was looking more and more like an ambush, and they'd chosen a good spot for it. The street was growing increasingly narrow, and was blocked off at both ends by market stalls. There were alleyways leading off to both sides, but none of them seemed to lead anywhere helpful. And the next main intersection was too far away, if it came to running. Besides, Hawk didn't believe in running. He let his hand fall casually to the axe at his side, and looked for the place to make a stand.

"I make it seven," said Burns quietly. "They picked us up not long after we left the baths."

"I wasn't sure you'd even noticed we were being followed."

"Working in the Westside, I spent a lot of time escorting gold- and silversmiths to the banks with their week's receipts. There's nothing like guarding large amounts of money in public to make you aware of when you're being followed. So what are we going to do? Make a stand?"

"I don't think we've much choice. And it's eight, not

seven. See that man in the doorway, just ahead, pretending not to watch us?"

"Yes. Damn. And if we can see eight, you can bet there are just as many more lurking somewhere handy out of sight, just in case they're needed. I don't like the odds, Hawk."

"I've faced worse."

"I wish you'd stop saying that. It's very irritating, and I don't believe it for a moment. Who do you think they are? Morgan's people?"

"Seems likely. He must have known I'd have to go to Saint Christophe eventually, so he just staked the place out and waited for us to turn up. Damn. I hate being predictable."

"We could go back to Saint Christophe and ask for protection."

"You have got to be joking. He'd love that. Besides, I have my reputation to think of."

"If we don't think of something fast, you're going to be the most reputable corpse in the Northside!"

"Calm down, Burns. You worry too much. If the fighting ground is unfavourable, then the obvious thing to do is change the fighting ground. You see that fire-escape stairway, to your right?"

"Yeah, what about it? Hey, wait a minute, Hawk. You can't be serious . . ."

"Shut up and run."

Hawk sprinted forward, with Burns only a pace or two behind. Their followers hesitated a moment, and then charged after them, forcing their way through the crowd with brutal efficiency. Hawk reached the metal stairway, and ran up it without slowing, taking the steps two at a time. Burns hurried after him, the fire escape shuddering under their combined weight. Hawk pulled himself up onto the roof and scurried across the uneven tilework to crouch beside the nearest chimney. Burns clattered unsteadily across to join him, and clutched at the chimney stack to steady himself. Hawk shot him a grin.

"Check the other side of the roof; see if there's any other way to get up here. I'll prepare a few nasty surprises."

"You're just loving this, aren't you?" said Burns through clenched teeth, hugging tight to the chimney.

"What's the matter with you?"

"I hate heights!"

"Oh, stop complaining, and get over to the other side. This is the perfect spot to take them on; lots of hiding places, and they're just as much at a disadvantage as we are. Trust me, I've done this before."

Burns scowled at him, reluctantly let go of the chimney, and moved cautiously across the tiles towards the spine of the roof. "All right, what's the plan, then?"

"Plan? What do we need a plan for? Just find something to hide behind, and jump out on anything that moves!"

Burns disappeared over the roof ridge, muttering to himself. Hawk looked quickly about him, taking in the gables, cornices, and chimney stacks that jutted from the undulating sea of roofs to either side. He drew his axe and waited patiently in the shadows of the chimney, listening for the first giveaway sound. It was at times like this that he wished he carried a length of tripwire.

He looked around him, taking in the state of the roof. A lot of snow had fallen away from the tiles, pulled loose by its own weight and the vibrations of passing traffic below, but there was enough left to make the tiles suitably treacherous. A sudden thud followed by muffled curses from the other side of the roof suggested that Burns had reached the same conclusion. Hawk grinned suddenly, as an idea hit him. He moved carefully away from the chimney, unbuttoned his fly and urinated over a stretch of apparently safe tilework. It steamed on the air, but froze almost as soon as it spread out across the tiles. Hawk finished and quickly buttoned up again, wincing at the cold. He looked round sharply as he caught the muffled sound of boots treading quietly on the metal stairway, and he scurried back to crouch down on the opposite side of the chimney stack. He breathed through his nose so that his steaming breath wouldn't give him away, and clutched his axe firmly.

He listened carefully as the first man stepped off the stairway onto the roof, hesitated, and then moved slowly forward. Timing his move precisely, Hawk suddenly emerged from behind the chimney, swinging his axe in both hands. Morgan's man spun round just in time to receive the heavy axehead in his shoulder. The blade sheared clean through his collarbone, and blood flew steaming on the bitter air. The impact drove the man to his knees. Hawk pulled the axe free, put a boot against the man's shoulder and pushed. The man-at-arms screamed once as he slid helplessly across the roof and over the side.

Hawk heard footsteps behind him and turned just in time to see the second man hit the patch of frozen urine. The swordsman's feet shot out from under him and he all but flew off the edge of the roof. The third man was standing by the fire escape with his mouth hanging open. Hawk bent down, snatched up a handful of snow, and threw it at him. As the man-at-arms raised his hand instinctively to guard his face, Hawk stepped carefully forward and swung his axe in a vicious sideways arc. The axehead punched clean through the man's rib cage and sent him flying backwards. He disappeared over the edge of the roof and fell back down the fire escape. There was a brief flurry of yells and curses from the other men coming up the stairway, and Hawk grinned. He hurried forward, and his feet shot out from under him.

He hit the roof hard, and slid kicking and cursing towards the edge of the roof. He threw aside his axe and grabbed at the iron guttering as he shot past it. He got a firm grip on the trough with both hands, and the sudden shock of stopping almost wrenched his arms from his sockets. The guttering groaned loudly, but supported his weight. Hawk hung there for a moment, breathing hard, his feet dangling above the street far below, and then he started to pull himself back up. The trough groaned again and shifted suddenly. There was a muffled pop as a rivet tore free, and Hawk froze where he was. The guttering didn't look at all secure, especially when seen from underneath, and he didn't think it would hold his weight much longer. On the other hand, one sudden movement might be all it would take to pull it away completely. He pulled himself up slowly and carefully, an inch at a time, ignoring the sudden groans and stirrings from the ironwork, and swung one leg up over onto the roof. A few moments later he was back on the roof, reaching for his axe and wiping sweat from his forehead. The sound of approaching feet on the fire escape caught his attention again and he grinned suddenly as a new idea came to him.

He moved carefully over to the metal stairway and

looked down. Seven men-at-arms were heading up towards him. They looked grim, and very competent. Hawk waved at them cheerfully, and then bent forward and stuck his axehead between the side of the stairway and the wall. He threw his weight against the axe, and the fire escape tore away from the wall with almost casual ease. The seven swordsmen screamed all the way down to the street below. Hawk put his axe away. Sometimes there was a lot to be said for cheap building practices.

He clambered up to the roof ridge and looked down the other side. Burns was crouching at the edge of the roof, sword in hand, keeping watch from behind a jutting gable. There was no sign of any more men-at-arms. Hawk called out to Burns, and he jumped half out of his skin. He spun round, sword at the ready, and then glared balefully as he saw it was only Hawk.

"Don't do that!"

"Sorry," said Hawk. "I take it none of the men-at-arms got this far?"

"Haven't seen hide nor hair of them. I don't think they were interested in me, only you. How many came after you?"

"Ten," said Hawk, casually.

"Bloody hell. What happened to them?"

Hawk grinned. "We had a falling out."

They made their way back to Headquarters, but though there were no further incidents, Hawk couldn't shake the feeling they were still being followed. He tried all the usual tricks to make a tail reveal himself, but he didn't see anyone, no matter how carefully he checked. It was always possible his current situation had him jumping at shadows, but he didn't think so. The crawling itch between his shoulder blades stayed with him all the way back to Guard Headquarters. He stopped at the main doors and peered wistfully down the street at The Cloudy Morning tavern. A drink would really hit the spot now, after the long day's exertions, but he could just visualize the look on Burns's face if he were to suggest it. All the partners he could have chosen, and he had to pick a saint in training. He strode scowling into Headquarters, and everyone hurried to get out of his way. Burns walked silently beside him, nodding casually to familiar faces. He'd been unusually quiet ever since Morgan's people jumped them. Hawk shrugged mentally. Apparently Burns was still mad at him for not trying to bring in his attackers alive. As if he'd had a choice, with ten-to-one odds.

They made their way through the building, going from department to department, ostensibly just passing the time of day with their co-workers, but always managing to slip in the occasional probing question. It was hard going. None of the Guards wanted to talk about Morgan or his drugs, and in particular no one wanted to be seen talking to Hawk. Overnight he'd become bad news, and no one wanted to get too close in case some of the guilt rubbed off on them. The sudden reticence was unnerving. Usually Headquarters was buzzing with gossip about everything under the sun, most of it unprovable and nearly all of it acrimonious, but now all Hawk had to do was stick his head round a door and silence would fall across the room. Hawk gritted his teeth and kept smiling. He didn't want anyone to think the silence was getting to him. And slowly, very slowly, he started getting answers. They were mostly evasive, and always hushed, but they often told as much by what they didn't say as what they did. And the picture that gradually emerged was more than a little disturbing.

Mistress Melanie of the Wardrobe department didn't know anything about Morgan or the missing drugs, but she did let slip that the campaign of silence was semiofficial in origin. Word had come down from Above that the Morgan case was closed. Permanently. Which suggested that someone High Up was involved, as well as someone at Headquarters. That was unusual; corruption in the higher ranks of the Guard tended to be political rather than criminal. A clerk in Intelligence quietly intimated that at least one Guard Captain was involved. And a pretty well-regarded Captain, too. He wouldn't even hint at a name.

Hawk and Burns hung around the Constables' cloakroom for a while, but it soon became clear that the Constables were uneasy in their company and had nothing to say. The Forensic Laboratory was up to its eyes in work, as usual, and the technicians were all too busy to talk. Vice, Forgery, and Confidence Tricks were all evasive and occasionally openly obstructive. Hawk had his enemies in the Guard, and some saw this as their chance to attack while he was vulnerable. Hawk just kept on smiling, and made a note of certain names for later.

Of all the departments, the Murder Squad turned out to be the most forthcoming—probably because no one was going to tell any of its members who they could and couldn't talk to. They were the toughest of the tough, took no nonsense from anyone, and didn't care who knew it. Unfortunately, what they knew wasn't really worth the telling. The crates of super-chacal had been taken down to the storage cellars, and signed in, all according to procedure. But when the time came to check the contents, there was no sign of the crates anywhere. Everyone in Stores swore blind that no one could have got to the drugs without breaking Stores' security, and all the wards and protections were still in place, undisturbed. Which meant it had to be an inside job. Someone in Stores had been got at. But when the Stores personnel were tested under truthspell, they all came out clean as a whistle. So whoever took the drugs had to be someone fairly high up in the Guard, with access to the right keys and passwords. Hawk mentioned the possibility of a Captain on the take. There was a lot of shrugging and sideways glances, but no one would admit to knowing anything definite. Hawk thanked them for their time, and left.

That just left the Drug Squad, but as Hawk expected, no one there would talk to him. They were already under suspicion themselves, and weren't about to make things worse by helping a pariah like Hawk. He nodded politely to the silent room, and then he and Burns left to do some hard thinking. They found an empty office, barricaded the door to keep out unwelcome visitors, and sat down with their feet propped up on either side of the desk.

"The more I learn, the less this case makes sense," said Hawk disgustedly. "There's no way anyone could have got those crates out of Stores without somebody noticing, passwords or no passwords. I mean, you'd have needed at least half a dozen people just to shift that many crates. Someone in Stores has got to be lying."

"But they all passed the truthspell."

"That doesn't necessarily mean anything. It's possible to beat the truthspell, if you know what you're doing."

"It could have been sorcery of some kind," said Burns. "Morgan had one sorcerer working for him in that factory; who's to say he doesn't have another one working for him?"

"Could be," said Hawk. "Hell, I don't know. I don't know anything anymore. Did you see their faces in the Drug Squad? I know those people. I've worked with practically everyone in that room at one time or another, and they looked at me like I was a stranger. It was the same with all the others; they don't trust me anymore, and the fact of the matter is, I don't trust them either. I don't know who to trust anymore. You heard what Intelligence said; it isn't just a Captain who's on the take, it's a well-respected Captain. There aren't too many of those."

"Maybe we should go talk to Commander Glen."

"No. I don't think so."

Burns looked at him. "Are you saying you don't trust Glen either? He's the one who gave you this brief, told you to find out what's going on!"

"He's also the one who let Morgan go. And it's clear there's been a lot of pressure coming down from Above to keep people quiet. What better way to conceal a potentially embarrassing investigation than to be the one who set it up?"

"But why would someone like Glen bother about a few missing drugs?"

"He wouldn't. More and more it seems to me the drugs are only a part of this. Something else is going on, something so big they can't afford for it to come to light."

"They?" said Burns.

Hawk shrugged. "Who knows how far up the corruption goes? Why stop at a Captain or a Commander? Morgan said there was a lot of money to be made out of this superchacal. Millions of ducats. And don't forget, most of the top people in the Guard are political appointees, and there's a damn sight more corruption in politics than there ever was in the Guard."

"Hawk," said Burns carefully, "this is starting to sound very paranoid. We're going to need an awful lot of hard evidence if we're to convince anyone else."

"We can't go to anyone else. We're all alone now. We can't trust anyone—not our colleagues, not our superiors, not our friends. Anyone could be working for the other side." Hawk hesitated, and looked intently at Burns. "You know, you don't have to stay with me on this. When I asked you to be my partner, I didn't know what we were getting into. There's still time for you to get out, if you want. Things could get very nasty very quickly once I start pushing this."

Burns smiled. "You're not getting rid of me that easily. Especially not now the case is getting so interesting. I'm not convinced about this massive conspiracy of yours, but there's no doubt something fascinating is going on. I'm with you all the way, until we break the case or it breaks us. Morgan's people killed my partner. I can't turn my back on that. So, what's our next step?"

"There's only one place we can go," said Hawk slowly. "The Guard Advisory Council."

Burns gaped at him for a moment. "You've got to be kidding! They're just a bunch of businessmen, Guard retirees and idealistic Quality who like to see themselves as a buffer between the Guard and the Council's politics. They mean well, but they're about as much use as a chocolate teapot. I mean, they're very free with their advice, but they don't have any real power. They're mostly just public relations. How can they help us?"

"They're all people in a position to have a finger on the pulse of what's happening in Haven. And just maybe they're divorced enough from both Guard and Council not to be tainted by the present corruption. Maybe we can get some answers there we won't get anywhere else. It's worth a try."

"Yes, I suppose it is." Burns hesitated a moment. "Hawk, this Captain who's working for Morgan. What if it turns out to be someone we know? Maybe even a friend?"

"We do whatever's necessary," said Hawk flatly. "Whoever it is."

Burns looked as though he was going to say something more, and then both he and Hawk jumped as someone knocked briskly on the office door. They both took their feet off the desk, and glanced at each other.

"Captain Hawk?" said a voice from outside. "I have a message for you."

"How did he know where to find me?" said Hawk quietly. "No one's supposed to know where we are."

"What do we do?" said Burns.

"Answer him, I suppose." Hawk got up and walked over to the barricaded door. "What do you want?"

"Captain Hawk? I have a message for you, sir. I'm supposed to deliver it in person."

Hawk hesitated, and then shrugged. He pulled away the chairs holding the door shut, drew his axe, and opened the door. A Guard Constable looked at him, and the axe, and nodded respectfully.

"Sorry to disturb you, Captain. It's about the child you rescued from under the collapsed tenement. The little girl."

"I remember her," said Hawk. "Has there been some improvement in her condition?"

"I'm sorry, sir. She's dead. I'm told she never regained consciousness."

"I see. Thank you." The Constable nodded and walked away. Hawk closed the door. "Damn. Oh damn."

Out in the corridor, the Constable smiled to himself. The news had obviously shaken Hawk badly. And anything that slowed Hawk down had to be good for Morgan and his backers. The Constable strode off down the corridor, patting the full purse at his belt and whistling cheerfully.

5

UNdER SieGE

Fisher peered out the study window, chewing thoughtfully on a chicken leg she'd liberated from the delegates' lunch time snack after they'd disappeared back into the pocket dimension. She'd spent the last half hour checking out the house security and searching for weak spots, but she had to admit ap Owen seemed to know what he was doing. Every door and window had locks or bolts or both, and they were all securely fastened. There were men-at-arms in servants' livery on every floor, making their rounds at random intervals so as not to fall into a predictable routine. Routines could be taken advantage of. There were caches of weapons stashed all over the house, carefully out of sight but still ready to hand in an emergency. Outside, the grounds were a security man's dream. All the approaches were wide open—nowhere for anyone to hide—and the thick covering of snow made the lawns impossible to cross without leaving obvious tracks.

All in all, everything was calm and peaceful, and showed every sign of staying that way. Which was probably why Fisher was so bored. Ap Owen's people seemed to regard her as an outsider, and her appointment as some kind of negative appraisal of their own abilities. As a result, none of them were talking to her. Ap Owen himself seemed friendly enough, but it was clear he was the worrying type, constantly on the move, checking that everything was running smoothly. Fisher wandered aimlessly around for a while, committing the layout of the house to memory and trying to get the feel of the place.

It was an old house, creaking and groaning under the weight of the winter cold, with a somewhat erratic design. There were rooms within rooms and corridors that led nowhere, and shadows in unexpected places. But everything that could be done to make the house secure had been done, and Fisher couldn't fault ap Owen's work. She should have felt entirely safe and protected, and it came as something of a surprise to her to find that she didn't. Deep down inside, where her instincts lived, she couldn't shake off the feeling she—and everyone else in the house—was in danger. No doubt part of that uneasiness came from knowing there was a pocket dimension nearby. After what had happened in the Hook she was more than a little leery of such magic, for all of ap Owen's reassurances. But more than that, she had a strong feeling of being watched, of being under siege. She had only to look out of a window to feel the pressure of unseen watching eyes, as though somewhere outside a cold professional gaze was studying her dispassionately, and considering options.

And so she'd ended up back in the study, staring out the wide window at the bare, innocent lawns and wondering if she was finally getting paranoid. Ap Owen acted as if he was expecting an attack at any moment, and she was beginning to understand why. There was a definite feeling of anticipation in the air, of something irrevocable edging closer; as though her instincts were trying to warn her of something her mind hadn't noticed yet. She threw aside her chicken leg, turned her back on the window defiantly, and looked around for something to distract her. Unfortunately, the study was briskly austere, with the bare minimum of chairs and a plain writing table. Bookshelves lined two of the walls, but their leather-bound volumes had a no-nonsense, businesslike look to them. There was one portrait, on the wall behind the desk, its subject a straight-backed, grim-faced man who apparently hadn't approved of such frivolities as having your portrait painted. The study had clearly been intended as a room for working, not relaxing.

Fisher leafed through some of the papers on the desk, but ap Owen's handwriting was so bad they might have been written in code for all she could tell. She looked thoughtfully at the wine decanters left over from the delegates' break, and then looked away. She'd been drinking too much of late. So had Hawk. Haven did that to you.

There was a definite crawling on the back of Fisher's neck, and she strode back to the window and glared out at the featureless scene again. The snow-covered lawns stretched away before her, vast and unmarked. There were no trees or hedges, nothing to hide behind. Everything was quiet. Fisher yawned suddenly, and didn't bother to cover her mouth. She'd been hoping to snatch a couple of hours' sleep here, but it seemed her nerves were determined to keep her restless and alert. She almost wished that someone would attack, just to get it over with.

She started to turn away from the window, and then stopped, startled, and looked quickly back again. The wide open lawns were empty and undisturbed; no one was there. But for a moment she could have sworn . . . It came again, a sudden movement tugging at the edge of her vision. She looked quickly back and forth, and pounded her fist on the windowsill in frustration. There couldn't be anyone out there. Even if they were invisible, they'd still leave tracks in the snow. Things moved at the corner of her eyes, teasing her with glimpses of shapes and movement that refused to come clear. She backed slowly away from the window and drew her sword. Something was happening out there. There was a sound behind her and she spun round, dropping into a fighter's crouch. Ap Owen raised an eyebrow, and she flushed angrily as she straightened up.

"Dammit, don't do that! Come and take a look, ap Owen. Something's going on outside."

"I know. Half my people are giving themselves eyestrain trying to get a clear look at it."

"Do you know what it is?"

"I have a very nasty suspicion," said ap Owen, moving over to join her before the window. "I think there's someone out there, hiding behind an illusion spell. It must be pretty powerful to hide his trail as well, but as he gets closer to the house the protective wards are interfering with the spell, giving us glimpses of what it's hiding."

"You think it's just one man?"

"Not really, no. Just wishful thinking. I've put my people on full alert, just in case."

"Does whoever's out there know we've spotted something?"

"Beats me. But they haven't tried anything yet, which suggests they still trust in the illusion to hide their true strength."

Fisher scowled out the window, and hefted her sword restlessly. "All right, what do we do?"

"Wait for them to come to us. Let's see if they can even get in here before we start panicking. After all, it would need a bloody army to take this house by force."

There was a sudden, vertiginous snap and the world jerked sideways and back again, as the house's wards finally broke down the illusion spell and showed what lay behind it. The wide lawns were covered with armed men, and more were pouring through the open gates. Dressed in nondescript furs and leathers, they advanced on the house in a calm, professional way. Fisher swore respectfully. There had to be at least two hundred men out there.

The four marble statues had come alive, and were cutting a bloody path through the invaders. They were coldly efficient and totally unstoppable, but were hard put to make any impression on so many invaders. Half a dozen guard dogs blinked in and out of existence as they threw themselves at the intruders, leaping and snapping and now and again tearing at a man on the ground, but again there were simply too few of them to make any real difference. No one had expected or planned for an invasion on such a scale as this.

"I don't want to disillusion you, ap Owen," said Fisher grimly, "but it looks to me like they've got a bloody army. We are in serious trouble."

"You could well be right. From the look of them, they're mercenaries." He yelled something out the study door, and four footmen burst in, each carrying a longbow and a quiver of arrows. Ap Owen grinned at Fisher. "They don't have much use for bows in the Guard, but I've always believed in them. You can do a lot of damage with a few bowmen who know what they're doing."

"No argument from me," said Fisher. "I've seen what longbows can do."

The footmen set up before the window, pulling off their long frock coats to give them more freedom of movement. Fisher and ap Owen struggled with the bolts that held the window shut, until Fisher lost her temper and smashed the glass with the hilt of her sword. Ap Owen threw the window open and stepped back to let the archers take up their position. Bitter cold streamed in from outside, and the ar-

chers narrowed their eyes against the glare of the snow.
The attacking force realised the grounds were no longer
hidden behind the illusion spell, and ran towards the house,
howling a dissonant mixture of war cries and chants. Sunlight flashed on swords and axes and morningstars. Fisher
couldn't even guess how many attackers there were anymore. The archers drew back and released their bowstrings
in a single fluid movement, and four of the attackers were
thrown backwards with arrows jutting from their bodies.
Their blood was vividly red on the snow. The archers let
fly again and again, punching holes in the attacking force,
but they just kept coming, ignoring their dead and
wounded.

"They're professionals, all right," said ap Owen calmly.
"Mercenaries. Could be working for any number of people.
Whoever it is must want us shut down really badly. An
army that size doesn't come cheap. I didn't think there
were that many mercenaries for hire left in Haven."

"How long before reinforcements can get here?" said
Fisher tightly.

"There aren't going to be any," said ap Owen. "We're
on our own. Low profile, remember? Officially, no one
knows we're here."

"And we're expendable," said Fisher.

"Right. We either win this one ourselves, or we don't
win it at all. What's the matter, don't you like a challenge?"

Fisher growled something under her breath. The first
handful of mercenaries to reach the window ducked under
the flight of arrows and clambered up onto the windowsill.
The archers threw aside their bows and grabbed for their
swords. Fisher thought briefly of the door behind her. She
didn't believe in suicide missions. On the other hand, she
didn't believe in running, either. She moved quickly forward to join ap Owen and the archers, and together they
threw the first mercenaries back in a flurry of blood and
gore. More of the attackers crowded in to take their place.
The war cries and chants were almost deafening at close
range. Fisher glanced at ap Owen, saw him palm a pill
from a small bottle, and swallow it. He caught her gaze
and smiled.

"Just a little something, to give me an edge. Want one?"

"No thanks. I was born with an edge."

"Suit yourself. Here they come again." He breathed deeply as the drug hit him, and smiled widely at the mercenaries. "Come and get it, you lousy bastards! Come one, come all!"

The main bulk of the attack force hit the window like a breaking wave, and forced the archers back by sheer force of numbers. Fisher was swept aside, fighting desperately against a forest of waving blades. In moments the room was full of mercenaries, most of whom ran past the small knot of beleaguered defenders and on into the house. Fisher and ap Owen ended up fighting back to back, carving bloody gaps in the shifting press of bodies. The archers fell one by one, and Fisher and ap Owen were slowly driven back across the room, away from the window, as more mercenaries poured in. There seemed no end to them.

Ap Owen laughed happily and mocked his opponents as he fought, and none of the mercenaries could get anywhere near him in his euphoric state. Fisher fought doggedly on. Mercenaries fell dead and dying around her, their blood staining the expensive carpet. Her footing became uncertain as bodies cluttered the floor, and it was getting harder to find room to swing her sword. She yelled at ap Owen to get his attention.

"We've got to get out of here, while we still can!"

"Right!" yelled ap Owen, grinning widely as he slit a mercenary's throat. "Follow me!"

They made a break for the door, ploughing through the startled mercenaries, and cutting down anyone who got in their way. They burst out into the hall, and Fisher was surprised to find it deserted. Ap Owen headed for the stairs, with Fisher close behind.

"They don't know where the Talks are really being held, so they're wasting time searching the house," said ap Owen breathlessly, as he took the steps two at a time. "But I know where there's an emergency entrance into the pocket dimension. We can hide out in there till the fighting's over."

"What about your people?" protested Fisher angrily. "You can't just abandon them!"

"They know where the entrance is, too. If they've got any sense, most of them are probably already there."

Fisher heard boots hammering on the stairs behind her,

and threw herself forward. The mercenary's sword swept past her head, the wind of its passing tugging at her hair. Fisher kicked backwards, and the swordsman's breath caught in his throat as the heel of her boot thudded solidly into his groin. Fisher turned around to finish him off, and found herself facing a dozen more mercenaries charging up the stairs towards her. She put a hand on the groaning swordsman's face and pushed him sharply backwards. He fell back down the stairs and crashed into his fellows, bringing them all to an abrupt halt. Fisher smiled angelically at the chaos, and turned her back on them. Ap Owen was nowhere to be seen.

She swore harshly, and hurried up the stairs to the landing. She paused at the top of the stairs to get her bearings, and an axe buried itself in the wall beside her. She ran along the hallway, glaring about her. Ap Owen couldn't have gone far. If he had, she was in trouble. He'd never got around to telling her where the doorway to the pocket dimension was. Sounds of hot pursuit grew louder behind her, and from all around came shouts and curses and war cries as the invaders spilled through the house, searching for the Peace Talks.

A mercenary burst out of a door just ahead of her, and Fisher ran him through while he was still gaping at her. She jerked the sword free and then had to back quickly away as two more men charged out of the room at her.

She put her back against the railing that ran the length of the hall and swung her sword in wide arcs to keep them at bay. Two-to-one odds didn't normally bother her, but this time she was facing two hardened professionals in very cramped surroundings, with nowhere to retreat and no one to guard her blind sides. It was at times like this that she realised how much she missed Hawk. She cut viciously at one mercenary's face, and he stepped back instinctively. Fisher darted for the gap that opened up, but the other swordsman was already there, forcing her back with a flurry of blows. Fisher fought on, but she could feel her chances of getting out alive slipping away like sand between her fingers.

And then one of the mercenaries went down in a flurry of blood, and ap Owen was standing over him, flashing his lunatic grin. Fisher quickly finished off the other mercenary, and the two Guards sprinted down the hallway, with more mercenaries in hot pursuit.

"Where the hell have you been?" demanded Fisher. "I turned my back on you for a moment and you were gone!"

"Sorry," said ap Owen breezily. "I didn't notice you weren't still with me. Now save your breath for running. We've got a way to go yet, and those bastards behind us are getting closer."

A mercenary appeared out of nowhere before them and ap Owen cut him down with a single slash. Fisher hurdled the writhing body without slowing, and followed ap Owen up a winding stairway. Footsteps hammered on the steps behind her, and she glanced back over her shoulder to see half a dozen mercenaries charging up the stairs after her. Fisher looked away and forced herself to run faster. She was already bone-tired after the long day, and her legs felt like lead, but somehow she forced out a little extra speed. Ap Owen, of course, was running well and strongly, buoyed up by his battle drug. Sweat ran down Fisher's face, stinging her eyes, and her sides ached as her lungs protested. She just hoped she wouldn't get a stitch. That would make it a perfect bloody day.

Ap Owen led her down a wide corridor at a pace she was hard pressed to match, but somehow she kept up with him. The growing crowd of mercenaries snapping at her heels helped. It worried her that she hadn't seen any of ap Owen's men. Surely some of them should have got this far. . . . A growing suspicion took root in her that they were all dead. That all the house's defenders were dead, apart from her and ap Owen. Which made it all the more urgent they reach the pocket dimension and warn the delegates.

Ap Owen darted suddenly sideways through an open doorway, and Fisher threw herself in after him. She whirled to slam the door shut, but three mercenaries forced their way in. Fisher cut down one with a single, economical stroke, and his blood flew on the air, but another swordsman darted in under her reach and cut at her leg. Her thick leather boot took most of the impact, but she could still feel blood trickling down her leg inside the boot. She drove the man back with a frenzied attack, and for a moment held off both opponents by the sheer fury of her attack.

And then ap Owen was with her, cutting and hacking like a madman, and between them they finished off the mercenaries, slammed the door shut, and bolted it. It rattled angrily in its frame as men on the other side put their shoulders to it.

The two Guards stood exhausted over the bodies for a moment, breathing harshly, and then ap Owen jerked his thumb over his shoulder. "Let's go. The doorway's here."

Fisher looked behind her, and saw an open door hanging unsupported in the air. Beyond the door there was only darkness. "About time. I just hope the pocket dimension turns out to be a damn sight more secure than this house."

"It is; I guarantee it. Now let's move it, please."

He grabbed her arm and hauled her through the doorway. The door slammed shut behind them, and disappeared from the room. There was a brief sensation of falling, and then Fisher was in the Peace Talks' hidden room. The delegates rose startled from their seats around a long table, staring at her and ap Owen. She quickly put up a hand to forestall their questions.

"The house is overrun with mercenaries. We had to cut and run. No choice. How many more of our people made it here?" She took in their blank faces, and looked away. "Damn. Then I think it's fair to assume they won't be coming. We're the only survivors."

She looked quickly round the sparsely furnished, medium-sized room, and then blinked as she found there was no sign of the doorway. All four walls were blank. She shrugged, and looked at ap Owen, who was sitting on the floor beside her with his head hanging down. He was deathly pale, with sweat streaming off his face, and obviously using all his willpower to keep from vomiting. Fisher smiled sourly. That was battle drugs for you. Great as long as adrenalin kept you going, but once you stopped there was hell to pay. She manhandled him onto a chair, and then turned back to the delegates. They were obviously waiting for a more detailed report, and it was clear from their faces that their patience had just about run out. Really, the report should come from ap Owen, as the senior Captain in charge of security, but since he was out of it and likely to stay that way for some time . . . Fisher realised she was still holding her sword, and sheathed it. She drew herself up to parade rest, thought briefly about saluting the delegates, and then decided the hell with it.

"We're in trouble," she said bluntly. "Someone hired a small army of mercenaries, backed them up with some heavy-duty sorcery, and sent them here looking for you. Our security forces didn't stand a chance; the mercenaries rolled right over us. Unless some more of our people arrive in the next few minutes, you'd better get used to the idea that your entire security force now consists of ap Owen and me. And there aren't going to be any reinforcements. We're trapped in here, and the house is crawling with mercenaries."

"It's not quite as bad as you make it sound, Captain," said Lord Regis calmly. "Firstly, we are quite safe here. The dimensional doorways won't open to the mercenaries, and the only other way in is to open a new doorway. Even a high-level sorcerer couldn't do that without first knowing the exact co-ordinates of this dimension, and those are, of course, only known to a select few. All we have to do is sit tight and wait for the mercenaries to leave. They won't hang around once they realise we're not in the house; an attack like this is bound to have been noticed, especially in Low Tory. I think we can be fairly confident that the Guard is on its way here even as we speak."

"Wait a minute," said Fisher. "How will we know when it's safe to leave?"

Lord Regis shrugged. "We'll just stick our heads out from time to time, and see what's happening."

Ap Owen chuckled harshly. "He means you and I will stick our heads out, Fisher. They're not going to take any risks. Right, my lord?"

"Of course," said Lord Regis. "That is what you're here for, isn't it?"

Fisher looked at ap Owen. His face was still pale, but he was sitting up straight and he looked a lot more composed. "How are you feeling?"

"Great. The side effects don't last long."

"Long enough to get you killed, if they hit you at the wrong moment."

Ap Owen shrugged.

"You're all missing the point," said Major de Tournay.

"How did the mercenaries know to look for us here? Our location was supposed to be secret."

"He has a point," said Lord Regis, looking heavily at ap Owen.

The senior Captain nodded unhappily. "Somebody must have talked. Someone always talks, eventually. But since they couldn't know about this dimension, it doesn't really matter. The mercenaries will just ransack the house, find no trace of the Talks, and report back to their masters that you weren't here. They'll be called off, and you can resume the Talks undisturbed, secure in the knowledge they won't be back again. And if the Guard reacts fast enough, they might even be able to follow the mercenaries back to their masters, and we can round them all up in one go."

"Excellent!" said Lord Nightingale. "This might turn out to have been all for the best, after all."

"Hold it just a minute," said Fisher, and there was a harshness in her voice that drew all eyes to her. "A lot of good men died out there, trying to protect you and your precious Talks. Doesn't that mean anything to you?"

The two merchants, Rook and Gardener, had the grace to look a little embarrassed. The two Majors stirred uncomfortably, but said nothing. Lord Regis looked thoughtfully at the floor. Lord Nightingale sniffed.

"They were just doing their job," he said flatly. "They understood they were expendable. As are we all."

"I'm sure that'll be a great comfort to their widows," said Fisher. "Those men never stood a chance, thanks to your insistence on low profile security."

"That's enough, Captain!" said Lord Regis sharply. "It's not your place to criticise your superiors. We have to consider the bigger picture."

Fisher gave him a hard look, and then turned away. Ap Owen relaxed slightly, and felt his heart start beating again. He didn't think Fisher would actually punch out a lord, but you could never tell with Fisher.

"His lordship is right, Fisher," he said carefully. "The safety of the delegates must come first. That's what they told us when we took on this job, remember? Now take it easy. We're all perfectly safe in here; nothing can reach us."

He broke off suddenly, as far away in the distance a bell tolled mournfully. The sound seemed to echo on and on, faint but distinct, as though it had travelled impossible distances to reach them. They all stood silently, listening. The bell tolled again and again, growing slowly louder and more mournful, like the bell from a forgotten church deep in the gulfs of hell. Fisher's breathing quickened, and her hand fell to her sword. Something was out there in the dark, she could feel it; something awful. The pealing of the bell grew louder still, painfully loud, until everyone in the hidden room had their hands pressed to their ears. And then the air split open above them, and nightmares spewed out into the waking world.

Creatures with insane shapes that hurt and disturbed the human eye fought and oozed and squirmed out of nowhere, and fell writhing to the floor. There were things with splintered bones and snapping mouths, and nauseating shapes that twisted through strange dimensions as they moved. Creatures with flails and barbs and elongating limbs. A monstrous slug with grinding teeth in its belly fell heavily onto the conference table, its weight cracking the thick wood from end to end. A clump of ropy crimson intestines squeezed out of the split in the air, and dropped squirming to the floor, where it dripped acid, eating holes in the carpet. The conference room rang to a cacophony of screams and howls and roars, drowning out the madly tolling bell.

For a moment everyone froze where they were, and then Fisher threw herself forward, swinging her sword in wide, vicious arcs. Strangely colored blood flew steaming on the air as her blade sank deep into unnatural flesh, and howling shapes rose up in fury all around her. Ap Owen was quickly at her side, and together they forced the demons back. Major Comber and Major de Tournay drew their swords and fought back to back, old enmities forgotten in the face of a common foe. They cut and thrust with professional efficiency, and nothing could stand against them for long.

The two traders, Rook and Gardener, retreated into a corner and defended themselves with unfamiliar swords as best they could. Creatures swarmed eagerly about them, scenting easy prey. Lord Regis fought stubbornly with his back to a wall, barely keeping the fangs and claws from his throat but determined not to give in. Lord Nightingale cleared a space around him with inspired swordsmanship, chanting all the while in a harsh forced rhythm. Human blood flowed as the creatures pressed closer, forcing their way past flashing steel by sheer force of numbers. And still more shapes poured through the split in the air, and there seemed no end to them.

"We've got to get out of here!" Fisher yelled to ap Owen.

"We can't," he answered, grunting with the effort of his blows. "Only Regis and Nightingale can open the door. And they both look a bit busy at the moment. See if you can work towards them, take some of the pressure off."

Fisher tried, but the growing tide of creatures forced her back foot by foot, and ap Owen had to struggle to keep his place at her side. A jagged cut on his forehead leaked blood steadily down one side of his face, and he had to keep blinking his eye to clear it. A raking claw suddenly opened up a long, curving gash across Fisher's hip and stomach, and she stumbled and almost fell as the pain flared through her. Ap Owen darted in to try and cover her, and a long, serrated tentacle whipped around his shoulders and snatched him up into the air. Fisher hacked at the tentacle, but it wouldn't let him go. Comber and de Tournay were soaked with blood from a dozen minor wounds, but were still holding their ground and grimly defying the creatures to move them. Rook and Gardener had already fallen and disappeared beneath a heaving throng of frenzied shapes. Lord Regis was struggling, tears of exhaustion running down his cheeks, but Lord Nightingale ignored him, concentrating on his rhythmic chanting.

And then Nightingale's voice rose sharply to a shout, and the split in the air slammed together and was gone. The creatures burst into flames, screaming and thrashing as a searing golden fire consumed them, leaving nothing but ash. The faraway bell was quiet, and the only sound in the hidden room was the harsh breathing and groans of the two Guards and the surviving delegates.

Fisher sat with her back braced against a wall, watching exhaustedly as ap Owen slowly picked himself up from where the burning tentacle had dropped him. The two Majors leaned on each other, exchanging quiet compliments. Lord Regis bent wearily over two bodies lying twisted and still in a corner, then straightened up and turned away. Rook and Gardener were beyond help. Regis looked across

at Lord Nightingale, calmly cleaning the blood from his
sword in the middle of the room,

"I didn't know you were a sorcerer, Nightingale."

The Outremer lord shrugged easily. "I'm not, really. I
just like to dabble."

"Still, I would have expected you to mention it," said
Regis. "Since one of the conditions for these Talks was that
none of the delegates be a sorcerer."

"I told you," said Nightingale. "I'm not a sorcerer. Just
a gifted amateur."

"That's not the point. . . ."

"Can we discuss this later?" said Fisher sharply. "We
need a doctor in here."

"I'm afraid that's out of the question," said Nightingale.
"We're under orders not to reveal our presence. Officially,
no one is to know we're here."

"You have got to be joking," said Fisher. "If there's one
thing we can be certain about, it's that our enemies know
where we are. Both the mercenaries and those stinking
creatures knew exactly how best to catch us off guard.
Somebody's talked. We're not a secret anymore. So forget
the low profile nonsense, and get some real protection in
here. We were lucky this time. We won't be again. And
get me a bloody doctor, dammit! If this wound gets in-
fected, I'll sue."

Some time later, after a number of hasty but effective healing spells, Fisher and ap Owen made their rounds of the
house, looking over their new, improved security force and
checking the faces of the dead mercenaries before they
were carried out. None of the mercenaries had been taken
alive. Those who hadn't managed to escape before Guard
reinforcements arrived killed themselves rather than be
captured.

"Which suggests to me they were under a geas," said ap
Owen. "It had to be some kind of magical compulsion.
Mercenaries don't believe in that kind of loyalty to a cause.
Any cause. We fight strictly for cash; nothing else. I had
wondered if I might know any of these poor bastards, but
I don't recognise any faces. Probably hired outside Haven,
to prevent any rumours of the attack from getting out. You

couldn't hope to hire this many men in Haven and keep it quiet."

"Right," said Fisher. "Somebody always talks. Which brings us back to the attack on the pocket dimension. Someone betrayed us. But who knew?"

"Not many. The delegates, you and I and the ten Guards working inside the house, and Commander Glen, of course." He stopped suddenly, and he and Fisher looked at each other. "Glen?" said ap Owen finally.

"Why not?" said Fisher. "He's the only one who had nothing to risk by talking."

Ap Owen shook his head firmly. "Glen's a hard bastard, but he's no traitor. Much more likely one of my people talked to the wrong person before they came here, and that person sold us out."

Fisher nodded unhappily. She couldn't ask any of ap Owen's people about it; none of them had survived the mercenaries' attack.

"That's not our only problem," said ap Owen dourly. "Nightingale's knowledge of magic has got everyone worked up. Admittedly he saved all our arses when the creatures broke through, but now Regis and Major Comber are worried sick he could be using his magic to influence their minds during the Talks. But they accepted him as a delegate and if they reject him now, Outremer will undoubtably retaliate in kind, and what progress they have achieved so far will all have been for nothing. So, for the moment the Talks are officially in abeyance until Rook and Gardener can be replaced. And you can bet Haven's replacement will know some sorcery, just to be on the safe side."

Fisher growled something unpleasant, and then shrugged. "At least the Talks will continue. That's something."

"Until the next attack."

"You think there'll be another one?"

"Bound to be. Too many interests want these Talks to fail. And we're stuck right in the middle. And I thought being a Guard would be a nice cushy number after being a mercenary. . . ."

6

Naming the Traitor

"This is where the Guard Advisory Council meets? I've seen more impressive outhouses." Hawk shook his head disgustedly. "Maybe you were right after all, Burns. Anyone who has to meet in a dump like this isn't going to be in any position to help us."

Burns kept a diplomatic silence, but his shrug spoke volumes. Hawk glared at the building before him, and wondered if there was any point in going inside. The Guard Advisory Council held its meetings in a rented room over a corner grocer's shop; the kind that stays open all hours and sells anything and everything. The two-storey building was fairly well-preserved, but looked like it hadn't seen a coat of paint in generations. Hawk peered into the shop through the single, smeared window, and one glance at the interior was enough to convince him he'd have to be bloody hungry before he ate anything that came from this grocer. He could practically see plague and food poisoning hiding in the shadows and giggling together. And he didn't want to think about what the unfamiliar cut of meat optimistically labelled "Special Offer" might be. He turned away and looked around the street. Passersby kept their heads down to avoid his gaze and hurried by the two Guards, trying hard to look innocent and failing miserably. Mostly they just succeeded in looking furtive. It was that kind of neighbourhood.

"I did try to tell you, Hawk," Burns said finally. "These people are Advisors, and that's all. They have no real power or influence, even if they like to think they have. They come up with the odd good idea on occasion, and they're good public relations, so the Guard tolerates them, but that's as far as it goes."

"Maybe," said Hawk. "But none of that's important.

What matters is that these people are connected to the Guard, but not a part of it. They ought to know some of what's going on but still be distanced enough that they can talk to us without fear of retribution. Dammit, Burns, I need someone to talk to me. I need information. We're flailing about in the dark and getting nowhere, and Morgan's sitting out there somewhere safe and secure, laughing at us. We need a lead, something to point us in the right direction at least."

"And you think we're going to get that from the Guard Advisory Council?"

"It's worth a try, dammit! We've got to do something!"

He strode angrily forward, ignored the shop doorway and stomped up the iron fire escape that clung uncertainly to the side of the building. Burns followed him silently. His partner was getting desperate, and it was beginning to show. Hawk stopped before the plain wooden door at the top of the fire escape, and banged loudly on it with his fist. Someone inside pulled back a sliding panel and studied Hawk for a long moment. Then the panel slid shut and there was the sound of bolts being drawn back. The door swung open, and Hawk and Burns stepped inside. The door closed quickly behind them.

The rented room turned out to be surprisingly cosy. Oil lamps shed a golden glow over the wood-panelled walls and chunky furniture, and large, comfortable-looking chairs had been set out before a crackling fire. Two men stood together by the chairs, facing Hawk and Burns with determined casualness. They looked embarrassed, and perhaps just a little frightened. Hawk studied them both, letting the silent moment stretch uncomfortably. Burns stirred at his side, but made no move to intervene. The man to their left coughed nervously.

"Good evening, Captains. It's good of you to visit us. It's not often the Guard takes an interest in our work. I'm Nicholas Linden, the lawyer. Perhaps you've heard of me. . . . And this is my associate, Michael Shire, once a Captain in the Guard, now retired."

Hawk nodded politely. Burns had already filled him in on who he'd be meeting, and he had no trouble recognising these two from Burns's descriptions. Nicholas Linden was tall and fashionably slender, with watchful eyes and a prac-

ticed smile. He'd started out as a meat-wagon chaser spe-
cialising in insurance cases, and had graduated through a
series of well-publicized cases and well-bribed juries to a
fairly successful practice in Low Tory. At which point he
suddenly developed a civic conscience, and started agitating
to put an end to the kind of sharp practices that had got
him where he was. His fellow lawyers had persuaded him
to join the Guard Advisory Council, in the hope of distracting him from things best left alone. To no one's surprise, it worked.

Michael Shire had been a Captain in the Guard for
twenty years, before taking early retirement to go into business for himself as a private security consultant. He'd done
well for himself over the past few years, and was now responsible for most of the hired muscle in the Westside.
He was a large, squarish man in his late forties, wearing
fashionably garish clothes that didn't suit him. He had a
calm, self-satisfied face, with cold, expressionless eyes.

And these were two of the people who'd set themselves
up as the Guard's conscience.

"Will any of the others be joining us?" Hawk said finally,
his voice flat and cold.

"I'm afraid not, Captain," said Linden, perhaps just a
little too quickly. "You must understand, we all lead very
busy lives outside the Advisory Council, and it isn't always
possible for all of us to attend meetings called at such short
notice. However, your message did say your business was
both urgent and important, so Michael and I agreed to . . .
represent the others. Do please sit down, Captains. And
help yourselves to some wine, if you will."

Hawk shook his head shortly, and sat down. Burns also
declined the wine, and he and the Advisors joined Hawk
in the chairs before the fire. Linden and Shire looked at
Hawk and Burns expectantly. Hawk set out the situation
as clearly and concisely as he could, taking it from the raid
on Morgan's factory to his growing belief that Morgan must
be bribing someone fairly high up in the Guard. There was
a pause, and then Shire snorted loudly.

"Don't see what all the fuss is about," he said gruffly,
meeting Hawk's gaze unflinchingly. "There's always been a
certain amount of . . . private enterprise in the Guard. It's
only natural for Guards to augment their income on occa-

sion, given the low wages. Everyone takes a special pay-
ment now and again; it's a sort of unofficial tax. If people
want real protection, they've got to be prepared to pay for
it. After all, a contented Guard is much more likely to look
out for you, isn't he? I think you're taking this too seriously, Captain Hawk."

"I'm not talking about half-arsed protection rackets,"
said Hawk. "I'm talking about a high-ranking Guard who's
been bought and paid for by one of the city's biggest
drug barons."

"So what?" said Shire flatly. "This is Haven, remember?
There are people here it doesn't pay to cross, and Morgan
is very definitely one of them. It's not in the Guard's interest to start a war it couldn't win."

"This time it's different," snapped Hawk. "Morgan's new
drug is too dangerous to be ignored. And whoever's helping
him in the Guard is putting the whole damned city at risk,
just to earn himself a nice little bonus. This isn't just corruption anymore; it's treason. I want this bastard, and
you're going to help me identify him. You're both in a
position to hear things, know things; people will talk to you
who wouldn't talk to me. I want to know what they've been
saying. I want the name."

Shire and Linden glanced at each other, and then Linden
leaned forward. He fixed Hawk with an earnest gaze, and
chose his words carefully. "You must understand, Captain,
that my associate and I are taking a not inconsiderable risk
in seeing you at all. You've made yourself dangerous to
know. You've been making enemies, the wrong sort of enemies. The word is that Morgan has important friends, very
well-connected people, who aren't taking kindly to your
enquiries. Anyone who openly helped you would be putting
his own neck in the noose."

"Refusing to talk to me can be pretty risky too," said
Hawk calmly. "I'm not playing by the rules anymore. I
don't have the time."

Shire sniffed. "Threats won't get you anywhere. To put
it bluntly, Morgan is connected to people who are scarier
than you'll ever be."

"Then why are you talking to us at all?" asked Burns.

"Because I was a Captain in the Guard for twenty
years . . ." said Shire slowly, ". . . and there are some things

I won't stand for. I might have taken the odd gratuity in my time, and looked the other way when I was told, but I was always my own man. No one tells me to roll over on my back and play dead, like a good dog. Not then or now. Linden came to see me earlier today. He was scared. He overheard something he shouldn't have, from one of Morgan's people, and he knew he wouldn't be safe as long as he was the only one who knew it. So he told me, and now he's going to tell you. There's no doubt that Morgan, or the people he's associated with, have infiltrated the Guard at practically every level. From the bottom right to the top. But for once, we have a name. Morgan's bought himself a Guard Captain, someone so loyal and honourable as to be above suspicion."

"Tell me the name," said Hawk.

Linden swallowed hard, and looked briefly at Shire for support. "You're not going to like this, Hawk. I don't have any proof or evidence; this is just what I heard. I could be wrong."

"Just tell me the bloody name!"

"Fisher," said Linden. "Captain Isobel Fisher."

Hawk launched himself out of his chair, both hands reaching for Linden. Burns grabbed at him, but Hawk shook him off. He took two handfuls of Linden's shirt and lifted him up into the air. The lawyer's face lost all its color, and his mouth worked soundlessly. Shire and Burns pulled at Hawk's arms, but he ignored them, thrusting his face close to Linden's.

"You're lying, you bastard. They put you up to this, didn't they? Didn't they! Tell me the name, you bastard. Tell me the real name!"

Linden struggled to get his breath, his eyes wide and staring. "Please . . . please don't hurt me. I'm sorry. . . ."

"He's telling the truth," said Shire urgently, almost shouting in Hawk's ear to get his attention. "Let him go, Hawk. He's just telling you what he heard."

"That's right," said Burns. "Let him go, Hawk. Come on, let him go."

Hawk dropped the lawyer back onto his chair, and turned away, breathing heavily. Linden clawed at his collar, trying to get some air into his lungs. Burns and Shire backed away from Hawk, watching him carefully.

"Take it easy, Hawk," said Burns soothingly. "It's just hearsay, that's all. They said themselves they had no proof or evidence."

"It's a lie," said Hawk.

"Of course it is."

"Don't use that tone of voice with me, Burns! I'm not a child. I'm not a fool, either. This is just something Morgan's come up with to try and slow me down, distract me from going after him. Well, it's not going to work. I know Isobel. It's impossible that she could be involved in anything like that. She wouldn't . . ."

"Of course not," said Burns. "Let's go, Hawk. We've got what we came for."

Hawk nodded, and headed for the door without even looking at Shire and Linden. Burns made a quick, placating gesture to them, and hurried out after his partner.

Down in the street, Hawk strode blindly through the snow and slush, staring straight ahead. People took one look at his face and hurried to get out of his way. Burns walked along beside him, studying his partner anxiously.

"We have to talk about this, Hawk," he said finally. "Of course the idea of Fisher being a rogue is ridiculous, but we can't just ignore it, either. Whoever the corrupt Captain is, it has to be someone who'd normally be above suspicion. Someone so honest and trustworthy no one would ever connect them with Morgan. Everyone we've talked to agrees on that, and it has to be said there aren't many Captains in the Guard who fill that description."

"It isn't Isobel," said Hawk.

"Then why name her in front of someone like Linden? Even if Morgan's people knew they were being overheard, how would they know you'd end up talking to Linden? You only decided to visit the Advisors a short time ago."

"He would have passed the word on, and it would have got round to me eventually. It's just a distraction, that's all."

"Sure," said Burns. "Look, whoever the rogue is, it has to be someone close to us. Close to you. Someone who knows you well enough to know the people you'd go to for answers. How else did Morgan's people know where to ambush us after we left Saint Christophe?"

"We're probably being watched," said Hawk.

"Not all the time; we'd notice."

"Well, maybe he's got a sorcerer watching us magically! He had a sorcerer at the factory; how do we know he hasn't got another magic-user working for him?"

"I think we'd better leave this till later," said Burns suddenly, his voice low. "We're being followed again. Look around you."

Hawk's preoccupation fell away in a moment, and he looked casually about him, his hand moving naturally to the axe at his side. "Hell's teeth, how did I miss them? They're not exactly professional quality, are they? That's what happens when you let yourself get distracted. There's a lot of them; I make it twenty-seven, most of them wearing gang colors. How about you?"

"I only see twenty-two, but I'll take your word for it. They must have known we were going to be here, Hawk; it's another bloody ambush. Better thought-out than the last one, too; they're all around us this time."

Hawk sniffed. "It doesn't matter. I'm just in the mood to cut up a few bad guys."

Burns looked at him sharply. "Wait a minute, Hawk; this is no time to start feeling heroic. We're outnumbered more than ten to one here."

"So what do you suggest? Put up our hands and surrender nicely, and hope we'll get taken as prisoners of war? This may be a war, Burns, but no one's taking any prisoners."

"We could always make a run for it."

"We could, but how far do you think we'd get? The streets are narrow and crowded, and we're both dog-tired while our pursuers look decidedly fresh. There aren't even any fire escapes in easy reach this time. They've planned this well, Burns, and we walked right into it."

The street grew increasingly quiet as they strode along, and passersby began moving into the shelter of doorways so as to be safely out of the way when the killing began. Everyone knew what was happening. The ambushers weren't even trying to hide themselves anymore.

Hawk stopped walking and looked openly around. Burns stopped beside him, and looked quickly about for any escape route he might have missed. The ambushers were everywhere, moving confidently forward. Now that they were all out in the open, Burns counted twenty-nine of them. They were dressed in ragged furs and leathers, and carrying clubs and swords and axes. Some had broken bottles and lengths of metal piping. They all looked lean and hungry and very dangerous. Burns looked to Hawk for support, and a sudden chill ran through him. Hawk was smiling, a cold and nasty death's-head grin. Burns felt an instinctive need to back away. He'd seen his partner go through many moods that day, but this was something new and awful, and for the first time Burns understood why Hawk was so widely feared in the Northside. At this moment, he looked vicious and deadly and totally unstoppable.

Burns made some kind of noise in his throat, and Hawk looked at him briefly. "These aren't Morgan's people," he said, his voice eerily calm and even. "These are street-gang toughs from the Devil's Hook. I beat up their leader, a piece of slime called Hammer, earlier on this morning. He must have declared vendetta on me. Knew I should have killed him."

He fell silent as one of the ambushers stepped forward, but his death's-head grin never wavered. He recognised the man as the gang leader, and drew his axe with a flourish. Hammer stopped where he was and called out to Hawk, his voice carefully loud and mocking.

"I've been looking for you, Hawk. No one messes with me and gets away with it, not even the high and mighty Captain Hawk. Don't look so tough now, do you? Now you're on your own and I've got my people here to back me up. You're going to die slow, Hawk. We're all going to take turns cutting on you; going to take our time and get real inventive. You're going to scream and cry and beg for death before we're through."

Hawk laughed at him, and there was enough naked violence in the sound to silence the gang leader almost in mid-word. The watching ambushers stirred uneasily. Hawk swept his axe back and forth before him. "Who's first?" he said mockingly. No one moved. Hawk glanced at Burns. "Get out of here while you can," he said quietly, his voice calm and conversational. "They don't care about you; they just want me. If you make a run for it, they'll probably let you go."

"Forget it," said Burns. "They'll kill me anyway, just for being a Guard, and being with you. Believe me, if I could see a way out of this mess, I'd take it. I'm not crazy. Do me a favour, Hawk: Next time you feel like punching out a gang leader, don't do it in front of witnesses. All right, you're supposed to be the expert on winning against impossible odds: What are we going to do? There's nowhere to run, and if we try and make a stand they'll roll right over us."

Hawk nodded, still grinning at the ambushers and hefting his axe. Burns looked away. The grin was starting to unnerve him. One of the toughs stepped forward. Hawk looked at him, and the tough stopped where he was.

"I think our best bet is to try and lose them in the side streets and alleyways," said Hawk calmly. "They're narrow and crowded, and the gang will only be able to come at us a few at a time. We should be able to take them easily, as long as we keep our heads."

"What if they've staked out the alleyways with more of their people?" said Burns tightly.

"Then we fight our way through and keep running. Maybe we can outrun them."

"What happens if we get trapped in a dead end?"

"Then we see how many of the bastards we can take with us. Think positive, Burns. We're not dead yet, and I've faced worse odds in my time."

"When?" demanded Burns. Hawk just grinned at him.

Hammer suddenly barked an order, and the toughs moved forward from every direction. Hawk lifted his axe threateningly and then sprinted towards the nearest side street. Burns charged after him, his stomach churning sickly. Three gang members made to block their way. Hawk cut down the first two with vicious sweeps of his axe, and hit the third man with a lowered shoulder. The massive tough was thrown aside like a child, and Burns hacked halfway through his waist without even slowing. He pounded after Hawk down the narrow street, with the gang howling behind them.

More gang members appeared out of darkened alley mouths, but somehow Hawk and Burns managed to cut a way through them and keep on running, leaving bodies lying in pools of vivid scarlet on the grimy snow. Hawk glared about him, trying to figure out exactly where he was. This wasn't an area he knew particularly well and he couldn't afford to stop and look for landmarks hidden or disguised by the recent snow. His breath burned in his chest, and he could feel the beginnings of a stitch in his side. Normally he prided himself on his stamina, but it had been a long day and it wasn't getting any shorter. From the sound of it, Burns was finding the going equally hard.

And then they rounded a sharp corner and skidded to a halt as they saw more gang members waiting for them. There were ten of them blocking the narrow alley, all armed with some kind of weapon and smiling confidently. Hawk glanced back over his shoulder. The pursuers were coming up fast, and there was no way out. Hawk felt more anger than anything. Being killed in a gang ambush was such a stupid way to go. And now he'd never get the chance to clear Fisher's name. He'd make them pay for that. He threw himself at the smiling faces before him, and laughed aloud as he saw their expressions change to shock and terror as his axe tore through them like firewood. He sensed Burns fighting desperately at his side, but Hawk had no room in him for anything but rage.

The first few died easily before his fury, but there were too many of them for him to break through, and soon the rest of the gang arrived. Hawk and Burns fought back to back, surrounded by screaming mouths and flailing weapons, hemmed in by the jostling press of bodies. The sheer number of attackers gave Hawk and Burns a fighting chance; the gang were so eager to get at their victims that they kept getting in each other's way and deflecting many of the blows meant for the two Guards. Hawk fought on fiercely, sending blood spraying through the freezing air, but knew it was only a matter of time before someone got in a lucky blow. Then his guard would drop, and he'd go down under a dozen swords. And if he was lucky, he'd die before Hammer could pull his people off. He was just sorry he'd dragged Burns into this. Hawk fought on, as much out of stubbornness as anything. If he had to die, he was going to make them work for it. A sword licked in past his defences, and punched through his side and out again. Blood ran thickly down his hip and leg, and the strength seemed to flow out of him along with the blood. He swung his axe clumsily, and the swords were everywhere.

A thick mist sprang up suddenly in the alleyway, diffusing the amber lamplight in strange ways, and misty grey ropes curled and tightened around the gang members' throats. They dropped their weapons to tear at the strangling mists with desperate hands, and fell gagging to the ground. Curling mists lashed viciously among the gang, sending them flying this way and that, and they fled screaming back down the alley and out into the surrounding streets. The mists flowed after them like a relentless river. Dead bodies littered the alley. Hammer stared uncomprehendingly about him, abandoned by his men, and then backed away as Hawk loomed up before him, grim and bloody, his gaze colder than the winter could ever be. He turned to run, and Hawk cut him down with one blow of his axe. Hammer fell dying to the ground, and there was enough anger still in Hawk for him to regret it was over so quickly.

He turned to see how Burns had fared, and fell back against a wall as the wound in his side caught up with him. The stabbing pain filled his mind, and then a strong arm curled around his shoulders, supporting him, and a cool hand pressed against his bloody side. There was a brief, crawling sensation as the wound knitted itself together, and then the sorceress Mistique stepped back and grinned at him.

"I thought I'd leave the gang leader for you to take care of personally. But I can't believe you just walked right into that ambush. If I hadn't been following you too, they'd have had to bury what was left of you in a closed coffin."

"I had a lot on my mind," said Hawk, feeling gingerly at his side. "And it must be said, this has not been one of my better days. Thanks for the rescue."

"You're welcome. But next time don't go dashing off like that. I nearly didn't catch up in time."

Hawk nodded, and looked across at Burns. The man's clothing was soaked in blood, but he nodded quickly to Hawk and Mistique to show he was all right. Hawk looked down at the gang leader, lying dead and broken on the dirty snow, and swore softly.

"I should have taken him alive. He might have been able to answer some questions."

Burns frowned. "What could he have known? He isn't connected with Morgan; he was just after you because you made him lose face in front of his people."

"Someone had to have told him where to find us! He couldn't have followed us all the way from the Hook."

"He didn't," said Mistique flatly. "I've been following you for some time, and they were already here waiting for you when you went in to talk to the Advisors."

Hawk looked at her narrowly. "I didn't see you following us."

Mistique smiled. "Well, after all, darling, I am a sorceress."

Hawk nodded slowly. "All right; want to tell me why you were following us? And why you dropped out of sight right after we left the Hook?"

The sorceress scowled, and leaned back against the alley wall with her arms folded. "I know something that certain important people don't want known. Something . . . dangerous. So I decided to disappear for a while, and do some hard thinking. I needed someone to talk to, someone I could trust. You were the obvious choice, Hawk, but I had to be sure you were what you were supposed to be. So I've been following you." She looked at him for a long moment. "Even now I'm not sure I'm doing the right thing. You're not going to like this, Hawk."

"Tell me," said Hawk. "Tell me what you know."

"I was talking to one of the prisoners we took in Morgan's factory, before we brought them back to Headquarters," said Mistique steadily. "He was mad as hell because the Guard Captain that Morgan had been paying off hadn't warned them about the raid. I asked him for the Captain's name, but he didn't know it. He knew what the Captain looked like, though. He recognised her when he saw her during the raid.

"It was Fisher, Hawk. Captain Isobel Fisher."

7

SCAPEGOAT

Fisher looked out the repaired study window and glowered sourly at the array of armed men camped out on the wide lawns. There had to be a hundred men out there now, wearing chain mail under their furs and warming their hands at the scattered iron braziers. If the Peace Talks had had this kind of protection before, two of the delegates and all of the original security force might still be alive. Fisher felt obscurely guilty that she hadn't got to know the men under her command before they were killed. As it was, it would take a hell of an army to get past the new security force; that, or a particularly nasty piece of magic. Fisher decided she wasn't going to think about that. She still got edgy every time she remembered the flood of twisted creatures that had come spilling out of the split in reality. She'd only just got over jumping at every sudden noise.

Raised angry voices cut across her reverie, and she turned her back on the window to study the squabbling delegates. Her mouth compressed into a thin, flat line as she realised they were going round and round in the same futile circles. The Peace Talks were becoming increasingly warlike, with the two lords blaming everyone and everything but themselves for the present sorry state of affairs. Lord Nightingale of Outremer was the loudest voice, quite openly determined to lay the blame for everything at Haven's door. Lord Regis was trying to be reasonable and diplomatic, but his temper was visibly shortening, and his voice had already risen to match Nightingale's.

The two Majors, Comber and de Tournay, had withdrawn from the fray and settled themselves in a corner with the drinks cabinet. They were busily comparing whiskies and doing their best to ignore the whole unpleasantness. They had no interest in recriminations or name-calling, and had said so loudly. Unfortunately, it hadn't been loud enough to compete with the racket Regis and Nightingale were making, so their objections had gone completely unnoticed by the two lords.

Captain ap Owen was standing with his back to the fireplace, watching everything and saying nothing. He hadn't spoken a dozen words to anyone since he'd overseen the new security force as they cleared up the mess left by the assault. Fisher understood. The men under his command had been longtime associates and friends, and now he'd lost them all in one brief clash of arms. The bodies were gone now, along with the dead mercenaries, but the smell of blood and death was still strong in the house.

Major Comber stirred suddenly, and slammed the flat of his hand against the top of a nearby table. It made a satisfyingly loud noise, and the two lords shut up and looked round to see what was happening. Comber carefully put down his whisky glass, and glared at each lord in turn.

"I think this nonsense has gone on long enough," he said firmly. "We're supposed to be here to discuss the border problem, not play at who can shout and stamp their foot the loudest. We'll probably never find out exactly who betrayed us, and it doesn't matter worth a damn anyway. The attack was a failure and the Talks can go on. Now, may I respectfully suggest that we get back to what we're supposed to be doing, and leave the squabbling and whining to the politicians. That's what they're paid for."

De Tournay started to nod vigorously in agreement, and then stopped as he realised both Nightingale and Regis were glaring at Comber.

"Your opinion is noted, *Major* Comber," said Lord Regis icily. "But allow me to remind you that your function at these Talks is to provide us with military information and advice. Nothing more. The Lord Nightingale and I are quite capable of deciding what is important here, and right now nothing is more important than determining who betrayed us. We could all have been killed, dammit, and I want to know who was responsible! Particularly since it seems we can't trust our own security people to keep us safe."

He glared at Fisher and ap Owen, who stared back calmly, fully aware that anything they said would only end up being used against them. Major de Tournay stirred in his corner, and then shrugged uncomfortably as Regis turned his glare on him.

"With respect, my lord, no security system is perfect. Fisher and ap Owen did their best, in extremely difficult circumstances."

He shut up as Nightingale turned to glare at him too. Nightingale's voice was low and deadly. "When I want your advice, *Major* de Tournay, I will ask for it. Until then you will oblige me by keeping your mouth shut. Is that clear?"

De Tournay and Comber looked at each other, nodded formally to their respective lords, and returned their attention to the whisky decanters. Regis sniffed, and looked back at Fisher and ap Owen.

"Now then, Captains, it cannot have escaped your attention that our security here has been hopelessly breached. Whether this was the result of internal treachery or simple incompetence on your part has yet to be determined. You can both be very sure there will be a full enquiry into your behaviour today. . . ."

"I don't think we can wait for that," said Nightingale flatly. "Someone has revealed to our enemies not only the location of this house, but also the coordinates of the pocket dimension. Quite a few people knew about the house—that was inevitable—but only a handful knew about the pocket dimension. Don't you find it interesting that our security problems only began after Captain Fisher joined us?"

"Oh, come on," said ap Owen immediately. "You're not seriously accusing Fisher? She's a legend in Haven! And she fought like hell against the mercenaries and the creatures in the dimension. In fact, if not for her, I wouldn't have lived long enough to reach the dimension, and you wouldn't have lived long enough to close the dimensional doorway. We owe her our lives!"

"Look at the facts," said Nightingale calmly. "The mercenaries didn't attack the house till she got here, and the creatures didn't attack us until she'd joined us in the pocket dimension. . . ."

"He has a point," said Regis slowly. "And it does seem

odd that Captain Fisher should have been in the middle of so much fighting, and come out of it with only minor, superficial wounds."

"She's a good fighter!" said ap Owen. "Everyone knows that."

"No one's that good," said Nightingale.

"And I must admit the new security forces have brought rather disquieting news concerning Fisher's partner, Captain Hawk," said Regis.

"Hawk?" said Fisher sharply. "What about Hawk?"

Regis fixed her with a steady gaze. "It appears that Captain Hawk is completely out of control. He's assaulted a superior officer and gone on a rampage through the city, attacking people in some kind of personal vendetta, and killing anyone who gets in his way. We don't know exactly how many people he's killed, but we have a confirmed account of more than thirty dead, and almost as many injured. At least a dozen were just innocent passersby."

"I don't believe it," said Fisher.

"In view of what you've just told me," said Lord Nightingale, ignoring Fisher, "I don't think I care to trust my well-being to any security force commanded by Captain Fisher. I'm afraid I must insist she be replaced, if the Talks are to continue."

"I have to agree," said Regis. "Well, Fisher, have you anything to say for yourself?"

"I didn't want to come here in the first place," said Fisher. "If you don't want me, I'll leave."

"It's not that simple," said Nightingale coldly. "We can't allow you to just walk out of here. You know too much. And besides, I don't believe in letting traitors walk free. Regis, I want this woman arrested, and held incommunicado till these Talks are over."

Regis nodded. "Fisher, hand over your sword. You're under arrest. The charge is treason."

Nightingale smiled at Fisher coldly. "I'll see you hanged for your part in this, bitch."

Fisher drew her sword and dropped into her fighting stance. "You and what army, Nightingale?"

"Fisher, that's enough!" snapped Regis. "Give your sword to ap Owen. That's an order!"

Fisher laughed at him. "Stuff your order. I may be slow,

but I'm not crazy. You're just desperate for a scapegoat, and I look like the best bet. Well, sorry, people, but I'm afraid I must decline the honour."

Regis looked at ap Owen. "Arrest her! Do whatever you have to, but stop her. She mustn't leave here alive!"

Ap Owen hesitated, and Fisher threw a chair at him. She was across the room and out the door before the two Majors could get to their feet and ap Owen could disentangle himself from the chair. Regis and Nightingale remained where they were, shouting orders. Fisher slammed the door shut behind her, grinned briefly as she heard someone crash into it, and then sprinted down the corridor to the front door. She yanked it open and charged out into the grounds. The new security people looked up in surprise, and moved towards her, anticipating some kind of emergency in the house. Fisher grabbed the first officer she saw, and pointed him at the front door.

"Block off that door and don't let anyone out, no matter what! Take as many men as you need. Everything depends on you! Move it!"

The officer threw her a quick salute, and charged towards the door, yelling for his men to follow him. Fisher ran for the front gate, breathlessly informing every man-at-arms she passed of the terrible emergency up at the house. The emergency became more and more terrible, and the details more and more fantastic, as she passed through the main body of men, determined to stir up the maximum confusion. She finally reached the gate, and paused a moment to look back. The men-at-arms were milling aimlessly back and forth, trampling the snow into slush, shouting incoherently to each other, and searching desperately for some sign of the enemy. Fisher grinned, and set off down the street at a fast but eminently respectable pace, so as not to attract too much attention.

First thing was to get rid of the Guard's uniform; it was too distinctive. Maybe change it for a long robe with a hood, something large and bulky enough to substantially alter her appearance. When word finally got out from the house, there were going to be an awful lot of people looking for Captain Fisher. There was no point in trying to protest her innocence. It was clear Nightingale had picked on her as the scapegoat, and the others would go along with him in order to keep the Talks going. As she'd been told from the beginning, the Peace Talks were far more important than any Guard Captain. She was expendable.

But she wasn't about to let anyone or anything get between her and her search for Hawk. From the sound if it, things had got really out of hand since she left him with Burns. She frowned. Strange there hadn't been any mention of Burns. She shook her head fiercely. That could wait. All that mattered was finding Hawk. If he really was out of control, she was the only one with any chance of stopping him. Whatever had happened between Hawk and Morgan, he'd listen to her.

And then they'd work together to find out who the real traitor was. Before, it had just been business. Now, it was personal.

In the study, Lord Regis and Lord Nightingale were taking turns shouting at Captain ap Owen. Outside in the grounds, Major Comber and Major de Tournay were trying desperately to restore some kind of order to the chaos Fisher had made out of the men-at-arms. Half of them were still running around like mad things, looking for something to hit and mistaking each other for the enemy as often as not. Ap Owen listened to the craziness outside, and somehow kept the smile from his lips. Eventually the lords ran out of accusations and curses, and stopped a moment to get their breath back. Ap Owen cleared his throat.

"What exactly do you want me to do, my lords? What are your orders?"

"Find Fisher!" snapped Nightingale, his cheeks mottled with rage. "I don't care how you do it, but find her!"

"Take twenty men and go out into the city," said Regis. "Spread the word among the Guard and on the streets. I'm authorizing you to offer a reward of five thousand ducats for Fisher's capture, dead or alive."

Ap Owen looked at him sharply. "But surely, my lord, we need her alive for questioning?"

"We need her stopped before she can do any more damage," said Nightingale. "As long as she's free, she's a threat. You know her reputation, Captain; if you try and take her alive she'll just kill your men and disappear again.

We can't risk that. If you find her, kill her. No quarter, no mercy."

Ap Owen looked at Regis, who nodded steadfastly. "Do whatever you have to, Captain, but don't bring her back alive."

8

Cutting Loose

Burns and Mistique followed Hawk silently as he led the way through a maze of narrow back streets and shadowed alleyways. He'd hardly said a word since Mistique reluctantly named Fisher as the traitor, and his cold, grim visage hadn't encouraged conversation. Burns and Mistique glanced at each other, but a few raised eyebrows and quick shrugs were enough to make it clear neither of them knew what was going through Hawk's mind. Given what he was capable of, his continued silence was worrying. Passersby hurried to get out of his way, but Hawk seemed totally oblivious of everything except his own thoughts. He walked unhurriedly through the shabby streets, staring straight ahead, his bloodied axe still in his hand.

They finally emerged into a quiet side street, and Hawk led his companions into a squalid little tavern called The Dragon's Blood. The air was thick with smoke, and the sawdust on the floor looked like it hadn't been changed in years. Mistique wrinkled her nose. Burns pushed the door closed with his fingertips, and then wiped his hand fastidiously on his cloak. The place was as dark as a coal cellar, with only occasional pools of dirty yellow light at the occupied tables, and two storm lanterns hanging over the bar. The window shutters had been nailed shut to ensure privacy. Shadowed drinkers watched silently as Hawk led his companions to a booth at the back of the room. Conversation slowly resumed as the three Guards seated themselves, but only as a bare murmur. The bartender emerged from behind his bar to serve them personally, and Hawk ordered three beers. They sat in silence until he came back with the drinks. Hawk paid him the exact amount and then dismissed him with a curt wave of his hand. The bartender shrugged, and went back to the bar to continue polishing his glasses with a dirty rag. Mistique looked dubiously at the drink in front of her, and decided that she wasn't thirsty. Hawk took two deep swallows from his beer, and then put the glass down and stared into it.

"The beer's safe enough here," he said quietly, "but don't touch the spirits. Half of it's made from wood alcohol."

Burns sipped at his beer to show willing, and his lips thinned away from his teeth at the bitterness. "Nice place you've chosen, Hawk. Great atmosphere. I'll bet plague rats stay away from here in case they catch something. Do you drink here often?"

"Only when I have some hard thinking to do. No one bothers me here." He drank from his glass again, and Burns and Mistique waited patiently for him to continue. Hawk wiped the froth from his mouth with the back of his hand, and leaned back in his chair, staring out into the gloom around them. "It all comes down to Morgan," he said finally. "He has all the answers. If we're ever going to get to the truth of what's really going on here, we have to find Morgan."

"Half the Guards in Haven are trying to do just that," said Burns. "But Morgan's always been able to disappear when he needed to. He could be anywhere in Haven. Our people are out leaning on every loose mouth in the city, but no one knows anything. Morgan's gone to ground so thoroughly this time that even his own people don't seem to know how to contact him. You must really have thrown a scare into him."

"He can't afford to be totally isolated," said Mistique. "He still has to move his super-chacal before word gets out how dangerous it is. And to do that, he must be doing business, however indirectly, with some distributor."

"Exactly," said Hawk. "Morgan may have crawled into his hole and pulled it in after him, but his lieutenants are still out there, doing business on his behalf. All we have to do is tail them, and eventually one of them will lead us to Morgan."

Burns shook his head. "Hawk, those people are professionals; they'll spot any tail we put on them."

"They won't spot a sorcerer," said Hawk. "How about it, Mistique? Can you follow these people with your magic?"

"There is a way . . ." said Mistique slowly. "But I don't know these lieutenants like you do. You'll have to open your minds so that I can learn what you know. Are you and Burns willing to do that?"

"No," said Burns flatly. "Sorry, Hawk, but there are some things I won't do, for you or anyone else. My thoughts are private, and my memories are my own."

"There's no need to be so defensive," said Mistique. "It's a comman reaction to my ability. Though why anyone should assume their secret thoughts are so fascinating I couldn't resist peeking, is beyond me."

"Take what you need from me," said Hawk. "But don't go wandering. There are things in my mind you don't want to know."

"I can believe that," said Mistique. She closed her eyes, and a cold breeze swept through Hawk's mind, ruffling his thoughts, and picking things up and putting them down again. Images flickered in Hawk's mind like flaring candles, come and gone so quickly he barely recognised them, and then Mistique opened her eyes, and his mind was quiet again. Mistique nodded, satisfied. "Got it. Names and faces for all twenty of his lieutenants. Now I need both of you to sit still and be quiet. This is going to be very difficult, and I can't afford any distractions."

She closed her eyes again and let her mind drift up and out, becoming one with the mists. Wherever mists and fogs rose throughout the city she had eyes and ears. She became the mists, flowing over houses and streets, through keyholes and under doors, and nothing was hidden from her. The mists carried her up into the sky, and she soared high above the city, seeing it spread out below her like a vast dark stone labyrinth of sudden turnings and endless possibilities. Lights burned in its darkness like furnaces in hell. She swooped down over the city, spreading her consciousness among the many streets and alleyways as mists curled everywhere in Haven. Buildings raced past her at bewildering speed, people appearing and disappearing in an instant, but all of them observed and studied and dismissed. Words from a thousand conversations battered her hearing like pounding waves on the rocks outside the harbour. Mistique let it all flow past and over her, sifting through the endless

noise and chaos until finally she found what she was looking for.

His name was Griff—a shabby, skinny man with long,
greasy dark hair, darting eyes, and a quick, unpleasant
smile. He wore a long frock coat mended at the collar and
elbows, and carried a quarterstaff. He didn't look like
much, but bigger men than he bobbed their heads and
smiled nervously in his presence. He was Morgan's eyes
and voice and executioner, and everyone knew it. Mistique
curled lazily on the air as Griff strode down a gloomy side
street, unobtrusively checking now and again that he wasn't
being followed. Mistique floated after him, everywhere and
nowhere, ahead and behind him.

Griff took a sudden turn into an alleyway and stopped
dead, just inside the alley mouth. He looked casually about
him to be sure he was unobserved, and then moved slowly
forward, counting the steps under his breath. He then
stopped, reached out and pressed five bricks in the left-
hand wall in a careful sequence. A door slowly appeared
in the wall, a great slab of solid steel, featureless save for
a single moulded handle, forming itself moment by moment
out of the dirty brickwork. Griff waited impatiently, his
gaze darting back and forth, and then he pulled the door
open, grunting with the effort. A bright crimson light flared
out into the alley, and Griff stepped forward into it. The
door slammed shut behind him, cutting off the bloody light,
and melted back into the brickwork. In the renewed gloom
of the alleyway, the roiling mists curled and twisted
triumphantly.

In the tavern, Hawk and Burns watched silently as Mistique closed her eyes and fell immediately into a trance
state. All trace of personality dropped out of her face as
her muscles relaxed completely. The air grew thick and
indistinct around her as wisps of mist seeped out of her
skin. The mists gradually thickened until they were boiling
up off her like ectoplasm at a séance. The tavern quickly
emptied as the other customers headed for the door at a
run. The bartender disappeared behind his bar. Burns
started to rise from his chair, and then sank reluctantly
back into it when Hawk glared at him. Hawk watched,
fascinated, as Mistique's eyes darted back and forth beneath her closed eyelids as though she were dreaming, and

then her eyes snapped open and personality flooded back into her face. The mists in the booth began to dissipate, stirred by a sourceless wind. Mistique fixed Hawk with her gaze.

"I've got him. Morgan's been hiding out in another pocket dimension, hidden off Packet Lane, not ten minutes' walk from here."

"Did you get a look inside?" said Hawk. "Did you see Morgan himself?"

"Not really. I could sense his presence, along with a dozen or so bodyguards, but when I tried to enter I brushed up against another sorcerer's wards, so I got the hell out of there before I gave myself away."

"Are you sure there's just the one sorcerer?" said Hawk.

Burns looked at him. "One is usually enough to screw up any mission."

Hawk ignored him, his gaze fixed on Mistique. "This is the second we've come across already. There might be more."

"No," said Mistique. "There's just the one."

"Good," said Hawk. "Burns and I will take care of the bodyguards. You handle the sorcerer. Only this time, let's all try really hard not to bring the pocket dimension down around our ears. All right?"

Mistique led the way to Packet Lane, striding confidently through the thickening fog. Hawk carried his axe at the ready and kept a careful watch, but no one seemed to be paying them any particular attention. People tended not to look at Guards if they could help it, on the grounds they didn't want Guards looking at them. Burns grumbled most of the way to Packet Lane, muttering that the odds stank, the whole idea was crazy, and they ought to call Headquarters for a backup. Eventually Hawk said *No* with enough force to prove that he meant it, and Burns shut up and sulked the rest of the way. As long as he did it quietly, Hawk didn't give a damn. He couldn't afford to have Headquarters involved at this stage. If they were, he'd have to tell them about Fisher.

Mistique finally brought them to Packet Lane, and they stood together in the alley mouth, staring into the gloom. Nothing moved in the alleyway, and the shadows lay quiet and undisturbed. Burns drew his sword, and the sudden grating noise was eerily loud in the quiet. He glanced at Hawk, who nodded to Mistique. She walked forward, counting out the steps, and pressed the five bricks in the correct sequence. The huge steel door appeared out of the brickwork, and swung open at Mistique's gesture. They stepped forward into the bright crimson light, and the door swung silently shut behind them.

The three Guards stood close together a moment, squinting into the crimson glare, and then Hawk hissed at Burns and Mistique to spread out. They made too good a target standing as a group. Their eyes quickly adjusted, and Hawk relaxed a little as he realised the long corridor before them was completely empty. The brilliant red light seemed to come from everywhere and nowhere, bathing everything in its bloody glow. The corridor had no furniture, no doors, and no visible turnings off. The walls and the floor were bare wood, not even varnished. Hawk took the point and led the way forward, axe at the ready. Burns and Mistique followed close behind. Their footsteps echoed loudly from the bare wooden floor, no matter how softly they trod.

The corridor seemed to go on forever. Hawk glanced back over his shoulder, and his hackles rose sharply as he saw the corridor stretching away behind him into the distance, with no sign of the door through which they'd entered. He shrugged uncomfortably, and trudged on down the corridor. It had to lead somewhere. The corridor suddenly rounded a corner and branched in two. Hawk looked down both paths, but there was nothing to choose between them. He looked back and forth while Burns and Mistique waited patiently for him to make up his mind, and then he tensed as he heard footsteps approaching. Hawk gestured quickly for the other two to fall back, and they retreated round the corner. Hawk eased back round the corner after them and stood poised, listening to the footsteps draw nearer. A man-at-arms rounded the corner, and Hawk whipped an arm round his throat before he had time to react. The man-at-arms started to call out, and Hawk tightened the hold until all that came out was a strangled croak.

"Don't move," said Hawk quietly. He waited till the man was perfectly still, and then eased his grip a little. The man-at-arms drew in a long, juddering breath. Hawk nodded to

Burns, and he stepped forward and took the man's sword. Hawk put his mouth close to his prisoner's ear.

"Morgan. Where is he?"

"Are you crazy? He'll have you killed for this. . . ." He broke off abruptly as the hold round his throat tightened harshly and then relaxed again.

"What's your name?" said Hawk.

"Justin."

"Do you know who I am?"

"No. Who are you?"

"I'm Hawk. Captain Hawk."

"Oh God."

"Where's Morgan?"

"It's not far. I'll lead you to him."

"That's a good boy. I'm going to let you go now. Behave yourself and you might come out of this alive."

He let go of the man-at-arms, and gestured for him to lead the way. Justin nodded jerkily, rubbed at his throat, and set off round the corner and down the left-hand path. Hawk and Mistique followed close behind, with Burns bringing up the rear. Hawk leaned in close to Mistique and spoke softly, so that only she could hear.

"Is there any way Morgan could know we're coming? Could his sorcerer have set up any protective wards in here?"

Mistique shook her head. "If he had, I'd know," she said softly. "There were wards and magical booby traps crawling all over the alleyway, but I defused them by summoning the door correctly. Keep your guard up, though, just in case. If I were Morgan, I'd have some kind of fall-back defences."

Hawk nodded. "That's probably what the dozen body-guards are supposed to be. I know how Morgan thinks; I've met his kind before. He thinks he's so big and powerful no one would dare just walk in on him. After all, he's got his own sorcerer and a dozen bodyguards to protect him. Who'd be crazy enough to come in here after him, in his own stronghold?"

Mistique looked at Hawk. "He might just have a point."

Hawk smiled. "I've faced worse odds. Morgan's just a cheap thug with delusions of grandeur. And I'm going to knock him down and rub his nose in it until he tells me what I want to know."

The man-at-arms led them through a short series of passageways to a pair of huge, polished oaken doors. Somewhere along the way, the sourceless crimson light had changed to a homely golden glow. There were expensive paintings and tapestries on the walls, and a deep-pile carpet on the floor. Hawk looked at the double doors for a long moment, and then turned and smiled at their guide.

"Well done, Justin. I'm very pleased with you. Mistique, put him to sleep for a while."

The sorceress locked eyes with Justin, and all the color drained out of his face. His eyes rolled up in his head and he fell limply backwards. Burns caught him and lowered him to the floor. Hawk hefted his axe, breathed deeply, and then reached forward and carefully opened one of the doors an inch. He looked back at Burns and Mistique.

"No mercy, no quarter—but whatever happens, I want Morgan alive. He's no use to me dead."

He turned back to the doors, kicked them open, and charged in, axe at the ready. Burns and Mistique charged in after him, eyes darting round the vast chamber as they searched for their first target. Morgan was reclining on embroidered cushions with a beautiful young woman, drinking wine from a silver goblet, and whispering something into her ear as she giggled helplessly. Half a dozen men-at-arms were playing cards at a table in a far corner. There was no sign of any sorcerer.

The men at the table looked round, startled, as the doors burst open, and then scrambled to their feet, grabbing for their swords. Morgan pushed aside his scantily clad companion and struggled to get to his feet, slipping and sliding on the cushions. Hawk sprinted forward, hoping to get to Morgan before the men-at-arms could reach him, but Morgan finally got his feet under him and ran for the far door. Thin streamers of mist shot past Hawk and wrapped themselves around Morgan, bringing him crashing to the floor. The far door flew open, revealing a tall, gaunt-faced man dressed in sorcerer's black. He gestured quickly, and the misty coils holding Morgan disappeared.

Hawk and Burns threw themselves at the charging men-at-arms. Hawk cut down the first two to reach him with savage sweeps of his axe. Blood pooled thickly on the floor as he stepped quickly over the writhing bodies to attack the next man. They stood face to face for a moment, exchanging cut and thrust and parry, but the man-at-arms was no match for Hawk's cold fury, and both of them knew it. The swordsman began to back away, and Hawk went after him. He swung his axe with vicious skill, and then caught a glimpse of flashing steel out of the corner of his eye. He threw himself to one side, and the young woman's sword just missed him. Hawk kicked the man-at-arms in the knee, elbowed him in the face, and turned quickly to face the young woman as she attacked him with just as much skill as the man-at-arms. Hawk wondered briefly where she'd hidden a sword in such a brief outfit, and then was forced to give her his full attention as she pressed home her attack.

She was good with a sword, and worse still, fresh and rested, while he was fighting off a long day's fatigue. He stood his ground, swinging his axe with both hands, but she deflected most of his blows and easily dodged the rest. Once again Hawk caught a glimpse of movement at his side, and sidestepped quickly as the man-at-arms he'd elbowed threw himself forward and accidentally impaled himself on the young woman's sword. She froze in shock, and Hawk slammed the butt of his axe against her head. She fell to the floor without a murmur and lay still. Hawk glowered down at her. If he'd had any sense, he'd have killed her while he had the chance, but he always was too chivalrous for his own good. Besides, he rationalized, she might answer questions that Morgan wouldn't.

He looked around him, suddenly aware the room was strangely quiet. Burns had dealt with the other men-at-arms, and was standing over his last kill, breathing heavily and checking himself for wounds. There didn't seem to be anything serious. Hawk grinned. There was a lot to be said for the advantage of surprise, not to mention the adrenalin provided by extreme desperation.

He looked across at Mistique, who was standing very still, her face cold, her eyes locked on the other sorcerer, still standing by the far door. Stray magic spat and sparkled on the air between them.

Mists curled and twisted around Mistique like unfinished ghosts, and then leapt forward with heart-stopping speed, only to dissipate and fall apart before they could reach the sorcerer. He raised his hand in a short, casual gesture and all around Mistique the floor bulged suddenly upwards, tearing itself apart. The jagged wood erupted up into thick twisting branches that clutched at the air like gnarled fingers. Barbed thorns thrust out of the crackling wood as the branches stretched towards Mistique. Thick tendrils of mist boiled off the sorceress, and shot forward to engulf the lengthening branches. The unliving wood cracked and splintered as the mists writhed, ripping the branches apart. Beads of sweat appeared on the sorcerer's face as the mists advanced on him. Sharp wooden stalagmites thrust out of the floor and wall around Mistique, piercing the air with razored points, but none of them came close to touching her. A pearly haze built around the sorcerer, thickening inexorably into a fog that swallowed him up. There was a single, choked cry from inside the fog, and then silence. The fog quickly cleared, dispersed by a sourceless wind, and there was no trace of the sorcerer anywhere. Hawk decided not to ask; he didn't think he wanted to know. Mistique glanced across at him.

"That's what comes of overspecialisation. If he hadn't limited himself to working with wood, he might have been able to do some real damage."

"You only work with mists," Hawk pointed out, striding quickly over to Morgan, who was still lying where he'd fallen.

"Mists are different," said Mistique. "You can do a lot with mists."

Hawk shrugged, grabbed Morgan by the collar, and dragged him to his feet. The drug baron twisted suddenly, a knife gleaming in his hand. Hawk let go and jumped back, sucking in his gut, and the knife ripped through his furs and out again without touching him. Morgan drew back his hand for another thrust, and Hawk caught him with a straight-finger jab just below the breastbone. Morgan's face paled, and the knife slipped from his numb fingers. Hawk grabbed him by the shirt-front and slammed him back against the nearest wall. He put his face close to Morgan's and showed the drug baron his death's-head smile.

"Talk to me, Morgan."

"What . . . what do you want to know?" Morgan fought to keep his voice even, but he couldn't face Hawk's cold gaze. He looked over Hawk's shoulder at Burns and Mistique, standing together, and his face paled even more.

"Let's start with the drug," said Hawk. "The super-chacal. Where is it?"

"In one of the back rooms here." Morgan looked reluctantly back at Hawk. "There are lots of empty rooms here. More than I can ever use."

"Have you started moving it yet?"

"No, we've been having difficulties setting up a new distribution network, thanks to your interference."

"It's nice to be appreciated," said Hawk. "Now let's talk about the drug itself. This super-chacal is something new. You didn't come up with it yourself. Developing a new drug takes lots of time and money, not to mention a staff of high-level alchemists in their own private lab. And that's out of your league, Morgan. So how did you get your hands on it?"

Morgan tried to shrug, but Hawk had too tight a hold on him. "It came in through the Docks, disguised as spices. All I had to do was make sure it hadn't been cut with anything, then package it and make the connection with the distributors. The drug itself was financed by outside money."

Hawk frowned thoughtfully. "Outside money . . . Outside Haven, or outside the Low Kingdoms?"

"Didn't know. Didn't care. Money's money; I don't give a damn where it comes from. This sounded like a good deal, so I went for it. I never got to talk to the real backers; they always worked through middlemen. I can give you their names if you want, but it won't do you any good. They'll have left Haven by now. I'd planned to be long gone myself, once the drug hit the streets."

"You really are a piece of slime, you know that?" Hawk thrust his face up close before Morgan's, and the drug baron tried to shrink back into the solid wall. Hawk's voice was calm and even, but his face held a bitter rage only barely held in check. "You knew what the drug was, and what it would do to anyone who took it. You knew that once the super-chacal hit the streets, there'd be a bloodbath that would tear Haven apart. But you went ahead with it anyway."

Morgan squirmed uncomfortably. "Come on, Hawk, if I hadn't gone for it, someone else would have. You're exaggerating the dangers. So we lose a few scum from the streets. So what? No one who really matters would have been hurt. And there's millions to be made from this drug. Once word gets out, everyone will want to try it. It gives a kind of hit no one's ever been able to deliver before. Even the weakest man can become strong enough and brave enough to get back at everyone who's ever done him down. Millions of ducats, Hawk. Think of it. It's not too late; you can still cut yourself in. There's enough money in this for everyone."

Hawk grinned at Morgan, and he shut up. "No deals, Morgan. Now then, you've done very well, so far. Just one more question, and I'll be finished with you. Answer it correctly, and you'll live to stand trial. You bought off a lot of people in the Guard while setting up this deal, but I'm interested in one name in particular. You bought yourself a Guard Captain. You know who I mean; the well-respected Captain, the one who no one would suspect. The one who made your drugs vanish from Guard Headquarters. I want to know who that Captain is. I want to know very badly. So you tell me the name, Morgan, or I swear I'll cut you into pieces right here and now."

"Hawk, you can't do this," said Burns. "It's inhuman."

"Shut up, Burns."

"He has to stand trial, Hawk. He'll tell us everything we need to know, under a truthspell."

"I need to know now! Talk to me, Morgan!"

"Stop it, Hawk! I won't stand for this!"

Hawk half turned to shout at Burns, and Morgan brought his knee up sharply into Hawk's groin. Air whistled in his throat as he fell backwards, momentarily paralysed by the pain. Morgan made a dash for the far door, but Mistique put herself between him and the door. Mists boiled up off her outstretched hands. Morgan produced another knife from somewhere and lunged at her. Burns ran him through from behind with his sword. Morgan sank slowly to his knees, still holding onto his knife. He coughed painfully, and blood ran thickly from his mouth. He fell forward and lay still, and Burns pulled his sword free. He knelt down beside the body, tried for a pulse at the neck, and shook his head. He got to his feet again, and a hand grabbed his shoulder from behind. He looked round, startled, and Hawk punched him in the mouth. Burns stumbled backwards, blood spilling down his chin. Hawk went after him, but Mistique grabbed him from behind and held him firmly.

"Stop it, Hawk! That's enough!"

Hawk struggled fiercely, but he was still weakened by Morgan's attack and he couldn't break her grip. His gaze was fixed on Burns. "You stupid bastard! I told you we needed him alive! How is he going to answer questions now?"

"I'm sorry," said Burns indistinctly, wiping blood from his mouth with the back of his hand. "I didn't think . . . I just saw him lunging at Mistique, and I really thought he was going to kill her. . . . ."

"I could have handled him," said Mistique.

"Yes, I'm sure you could have," said Burns, looking at the blood smeared across his hand. "I didn't think . . . I'm sorry."

"Damn you," said Hawk. "What are we going to do now? He was the only one who knew all the names." He shook his head sickly, then took a deep breath and let it out slowly. "It's all right, Mistique, you can let me go now. I'm all right."

She let him go, and stood back. Hawk moved over to Morgan's body and knelt down beside it, wincing as pain shot through him. He'd managed to take some of Morgan's kneeing on his thigh, but the pain was still bad enough to make him move like an old man. He tried for a pulse, but couldn't find one. He searched the body slowly and methodically, but didn't come up with anything useful, apart from a small bunch of keys. He got to his feet again, with a little help from Mistique.

"At least we've got the drugs back," he said brusquely. "And this time I'll make sure they don't go missing, even if I have to feed every damn package to the incinerator myself."

"We ought to search the place before we go," said Burns. "There's always the chance he kept records of who was working for him, and who he was paying off."

Hawk nodded curtly. "He probably had more sense than to leave something like that just lying about, but it's worth a look. Don't move anything, though. We'll leave the real search to the experts. Place is probably rigged with booby traps." A sudden thought struck him and he looked quickly at Mistique. "Or is this place going to collapse around our ears like the other one?"

The sorceress shook her head. "Solid as rock. Whoever set up this place knew what he was doing."

They headed for the far door, Mistique staying close by Hawk in case he needed to lean on her again. Burns kept a tactful distance. The sorceress cleared her throat uncertainly.

"Hawk . . . would you really have used your axe on Morgan?"

He smiled slightly. "I was bluffing. Mostly. I'm not really as bad as my reputation makes out."

"You convinced me," said Mistique. "I've never seen anyone look so mad."

"I wanted the name."

"Hawk," said Mistique gently. "We already know the name."

"So, did you find anything?" asked Commander Glen, leaning forward over his desk and staring intently at Hawk and Burns.

Hawk shook his head. "Nothing useful. And Morgan didn't strike me as dumb enough to commit anything incriminating to paper anyway."

Glen sniffed, and leaned back in his chair. "You're probably right. At least you had enough restraint not to wreck the place, for a change—even if you didn't leave anyone alive to answer questions."

"What about the man-at-arms Mistique put to sleep?" said Burns. "And the woman Hawk knocked out?"

"Hired muscle," said Glen dismissively. "They weren't far enough in to know anything useful. And speaking of Mistique, where is she? I want to hear her report, too."

Hawk and Burns stared over Glen's head at the wall behind him. "She said she'd look in later," said Hawk. "She's . . . rather busy at the moment." He lowered his gaze abruptly, and fixed Glen with his single, cold eye.

"Commander, there's something I need to discuss with you."

"Yes," said Glen. "We have to talk about Captain Fisher. I've been hearing stories about her for some time now. As long as they were just stories I could afford to ignore them. You and Fisher were a good team; you got results. But I can't ignore this, Hawk. She's betrayed the security of the Peace Talks, and gone on the run. We have no idea where she is, or what she might be planning. And now there's mounting evidence that she's been working for Morgan all along."

"I don't believe that," said Hawk. "I don't believe any of it."

Glen looked at him steadily. "She's gone rogue, Hawk. I have issued a warrant for her arrest. There's a reward of five thousand ducats for anyone who brings her in, dead or alive."

For a moment Hawk just looked back at him, his scarred face cold and impassive, saying nothing. "I'll find her," he said finally. "I'll find her, and bring her in. Call off your dogs, Commander."

"I can't do that, Hawk. It's out of my hands now. And I can't let you go, either. You did a good job in recovering the super-chacal, but you upset a great many prominent people in the process. If you'd brought Morgan in alive, no one would have said anything, but as it is . . ."

"That was my fault, Commander," said Burns, but Hawk and Glen didn't even look at him.

"Now that Fisher's gone rogue," said Glen, "you've become suspect too, Hawk, through your relationship with her. Too many things have gone wrong around you just lately. No one trusts you anymore. I have a warrant for your arrest too, Hawk. I'm sorry."

"You've got to let me find Fisher," said Hawk. "Please. Let me bring her in, and we'll prove our innocence."

"I'm sorry," said Glen. "I have my orders. Give me your axe, please."

Hawk drew his axe, and the room suddenly became very tense. He hefted the weapon in his hand a moment, and then put it down on Glen's desk. The Commander relaxed a little, and Hawk hit him with a vicious left uppercut. Glen flew backwards out of his chair, slammed into the wall behind his desk, and slid unconscious to the floor. Burns opened his mouth to yell something, his hand already reaching for his sword. Hawk spun round, grabbed up his axe, and hit Burns across the head with the flat of the blade while Burns was still drawing his sword. He fell to the floor and lay there motionless, groaning quietly.

Hawk would have liked to tie them both up, but a quick glance around showed him nothing he could use as a rope, and he didn't have the time, anyway. He hauled them both into Glen's private washroom, and locked the door on them. He took a last quick look round, and then left Glen's office and made his way casually through Headquarters to the main entrance. He smiled and nodded to people he passed, and they smiled and muttered automatically in return. Hawk kept his face calm, but his thoughts were in a turmoil. He had to find Isobel before anyone else did. He couldn't trust anyone else with the job.

Isobel . . . I'm coming for you.

9

Under the Masks

Fisher moved quietly through the back streets, trudging doggedly through the snow and slush, with her head bowed. The tattered grey cloak didn't do much to keep out the cold, but with the hood pulled well forward there was no way anyone was going to recognise her. After all, who would expect the bold and dashing Captain Fisher to be skulking through the worst part of town in rags she wouldn't normally have used to polish her boots? She seethed inwardly at the indignity, but kept her outer demeanour carefully calm and unobtrusive. Her disguise would only hold up as long as no one challenged it, and there were a hell of a lot of people who'd be only too happy to turn her in for whatever reward was currently on her head.

Fisher had no doubt there was a reward. The Powers That Be needed a scapegoat, and she was tailor-made for the role. She could plead her innocence till she was blue in the face, but no one would give a damn. She had to be found guilty so that the Outremer delegates would be reassured and the Peace Talks could go on. They'd told her right from the beginning that she was expendable. Fisher grinned fiercely. That was their opinion. If they wanted her to be a rogue, she'd be one. And anyone who got in her way was going to regret it.

She slowed her pace slightly as two ragged figures appeared out of a dark alley mouth and moved casually towards her. She caught brief glimpses of the knives half hidden under their cloaks, and turned to face them. She'd obviously overdone the unthreatening aspect of her disguise and made herself look an easy target. Fisher scowled. She couldn't afford to fight them; at best it would draw attention to her, particularly when she won, and at worst it might actually give away who she was. But she couldn't hope for any help, either. Not in the Northside. She swore under her breath, and let her hand move to her sword under cover of the cloak. There was never a bloody Constable around when you needed one.

The two bravos moved to block her path, and she came to a halt. She pushed back her cloak to reveal the sword at her side, and lifted her head to give them her best glare. She'd put a lot of work and practice into that glare, and it had always served her well in the past. It suggested she was one hundred percent crazy, barely under control, and violent with it. The two bravos took in the glare and the sword, looked at each other, and then made their knives disappear, and moved casually off in another direction, as though they'd intended to go that way all along. Fisher let her cloak fall back to cover the sword, pulled her hood even lower over her face, and continued on her way, trying not to look too much in a hurry.

She had to think of somewhere to go, somewhere she could hole up for a while till she could figure some way to get out of the city. She couldn't go home; it was the first place they'd think of, and was probably crawling with Guards by now, ransacking every room in search of evidence that wasn't there. A slow, sullen anger burned in her, at the thought of strangers trampling through her house, but she knew there was no point in brooding over it. Or the treasured possessions she'd have to leave behind when she finally found a way out of the city.

She had to find somewhere she could stop and think, somewhere safe. And there were all sorts of things she'd have to get her hands on, things she'd need just to survive out in the wilds of the Low Kingdoms, in the dead of winter. Starting with a decent fur cloak. The cold cut right through the thin grey one she had now. And she'd need a horse and provisions . . . and a dozen other things, none of which she had the money to buy. Her money was back at the house. What there was of it.

Her pace slowed as her thoughts churned furiously. She wasn't used to having to plan ahead. That had always been Hawk's responsibility. Hawk. The name cut at her briefly, like a razor drawn against unsuspecting skin. She wanted to go to him so badly, but she didn't dare. Everything she'd

heard since she hit the streets suggested that Hawk had
gone berserk, fighting and killing anyone who got between
him and Morgan. Something bad must have happened,
something so awful he no longer cared what happened to
him as long as he got to Morgan. Her first impulse had
been to find him and fight at his side, but she couldn't do
that. By now there had to be a small army of Guards on
her tail, and she'd be leading them straight to Hawk. And if
he really had gone berserk, he'd die rather than be stopped.

She couldn't let that happen.

There must be somewhere she could go, somewhere they
wouldn't think of looking. She trudged on, head down, not
looking where she was going, as her mind floundered from
one possibility to another before finally, reluctantly, settling
on one. The Tolling Bell was a rancid little tavern, tucked
away at the back of nowhere. The kind of place where
they sold illegally strong drinks and the bartender had little
conversation and even less of a memory for faces. Fisher
had used the place before, when she needed to get away
by herself for a while. When she'd had a row with Hawk,
or just needed to be alone with her thoughts. She'd always
taken pains to disguise her identity, so no one could find
her till she was ready to be found. The Tolling Bell . . .
Yes . . . she could be there in half an hour.

Her head snapped up, suddenly alert as she heard tramp-
ing feet heading towards her. Six Guard Constables were
moving purposefully in her direction. She quickly dropped
her head again, and hunched over under her cloak to make
herself look smaller. Her hand moved unobtrusively to the
sword at her side. Six-to-one odds, and no one to watch
her back. Bad odds, but she'd faced worse in her time. She
glanced cautiously around for possible escape routes, and
only then realised the Guards weren't actually looking at
her. Hope flared in her again, and she shrank back against
the wall as the Guards tramped past, doing her best to look
insignificant and harmless. The Constables hardly glanced
at her as they passed, and continued on their way. Fisher
waited where she was, listening to the sound of the footsteps dying gradually away, and then moved slowly on,
careful not to look behind her. Her back crawled in anticipation of a sudden sword thrust, but it never came. She
finally allowed herself to glance back over her shoulder,

and found the Constables were almost out of sight at the end of the street. Her breath began to come a little more easily, and she increased her pace. She'd be safe at The Tolling Bell. For a while. She could sit down, and rest, and think. And just maybe she'd be able to see a way out of this mess.

Hawk strode angrily down the main street, pulling his ratty brown cloak tightly about him. The cold cut through the ragged cloth as though it weren't there, but at least the hood concealed his face, as long as he remembered to keep his head bowed. Someone had to have found Glen and Burns by now, which meant word would soon be circulating on the streets that Hawk was fair game for anyone who felt like going after him. And with the kind of reward the Guard would be offering, there'd be no shortage of volunteers. Most of the usual bounty hunters would have more sense than to go after Captain Hawk, but there were always some stupid enough to take any risk, for a chance at the big money. And if enough of them got together, they might just manage it.

Hawk scowled, and peered unobtrusively about him. They were after Fisher too. He had to find her, before anyone else did. Find her, and find out what had happened. Why she'd betrayed Haven, and the Guard. And him. There had to be a reason, a good reason. He believed that implicitly, because to think anything else would drive him insane. He trusted Isobel, but all the evidence pointed to her guilt. As a Guard, he'd learned to rely on the evidence before anything else, and never to trust his instincts or his feelings until he had hard evidence to back them up. But this was different. This was Isobel. He had to find her and hear her explanation. And then he'd know what to do next.

Though really, deep down, he'd already decided what he was going to do. Whatever she said, whatever she'd done; it didn't matter. Once before he'd given up everything he had for her sake, and he wouldn't hesitate to do it again if he had to. There were other cities, other countries they could go to, and it wouldn't be the first time they'd had to change their names.

But he had to find her soon, before the Guard did. She wouldn't go to any of her usual haunts; too many other people knew about them. There had to be some place she'd regard as safe, some place she'd think no one knew about but her. . . . The Tolling Bell. That had to be it. Isobel often disappeared there when she lost an argument or was feeling broody.

A shout went up not too far away, as a sudden gust of wind caught the edge of his hood and flipped it back, revealing his face. Hawk pulled the hood back into position, but the damage had been done. Two Guard Constables were running towards him, swords drawn. Hawk looked quickly around for an escape route, but they were all blocked by curious onlookers eager for some free entertainment. Hawk cursed unemotionally, straightened up, and drew his axe. He shrugged his cloak back out of the way and stamped the snow flat to give him better footing. He hefted his axe thoughtfully, and waited for the two Constables to come within range. He didn't want to kill them if he could avoid it. They were just doing their job. As far as they were concerned, he was a rogue and a traitor. But he couldn't let them stop him. Isobel's life might depend on his getting to her before anyone else did.

The Constables slowed their pace as they drew near Hawk, and moved apart to take him from two directions at once. Hawk picked the nearest one, and launched himself forward. He ducked under the Constable's wild swing, the sword blade tugging briefly at the top of his hood, and slammed his shoulder into the Constable's gut. The man folded in half and fell away, gasping for air. Hawk clubbed him forcefully across the back of the head with the butt of his axe, and then spun round just in time to block an attack from the other Constable.

The two of them stamped back and forth, feinting and withdrawing, each trying to make the other commit himself. Hawk faked a stumble, and went down on one knee. The Constable immediately fell back a step, too old a hand to be taken in by such an obvious stunt, and Hawk hit him in the face with the handful of snow he'd palmed when he went down. The Constable staggered back, lashing out blindly with his sword while he tried to claw the snow out of his eyes with his free hand. Hawk timed it carefully, stepped in during a brief moment when the Constable left himself open, and kicked him in the groin.

The Constable went down without a sound, and Hawk clubbed him unconscious. He nodded once, satisfied, and then froze as a shout went up again, some way behind him. He looked round and saw six more Constables charging down the street towards him. Hawk turned on his heel and ran for the nearest alleyway. If he had to take on six-to-one odds with no one to guard his back, someone was definitely going to end up dead. Quite possibly him. The people in the alley mouth scattered as he bore down on them axe in hand, and he plunged past them into the concealing gloom of the narrow passageway. His best bet was to try and lose his pursuers in the maze of back streets and cul de sacs. He knew this area, and the odds were they didn't. He just hoped he wouldn't have to outrun them. He was already short of breath. It had been a long day, and the end was nowhere in sight.

He scowled to himself as he ran. Running from a mere six-to-one odds. If this got out, he'd never live it down.

Captain ap Owen watched with interest as Commander Glen sat glowering behind his desk, painfully growling orders to a steady stream of visitors. He kept an ice pack pressed against his face. A quite spectacular bruise was spreading across his jaw and peeking round the edges of the ice pack. People came and went in sudden rushes and flurries, darting into the office to deliver updated reports and possible sightings, and then quickly disappearing before Glen could turn his glare on them. But for all their bustle and effort, it was clear they were no nearer locating Hawk or Fisher.

"They can't just have vanished," protested Captain Burns, pacing back and forth, and occasionally raising a hand to feel gingerly at the back of his head. He claimed to have a hell of a bump there, but no one else had seen it. Ap Owen thought it was probably more hurt pride than anything else. Burns glared at ap Owen as though it were all his fault, and ap Owen quickly looked away, somehow keeping a smile off his face. It had to be said, he'd never much cared for Burns. Too interested in looking good, that one. Probably had a great career ahead of him—in administration.

"We'll find them," said Glen slowly, trying hard not to

move his mouth when he spoke. "We've got their house staked out, and all their usual haunts. The city Gates have been sealed, so they can't get out of Haven. All we have to do now is run them to ground . . ." He broke off abruptly as a wave of pain hit him, but his eyes were still hot and furious.

"We're leaning on all the usual informants," said ap Owen. "Most of them are falling over themselves at a chance to do Hawk and Fisher some dirt. Those two have made an awful lot of enemies during their short time in Haven."

Burns sniffed. "No honour among thieves. Or traitors."

Ap Owen raised an eyebrow. "That's hardly fair, Burns. Up until now, Hawk and Fisher have always had an exemplary reputation."

"You have got to be joking. Everyone knows about the brutal tactics they use. They don't care who they hurt or intimidate, and they kill anyone who gets in their way. I've even heard it said they plant evidence and manufacture confessions, just to make their arrest rate look good. They're no better than thugs in uniform."

"They always upheld the law."

"When it suited them," said Burns. "Anybody can be bought, for the right price."

Ap Owen shrugged unhappily, and looked across at Glen. "With respect, Commander, I think our quarry have more than enough sense to keep clear of all their usual haunts. Is there anywhere they might go, that they might think we don't know about? You were with Hawk all day, Burns. Did he mention any place to you?"

"If he had, I'd have said so!" snapped Burns. "Why aren't you out there looking for them? You've got twenty men under you. Why aren't you out combing the streets?"

"What's the point?" said ap Owen mildly. "We've got half an army out there as it is; adding my people to that pack would only give them someone else to trip over. Besides, I don't want my men wandering aimlessly about in the cold, or they won't be worth spit when we finally get a chance to arrest Hawk or Fisher. Or both. In fact, the more I think about it, the more sure I am they'll have joined up by now. They always were very devoted to each other."

"I don't know," said Glen indistinctly, from behind his

ice pack. "Hawk seemed honestly shocked when he heard the news about Fisher's treachery. I think there's a real chance he may not be involved in the treason himself."

"If he wasn't a traitor before, he is now," said Burns. "He's defied lawful orders and assaulted a superior officer. And right now you can bet he's doing his utmost to help the traitor Fisher to escape justice. Even though her actions may have helped to start a war."

"Calm down," said ap Owen. "It isn't that bad. Yet. The delegates are still talking to each other, even if it's not on an official basis at the moment. There's still hope. In the meantime, guilty or not, I think we can assume Hawk is doing his best to locate Fisher. And since he's much more likely to figure out where she's hidden herself than we are, I think we can also assume that when we finally catch up with them, they're going to be together. And together, they're the most formidable fighting machine Haven has ever seen. I'm not sure I can take them, even with twenty men under me. Which is why, Captain Burns, my men are staying here, warm and rested, until they're needed. I don't want them worn out from chasing round Haven after every unconfirmed sighting."

"Thank you, Captain," said Glen heavily. "I think you've made your point." He scowled at ap Owen and Burns, and then stared unseeingly at the papers on his desk, his fingers drumming quietly as he thought. "Hawk said something once, about Fisher having a special place to go to be on her own, when she wanted to get away from everything. He told me about it one time, when we were looking for her in an emergency and couldn't find her. It was an inn. The something Bell. The Tolling Bell, that was it."

"What district?" said ap Owen.

"How the hell should I know? Find out!"

Ap Owen rose to his feet. "It's got to be somewhere near their home. Shouldn't be too hard to find someone here who lives in that area. I'll let you know the minute I've got word, Commander; then I'll move in with my men while you have the area surrounded. Maybe we can talk Hawk and Fisher into giving up. I don't see any point in getting my people killed if I can avoid it."

"It's not as simple as that," said Glen slowly. "I have my orders, Captain ap Owen, and I'm passing them on to

you. Hawk and Fisher are to be brought in dead. We're
not interested in their capture or surrender. Our superiors
have decided that they can't be allowed to stand trial. They
know too many secrets, too many things the Council can't
afford to have discussed in public. So Hawk and Fisher are
going to die resisting arrest. That's the way our superiors
want it, and that's the way it's going to be. Understand?"

"Yes, Commander," said ap Owen. "I understand. Now,
if you'll excuse me . . ."

"I'm going with you," said Burns. "I have a personal
stake in this."

Ap Owen glanced at Commander Glen, who nodded
brusquely. Ap Owen crossed over to the door without looking at Burns, and left the Commander's office. Burns followed him out. Glen stared at the papers on his desk for
a long time before returning to his work.

Fisher slipped into The Tolling Bell tavern with her hood
pulled low, and ordered an ale by pointing and grunting.
The bartender drew her off a pint without commenting.
You got all sorts in The Tolling Bell. Fisher paid for her
drink and quickly settled herself in a dark corner, careful
to avoid her usual booth. She took a long swallow of the
bitter ale, wiped the froth from her upper lip with care, so
as not to disturb her hood, and only then allowed herself
to relax a little. She'd always thought of The Bell as a
sanctuary, a place apart from the cares and duties of her
life, and now she needed that feeling more than ever. She
looked around casually, checking the place out.

The inn was quiet, not surprising given the time of day,
with only a dozen or so customers. Fisher recognised all of
them as regulars. They'd mind their own business. They
always did.

*Hawk's gone berserk. He's killing anyone who gets in
his way.*

Fisher squeezed her eyes shut. She didn't want to believe
that what she'd heard was true, but it could be. It could
be. And if it were . . . she didn't know what to do for the
best. She couldn't let him go on as he was. If he really had
gone berserk, innocent people might get hurt, even killed.
She couldn't risk looking for him herself; she might un-
knowingly lead the Guard right to him. But she couldn't

just abandon him, either. She had to do something . . . something, while there was still time.

In the street outside, Hawk leaned against a wall and looked casually about him. No one seemed to be paying him any untoward attention. He was pretty sure he hadn't been followed since he shook off the pursuing Constables, but he wasn't taking any chances. He approved of Fisher's choice of inn. The Tolling Bell was quiet, off the beaten track and nicely anonymous. Not at all the kind of place you'd expect to find Captains Hawk and Fisher. He took one last look around, pulled his hood even lower, and ducked in through the open doorway.

He strolled over to the bar, and ordered a beer by grunting and pointing. The bartender looked at him for a moment, and then drew him a pint. Hawk paid the man, put his back against the bar, and sipped his beer thoughtfully as he looked about him. The other customers ignored him completely, but one figure near the back seemed to be going out of its way to avoid looking in his direction.

Fisher's heart beat painfully fast, and she clutched her glass until her knuckles showed white. She had recognised Hawk the moment he entered the inn. She knew the way he walked, the way he moved. . . . He'd spotted her. She could tell from the way his stance suddenly changed. Her thoughts raced furiously. Why was he just standing there? Had he come to take her in? Did he want Morgan so badly now, he'd even sacrifice her in return for a clear shot at the drug baron? *He's gone rogue. Killing anyone who gets in his way. Anyone.*

She shoved her chair back from the table and sprang to her feet. She swept her cloak over her shoulders, out of the way, and drew her sword. She couldn't let Hawk take her in. He didn't understand what was going on. They'd kill her, once she was safely out of the public eye, to be sure of appeasing the Outremer delegates. She couldn't let Hawk take her in.

Hawk shrugged his own cloak back out of the way, and drew his axe as she drew her sword. What little he could see of her face looked strained and desperate. *She must be a traitor. She's betrayed everyone. She betrayed you.* There were frantic scrambling sounds all around as the other customers hurried to get out of the way. A tense, echoing silence filled the room.

She's a traitor. All the evidence proves it. She drew a sword on you. You can't trust her anymore.

He's a rogue. He's gone berserk, out of control. He's killed people all over Haven. You can't trust him anymore.

Hawk slowly straightened up out of his fighting stance, and put away his axe. He pushed back his hood, and walked slowly towards Isobel. She straightened up and lowered her sword. Hawk stopped before her, easily in reach of her sword, and smiled at her.

"It's all right, Isobel. I don't care what you've done. You must have had a good reason for it. If you don't want me with you, if you feel you have to . . . leave me behind, that's all right. I'll understand. All that matters to me is that you're safe."

Fisher slammed her sword back into its scabbard, and hugged Hawk fiercely, crushing the breath out of him. "You damned fool, Hawk! As if I could ever leave you . . ."

They clung together for a while, happy and secure in each other's arms, eyes squeezed shut, as if they could close out everything in the world except the two of them. The other customers slowly began to settle down again, though still keeping a wary eye on the embracing couple. Eventually, reluctantly, Hawk and Fisher broke apart, and stepped back to look at each other properly. Hawk's mouth twitched.

"That is a really horrible-looking cloak, Isobel."

"You should talk. What the hell have you been up to, Hawk? I've been hearing all kinds of crazy things about you."

Hawk grinned. "Most of them are probably true. You should hear what they've been saying about you."

They sat down together at Fisher's table, and brought each other up to date on the day's events. It took a while, not least because there were a lot of things they weren't too sure about themselves, but eventually they both ran down, and sat quietly, thinking hard. A growing murmur of conversation rose around them, as the inn's customers disappointedly decided that there wasn't going to be any more action after all.

"Somebody's been setting us up," said Hawk finally.

"Both of us. We've been led around by the nose all day long, and we were so tied up in our own concerns we never even noticed. But the way things are, no one's going to believe us, no matter what we say. You know, we could still make a run for it. I know a forger who could knock us out new identities in under an hour."

Fisher looked at him. "Do you want to run?"

"Well, no, not really, but I thought you . . ."

"That was different. I thought I was on my own then. But now . . ."

"Right," said Hawk. "No one sets us up and gets away with it. The trouble is, who the hell did it to us? I thought for a long time it was Morgan, but that turned out not to be the case."

"Pity," said Fisher. "It would have simplified things. He said the drug was developed by *outside* money . . . so presumably the people behind Morgan are our real enemies. Whoever they are. It's not just the drug; they've got to be connected with the Peace Talks in some way as well. Maybe they were banking on the chaos the super-chacal would cause to break up the Talks, or at least keep the Guard so occupied they couldn't protect the delegates properly. Wait a minute . . . wait just a minute. All that talk of *outside* money could refer to outside the Low Kingdoms; meaning Outremer."

"Right," said Hawk. "I thought that as well. We need a wedge, something or someone we can use to force open this case and let in a little light. Look, just because you're not a traitor, it doesn't mean there isn't one. Someone removed those drugs from Headquarters, and sabotaged the Talks by revealing the house's location and the co-ordinates of the pocket dimension. Who is there that's been as closely involved in this case as you and I, and had the opportunity to do all the things you've been accused of doing?"

"If the rumours are to be believed, it's a Guard Captain," said Fisher, scowling thoughtfully into her drink. "A well-respected Captain, too honest and too trusted ever to be suspected. But the only other Captain in this case is . . ." A sudden inspiration stirred in her, and she stared at Hawk, her eyes widening. "No, it couldn't be. Not him. Not *Burns.*"

"Why not? He had the opportunity." Hawk nodded

grimly, his thoughts racing furiously. "It has to be him; he fits all the facts. And remember, one of Morgan's people at the drug factory said he recognised one of the Captains who took part in the raid as someone who worked for Morgan. He actually fingered you, but presumably by then he'd been got at. So, if it wasn't you, it had to be one of the other Captains. We can forget Doughty because he's dead, and we know it wasn't us, so that just leaves Burns! Dammit, I always thought he was too good to be true!"

"Wait a minute," said Fisher. "Let's not get carried away with this. How could Burns have sabotaged the Peace Talks?"

Hawk frowned. "It wouldn't have been difficult for him to get the information. He's been in and out of Headquarters all day, just like us. I feel like an idiot, Isobel. It's no wonder I've been walking into traps all day; Burns must have been reporting our position every time my back was turned!"

"It also explains why he killed Morgan," said Fisher. "He was afraid Morgan might finger him, as a way of saving his own neck. We've found our traitor, Hawk. Burns is behind everything bad that's happened to us today."

"Never liked him," said Hawk. "I wish now I'd hit him harder, when I had the chance."

"A well-respected Captain that no one would suspect. The rumours were right about that, at any rate. I never even heard a whisper about corruption concerning Burns." Fisher frowned suddenly. "You know, Hawk, this isn't going to be easy to prove. Who's going to take the word of two suspected traitors and renegades like us against a paragon of virtue like Burns?"

"We'll just have to find him, and persuade him to tell them the truth."

"No rough stuff, Hawk. He'd only claim he was intimidated into saying what we wanted him to say, and with our reputation, they'd believe him. We need evidence. Hard evidence."

"All right, but first we've got to find him. And that's not going to be easy either. He could be anywhere in Haven. Where are we supposed to start looking?"

"Right here," said Burns.

They looked up quickly, hands dropping to their weapons, and there was Burns standing by the bar, with ap Owen beside him. Guard Constables were filing quickly into the inn, swords at the ready. Once again the customers scrambled to get out of the way. Hawk and Fisher rose slowly to their feet and moved away from the table, ostentatiously keeping their hands well away from their weapons. More Guards entered the inn. Hawk counted twenty in all. If the situation hadn't been so grim, Hawk might have felt flattered they'd felt it necessary to send so many men after him and Isobel. As it was, he was more interested in trying to spot a quick escape route.

"Getting old, Hawk," said Burns casually. "You weren't even bothering to watch the door. There was a time we wouldn't have caught you this easily."

"We're not caught yet," said Hawk. "But I'm glad you're here, Burns. There's a lot of things Isobel and I want to discuss with you."

"The time for talk is over," said Burns. "In fact, your time has just run out."

"Drop your weapons on the floor, please," said ap Owen steadily. "You're under arrest, Captains."

Burns looked around, startled, and glared at ap Owen. "Those were not our orders! You obey Commander Glen's orders, or I'll have you put under arrest!" He gestured quickly to the watching Constables. "You have your instructions. Kill them both."

Hawk's axe was suddenly in his hands, the heavy blade gleaming hungrily in the lamplight. Fisher stood at his side, sword at the ready. Hawk grinned nastily at the other Guards.

"When you're ready, gentlemen. Who wants to die first?"

The Guards looked at each other. Nobody moved.

"I think we'll be leaving now," said Hawk calmly. "If anyone tries to follow us, I'll take it as a personal insult. Now, stand clear of the door."

He almost brought it off. He was Hawk, after all. But Burns suddenly stepped forward, sword in hand, and his angry voice broke the atmosphere.

"What the hell are you waiting for?" he said to his men. "You outnumber them ten to one, and they're both dog-tired from chasing round the city all day! Now carry out your orders, or I swear I'll see every man of you arrested for aiding and abetting known traitors!"

The Constables' faces hardened, and they moved slowly forward, fanning out to attack Hawk and Fisher from as many sides as possible. Hawk and Fisher moved quickly to stand back to back. Fisher looked appealingly at Captain ap Owen.

"Listen to me, ap Owen. You know this isn't right. This whole thing's a setup. There are things going on here you don't know about. Listen to me, please, for Haven's sake."

Ap Owen looked at her uncertainly. Burns glared at ap Owen.

"Don't listen to her. The bitch would say anything to save her neck."

"Watch your mouth, Burns," said ap Owen. "Stay where you are, men. No one is to start anything without my order. Unless any of you really want to go one-on-one with Captain Hawk."

The Constables lowered their swords and relaxed a little, some of them looking openly relieved. Burns started to say something angrily, and then stopped when he realised ap Owen's sword was pressed against his side.

"I think we've heard enough from you, Captain Burns," said ap Owen. "Now please be quiet, while I listen to what Captain Fisher has to say."

"To start with," said Fisher, "take a look at Hawk. Does he really look like he's gone kill-crazy? The only person here who fits that description is Burns, the very person who's been supplying all the evidence against Hawk. As for me, I was set up. Do you really think I'd have stuck around to defend the Talks if I'd known there was an army of mercenaries on the way? Or retreated into the pocket dimension with you if I'd known it was going to be under attack, too? No, there's only one traitor here, and he's standing right beside you."

"You see," said Burns. "I told you she'd say anything. She'll be accusing you next. We have to kill them, or the Outremer delegates will walk out! Dammit, ap Owen, you follow your orders or I swear I'll see you hanged as a traitor yourself!"

"Oh, shut up," said ap Owen. "I'm getting really tired of the sound of your voice, Burns." He looked at Hawk and Fisher. "Let's assume, just for the moment, that there may be something in what you say. That buys you a reprieve. But I've still got to take you in. If you'll hand over your weapons, I give you my word that I'll get you back to Headquarters alive and unharmed, and you can tell your story to Commander Glen. Sound fair to you?"

"Very fair," said Fisher. "I promise you, you won't regret this."

Ap Owen smiled slightly. "I'm already regretting it. Ah hell; I was never that interested in promotion anyway."

Burns stepped forward suddenly and addressed the Constables, who were stirring uneasily and looking at each other. "Men, Commander Glen himself put me in charge of you, along with ap Owen. You know what your orders are. Now, whose orders are you going to follow—your Commander's, or a Captain who is clearly allied with the traitors Hawk and Fisher?"

The Guards looked at ap Owen, and then back at Burns. They didn't have to say anything; Burns could see the decision in their faces. They didn't trust him, and they weren't going to take on Hawk and Fisher if they didn't have to. Burns turned suddenly, slapped ap Owen's sword aside, and ran for the door. The Constables moved instinctively to stop him, and Burns cut about him viciously with his sword. Hawk and Fisher charged after him. Men fell screaming as blood flew on the air. Burns plunged forward, his eyes fixed on the door.

He'd almost made it when Hawk brought him down with a last, desperate leap. They rolled back and forth on the floor, kicking and struggling. The Constables crowded in around them, hacking and cutting at Burns, furious at his treacherous attack. Hawk fought back with his axe, as much to protect himself as Burns. He shouted that they needed Burns alive, but the Guards were too angry to care. Ap Owen yelled orders that no one listened to. Fisher threw herself into the fray, hauling Guards away from the fight by main force and sheer determination, but there were too many Guards between her and Hawk, and she knew it. The Constables fought each other to get at Burns, blinded by blood and rage. Hawk tried to get his feet under him, and failed. Swords flew all around him, and blood pooled on the floor. He braced himself for one last effort, and hardened his heart at the thought of the innocent Guards he'd have to kill. He couldn't let Burns die.

And then a thick fog boiled in through the open door, filling the inn in a matter of moments. A hundred clammy tentacles tore the combatants apart and held them firmly in unyielding misty coils. There was a pause as they all struggled futilely, and then the sorceress Mistique stepped delicately in through the open door. Hawk relaxed and grinned at her.

"I was wondering when you were going to turn up again."

"You didn't think I was going to miss out on the climax, after all I've been through today, did you, darling?" Mistique smiled back at him, and then looked around sternly. "I'm going to let you go now. But anyone who misbehaves will regret it. Is that understood?"

The Constables nodded, their anger already cooling rapidly. Some of them realised they'd been fighting Hawk and Fisher, and went pale as they considered how lucky they were to still be alive. Mistique gestured gracefully, and the mists fell away from everyone, dissipating quickly on the warm air. Hawk and Fisher pushed the Guards out of the way and knelt down beside Burns. There was a gaping wound in his side, and a lot of blood on the floor around him. Fisher pulled out a clean folded handkerchief and pressed it against the wound, but it was clearly too little too late. Burns turned his head slightly, and looked at Hawk. His face was very pale, but his mouth and chin were red with blood.

"Almost had you," he said quietly.

"Why, Burns?" said Hawk. "You were one of the best. Everyone said so. Why betray everything you ever believed in?"

"For the money, of course. I spent years overseeing transactions of gold and silver and precious stones, protecting men who had more money than they knew what to do with, and eventually I just decided I wanted some of that wealth for myself. I wanted some of the luxuries and comforts I saw every day and couldn't touch. Honour and honesty are all very well, but they don't pay the bills. I was going to be rich, Hawk, richer than you've ever dreamed of. Almost made it. Would have, too, if it hadn't been for you and that bitch."

"You were Morgan's contact inside the Guard, weren't you?" said Fisher impatiently.

"Of course," said Burns. "I went to Morgan and suggested it. It was perfect. Who would ever have suspected me?"

"People died because of you," said Hawk. "People who trusted you."

Burns grinned widely. There was blood on his teeth. "They shouldn't have got in my way. I killed Doughty, you know. He was there when that little bastard at the drug factory recognised me. So I killed him, and persuaded the informant to implicate Fisher instead."

"You killed your own partner?" said Fisher, shocked.

"Why not?" said Burns. "I was going to be rich. I didn't need him anymore."

"Why did you betray the Peace Talks?" said Hawk.

Burns chuckled painfully, and fresh blood spilled down his chin. "I didn't. That wasn't me. See, you're not as smart as you thought you were, are you?"

"Who was it, Burns?" said Hawk. "Who were you working for?"

"Go to hell," said Burns. He reared up, tried to spit blood at Hawk, and then the light went out of his eyes and he fell back and died.

"Great," said Hawk. "Bloody marvelous. Every time I think I've found someone who can explain what the hell's going on, they bloody up and die on me."

He closed Burns's staring eyes with a surprisingly gentle hand, and got to his feet again. He made to offer ap Owen his axe, but ap Owen shook his head. Fisher stood up, looked down at Burns a moment, and then kicked the body viciously.

"Don't," said Hawk. "He was a good man, once."

"I'm damned if I know what's happening anymore," said ap Owen. "But Burns's dying confession seemed straightforward enough, so as far as I'm concerned, you're both cleared. But you'd better stick with me until we can get back to Headquarters and make it official. There's still a lot of people out on the streets looking for you, with swords

in their hands and blood in their eyes. The Council has
done everything but declare open season on you both."

"We can't go back," said Hawk. "It's not over yet. You
heard what Burns said; he didn't betray the Peace Talks.
Someone else did that. Which means the delegates are still
in danger. And the two people who should be in charge of
protecting them are right here in this room with me. It's
more than possible that Isobel was deliberately set up to
draw attention away from the real traitor, so that security
round the delegates would be relaxed."

"We've got to get back there," said Fisher. "Those poor
bastards think they're safe, now I'm not there! They're
probably not even bothering with anything more than
basic security."

"Let's go," said ap Owen. "Anything could be happening
while we're standing around being horrified." He turned to
the silently watching Constables. "You stick with us. From
now on, you do whatever Hawk and Fisher say. They're in
charge. Anyone have any problems with that?" The Guards
coughed and shrugged and looked at their boots. Ap Owen
smiled slightly. "I thought not. All right, let's move it. Follow me, people."

He led the way out of the inn at a quick, impatient pace,
followed resignedly by the Guards. Hawk and Fisher
brought up the rear, along with Mistique. Hawk cleared
his throat.

"Thanks for the help," he said brusquely. "Of course, we
could have beaten the Guards by ourselves, if we'd had to."

"Oh, of course you could, darling," said Mistique. "But
you wouldn't have wanted to hurt all those innocent people, would you?"

"Of course not," said Fisher, looking straight ahead.
"That's why we were holding back. Otherwise, we could
have beaten them easily."

"Of course," said Mistique.

The Peace Talks had ground to a halt yet again, and the
four remaining delegates were taking another break in the
study. None of them minded much; they all knew nothing
important was going to be decided until the new delegates
arrived to replace the two who'd died. And in particular,
the Haven delegation wasn't going to agree to anything

until they had a sorcerer on their side who could counteract any subtle magics the Lord Nightingale might or might not be using to influence things. No one admitted any of this out loud, of course, but everyone understood the situation. They still kept the Talks going. They were, after all, politicians, and there was always the chance someone might be manoeuvred into saying something they hadn't meant to. Careers could be built by pouncing on lapses like that.

Lord Nightingale selected one of the cut-glass decanters and poured out generous measures for them all. The mood was generally more relaxed than it had been, now that the traitor Fisher had been exposed, and they shared little jokes and anecdotes as they emptied their glasses. Nothing like talking for ages and saying nothing to work up a really good thirst. Their murmured conversation wandered aimlessly. None of them were in any particular hurry to get back to the Talks. The chairs were comfortable, the room was pleasantly warm, and in a while it would be time to take a break for dinner anyway.

Lord Nightingale looked at the clock on the mantelpiece, heaved himself out of his chair and left the room on a muttered errand. He shut the door, smiled broadly, and then froze as someone in the hall behind him cleared his throat politely. He looked round sharply, and found himself facing ap Owen and Fisher, someone who by his appearance had to be Hawk, and a woman in sorcerer's black. For a moment Nightingale just stood there, his face and mind utterly blank, and then he drew himself up, and nodded quickly to ap Owen.

"Well done, Captain. You've apprehended the traitor Fisher. I'll see you receive a commendation for this."

Ap Owen stared at him stonily. "I'm afraid that's not why we're here, my lord. It is my duty to inform you that you are under arrest."

"If this is some kind of joke, *Captain,* it's in very bad taste. I shall inform your superiors about this."

Ap Owen continued as if he'd never been interrupted. "We've been here some time, my lord, searching the house. Among your belongings we discovered—"

"You searched my room? How dare you! I have diplomatic immunity from this sort of petty harassment!"

"Among your belongings, hidden inside the handle of

one of your trunks, we found a quantity of the super-chacal drug."

"A lot of things made sense, once we found the drug," said Fisher. "We knew the drug tied into the Talks somehow, but we didn't have a connection, until we found you. And once we started looking at you closely, all kinds of things became clear. You gave away the location of the house, because you knew you'd be safe inside the pocket dimension. When that didn't work as well as you'd hoped, you used your sorcery to open a door into the dimension, knowing your sorcery would protect you from the creatures you'd summoned. And of course you were able to close the door once it became clear the creatures were getting out of hand and might pose a threat to you. Finally, you've been subtly using your magic all along, influencing the delegates to make sure nothing would ever be agreed. You've gone very quiet, my lord. Nothing to say for yourself?"

"I admit everything," said Lord Nightingale calmly. "I'll admit anything you like, here, in private. It doesn't matter anymore. You can't prove any of it, and even if you could, I have diplomatic immunity from arrest. And I'm afraid the whole matter is academic now, anyway. My fellow delegates have just drunk a glass of wine from a decanter I dosed rather heavily with the super-chacal drug. My sorcery protected me from suffering any effects, but we should begin to hear the results on them any time now. They'll tear each other to pieces in an animal frenzy, and that will be the end of the Peace Talks. Evidence is already being planted in the right places that this was the work of certain leading factions in Haven, to express their opposition to the thought of peace with Outremer."

"Why?" said Hawk. "Why have you done all this? What sane man wants to start a war?"

Lord Nightingale smiled condescendingly. "There's money to be made in a war, Captain. A great deal of money. Not to mention political capital, and military advancement. A man in the right place at the right time, if properly forewarned, can rise rapidly in wartime, no matter who wins. Whatever the outcome of the war, my associates and I will end up a great deal richer and more powerful than we could ever have hoped to be under normal conditions. The super-chacal was my idea. I helped fund its creation, and oversaw its introduction into Haven. You can think of this city as a testing ground for the new drug. If it does as well here as we expect, it should prove an excellent means of sabotaging the Low Kingdoms. We'll introduce the drug into selected foods and wines, poison some strategic wells and rivers, and then just sit back and watch as your country tears itself apart. All we'll have to do is come in afterwards and clean up the mess. It could be the start of a whole new form of warfare.

"I hope you've all been listening carefully. It's so nice to be appreciated for one's work. And it's not as if you'll ever get a chance to tell anyone else. My fellow delegates should see to that."

He reached to open the study door, and then hesitated, listening. Hawk smiled coldly.

"That's right, my Lord. Quiet in there, isn't it? Like ap Owen said, we've been here for some time. Mistique's magic revealed that one of the decanters had been drugged, so we switched it for another one. The original should make good evidence at your trial. As for your citywide test of the drug, you can forget that, too. We got it all back before it could hit the streets, and it's currently being protected by some very trustworthy Guards. Morgan is dead. So is Burns. You're on your own now, Nightingale."

"You can't arrest me," said Lord Nightingale. "I have diplomatic immunity."

"I think your people can be persuaded to waive that," said Hawk. "You'll be surprised how fast they disown you, to avoid being implicated themselves. After all, no one loves a failure. They'll probably let us hang you right here in Haven, if we ask them nicely."

Lord Nightingale suddenly raised his hands and spoke a Word of Power, and halfway down the hall the air split open. A howling wind came roaring out of the widening split, carrying a rush of thick snow and a bitter blast of cold. Within seconds, a blizzard raged in the narrow hallway, and the temperature plummeted. Ice formed thickly on the doors and walls, and made the floor treacherous underfoot. Hawk raised an arm to protect his face as the freezing wind cut at his exposed skin like a knife. The cold was so intense it burned, and even the shallowest breath was painful.

Hawk glared about him into the swirling snow, trying to

locate Lord Nightingale, but he and everyone else had become little more than shadows in the roaring white. From behind him, he could hear something howling in the world beyond the gateway that Nightingale had opened. It sounded huge and angry and utterly inhuman. More howls sounded over the roaring of the blizzard and the buffeting wind, growing louder all the time, and Hawk realised the creatures were slowly drawing nearer. He staggered forward, head bent against the wind, until his flailing arms found the nearest wall. Nightingale would be just as blind in this storm as everyone else, so he had to be following the wall to find his way out. All Hawk had to do was make his way down the wall after him—assuming he hadn't got so turned around in the blizzard that he'd ended up against the wrong wall. . . . Hawk decided he wasn't going to think about that. He had to be right.

And then his heart leapt in his chest as a door suddenly opened to his right, revealing the startled faces of the other delegates. The force of the storm quickly threw them back into the study, where they struggled to close the door again, but Hawk took little notice. He knew now that he'd found the right wall. The howling of the creatures came again, rising eerily over the sound of the storm. They sounded very close. Hawk ran down the corridor, slipping and sliding on the ice, his shoulder pressed against the wall. A shadow loomed up before him. Hawk threw himself forward, grabbed the figure by the shoulder, and slammed it back against the wall. He thrust his face close up against the other's, and smiled savagely as he recognised Nightingale's frightened face.

"We've got to get out of here!" shouted Nightingale, his voice barely audible over the roar of the blizzard. "The creatures will be here soon!"

"I've got a better idea," said Hawk, not caring if the Outremer lord heard him. He took a firm hold of Nightingale's collar and dragged him kicking and struggling back down the corridor towards the gateway he'd opened.

Hawk had to fight the force of the storm with every step, as well as hang on to Nightingale with a hand so numb he could barely feel his grip anymore, and he thought for a while that he wasn't going to make it. But then suddenly he was close enough to make out the split in the air, stretching from floor to ceiling, and he lurched to a halt. The split was wider now. Huge dark shadows moved in the blizzard beyond the gateway. The creatures were almost there. Their howls were deafening. Hawk put his mouth against Nightingale's ear.

"Close the gateway! Close it, or I swear I'll throw you through that opening and let those things have you!"

Nightingale lifted his hands and chanted something, the words lost in the tumult of the blizzard and the creatures' incessant howling. For a long, heart-stopping moment nothing happened, and then the split in the air snapped together and was gone, and the blizzard collapsed. The sudden silence was shocking, and everyone just stood where they were, numbly watching the last of the snow drift lazily on the air before falling to the floor. The corridor seemed a little less cold, but their breath still steamed on the air before them. Nightingale lurched away from Hawk, and headed down the corridor at a shaky run. Hawk caught up with him before he'd gone a dozen paces, and clubbed him from behind with the butt of his axe. Nightingale fell limply into the thick snow on the floor, and lay still. Hawk leaned over him and hit him again, just to be sure. Then he dragged him back to the others. Ap Owen shook his head unhappily.

"They won't let us put him on trial, you know. He'd be an embarrassment to both sides, and probably prevent any future Talks. And besides, diplomatic immunity's too important a concept in troubled times like these. They'll never allow it to be waived, no matter what the crime."

"You mean he's going to get away with it?" said Fisher, scowling dangerously.

Ap Owen shrugged. "Like I said; he's an embarrassment. His own people will probably take away his position and privileges and send him into internal exile, but that's about it."

"Right," said Hawk. "Technically, for what he tried to do, he should be executed, but there's no way that will happen. Aristocrats don't believe in passing death sentences on their own kind if they can avoid it. It might give the peasants ideas." He looked down at Nightingale's unconscious body, his face set and cold. "So many people dead, because of him. All the people who might have died. And

I almost raised my axe against Isobel. . . . If I killed him now, no one would say anything. They'd probably even thank me for getting rid of such an embarrassment."

"You can't just kill him in cold blood!" protested ap Owen.

"No," said Hawk finally. "I can't. Even after all these years in Haven, I still know what's right and what's wrong. I only kill when I have to. I know my duty."

"Look on the bright side," said Mistique cheerfully. "You found the drug before it hit the streets, exposed the traitor in the Guard, and with Nightingale removed from the Talks, they might actually start agreeing on things. You've saved the city and possibly averted a war. What more do you want?"

Hawk and Fisher looked at each other.

"Overtime," said Hawk firmly.

10

Loose Ends

As prisons went, it wasn't too bad. Certainly Lord Nightingale had spent longer periods under far worse conditions during his travels. He'd known some country inns that boasted accommodations so primitive even a leper would have turned up what was left of his nose at them. His present circumstances were surprisingly pleasant, and, all things considered, the Outremer Embassy in Haven had gone out of its way to treat him with every courtesy. He was confined in one of the Embassy's guest rooms, with every comfort the staff could provide, until such time as he could be escorted back to Outremer. And given the current appalling weather conditions, that could be quite some time.

Nightingale didn't mind. The longer the better, as far as he was concerned. He was already filling his time writing carefully worded letters to certain people of standing and influence back in Outremer. There were quite a few who shared his feelings about the coming war, people who could be trusted to see that his cause was presented to the King in its most positive light. He'd have to spend some time in internal exile, of course; that was only to be expected. But once the war began, as it inevitably would, and his associates became men of power at Court, he would undoubtably be summoned again, and his present little setback would be nothing more than an unfortunate memory. In the meantime, his current captors were being very careful to treat him with the utmost respect, for fear of alienating the wrong people. You could always rely on diplomats to appreciate the political realities; particularly when their own careers might be at risk.

So, for the moment, Nightingale bided his time and was the perfect prisoner, never once complaining or making any fuss, and the time passed pleasantly enough. There were books to read and letters to write, and a steady stream of visitors from among the Embassy staff, just stopping by for a chat, and dropping not especially subtle hints of encouragement and support, in the hope of being remembered in the future. True, his door was always locked, and there was an armed guard in the corridor outside his room, but given the current circumstances, Nightingale found that rather reassuring. If word of what he'd intended were to get out in Haven, the populace would quite probably attempt to storm the building and drag him out to hang him from the nearest lamppost. You couldn't expect the rabble to understand the importance of concepts like diplomatic immunity.

There was a sudden knocking at the door, and Nightingale jumped in spite of himself. He cleared his throat carefully, and called for his visitor to enter. A key turned in the lock, and the heavy door swung open to reveal Major de Tournay, carrying a bottle of wine. Nightingale was somewhat surprised to see the Major, but kept all trace of it from his face. De Tournay had taken the news of Nightingale's treachery surprisingly calmly, given that his life had been one of those threatened, but even so he was one of the last people Nightingale had expected to drop by for a chat. Still, recent events had done much to turn up unexpected allies.

"Come in, my dear Major," he said warmly. "Is that wine for me? How splendid." He studied the bottle's label, and raised an appreciative eyebrow. "I'm obliged to you, de Tournay. The Ambassador means well, but his cellar is shockingly depleted."

"I need to talk to you, my lord," said de Tournay bluntly. He looked vaguely round the room, as though embarrassed to be there and unsure how to proceed. Nightingale waved for him to sit down on a chair opposite, and the Major did so, sitting stiffly and almost at attention. "We need to discuss the present situation, my lord. There are matters which need to be . . . clarified."

"Of course, Major. But first, let us sample this excellent wine you've brought me."

De Tournay nodded, and watched woodenly as Nightingale removed the cork, sniffed it, and poured them both a generous glass. They toasted each other politely, but though de Tournay drank deeply, his attention remained fixed on Nightingale rather than the wine.

"Before we begin, Major," said Nightingale, leaning elegantly back in his chair, "perhaps you would oblige me by bringing me up to date on what is happening with Captains Hawk and Fisher. I must confess I half expect every knock at my door to be them, come to drag me off in chains to face Haven justice, or worse still, administer it themselves."

"You needn't worry about them," said de Tournay. "They had their chance to kill you, and chose not to. They understand the realities of the situation. And since they've been cleared of all charges, they're not foolish enough to risk their necks again by harassing you."

"I'm relieved to hear it." Nightingale drank his wine unhurriedly, ignoring de Tournay's impatience to get to the point of his visit. Nightingale smiled. It was very good wine. "Now then, Major, what exactly did you want to see me about?"

"Are there really plans to use this super-chacal drug as a weapon in a war against Haven?"

"Of course. I feel sure it will be very effective. The few test results we've seen have been very promising."

"It's a dishonourable way to fight a war," said de Tournay flatly.

Nightingale laughed, honestly amused. "There's nothing honourable about war, Major. It's nothing but slaughter and destruction on a grand scale, and the more efficiently it's pursued, the better. The drug is just another weapon, that's all."

"But your way leaves no room for heroes or triumphs. Only the spectacle of mad animals, tearing each other to pieces."

Nightingale poured himself another glass of wine, and topped up de Tournay's. "I take it you're one of those people who doesn't want this war, de Tournay. Allow me to remind you that a war is vital if your career is to advance at all. There's no other way for you to gain rank or position so quickly. Or are you content to be a Major all your life?"

"I have ambitions. But I'd prefer to obtain my advances cleanly and honourably."

"Oh, don't worry, Major. There will be plenty of honest slaughter for you and your troops to get involved in. The drug will be used mainly against the civilian population, as a means of destroying morale. You should be grateful, Major. The drug will make your job a great deal easier. Leave policy to the politicians, de Tournay. It's not your province to worry about such things."

De Tournay shrugged. "Maybe you're right." He rose abruptly to his feet, gulped down the last of his wine, and put down the empty glass with unnecessary force. "I'm afraid I can't stay any longer, my lord. Business to attend to. Enjoy your wine." He bowed formally and left, shutting the door quietly behind him.

Nightingale listened to the key turning in the lock, and shrugged. Poor, innocent Major de Tournay. A good judge of wine, though. He raised his glass in a sardonic toast to the closed door.

De Tournay walked unhurriedly down the corridor, and nodded to the bored guard standing at the far end. "The Lord Nightingale doesn't wish to be disturbed for the rest of the afternoon. See to it, would you?"

The guard nodded, and then smiled his thanks at the Major's generous tip. De Tournay made his way through the bustling corridors of the Embassy and out into the packed streets, paying no attention to anyone he passed, lost in his own thoughts. The wine should be taking effect soon. There was a certain ironic justice in Nightingale's falling prey to the very drug he'd championed so highly. It hadn't been too difficult to obtain a small supply of the super-chacal from Guard Headquarters, though procuring an antidote he could take in advance had proved rather expensive. But he'd known he'd have to drink the wine too, so Nightingale wouldn't be suspicious. The drug should be raging through Nightingale's system by now. Left alone, locked in his room, Lord Nightingale would tear himself apart, victim of his own murderous intentions. Which only went to prove there was some justice in the world. You just had to help it along now and again.

De Tournay smiled briefly, and walked off into the city, disappearing into the milling crowds.

Hawk and Fisher stood together outside Guard Headquarters, watching the crowds. They'd been officially cleared of all outstanding charges, officially yelled at for getting themselves into such a mess in the first place by going off on their own, officially congratulated for exposing the traitors Burns and Nightingale, and very officially refused any extra overtime payments. At which point Hawk and Fisher had decided it was time to leave, before things got even more complicated. Hawk thought briefly about apologising to Commander Glen for hitting him, but one look at Glen's simmering glare was enough to convince him it might not be the best time to bring the matter up.

He smiled regretfully, and looked about him. The streets were packed with people trudging determinedly through the snow and slush, none of them paying Hawk and Fisher any attention at all. Hawk grinned. He liked it that way. After everything they'd been through, it made a pleasant change.

"I still can't believe how quickly everyone believed you were crazy and I was a traitor," said Fisher. "When you consider everything we've done for this city . . ."

"Yeah, well," said Hawk. "That's Haven for you. And it has to be said, our reputations didn't help. Half of Haven thinks we're crazy anyway for being so honest, and thinking we can change things, and the other half is scared stiff we're going to kill them on sight."

"We need our reputations; we couldn't get any work done without them. It's still no reason to turn on us like that. You know, Hawk, the more I think about it, the more I think Haven is such a worthless cesspool it's not worth saving. It's crooked and corrupt and so steeped in sin we might have done the Low Kingdoms a favour by just staying out of things and letting Morgan dump his drugs onto the streets."

"Now don't be like that, Isobel. Most people in Haven are just like anyone else in any other city—good people struggling to make ends meet, keep their heads above water, and hold their families together. They're too busy working all the hours God sends to think about making trouble. That's why we do this job; because they're worth protecting from the scum out there who try to steal what little those people have. Most people here are all right."

"Yeah?" growled Fisher. "Name two."

She broke off as a woman wrapped in tattered furs waded through the thick slush to get to them. She was hauling along by one hand a little girl of about five or six, so buried under mismatched furs as to be little more than a bundle on legs. The mother lurched to a halt before Hawk and Fisher and stopped for a moment to get her breath. The little girl looked up at Hawk, smiled shyly, and then hid her face behind her mother's leg. The mother nodded to Fisher, and smiled broadly at Hawk.

"I just wanted to say thank you, Captain. For going down into the rubble after the tenement collapsed, and bringing out my little Katie safe and sound. She'd have died, if it hadn't been for you. Thank you."

Hawk looked down at the little girl, and smiled slowly. "They told me she was dead."

"Bless your heart, no, Captain! Someone found her foot in the rubble, and the doctors stuck it back on with a healing spell! And the Guard is paying the bill! Almost makes you believe in miracles. She's right as rain now. Thanks to you, Captain. I never did believe all the terrible things they say about you."

She plunged forward, hugged him tight, kissed him quickly and stepped back again. She nodded to Fisher and set off down the street, hauling her daughter along behind her. The little girl looked back briefly and waved goodbye, and then mother and child disappeared into the crowd and were gone. Fisher looked at Hawk.

"All right, that's two."

The Bones of Haven

The book is dedicated to Grant Morrison, boy genius, and The Waterboys, sui generis, without whose inspiration this book could not have been written.

Haven is an old city, but still growing, with new houses built on the bones of the old. But some parts of Haven are older than others and have never been properly put to rest. Down below the surface of the city, the remains of older structures stir uneasily in their sleep and dream dark thoughts of the way things used to be. There are new buildings all over Haven, and some of them stand on unquiet graves. . . .

1

Hell Wing

Rain had come to Haven with the spring, and a sharp, gusting wind blew it in off the sea. The rain hammered down with mindless ferocity, bouncing back from the cobbles and running down the gutters in raging torrents. Water dripped from every surface, gushed out of drainpipes, and flew in graceful arcs from carved gargoyle mouths on the smarter buildings. It had been raining on and off for weeks, despite everything the city weather wizards could do, and everyone was heartily sick of it. The rain forced itself past slates and tiles and gurgled down chimneys, making fires sputter and smoke. Anyone venturing out into the streets was quickly soaked, and even inside the air seemed saturated with moisture. People gritted their teeth and learned to ignore damp clothing and the constant drumming of rain on the roof. It was the rainy season, and the city endured it as the city endured so many other afflictions—with stubborn defiance and aimless, sullen anger.

And yet things were not as gloomy in the port city of Haven as they might have been. The rain-soaked streets were decked with flags and bunting and decorations, their bright and gaudy colors blazing determinedly through the grayness of the day. Two Kings had come to Haven, and the city was putting on an attractive face and enjoying itself as best it could. It would take more than a little rain to dampen Haven's spirits when it had an excuse to celebrate. A public holiday had been declared from most jobs, on the grounds that the eager citizens would have taken one anyway if it hadn't been granted, and people held street parties between the downpours and boosted the takings at all the inns and taverns. Tarpaulins were erected in the streets wherever possible, to ward off the rain, and beneath them could be found street fairs and conjurers and play-actors and all manner of entertainments.

Of course, not everyone got to take the day off. The city Guard still went about its business, enforcing the law and protecting the good citizens from pickpockets and villains and outrages, and, most important of all, from each other. Haven was a harsh, cruel city swarming with predators, even during a time of supposedly universal celebration. So Hawk and Fisher, husband and wife and Captains in the city Guard, made their way through the dismal gray streets of the Northside and wished they were somewhere else. Anywhere else. They huddled inside their thick black cloaks, and pulled the hoods well forward to keep the rain out of their faces.

Hawk was tall, dark, and no longer handsome. He wore a black silk patch over his right eye, and a series of old scars ran down the right side of his face, giving him a cold, sinister look. Huddled inside his soaking wet black cloak, he looked like a rather bedraggled raven that had known better days. It had to be said that even when seen at his best, he didn't look like much. He was lean and wiry rather than muscular, and was beginning to build a stomach. He wore his dark hair at shoulder length, swept roughly back from his forehead and tied at the nape of his neck with a silver clasp. He'd only just entered his thirties, but already there were streaks of gray in his hair. It would have been easy to dismiss him as just another bravo, perhaps already past his prime, but there was a dangerous alertness in the way he carried himself, and the cold gaze of his single eye was disturbingly direct. He carried a short-handled axe on his right hip, instead of a sword. He was very good with an axe. He'd had lots of practice.

Isobel Fisher walked at his side, unconsciously echoing his pace and stance with the naturalness of long companionship. She was tall, easily six foot in height, and her long blond hair fell to her waist in a single thick plait, weighted at the tip with a polished steel ball. She was in her late twenties, and handsome rather than beautiful, with a raw-boned harshness to her face that contrasted strongly with her deep blue eyes and generous mouth. Some time ago, something had scoured all the human weaknesses out of her, and it showed. Even wrapped in her thick cloak against the driving rain, she moved with a determined, aggressive grace, and her right hand never strayed far from the sword on her hip.

People gave them plenty of room as they approached, and were careful to look away rather than risk catching the Guards' eyes. None of them wanted to be noticed. It wasn't healthy. Hawk and Fisher were feared and respected as two of the toughest and most honest Guards in Haven, and everyone in the Northside had something to hide. It was that kind of area. Hawk glared balefully about him as he and Fisher strode along, and stamped his boots unnecessarily hard on the water-slick cobbles. Fisher chuckled quietly.

"Cheer up, Hawk. Only another month or so of utter misery, and the rainy season will be over. Then you can start looking forward to the utter misery of the boiling hot summer. Always something to look forward to in Haven."

Hawk sniffed. "I hate it when you're this cheerful. It's not natural."

"Me, or the rain?"

"Both." Hawk stepped carefully over a tangled mass of bunting that had fallen from a nearby building. "I can't believe people are still going ahead with celebrations in this downpour."

Fisher shrugged. "Any excuse for a holiday. Besides, they can hardly postpone it, can they? The Kings will only be here two more days. Then it'll all be over, and we can get back to what passes for normal here in the Northside."

Hawk just grunted, not trusting himself to any more than that. His job was hard enough without extra complications. Haven was without doubt the most corrupt and crime-ridden city in the Low Kingdoms, and the Northside was its dark and rotten heart. No crime was too vile or too vicious to be overlooked, and if you could make any kind of profit out of it, you could be sure someone was doing it somewhere. And double-crossing his partner at the same time, like as not. Violence was commonplace, along with rape and murder and protection rackets. Conspiracies blossomed in the shadows, talking treason in lowered voices behind locked doors and shuttered windows. Throughout Haven, the city Guard was stretched thin to breaking point and beyond, but somehow they managed to keep a lid on things, most of the time. Usually by being even harsher and more violent than the people they fought. When they weren't taking sweeteners to look the other way, of course. All of which made it increasingly difficult for anyone to figure out why the Parliaments of both the Low Kingdoms and Outremer had insisted on their respective Kings coming to Haven to sign the new Peace Treaty between the two countries.

It was true that the Peace Talks at which the Treaty had been hammered out had taken place in Haven, but only after the Guard had protected the negotiators from treacherous assault by mercenaries and terrorists. There were a great many people in both countries who had vested interests in seeing the Peace Talks fail, and they'd shown no hesitation in turning Haven into their own private battleground. Hawk and Fisher had managed to smash the worst conspiracy and preserve the Talks, but it had been a very close thing, and everyone knew it. Everyone except the two Parliaments apparently. They'd set their minds on Haven, and weren't going to be talked out of it. Probably because they simply couldn't believe what their Advisors were telling them about the city.

Upon hearing of the singular honour being bestowed on their fair city, Haven's city Councillors practically had a collective coronary, and then began issuing orders in a white-hot panic. No one had ever seen them do so much so quickly. One of the first things they did was to give the Guard strict instructions to get all the villains off the streets as quickly as possible, and throw the lot of them in gaol, for any or no reason. They'd worry about trials and sentences later, if at all. For the moment, all that mattered was rounding up as many villains as possible and keeping them safely out of the way until the Kings had left Haven. The prison Governor came closer to apoplexy than a coronary, though it was a near thing, and demanded hysterically where he was supposed to put all these extra bodies in his already overcrowded prison. That, he was curtly informed, was his problem. So the Guards had gone out into the streets all over the city, backed up by as many men-at-arms and militia as the Council could put together, and started picking up villains and hauling them away. In some cases where their lawyers objected strongly, the Guards took them in as well. Word soon got around, and those miscreants who managed to avoid the sweeps decided it would be wisest to keep their heads down for a while, and quietly disappeared. The crime rate plummeted, overnight.

Which is not to say the city streets suddenly became peaceful and law-abiding. This was Haven, after all. But the usual petty crimes and everyday violence could be more or less controlled by the Guard and kept well away from the Kings and their retinues, which was all that mattered as far as the Council was concerned. No one wanted to think what the city would be like after the Kings had left and most of the villains had to be released from prison due to lack of evidence. To be honest, few people in Haven were thinking that far ahead. In the meantime, Hawk and Fisher patrolled their usual beat in the Northside, and were pleasantly surprised at the change. There were stretches when no one tried to kill anyone else for hours on end.

"What do you think about this Peace Treaty?" said Hawk idly. "Do you think it's going to work?"

Fisher shrugged. "Maybe. As I understand it, the two sides have hammered out a deal that both of them hate but both of them can live with, and that's the best anyone can hope for. Now that they've agreed on a definitive boundary line for the first time in centuries, it should put an end to the recent border clashes at least. Too many good men were dying out there in the borderlands, defending a shaky line on a faded old map to satisfy some politician's pride."

Hawk nodded. "I just wish they'd chosen somewhere else for their signing ceremony. Just by being here, the Kings are a magnet for trouble. Every fanatic, assassin, and terrorist for miles around will see this as their big chance, and head straight for Haven with blood in their eyes and steel in their hands."

"Come on," said Fisher. "You've got to admit, the Kings' security is pretty impressive. They've got four heavy-duty sorcerers with them, a private army of men-at-arms, and a massive deputation of honour guards from the Brotherhood of Steel. I could conquer a minor country with a security force that size."

Hawk sniffed, unimpressed. "No security is ever perfect; you know that. All it needs is one fanatic with a knife and a martyr's complex in the right place at the right time, and we could have two dead Kings on our hands. And you can bet Haven would end up taking all the blame, not the security people. They should never have come here, Isobel. I've got a real bad feeling about this."

"You have bad feelings about everything."

"And I'm usually right."

Isobel looked at him knowingly. "You're just miffed because they wouldn't let any Haven Guards into their security force."

"Damn right I'm annoyed. We know the situation here; they don't. But I can't really blame them, much as I'd like to. Everyone knows the Guard in this city is rife with corruption, and after our last case, no one trusts anyone anymore. After all, if even we can come under suspicion . . ."

"We proved our innocence, and exposed the real traitor."

"Doesn't make a blind bit of difference." Hawk scowled and shook his head slowly. "I still can't believe how ready everyone was to accept we were guilty. After all we've done for this city. . . . Anyway, from now on, there'll always be someone ready to point the finger and mutter about no smoke without fire."

"Anyone points a finger at me," said Fisher calmly, "I'll cut it off, and make him eat it. Now, stop worrying about the Kings; they're not our responsibility."

They walked a while in silence, kicking occasionally at loose debris in the street. The rain seemed to be letting up a bit. Every now and again someone up on a roof would throw something down at them, but Hawk and Fisher just ignored it. Thanks to the overhanging upper floors of the buildings, it was rare for anything to come close enough to do any harm, and there was no point in trying to chase after whoever was responsible. By the time the Guards could get up to the roof, the culprits would be gone, and both sides knew it. They were in more danger from a suddenly emptied chamber pot from an upper window. You had to expect that kind of thing in the Northside. Even if you were the infamous Hawk and Fisher.

Hawk scowled as he strode along, brooding over recent events. It wasn't that long ago that most of Haven had been convinced he'd gone berserk, killing anyone who got in the way of his own personal vendetta outside the law. It hadn't been true, and eventually he'd proved it, but that wasn't the point. He knew he had a reputation for violence; he'd gone to great pains to establish it. It kept the villains and the hardcases off his back, and made the small fry too nervous to give him any trouble. But even so, the speed with which people believed he'd gone bad had disturbed him greatly. For the first time, he'd seen himself as others saw him, and he didn't like what he saw.

"We never used to be this hard," he said quietly. "These days, every time I look at someone I'm thinking about the best way to take them out before they can get to me. Whether they're behaving aggressively or not. Whenever I talk to someone, part of me is listening for a lie or an evasion. And more and more, I tend to assume a suspect is bound to be guilty, unless hard evidence proves them innocent."

"In the Northside, they usually are guilty," said Fisher.

"That's not the point! I always said I'd never laid a finger on an honest man, or killed anyone who didn't need killing. I'm not so sure of that anymore. I'm not infallible. I make mistakes. Only thing is, my mistakes could cost someone their life. When we first took on this job, I really thought we could do some good, make a difference, help protect the people who needed protection. But now, everyone I meet gets weighed as a potential enemy, and I care more about nailing villains than I do about protecting their victims. We've changed, Isobel. The job has changed us. Maybe . . . we should think about leaving Haven. I don't like what we've become."

Fisher looked at him anxiously. "We're only as hard as we need to be to get the job done. This city is full of human wolves, ready to tear us apart at the first sign of weakness. It's only our reputation for sudden death and destruction that keeps them at bay. Remember what it was like when we first started? We had to prove ourselves every day, fighting and killing every hardcase with a sword and a grudge, just to earn the right to walk the streets in peace. Now they've learned to leave us alone, we can get things done. Look, we're a reflection of the people we're guarding. If they start acting civilized and playing by the rule book, so will I. Until then, we just do what we have to, to get the job done."

"But that's the point, Isobel. Why do the job? What difference does it make? For every villain we put away, there are a dozen more we can't touch who are just waiting to take his place. We bust our arses every day, and nothing ever changes. Except us."

"Now, don't start that again. We have made a difference. Sure, things are bad now, but they were much worse before we came. And they'd be worse again if we left. You can't expect to change centuries of accumulated evil and despair in a few short years. We do the best we can, and protect the good people every chance we get. Anything above and beyond that is a bonus. You've got to be realistic, Hawk."

"Yeah. Maybe." Hawk stared straight ahead of him, looking through the driving rain without seeing it. "I've lost my way, Isobel. I don't like what I am, what I'm doing, what I've become. This isn't what I meant to do with my life, but I don't know what else to do. We are needed here; you're right about that. But some days I look in the mirror and I don't recognize my face at all. I hear people talking about things I've done and it doesn't sound like me. Not the me I remember being, before we came here. I've lost my way. And I don't know how to find it again."

Fisher scowled unhappily, and decided she'd better change the subject. "I know what your problem is. You're just brooding because I've put you on another diet."

Hawk smiled in spite of himself. "Right. I must be getting old, lass; I never used to put on weight like this. I can't believe I've had to let my belt out *another* notch. When I was younger I had so much energy I used to burn off food as fast as I could eat it. These days, I only have to look at a dessert and my waistline expands. I should never have admitted turning thirty. That was when the rot set in."

"Never mind, dear," said Fisher. "When we get back home tonight I'll put out your pipe and slippers, and you can have a nice doze in your chair by the fire before dinner."

Hawk looked at her. "Don't push your luck, Isobel."

She laughed. "Well, it serves you right. Anyone would think you were on your last legs and doddering towards the grave, to hear you talk. There's nothing wrong with you that a good fight in a good cause couldn't put right. In the meantime, no desserts, cut down on the meat, and lots of nice healthy salads. And no more snacks in between meals, either."

"Why does everything that's good for you have to taste so damned bland?" complained Hawk. "And I don't care if lettuce is good for me; I'm not eating it. Flaming rabbit food . . ."

They continued on their way through the Northside, doing their rounds and showing their faces. Hawk seemed in a somewhat better mood but was still unusually quiet. Fisher decided to let him brood, and not push it. He'd had these moods before, and always snapped out of it eventually. Together, they checked out three burglaries, and lectured one shopkeeper on the need for bolts as well as locks on his doors and window shutters. None of the burglaries were anything special, just routine break-ins. Not much point in looking for clues. Sooner or later they'd catch someone in the act, and he'd confess to a whole bunch of others crimes and that would be that. After the burglaries, they got involved in a series of assaults, sorting out tavern brawls, muggings, and finally a domestic dispute. Hawk hated being dragged into domestic quarrels. You couldn't win. Whatever you did was bound to be wrong.

They approached the location of the domestic dispute cautiously, but at least this time there was no flying crockery to dodge. Or flying knives. The address was a poky little apartment in the middle of a row of shabby tenements. Neighbors watched silently as the two Guards entered the building. Hawk took the lead and kept a careful eye on the house's occupants as they made way before him. Guards were the common enemy of all Northsiders; they represented and enforced all the laws and authority that kept the poor in their place. As a result, Guards were targets for anyone with a grudge or a mad on, and one of the nastier surprise attacks these days was the Haven mud pie—a mixture of lye and grease. Thrown at close range, the effect could be devastating. The lye burned through clothing as though it wasn't there, and if it hit bare skin it could eat its way right down to the bone. The grease made the lye stick like glue. Even a small mud pie could put a Guard in hospital for weeks, if his partner didn't get him to a doctor fast enough. And doctors tended to be few and far between in the Northside. The last man to aim a mud pie at Hawk had got both his arms broken, but there were any number of borderline crazies in the Northside, just waiting to be pushed over the edge by one frustration too many. So Hawk and Fisher stayed close together and kept a wary eye on shadowed corners and doors left just a little too far ajar.

They made their way through the hall and up the narrow stairs without incident. Mothers and small children watched in stony silence, while from above came the sound of domestic unrest. A man and a woman were shouting and screeching at the tops of their voices, but Hawk and Fisher didn't let themselves be hurried. As long as the couple were still shouting they weren't searching for blunt instruments or something with a sharp edge. It was when things went suddenly quiet that you had to worry. Hawk and Fisher reached the landing and strode down the hall, stepping over small children playing unconcernedly on the floor. They found the door with the right number, the sounds from within made it pretty hard to miss. Hawk hammered on the door with his fist, and an angry male voice broke off from its tirade just long enough to tell him to go to hell. Hawk tried again, and got a torrent of abuse for his trouble. He shrugged, drew his axe, and kicked the door in.

A man and a woman looked round in surprise as Hawk and Fisher stood in the doorway taking in the scene. The woman was less than average height, and more than a little undernourished, with a badly bruised face and a bloody nose. She was trying to stop the flowing blood with a grubby handkerchief, and not being very successful. The man was easily twice her size, with muscles on his muscles, and he was brandishing a fist the size of a mallet. His face was dark with rage, and he glared sullenly at Hawk and Fisher as he took in their Guards' cloaks.

"What are you doing here? You've no business in this house, so get out. And if you've damaged my door I'll see you pay for the repairs!"

Hawk smiled coldly. "If you've damaged that woman, you'll pay for it. Now, stand back from her and put down that fist, and we'll all have a nice little chat."

"This is family business," said the man quickly, before the woman could say anything. He lowered his fist, but stood his ground defiantly.

Fisher moved forward to speak to the woman, and the man fell back a step in spite of himself. She ignored him, and spoke softly to the woman. "Does this kind of thing happen often?"

"Often enough," said the woman indistinctly, behind her handkerchief.

Fisher frowned. "Just say the word, and we'll drag him off to gaol. You don't have to put up with this. Are you married to him?"

The woman shrugged. "More or less. He's not so bad, most of the time, but he can't keep a job because of his temper. He just lost another one today."

"So he comes home and takes it out on you." Fisher nodded understandingly.

"That's enough!" snapped the man suddenly, stung at being talked about as though he wasn't there. "She's got nothing more to say to you, Guard, if she knows what's good for her. And you two can get out now, or I'll throw you out."

Hawk stirred, and looked at him with interest. "You and what army?"

"I really think you should swear out a complaint against him," said Fisher. "Next time he might not just break your nose. A few nights in gaol might calm him down a bit, and if nothing else, it should make him think twice about hitting you again."

The woman nodded slowly. "You're right. I'll swear out a complaint."

"You lousy bitch!" The man lurched forward, raising his huge hands menacingly. Fisher turned and smacked him solidly between the eyes with her fist. The man fell back a step and then sat down abruptly, blinking dazedly. Fisher looked at Hawk.

"We'd better get him downstairs. You take one arm and I'll take the other."

"Right," said Hawk. "There's some railings outside we can chain him to until we can find a Constable to take him back to Headquarters for charging."

They got him to his feet easily enough and were heading for the door when Hawk, hearing a muffled cry behind them, looked back just in time to see the woman heading straight for him with a knife in her hand. Hawk dropped

the man and stepped quickly to one side, but the woman
kept coming at him, her eyes wild and desperate. Fisher
stuck out a leg and tripped her. The woman fell heavily
and lost her grip on the knife. Hawk stepped forward and
kicked it out of reach. The woman burst into tears. Hawk
looked at Fisher.

"What the hell was that all about?"

"She loves him," said Fisher, shaking her head sadly.
"She might not like the treatment, but she loves him just
the same. And when she saw us hauling him off to gaol,
she forgot how angry she was and decided we were the
villains of the piece, for threatening her man. . . . Now we
have to take them both in. Can't let anyone get away with
attacking a Guard, or we'll never have any peace."

Hawk nodded reluctantly, and they set about manhandling the man and the woman down the stairs and out into
the street.

They found a Constable, eventually, and let him take
over, then set off on their beat again. The rain continued
to show signs of letting up without ever actually doing anything about it. The day wore slowly on, fairly quiet by
Northside standards. Hawk and Fisher broke up half a
dozen fights, ran off a somewhat insecure flasher, and
helped talk a leaper out of jumping from a second-story
building. The city didn't really care if a leaper killed himself
or not, but there was always the chance he might land on
someone important, so official policy in such cases was to
clear the street below and then just let the would-be suicide
get on with it. As in many other things, Hawk and Fisher
ignored official policy and took the time to talk quietly and
encouragingly to the man, until he agreed to go down the
normal way, via the stairs. The odds were that by tomorrow
he'd be back up on the roof again, but at least they'd
bought him some time to think it over. Working in the
Northside, you learned to be content with little victories.

"You know," said Hawk as he and Fisher walked away,
"sometimes, when I'm up on a roof with a leaper, I have
an almost overwhelming urge to sneak up behind him and
shout Boo! in his ear. Just to see what would happen."

"You're weird, Hawk," said Fisher, and he nodded solemnly. At which point a rush of gentle flute music poured

through their minds, followed by the dry, acid voice of the Guard communications sorcerer.

All Guards in the Northern sector, report immediately to Damnation Row, where there is a major riot in progress. This order supersedes all other instructions. Do not discuss the situation with anyone else until you have reported to the prison Governor. That is all.

Hawk scowled grimly as he and Fisher turned around and headed back down the street shoulders hunched against the renewed heavy rain. Damnation Row was Haven's oldest and largest prison, as well as the most secure. A great squat monstrosity of basalt stone, surrounded on all sides by high walls and potent sorceries, it was infamous throughout the Low Kingdoms as the one prison no one ever escaped from. Riots were almost unknown, never mind a major riot. No wonder they'd been instructed not to talk about it. The prison's reputation was part of its protection. Besides, if word did get out, the streets would be thronged with people heading for the prison to try and help the inmates break out. Most people in Haven knew someone in Damnation Row.

The prison itself stood jammed up against the city wall on the far boundary of the Northside, and Hawk and Fisher could see its outline through the driving rain long before they got to its gatehouse. The exterior walls were huge, dark, and largely featureless, and seemed especially grim and forbidding through the downpour. Hawk hauled on the steel bell pull at the main gate, and waited impatiently with Fisher for someone to answer. He'd never been inside Damnation Row before and was curious to see if it was as bad as everyone said. Conditions inside were supposed to be deliberately appalling. Haven had nothing but contempt for anyone dumb enough or unsuccessful enough to get caught, and the idea was that a stay in Damnation Row would scare the offender so much he'd do anything rather than be sent back—including going straight. The prison's excellent security record also made it a useful dumping ground for dangerous lunatics, untrustworthy magic-users, and political and religious embarrassments. The city firmly believed in taking revenge on its enemies. All of them.

Hawk yanked on the bell pull again, hammered on the door with his fist, and kicked it a few times for good measure. All he got out of it was a stubbed toe and an unsympathetic glance from Fisher. Finally a sliding panel in the door jerked open and a grim-faced prison guard studied their Guards' uniforms for a long moment before slamming the panel shut and opening the judas gate in the main door to let them in. Hawk and Fisher identified themselves, and weren't even given time to dump their dripping wet cloaks before being hustled through the outer precincts of the prison to the Governor's office. Everywhere they looked there was bedlam, with prison guards running this way and that, shouting orders no one listened to and getting in each other's way. Off in the distance they could hear a dull roar of raised voices and the hammering of hard objects on iron bars.

The Governor's office was comfortably furnished, but clearly a place of work rather than relaxation. The walls were bare save for a number of past and present *Wanted* posters, and two framed testimonials. The plain, almost austere desk was buried under paperwork, split more or less equally into two piles marked "Pending" and "Urgent." The Governor, Phillipe Dexter, stood up from behind his desk to shake hands briefly with Hawk and Fisher, gestured for them to take a seat, and then returned to his own chair quickly, as though only sheer willpower had kept him on his feet that long. He was an average-looking man in his late forties, dressed fashionably but conservatively, and had a bland, politician's face. At the moment he looked tired and drawn, and his hand had trembled slightly with fatigue when Hawk shook it. The two Guards took off their cloaks and draped them over the coat rack before sitting down. The Governor watched the cloaks dripping heavily on his carpet, and closed his eyes for a moment, as though that was definitely the last straw.

"How long has this riot been going on?" asked Hawk, to get the ball rolling.

"Almost four hours now." The Governor scowled unhappily, but his voice was calm and measured. "We thought we could contain it at first, but we just didn't have the manpower. This prison has always suffered from overcrowding, with two or even three inmates locked up in a cell originally meant for one. Mainly because Haven has almost doubled in size since this prison was built. But we coped, because we had to. There was nowhere else to put the prisoners; all the other gaols in Haven are just holding pens and debtors' prisons, and they face the same problem as us. But, thanks to the Council's ill-advised purge of the streets, we've had prisoners arriving here in the hundreds over the last week or so, and my staff just couldn't cope with the resulting crush. We had four, sometimes five, to a cell in some places, and not even enough warning to allow for extra food and blankets. Something had to give.

"The prisoners decided this morning that they couldn't be treated any worse than they already were, and attacked the prison staff during breakfast and slopping-out. The violence soon spread, and we didn't have enough manpower to put it down. Essentially, we've lost half the prison. Barricades and booby traps have been set up by the inmates in all the approaches to two of the main Wings, and they've been throwing everything they can get their hands on at us to make us keep our distance. They've started several fires, but so far the prison's security spells have been able to stamp them out before they could get out of control. So far, no one's actually escaped. Our perimeter is still secure.

"We've tried to negotiate with the inmates, but none of them have shown any interest in talking. Pretty soon the Council is going to order me to take the occupied Wings back by force, before the Kings get to hear about the riot and start getting worried. But that, believe it or not, isn't the main problem. Adjoining the two occupied Wings is Hell Wing, where we keep our supernatural prisoners. Creatures of power and magic, locked away here while awaiting trial. Hell Wing is in its own pocket dimension, surrounded by powerful wards, so it should still be secure. But there are reported to be several magic-users among the rioters, and if they find a way into Hell Wing and set those creatures loose, a whole army of Guards wouldn't be enough to control them."

Hawk and Fisher looked at each other, and then back at the Governor. "If it's as serious as all that," said Hawk, "why are you wasting time talking to us? You need somebody with real power, like the God Squad, or the SWAT team."

The Governor nodded quickly. "The God Squad have been alerted, but at present they're busy coping with an

emergency on the Street of Gods. I've sent for the Special
Wizardry and Tactics team; they're on their way. When
they get here, I want you two to work with them. You've
both worked with the God Squad in the past, you have
experience coping with supernatural creatures, and you
have a reputation for salvaging impossible situations. And
right now, I'm so desperate I'll grab at any straw."

There was a brief knocking at the door, and it swung
open before the Governor could even ask who it was. A
woman and three men filed into the office and slammed
the door shut behind them. The woman fixed the Governor
with a harsh gaze.

"You sent for the SWAT team. We're here. Don't worry,
we've been briefed." She looked at Hawk and Fisher.
"What are they doing here?"

"They'll be working with you on this," said the Governor
firmly, trying to regain control of the situation. "The God
Squad's been delayed. These two officers are . . ."

"I know who they are." The woman nodded briskly to
Hawk and Fisher. "I'm Jessica Winter, team leader and
tactician. My associates are Stuart Barber, weaponmaster;
John MacReady, negotiator; and Storm, sorcerer. That
takes care of introductions; anything more can wait till
later; we're on a tight schedule and time's running out.
Let's go. Sit tight, Governor; you'll have your prison back
in a few hours. Oh, and if any more Guards arrive, keep
them out of our way."

She smiled briefly, and hustled her people out of the
office before the Governor could work up a reply. Hawk
and Fisher nodded to him and hurried out after the SWAT
team. Jessica Winter led the way down the corridor with
casual confidence, and Hawk took the opportunity to surreptitiously study his new partners. He knew them all by
reputation but had never worked with any of them before.

Winter was a short, stocky woman with a determined,
friendly manner that reminded Hawk irresistibly of an amiable bulldog. She was in her early thirties and looked it,
and clearly didn't give a damn. She'd been through two
husbands that Hawk knew of, and was currently pursuing
her third. She moved and spoke with a brisk, no-nonsense
efficiency, and by all accounts could be charming or overwhelming as the mood took her. She was dressed in a sim-

ple shirt and trousers, topped with a chain-mail vest that had been polished within an inch of its life, and wore a sword on her hip in a plain, regulation issue scabbard. She'd been with the SWAT team for seven years, two of them as leader and tactician. She had a good if somewhat spotty record, and preferred to dismiss her failures as learning experiences. Given that her team usually wasn't called in until things had got totally out of hand, Winter had built up a good reputation for finding solutions to problems at the last possible moment. She also had a reputation for convoluted and devious strategies, which Hawk felt might come in very handy just at the moment. He had a strong feeling there was a lot more to this situation than met the eye.

He glanced across at Stuart Barber, the weaponmaster, and felt a little reassured. Even walking down an empty corridor in the midst of friends and allies, Barber exuded an air of danger and menace. He was a tall, powerfully-built man in his mid-twenties, with arms so tightly muscled the veins bulged fiercely even when his arms were apparently relaxed. He had a broad, brutal-looking sword on his hip, in a battered leather scabbard, and wore a long chain-mail vest that had been repaired many times, not always neatly. He had a long, angular head, with pale, pinched features accentuated by dark hair cropped short in a military cut. He had a constant slight scowl that made him look more thoughtful than bad-tempered.

John MacReady, the negotiator, looked like everyone's favourite uncle. It was his job to talk people out of things before Winter let Barber loose on them. MacReady was average height and well-padded, in a friendly, non-threatening way. He smiled a lot, and had the charming gift of convincing people he was giving them his entire attention while they were talking. He was in his mid-forties, going bald, and trying to hide it with a somewhat desperate hairstyle. He had an easy, companiable way about him that made him hard to distrust, but Hawk decided to try anyway. He didn't put much faith in people who smiled too much. It wasn't natural.

The sorcerer called Storm was a large, awkward-looking man in his late twenties. He was easily six foot six inches, and his broad frame made him look even taller. His robe of sorcerer's black looked as if it hadn't been cleaned in months, and the state of his long black hair and beard suggested they'd never even been threatened with a comb. He scowled fiercely at nothing and everything, and just grunted whenever Winter addressed him. His hands curled and uncurled into fists at his side, and he strode along with his beard jutting out before him, as though just waiting for some fool to pick a quarrel with him. All in all, he looked rather like some mystical hermit who'd spent years in a cave meditating on the nature of man and the universe, and came up with some very unsatisfactory answers. The sorcerer looked round suddenly, and caught Hawk's eye.

"What are you staring at?"

"I was just wondering about your name," said Hawk easily.

"My name? What about it?"

"Well, Storm's not exactly a usual name for a sorcerer. A weather wizard, maybe, but . . ."

"It suits me," said the sorcerer flatly. "Want to make something of it?"

Hawk thought about it for a moment, and then shook his head. "Not right now. I was just curious."

Storm sniffed dismissively, and looked away. Jessica Winter fell back a few steps to walk alongside Hawk. She smiled at him briefly. "Don't mind Storm," she said briskly, not bothering to lower her voice. "He's a gloomy bugger, but he knows his job."

"Just what kind of a setup are we walking into?" asked Fisher, moving up on Hawk's other side. "As I understand it, you've had a full briefing. We just got the edited highlights."

Winter nodded quickly. "Not surprisingly, the situation isn't as simple and straightforward as it appears. The riot broke out far too suddenly and too efficiently for it to have been entirely spontaneous. Somebody had to be behind it, pulling the strings and pointing people in the right direction. But the Governor's attempts to negotiate got nowhere, because the rioters couldn't agree on a leader to represent them. Which suggests that whoever is behind the riot is keeping his head down. Which in turn suggests that person had his own reasons for starting it."

"Like breaking someone out, under cover of the chaos?" said Fisher.

"Got it in one," said Winter. "But so far no one's got out over the walls or through the gates; the prison guards have seen to that. The Governor's insistence on regular panic drills seems to have paid off. The real problem lies with Hell Wing, which is where we come in. If someone's managed to get in there and bust any of those creatures loose, we could be in real trouble. You could break out any number of people in the chaos that would cause. And if that someone's let them all loose . . . we might as well evacuate the entire city."

"That bad?" said Hawk.

"Worse."

Hawk thought about it. "Might this be a good time to suggest a strategic retreat, so we can wait for the God Squad to back us up?"

Storm sniffed loudly. "The word retreat isn't in our vocabulary."

"It's in mine," said Hawk.

"Just how well-confined are these supernatural prisoners?" asked Fisher hurriedly.

"Very," said Winter. "Hell Wing is a separate pocket dimension linked to Damnation Row by a single doorway, protected by armed guards and a number of powerful magical wards. Each inmate is confined separately behind bars of cold iron, backed up by an individually tailored geas, a magical compulsion that prevents them from escaping. There's never been an escape from Hell Wing. The system's supposed to be foolproof."

"Unless it's been sabotaged from inside," said Hawk.

"Exactly."

Fisher frowned. "All of this suggests the riot was planned well in advance. But the prison didn't become dangerously overcrowded until just recently."

"It was a fairly predictable situation," said Winter. "Once it was known the Kings were coming here. Especially if our mysterious planners knew of that in advance."

From up ahead came the sound of ragged cheering, interspersed with occasional screams and catcalls.

"We'll have to take it carefully from here on in," said MacReady quietly. "We're getting close to the occupied

Wings. We have to pass right by them to get to Hell Wing. The Governor's going to try and distract them with new attempts at negotiating, but there's no telling how long that will last. It's bedlam in there."

A scream rose suddenly in the distance, drowned out quickly by stamping feet and baying voices. Fisher shivered despite herself.

"What the hell are they doing?"

"They'll have got to the sex offenders by now," said MacReady. "There's a social status among criminals, even in Damnation Row, and sex offenders and child molesters are right at the bottom of the list. The other prisoners loathe and despise them. They call them beasts, and assault them every chance they get. Mostly they're held in solitary confinement, for their own protection. But right now the prisoners are holding mock trials and killing the rapists and child abusers, one by one.

"Of course, when they've finished with that, there are various political and religious factions, all eager to settle old grudges. When the dust's settled from that, and the prisoners have demolished as much of the prison building as they can, they'll turn on the seventeen prison staff they were able to get their hands on, and try and use them as a lever for an escape. When that doesn't work, they'll kill them too."

"We can't let that happen," said Fisher. "We have to put a stop to this."

"We will," said Winter. "Once we've made sure Hell Wing is secure. I know, Fisher, you want to rush in there and rescue them, but we can't. Part of this job, perhaps the hardest part, is learning to turn your back on one evil so you can concentrate on a greater one."

It was ominously quiet in the distance. Hawk scowled. "Should have put a geas on the lot of them. Then there wouldn't have been all this trouble in the first place."

"It's been suggested many times," said Winter, "but it would cost like hell, and the Council won't go for it. Cells and bars come a lot cheaper than magic."

"Hold it," said Storm suddenly, his voice so sharp and commanding that everyone stopped dead where they were. The sorcerer stared silently at the empty corridor ahead of them, his scowl gradually deepening. "We're almost there," he said finally, his voice now low and thoughtful. "The next bend leads into Sorcerers' Row, where the magic-users are confined. They're held in separate cells, backed up by an individual geas. After that, there's nothing between us and Hell Wing."

"Why have we stopped?" said Winter quietly. "What's wrong, Storm?"

"I don't know. My inner Sight's not much use here. Too many security spells. But I ought to be picking up some trace of the magic-users on Sorcerers' Row, and I'm not getting anything. Just traces of stray magic, scattered all over the place, as though something very powerful happened here not long ago. I don't like the feel of it, Jessica."

"Draw your weapons," said Winter, glancing back at the others, and there was a quick rasp of steel on leather as the team's swords left their scabbards. Hawk hefted his axe thoughtfully, and then frowned as he realised MacReady was unarmed.

"Where's your sword?" he said quietly.

"I don't need one," said the negotiator calmly. "I lead a charmed life."

Hawk decided he wasn't going to ask, if only because MacReady was obviously waiting for him to do so. He nodded calmly to the negotiator, and moved forward to join Winter and Storm.

"I don't like standing around here, Winter. It makes us too good a target. If there's a problem with Sorcerers' Row, let's check it out."

Winter looked at him coolly. "I lead the team, Captain Hawk, and that means I make the decisions. We're going to take this slow and easy, one step at a time. I don't believe in rushing into things."

Hawk shrugged. "You're in charge, Winter. What's the plan?"

Winter frowned. "It's possible the rioters could have broken the magic-users out of their cells, but not very likely; the geas should still hold them. Captain Hawk, you and your partner check out the situation. Barber, back them up. Everyone else stays put. And Hawk, no heroics, please. Just take a quick look around, and then come back and tell me what you saw. Got it?"

"Got it," said Hawk.

He moved slowly forward, axe held at the ready before him. Fisher moved silently at his side, and Barber brought up the rear. Hawk would rather not have had him there, on the grounds that he didn't want to be worrying about what Barber was doing when he should be concentrating on getting the job done, but he couldn't say no. He didn't want to upset Winter this early in their professional relationship. Or Barber, for that matter. He looked like he knew how to use that sword. Hawk sighed inaudibly and concentrated on the darkening corridor ahead. Some of the lamps had gone out, and Hawk's gaze darted from shadow to shadow as he approached the bend in the corridor. The continuing silence seemed to grow thicker and more menacing, and Hawk had a growing conviction that someone, or something, was waiting for him just out of sight round the corner.

He eased to a halt, his shoulder pressed against the wall just before the bend, then glanced back at Fisher and Barber. He gestured for them to stay put, took a firm grip on his axe, and then jumped forward to stare down the side corridor into Sorcerers' Row. It stretched away before him, all gloom and shadow, lit only by half a dozen wall lamps at irregular intervals. The place was deserted, but all the cell doors had been torn out of their frames and lay scattered across the floor. The open cells were dark and silent, and reminded Hawk unpleasantly of the gap left after a tooth has been pulled. He stayed where he was, and gestured for Fisher and Barber to join him. They did so quickly, and Fisher whistled softly.

"We got here too late, Hawk. Whatever happened here is over."

"We don't know that yet," said Hawk. "We've still got to check the cells. Fisher, watch my back. Barber, stay put and watch the corridor. Both ends. And let's all be very careful. I don't like the feel of this."

"Blood has been spilled here," said Barber quietly. "A lot of it. Some of it's still pretty fresh."

"I don't see any blood," said Fisher.

"I can smell it," said Barber.

Hawk and Fisher looked at each other briefly, and then moved cautiously towards the first cell. Fisher took one of the lamps from its niche in the wall and held it up to give

Hawk more light. He grunted acknowledgment, and glanced down at the solid steel door lying warped and twisted on the floor before him. At first he thought it must have been buckled by some form of intense heat, but there was no trace of any melting or scorching on the metal. The door was a good two inches thick. Hawk didn't want to think about the kind of strength that could warp that thickness of steel.

There were a few small splashes of blood in the cell doorway, dry and almost black. Hawk eased forward a step at a time, ready for any attack, and then swore softly as the light from Fisher's lamp filled the cell. The cell's occupant had been nailed to the far wall with a dozen daggers and left to bleed to death. Given the amount of blood soaking the floor below him, he'd taken a long time to die.

Hawk moved quickly from cell to cell, with Fisher close behind him. Every cell held a dead man. They'd all been killed in different ways, and none of them had died easily. They all wore sorcerer's black, but their magic hadn't protected them. Hawk sent Barber back to fetch the rest of the team while he and Fisher dutifully searched the bodies for any sign of life. It didn't take long. Winter walked slowly down Sorcerers' Row, frowning, with MacReady at her side. Storm darted from cell to cell, muttering under his breath. Barber sheathed his sword and leaned against the corridor wall with his arms folded. He looked completely relaxed, but Hawk noted that he was still keeping a careful watch on both ends of the corridor. Storm finally finished his inspection and stalked back to report to Winter. Hawk and Fisher joined them.

"What happened here?" said Hawk. "I thought they were supposed to be magic-users. Why didn't they defend themselves?"

"Their geas wouldn't let them," said Storm, bitterly. "They were helpless in their cells when the killers came."

"Why kill them at all?" said Fisher. "Why should the rioters hate magic-users enough to do something like this to them?"

"There was no hate in this," said Storm. "This was cold and calculated, every bloody bit of it. It's a mass sacrifice, a ritual designed to increase magical power. If one sorcerer sacrifices another, he can add the dead man's magic to his own. And if a sorcerer were to sacrifice all these magic-users, one after another . . . he'd have more than enough magic to smash through into Hell Wing, and make a new doorway."

"Wait a minute," said Hawk. "All the sorcerers in this prison were held here, on Sorcerers' Row, and none of them are missing. There's a dead body in every cell."

"Someone must have smuggled a sorcerer in, disguised as a prisoner," said Winter. "Probably bribed a guard to look the other way. This riot was carefully planned, people, right down to the last detail."

Fisher frowned. "So someone could have already entered Hell Wing and let the creatures out?"

"I don't know," said Storm. "Maybe. I can tell there's a new dimensional doorway close at hand, now I know what I'm looking for, but I can't tell if anyone's been through it recently."

"Great," said Fisher. "Just what this case needed, more complications." She looked at Winter. "All right, leader, what are we going to do?"

"Go into Hell Wing, and see what's happened," said Winter evenly. "Our orders were to do whatever is necessary to prevent the inmates of Hell Wing from breaking out. Nothing has happened to change that."

"Except we now face a rogue sorcerer and an unknown number of rioters as well as whatever's locked up in there," said Hawk. "I didn't like the odds when we started, and I like them even less now. I can't do suicide missions."

"Right," said Fisher.

Winter looked at them both steadily. "As long as you're a part of the SWAT team, you'll do whatever I require you to do. If that isn't acceptable, you can leave any time."

Hawk smiled coldly. "We'll stay. For now."

"That isn't good enough, Captain."

"It's all you're going to get."

Fisher pushed in between Hawk and Winter, and glared at them both impartially. "If you two have quite finished flexing your muscles at each other, may I remind you we've still got a job to do? You can butt heads later, on your own time."

Winter nodded stiffly. "Your partner is right, Captain

Hawk; we can continue this later. I take it I can rely on your cooperation for the remainder of this mission?"

"Sure," said Hawk. "I can be professional when I have to be."

"Good." Winter took a deep, steadying breath and let it out slowly. "The situation isn't necessarily as bad as it sounds. I think we have to assume some of the rioters have entered Hell Wing, presumably to release the inmates in the hope that they'd add to the general chaos. But if the fools have managed to break any of the geases and some of the creatures are loose, I think we can also safely assume that those rioters are now dead. Which means we're free to concentrate on recapturing those creatures that have broken loose."

"Just how powerful are these . . . creatures?" asked Fisher.

"Very," said Storm shortly. "Personally, I think we should just seal off the entire Wing, and forget how to find it."

"Those are not our orders," said Winter. "They have a right to a fair trial."

Storm sniffed. "That's not why our Lords and masters want these things kept alive. Creatures of Power like these could prove very useful as weapons, just in case the Peace Treaty doesn't work out after all. . . ."

"That's none of our business, Storm!"

"Wait a minute," said Hawk. "Are you saying we're supposed to take these things alive?"

"If at all possible, yes," said Winter. "Do you have a problem with that?"

"This case gets better by the minute," growled Hawk. "Look, before we go any further, I want a full briefing on these Creatures of Power. What exactly are we going to be facing in Hell Wing?"

"To start with, there's the Pale Men," said Winter steadily. "They're not real, but that just makes them more dangerous. They can take on the aspect of people you used to be but no longer are. The longer they hold the contact, the more real they become, while you fade into a ghost, a fancy, a might-have-been. Sorcerers create Pale Men from old love letters, blood spilled in anger, an engagement ring from a marriage that failed, or a baby's shoes bought for a child that was never born. Any unfinished emotion that can still be tapped. Be wary of them. They're very good at finding chinks in your emotional armour that you never knew you had."

"How many of them are there?" said Fisher.

"We don't know. It tends to vary. We don't know why. Then there's Johnny Nobody. We think he used to be human, perhaps a sorcerer who lost a duel. Now he's just a human shape, consisting of guts and muscle and blood held together by surface tension. He has no skin and no bones, but he still stands upright. He screams a lot, but he never speaks. When we caught him, he was killing people for their skin and bones. Apparently he can use them to replace what he lost, for a time, but his body keeps rejecting them, so he has to keep searching for more."

"I'm surprised he hasn't killed himself," said Fisher.

"He's tried, several times," said Winter. "His curse won't let him die. Now, if I may continue . . . Messerschmann's Portrait is a magical booby trap left behind by the sorcerer Void when he had to leave Haven in a hurry earlier this year, pursued by half the sorcerers in Magus Court. We still don't know what he did to upset them, but it must have been pretty extreme. They're a hard-boiled bunch in Magus Court. Anyway, the Portrait was brought here for safekeeping, and it's been in Hell Wing ever since. The creature in the Portrait may have been human once, but it sure as hell isn't now. According to the experts who examined the Portrait, the creature is actually alive, trapped in the Portrait by some powerful magic they don't fully understand. And it wants out. Apparently, if it locks eyes with you long enough, it can walk out into the world, and you would be trapped in the Portrait, in its place. So don't get careless around it."

"You should be safe enough, Hawk," said Fisher. "It'd have a hard job locking eyes with you."

Hawk winked his single eye. Winter coughed loudly to get their attention.

"Crawling Jenny is something of an enigma. It's a living mixture of moss, fungi, and cobwebs, with staring eyes and snapping mouths. It was only five or six feet in diameter when it was first removed from the Street of Gods because it was menacing the tourists. Now it fills most of its cell. If some fool's let Crawling Jenny loose and it's been feeding all this time, there's no telling how big it might be by now.

"The Brimstone Boys are human constructs, neither living nor dead. They smell of dust and sulphur, and their eyes bleed. Their presence distorts reality, and they bring entropy wherever they go. There are only two of them, thank all the Gods, but watch yourselves; they're dangerous. We lost five Constables and two sorcerers taking them. I don't want to add to that number.

"And finally, we come to Who Knows. We don't know what that is. It's big, very nasty, and completely invisible. And judging by the state of its victims' bodies, it's got a hell of a lot of teeth. They caught it with nets, pushed it into its cell on the end of several long poles, and nobody's gone near it since. It hasn't been fed for over a month, but it's still alive—as far as anyone can tell."

"I've just had a great idea," said Fisher, when Winter finally paused for breath. "Let's turn around, go back, and swear blind we couldn't find Hell Wing."

"I'll go along with that," said Barber.

Winter's mouth twitched. "It's tempting, I'll admit, but no. We're SWAT, and we can handle anything. It says so in our contract. Listen up, people. This is how we're going to do it. Storm, you open up the gateway and then stand back. Barber, Hawk, and Fisher—you'll go through first. If you see something and it moves, hit it. Hard. Storm will be right behind you, to provide whatever magical support you need. I'll bring up the rear. Mac, you stay back here and guard the entrance. I don't want anyone sneaking up on us from behind."

"You never let me in on the exciting stuff," said Mac-Ready.

"Yes," said Winter. "And aren't you grateful?"

"Very."

Winter smiled, and turned back to the others. "Take your places, people. Storm, open the gateway."

The sorcerer walked a few steps down the corridor and began muttering to himself under his breath. Barber stepped forward to take the point, and Hawk and Fisher moved in on either side of him. Barber glanced at them briefly, and frowned.

"Don't you people believe in armour? This isn't some bar brawl we're walking into."

"Armour just slows you down," said Hawk. "The Guard experiments with it from time to time, but it's never caught on. With the kind of work we do, it's more important for us to be able to move freely and react quickly. You can't chase a pickpocket down a crowded street while wearing chain mail. Our cloaks have steel mesh built into them, but that's it."

"And you don't even wear that, most of the time, unless I nag you," said Fisher.

Hawk shrugged. "Don't like cloaks. They get in the way while I'm fighting."

"I've always believed in armour," said Barber, swinging his sword loosely before him. He seemed perfectly relaxed, but his gaze never left Storm. "It doesn't matter how good you are with a blade, there's always someone better, or luckier, and that's when a good set of chain mail comes into its own."

He broke off as the sorcerer's voice rose suddenly, and then cut off sharply. The floor lurched and dropped away beneath their feet for a heart-stopping moment before becoming firm again. A huge metal door hung unsupported on the air right in front of them, floating two or three inches off the ground. An eight-foot-tall slab of roughly beaten steel, it gleamed dully in the lamplight, and then, as they watched, it swung slowly open to reveal a featureless, impenetrable darkness. A cold breeze blew steadily from the doorway, carrying vague, blurred sounds from off in the distance. Hawk thought he heard something that might have been screaming, or laughter, but it was gone too quickly for him to identify it.

"Move it," said Storm tightly. "I don't know how long I can keep the gateway open. There's so much stray magic around, it's distorting my spells."

"You heard the man," said Winter. "Go go go!"

Barber stepped through the doorway, and the darkness swallowed him up. Hawk and Fisher followed him in, blades at the ready. The darkness quickly gave way to a vague, sourceless silver glow. Barber, Hawk, and Fisher moved immediately to take up a defensive pattern, looking quickly about them for possible threats. They were standing in a narrow corridor that seemed to stretch away forever. The walls and the low ceiling were both covered with a thick mass of dirty grey cobwebs. The floor was a pale, pockmarked stone, splashed here and there with dark spots of dried blood. There was a brief disturbance in the air behind them as first Storm and then Winter appeared out of nowhere to join them.

"All clear here, Jessica," said Barber quietly. "No sign of anyone, or anything."

"If this is Hell Wing, I don't think much of it," said Fisher. "Don't they ever clean up in here?"

"I'm not sure where or what this is," said Storm. "It doesn't feel like Hell Wing. The air is charged with magic, but there's no trace of the standard security spells that ought to be here. Everything . . . feels wrong."

"Are you saying you've brought us to the wrong place?" asked Hawk dangerously.

"Of course not!" snapped the sorcerer. "This is where Hell Wing used to be. This is what has . . . replaced Hell Wing. I think we have to assume the creatures have broken loose. All of them."

Barber cursed softly, and hefted his sword. "I don't like this, Jessica. They must have known somebody would be coming. Odds are this place is one big trap, set and primed just for us."

"Could be," said Winter. "But let's not panic just yet, all right? Nothing's actually threatened us so far. Storm, where does this corridor lead?"

Storm shook his head angrily. "I can't tell. My Sight's all but useless here. But there's something up ahead; I can feel it. I think it's watching us."

"Then let's go find it," said Winter briskly. "Barber, you have the point. Let's take this one step at a time, people. And remember, we're not just looking for the creatures. The rioters who opened the gateway have got to be here somewhere. And, people, when we find them, I don't want any heroics. If any of the rioters wants to surrender, that's fine, but no one's to take any chances with them. All right; move out. Let's get the job done."

They moved off down the corridor, and the darkness retreated before them so that they moved always in the same sourceless silver glow. The thick matted cobwebs that

furred the walls and ceiling hung down here and there in
grimy streamers that swayed gently on the air, stirred by
an unfelt breeze. Noises came and went in the distance,
lingering just long enough to chill the blood and disturb
the mind. Hawk held his axe before him, his hands clutching the haft so tightly that his knuckles showed white. His
instincts were screaming at him to get out while he still
could, but he couldn't just turn tail and run. Not in front
of Winter. Besides, she was right; even if this place was a
trap, they still had a job to do. He glared at the darkness
ahead of them, and then glanced back over his shoulder.
The darkness was there too, following the pool of light the
team moved in. More and more it seemed to Hawk that
they were moving through the body of some immense unnatural beast, as though they'd been swallowed alive and
were soon to be digested.

Barber stopped suddenly, and they all piled up behind
him, somehow just managing to avoid toppling each other.
Barber silently indicated the right-hand wall, and they
crowded round to examine it. There was a ragged break in
the thick matting of dirty grey cobwebs, revealing a plain
wooden door, standing slightly ajar. The wood was scarred
and gouged as though by claws, and splashed with dried
blood. The heavy iron lock had been smashed, and was half
hanging away from the door. Winter gestured for them all
to move back, and they did so.

"It seems my first guess was wrong," said Storm quietly.
"This is Hell Wing, after all, merely hidden and disguised
by this . . . transformation. The lock quite clearly bears the
prison's official mark. Presumably the door leads to what
was originally one of the cells."

"Any idea what's in there?" asked Winter softly.

"Something magical, but that's all I can tell. Might be
alive, might not. Again, there's so much stray magic floating
around, my Sight can't see through it."

"Then why not just open the door and take a look?"
said Hawk bluntly. "I've had it up to here with sneaking
around, and I'm just in the mood to hit something. All we
have to do is kick the door in, and then fill the gap so that
whatever's in there can't escape."

"Sounds good to me," said Fisher. "Who gets to kick the
door in?"

"I do," said Barber. "I'm still the point man."

He looked at Winter, and she nodded. Barber moved silently back to the door and the others formed up behind him, weapons at the ready. Barber took a firm grip on his sword, lifted his left boot, and slammed it hard against the door. The heavy door swung inward on groaning hinges, revealing half of the small, gloomy cell. Barber hit the door again and it swung all the way open. Everybody tensed, ready for any sudden sound or movement, but nothing happened. The cell wasn't much bigger than a privy, and it smelled much the same. The only illumination was the silver glow falling in from the corridor outside, but it was more than enough to show that the cell was completely empty. There was no bed or other furnishings—only some filthy straw on the floor.

Some of the tension went out of Hawk, and he lowered his axe. "Looks like you got it wrong this time, Storm; no one's home. Whoever or whatever used to be locked up in here is long gone now."

"With a trusting nature like yours, Captain, I'm astonished you've lasted as long as you have," the sorcerer said acidly. "The cell's occupant is quite likely still here, held by its geas, even though the lock has been broken. You just can't see it, that's all."

Anyone else would have blushed. As it was, Hawk spent a moment looking down at his boots before nodding briefly to the sorcerer and then staring into the cell with renewed interest. "Right. I'd forgotten about Who Knows, the invisible creature. You're sure the geas is still controlling it?"

"Of course!" snapped Storm. "If it wasn't, the creature would have attacked us by now."

"Not necessarily," said Winter slowly. "It might just be waiting for us to lower our guard. Which presents us with something of a problem. If it isn't still held by its geas, we can't afford to just turn our backs and walk away. It might come after us. The reports I saw described it as immensely strong and entirely malevolent."

"Which means," said Barber, "someone's going to have to go into that cell and check the thing's actually there."

"Good idea," said Fisher. "Hawk, just pop in and check it out, would you?"

Hawk looked at her. "*You* pop in and check it out. Do I look crazy?"

"Good point."

"I'll do it," said Barber.

"No you won't," said Winter quickly. "No one's going into that cell. I can't afford to lose any of you. Barber, hand me an incendiary."

Barber smiled briefly, and reached into a leather pouch at his belt. He brought out a small smooth stone that glowed a dull, sullen red in the gloom, like a coal that had been left too long in the fire, and handed it carefully to Winter. She hefted it briefly, and then tossed it casually from hand to hand while staring into the apparently empty cell. Barber winced. Winter turned to Hawk and Fisher, and gestured with the glowing stone.

"I don't suppose you've seen one of these before. It's something new the Guard sorcerers came up with. We're field-testing them. Each incendiary is a moment taken out of time from an exploding volcano; an instant of appalling heat and violence fixed in time like an insect trapped in amber. All I have to do is say the right Word, throw the damn thing as far as I can, and a few seconds later the spell collapses, releasing all that heat and violence. Which is pretty unfortunate for anything that happens to be in the vicinity at the time. If Who Knows is in that cell, it's about to get a very nasty surprise. Stand ready, people. As soon as I throw this thing, I want that door slammed shut fast and everyone out of the way of the blast."

"What kind of range does it cover?" said Hawk.

"That's one of the things we're testing."

"I had a suspicion you were going to say something like that."

Winter lifted the stone to her mouth, whispered something, and then tossed the incendiary into the cell. She stepped quickly back and to one side. Hawk and Barber slammed the cell door shut and put their backs to the wall on either side of it. A moment later, the door was blown clean off its hinges by a blast of superheated air and hurled into the corridor. Hawk put up an arm to protect his face from the sudden, intense heat, and a glaring crimson light filled the corridor. The wooden door frame burst into flames, and the cobwebs on the corridor wall opposite scorched and blackened in an instant. In the heart of the leaping flames that filled the cell something dark and shapeless thrashed and screamed and was finally still. The temperature in the corridor grew intolerably hot, and Hawk backed away down the corridor, mopping at the sweat that ran down his face. The others moved with him, and he was about to suggest they all run like hell for the gateway, when the flames suddenly died away. The crimson glare disappeared, and the temperature dropped as quickly as it had risen. There was a vile smell on the smoky air, but the only sound was the quiet crackling of the flames as they consumed the door frame. Hawk moved slowly forward and peered cautiously into the cell. The walls were blackened with soot, and smoke hung heavily on the still air, but there was no sign of the cell's occupant, dead or alive.

"Think we got it?" asked Fisher, just behind him.

Hawk shrugged. "Who knows? But we'd better hope so. If the incendiary didn't kill it, I'd hate to think of the mood it must be in."

"It's dead," said Storm shortly. "I felt it die."

"Handy things, those incendiaries," said Hawk casually as he and Fisher turned back to face the others. "How long do you think it'll be before they're released to the rest of the Guard?"

"Hopefully never, in your case," said Storm. "Given your reputation for death and destruction."

"You don't want to believe everything you hear," said Hawk.

"Just the bad bits," said Fisher.

Hawk looked at her reproachfully. Winter coughed behind a raised hand. "Let's move it, people. We've got a lot more ground to cover yet. Barber, take the point again. Everyone else as before. Let's go."

They moved on down the corridor, and the sourceless silver glow moved with them. Hawk glanced back over his shoulder, expecting to see the burning door frame glowing in the gloom, but there was only the darkness, deep and impenetrable. Hawk turned away, and didn't look back again. The corridor seemed to go on forever, and without any way of judging how far they'd come, Hawk began to lose his sense of time. It seemed like they'd been walking for hours, but still the corridor stretched away before them, the only sound the quiet slapping of their boots on the stone floor. The dense growth of filthy matted cobwebs on the walls and ceiling grew steadily thicker, making the corridor seem increasingly narrow. Storm had to bend forward to avoid brushing the cobwebs with his head. All of them were careful to avoid touching the stuff. It looked diseased.

They finally came to another cell, with the door standing slightly open, as before. Storm stared at it for a long time, but was finally forced to admit he couldn't See anything anymore. Magic was running loose in Hell Wing, and he had become as blind as the rest of them. In the end, Barber kicked the door in, and he and Hawk charged in with weapons at the ready. The cell looked much like the last one, save for a canvas on an easel standing in the middle of the room, facing the back wall. Averting their eyes from the painting, Hawk and Barber checked the cell thoroughly, but there was nothing else there. Winter directed the others to stay out in the corridor and told Hawk to inspect the canvas. If it was what they thought it was, his single eye should help protect him from the painting's curse. Barber stood by, carefully watching Hawk rather than the painting, so that if anything went wrong he could pull Hawk away before the curse could affect him. That was the theory, anyway.

Hawk glanced out the cell door, and nodded reassuringly to Fisher. She wasn't fooled, but gave him a smile anyway. Hawk stepped in front of the easel, and looked for the first time at Messerschmann's Portrait. The scene was a bleak and open plain, arid and fractured, with no trace of life anywhere, save for the single figure of a man in the foreground. The man stared wildly out of the Portrait, so close it seemed Hawk could almost reach out and touch him. He was wearing a torn and ragged prison uniform, and his face was twisted with terror and madness.

"Damn," said Hawk, hardly aware he'd spoken aloud. "It's got out."

The background scene had been painted with staggering realism. Hawk could almost feel the oppressive heat wafting out of the painting at him. The figure in the foreground was so alive he seemed almost to be moving, drawing closer. . . . Suddenly Hawk was falling, and he put out his hands instinctively to break his fall. His palms slapped hard against the cold stone floor of the cell, and he was suddenly shocked into awareness again. His gaze fell on the Portrait, and he scrabbled backwards across the floor away from it, his gaze averted, until his back was pressed against the far cell wall.

"Take it easy," said Fisher, kneeling down beside him. "Barber spotted something was wrong, and pulled you away from the Portrait when you wouldn't answer him. You feeling all right now?"

"Sure," said Hawk quickly. "Fine. Help me up, would you?"

Fisher and Barber got him on his feet again, and he smiled his thanks and waved them away. He was careful not even to glance in the Portrait's direction as he left the cell to make his report to Winter.

"Whatever was in the Portrait originally has got out and is running loose somewhere in Hell Wing. One of the rioters has taken its place. Is there any way we can get him out?"

"Only by replacing him with someone else," said Storm. "That's the way the curse works."

"Then there's nothing more we can do here," said Winter. "If you've fully recovered, Captain, I think we should move on."

Hawk nodded quickly, and the SWAT team set off down the corridor again.

"At least we've got one less rioter to worry about," said Hawk after a while. The others looked at him. "Just trying to look on the bright side," he explained.

"Nice try," said Winter. "Hang on to that cheerfulness. You're going to need it. From what I've heard, we'd be better off facing a dozen rioters with the plague than the Portrait's original occupant. It might have been human once, but its time in the Portrait changed it. Now it's a nightmare in flesh and blood, every evil thought you ever had given shape and form, and it's running loose in Hell Wing with us. So, along with all our other problems, we're going to have to track it down and kill it before we leave. Assuming it can be killed."

"Are you always this optimistic?" asked Fisher.

Winter snorted. "If there was any room for optimism, they wouldn't have called us in."

"Something's coming," said Storm suddenly. "I can't see it, but I can feel it. Something powerful . . ."

Winter barked orders, and the SWAT team fell quickly into a defensive formation, with Barber, Hawk, and Fisher at the point, weapons at the ready. Hawk glanced thoughtfully at Barber. Now that there was finally a chance at some action, the weaponmaster had come fully alive. His dark eyes were fixed eagerly on the gloom ahead, and his grin was disturbingly wolfish. A sudden conviction rooted itself in Hawk that Barber would look just the same if the order ever came down for the weaponmaster to go after him or Fisher. Barber didn't give a damn for the law or for justice. He was just a man born to kill, a butcher waiting to be unleashed, and to him one target was as good as any other. There was no room in a man like Barber for conscience or ethics.

A sudden sound caught Hawk's attention, and his thoughts snapped back to the situation at hand. Something was coming towards them out of the darkness. Hawk's grip tightened on his axe. Footsteps sounded distinctly in the gloom, drawing steadily closer. There were two separate sets of footsteps, and Hawk smiled and relaxed a little. It was only a couple of rioters. But the more he listened, the more it seemed to him there was something wrong with the footsteps. They were too slow, too steady, and they seemed to echo unnaturally long on the quiet. The air was tense, and Hawk could feel his hackles rising. There was something bad hidden in the darkness, something he didn't want to see. A slight breeze blew out of the gloom towards him. It smelt of dust and sulphur.

"They're coming," said Storm softly. "The chaos bringers, the lords of entropy. The dust and ruins of reality. The Brimstone Boys."

Hawk glared at the sorcerer, and then back at the darkness. Storm had sounded shaken, almost unnerved. If just the approach of the Brimstone Boys was enough to rattle a hardened SWAT man, Hawk had a strong feeling he didn't want to face them with nothing but his axe. He fell back a step and glanced across at Winter.

"Might I suggest this would be a good time to try out another of those incendiary things?"

Winter nodded sharply and gestured to Barber. He took

another of the glowing stones from his pouch, whispered the activating Word, and threw the stone into the darkness. They all tensed, waiting for the explosion, but nothing happened. Storm laughed brusquely, a bleak, unpleasant sound.

"That won't stop them. They control reality, run rings round the warp and weft of space itself. Cause and effect run backwards where they look. They're the Brimstone Boys; they undo natural laws, turn certainties into whims and maybes."

"Then do something!" snapped Winter. "Use your magic. You're supposed to be a top-level sorcerer, dammit! You didn't sound this worried when you first told us about them."

"I didn't know," whispered Storm, staring unseeingly at the gloom. "I couldn't know. They're too big. Too powerful. There's nothing we can do."

Winter grabbed him by the shoulder and hauled him back out of the way. "His nerve's gone," she said shortly to the others. "The Brimstone Boys must have got to him somehow. I'm not taking any chances with these bastards. The minute you see them, kill them."

"We're supposed to take these creatures alive, remember?" said Barber mildly.

"To hell with that," Winter snapped. "Anything that can take out an experienced sorcerer like Storm so easily is too dangerous to mess about with."

Hawk nodded, and he and Fisher moved forward to stand on either side of Barber. The weaponmaster was quivering slightly, like a hound straining at the leash, or a horse readying for a charge, but his sword hand was perfectly steady. Hawk glared into the darkness, and then looked down suddenly. The corridor floor seemed to be shifting subtly under his feet, stretching and contracting. His boots were sinking into the solid stone floor as though it had turned to mud. He looked across at Barber and Fisher to see if they'd noticed it too, and was shocked to discover that they were now yards away, as though the corridor had somehow expanded vastly while he wasn't looking. He jerked his boots free from the sticky stone, and backed away. The ceiling was impossibly far above him, and the wall was running with boiling water that steamed and spat at him. Birds were singing, harsh and raucous, and somewhere children screamed in agony. The light changed to golden summer sunlight, suffusing the air like bitter honey. Hawk smelled dust and sulphur, so strong he could hardly breathe. And out of the darkness, stepping slow and somber, came the Brimstone Boys.

They might have been human once, but now they were impossibly, obscenely old. Their bodies were twisted and withered, turned in upon themselves by time, and there were gaping holes in their anatomy where skin and bone had rotted away to dust and nothingness. Their wrinkled skin was grey and colorless, and tore when movement stretched it. Their faces were the worst. Their lips were gone, and their impossibly wide smiles were crammed with huge blocky teeth like bony chisels. Blood ran constantly from their dirty yellow eyes and dropped from their awful smiles, spattering their ancient tattered skin.

Barber shouted something incoherent, and launched himself at the nearest figure. His sword flew in a deadly pattern, but the blade didn't even come close to touching the creature. Barber strained and struggled, but it was as though he and the ancient figures, only a few feet apart, lived in separate worlds, where they could see each other but not touch. Fisher drew a knife from her boot and threw it at the other figure. The knife tumbled end over end, shrinking slowly as though crossing some impossible distance but still not reaching its target. The withered creature looked at Fisher with its bleeding eyes, and she cried out as she began to sink into the floor. Despite all her struggles to resist, the flagstones sucked her down into themselves like a treacherous marsh. She struck at the floor with her sword, and sparks flew as the steel blade hit solid stone.

Hawk ran towards her, but she seemed to recede into the distance as he ran. He pushed himself harder, but the faster he ran, the further away she seemed to be. Somewhere between the two of them, Barber sobbed with helpless rage as he struggled futilely to touch the Brimstone Boys with his sword. Hawk could vaguely hear Winter shouting something, but all he could think of was Fisher. The stone floor was lapping up around her shoulders. The light was growing dimmer. Sounds echoed strangely. And then something gold and shining flew slowly past him, gleaming richly in the fading light, and landed on the floor between the Brimstone Boys. They looked down at it, and despite himself, Hawk's gaze was drawn to it too. It was a pocket watch.

He could hear it ticking in the endless quiet. Ticktocking away the seconds, turning past into present into future. The Brimstone Boys raised their awful heads, their grinning mouths stretched wide in soundless screams. Dust fell endlessly through golden light. The floor grew solid again, spitting out Fisher, and the walls rushed in on either side. The ceiling fell back to its previous height. And the Brimstone Boys crumbled into dust and blew away.

Hawk looked around him, and the corridor was just as it had always been. The silver light pushed back the darkness, and the floor was solid and reliable under his feet. Fisher picked up the throwing knife from the floor before her, looked at it for a moment, and then slipped it back into her boot. Barber put away his sword and shook his head slowly, breathing heavily. Hawk turned and looked back at Winter and the sorcerer Storm, who seemed to have completely recovered from his daze. In fact, he was actually smiling quite smugly.

"All right," said Hawk. "What happened?"

Storm's smile widened. "It's all very simple and straightforward, really," he said airily. "The Brimstone Boys distorted reality wherever they went, but they weren't very stable. They could play all kinds of tricks with space and probabilities and the laws of reality, but they were still vulnerable to time. The ordered sequence of events was anathema to their existence. It was already eroding away at them; that's why they looked so ancient. I just speeded the process up a bit, with an augmented timepiece whose reality was a little bit stronger than theirs."

"What was all that nonsense you were spouting before?" demanded Fisher. "I thought you'd gone off your head."

"That was the idea," said Storm smugly. "They didn't see me as a threat, so they ignored me. Which gave me time to work my magic on the watch. I could have been an actor, you know."

He stretched out his hand, and the watch flew through the air to nestle snugly in his hand. Storm checked the time, and put the watch back into his pocket.

"Heads up," said Barber suddenly. "We've got company again."

"Now what?" demanded Hawk, spinning round to face the darkness, and then freezing on the spot as he saw what was watching them from the edge of the silver glow. A human shape, formed of bloody organs and viscera, but no skin, stood trembling on legs of muscle and tendons but no bones. Its naked eyes stared wetly from a flat crimson mess that might once have been its face. It breathed noisily, and they could see its lungs rising and falling in what had once been its chest.

"Johnny Nobody," said Hawk. "Poor bastard. Are we going to have to kill him too?"

"Hopefully not," said Winter. "We're going to be in enough trouble over Who Knows and the Brimstone Boys. With a little luck, we might be able to herd this thing back into its cell. It's supposed to be strong and quick, but not very bright."

And then something pounced on Johnny Nobody from behind and smashed it to the floor. Blood spurted through the air as its attacker tore it apart and stuffed the gory chunks into its mouth. The newcomer looked up at the SWAT team, its mouth stretched in a bloody grin as it ate and swallowed chunks of Johnny Nobody's unnatural flesh. What upset Hawk the most was how ordinary the creature looked. It was a man, dressed in tatters, with wide, staring eyes you only had to meet for a moment to know their owner was utterly insane. Just looking at him made Hawk's skin crawl. What was left of Johnny Nobody kicked and struggled, unable to die despite its awful wounds, but incapable of breaking its attacker's hold. The crazy man squatted over the body, ripping out strings of viscera and giggling to himself in between bloody mouthfuls.

"Who the hell is that?" asked Fisher softly. "One of the rioters?"

"I don't think so," said Winter. "I think we're looking at the original occupant of Messerschmann's Portrait."

"I thought he was supposed to be some kind of monster," said Hawk.

"Well, isn't he?" said Winter, and Hawk had no answer. The SWAT leader looked at Barber. "Knock him out, Barber. Maybe our sorcerers can do something to bring his mind back."

Barber shrugged. "I'll do what I can, but bringing them in alive isn't what I do best."

He advanced slowly on the madman, who looked up sharply and growled at him like an animal. Barber stopped where he was and sheathed his sword. Moving slowly and carefully, he reached inside one of his pockets and brought out a small steel ball, no more than an inch or so in diameter. He hefted it once in his hand, glanced at the madman, and then snapped his arm forward. The steel ball sped through the air and struck the madman right between the eyes. He fell backwards and lay still, without making a sound. Barber walked over to him, checked his pulse, and then bent down beside him to retrieve his steel ball. Johnny Nobody twitched and shuddered, leaking blood and other fluids, and Barber's lips thinned back from his teeth as he saw the raw wounds slowly knitting themselves together. He moved quickly back to the others, dragging the unconscious madman with him.

"About time we had a little luck," said Winter. "Johnny Nobody's in no shape to give us any trouble, and we've got ourselves a nice little bonus in the form of our unconscious friend here. At least now we'll have something to show for our trouble."

"Winter," said Fisher slowly, "I think we've got another problem."

There was something in the way she said it that made everyone's head snap round to see what she was talking about. Thick tendrils of the dirty grey cobwebs had dropped from the ceiling and were wriggling towards Johnny Nobody. The bloody shape struggled feebly, but the grey strands whipped around it and dragged the body slowly away along the floor into the darkness, leaving a trail of blood and other things on the stone floor. Hawk looked at the thick mass of cobwebs covering the walls and ceiling, and made a connection he should have made some time back. He looked at Winter.

"It's Crawling Jenny, isn't it? All of it."

"Took you long enough to work it out," said Winter. "The rioters must have opened its cell and let it out. Which is probably why we haven't seen any of them since. According to the reports I saw, Crawling Jenny is carnivorous, and always ravenously hungry."

"Are you saying this stuff ate all the rioters?" said Fisher, glaring distrustfully at the nearest wall.

"It seems likely. Where else could it have got enough mass to grow like this? I hate to think how big the creature must be in total."

"Why didn't you tell us what this stuff was before?" said Hawk. "We've been walking through it all unknowing, totally at its mercy. It could have attacked us at any time."

"No it couldn't," said Storm. "I've been shielding us. It doesn't even know we're here."

"There wasn't any point in attacking its outer reaches," said Winter. "It'd just grow some more. No, I've been waiting for something like this to happen. Since Johnny Nobody is undoubtedly heading for the creature's stomach, all we have to do is follow it. I'm not sure if Crawling Jenny has any vulnerable organs, but if it has, that's where they'll be."

She set off down the corridor without looking back, hurrying to catch up with the dragging sounds ahead. The others exchanged glances and moved quickly after her. Barber carried the unconscious madman over his shoulder in a fireman's lift. It didn't seem to slow him down any. Hawk glared suspiciously at the thick mass of cobwebs lining the corridor, but it seemed quiet enough at the moment. Which was just as well, because Hawk had a strong feeling his axe wasn't going to be much use against a bunch of cobwebs.

They soon caught up with the tendrils dragging the body, and followed at a respectful distance. Storm's magic kept them unseen and unheard as far as Crawling Jenny was concerned, but no one felt like pushing their luck. Hawk in particular was careful to keep to the center of the corridor, well away from both walls. He found it only too easy to visualize hundreds of tentacles suddenly lashing out from the walls and ceiling, wrapping up victims in helpless bundles and dragging them off to the waiting stomach.

Eventually, the tendrils dragged the body into a dark opening in the wall. Winter gestured quickly for everyone to stay where they were. Barber lowered the unconscious madman to the floor, and stretched easily. He wasn't even breathing hard. Winter moved slowly forward to peer into the opening, and the others moved quietly in behind her, careful not to crowd each other so that they could still retreat in a hurry if they had to. The silver light from the corridor shone brightly behind them, and Hawk's lip curled in disgust at the sight ahead. The narrow stone cell was filled with a soft, pulsating mass of mold and fungi studded with lidless, staring eyes that burned with a horrid awareness. Sheets of gauzy cobwebs anchored the mass to the walls and ceiling, and frayed away in questing tendrils. As the team watched, two of the tendrils dropped Johnny Nobody's writhing body onto the central mass, and a dozen snapping mouths opened, crammed with grinding yellow teeth. They tore the body apart and consumed it in a matter of seconds.

"Damn," said Winter. "We've lost another one."

"So much for Johnny Nobody," said Barber quietly. "Poor Johnny, we hardly knew you."

"I don't know about you," said Hawk quietly to Winter, "but it seems to me that swords and axes aren't going to be much use against something like that. You could hack at it for hours and still not know if you'd hit anything vital."

"Agreed," said Winter. "Luckily, we should still have one incendiary left." She looked at Barber, who nodded quickly, and produced another of the glowing stones from his pouch. Winter nodded, and looked back at the slowly pulsating mass before her. "When you're ready, Barber, throw the incendiary into one of those mouths. As soon as the damned thing's swallowed it, everyone turn and run like a fury. I'm not sure what effect an incendiary will have on a creature like that, but I don't think we should hang around to find out. And Barber—don't miss. Or you're fired."

He grinned, murmured the activating Word, and tossed the glowing stone into one of the snapping mouths. It went in easily, and Crawling Jenny swallowed the incendiary reflexively. The SWAT team turned as one and bolted back down the corridor, Barber pausing just long enough to sling the unconscious madman over his shoulder again. A muffled explosion went off behind them, like a roll of faraway thunder, quickly drowned out by a deafening keening that filled the narrow corridor as the creature screamed with all its many mouths. A blast of intense heat caught up with the running figures and passed them by. Hawk flinched instinctively, but Storm's magic protected them.

Rivulets of flame ran along the walls and ceiling, hungrily consuming the thick cobwebs. Burning tendrils thrust out of the furry mass and lashed blindly at the running SWAT team. Hawk and Fisher cut fiercely at the tendrils, slicing through them easily. Burning lengths of cobwebs fell to the corridor floor, writhing and twisting as the flames consumed them. Charred and darkened masses of cobwebs fell limply from the wall and ceiling as a thick choking smoke filled the corridor. Storm suddenly stumbled to a halt, and the others piled up around him.

"What is it?" yelled Hawk, struggling to be heard over the screaming creature and the roaring of the flames.

"The exit's just ahead," yelled Storm, "but something's got there before us."

"What do you mean, 'something'?" Hawk hefted his axe and peered through the thickening smoke but couldn't see anything. The flames pressed closer.

Storm's hands clenched into fists. Stray magic sputtered on the air before him. "Them. They've found us. The Pale Men."

They came out of the darkness and into the light, shifting forms that hovered on the edge of meaning and recognition. Smoke drifted around and through them, like ghostly ectoplasm. Hawk slowly lowered his axe as it grew too heavy for him. His vision grayed in and out, and the roar and heat of the fire seemed far away and unimportant. The world rolled back upon itself, back into yesterday and beyond.

Memories surged through him, of all the people he'd been, some so strange to him now he hardly recognized them. Some smiled sadly at what he'd become, while others pointed accusing fingers or turned their heads away. His mind began to drift apart, fragmenting into forgotten dreams and hopes and might-have-beens. He screamed soundlessly, a long, wordless howl of denial, and his thoughts slowly began to clear. He was who he was because of all the people he'd been, and even if he didn't always like that person very much, he knew he couldn't go back. He'd paid too high a price for the lessons he'd learned to turn his back on them now. He concentrated on his memories, hugging them to him jealously, and the ghosts of his past faded away and were gone. He was Hawk, and no one was going to take that away from him. Not even himself.

The world lurched and he was back in the narrow stone corridor again, choking on the thick smoke and flinching away from the roaring flames as they closed in around him. The rest of the team were standing still as statues, eyes vague and far away. Some of them were already beginning to look frayed and uncertain, their features growing indistinct as the Pale Men leeched the pasts out of them. Hawk glared briefly at the shifting figures shining brightly through the smoke and grabbed Storm's shoulder. For a moment his fingers seemed to sink into the sorcerer's flesh, and then it suddenly hardened and became solid, as though Hawk's touch had reaffirmed its reality. Shape and meaning flooded back into Storm's face, and he shook his head sharply, as though waking from a nagging dream. He looked at Hawk, and then at the Pale Men, and his face darkened.

"Get out of the way, you bastards!"

He thrust one outstretched hand at the drifting figures, and a blast of raw magic exploded in the corridor. It beat on the air like a captured wild bird, and the Pale Men were suddenly gone, as though they'd never been there at all. Hawk looked questioningly at Storm.

"Is that it? Wave your hand and they disappear?"

"Of course," said Storm. "They're only as real as you allow them to be. Now help me get the others out of here."

Hawk nodded quickly, and started pushing the others down the corridor. Their faces were already clearing as they shook off their yesterdays. Smoke filled the corridor, and a wave of roaring flame came rushing towards them. Storm howled a Word of Power, and gestured sharply with his hand, and a solid steel door was suddenly floating on the air before them. It swung open, and the SWAT team plunged through. They fell into the corridor beyond, and the door slammed shut behind him.

For a while, they all lay where they were on the cool stone floor, coughing the smoke out of their lungs and gasping at the blessedly fresh air. Eventually, they sat up and looked around them, sharing shaken but triumphant smiles. Hawk knew he was grinning like a fool, and didn't give a damn. There was nothing like almost dying to make you feel glad to be alive.

"Excuse me," said a polite, unfamiliar voice, "but can anyone tell me what I'm doing here?"

They all looked round sharply, and found that the madman Barber had brought out with them was now sitting up and looking at them, his eyes clear and sane and more than a little puzzled. Storm chuckled suddenly.

"Well, it would appear the Pale Men did some good, in spite of themselves. By calling back his memories, they made him sane again."

The ex-madman looked around him. "I have a strong feeling I'm going to regret asking this, but by any chance are we in prison?"

Hawk chuckled. "Don't worry about it. It's only temporary. Who are you?"

"Wulf Saxon. I think."

Winter rose painfully to her feet and nodded to Mac-Ready, who had been standing patiently to one side, waiting for them to notice him. As far as Hawk could tell, the negotiator hadn't moved an inch from where they'd left him.

"Mission over," said Winter, just a little breathlessly. "Any trouble on your end, Mac?"

"Not really."

He glanced back down the corridor. Hawk followed his gaze and for the first time took in the seven dead men, dressed in prisoner's uniforms, lying crumpled on the corridor floor. Hawk gave the unarmed negotiator a hard look, and he smiled back enigmatically.

"Like I said: I have a charmed life."

I'm not going to ask, thought Hawk firmly. "Well," he said, in the tone of someone determined to change the subject. "Another successful mission accomplished."

Winter looked at him. "You have got to be joking. All the creatures we were supposed to capture are dead, and Hell Wing is a blazing inferno! It'll cost a fortune to rebuild. How the hell can it be a success?"

Fisher grinned. "We're alive, aren't we?"

Back in the Governor's office, the SWAT team stood more or less at attention, and waited patiently for the Governor to calm down. The riots had finally been crushed, and peace restored to Damnation Row, but only after a number of fatalities among both inmates and prison staff. The damage to parts of the prison was extensive, but that wasn't too important; it would just give the inmates something to do to keep them out of mischief. Nothing like a good building project to keep prisoners busy. Not to mention too exhausted to think about rioting again.

Even so, it probably hadn't been the best time to inform the Governor that all his potentially valuable Hell Wing inmates were unfortunately deceased, and the Wing itself was a burnt-out ruin.

The Governor finally stopped shouting, partly because he was beginning to lose his voice, and threw himself into the chair behind his desk. He glared impartially at the SWAT team, and drummed his fingers on his desk. Hawk cleared his throat cautiously, and the Governor's glare fell on him like a hungry predator just waiting for its prey to provide an opening.

"Yes, Captain Hawk? You have something to say, perhaps? Something that will excuse your pitiable performance on this mission, and give some indication as to why I shouldn't lock you all up in the dirtiest, foulest dungeon I can find and then throw the key down the nearest sewer?"

"Well," said Hawk, "things could have turned out worse." The Governor's face went an interesting shade of puce, but Hawk pressed on anyway. "Our main objective, according to your orders, was to prevent the inmates of Hell Wing from escaping and wreaking havoc in the city. I think we can safely assume the city is no longer in any danger from those inmates. Hell Wing itself is somewhat scorched and blackened, I'll admit, but solid stone walls are pretty fire-resistant, as a rule. A lot of scrubbing and a lick of paint, and the place'll be as good as new. And on top of all that, we managed to rescue Wulf Saxon from Messerschmann's Portrait, and restore his sanity. I don't think we did too badly, all things considered."

He waited with interest to see what the Governor's response would be. The odds favored a coronary, but he wouldn't rule out a stroke. The Governor took several deep breaths to calm himself down, and fixed Hawk with a withering stare.

"Wulf Saxon has disappeared. But we were able to learn a few things of interest about him, by consulting our prison records. In his time, some twenty-three years ago, Saxon was a well-known figure in this city. He was a thief, a forger, and a confidence trickster. He was also an ex-Guard, ex-city Councillor, and the founder of three separate religions, two of which are still doing very well for themselves on the Street of Gods. He's a confirmed troublemaker, a revolutionary, and a major pain in the arse, and you've let him loose in the city again!"

Hawk smiled, and shook his head. "We had him captured. Your people let him loose."

"He's still an extremely dangerous individual that this city was well rid of, until you became involved!"

Fisher leaned forward suddenly. "If he's that dangerous, does that mean there's a reward for his capture?"

"Good point, Isobel," said Hawk, and they both looked expectantly at the Governor.

The Governor decided to ignore both Hawk and Fisher, for the sake of his blood pressure, and turned to Winter. "Regretfully, I have no choice but to commend you and your SWAT team for your actions. Officially, at least. The city Council has chosen to disregard my objections, and has ordered me to congratulate you on your handling of the situation." He scowled at Winter. "Well done."

"Thank you," said Winter graciously. "We were just doing our job. Have you discovered any more about the forces behind the riot?"

The Governor sniffed, and shuffled through the papers on his desk. "Unlikely as it seems, the whole thing may have been engineered to cover a single prisoner's escape. A man named Ritenour. He disappeared early on in the riot, and there's a growing body of evidence that he received help in doing so from both inside and outside the prison."

Winter frowned. "A riot this big, and this bloody, just to free one man? Who is this Ritenour? I've never heard of him."

"No reason why you should have," said the Governor, running his eyes quickly down the file before him. "Ritenour is a sorcerer shaman, specializing in animal magic, of all things. I wouldn't have thought there was much work for him in a city like Haven, unless he likes working with rats, but he's been here three years to our certain knowledge. He's worked with a few big names in his time, but he's never amounted to anything himself. He was in here awaiting trial for nonpayment of taxes, which is why he wasn't guarded as closely as he might have been."

"If he worked for big names in the past," said Hawk slowly, "maybe one of them arranged for him to be sprung, on the grounds he knew something important, something they couldn't risk coming out at his trial. Prisoners tend to become very talkative when faced with the possibility of a long sentence in Damnation Row."

"My people are busy checking that connection at this moment, Captain," said the Governor sharply. "They know their job. Now then, I have one last piece of business with you all, and then with any luck I can get you out of my life forever. It seems the security forces protecting the two Kings and the signing of the Peace Treaty have decided there might just be some connection between Ritenour's escape and a plot against the two Kings. I can't see it as very likely myself, but, as usual, no one's interested in my opinions. The SWAT team, including Captains Hawk and Fisher, are to report to the head of the security forces at Champion House, to discuss the situation. That's it. Now get out of my office, and let me get back to clearing up the mess you people have made of my prison."

Everyone bowed formally, except for the Governor, who ostentatiously busied himself with the files before him. Hawk and Fisher looked at each other, nodded firmly, and advanced on the Governor. They each took one end of his desk, lifted it up, and overturned it. Papers fluttered on the air like startled butterflies. The Governor started to rise spluttering from his chair, and then dropped quickly back into it as Hawk and Fisher leaned over him, their eyes cold and menacing.

"Don't shout at us," said Hawk. "We've had a hard day."

"Right," said Fisher.

The Governor looked at them both. At that moment, all the awful stories he'd heard about Hawk and Fisher seemed a lot more believable.

"If you've quite finished intimidating a superior officer,

can we get out of here?" said Winter. "Those security types don't like to be kept waiting. Besides, if we're lucky, we might get to meet the Kings themselves."

"That'll make a change," said Hawk as he and Fisher headed unhurriedly for the door.

"Yeah," said Fisher. "If we're really lucky, maybe we'll get to intimidate them too."

"I wish I thought you were joking," said Winter.

2

SOMETHING TO BELIEVE IN

When it rains in Haven, it really rains. The rain hammered down without mercy, beating with spiteful persistence at every exposed surface. Ritenour—sorcerer, shaman, and now ex-convict—looked around him with interest as he strode along behind the taciturn man-at-arms called Horn. They were both protected by Ritenour's rain-avoidance spell, but everyone else in the crowded street looked like so many half-drowned sewer rats. The rains had barely begun when Ritenour had been thrown into Damnation Row, but they were in full force now, as blindly unstoppable as death or taxes. A continuous wave of water three inches deep washed down the cobbled street, past the overflowing gutters. Ritenour stamped enthusiastically through the water, smiling merrily at those people he splashed. He ignored the furious looks and muttered curses, secure in the knowledge that Horn wouldn't allow him to come to any harm.

Ritenour's smile widened as they made their way through the Northside. He didn't know where he was going, but he didn't give a damn. He was back in the open air again, and even the stinking streets of the Northside seemed light and fresh after the filthy rat-hole he'd shared with three other magic-users on Sorcerers' Row. In fact, he felt so good about things in general, he didn't even think about killing the insensitive men and women who crowded around him in the packed street. There'd be time for such things later.

He studied the back of the man in front of him thoughtfully. Horn hadn't said much to him since collecting him from the professionally anonymous men who'd smuggled him out of Damnation Row under cover of the riot. Apparently Horn fancied himself as the strong, silent type. Deeds, not words—that sort of thing. Ritenour sighed happily.

Such types were delightfully easy to manipulate. Not that he had any such thing in mind at the moment, of course. Horn was taking him to Daniel Madigan, and you don't kill the goose that may produce golden eggs. Not until you've got your hands on the golden eggs, anyway.

Ritenour wondered, not for the first time, what a terrorist's terrorist like Madigan wanted with a lowly sorcerer shaman like him. Arranging the prison riot must have cost Madigan a pretty penny; he had to be expecting Ritenour to provide something of more than equal value in return. Ritenour shrugged. Whatever it was, he was in no position to argue. He'd only been in gaol for tax evasion, but all too soon he'd have ended up in Court under a truthspell, and then they'd have found out all about his experiments in human as well as animal vivisection. They'd have hanged him for that, even though his experiments had been pursued strictly in the interests of sorcerous research. Madigan had rescued him in the very nick of time, whether the terrorist knew it or not.

He let his mind drift on to other matters. Horn had promised him, on Madigan's behalf, a great deal of money if he would agree to work with the terrorist on a project of mutual interest. Ritenour was always interested in large amounts of money. People had no idea how expensive sorcerous research was these days, particularly when your subjects insisted on dying. But it had to be said that Madigan was not the sort of person Ritenour would have chosen to work with. The man was an idealist, and fanatically devoted to his Cause: the overthrowing and destruction of Outremer. He was very intelligent, inhumanly devious and determined, and had raised violence and murder to a fine art. Ritenour frowned slightly. Whatever Madigan wanted him for, it was bound to be unpleasant and not a little dangerous. In the event he decided to go through with this project, he'd better be careful to get most of his money up front. Just in case he had to disappear in a hurry.

Horn stopped suddenly before a pleasantly anonymous little tavern tucked away in a side court. Ritenour looked automatically for a sign, to see what the place was called, but there didn't seem to be one. Which implied the tavern was both expensive and exclusive (you either knew about it already or you didn't matter), and therefore very security conscious. Just the sort of place he'd expect to find Madigan. The best place to lie low was out in the open, hidden behind a cloud of money and privilege.

Horn held open the door for him, and then followed him into the dimly lit tavern. People sat around tables in small, intimate groups, talking animatedly in lowered voices. No one looked up as Horn led the way through the tables to a hidden stairway at the back of the room. The stairs led up to a narrow hallway, and Horn stopped before the second door. It had no number on it, but there was an inconspicuous peephole. Horn knocked three times, paused, and then knocked twice. Ritenour smiled. Secret knocks, no less. Terrorists did so love their little rituals. He wondered hopefully if there'd be a secret password as well, but the door swung open almost immediately, suggesting someone had already studied Horn through the peephole. Ritenour assumed a carefully amiable expression and followed Horn in. The door shut firmly behind him, and he heard four separate bolts sliding into place. He didn't look back, and instead put on his best open smile and looked casually about him.

The room was surprisingly large for tavern lodgings, and very comfortably furnished. Apparently, Madigan was one of those people who believed the mind works best when the body is well cared for. Ritenour was glad they had something in common. Most of the fanatics he'd had dealings with in the past had firmly believed in the virtues of poverty and making do with the barest essentials. Luxuries were only for the rich and the decadent. They also believed in compulsory hair shirts and cold baths, and had shown no trace whatsoever of a sense of humor. Ritenour wouldn't have dealt with such killjoys at all if his experiments hadn't required so many human subjects. His main problem had always been obtaining them discreetly. After all, he couldn't just go out into the streets and drag passersby into his laboratory. People would talk.

A young man and attractive woman, seated at a table at the far end of the room, were keeping a watchful eye on him. Ritenour gave them his best charming smile. Another man was standing guard by the door, arms folded across his massive chest. He had to be the largest man Ritenour had ever seen, and he was watching Ritenour closely. The sorcerer nodded to him politely, uncomfortably aware that Horn hadn't moved from his side since they'd entered the room. Ritenour didn't need to be told what would happen if Madigan decided he couldn't use him after all. Or, to be more exact, what might happen. Ritenour might be unarmed, but he was never helpless. He always kept a few nasty surprises up his metaphorical sleeves, just in case of situations like this. You met all sorts, as a working sorcerer.

One man was standing on his own before the open fireplace, his face cold and calm, and Ritenour knew at once that this had to be Daniel Madigan. Even standing still and silent, he radiated power and authority, as though there was nothing he couldn't do if he but put his mind to it. He stepped forward suddenly, and Ritenour's heart jumped painfully. Although Madigan wore no sword, Ritenour knew the man was dangerous, that violence and murder were as natural to him as breathing. The threat of sudden death hung about him like a bloodied shroud. Ritenour felt an almost overwhelming urge to back away, but somehow made himself hold his ground. Out of the corner of his eye, he could see the other terrorists looking at Madigan with respect, and something that might have been awe or fear. Or both. Madigan held out a hand for Ritenour to shake, and the sorcerer did so, finding a small satisfaction in the knowledge that his hand wasn't shaking. Madigan's hand was cold and hard, like a store mannequin's. There was no warmth or emotion in the handshake, and Ritenour let go as soon as he politely could. Madigan gestured at the two chairs before the open fire.

"Good of you to come and see me, sir sorcerer. Please; take a seat. Make yourself comfortable. And then we can have a little talk, you and I."

"Of course," said Ritenour, bowing formally. His mind was racing. When in doubt, take the initiative away from your opponent. "I wonder if I could prevail on you for a bite of something, and perhaps a glass of wine? Prison fare tends to be infrequent, and bordering on inedible."

There was a moment of silence as Madigan stared at him impassively, and Ritenour wondered if he'd pushed it too far, too early. Everyone else in the room seemed to have gone very still. And then Madigan bowed slightly, and everyone relaxed a little. He nodded to the young man sitting at the table, and he rose quickly to his feet and left the room, fumbling at the door's bolts in his haste. Ritenour followed Madigan to the two chairs by the fire, and was careful to let Madigan sit down first. Horn moved in to stand beside Madigan's chair.

"Allow me to introduce my associates in this glorious venture," said Madigan mildly. "You've already met Horn, though I doubt he's told you much about himself. He is the warrior of our little group, a most excellent fighter and an experienced killer. His family were deported from Outremer some generations ago, stripped of title and land and property. Horn has vowed to avenge that ancient insult.

"The young lady watching you so intently from that table is Eleanour Todd, my second-in-command. When I am not available, she is my voice and my authority. Her parents died in an Outremer cell. She fought as a mercenary for the Low Kingdoms for several years, but now they have betrayed her by seeking peace with Outremer she has joined me to exact a more personal revenge.

"The large gentleman at the door is Bailey. If he has another name, I've been unable to discover it. Bailey is a longtime mercenary and a seasoned campaigner. And yet despite his many years of loyal service to both Outremer and the Low Kingdoms, he has nothing to show for it, while those he served have grown fat and rich at his expense. I have promised him a chance to make them pay in blood and terror."

Someone outside the door gave the secret knock. Bailey looked through the peephole, and then pulled back the bolts and opened the door. The young man who'd left only a few moments before bustled in carrying a tray of cold meats and a glass of wine. He set down the tray before Ritenour, who smiled and nodded his thanks. The young man grinned cheerfully, and bobbed his head like a puppy that's just got a trick right, then looked quickly at Madigan to check he'd done the right thing.

"And this young gentleman is Ellis Glen," said Madigan dryly. "One of the most savage and vicious killers it has ever been my good fortune to encounter. You must let him show you his necklace of human teeth some time. It's really quite impressive. I have given his life shape and meaning, and he has vowed to obey me in everything. I expect great things of Ellis."

He tilted his head slightly, dismissing Glen, and the young man scurried over to sit at the table, blushing like a girl who'd been complimented on her beauty. Madigan settled back in his chair and waved for Ritenour to begin his meal. The sorcerer did so, carefully not hurrying. More and more it seemed to him he couldn't afford to seem weak in front of these people. Madigan watched him patiently, his face calm and serene. Ritenour could feel the pressure of the others' watching eyes, and took the opportunity his meal provided to study them unobtrusively.

Horn looked to be standard hired muscle, big as an ox and nearly as smart. You could find a dozen like him in most taverns in the Northside, ready for any kind of trouble as long as it paid well. He had a square, meaty face that had taken a few too many knocks in its time. He wore a constant scowl, aimed for the moment at Ritenour, but its unvarying depth suggested it was probably his usual expression anyway. And yet there was something about the man that disturbed the sorcerer on some deep, basic level. He had the strong feeling that Horn was the kind of warrior who would just keep coming towards you, no matter how badly you injured him, until either you were dead or he was.

Ritenour suppressed a shudder and switched his gaze to Eleanour Todd. She was altogether easier on the eye, and Ritenour flashed her his most winning smile. She looked coldly back, her gaze fixed unwaveringly on him as he ate. Judging by the length of her splendid legs, she would be easily his height when standing, and her large frame was lithely muscular. She wore a standard mercenary's outfit, hard-wearing and braced with leather in strategic places for protection, but cut tightly here and there to emphasize her femininity. With her thick mane of long black hair and calm dark eyes, she reminded Ritenour of nothing so much as a trained fighting cat, awaiting only her master's instruction to leap upon her prey and rend it with slow, malicious glee. She held his gaze for a moment, and then smiled slowly. Ritenour's stomach muscles tightened. Her front teeth had been filed to sharp points. Ritenour nodded politely and

ooked away, making a firm mental note never to turn his
back on her.

The huge warrior, Bailey, could well be a problem. He
had to be in his late forties, maybe even early fifties, but
he was still in magnificent shape, with a broad muscular
chest and shoulders so wide he probably had to turn sideways when he walked through a doorway. Even standing
still on the other side of the room, he seemed to be looming
over everyone else. He made Horn look almost petite. And
yet his face was painfully gaunt, and there were dark shadows under his eyes, as though he'd been having trouble
sleeping. Ritenour shrugged inwardly. Any mercenary Bailey's age was bound to have more than a few ghosts
haunting his memories. Ritenour studied the man's face
thoughtfully, searching for clues. Bailey's hair was iron-
grey, cropped short in a military cut. His eyes were icy
blue, and his mouth was a thin line like a knife-cut. Ritenour could see control in the face, and strength, but his cold
mask hid everything else. Ritenour decided he wouldn't
turn his back on this one either.

Despite Madigan's unsettling praises of the young man,
Ritenour didn't see Ellis Glen as much of a problem. He
was barely out of his teens, tall and gangling and not yet
into his full growth. His face was bright and open, and he
was so full of energy it was all he could do to sit still at
his table while Ritenour ate. He was probably only there
to run errands and take care of the scutwork no one else
wanted to be bothered with. Useful battle fodder too;
someone expendable Madigan could send into dangerous
situations to check for traps and ambushes.

And finally, of course, there was Daniel Madigan himself.
You only had to look at him for a moment to know he
was the leader. He was darkly handsome and effortlessly
charismatic, and even sitting still and silent, he radiated
strength and authority and presence. He was the first person everyone's eyes went to on entering a room, drawing
attention in much the same way a wolf would, or any other
predator. Looked at coolly, he wasn't physically all that
outstanding. He was slightly less than average height, and
certainly not muscular, but still he was the most dangerous
man in the room, and everyone knew it. Ritenour felt increasingly unsettled by Madigan's gaze, but forced himself

to continue his meal and his appraisal of the terrorist leader.

The more he studied Madigan, the clearer it became that violence of thought and deed was always simmering just below a calm surface. And yet there was nothing special you could put your finger on about his face or bearing. Ritenour had heard it said that Madigan, when he felt like it, could turn off his personality in a moment, and become just another anonymous face in the crowd. It was an attribute that had enabled him to escape from many traps and tight corners in his time. Ritenour studied the man's features carefully. Just now, Madigan was showing him a cool unemotional politician's face, half hidden behind a neatly trimmed beard. His eyes were dark and unwavering, and his occasional smile came and went so quickly you couldn't be sure whether you'd seen it or not. He looked to be in his early thirties, but had to be at least ten years older unless he'd started his career of death and terror as a child. Not that Ritenour would put that past him. If ever a man had been born to violence and intrigue and sudden death it was Daniel Madigan. No one knew how many people he'd killed down the years, how many towns and villages he'd destroyed in blood and fire, how many outrages he'd committed in the name of his Cause.

He had vowed to overthrow and destroy Outremer. No one knew why. There were many stories, mostly concerning the fate of his unknown family, but they were only stories. The Low Kingdoms had long since disowned him and his actions. He was too extreme, too ruthless . . . too dangerous to be associated with, even at a distance. Madigan didn't care. He went his own way, following his own Cause, ready to kill or destroy anyone or anything that got in his way.

And now he was sitting opposite Ritenour, studying him coolly and waiting to talk to him. With a start, Ritenour realised he'd finished his meal and was staring openly at Madigan. He buried his face in his wineglass and fought his way back to some kind of composure. He finally lowered his glass and put it carefully down on the arm of his chair, aware that the other terrorists were watching him with varying shades of impatience.

"Did the vintage meet with your approval?" asked Madigan.

"An excellent choice," said Ritenour, smiling calmly back. In fact, he'd been so preoccupied he hadn't a clue as to what he'd just drunk. It could have been dishwater for all he knew. He braced himself, and met Madigan's unnerving gaze as firmly as he could. "What do you want with me, Madigan? I'm no one special, and we both know it. I'm just another mid-level sorcerer, in a city infested with them. What makes me so important to you that you were ready to start a riot to break me out of Damnation Row?"

"You're not just a sorcerer," said Madigan easily. "You're also a shaman, a man with intimate knowledge of the life and death of animals and men. I have a use for a shaman. Particularly one who's followed the path of your recent experiments. Oh yes, my friend, I know all the secrets of your laboratory. I make it my business to know such things. Relax; no one else need ever know. Providing you do this little job for me."

"What job?" said Ritenour. "What do you want me to do?"

Madigan leaned forward, smiling slightly. "Together, you and I are going to rewrite history. We're going to kill the Kings of Outremer and the Low Kingdoms."

Ritenour looked at him blankly, too stunned even to register the shock that he felt. He'd known the Kings had arrived in Haven. That news had penetrated even Damnation Row's thick walls. But the sheer enormity of the plan took his breath away. He realized his mouth was hanging open, and shut it with a snap.

"Let me get this right," he said finally, too thrown even to care about sounding respectful. "You're planning to kill *both* Kings? Why both? I thought your quarrel was just with Outremer?"

"It is. I have dedicated my life to that country's destruction."

"Then why the hell . . . ?" Horn stirred suddenly at Madigan's side, reacting to the baffled anger in Ritenour's voice, and he shut up quickly to give his mind a chance to catch up with his mouth. There had to be a reason. Madigan did nothing without a reason. "Why do you want to kill your own King?"

"Because the Low Kingdoms' Parliament has betrayed us all by agreeing to his new Peace Treaty. Once this worthless scrap of paper has been signed, land that is rightfully ours and has been for generations will be given away to our hereditary enemies. I will not allow that to happen. There can be no peace with Outremer. As long as that country exists, it is an abomination in the sight of the Gods. That land was ours, and will be again. Outremer must be brought down, no matter what the price. So, both their King and ours must die, and in such a fashion that no one knows who is responsible. Both Parliaments will blame the other, both will deny any knowledge of any plot, and in the end there will be war. The people of both countries will demand it. And Outremer will be wiped from the face of the earth."

"We're going to do all this?" said Ritenour. "Just the six of us?"

"I have a hundred armed men at my command, hand-picked and assembled just for this project. But if all goes well, we shouldn't even need them much, except to ensure our security once we've taken control of Champion House. You must learn to trust me, sir sorcerer. Everyone in this room has committed their lives to carrying out this plan."

"You're committed to your Cause," said Ritenour bluntly. "I'm not. I'm here because I was promised a great deal of money. And all this talk of dying for a Cause makes me nervous. Dead men are notorious for not paying their bills."

Madigan chuckled briefly. It wasn't a pleasant sound. "Don't worry, my friend. You'll get your money. It's being held in a safe place until after this mission is over. And to answer the question you didn't ask; no, you will not be required to die for our Cause. Once you have performed the task I require of you, you are free to leave."

There was a knock at the door, an ordinary, everyday knock, and Madigan's people tensed, their hands moving quickly to their weapons. Bailey stared through the peephole, grunted once and relaxed. "It's all right. It's just the traitor." He unbolted the door and pulled it open, and a young nobleman strode in as if he owned the place.

He was tall and very slender, with a skin so pale it all but boasted that its owner never voluntarily put a foot outdoors. His long, narrow face bore two beauty spots and a look of utter disdain. He was dressed in the latest fashion.

with tightly cut trousers and a padded jerkin with a chin-high collar. He had the kind of natural poise and arrogance that comes only with regular practice since childhood, and his formal bow to Madigan bordered on insolence. He swept off his wet cloak and handed it to Bailey without looking at him. The old warrior held the dripping garment between thumb and forefinger, and for a moment Ritenour thought Bailey might tell the young nobleman what he could do with it. But Madigan glanced briefly at him, and Bailey hung the cloak carefully on the rack by the door. The young noble strutted forward, ostentatiously ignoring everyone, and warmed his hands by the fire.

"Beastly weather out. Damned if I know why your city weather wizards allow it. My new boots are positively ruined." He glared at Ritenour as though it was his fault. The sorcerer smiled in response, and made a mental note of the young man's face for future attention. The nobleman sniffed loudly and turned his glare on Madigan. "This is the sorcerer fellow, is it? Are you sure he's up to the job? I've seen better dressed scarecrows."

"I don't need him for his fashion sense," said Madigan calmly. "Have you brought the information I require, Sir Roland?"

"Of course. You don't think I'd venture out in this bloody downpour unless it was absolutely necessary, do you?"

He pulled a roll of papers from inside his jerkin, and moved over to spread them out on the table, scowling at Glen and Eleanour Todd until they stood up and got out of the way. Ritenour and Madigan got up and went over to join him at the table. The sorcerer studied Sir Roland with interest. Either the man had nerves of steel, or he was totally insensitive to the fact that he was making enemies of some very dangerous people. Sir Roland secured his papers at the corners with the terrorists' wineglasses, and gestured impatiently for Madigan to move in beside him. He did so, and everyone else crowded in behind him.

"These are the floor plans for Champion House," said Sir Roland brusquely. "All the details you'll need are here, including the location and nature of all the security spells. I've also marked the routes of the various security patrols, and how many men-at-arms you can expect to encounter at each point. You'll find details of their movements, a timetable for each patrol and so on, in the other papers. I don't have time to go through those with you now. I've also got you the plans you requested for the cellar, though what good that's going to do you is beyond me. No one's been down there for simply ages, and the whole place is a mess. It's full of rubbish and probably crawling with rats. And if you're thinking of breaking in that way, you can forget it. The cellar was built on solid concrete, and there are unbreakable security wards to prevent anyone from teleporting into the House.

"Now then, this sheet gives you both Kings' separate schedules, inside and outside the building, complete with details of how much protection they'll have. With these schedules, you'll be able to tell exactly where each King should be at any given moment. There are bound to be alterations from time to time, to accommodate any whims or fears of the Kings' security people, but I'll see you're kept up to date as much as possible. For the moment, everyone's so afraid of offending somebody that they're all following their schedules to the letter, but you know how paranoid security people can get. You'd almost think they had something to worry about. Finally, this sheet gives you the names of those people who can be trusted to support you, once the operation is underway. You'll notice the list includes names from the parties of both countries." The young noble smiled slightly. "Though of course they won't reveal themselves unless it becomes absolutely necessary. Still, I think you can rely on them to keep their fellow hostages in line, prevent any heroics, that sort of thing.

"I think you'll find everything you need in here. I must say I'm rather looking forward to seeing Their Majesties' faces when they discover they're being held for ransom. Glorious fun. Now then, I must be off. I have to get back before I'm missed. I don't see any need for us to meet again, Madigan, but if you must contact me, do be terribly discreet. We don't want anything to go wrong at this late stage, now do we?"

He turned away from the table, and gestured imperiously for Bailey to fetch him his cloak. Bailey did so, after a look at Madigan, and Sir Roland swung the cloak around his shoulders with a practised dramatic gesture. Ritenour almost felt like applauding. Sir Roland bowed briefly to Madigan, ignored everyone else, and left. Bailey closed and bolted the door behind him. Ritenour looked at Madigan.

"Dear Roland doesn't know what's really going on, does he?"

Madigan's smile flickered briefly. "He and his fellow conspirators believe they're part of a plot to disrupt the Peace Signing with a kidnapping. They believe this will delay the Signing, buy them time to sow seeds of doubt in their precious Parliaments, and generally stir up bad feeling on both sides. They also expect a large share of the ransom money to find its way into their hands. I fear they're going to be somewhat disappointed. I'm rather looking forward to seeing their faces when we execute the two Kings right before their eyes."

"Glorious fun," said Eleanour Todd, and everyone laughed.

"About these conspirators," said Ritenour diffidently, indicating the relevant page. "You do realize that all of them, and most particularly including Sir Roland, will have to die? Along with everyone who could identify us."

Madigan nodded. "Believe me, sir sorcerer, no one will be left alive to point the finger, and no one will pursue us. Haven . . . will have its own problems."

Ritenour looked around him, taking in the mocking smiles on the terrorists' faces, and a sudden chill clutched at his heart. "What exactly are you planning, Madigan? What do you want from me?"

Madigan told him.

Wulf Saxon strode through the old familiar district he used to live in, and no one knew him. The last time he'd walked these streets, twenty-three years ago, people had waved and smiled and some had even cheered. Everyone wanted to know him then—the local lad who'd made good. The city Councillor who'd started out in the same mean streets as them. But now no one recognised his face, and in a way he was glad. The Northside had always been rough and ready, shaped by poverty and need, but it had never seemed this bad. There was no pride or spirit left in the quiet, defeated people who scurried through the pouring rain with their heads bowed. The once brightly painted buildings were grey and faceless with accumulated soot and filth. Garbage blocked the gutters, and sullen-eyed bravos shouldered their way through the crowds without anyone so much as raising a murmur of protest.

Saxon had expected some changes after his long absence, but nothing like this. The Northside he remembered had been vile, corrupt, and dangerous, but the people had a spark then, a vitality that enabled them to rise above all that and claim their own little victories against an uncaring world. Whatever spark these people might once have possessed had been beaten out of them. Saxon trudged on down the street, letting his feet guide him where they would. He should have felt angry or depressed, but mostly he just felt tired. He'd spent the last few hours tracking down names and memories, only to find that most of the people he'd once known were now either missing or dead. Some names only produced blank faces. It seemed many things could change in twenty-three years.

He found himself standing in front of a tavern with a familiar name, the Monkey's Drum, and decided he could use a drink. He pushed the door open and stepped inside, his eyes narrowing against the sudden gloom. He took off his cloak and flapped it briskly out the open door a few times to lose the worst of the rain, and then hung it on a nearby peg. He shut the door and turned to study the tavern's interior with a critical eye.

It was fairly clean, in an absent-minded sort of way, and half-full of patrons sitting quietly at their tables, talking in lowered voices. None of them looked at Saxon for more than the briefest of moments, to make sure he wasn't the Guard. He smiled sourly, and headed for the bar. It seemed some things never changed. The Monkey's Drum had always been a place where you could buy and sell and make a deal. He made his way through the closely packed tables and ordered a brandy at the bar. The price made him wince, but he paid it with as much good grace as he could muster. Inflation could do a lot to prices in twenty-three years. The money he'd set aside in his secret lock-up all those years ago wasn't going to last nearly as long as he'd hoped. Twenty-three years . . . He kept repeating the number of years to himself, as though he could make himself believe it through sheer repetition, but it didn't get any easier. It was as though he'd gone to sleep in one world and awakened in another that bore only a nightmarish resemblance to the one he remembered.

That would teach him to try and steal a sorcerer's painting.

He smiled, and shrugged resignedly. Being a city Councillor had proved surprisingly expensive, and the pittance the city paid wasn't nearly enough to keep him in the style to which he intended to become accustomed. So he'd gone back to his previous occupation as a gentleman crook, a burglar with style and panache, and had broken into the house of a sorcerer he'd known was currently out of town. He'd been doing quite well, sidestepping all the sorcerer's protective wards with his usual skill, only to end up being eaten by Messerschmann's bloody Portrait. Sometimes there's no justice in this world.

Saxon put his back against the bar and looked round the room, sipping at his brandy while he wondered what to do next. He couldn't stay here, but he didn't know where else to go. Or even if there was any point in going anywhere. His ex-wife was probably still around somewhere, but there was nothing he wanted to say to her. She was the only woman he'd ever wanted, but it had only taken her a few years of marriage to decide that she didn't want him. No, he didn't want to see her. Besides, he owed her twenty-three years of back alimony payments. And then his gaze stumbled across a familiar face, and he straightened up. The years had not been kind to the face, but he recognized it anyway. He strode through the tables, a smile tugging at his lips, and loomed over the figure drinking alone at a table half hidden in the shadows.

"William Doyle. I represent the city auditor. Taxes division. I want to see all your receipts for the last four years."

The man choked on his drink and went bright red. He coughed quickly to get his breath back, and tried on an ingratiating smile. It didn't suit him. "Listen, I can explain everything. . . ."

"Relax, Billy," said Saxon, dropping into the chair opposite him. "You always were easy to get a rise out of. It's your own fault, for having such a guilty conscience. Well, no words of cheer and greeting for an old friend?"

Bill Doyle looked at him blankly for a long moment, and then slow recognition crept into his flushed face. "Wulf . . .

Wulf Saxon. I'll be damned. I never thought to see you again. How many years has it been?"

"Too many," said Saxon.

"You're looking good, Wulf. You haven't changed a bit."

"Wish I could say the same for you. The years have not been kind to you, Billy boy."

Doyle shrugged, and drank his wine. Saxon looked at him wonderingly. The Billy Doyle he remembered had been a scrawny, intense young man in his early twenties. Not much in the way of muscle, but more than enough energy to keep him going long after most men gave up and dropped out. Billy never gave up. And now here he was, a man in his late forties, weighing twice what he used to and none of it muscle. The thinning hair was still jet-black, but had a flat, shiny look that suggested it was probably helped along with a little dye. The face that had once been so sharp and fierce was now coarse and almost piggy, the familiar features blurred with fat like a cheap caricature. He looked like his own father. Or like his father might have looked after too many good meals and too many nights on booze. His clothes might once have been stylish, but showed signs of having been washed and mended too many times. Without having to be told, Saxon knew that Billy Doyle was no longer one of life's successes.

Doyle looked at him, frowning. "You haven't changed at all, Wulf. It's uncanny. What happened. You raise enough money for a rejuvenation spell?"

"In a way. So, what's been happening in your life, Billy? What are you doing these days?"

"Oh, this and that. Wheeling and dealing. You know how it is."

"I used to," said Saxon, slumping unhappily in his chair. "But things have changed while I was away. I went to where my old house used to be, and they'd torn it down and replaced it with some mock-Gothic monstrosity. The people who lived there had never even heard of me. I went to the old neighborhood and there was no trace of my family anywhere. Everyone I ever knew is either dead or moved on. You're the first friendly face I've seen all day."

Doyle looked at the clock on the wall, and gulped at his drink. "Listen," he said, trying hard to sound casual, "I'd love to sit and chat about the old days, but I'm waiting for someone. Business; you know how it is."

"You're nervous, Billy," said Saxon thoughtfully. "Now, what have you got to be nervous about? After all, this is me, your old friend Wulf. We never used to have secrets from each other. Or can it be that this particular piece of business you're involved in is something you know I wouldn't approve of?"

"Listen, Wulf . . ."

"Now, there aren't many things I don't approve of. I've tried most things once, and twice if I enjoyed it. And I was, after all, a gentleman thief, who robbed from the rich and kept it. But there was one thing I never would look the other way for, and that hasn't changed. Tell me, Billy boy, have you got yourself involved in childnapping?"

"Where do you get off, coming on so self-righteous?" said Doyle hotly. "You've been away; you don't know what it's like here these days. Things have changed. It's always been hard to make a living here, but these days there's even less money around than there used to be. You've got to fight for every penny and watch your back every minute of the day. If you won't take on a job, there are a dozen men waiting to take your place. There's a market for kids—brothels, fighting pits, sorcerers, you name it. And who's going to miss a few brats from the streets, anyway? Their parents are probably glad they've got one less mouth to feed. I can't afford to be proud anymore. The money's good, and that's all I care about."

"You used to care," said Saxon.

"That was a long time ago. Don't try and interfere, Wulf. You'll get hurt."

"Are you threatening me, Billy?"

"If that's what it takes."

"You wouldn't hurt me, Billy boy. Not after everything we've been through together."

"That was someone else. Get out of here, Wulf. You don't belong here anymore. Times have changed, and you haven't changed with them. You've got soft."

He looked past Saxon's shoulder, and rose quickly to his feet. Saxon got up too, and looked around, carefully moving away from the table so that his sword arm wouldn't be crowded. Two bravos were standing by the table, staring at him suspiciously. One of them was holding a young boy by the arm, as much to hold him up as prevent him escaping. He couldn't have been more than nine or ten years old, and his blank face and empty eyes showed he'd been drugged. Saxon looked at the bravos thoughtfully. They were nothing special; just off-the-shelf muscle. He looked at Doyle.

"Can't let you do this, Billy. Not this."

"It's what I do now, Wulf. Stay out of it."

"We used to be friends."

"And now you're just a witness." Doyle looked at the two bravos and gestured jerkily at Saxon. "Kill him, and dispose of the body. I'll take care of the merchandise."

The bravos grinned, and the one holding the boy let go of his arm. The child stood still, staring at nothing as the bravos advanced on Saxon. They went to draw their swords, and Saxon stepped forward to meet them with empty hands. He smiled once, and then his fist lashed out with supernatural speed. The first bravo's head whipped round as the force of the blow smashed his jaw and broke his neck, and he crumpled lifelessly to the floor. The other bravo cried out with shock and rage, and Saxon turned to face him.

The bravo cut at him with his sword, and Saxon's hand snapped out and closed on the man's wrist, bringing the sword to a sudden halt. The bravo strained against the hold, but couldn't move his arm an inch. Saxon twisted his hand, and there was a sickening crunching sound as the man's wrist bones shattered. All the color went out of his face, and the sword fell from his limp fingers. Saxon let go of him. The bravo snatched a knife from his belt with his other hand, and Saxon slammed a punch into his gut. His hand sank in deeply, and blood burst from the man's mouth. Saxon pulled back his hand, and the bravo fell to the floor and lay still. Saxon heard a footstep behind him, and turned round to see Billy Doyle backing slowly away, a sword in his hand. Saxon looked at him, and Doyle dropped the sword. His eyes were wide and frightened, and his hands were trembling.

"You're not even breathing hard," he said numbly. "Who are you?"

"I'm Wulf Saxon, and I'm back. My time away has . . .

changed me somewhat. I'm faster, stronger. And I don't have a lot of patience anymore. But some things about me haven't changed at all. You're out of the childnapping business, Billy. As of now. I'll hand the boy over to the Guard. You'd better start running."

Doyle stood where he was, deathly pale. He licked his lips, and shifted his feet uncertainly. "You wouldn't set the Guard on me, Wulf. You wouldn't do that to me. We're old friends, remember? You were never the sort to betray a friend."

"That was someone else," said Saxon. "One question, and then you can go. The correct answer buys you a half-hour start. If you lie to me, I'll hunt you down and kill you. Where's my sister, Billy? Where's Annathea?"

Doyle smiled. "Yeah, figures you'd have a job tracking her down. She doesn't use that name anymore. Hasn't for a long time. Ask for Jenny Grove, down on Cheape Street. Grove used to be her old man. Ran off years ago. He never was worth much."

"Where on Cheape Street?"

"Just ask. They all know Jenny Grove round there. But you aren't going to like what you'll find, Wulf. I'm not the only one that's changed. Your precious sister's been through a lot since you abandoned her."

"Start running, Billy. Your half hour starts now. And pass the word around. Wulf Saxon is back, and he's in a real bad mood."

Billy Doyle took in Saxon's icy blue eyes and the flat menace in his voice, and nodded stiffly, the smile gone from his mouth as though it had never been there. He was very close to death, and he knew it. He turned and headed for the door at a fast walk that was almost a run. He grabbed a drab-looking cloak from the rack, pulled open the door, and looked back at Saxon. "I'll see you regret this, Wulf. I have friends, important people, with connections. They aren't going to like this at all. Haven's changed since your day. There are people out there now who'll eat you alive."

"Send them," said Saxon. "Send them all. Twenty-eight minutes left, Billy boy."

Doyle turned and left, slamming the door behind him. Saxon looked around him unhurriedly, but no one moved at their tables. The tavern's patrons watched in silence as

Saxon took the drugged boy by the arm and headed for the door. He collected his cloak, slung it round his shoulders, and pulled open the door. It was still raining. He looked back into the tavern, and the patrons met his gaze like so many wild dogs, cowed for the moment but still dangerous. Saxon bowed to them politely.

"You've got five minutes to get out of here by the back door. Then I'm setting fire to the tavern."

He handed the boy over to a Guard Constable who came to watch the fire brigade as they tried to put out the blazing tavern. The driving rain kept the fire from spreading, but the Monkey's Drum was already beyond saving. There were occasional explosions inside as the flames reached new caches of booze. Saxon watched for a while, enjoying the spectacle, and then got directions to Cheape Street from the Constable and set off deeper into the Northside.

He didn't know this particular area very well, except by reputation, and undoubtedly that had also changed in the past twenty-three years, along with everything else. Certainly the streets he passed through seemed increasingly dingy and squalid, and he grew thankful for the heavy rain that hid the worst details from him. A slow, sick feeling squirmed in his gut as he wondered what Doyle had meant in his comments about Annathea. And why should she have changed her first name, just because she got married? It didn't make sense. Anyone would think she was hiding from someone.

It didn't occur to him until some time later that she might have been hiding from him.

Cheape Street turned out to be right on the edge of the Devil's Hook, a square mile of slums and alleyways bordering the Docks. The Hook was where you ended up when you'd fallen so far there was nowhere else to go but the cemetery. Poverty and suffering were as much a part of the Devil's Hook as the filthy air and fouled streets. Death and sudden violence were a part of everyday life. Saxon kept his hand conspicuously near his sword, and turned a hard glare on anyone who even looked like they were getting too close. He had no trouble in finding the address he'd been given, and stared in disbelief at the sagging tenements huddled together in the rain. This was the kind of place where absentee landlords crammed whole families into one room, and no one could afford to complain. What the hell was Annathea doing here? He stopped a few people at random, using the Jenny Grove name, and got directions to a second-floor flat right at the end of the tenement building.

Saxon found the right entrance and strode into the narrow hallway. Four men were sitting on the stairs, blocking his way. They were pretty much what he expected. Young, overmuscled, and out of work, with too much time on their hands and nothing to do but make trouble to relieve the endless boredom. Probably saw this filthy old fleatrap as their territory, and were glad of a chance to manhandle an outsider. Unfortunately for them, Saxon wasn't in the mood to play along. He strode towards them, smiling calmly, and they moved to block off the stairs completely. The oldest, who couldn't have been more than twenty, grinned insolently up at Saxon. He wore battered leathers pierced with cheap brass rings in rough patterns, and made a big play out of pretending to clean his filthy nails with the point of a vicious-looking knife.

"Where do you think you're going?"

"I'm visiting my sister," said Saxon. "Is there a problem?"

"Yeah. You could say that. You're not from around here, not with fancy clothes like those. You don't belong here. This is Serpent territory. We're the Serpents. You want to walk around where we live, that's going to cost you. Think of it as an informal community tax."

The others laughed at that, a soft dangerous sound, and watched Saxon with dark, unblinking eyes. Saxon just nodded, unmoved.

"And how much would this tax be?"

"Everything you've got, friend, everything you've got."

The young tough rose lithely to his feet, holding his knife out before him. Saxon stepped forward, took him by the throat with one hand, and lifted him off his feet. The Serpent's eyes bulged and his grin vanished. His feet kicked helplessly inches above the floor. He started to lift his knife, and Saxon turned and threw him the length of the hall. He slammed into the end wall by the door, and slid unconscious to the floor. Saxon looked at the Serpents still blocking the stairs, and they scrambled to get out of his way.

He started up the stairs, and one of them produced a length of steel chain from somewhere and whipped it viciously at Saxon's face, aiming for the eyes. The other two produced knives and moved forward, their eyes eager for blood. Saxon swayed easily to one side and the chain missed, though he felt the breath of its passing on his face. His attacker stumbled forward, caught off balance, and Saxon took the Serpent's throat in his hand and crushed it. Blood flew from the man's mouth, and he fell dying to the floor. Saxon kicked him out of the way. That left two.

He slapped the knife out of one Serpent's hand, and kicked the other in the leg. He felt, as well as heard, the bone break beneath his boot. The man fell back, screaming and clutching at his leg. The other was down on one knee, scrabbling frantically for his knife. Saxon kicked him in the face. The Serpent's neck snapped under the impact, and he flew backwards to lie unmoving on the hall floor. Saxon turned and looked at the last Serpent, who cringed from him, his back pressed against the stairway banisters. Saxon reached down, grabbed a handful of the man's leathers, and lifted him up effortlessly, so that they were face to face. Sweat ran down the Serpent's face, and his eyes were wide with shock and fear.

"Who are you?"

"I'm Saxon. Wulf Saxon. I've been away, but now I'm back. I'm going up to visit my sister now. If anyone feels like coming up after me and disturbing my visit, I'm relying on you to convince them that it's a bad idea. Because if anyone else annoys me, I'm going to get really unpleasant."

He dropped the Serpent, and continued on up the stairs without looking back. The second floor was dark and gloomy. The windows had been boarded up, and there were no lamps. The doors all looked much the same, old and hard-used and covered with an ancient coat of peeling paint. The numbers had been crudely carved into the wood, probably because any attached number would have been pried off and stolen in the hope someone would pay a few pennies for it. In this kind of neighborhood, anything that wasn't actually nailed down and guarded with a drawn sword was considered fair game.

He found the right door, raised a hand to knock, and then hesitated. He wondered suddenly if he wanted to meet the person his sister had become. Billy Doyle had been a good sort once; brave, reliable, honourable. Saxon slowly lowered his hand. His sister was Annathea, not this Jenny Grove; whoever she was. Perhaps the best thing would be to just turn around and leave. That way he'd at least have his memories of Annathea. He pushed the temptation aside. He had to know. Whatever she'd done, whoever she'd become, she was still family, and there might be something he could do to help. He knocked briskly at the door. There was a pause, and then he heard the muffled sound of footsteps from inside.

"Who is it?"

Something clutched at Saxon's heart like a fist. The voice had been that of an old woman. He had to cough and clear his throat before he could answer.

"It's me, Anna. It's your long-lost brother, Wulf."

There was a long pause, and then he heard the sound of bolts being drawn, and the door opened to reveal a faded, middle-aged woman in a shapeless grey robe. Her thin grey hair had been pulled back into a tight bun, and he didn't know her face at all. Saxon relaxed a little, and some of the weight lifted from his heart. He had come to the wrong place after all. He'd make his excuses, apologise for disturbing the old lady, and leave. And then she leaned forward, and raised a veined hand to touch his arm, her face full of wonder.

"Wulf? Is it really you, Wulf?"

"Annathea?"

The woman smiled sadly. "No one's called me that in years. Come in, Wulf. Come in and tell me why you abandoned your family all those years ago."

She stepped back while he was still searching for an answer, and gestured for him to enter. He did so, and she shut the door, carefully pushing home the two heavy bolts. Saxon stood uncertainly in his sister's single room and looked around him, as much to give him an excuse for not speaking as anything else. It was clean, if not particularly tidy, with a few pieces of battered old furniture that wouldn't have looked out of place in the city dump. Which was probably where they'd come from. A narrow bed was pushed up against the far wall, the bedclothes held together by patches and rough stitching.

The woman gestured for him to sit down on one of the uncomfortable-looking chairs pulled up to the fire. He did so, and she slowly lowered herself into the facing chair. Her bones cracked loudly in the quiet, sounding almost like the damp logs spitting in the fire. For a while Saxon and the woman just sat there, looking at each other. He still couldn't see his sister in the drawn, wrinkled face before him.

"I hear you used to be married," he said finally.

"Ah yes. Dear Robbie. He was so alive, always joking and smiling and full of big plans. Sometimes I think I married him because he reminded me so much of you. That should have warned me, but I was lonely and he was insistent. He ran through what was left of the family fortune in twelve months, and then I woke up one morning and he was gone. He left me a nice little note, thanking me for all the good times. I never saw him again. Things were hard for a while after that. I had no money, and Robbie left a lot of debts behind him. But I coped. I had to."

"Wait a minute," said Saxon, confused. "What about the rest of the family? Why didn't they help you?"

Jenny Grove looked at him. "I thought you'd know by now. They're all dead, Wulf. It broke mother's heart when you ran off and left us without even a word or a note. Father spent a lot of money hiring private agents to try and track you down, but it was all money wasted. Your friends were convinced something must have happened to you, but they couldn't find out anything either. Mother died not long after you left. She was never very strong. Father faded away once she was gone, and followed her a year later. George and Curt both became soldiers. George joined the army, and Curt became a mercenary. You know they never could agree on anything. They died fighting on opposite sides of the same battle, over fifteen years ago. That just left me. For a long time I clung to the hope that you might come back to help me, but you never did. After a while, after a long while, I stopped hoping. It hurt too much. How could you do it, Wulf? You meant so much to us; we were all so proud of you. How could you just run off and leave us?"

"I didn't," said Saxon. "I got caught in a sorcerer's trap.

I was only released today. That's why I haven't aged. For me, twenty-three years ago was yesterday."

"Stealing," said Jenny Grove. "You were out stealing again, weren't you? Everything you had, wealth and power and position; that wasn't enough for you, was it? You had to have your stupid little thrills as well, didn't you?"

"Yes. I'm sorry."

She looked at him, too tired and beaten down even to be bitter, and he had to look away. There was a long, awkward silence as he searched for something to say.

"Why . . . Jenny Grove?" he said finally.

She shrugged. "Your money took us out of the Northside, and let us live the good life, for a while. I wish it hadn't. It made it so much harder to go back to being nothing again. Annathea and her life became just a dream, a dream I wanted to forget, because it drove me mad. So I became Jenny Grove, who'd never been anything but poor, and had no memories to forget."

"But what about our friends? Did none of them help you?"

"Friends . . . you'd be surprised how quickly friends disappear once the money's run out. And you made a lot of enemies when you disappeared so suddenly. Friends who'd been as close as family wouldn't even speak to us, because of the way you left them in the lurch. They were convinced we must have known about it, you see. Not everyone turned their back on me. Billy Doyle—you remember Billy—he helped sort out the debts Robbie left me, and helped me start a new life. I drove him away in the end. He was part of the old days, and I just wanted to forget. Dear Billy; he had such a crush on me when we were younger. I don't suppose you remember that."

"I remember," said Saxon. "He told me where to find you."

"That was good of him."

"Yes, it was. He said . . . everyone around here knew you. What do you do, these days?"

"I read the cards, tell fortunes, that sort of thing. Father would never have approved, but it's harmless enough. Mostly I just tell them what they want to hear, and they go away happy. I have my regular customers, and they bring me enough to get by on."

Saxon smiled for the first time. "That's a relief, at least. From the way Billy said it, I was afraid you might have been a . . . well, a lady of the evening."

"You mean a whore. I was, dear. What else was there for me, then? But I got too old for that. I decided I'd spent enough time staring at my bedroom ceiling, and took up the cards instead. Dear me, Wulf, you look shocked. You shouldn't. There are worse ways to make money, and you'll find most of them here in the Hook. Why did you come here, Wulf? What do you want from me?"

Saxon looked at her. "You're my sister."

"No," said Jenny Grove flatly. "That was someone else. Annathea Saxon died years ago—of a broken heart, like her parents. Go away, Wulf. We've nothing to say to each other. All you can do is stir up memories best forgotten by both of us. Go away, Wulf. Please."

Saxon rose slowly to his feet. He felt so helpless it hurt. "I'll get some money together, and then I'll come back and see you again."

"Goodbye, Wulf."

"Goodbye, Anna."

He left without saying any more, and without looking back. Jenny Grove stared into the crackling fire, and wouldn't let herself cry until she was sure he'd gone.

Saxon stomped down the stairs, scowling angrily. There had to be someone left from his past who'd be glad to see him. Someone he'd started on the road to success . . . He smiled suddenly. Richard Anderson. Young Richard had been just starting out in Reform politics twenty-three years ago, and Saxon had provided both financial and personal backing when no one else believed in Anderson at all. Saxon had believed in him. Richard Anderson had shown drive and ambition and an almost savage grasp of how to play the political game. If anyone had succeeded and prospered in Saxon's absence, it would be Anderson. And someone with his genius for keeping a high profile shouldn't be that difficult to track down.

He started down the stairs that led to the ground floor, and then stopped suddenly, his hand dropping to his sword. The entry hall was crammed with a dozen young toughs and bravos, all wearing the same leathers as the four Serpents he'd encountered earlier. Apparently the survivor had gone running for his friends. Well, crawling anyway. They carried knives and clubs and lengths of steel chains, and they looked at Saxon with mocking grins and hungry eyes. Saxon looked calmly out at them.

"I've had a bad day, my friends. You're about to have a worse one."

He ran down the last few stairs and launched himself into their midst. He landed heavily on two Serpents, and his weight threw them all to the floor. He lashed out with his fist, and one Serpent's face disappeared in a mess of blood and broken bone. Stamping down hard as he rose to his feet, Saxon felt the other Serpent's ribs break and splinter under his boot. Knives and bludgeons flailed around him, but he was too fast for them. He moved among the Serpents like a deadly ghost, his fists lashing out with supernatural strength and fury. He picked up one of his assailants and used him as a living flail with which to batter his fellows. The Serpent screamed at first, but not for long. Bones broke and splintered, blood flew on the air, and Serpents fell to the floor and did not rise again. Saxon soon tired of that, and threw the limp body away. He needed it to be more personal. He needed to get his hands on them.

But the few remaining Serpents turned and ran rather than face him, and he was left alone in the hallway, surrounded by the dead and the dying. Blood pooled on the floor and ran down the walls, the stink of it heavy on the air. Saxon looked slowly around him, almost disappointed there was no one left on whom he could take out his frustration, and realised suddenly that he wasn't even breathing hard. Something strange had happened to him during his time in the Portrait. He'd lost his mind, and recovered it in some fashion he didn't really understand, but he'd gained something too. Not only had he not aged, but when he fought it was as though all the lost years burned in him at once. He was stronger and faster than anyone he'd ever known. The Serpents hadn't been able to lay a finger on him. His gaze moved slowly over the broken and bloodied bodies that lay scattered across the hallway, and he grinned suddenly. He'd been away, but now he was back, and he wasn't in the mood to take any shit from anyone. Haven might have gone to hell while he was away, but he was going to drag it back to civilisation, kicking and screaming all the way if necessary.

He left the tenement building and strode off into the Northside, in search of Richard Anderson.

"Councillor Anderson," said Saxon. "I'm impressed, Richard; really. You've come up in the world."

Saxon leaned back in his chair and puffed happily at the long cigar he'd taken from the box on Anderson's desk. The rich smell of cigar smoke filled the office, obliterating the damp smell from Saxon's clothes. There were fresh bloodstains on his clothes too, but so far, Anderson had carefully refrained from mentioning them. Saxon looked around the office, taking his time. He liked the office. It had been his once, back when he'd been a Reform Councillor. One of the first Reform Councillors, in fact. The office had been extensively renovated and refurnished since then, of course, and it looked a hundred times better. Everything was top quality now, including the paintings on the walls. Saxon could remember when the only painting had been a portrait of their main Conservative rival. They'd used it for knife-throwing practice. Saxon sighed, and looked down at the floor. There was even a fitted carpet now, with an intimidatingly deep pile. He looked back at the man sitting on the opposite side of the desk, and tried hard to keep the frown off his face.

Councillor Richard Anderson was a stocky, tolerably handsome man in his middle forties, dressed in sober but acceptably fashionable clothes. Saxon thought he looked ridiculous, but then fashions had changed a lot in the past twenty-three years. Anderson looked impassively back at Saxon, wearing a standard politician's face—polite but uninvolved. There was nothing in his expression or posture to show how he felt about seeing the man who had once been his closest friend and colleague, back from the dead after all the long years. Nothing except the slow anger in his eyes.

"What the hell happened to you, Richard?" said Saxon finally. "How did you of all people end up as a Conservative Councillor? You used to be even more of a Reformer than I was; a hotheaded rebel who couldn't wait to get into politics and start making changes. What happened?"

"I grew up," said Anderson. "What happened to you?"

"Long story. Tell me about the others. I assume they haven't all become Conservatives. What's Dave Carrera doing these days?"

"He's an old man now. Sixty-one, I think. Left politics after he lost two elections in a row. Runs a catering business in the Eastside."

"And Howard Kilronan?"

"Runs a tavern, the Inn of the Black Freighter."

"Aaron Cooney, Padraig Moran?"

"Aaron was killed in a tavern brawl, twenty years ago. I don't know what happened to Padraig. I lost touch over the years."

Saxon shook his head disgustedly. "And we were going to change the world. We had such hopes and such plans. . . . I take it there is still a Reform movement in Haven?"

"Of course. It's even had a few successes of late. But it won't last. Idealists don't last long in Haven as a rule. What are you doing here, Wulf?"

"I came to see a friend," said Saxon. "I don't seem to have many left."

"What did you expect, after running out on us like that? All our plans fell apart without you here to lead us. You were a Councillor, Wulf; you had responsibilities, not just to us but to all the people who worked and campaigned on your behalf. When you just up and vanished, a lot of people lost heart, and we lost the Seat on the Council back to the Conservatives. All of us who'd put money into the Cause lost everything. Billy Doyle spent a year in a debtors' prison. You know how he felt about you, and your sister. Have you seen her yet?"

"Yes. Why didn't you do something to help her?"

"I tried. She didn't want to know."

They sat in silence for a while, both of them holding back angry words. Saxon stubbed out his cigar. The taste had gone flat. He rose to his feet and nodded briskly to Anderson. "Time to go. I'll see you again, Richard; at the next election. This is my office, and I'm going to get it back."

"No, wait; don't go." Anderson rose quickly to his feet and gestured uncertainly. "Stay and talk for a while. You still haven't told me how you've stayed so young. What have you been doing all these years?"

Saxon looked at him. Anderson's voice had been carefully casual, and yet there had been a definite wrong note; a hint of something that might have been alarm, or even desperation. Why should it suddenly matter so much to Anderson whether he left or not? A sudden intuition flared within him, and he moved over to look out the window. In the street below, Guard Constables were gathering outside the house. Saxon cursed dispassionately, and turned back to look at Anderson.

"You son of a bitch. You set me up."

Anderson's face paled, but he stood his ground. "You're a wanted criminal, Wulf. A common murderer and arsonist. I know my duty."

Saxon stepped forward, his face set and grim. Anderson backed quickly away, until his back slammed up against the wall. Saxon picked up the heavy wooden desk between them and threw it effortlessly to one side, and then stood still, staring coldly at Anderson.

"I ought to tear your head right off your shoulders. After all the things I did for you . . . But it seems I'm a bit pressed for time at the moment. I'll see you again, Richard; and then we'll continue this conversation."

He turned away and headed for the door. Anderson struggled to regain his composure.

"They'll find you, Saxon! There's nowhere you can hide. They'll hunt you down and kill you like a rabid dog!"

Saxon smiled at him, and Anderson flinched. Saxon laughed softly. "Anyone who finds me will regret it. I've got nothing left to lose, Richard; and that makes me dangerous. Very dangerous."

He left the office, not even bothering to slam the door behind him. He ran down the stairs to meet the Guard, feeling his new strength mount within him like a fever. He wasn't going to let the Guard stop him. He had things to do. He wasn't sure what they were yet, but he was sure of one thing: someone was going to pay for all the years he'd lost, for all the friends and hopes that had been taken from him. The first of the Guard Constables appeared at the bottom of the stairs, and Saxon smiled down at him.

"You know something? I've had a really bad day. You're about to have a worse one."

The other Guards arrived, and he threw himself at them.

The cemetery wasn't much to look at, just a plot of open land covered with earth mounds and headstones. Incense sticks burned at regular intervals, but the smell was still pretty bad. Saxon stood looking down at the single modest stone bearing both his parents' names, and felt more numb than anything. He'd never meant for them to be buried here. He'd always intended they should be laid to rest in one of the more discreet, upmarket cemetaries on the outskirts of the city. But by the time they died, most of the money he'd brought to the family was gone, and so they were buried here. At least they were together, as they'd wanted.

The rain had died away to a miserable drizzle, though the sky was still dark and overcast. Saxon stood with his head bare, and let the rain run down his face like tears. He felt cold, inside and out. He knelt down beside the headstone, and set about methodically clearing the weeds away from the stone and the grave. He'd known his parents would probably be dead, as soon as he was told how many years he'd been away, but he hadn't really believed it. Then Anna told him they'd died, but he still didn't believe it, not really. For him it was only yesterday that they'd both been alive and well, and proud of him. Their son, the city Councillor. And now they were gone, and they'd died believing he deserted them, and all the people who depended on him. He stopped weeding and sat still, and the tears burst from him with a violence that shook him.

They finally passed, leaving him feeling weak and drained. He'd never felt so alone. In the past, there had always been family and friends to look out for him, to pick him up when he fell over his own feet from trying to run too fast. They'd always been there when he needed them, family and friends, and Mum and Dad. Now they were gone, and there was no one left but him. So that would have to be enough.

He'd drifted into Reform politics because he thought people needed him, to protect them from the scum who preyed on them, both inside and outside the law. That seemed more true than ever now. Except that things had got so bad he couldn't tell the guilty from the innocent anymore. Something had to be done, but he no longer had any faith in politics; he needed to take a more personal stand. To get his hands on the bad guys and make them hurt, the way he was hurting. He could do that. He was different now; stronger, faster, maybe even unbeatable. He could find the people responsible for making Haven what it had become, and exact vengeance for himself and everyone else who'd lost all hope and faith in the future. He smiled slowly, his eyes cold and savage. He would have his vengeance, and the Gods help anyone who got in his way.

He rose to his feet, and took one last look at the headstone. Whatever happened, he didn't think he'd be coming back.

"Goodbye, Mum, Dad. I'll make you proud of me again. I'll put things right. I promise."

He turned and left the cemetery, and walked back into the unsuspecting city.

3

HOSTAGES

The rain was still hammering down, and Hawk was getting distinctly tired of it. He pulled his hood well forward and ran after Jessica Winter as she led the SWAT team down the wide, empty road that led into Mulberry Crescent. They'd been running flat out for the last five streets, ever since Winter got the emergency call from the Guard communications sorcerer. She was still running well and strongly, but Hawk was starting to find it hard going. Personally, he thought she was just showing off. Whatever the emergency was, it couldn't be so important they had to sprint all the way there. Hawk had never been much of a one for running, mainly because he'd always tended towards stamina rather than speed. But he couldn't afford to look bad before the rest of the team, so he gritted his teeth and pounded along in Winter's wake, glaring at her unresponsive back.

He still found the time to keep a wary eye on his surroundings, and was surprised to find the street was totally empty. Even allowing for the foul weather, there should have been some kind of crowd out on the street, celebrating the Peace Treaty. But though strings of brightly colored bunting hung damply above them, and flags flapped limply in the gusting wind, the SWAT team were alone in the middle of the fashionable Westside street. And that was strange in itself. Guards weren't usually welcome in the Westside. The well-to-do and high-placed families who lived there tended to prefer their own private guards when it came to keeping the peace; men who knew where their loyalties lay, and could be relied on to look the other way at the proper moments. Hawk smiled sourly. It would appear the private guards had run into something they couldn't handle, and then been forced to call in the SWAT

team. Hawk's grin widened at the thought. He bet that had
rankled. Hawk didn't have much use for private guards. In
his experience, they tended to be overpaid, overdressed,
and about as much use as a chocolate teapot.

Winter finally slowed to a halt at the end of the street,
and looked out over Mulberry Crescent. The rest of the
team formed up around her. Hawk did his best to hide his
lack of breath, and squinted through the rain at the killing
ground before him. Bodies lay scattered the length of the
Crescent. Men, women, and children lay twisted and broken, like discarded toys a destructive child had tired of.
Water pooled around the bodies, tinted pink with blood.
Hawk counted twenty-nine in plain sight, and had a sick
feeling there were probably more he couldn't see yet. No
one moved in the Crescent, and no one stared from the
windows. If there was anybody left alive, they were keeping
their heads well down. Which suggested that whatever had
happened here, it wasn't over yet.

There was still no sign anywhere of the private guards,
which didn't surprise Hawk one bit. They were all very well
when it came to moving on undesirables and manhandling
the occasional troublemaker, but show them a real problem
and they tended to be suddenly scarce on the ground. He
looked at the pathetic contorted bodies lying abandoned in
the rain, and his hands curled into fists. Someone was going
to pay for this. One way or another. He looked at Winter,
who was standing silently beside him.

"I think it's time you filled us in on why we're here,
Winter. The Crescent looks like it was ambushed. What
exactly are we dealing with here?"

"A sniper," said Winter, not taking her eyes off the scene
before her. "He's been active for less than forty minutes,
but there are already thirty-two dead that we know of. No
wounded. He kills every time. And just to complicate
things, he's a magic-user, and a pretty powerful one at that.
He's holed up in an upper story of one of these houses,
somewhere down the far end. He's been using his magic to
blast everything that moves, irrespective of who or what it
might be. Local guards have cleared the streets, but it's up
to us to do something about the sniper." She glanced briefly
at Storm. "Well, do you See anything useful?"

"Not really," said Storm, scowling unhappily. "He's in

the third house from the end, down on the left, but he's protected himself very thoroughly against any form of magical attack. I can break through his wards, given enough time, but he could do a hell of a lot of damage to the surrounding area before I took him out."

"Be specific. How much damage?"

"He could demolish every building for at least four blocks in every direction, and kill hundreds of people. That specific enough for you?"

Winter scowled, and rubbed her chin thoughtfully with a thumb knuckle. "What kind of magic has he been using?"

"All sorts. For a psychotic killer, he's very versatile. The air's heavy with unexpended magic. I can still See his victims dying as they ran for safety. Some had all the life drained out of them, so they could feel themselves dying. Others were transformed into things that didn't live long. Luckily. And some were just blown apart, for the fun of it. We've got a bad one here, Jessica. He's powerful, versatile, and ready to do anything to get what he wants."

Winter nodded. "Question is, what does he want? Attention, revenge; what?"

Hawk spun round suddenly, his axe flashing out to stop a finger's breadth from the throat of a private guard behind him. All the color drained from the man's face, and Hawk grinned at him nastily. "I don't like people sneaking up on me, particularly when they do it so badly. Takes all the challenge out of it. I could hear you coming even through the pouring rain." He lowered his axe but didn't put it away. "All right; who are you, and what do you want?"

The private guard swallowed hard. Color was slowly seeping back into his face, but it was still pale enough to clash interestingly with the vivid vermilion and green of his uniform. He cleared his throat and looked pleadingly at Winter. "Corporal Guthrie, of Lord Dunford's guards, ma'am. I'm your local liaison officer."

"About time you got here," said Winter. "Fill us in. What's the background on this case?"

Corporal Guthrie moved over to join her, giving Hawk and his axe a wide berth.

"The sorcerer Domain has been a resident of Mulberry Crescent for years. Always quiet and polite. Never any trouble. But about three-quarters of an hour ago, he suddenly appeared at a window on the upper floor of his house and started screaming at people down in the street. We don't know about what. Everybody who was in the street at that time is dead. According to one eyewitness who watched from his window, Domain just lashed out with his magic for no reason, killing everyone in sight. No one's dared leave their houses since. We've sealed off the Crescent at both ends, and evacuated the houses farthest from Domain, but we daren't get too close for fear of starting him off again. A doctor went in a while ago under a white flag to check the bodies, just in case there was anyone alive. There wasn't, so he approached Domain's house, to try and reason with him. The sorcerer told the doctor he wanted to be left alone, and that he'd kill anyone who tried to interfere with him."

"I'd like to talk to this doctor," said Winter. "He might be able to tell us all kinds of useful things."

"I don't think so," said Guthrie. "Domain destroyed his mind. All he does is repeat the sorcerer's message, over and over again."

Fisher swore harshly. "Let's just take the bastard out. Storm can protect us with his magic, and Hawk and I will go in and carve him up. It'll be a pleasure."

"It's not as simple as that," said Guthrie.

"I had a feeling he was going to say that," said Hawk.

"Domain has a hostage," said Guthrie. "Susan Wallinger, twenty-one years old. She was Domain's lady friend. We have reason to believe she wished to end the relationship, and had gone to his home to tell him so. It would appear Domain took this rather badly. He's threatened to kill her if she tries to leave, or if we send anyone in after her."

"You know the city's policy on hostages," said Winter. "They're expendable."

"Yes, ma'am. But Susan Wallinger is Councillor Wallinger's daughter."

"That is going to complicate things," said Fisher.

Hawk nodded grimly. Councillor Wallinger was one of the leading lights of the Conservatives, and his many businesses helped to provide a large part of the Party's funds. No wonder the Council had called in the SWAT team so quickly. They were expected to save the hostage as well as take out the sniper. Which, as Fisher pointed out, complicated the hell out of things. Hawk looked out over the corpse-strewn street, and his mouth tightened. As long as Domain was running loose, he was a menace. From the sound of his mental state, anything might set him off again, and next time he might not limit himself to the people in plain sight. He might decide to blow up every house in the Crescent, along with everyone in them. He might do something even worse. He was a sorcerer, after all, and they had no idea as to the limits of his power. One way or another, Domain had to be stopped. Hawk hefted his axe and studied the sorcerer's house. He'd get the girl out alive if he could, but if push came to shove, she was expendable—and to hell with who her father was.

Poor lass.

"We have a standard routine for handling hostage situations," said Winter, looking hard at Hawk and Fisher. "And we're going to follow it here, by the numbers. I don't want either of you doing anything without a direct order from me first. Is that clear?"

"Oh sure," said Hawk. Fisher nodded innocently. Winter glared at them both, unimpressed.

"I'm not unfamiliar with your reputations, Captains. Common belief has it that you're as dangerous as the black death, and about as subtle. You'll find we do things differently on the SWAT team. Whenever possible, our job is to resolve a crisis situation without resorting to violence. Nine times out of ten we get better results by talking and listening than we would if we used force. MacReady is our negotiator, and a damned good one. Until he's tried everything he can think of, and they've all failed, no one else does squat. Is that clear?"

"And if he does fail?" said Fisher.

"Then I'll unleash you and Hawk and Barber, and you'll go in after Domain, under Storm's protection. But that's as a last resort only." She looked at Corporal Guthrie. "You'd better get back to your people and tell them what's happening. I'll be sending Mac down to talk to Domain in a few moments. Tell everyone to get their heads down and keep them down. Just in case."

The Corporal nodded jerkily, and hurried off into the rain. Hawk stared after him.

"Nice uniform," he said solemnly. "Vermilion and green. Cute."

Winter's mouth twitched. "Maybe he just wants to be sure he can be seen at night. All right, Mac; let's do this by the numbers, nice and easy. Your first job is to persuade him to let the girl go. Promise him whatever it takes. Councillor Wallinger will make good on practically anything, if it will get him his daughter back safe and sound. Once she's safely out of the way, then you can concentrate on trying to talk him down."

MacReady looked at her steadily. "Assuming he won't give up the girl, which has priority: getting her out or getting him down?"

"If it comes to that, the girl is expendable," said Winter. "Why do you think I sent Guthrie away before I briefed you? Now get going. We're wasting time."

MacReady nodded, and headed unhurriedly down the street towards Domain's house. Hawk looked sharply at Storm. "Aren't you going to give him any protection?"

"He doesn't need any," said Storm. "He's protected by a Family charm; magic can't touch him, swords can't cut him, and drugs won't poison him. You could drop him off a ten-story building, and he'd probably just bounce. At the same time, the charm doesn't allow him to use any offensive weapons, which is just as well, or he'd have taken over the whole damn country by now. As it is, he makes a damned good negotiator."

He fell silent as a low, rumbling sound trembled in the ground under their feet. Hawk looked quickly about him, but the street was still empty. The rumbling grew louder and more ominous, and then the street next to MacReady exploded. Solid stone tore like paper, and cobbles flew through the air like shrapnel. Hawk held up his cloak as a shield, and cobblestones pattered against it like hailstones in a sudden storm. It was all over in a few seconds, and Hawk slowly lowered his cloak and looked around him. None of the others were hurt. Fisher had her sword in her hand, and was glaring about her for someone to use it on. She looked down the street, and her eyes widened. Hawk followed her gaze.

MacReady was standing unharmed amid vicious-looking fragments of broken stone and concrete, staring calmly into jagged rent in the ground. The explosion didn't seem to ave harmed him at all, even though it must have gone off ractically in his ear. His clothing wasn't even mussed. He hook his head, turned his back on the gaping fissure, and valked on down the street. The outer wall of a nearby ouse bulged suddenly outwards and collapsed over him. Vhen the dust cloud settled, washed quickly out of the air y the driving rain, MacReady was still standing there, enirely unhurt, surrounded by rubble. He clambered awkvardly over some of the larger pieces, and continued on is way. Lightning stabbed down from the overcast sky, gain and again, but didn't even come close to touching im. Magic spat and sparkled around him, scraping across he air like fingernails on a blackboard, but MacReady valked steadily on. He looked almost bored. Eventually he ame to the third house from the end on the left, and ɔoked up at the top floor. A dark shape showed briefly at ɔne of the windows, and then was gone. MacReady pushed ɔpen the front door and walked inside.

Winter stirred at Hawk's side. "Well, if nothing else, I hink we can be fairly sure that Domain knows he's oming."

It was very quiet inside the house, out of the driving rain, nd MacReady paused in the gloomy hallway to take off iis cloak and hang it neatly on the wall rack. A woman's loak was already hanging there, barely damp to his touch. Presumably Susan Wallinger's. He looked around him. All vas still except for the loud ticking of a clock somewhere lose at hand, and an occasional quiet creaking as the old iouse settled itself. MacReady moved over to the nearest loor. It was standing slightly ajar, and he pushed it open. A headless body lay sprawled before the open fireplace. 3lood and gore had soaked into the rich pile carpet where iis head should have been. There was no sign of the head tself. Judging by the ragged state of the neck, the head iadn't been neatly severed with a blade. It had been torn ɔff by brute force. MacReady stepped back into the hall nd headed for the stairs. The body might have been a ailed negotiator, or someone who lived in the house. It night even have been a friend of Domain's.

Hello, Domain. Guess what? I'm going to be your friend.

*I'm going to win your trust and then abuse it. I'm going to
persuade you to give up your hostage and come down peace-
fully, so that we can put you on trial, find you guilty, and
execute you. I won't tell you that, of course. I'll tell you
comforting lies and make you think they're true. Why? Because it's my job, and I'm good at it.*

*And because I get so horribly bored waiting to die, and
outwitting kill-crazy lunatics like you is the only fun I
have left.*

He made his way up the stairs, making no attempt to be
quiet. He wanted Domain to know he was coming. If the
sorcerer thought he was sneaking up on him, he might
panic and harm the girl. MacReady shook his head in mock
disapproval. He couldn't allow that. Getting the girl out
alive was part of the game, and he didn't like to lose. He
stepped onto the dimly lit landing, bracing himself mentally
against any further sorcerous attacks, but nothing happened. There was a door at the end of the hall with a light
showing round its edges. He started towards the door, and
it flew open suddenly as Domain lurched out into the hall.

His robe of sorcerer's black was torn and ragged, and
there was dried blood on his sleeves and hands. He was
tall and painfully thin, and barely into his early twenties.
His face was deathly pale, split almost in two by a wide
death's-head grin. His eyes were wide and staring, and they
didn't blink often enough. He was shaking with suppressed
emotion, ready to lash out at anyone or anything that
seemed to threaten him. MacReady stayed where he was,
and smiled calmly at the sorcerer.

"Stay where you are!" snapped Domain, his voice harsh
and tinged with hysteria. "One step closer and I'll kill her!
I will!"

"I believe you," said MacReady earnestly. "I'll do whatever you say, sir sorcerer. You're in charge here. My name
is John MacReady. I've come to talk to you and Susan."

"You've come to take her away from me!"

"No, I'm just here to talk to you, that's all. You've got
yourself in a bit of a mess, Domain. I'm here to help you
find a way out of it. The authorities have promised not to
interfere. You just tell me what you want, and I'll tell them.
There must be something you want. You don't want to stay
here, do you?"

"No. Something bad happened here." Domain's gaze turned inward for a moment, and then the crazy glare was back in his eyes, as though he couldn't bear to think about what he'd seen in that moment. "I'm getting out of here, and Susan's coming with me. I'll kill anyone who tries to stop us!"

"Yes, Domain. We understand that. That's why I'm here. We don't want any more deaths. Could I speak to Susan? Perhaps between the three of us we can come up with a plan that will get you both out of the city without anyone else having to be hurt."

The sorcerer studied him suspiciously for a dangerously long moment, and then jerked his head at the open door behind him. "She's in here. But no tricks. I may not be able to hurt you, but I can still hurt her. I'll kill her if I have to, to keep her with me!"

"I'll do exactly as you say, Domain. Just tell me what to do. You're in charge here."

MacReady kept up a low, soothing monologue as he slowly approached Domain. It didn't really matter what he said. The man had clearly gone beyond the point where he could be reached with logic, but he could still be soothed, charmed, manipulated. The important thing now was to keep pressing home the idea that Domain was in charge of the situation, and MacReady was only there to carry out his wishes. As long as Domain was feeling confident and in control, he shouldn't feel the need to lash out with his magic. And then MacReady entered the room, and his words stuck in his throat.

Blood had spattered the walls and pooled on the floor. Dark footprints showed where Domain had walked unheedingly through the blood. The corpse of a young woman stood unsupported in the middle of the room, her head hanging limply to show a broken neck. Her eyes were open, but they saw nothing at all. Blood had run thickly from her nose and mouth, and dried blackly on her neck and chest. Flies buzzed around her. MacReady wondered briefly if she'd died before or after Domain lost his mind.

I'll kill her if I have to, to keep her with me.

"It's all right, darling," said Domain to the dead woman. "Don't be frightened. This is John MacReady. He's just come to talk to us. I won't let him take you away. You're safe here, with me."

The corpse walked slowly towards him, her head lolling limply from side to side. The corpse stood beside the sorcerer, and he put a comforting arm round its shoulders, and hugged it to him. MacReady smiled at them both, his face open and guileless.

"Hello, Susan; it's nice to meet you. Well, the first thing I have to do is report back to my superiors that you're alive and well, and with Domain of your own free will."

"Of course she is," said Domain. "We love each other. We're going to be married. And nothing will ever part us. Nothing . . ." His voice trailed away, and his gaze became troubled for a moment, as though reality was nudging at his mind, but the moment passed and he smiled fondly at the dead woman, animated only by his magic. "Don't worry, darling. I won't let them hurt you."

"Is there anything you want me to tell the authorities?" said MacReady carefully. The response would tell him a lot about what was going on in the madman's mind.

"Yes," said Domain flatly. "Tell them to go away and leave us alone. Susan and I will be leaving here soon. If anyone gets in our way, I'll kill them. Tell them that, John MacReady."

"Of course." MacReady bowed formally. "May I go now, sir sorcerer?"

Domain dismissed him with a wave of his hand, all his attention fixed on the dead woman at his side. Quiet music rang out on the air from nowhere, some pleasant, forgettable melody that had been popular recently. Domain took the dead woman in his arms and they danced together to music that had been their song, once.

The SWAT team had found a columned porch to shelter under, and stood huddled together in the narrow space, staring out into the rain. Hawk scowled, and shifted impatiently from foot to foot. He hated standing around doing nothing. A thought struck him, and he looked suddenly at Winter.

"If MacReady's immune to any kind of attack, why doesn't he just grab the girl and punch out Domain?"

"The charm won't let him," said Winter sharply. "If he

behaves aggressively, the charm stops working. If he tried anything with Domain, he'd be dead in a second. His job is to talk to Domain, and that's all. Don't worry about it, Captain; he's very good at his job. He'll get the girl out alive if anyone can."

"Something's happening," said Fisher. "There's movement down the street."

They all turned to look. A stream of people were pouring out of a house halfway down the street and running towards the SWAT team. Some of them glanced back at Domain's house, or at the bodies lying sprawled in the rain, but for the most part the only thing in their minds was flight. Their eyes were fixed and staring, and they ran with the awkward, determined speed of desperation and sheer terror.

"They must have been caught in the street when people started dying," said Winter. "Dammit, why couldn't they have stayed in the house? Do they think it's all over, just because it's been quiet for a while?"

"You have to stop them," said Storm. "If Domain should see them . . ."

"There's nothing I can do," said Winter. "Nothing anyone can do now."

They stood together, watching the group run, hoping they'd make it to safety and knowing the odds were they wouldn't. They were close enough now for the SWAT team to hear their pounding footsteps on the broken ground, even through the rain.

"Run," said Storm quietly. "Run your hearts out, damn you."

There were seven men in the group, and three women. Hawk could just make out their faces through the rain. His breathing speeded up as he silently urged the runners on. They were closer now, only a few seconds from safety. The man in the lead faltered suddenly, frowning as though confused, and his head exploded in a flurry of blood and gore. His body stumbled on for a few more steps, and then fell twitching to the blood-slick cobbles. The woman behind him screamed shrilly, but ran on through his blood and brains. Her screams were cut off suddenly as she was jerked up off the ground and high up into the air. She clawed desperately at her throat, as though pulling at some invisible noose. Her eyes bulged, and her tongue protruded from her mouth. She fell back towards the ground, gathering speed with every second until she was falling impossibly fast. She hit the street with a sickening sound, her body crushed by the impact into something no longer human. The others kept running.

One woman just disappeared. For a moment the rain outlined an empty silhouette, and then there was a flat, popping sound as air rushed in to fill the space where she'd been. Two men collapsed and fell screaming to the cobbles. Their bodies melted and ran away in the rain, leaving nothing behind. Their screams seemed to echo on the air long after they'd gone. The five surviving runners suddenly stumbled to a halt, four men and a woman soaked to the skin by the pouring rain. They looked at each other, and started laughing. They stood together in the rain, their faces blank and their eyes empty, and laughed their minds away.

Hawk beat at one of the portico's columns with his fist. Fisher was cursing in a flat, angry whisper. Storm had looked away, but Winter watched the scene before her with a cold, detached professionalism. Barber was still watching Domain's house at the end of the street. The front door opened, and MacReady stepped out into the rain. He pulled the hood of his cloak well forward and walked unhurriedly back up the street, stepping carefully to avoid the pools of blood. He gave the laughing group a wide berth, but they didn't even know he was there. Hawk looked at Storm.

"Wasn't there anything you could have done to protect them?"

"No," said Winter. "There wasn't. Domain mustn't know about Storm yet. He's our ace in the hole, in case we have to end this siege the hard way. How many times do I have to say it, Captain Hawk? Our responsibility is to the city, not individuals. Compared to the hundreds Domain could kill if we don't stop him, those few people were expendable. They should have stayed where they were. There's no room in a SWAT team for sentiment, Captain; we have to take the long view."

"Is it all right if I feel sorry for the poor bastards?" said Fisher tightly.

"Of course. As long as it doesn't get in the way of the job."

The SWAT team watched in silence as MacReady made his way through the rain to join them. He stepped into the porticoed shelter, shook himself briskly, then looked at Winter and shook his head.

"How bad is it?" said Winter.

"About as bad as it could be. Susan Wallinger is dead. Domain has animated her corpse, and talks to it as if it were alive. He's quite mad. There's no way I can reach him with logic or promises. I hate it when they're mad. Takes all the fun out of it. I was really looking forward to rescuing the girl." He looked back at Domain's house. "Bastard."

"What's the present situation?" said Winter, ignoring his bad temper.

MacReady sniffed and shrugged. "At the moment I'm supposed to be negotiating a safe passage for Domain and Susan to leave the city. But you can forget that. In his present condition he's too dangerous to be allowed to run loose, even if we were leading him into a trap. He could lash out at anyone or anything, for any reason. In his madness he's tapping into levels of power that would normally be far beyond him. As long as we've got him bottled up here, there's a limit to the damage he can do."

"So we're going to take him out," said Barber showing an interest in the proceedings for the first time. "Good. I haven't killed a sorcerer in ages."

Storm gave him a sideways look but said nothing. Hawk coughed loudly, to get everyone's attention.

"I think we can safely assume that the time for negotiations has passed. From the sound of it, Domain very definitely doesn't have both his oars in the water anymore. So what's the procedure, Winter? Do we just burst in under Storm's protection and kill Domain?"

"Not exactly," said Winter. "You and Fisher will go in first, making as much noise as possible, and hold Domain's attention while Barber sneaks in the back and cuts him down from behind. Not very sporting, I'll admit, but I'm not taking any chances with this one. He could do a lot of damage before we take him down. So please; no heroics, from anyone. If you screw up on this, you won't be the only ones to suffer."

"Wait a minute," said Fisher, frowning. "What can go wrong? I thought Storm was going to protect us against Domain's magic?"

"I can protect you from any direct magical attack," said Storm quickly, "but Domain's a very versatile sorcerer. He'll almost certainly animate the bodies of those he killed and use them to defend himself. He might even animate the physical structure of the house itself. I can't protect you from things like that without dropping the wards that protect you from his magic."

"Relax," said Fisher. "We can look after ourselves."

"I'm sure you can," said Winter. "After all, you're the infamous Hawk and Fisher, aren't you? If you're as good as your reputation, this should be a walk in the park for you."

Hawk smiled coldly. "We're not as good as our reputation. We're better."

"Then this is your chance to prove it."

Fisher glared at Winter, her hand resting on her sword hilt. Hawk drew his axe. Barber stirred, and moved a little closer to Winter. The atmosphere on the crowded porch was suddenly uncomfortably tense. Hawk smiled coldly at Winter, and looked across at Barber.

"I don't suppose you've any of those incendiaries left?"

"Sorry. They were only experimental prototypes, and I used them all in Hell Wing."

"Got anything else we could use?"

Barber shrugged. "Nothing you could learn to use quickly, and like Winter said, we're pushed for time. You just go in there and do what you're good at; hit anything that moves. I'll be around, even if you can't see me. Now let's go, before Domain figures out he's not going to get what he's waiting for."

Hawk nodded, pulled his hood up over his head and stepped out into the rain. Fisher gave Winter one last glare, and hurried after him. She sniffed loudly.

"Walk in the park," she growled to Hawk. "Has she seen the park lately?"

They strode down the middle of the street, not bothering to hide themselves. Domain would know they were coming. They avoided the laughing victims, staring sightlessly ahead as the rain ran down their contorted faces like tears. They stepped carefully over and around the dead bodies, and

Hawk gripped his axe tightly. He looked constantly around him, but there was no sign of movement anywhere in the street, and the roar of the rain cut off every other sound. The first he and Isobel would know about any attack was when it hit them.

Hawk and Fisher were almost halfway down the street when the sky opened up. Lightning stabbed down, dazzling them both with its glare. The cobbled street split open under the bolt's impact, sending Hawk and Fisher staggering sideways as the ground heaved beneath them, but the lightning didn't even come close to touching them. Hawk broke into a run, with Fisher right beside him. Storm's magic might be able to protect them as thoroughly as MacReady's charm had protected him, but Hawk didn't feel like putting it to the test. Domain's house loomed up before them, strange lights glowing at its windows. Hawk kicked in the front door, and they darted into the hallway while lightning flared impotently in the street outside. Hawk slammed the door shut behind them, and put his back against it.

They stood together a moment, getting their breath back and staring round the gloomy hall. Hawk pointed at the stairs, and Fisher nodded. They moved forward silently and took the steps one at a time, checking for booby traps and keeping a careful watch on the dark shadows around them. They'd barely reached the halfway mark when the front door slammed open behind them. Hawk and Fisher looked back, blades at the ready. A dead man stood in the doorway, rain running down its face and trickling across its unblinking eyes.

Hawk ran back down the stairs and threw himself at the lich. His axe flashed briefly as he buried it in the lich's chest. The dead man staggered back under the impact, but didn't fall. It reached for Hawk with clutching hands, its colorless lips stretching slowly in another man's smile. Domain's smile. Hawk wrenched his axe free and struck at the lich again, this time aiming for the hip. The impact drove the lich to the ground this time, and Hawk bent over it. He pressed a boot on its chest to hold it down, and jerked the axehead free. The lich grabbed his ankle with a pale hand, the dead fingers closing like a vise. Hawk grimaced as pain shot up his leg, and swung his axe with both hands. The heavy axehead tore through the lich's throat and sank into the cobbles beneath. The dead hand's hold tightened, and Hawk had to grit his teeth to keep from crying out. He used the axe as a lever and tore the lich's head from its body. The head rolled away into the rain, its mouth working soundlessly. The grip on Hawk's ankle didn't loosen, and the body heaved beneath his foot as it tried to rise again.

Fisher was suddenly at his side, and her sword sliced through the lich's wrist, severing the gripping hand. Hawk staggered back, and between them, he and Fisher pried the hand from his ankle. It fell away into the street, its fingers still flexing angrily, like a huge fleshy spider. The headless body heaved itself up onto its knees. Fisher moved in behind it, and cut through its leg muscles. More dark shadows appeared in the rain, heading towards Hawk and Fisher with fixed eyes and reaching hands.

Hawk cursed quickly and darted back through the open front door. Fisher glared at the approaching liches, and then hurried into the house after him. The dead moved purposefully forward. Hawk pushed the door shut and slammed the bolts home. There were only two, and neither of them looked particularly sturdy. Hawk looked quickly about him.

"I wonder if there's a back door to this place?"

Fisher raised an eyebrow. "Are you suggesting we make a run for it?"

"The thought had occurred to me. I don't like the situation, and I definitely don't like the odds."

"It's going to make a bad impression on the SWAT team if we run away."

"It'd make an even worse impression if we got killed." Hawk scowled. "But you're right. We can't leave. We've got to hold Domain's attention until Barber can get to him. Or there's no telling how many more Domain might kill."

"So what's the plan?" said Fisher. "Make a stand here, and hope we can hold off the liches until Barber makes his move?"

"To hell with that," said Hawk. "There's too many of the damn things, and if they're all as determined as that first one, they're going to take a lot of stopping. All it needs is for one of them to get in a lucky blow, and we could be in real trouble. We can't even keep them out of the house. That door won't last five minutes against a determined assault. I've got a better idea. Let's head up those stairs, find Domain, and cut him into little pieces. That should hold his attention."

"Sounds good to me," said Fisher. "Assuming Storm's protection holds up under attack at such close quarters."

"Would you rather face the liches?" asked Hawk.

"Good point," said Fisher. "Let's go."

A headless body lurched out of the room to their left, reaching for them with blindly grasping hands. Hawk and Fisher separated, and hit it from different sides. Hawk slammed his axe into the lich's ribs, throwing the dead thing back against the wall. Fisher's sword licked out and sliced through the back of the lich's left leg, and the creature sank to one knee. Hawk pulled his axe free, and swung it with both hands. The heavy blade all but severed the lich's right leg below the knee, and the dead man sprawled helplessly on the floor. Hawk indicated the stairs with a jerk of his head, and Fisher nodded quickly. Hawk kicked the headless body aside, and ran for the stairs with Fisher right beside him. Behind them, the lich scrabbled furiously on the floor, trying to pull itself after them with its arms. The front door shuddered suddenly in its frame as dead fists hammered on it. A window shattered somewhere close at hand. Hawk and Fisher pounded up the stairs, and didn't look back.

Barber made his way unhurriedly down the rain-swept street, and neither the living nor the dead saw him pass. He carried his sword at the ready, but he didn't expect to have to use it yet. No one knew he was there, and no one would, until he'd thrust his sword into Domain's back and put an end to all this nonsense. In the end, as in so many SWAT operations, it all came down to him and his sword. Storm could cast his spells, and MacReady could talk, and Winter could plot her strategies, but in the end they always turned to him and his sword. Which was why he stayed with them. He needed to kill just as much as they needed him to put an end to killers.

Not that he enjoyed the killing; he took no pleasure in death or suffering. It was simply that he was so very good at what he did, and he took a real satisfaction in doing a

difficult job that no one else could do, and doing it su-
perbly. He didn't care who he killed; he barely remembered
their faces, let alone their names. He didn't even care what
they'd done; their various crimes or outrages were of no
interest to him. All that mattered was the opportunity to
kill; to kill with a style and expertise that no one else
could match.

And the Council actually paid him to do it.

He drifted down the street, unseen and unheard, and
made his way round to the rear of Domain's house, searching for the back door. The door stuck when he tried it, but
it swung open easily enough when he put his shoulder to
it. He stepped into the gloom, wary but unconcerned, and
pushed the door shut behind him. He wasn't expecting any
trouble. When he was working, no one could see or hear
him, unless he wanted them to. A useful talent for an
assassin.

Domain would never even know what hit him.

Hawk and Fisher were only halfway up the stairs when the
front door burst open, and dead things spilled into the hall.
Hawk pressed on, heading for the narrow landing with
Fisher only a step or so behind him. The stairs suddenly
lurched and heaved beneath them like a ship at sea, and
they had to fight to keep their balance. Jagged mouths and
staring eyes formed in the wall beside them. The wooden
panelling steamed and bubbled. Hawk moved to the middle
of the stairs, away from the manifestations, and glanced
back over his shoulder. The first of the dead had reached
the stairs. The hall was full of liches, soaked and dripping
with rainwater that couldn't entirely wash away the blood
from their wounds, their empty eyes fixed unwaveringly on
the two Guards.

The stairs lurched again, and Hawk grabbed at the banister to steady himself. It writhed under his hand like a huge
worm; all cold and slimy and raised segments. Hawk
snarled and snatched his hand away, and plunged forward,
heading for the landing. Fisher called out behind him, and
he looked back to see her struggling to pull her foot free
from a step that had turned to bottomless mud. She cut at
the step with her sword, but the blade swept through the
thick mud and out again without even slowing. Hawk

grabbed her arm and pulled hard, and her foot came free with a slow, sucking sound. They threw themselves forward and out onto the landing, and ran towards the door Mac-Ready had described in his briefing.

Blood ran down the wall in thick streams, and a dirty yellow mist curled and twisted on the air, hot and acrid. Jagged holes appeared in the floor beneath their feet, falling away forever. Hawk and Fisher jumped over them without slowing. Behind them, something large and awful began to form out of the shadows. The air was suddenly full of the stench of decaying meat and freshly spilled blood, and something giggled softly in anticipation. Hawk and Fisher reached Domain's door and Fisher kicked it open. They ran into the room, and Hawk slammed the door shut behind them.

Everything seemed still and calm and quiet in the comfortable, cozy little room. For a moment it seemed almost a sanctuary from the madness running loose in the house, until Hawk took in the blood splashed across the wall and floor, and the dead woman standing beside the seated sorcerer, one hand resting on his shoulder. Hawk met Domain's gaze, and knew the real madness was right there in the room with him, held at bay only by Storm's protection. Outside in the hallway, heavy footsteps moved slowly closer, the floor trembling slightly with each impact. Fisher glanced back at the door.

"Call it off, Domain," she said harshly.

"Or what? Do you really think you can do anything to threaten me?" Domain smiled, the same smile Hawk had seen on the faces of the dead men. "This is my house, and I don't want you here. You've come to take Susan away from me."

"That's why you have to stop whatever's out there," said Hawk quickly. "If it comes in here after us, Susan could get hurt. Couldn't she?"

Domain nodded reluctantly, and there was a sudden silence as the heavy footsteps stopped, followed by a small clap of thunder as air rushed in to fill a gap where something large had been only a moment before. The sorcerer leaned back in his chair as though it were a throne, and looked crossly at Hawk and Fisher.

"I thought I'd made it clear I didn't want to be disturbed.

How many people do I have to kill to make you leave us alone?"

"We don't want you to kill anyone," said Hawk. "That's why we're here."

Domain made a dismissive gesture, as though he'd caught them in an obvious lie. "I know why you're here. Perhaps if I changed you into something amusing, and sent you back that way, then they'd understand not to play games with me."

"You can't hurt us," said Fisher. "We're protected."

Domain looked at her narrowly, and then at Hawk. "So you are. A very sophisticated defense, too. I could break it, but that would take too much out of me. I have to keep something back to protect Susan. So unless you're stupid enough to attack me, I'll just wait, and let the things I've called up come and take you." He scowled suddenly. "I should have known I couldn't depend on the city to bargain in good faith. I'll punish them for this. I'll turn their precious city into a nightmare they'll never forget."

In the corners of the room, the shadows grew darker. A presence was gathering in the room, something huge and awful pressing against the walls of reality. And beyond that, Hawk could hear dead feet ascending the stairs and making their way onto the landing. The dead woman standing beside Domain's chair smiled emptily at nothing, like a hostess waiting to greet expected guests. Hawk and Fisher looked desperately at each other, but saw no answer in each other's faces. The presence growing in the shadows was almost overpowering, and the dead were almost outside the door.

"Don't worry, Susan," said Domain comfortingly to the dead woman. "It'll all be over soon, and then we'll be together, forever. No one's ever going to take you away from me."

The door swung silently open, and Barber eased into the room, his sword at the ready. Hawk and Fisher looked quickly away, to avoid drawing Domain's attention to him. They'd been briefed on Barber's special talent, but it was still hard to believe Domain couldn't see him. Barber moved slowly forward across the room, making no more noise than a breath of air. Hawk found he was holding his breath. The sorcerer smiled at his dead love, unconcerned.

Barber moved in behind Domain and raised his sword. And then Domain raised his left hand. Light flared briefly around the upraised fingers, and Barber froze where he was, unable to move. Domain turned unhurriedly in his chair to look at him.

"Did you really think you could break into my house, and I wouldn't know? There's a power in me, assassin, a power beyond your worst nightmares, and it's more than enough to see through your simple glamour. I knew the city would send someone like you. They want to take my love away from me. I won't let them. I'll destroy this whole stinking city first!"

He gestured sharply, and Barber flew across the room to crash into the opposite wall. He slid to the floor, only half conscious but still somehow hanging onto his sword. Footsteps clumped heavily in the hallway outside, and Domain smiled broadly as the dead spilled into the room. Fisher raised her sword and went to meet them. Hawk lifted his axe and threw it in one swift motion, with all his strength behind it. The axe flew through the air and buried itself to the haft in Susan's skull. The impact slammed the dead woman backwards, and she staggered clumsily in a circle. Domain screamed, and jumped out of his chair to grab her by the arms. He howled wordlessly in horror and despair, and the dead woman crumpled limply to the floor, no longer sustained by the sorcerer's will. Domain sank to his knees beside her, and started to cry. The dead men in the doorway fell to the floor and lay still, and the invading presence was suddenly gone. The room seemed somehow lighter, and the shadows were only shadows. The only sound in the small, unexceptional room were the anguished sobs of a heartbroken young man crying for his lost love.

Fisher lowered her sword, and nodded to Hawk. "Nice thinking. Even he couldn't believe she was still alive with an axe buried between her eyes."

"Right. He's no danger anymore. Poor bastard. Though I think we'd better get Storm in here as soon as possible, just in case." He shook his head slowly. "What a mess. So many dead, and all for love."

"I'm fine, thank you," said Barber, getting slowly and painfully to his feet.

Hawk turned and grinned at him. "Next time, try not to make so much noise."

Barber just looked at him.

The beggars sat clustered together outside the main gate of Champion House, lined up ten or twelve deep in places. They were of all ages, from babes to ancients, and wore only the barest rags and scraps of clothing, the better to show off their various diseases and deformities. Some were clearly on the edge of starvation, little more than skin stretched over bone, while others lacked legs or hands or eyes. The rain poured down upon their bare heads, but they paid it no attention. It was the least of their troubles. Some wore the vestiges of army uniforms, complete with faded campaign ribbons. They stood out from the others, in that they seemed to have a little pride left. If they were lucky, they'd soon lose it. It just made being a beggar that much harder.

The beggars huddled together, as much for company as comfort, their eyes fixed on the main gate, waiting patiently for someone to go in or out. The honour guards supplied by the Brotherhood of Steel for the two Kings' protection stared out over the beggars, ignoring them completely. They posed no threat to the House's security, as long as they continued to keep a respectable distance, and were therefore of no interest. The beggars sat together in the rain, heads bowed, and among them sat Wulf Saxon.

He watched the main gate carefully, from beneath lowered brows. He'd been there almost two hours, shivering in the damp and the cold, and had put together a pretty good picture of the House's outer security system. The honour guards were everywhere, watching all the entrances and checking everyone's credentials carefully before allowing them to enter. They took their time and didn't allow anyone to hurt them, no matter how important-seeming or obviously aristocratic the applicant might be. The Brotherhood of Steel trained its people well. Saxon frowned, thinking his way unhurriedly through the problem. There had to be magical protections around the House as well, which suggested that the successful applicants had been issued charms of some kind which allowed them to enter the grounds without setting off the alarms. He'd have to acquire one. After he found a way in.

He hugged his knees to his chest, and ignored the rain trickling down his face with proper beggarlike indifference. He'd suffered worse discomfort in his early career as a confidence trickster, before he discovered politics. Though there were those who'd claimed he'd just graduated from the smaller arena to the large. He smiled to himself, and his fingers drifted casually over his left trouser leg, pressing against the long leather canister strapped to his shin. The baggy trousers hid it from view, but he liked to remind himself of its presence now and again. It helped fuel his anger. The contents of the canister would be his revenge against the two Kings. The first of many blows against the heartless and corrupt authorities who'd made Haven the hellhole it was and kept it that way because it suited their interests to do so. He was going to hurt them, hurt them all in the ways that would hurt them the most, until finally his vengeance forced them to make reforms, for fear of what he'd do next.

He made himself concentrate on the problem at hand, and reluctantly decided against a frontal assault. No matter how good his disguise, or how persuasive his arguments, there were just too many guards at the main gate and too many ways for things to go wrong. Not to mention too many witnesses. Fouling up in public would destroy his reputation before he even had a chance to re-establish it. And there was still the problem of the House's protective wards. He wasn't going to get anywhere without the right charms. Saxon shrugged. Fate would provide, or she wouldn't. He tended to prefer simple plans, whenever possible, mainly because they allowed more room for improvisation if circumstances suddenly changed. Though he could be as obscure and devious as the next man, when he felt like it. The more intricate schemes appealed to his creative nature, if not his better judgment.

He rose to his feet and stumbled off through the crowd of beggars, his head carefully bowed, his whole attitude one of utter dejection. No one looked at him. Beggars tended to be invisible, except when they got under people's feet. Saxon made his way into a nearby dark alley, listened for a long moment to be sure he was alone, and then straight-

ened up with a low sigh of relief. All that bowing his head
and hunching over was doing his back no good at all. He
stepped briskly over to the nearest drainpipe, took a firm
grip, and climbed up onto the roof. The pipe creaked
threateningly under his weight, but he knew it would hold.
He'd checked it out earlier, just to be on the safe side. He
pulled himself up over the guttering and onto the sloping
roof in one easy motion, so quietly he didn't even disturb
a dozing pigeon in the eaves. He padded softly over the
rain-slick slates to the far edge of the roof, and jumped
easily onto the adjoining roof. The gap was only a few feet,
and he didn't look down. The length of the drop would
only have worried him; he was better off not knowing. He
crossed two more roofs in the same fashion, and crouched
down on the edge of the final roof, a ragged gargoyle in
the driving rain. A narrow alley was all that separated him
from Champion House.

The wall surrounding the grounds stared aggressively
back at him: ten feet of featureless stone topped with iron
spikes and a generous scattering of broken glass. A single
narrow gate looked out onto the alley, a tradesman's entrance manned by two large, professional-looking men-at-
arms. They both wore chain mail, and had long, businesslike swords on their hips. Saxon had spotted the gate on
his first reconnoitre, and had marked it down in his memory
as a definite possibility. Tradesmen had been in and out of
Champion House all morning, bringing extra supplies for
the new guests and their entourages. At the moment, a
large confectioner's cart was parked at the end of the alley,
and a stream of white-coated staff were carrying covered
trays past the men-at-arms. Saxon grinned. Perfect. The
confectioner hadn't even questioned the unexpected order
when Saxon delivered it to him, clad in his most impressive-
looking footman's outfit. Of course, it had helped that the
order had been written on engraved notepaper bearing the
Champion House crest. Saxon believed in getting all the
details right.

He was just grateful he'd had the foresight to store all
his con man's props in his secret lock-up all those years
ago. Actually, it hadn't really been foresight. He just hadn't
wanted to take a chance on any of them turning up unex-

pectedly to embarrass him after he'd become an eminently respectable Councillor. . . .

And he never could bear to throw anything away.

He slid silently over the edge of the roof, and padded quickly down the fire escape, the few unavoidable sounds drowned out by the pounding rain. He stood very still in the shadows, under the fire escape, and waited patiently for just the right moment. A white-coated confectioner's assistant came out of the side gate with his hands in his pockets, and headed unhurriedly for the cart at the end of the alley. He passed by the fire escape, whistling tunelessly, and two strong hands shot out of nowhere and dragged him into the shadows.

Saxon emerged from the shadows a few moments later wearing a white coat, and headed for the confectioner's cart. The coat fit like a tent, but you couldn't have everything. More's the pity. At the cart, a harried-looking supervisor handed him down a covered tray, and Saxon balanced it on his shoulder as he'd seen the others do. He kept his face carefully averted, but the supervisor was too busy to notice anyway.

"Get a move on," he growled to Saxon, without looking up from the list he was checking. "We're way behind schedule, and if the boss chews on my arse because we got back late, you can bet I'm going to chew on yours. And don't think I didn't spot you sloping off to lounge about behind the fire escape. You pull that again, and I'll have your guts for garters. Well, don't just stand there; get the hell out of here! If those pastries are ruined, it's coming out of your wages, not mine!"

Saxon grunted something vaguely placating, and headed for the side gate. The men-at-arms didn't even look at him, just at the white coat. Saxon timed his pace carefully, not too slow and not too hurried, and tucked his chin down against his chest, as though trying to keep the rain out of his face. As he neared the gate, one of the men-at-arms stirred suddenly, and Saxon's heart jumped.

"Stay on the path," said the man-at-arms in a bored monotone, as though he'd said it before many times, and knew he'd have to say it a great many more times before the day was over. "As long as you stay on the path the alarms won't go off. If you do set off an alarm, stay where you are till someone comes to get you."

Saxon grunted again, and passed between the two men-at-arms. He braced himself for a last-minute shout or blow, but nothing happened. He strode quickly along the gravel path, speeding up his pace as much as he dared. The path led him through the wide-open grounds to a door at the rear of the House. He followed slow-moving white coats into the kitchens, put down his tray with the others, and leaned against a wall to get his breath back and wipe the rain from his face, surreptitiously taking in the scene as he did so. The kitchen was bigger than some houses he'd known, with ovens and grills on all sides, and a single massive table in the middle of everything, holding enough food to feed a medium-sized army. The air was full of steam and the smells of cooking, and a small battalion of servants bustled noisily back and forth, shouted at impartially by the three senior cooks. A single guard was leaning easily against the far door, gnawing on a pork rib and chatting amiably with a grinning servant girl. Saxon smiled. Just what the doctor ordered. He headed straight for the guard, oozing confidence and purpose, as though he had every right to be there, and people hurried to get out of his way. He came to a halt before the guard and coughed meaningfully. The guard looked at him.

"Yeah? You want something?"

"Through here," said Saxon crisply. "You'd better take a look at this."

He pushed open the door behind the guard, stepped through, and held the door open for the guard to follow him. The guard shrugged, and smiled at the servant girl. "Don't you move, little darling. I'll be back before you know it. And don't talk to any strange men. That's my job." He stepped out into the corridor, and Saxon pulled the door shut behind him. The guard glared at him. "This had better be important."

"Oh, it is," said Saxon. "You have no idea." He looked quickly around to be sure no one was looking, then briskly kneed the guard in the groin. The guard's eyes bulged, and he bent slowly forward. His mouth worked as he tried to force out a scream and couldn't. Saxon took him in a basic but very efficient stranglehold, and a few seconds later lowered the unconscious body to the floor. It was good to know he hadn't lost his touch. He dragged the body over to a cupboard he'd spotted, and yanked it open. From now on, speed was of the essence. Anyone could come along, at any moment. The cupboard proved big enough to take both of them easily, and he took the opportunity to change his white coat and beggar's rags for the guard's honour outfit and chain mail. Leaving the door open a crack provided all the light he needed. The mail fit tightly in all the most uncomfortable places, but it would do. He kicked the guard spitefully for being the wrong size, and strapped the man's sword to his own hip. He wished briefly for a mirror, and then pushed open the cupboard door and stepped out into the corridor. A passing servant stopped in his tracks and stared blankly at Saxon.

"Excuse me . . . this is probably a silly question, but what were you doing in the cupboard?"

"Security," said Saxon darkly, closing the door. "You can't be too careful."

He met the servant's gaze without flinching, and the man decided to continue about his business and not ask any more stupid questions. Saxon grinned at the servant's departing back. It was his experience that people will believe practically anything you care to tell them, as long as you say it firmly enough. He fingered the bone medallion he'd found on the guard, and which was now hanging round his own neck. Presumably this was the charm that protected the guard against the House's protective wards. With it, he should be able to go anywhere he wanted. Of course, if it wasn't the charm, or the right charm, he was about to find out the hard way. He shrugged. Whatever happened, he'd think of something. He always did.

He strode leisurely through the House as though he belonged there, nodding to people as they passed. They nodded back automatically, seeing only his uniform, sure he must have a good reason for being where he was. Saxon smiled inwardly, and studied his surroundings without seeming to do so. Everywhere he looked there was luxury, in the thick carpets and antique furniture, and the portraits and tapestries covering the walls. And so much space. He remembered the single room where his sister now lived, and his fury burned in him.

He had to find the two Kings. He needed to see them, study their faces, look into their eyes. He wanted to know the people he was going to destroy. There was no satisfaction in taking vengeance on faceless people, on titles and positions rather than individuals. He wanted this first act of revenge to be entirely personal. He stepped out of a side corridor into a high-ceiling hall, and stopped to get his bearings. Servants scurried back and forth around him, intent on their various missions. He couldn't just stand around watching without appearing conspicuous. So, when in doubt, be direct. Saxon stepped deliberately in front of a hurrying footman, and gave the man his best intimidating scowl.

"You; where are the Kings?"

"Fourth floor, in the main parlour, sir. Where they've been for the past two hours."

There had been more than a hint of insolence in the footman's tone, so Saxon cranked up his scowl another notch. "And how do you know I'm not some terrorist spy? Do you normally give away vital information to the first person who walks up to you and asks? Shape up, man! And stay alert. The enemy could be anywhere."

Saxon stalked off in the direction of the stairs, leaving a thoroughly confused and worried footman behind him. He threaded his way through the bustling crowd, nodding briskly to the few guards he passed. He'd almost reached the stairs when a guard officer appeared out of nowhere right in front of him, and he had to stop or run the man down. The officer glared at him, and Saxon remembered just in time to salute him. The officer grunted and returned the salute.

"What the hell do you think you're doing, appearing on duty looking like that? Your uniform's a disgrace, your chain mail looks like it was made for a deformed dwarf, and that was the sloppiest damn salute I've ever seen. What's your name and your unit?"

Oh, hell, thought Saxon wearily. *I don't need this. I really don't.*

He glanced quickly around to be sure no one was looking and then gave the officer a vicious punch well below the belt. All the color drained out of the officer's face, and his legs buckled. Saxon grabbed him before he fell and quickly walked him across the hall and back into the side corridor. He shook his head woefully at a passing guest.

"Don't touch the shellfish."

The guest blinked, and hurried on his way. Saxon waited a moment till the corridor was deserted, and then knocked the officer out with a crisp blow to the jaw. It was only a matter of a few seconds to stuff him into the cupboard along with the first guard. He considered for a moment whether to swap his outfit for the officer's, but decided against it. Officers tended to stand out; the rank and file drew less notice. He hurried back down the corridor into the hall, and ran straight into another officer. This time he remembered to salute. The new officer returned it absent-mindedly.

"I'm looking for Major Tierman. Have you seen him?"

"No, sir. Haven't seen him all day."

"What do you mean, you haven't see him all day? This is your commanding officer we're talking about! What's your name and unit?"

Oh, hell.

"If you'll follow me, sir, I think I can take you right to the Major."

Back in the side corridor, Saxon finished stuffing the un-conscious officer into the cupboard, and forced the door shut. He'd better not run into any more officers, or he'd have to find another cupboard. He set off again at a brisk walk, with a very determined expression that he hoped sug-gested he was going somewhere very important and shouldn't be detained. He flexed the fingers of his right hand thoughtfully. There was one thing to be said for his new strength: when he hit someone they stayed hit. He doubted the two officers and the guard would be waking up for a good few hours yet. More than enough time for him to take his vengeance on the two Kings and depart.

The main parlour turned out to be full of people trying to look important. The two Kings sat in state at the back of the room, surrounded by an ever-shifting mob of court-iers, local Quality, and guards. Any assassin trying to get close to the monarchs would probably have been trampled underfoot in the crush long before he got anywhere near his targets. Politicians and military mixed more or less ami-cably around the punch bowl, while merchants and nouveau riche Quality hovered desperately on the edges of conversations, angling hopefully for introductions to the right people. Polite conversation provided a steady roar of noise, easily drowning out the string quartet murdering a classical piece in the corner. No one even noticed Saxon's entrance. He took up a position by the door, not too far from the buffet table, and studied the layout of the room. No one paid him any attention. He was just another guard.

He watched the two Kings for a time. They didn't look like much. Take away their crowns and their gorgeous robes of state, and you wouldn't look at them twice in a crowd. But those two men, both in their late forties, were symbols of their countries and the Parliaments that governed them. A blow struck against them would be heard across the world. But of even more importance was the Peace Treaty, standing on display in a simple glass case between the two Kings.

There were two copies of the Treaty, standing side by side under the glass; one for each Parliament. Two sheets of pale-cream parchment covered with the very best copperplate calligraphy, awaiting only the Kings' signatures to make them law. Saxon smiled slowly. He flexed his leg, and felt the leather canister press against his bare skin. Inside the canister were two sheets of pale-cream parchment, carefully rolled, and protected by padding. From a distance, they looked exactly like the Treaty. And once Saxon had swapped them for the real Treaty, no one would be able to tell the difference. At least, not until it was far too late.

Saxon had put a great deal of thought into his first act of vengeance. It wasn't enough just to hurt those in authority; they had to be publicly humiliated. His two sheets of parchment were covered with copperplate calligraphy, but a minor avoidance spell which Saxon had purchased from the son of one of his old contacts would ensure that no one studied the text too closely. The spell was too subtle and too minor to set off any security alarms and would fade away completely in a matter of hours anyway, but by then the damage would have been done. Both the Kings would have put their signatures, and thereby their Parliaments' approval, to a Treaty that declared the authorities of both countries to be corrupt, incompetent, and complete and utter bastards without a single trace of human feeling.

The text went on like that for some time, in increasingly lengthy and insulting detail. Saxon had written it himself in a fury of white-hot inspiration, and was rather proud of it.

And the Kings were going to sign it. Right there in public, with everyone watching. They'd never live it down. When word got out, as it inevitably would, as to exactly what they'd put their names to, a shock wave of incredulous laughter would wash across Outremer and the Low Kingdoms. The more the authorities tried to suppress and deny the story, the more people would flock to read or listen to pirated copies of the false Treaty, and the wider the story would spread. The first part of Saxon's vengeance would have begun. More practical jokes and humiliations would follow, and no one would be safe from ridicule. Powers that would stand firm against intrigue and violence were helpless when it came to defending themselves against derisive laughter. It's hard to be scared of someone when their very appearance is enough to start you giggling. Saxon's grin broadened. After today, both the Kings and their Parliaments were going to be laughingstocks.

He looked around one last time, and let his hands drift casually into his trouser pockets, reaching for the smoke bombs he'd put there. One to go into the open fire, and the second for an emergency exit, if necessary. Under cover of the smoke and chaos, and while the security people were busy protecting the Kings from any attack, it would be child's play for him to open the glass case and make the substitution. The real parchments would disappear into his leather canister, and it would all be over before the smoke cleared. And afterwards it should be easy enough for a single guard to disappear in all the confusion.

It was a superb plan; simple but elegant. Nothing could go wrong.

Daniel Madigan stood openly in the street under a rain avoidance spell, watching Champion House from the middle of a crowd of onlookers waiting patiently for a glimpse of the two Kings. Horn and Eleanour Todd stood on either side of him, watching the crowd. Just in case. The young killer Ellis Glen stood beside Todd, shifting impatiently from foot to foot. They'd been watching the House for the best part of an hour, waiting for a signal from the traitors inside the House. The signal would tell them that the protective wards had been temporarily lowered, and then the fun could begin. But until then, they could only wait and watch. Even with the sorcerer shaman Ritenour working for him, Madigan wasn't prepared to take on the kind of magical defenses the Kings' sorcerers would have set up. He hadn't made his reputation by being stupid. Or impatient.

Ritenour himself stood a little away from his new associates. Their constant aura of suppressed violence disturbed him. To his eyes, the House was surrounded by an ever-shifting aurora of lights and vibrations, flaring here and there with deadly intent. The magic within him stirred at the sight of it. He looked thoughtfully at the terrorists. He still wasn't sure why he was there. The more he thought about what Madigan had planned, the less tempting the money seemed. He could still leave. Ritenour had no loyalty to anyone save himself, let alone anything as nebulous as a Cause. And he didn't trust fanatics, particularly when it came to their paying their bills. But when all was said and done, he was intrigued, curious to see if Madigan could bring off his plan. And perhaps, just perhaps, he stayed with Madigan because he knew the terrorist would kill him if he tried to back out now.

"Can't keep still for a moment, can you?" said Horn to Glen, as the young man shifted his position yet again. "Like a big kid, aren't you, Alice?"

"Don't call me that," said Glen. He was blushing despite himself, but his eyes were cold. "I've told you; my name is Ellis."

"That's what I said, Alice. It's a nice name; suits a good looker like you. Tell you what: you do good in there today and I'll get you a nice big bunch of flowers and a ribbon for your hair. How about that?"

"If you don't shut up, I'm going to kill you, Horn. Right here and now."

"Now, Alice, behave yourself, or I'll have to spank you."

Glen's hand dropped to the sword at his side, and Todd glanced at Horn. "That's enough. Leave the boy alone."

Glen shot her a look of almost puppyish adoration and gratitude, and looked away. Horn chuckled.

"I think he fancies you, Eleanour. Isn't that nice? All girls together."

Todd glared at him, and Horn looked away, still chuckling. He didn't say anything more. Much as he enjoyed teasing Glen and challenging Todd's authority, he knew he could only push it so far before Madigan would step in. Horn wasn't stupid enough to upset Madigan. Over anything. He glanced surreptitiously at Eleanour Todd. Before Madigan brought her into the group, he'd been second-in-command, Madigan's voice. And if something were to happen to her, he might be again. Of course, he'd have to be very careful. If Madigan even suspected he was plotting something against another member of the group . . . The thought alone was enough to stop him chuckling, and he went back to studying the House.

Glen stared straight ahead of him, not really seeing the crowd or the House. He could feel the warmth of the betraying blush still beating in his face, and his hands had clenched into fists at his sides. The need to cut and thrust and kill was almost overpowering, but he held it back. If he let it loose too soon, Madigan would be disappointed in him, and Glen would have cut off his own hand rather than disappoint Madigan. He had turned Glen's life around, given him a Cause and a purpose. Told him that his talent for death was a skill and an asset, not something to hide or be ashamed of. Madigan understood his dark needs and bloody dreams, and had taught him to control and channel them. Now he killed only at Madigan's order, and the joy was that much sweeter.

He wondered if Eleanour had seen him blushing. He worshipped her almost as much as he did Madigan, though for different reasons. He'd kill for Madigan, but he'd die for Eleanour. She was everything he dreamed of being—a cool professional killer who stood at Madigan's right hand, his trusted support and confidante. She was also heart-stoppingly beautiful, and on the few occasions when she actually smiled at him, he walked around in a daze for minutes on end. He'd never told her how he felt, of course. He'd seen the way she looked at Madigan. But still he dreamed. And it was only in his dreams that it occurred to him that Eleanour might look more kindly on him if Madigan wasn't around any longer. . . .

Bailey strode through the crowd to rejoin his associates, and people hurried to get out of his way. His huge frame was intimidating, even when he was trying his best to be inconspicuous. Ritenour was glad to see the big man back again, even though he couldn't stand the fellow. Madigan had sent the warrior out on reconnaissance almost an hour ago, and the long wait had been wearing at everyone's nerves. Everyone except Madigan, of course. Bailey ground to a halt before Madigan, and nodded briefly.

"Everything's set. The men are all in position, awaiting your signal to begin."

"Are you sure we can trust these men?" said Ritenour. "If they let us down, or turn against us, we're dead."

"Relax, shaman," said Madigan easily. "These are professional fighting men, every one; a hundred of the very best, gathered and placed under contract outside Haven so as not to draw unwelcome attention. We can trust them to fight and die like any other mercenary, particularly on the wages they've been promised."

"I'd have thought you'd be happier with fanatics, ready to die for their Cause."

"I don't want men who can die; I want men who can win. That's enough questions for now, shaman. We have work to do."

"If you'd take the time to fill me in on what's happening, I wouldn't have to keep asking questions."

"You know all you have to. Now be quiet. Or I'll have Bailey remonstrate with you."

Ritenour looked at the huge warrior looming over him, and decided there was nothing to be gained by pushing Madigan any further. He had to know more about the terrorists' plans if he was to know the best time to cut and run, but that could wait. He had no intention of leaving without his money, anyway, and he also had to be sure that Madigan was in no position to come after him. He gazed haughtily up at Bailey, and turned his back on him. The huge warrior chuckled quietly. Ritenour pointedly ignored him, and fixed his attention on Champion House. A light flared briefly in an upper window. There was a slight pause, and then it flashed again. Madigan nodded calmly.

"About time, Sir Roland. Bailey, give the signal. The wards are finally down, and we can proceed."

Bailey waved his hand over his head, and the mercenaries appeared from everywhere, with swords and axes in their hands. They came from among the gawking crowd, from the beggars at the main gate, and from every side street and alleyway. They were in a multitude of disguises, but all of them wore the identifying black iron torc of the mercenary on their wrist. They howled a deafening mixture of battle cries, and threw themselves at the various gates in the House's outer walls. The honor guards fought well and valiantly, but were quickly overwhelmed by the sheer number of their attackers. The mercenaries hurdled their twitching bodies and raced on into the grounds.

Madigan led his people through the panicking crowd, and approached the main gate. A small band of guards had slammed the gate in the mercenaries' faces, and were somehow still holding their ground behind the gate's heavy steel framework. Madigan looked at Ritenour, who nodded quickly. He gestured at the guards and spoke a minor Word of Power. The guards fell screaming to the ground as the blood boiled like acid in their veins. Steam rose from their twisting bodies as the acid ate holes in their flesh. Ritenour gestured again, and the gate swung open, pushing the guards' bodies out of the way. Madigan led his people though the open gate and into the grounds, smiling quietly at the chaos his mercenaries had caused.

A small army of guards and men-at-arms spilled out of the House and stared wildly about them, confused and disoriented because the security wards had failed them. The mercenaries fell upon them like starving wolves, and blades flashed dully in the rain. The air was full of screams and war cries, and blood pooled thickly on the sodden ground. Madigan cut down the first defender to get in his way with a single stroke of his sword, and passed on without slowing. Bailey strode at his side, wielding his great sword with casual, professional skill. No one could stand against his strength and skill, and only the desperate or the foolish even tried. Horn and Eleanour Todd busied themselves opening up a bloody path for Madigan to walk through. Glen fought where he would, cutting down opponents as fast as he could reach them. His face was wild and horribly happy, and his chain mail was thickly spattered with other men's blood. He was always in the thick of the fighting, but no one could touch him. He killed wherever his eyes fell, and it was never enough. Ritenour hurried to keep up with the others, saving his magic as much as he could. He was going to need all his power for the horrible thing Madigan wanted him to do later.

Men-at-arms and honour guards threw themselves at the advancing terrorists, and fell back dead and dying. All across the grounds the defenders were being killed or beaten back, and mercenaries were streaming into the House itself. Madigan led his people through the open front door, and into the entrance hall. He paused just long enough to congratulate the mercenaries who were guarding the door, and then led his people quickly through the panic-filled corridors, ignoring the screaming servants who scattered before the terrorists' bloody blades like startled geese. A small group of men-at-arms tried to ambush them in an open hall, and the terrorists quickly closed around Madigan to protect him. Bailey scattered the men-at-arms with wide sweeps of his great sword, and Glen and Eleanour Todd cut them down with savage efficiency. The last remaining man-at-arms tried to turn and run, and Horn disemboweled him with a casual sideways sweep of his sword. The man sank to his knees, and tried to stuff his bloody guts back into his stomach. The terrorists left him sitting there, and continued on their way. Ritenour hurried along in the rear, fighting for breath but not wanting to be left behind. Here and there the House's defenders still struggled with Madigan's mercenaries, but they were clearly outnumbered and outmatched. Blood and gore soaked the thick pile carpets and spattered the priceless tapestries.

Finally they came to the main parlour on the fourth floor, and Madigan stood for a moment in the doorway, smiling round at the terrified guests. The guards and men-at-arms in the room were all dead, the bodies left to lie where they had fallen. Twenty mercenaries surrounded the guests with drawn swords, and a small pile of mostly ceremonial swords and daggers at one side showed that the prisoners had already been disarmed. Madigan nodded approvingly, and walked unhurriedly into the room, flanked by Horn and Eleanour Todd. He stopped before the two Kings, sitting stiffly in their chairs with knives at their throats, and bowed politely. His voice was smooth and assured and only lightly mocking.

"Your Majesties, I do beg your pardon for this intrusion. Allow me to assure you that as long as you and your guests behave yourselves, there is no reason why most of you shouldn't leave this room alive. Please don't delude yourselves with any thought of rescue. My men now control this House and its surrounding grounds. Your men are dead."

"You won't get away with this!" A gray-haired General from the Outremer delegation stepped forward, ignoring the swords that moved to follow him. His uniform had been pressed within an inch of its life, and his right breast bore ribbons from a dozen major campaigns. His face was flushed with anger, and his eyes met Madigan's unflinchingly. "By now this whole area is surrounded by enough armed men to outnumber your little army a hundred times over. You don't have a hope in hell of getting out of here alive. Surrender now, and I'll see you get a fair trial."

Madigan nodded to Horn, who stepped forward and plunged his sword into the General's belly. There were muffled screams from some of the ladies, and gasps from the men. The General looked down at the sword unbelievingly. Horn twisted the blade, and blood poured down between the General's legs. He groaned softly and sank to his knees. Horn withdrew the blade, and the General fell forward onto the bloody carpet. Over by the door, Glen giggled quietly. Madigan looked calmly about him.

"I trust there'll be no more outbursts. Any further unpleasantness will be dealt with most firmly."

No one said anything. The General was breathing heavily as blood pooled around him, but no one dared approach him. Ritenour took advantage of the pause to surreptitiously study four bodies in sorcerer's black that had been dumped unceremoniously in a pile by the door. Their faces were pale, their eyes bulged unseeing from their sockets, and their lips were tinged with blue.

Poison, thought Ritenour approvingly. *No wonder the Kings' sorcerers were unable to maintain the House's wards or defend against the mercenaries' attack. Madigan's pet traitors must have doctored their wine.*

He looked up quickly as a mercenary came running into the room and whispered at length to Bailey. The big man nodded, and moved forward to murmur in Madigan's ear. The terrorist smiled and turned back to face his reluctant audience.

"You'll no doubt be relieved to hear that the authorities have been informed of your plight and negotiations for your release will soon begin. Now, I suppose you're wondering what this is all about. It's really very simple. Everyone here will be released unharmed when the authorities agree to meet my demands, which are very reasonable under the circumstances. I want one million ducats in gold and silver, carts to transport it, and a ship waiting at the docks to carry us away from Haven. I also want a number of political prisoners freed from jails in the Low Kingdoms and Outremer. A list of names and locations will be provided."

King Gregor of the Low Kingdoms leaned forward slightly, careful of the knife at his throat. His narrow, waspish features did little to hide the anger boiling within him, but when he spoke his voice was calm and even. "And if our respective Parliaments should refuse to go along with your demands; what then?"

King Louis of Outremer nodded firmly, imperiously ignoring the knife at his throat. His unremarkable face had the constant redness that comes from too much good food and drink, but his smile was unflinchingly arrogant, and his eyes were full of a cold, contemptuous fury. "They won't pay. They can't afford to give in to terrorist scum. Not even for us." His smile widened slightly. "If we'd been the Prime Ministers you might have got away with it. But our Parliaments won't pay a single penny for us, or release a single prisoner. They can't afford to look weak, or they'd end up a target for every terrorist group with a grudge or a Cause."

"I hope for your sake that you're wrong," said Madigan calmly. "If my demands are not met before the deadline I've set, I'll have no choice but to begin by killing your guests, one at a time, and sending out the bodies to convince the authorities I mean business. If that doesn't impress them, I'll start sending out pieces of your royal anatomy. I think I'll begin with the teeth. They should last a while." He looked away from the silent Kings and smiled at the assembled guests, who shrank before his cold gaze. "Do make yourselves comfortable, my friends. We're in for

omething of a wait, I fear, before Haven's authorities can
et their scattered wits together enough to begin negotia-
ons. Remember: as long as you behave yourselves, you'll
e well treated. annoy me, and I'll have my men hurt some
f you severely, as an example to the others. And please;
ut all thoughts of rescue out of your minds. You're mine
ow."

He looked at Horn and Todd. "Take them into the ad-
oining rooms in small groups, and have the mercenaries
earch them thoroughly. I don't want anyone harboring any
asty surprises. Strip them if necessary, and confiscate any-
hing that even looks dangerous." He looked back at the
hite-faced guests. "Anyone who wishes to give up their
ttle secrets now, to avoid any unpleasantness, is of course
elcome to do so."

There was a pause, and then several men and a few of
he ladies produced hidden knives and dropped them on
he floor. Two mercenaries quickly gathered up the weap-
ns and put them with the other confiscated blades. Madi-
an waited patiently, and one lady pulled a long hat pin
om her hair and offered it to the nearest mercenary, who
ook it with a grin and a knowing wink. The lady ignored
im. Wulf Saxon raised his hand politely. Madigan looked
t him.

"If you want to visit the jakes, you'll have to wait."

"I have a document container strapped to my leg," said
axon. "I don't want it confused for a weapon."

"Then I think we'd better have a look at it, just to be
ure," said Madigan. "Drop your trousers." Saxon looked
round him, and Madigan smiled. "We're all friends to-
ether here. Now take them off, or I'll have someone take
em off for you."

Saxon undid his belt, and lowered his trousers with im-
ense dignity. Madigan approached him, and prodded the
eather canister with the tip of his sword. Saxon didn't
inch.

"What's in the container?" said Madigan, not looking up.

"Documents," said Saxon vaguely. "I'm a courier."

"Take it off and give it to me."

Saxon did so, as slowly as he dared. He'd hoped that by
evealing the canister openly, he could bluff them into
inking it was unimportant and therefore not worth open-

ing, but he couldn't refuse a direct order from Madigan
Not if he wanted to keep his teeth where they were. On
the other hand, he couldn't afford to hand over the fake
Treaties. They'd break the avoidance spell easily, once they
realized what it was, and once they read the parchment
they'd be bound to ask all sorts of awkward questions. And
whatever happened then, his chance of vengeance would
be gone. Terrorists! He'd planned for anything but that
He still had his smoke bombs, but it was a long way to the
door, and the solitary double windows overlooked a hell of
a long drop to the unforgiving flagstones below. Even he
might not survive a fall of four stories. Besides, both the
house and the grounds were apparently occupied by merce
naries. There could be a whole army out there for all he
knew. And there were definite limits to his new strength
and speed . . . especially with his trousers round his ankles

He handed the leather canister over to Madigan as casu
ally as he could. There was a way out of this. There had
to be. A dozen possible stratagems ran through his mind
as Madigan opened the canister, looked briefly at the
parchments, and then turned the receptacle upside down
and shook it, to check there was nothing else inside but
the padding. He sniffed, unimpressed, and dropped the can
ister and parchments onto the buffet table. Saxon almost
gaped at him. The terrorist obviously considered him com
pletely harmless and unimportant. The nerve of the man
Saxon was so outraged, he almost forgot to be relieved
about the parchments. He'd make the terrorist pay for this
insult. He didn't know how yet, but he'd think of some
thing. In the meantime . . . He coughed loudly.

"Excuse me, but can I pull my trousers back up?"

"Of course," said Madigan. "we're not barbarians."

Saxon pulled his pants back up, and forced the belt shut
regretting once again that he couldn't have found a larger
guard to steal a uniform from. It suddenly struck him that
it was only a matter of time before Madigan's people dis
covered the guard and the two officers he'd stuffed into the
closet. And Madigan didn't look the type to suffer myster
ies long. Saxon scowled mentally. The sooner he figured
out a way to shake off the terrorists and disappear, the
better. Not that he had any intention of leaving Champion
House just yet. No one insulted him and ruined one of his

cams and got away with it. He had his reputation to think
of. The Kings could wait. Madigan and his terrorists were
going to rue the day they ever crossed Wulf Saxon.

Ritenour found himself a comfortable chair, and gave
some serious attention to the plateful of food he'd gathered
from the buffet. Nothing like hard work to give you a good
appetite. He offered a chicken leg to Bailey, but the big
man ignored him, presumably too professional to allow
himself to be distracted while on duty. Idiot. Ritenour took
a healthy bite from the chicken leg, and chewed thoughtfully as he studied his fellow conspirators.

Glen was almost falling over himself trying to impress
Bailey with accounts of his part in the storming of Champion House. Bailey was listening indulgently, though his
gaze never left the captives. Madigan and Todd were talking quietly together. Ritenour still wasn't sure about them.
Sometimes they seemed like partners, or even lovers, but
at other times Madigan treated her as just another follower.
Horn was watching the two of them covertly, clearly jealous
of the attention Todd was getting from Madigan. Ritenour
filed the thought away for future reference. It might come
in handy to have something divisive to use against his new
associates. They were all too eager to give everything for
their precious Cause, for his liking. Ritenour had no intention of giving anything that mattered for anybody's Cause.

He thought again of what Madigan wanted him to do,
down in the cellar, and the parlour seemed suddenly colder.

4

Something in the Dark

Hawk waded slowly through dark, knee-high water in the sewers under the Westside, and tried hard not to recognise some of the things that were floating on the surface. Fisher moved scowling at his side, holding her lantern high to spread the light as far as possible. She kept a careful eye on the flame. If it flickered and changed color, it meant the gases in the air were growing dangerously poisonous. There were supposed to be old spells built into the sewers to prevent the build-up of such gases, but judging by the smell, they weren't working too well. Hawk wrinkled his nose and tried to breathe only through his mouth. If the air had been any thicker, he could have cut it with his axe.

He glared about him, searching the low-ceilinged tunnel for signs of life, but everything seemed still and quiet. The only sounds came from the SWAT team splashing along behind him, and Fisher cursing monotonously under her breath. The lantern's golden light reflected back from the dark water and glistened on moisture running down the curved brick walls, but it didn't carry far down the tunnel, and the shadows it cast were lengthened and distorted by the curving brickwork. Hawk glowered unhappily, and pressed on through the filthy water and the stench. It was like moving through the bowels of the city, where all the filth and evil no one cared about ended up.

Jessica Winter plodded along just behind the two Guards, looking around her with interest. If the smell bothered her, it didn't show in her face. Hawk smiled slightly. Winter wasn't the sort to admit to any weakness, no matter how trivial. Barber and MacReady brought up the rear, ploughing steadily along in Winter's wake. Barber carried his sword at the ready, and studied every side tunnel and moving shadow with dark suspicion. MacReady held the other lantern, his eyes thoughtful and far away. Nothing much bothered MacReady, but then if Storm's explanation about his charmed life was right, he didn't have much to worry about. Storm . . . Hawk scowled. While they were all up to their knees in it and gagging on the stench, the sorcerer was probably sitting in some nice dry office with his feet up, following it all with his Sight and grinning a lot. He couldn't go with them, he'd explained in a voice positively dripping with mock disappointment, because the terrorists had raised the House's defensive wards again, and no sorcerer could even approach Champion House without setting off all kinds of alarms.

Hawk's scowl deepened. The situation got more complicated every time he looked at it. The city negotiators had been talking earnestly with the terrorists from the moment they made their first demands, but so far they hadn't got anywhere. The terrorists wouldn't budge an inch in their demands, and the city Council couldn't agree to meet them because both Parliaments were still arguing over what to do. Sorcerers were working in relays passing messages back and forth across the two countries, but so far nothing had been decided. Some factions were pressing for a full-scale assault on Champion House, arguing that a powerful enough force could smash through the House's defences and reach the hostages before the terrorists even knew what was happening. Fortunately for the hostages, no one was listening to these people. Apart from the obvious danger to the two Kings, most of the hostages were extremely well-connected—socially, politically, or economically—and those connections were making it clear to both Parliaments that they would take it very badly if any kind of force was used before every other avenue had been investigated.

So the negotiators talked and got nowhere, the city men-at-arms trained endlessly for an attack they might never make, and the Brotherhood of Steel told anyone who'd listen that this insult to the honour guards they'd provided would be avenged in blood, whatever happened. It wasn't clear whether the Brotherhood was referring to the terrorists or the people who wouldn't let them send in a rescue force, and no one liked to ask. On top of all that, the city's sorcerers couldn't do a damned thing to help because the House's wards were apparently so powerful it would have taken every sorcerer in the city working together to breach them, and the terrorists had threatened to kill both Kings if the wards even looked like they were going down. Champion House was an old house, with a great deal of magic built into its walls. It had been built to withstand a siege, and that was exactly what it was doing.

The city Council listened to everyone, had a fit of the vapours, threw its collective hands in the air, and called in the SWAT team. Wild promises and open threats were made. And that was why Hawk was up to his knees in stinking water and wishing he was somewhere else. Anywhere else. A study of the House's architectural plans revealed it had been built directly over the ruins of an old slaughterhouse (the Westside hadn't always been fashionable), and supposedly there were still tunnels leading from the cellar straight into the sewers. So, theoretically it should be possible for the SWAT team to break into the cellar from the sewers without being noticed. The wards were worn thin down there, for some reason Storm didn't understand, and could be breached by a small force that had been suitably prepared.

Hawk had pressed Storm on this point, but the sorcerer had been unusally evasive. He just insisted that he could keep any alarms from going off, and that was all that mattered. And then he looked away, and said quietly that the cellar had originally belonged to another, even older building, and the slaughterhouse had been built on its ruins. He didn't know what the original building had been, but just making mental contact with the cellar had made his skin crawl. Storm didn't tell Hawk to be careful. He didn't have to. All of which hadn't exactly filled Hawk with confidence, but as Winter kept pointing out, she was the team leader, and she was determined to go in. So they went in.

Hawk studied the sewer tunnel as he trudged along, and supposed he ought to be impressed. There were said to be miles of these tunnels, winding back and forth under the better parts of the city before carrying the wastes out to sea. Of course such tunnels are expensive, which is why you only found them beneath the better parts of the city. Everyone else had to make do with crude drains, runoffs, and sinkholes. Which is why you always knew which way the downmarket areas of the city were, especially when the

wind was blowing. The thought made Hawk aware of the
sewer's stench again, and he made a determined effort to
think about something else. He and the rest of the team
had been given the House's plans and the sewers' layout
as a mental overlay before they left, and he could tell they
were getting close to the right area. The tunnels leading up
to the cellar weren't actually marked on either set of plans,
but they had to be around here somewhere.

Hawk smiled sourly. Actually, there were lots of things
about the sewers that weren't on any map. Half the sorcerers and alchemists in Haven flushed their failed experiments down into the sewers, producing an unholy mixture
of chemicals and forces that gave nightmares to anyone
who thought about it too much. Oversized rats were the
least of the unpleasant things said to prowl the sewer darkness. There were cobwebs everywhere, strung across the
walls and beaded here and there with moisture. Hanging
strands of slimy gossamer twitched occasionally as wafts of
warm air moved through the tunnels. In places the webs
became so thick they half blocked the tunnels, and Hawk
had to cut his way through with his axe. Sometimes he
found the remains of dead rats and tiny homunculi co-
cooned in the webbing, along with other things he couldn't
identify, and wasn't sure he wanted to. He tried hard not
to think about Crawling Jenny, or how big a spider would
have to be to produce such webs.

He'd never liked spiders.

Fisher moved in close beside him, so that they could talk
quietly without being overheard. "I once talked with one
of the maintenance men whose job it is to clean out these
tunnels twice a year. He said there wasn't enough money
in the world to get him to come down here more often
than that. He'd seen things, heard things. . . ."

"What sort of things?" said Hawk, casually.

Fisher moved in even closer, her voice little more than
a murmur. "Once, they found a blind angel with tattered
wings, from the Street of Gods. They offered to guide it
out, but it wouldn't go. It said it was guilty. It wouldn't say
what of. Another time, the slime on top of the water came
alive and attacked them. Someone smashed a lantern
against it, and it burst into flames. It rolled away into the
darkness, riding on top of the water, screaming in a dozen

voices. And once, they saw a spider as big as a dog, spinning a cocoon around something even larger."

"Anything else?" asked Hawk, his mouth dry.

Fisher shrugged. "There are always stories. Some say this is where all the aborted babies end up, neither living nor dead. They crawl around in the tunnels, in the dark, looking for a way out and never finding it."

"If you've got any more cheerful stories, do me a favour and keep them to yourself," said Hawk. "They're just stories. Look, we've been down here almost an hour now, and we haven't seen a damned thing so far. Not even a rat."

"Yeah," said Fisher darkly. "Suspicious, that."

Hawk sighed. "Whose stupid idea was this, anyway?"

"Yours, originally."

"Why do you listen to me?"

Fisher chuckled briefly, but didn't stop frowning. "If there aren't any rats, it can only be because something else has been preying on them." She stopped suddenly, and Hawk stopped to look at her. She cocked her head slightly to one side, listening. "Hawk, can you hear something?"

Hawk strained his ears against the quiet. The rest of the team had stopped too, and the last echoes from their progress through the water died away into whispers. The silence gathered around them like a watchful predator, waiting for them to make a mistake. Fisher held her lantern higher, her hand brushing against the tunnel roof, but the light still couldn't penetrate far into the darkness. Winter moved forward to join them.

"Why have we stopped?"

"Isobel thought she heard something ahead," said Hawk.

"I did hear something," said Fisher firmly.

Winter nodded slowly. "I've been aware of something too, just at the edge of my hearing. Sometimes I think it's behind us, sometimes out in front."

"There's something out there," said MacReady flatly. "I can feel its presence."

They all looked at him. "Any idea what it is?" asked Hawk.

"No. But it's close now. Very close."

"Great. Thanks a lot, MacReady." Hawk reached out with his mind to Storm, using the mental link the sorcerer had established with the team before they left. *Hey, Storm. You there?*

For the moment, Captain Hawk. The closer you get to the House's wards, the harder it is for me to make contact.

Can you tell what's ahead of us in the dark?

I'm sorry, Captain. My Sight is useless under these conditions. But you should all be wary. There's a lot of magic in Champion House, old magic, bad magic, and its proximity to the sewers is bound to have had unfortunate effects on whatever lives there.

A lot of help you are, sorcerer. Hawk broke the contact, and hefted his axe. "Well, we can't go back, and according to the plans, there's no other way that'll get us where we're going. So we go on. And if there *is* anything up ahead, we'd better hope it's got enough sense to stay out of our way."

"Everyone draw their weapons," said Winter crisply. "And Hawk, since you're so keen to make all the decisions, you can lead the way."

"You're so good to me," said Hawk. "Let's go, people."

He led the way forward into the dark, feeling Winter's angry look burning into his back. He didn't mean to keep undermining her position as leader, but he wasn't used to taking orders. And he couldn't wait around and keep quiet while she made up her mind. It wasn't in his nature. Fisher waded along beside him, holding her lantern in one hand and her sword in the other. The rest of the team ploughed along behind them, spread out enough not to make a single target, but not so far apart they could be picked off one at a time without the others noticing. The silence pressed in close around them, weighing down so heavily it was almost like a physical presence. Hawk had an almost overpowering urge to shout and yell, to fill the tunnel with sound, if only to emphasise his presence. But he didn't. He had an unsettling feeling his voice would sound small and lost in this vast network of tunnels, no matter how loudly he shouted. And apart from that, there was also the rumour he'd heard that any loud sound in the tunnels never really died away. It just echoed on and on, passing from tunnel to tunnel, growing gradually quieter and more plaintive but never fully fading away. Hawk didn't like the idea of any part of him being trapped down here in the dark forever, not even just his voice.

After a while, it seemed to him he could hear something moving in the tunnel up ahead, a sound so faint and quick he could only tell it was there by the deeper silence that came when it stopped. His instincts were clawing at his gut, urging him to get the hell out of there while he still could, and he clutched the haft of his axe so tightly his fingers ached. He made himself loosen his grip a little, but the faint sounds in the dark wore at his nerves like sandpaper. He took to checking each new side tunnel thoroughly before he'd let the others pass it, torn between his need for action and the urgency of their mission, and the necessity of not allowing himself to be hurried. Hurried people make mistakes. He couldn't help the hostages if he got himself killed by acting carelessly.

The sounds grew suddenly louder and more distinct and he stopped, glaring ahead into the gloom. The others stopped with him, and Fisher moved in close beside him, her sword at the ready. Something was coming towards them out of the darkness, not even bothering to hide its presence anymore, something so large and heavy its progress pushed the air before it like a breeze. Hawk could feel the air pressing against his face.

A dozen red gleams appeared high up in the gloom before him, shining like fires in the night. Hawk lifted his axe as a horrid suspicion stirred within him. The glaring eyes, the soft sounds, and everywhere he looked, the endless webbing. . . . Oh hell, no. Anything but that. The blazing eyes drew closer, hovering up by the tunnel roof, and then the huge spider burst out of the darkness and lurched to a stop at the edge of the lantern light, its eight spindly legs quivering like guitar strings. It swayed silently before them, the top of its furry body pressing against the roof, its legs splayed out into the water and pressing against the tunnel walls. The vast oval body all but filled the tunnel, its thick black fur matted with water and slime. Its red eyes glared fiercely in the lantern light, watchful and unblinking. Thick gobbets of saliva ran from its twitching mandibles. Hawk stood very still. There was no telling what sudden sound or movement might prompt it to attack.

What the hell, he thought firmly. *You can handle this. You've faced a lot worse in your time.*

That was true, but not particularly comforting. Truth be

old, he'd never liked spiders, and in particular he'd never
liked the sudden darting way in which they moved. If he
found one in the jakes, he usually called for Isobel to come
and get rid of it. Of course, she was so softhearted she
couldn't bear to kill a helpless little insect, so she just
dumped it outside, whereupon it immediately found its way
back inside again to have another go at terrorizing him. He
realized his thoughts were rambling, and brought them
firmly back under control. He could handle this. He looked
surreptitiously back at the others, and was a little relieved
to see that they looked just as shaken as he was.

"Well?" he said steadily. "Anyone got any ideas?"

"Let's cut its legs off, for a start," said Barber. "That
should ruin its day."

"Sounds good to me," said Fisher. "I'll go for the head.
Hack its brain into mincemeat, and it's got to lie down and
die. Hasn't it?"

"Strictly speaking," said Hawk, "it doesn't appear to
have a head. The eyes are set in the top part of its body."

"All right. I'll go for the top part of its body, then. God,
you can be picky sometimes, Hawk."

"That's enough!" hissed Winter sharply. "Keep your
voices down, all of you. I don't want it panicked into attacking before we're ready to handle it. Or hasn't it occurred to you that the bloody thing is hardly going to just
stand there and watch while you step forward and take a
hack at it? If it can move as fast as its smaller cousins, we
could be in big trouble."

"It might also be poisonous," said MacReady.

They all looked at him. "Something that big doesn't need
to be poisonous," said Fisher, uncertainly.

"Are you willing to bet your life on that?" asked
MacReady.

"We're wasting time," said Winter. "While we're standing around here arguing, the terrorists could be killing hostages. We've got to get past this thing, no matter how
dangerous it is. We need someone to hold the creature's
attention while Barber and Fisher attack its weak spots.
Hawk, I think it's time we found out just how good you
are with that axe."

Hawk nodded stiffly. "No problem. Just give me some
room."

He moved slowly forward, the scummy waters swirling about his knees. The tunnel floor was uneven, and he couldn't see where to put his feet. Not exactly ideal fighting conditions. The spider's huge body quivered suddenly, its legs trembling, and Hawk froze where he was. The serrated mandibles flexed silently, and Hawk took a firmer grip on his axe. He stepped forward, and the spider launched itself at him, moving impossibly fast for its bulk. He braced himself, and buried his axe in the spider's body, just above the mandibles. Thick black blood spattered over his hands, and he was carried back three or four feet by the force of the spider's charge before he could brace himself again. He could hear the SWAT team scattering behind him, but couldn't spare the time to look back. The spider shook itself violently, and Hawk was lifted off his feet. He clung desperately to his axe with one hand, and grabbed the mandibles with the other, keeping them at arm's length from his body. At his side, Barber cut viciously at the creature's nearest leg, but the spider lifted it out of the way with cat-quick reflexes. Barber stumbled, caught off balance by the force of his own blow, and the leg lashed out and caught him full in the chest, sending him flying backwards into the water. He disappeared beneath the surface, and reappeared coughing and spluttering but still hanging onto his sword.

Fisher cut at the spider's eyes with the tip of her sword, and it flinched back, dragging Hawk with it as he tried to tear his axe free. The spider's body had seemed as soft as a sponge when he hit it, but now the sides of the wound had closed on the axehead like a living vise. He braced one foot against the tunnel wall and pulled hard with both hands, putting his back into it. The axe jerked free with a loud, sucking sound and he fell back into the water, just managing to keep his feet under him. The spider reared up over him, and he swung his axe double-handed into the creature's belly. The heavy weapon sank into the black fur, the force of the blow burying the axe deep into the spider's guts. Thick blood drenched Hawk's arms and chest as he wrenched the axe free and struck at the belly again.

Barber coughed up the last of the water he'd swallowed and staggered back into the fight. Winter was trying to cut through the spider's front legs, but it always managed to pull them out of reach at the last moment, and she had to throw herself this way and that to avoid the legs as they came swinging viciously back. Barber chose his moment carefully, and cut at one leg just as it lashed out after Winter. His blade sank deep into the spindly leg and jarred on bone. He pulled the sword free and cut again, and the leg folded awkwardly in two, well below the joint.

The spider lurched to one side, and Fisher scrambled up on top of it, grabbing handfuls of the thick fur as she went. She thrust her sword in between the glaring red eyes again and again, burying the blade to the hilt. The edge of the sword burst one of the eyes and its crimson light went out, drowned in black blood. The spider reared beneath her, slamming her against the tunnel roof and trying to throw her off. She hung on grimly, probing for the creature's brain with her sword. Barber and Winter cut through another leg between them, and the spider collapsed against the tunnel wall, thrown off balance by its own weight. Hawk cut deeply into the spider's belly above him, kneeling in the water to get more room to swing his axe. Blood and steaming liquids spilled over him as he hacked and tore at the creature's guts. Barber severed a third leg, and Fisher slammed her sword into a glaring red eye. The spider reared up, crushing Fisher against the tunnel roof, and then collapsed on top of Hawk. He just had time to see the great bulk coming down on top of him, and then the spider's great weight thrust him down beneath the surface of the water and held him there.

The spider's last breath went out of it in a long shuddering sigh, its mandibles clattering loudly, and then it was still. The light went out of its remaining eyes, and black blood spilled out into the filthy water. Winter and Barber leaned on each other for support while they got their breath back. Fisher clambered slowly down off the spider's back, wincing at the bruises she'd got from being slammed against the tunnel roof. She dropped back into the water, and looked around her.

"Where's Hawk?"

Winter and Barber looked at each other. "I lost track of him in the fight," said Winter. "Mac, did you see what happened to him?"

MacReady looked at Fisher. "I'm very sorry. Hawk was trapped beneath the water by the spider when it collapsed."

Fisher looked at him speechlessly for a moment, then demanded, "Why the hell didn't you say something? We can still get him out! There's still time. Help me, damn you!"

She splashed back through the water and tried to grab the spider's side to lift it, but her hands sank uselessly into the spongy mass. Barber and Winter moved in on either side of her to help, but even when they could find a hold, they couldn't lift the spider's body an inch. They couldn't shift the immense weight without leverage, and the soft yielding body wouldn't allow them any.

"There's nothing you can do, Isobel," said MacReady. "If there was, I'd have done it. I'm sorry, but it was obvious Hawk was a dead man from the moment the spider collapsed on top of him."

"Shut up!" said Fisher. "And get over here and help, damn you, or I swear I'll cut you down where you stand, charm or no bloody charm!"

MacReady shrugged, and moved in beside Barber. Fisher sank her arms into the spider's body up to her elbows, and strained upwards with all her strength, but the body didn't move. She tried again and again, hauling at the dead weight till her back screamed and sweat ran down her face in streams, but it was no use. Finally she realised that the others had stopped trying and were staring at her compassionately. She stumbled back from the dead spider, shaking her head slowly at the words she knew were coming.

"It's no good," said Barber. "We can't lift it, Isobel. We'd need a dock crane just to shift the bloody thing. And it's been too long anyway. He's gone, Isobel. There's nothing more we can do."

"There has to be," said Fisher numbly.

"I'm sorry," said Winter. "He was a good fighter, and a brave man."

"You couldn't stand him!" said Fisher. "You thought he wanted your stupid command! If you hadn't sent him in first, on his own, he might still be alive!"

"Yes," said Winter. "He might. I'm sorry."

Storm! yelled Fisher with her mind. *You're a sorcerer! Do something!*

There's nothing I can do, my dear. This close to the House, my magic is useless.

"Damn you! Damn you all! He can't die here. Not like this."

They stood for a while in the tunnel, saying nothing.

"It's time to go," said Winter finally. "We still have our mission. The hostages are depending on us. Hawk wouldn't have wanted them to die because of him."

"We can't just leave him here," said Fisher. "Not alone. In the dark."

"We'll send someone back for him later," said Barber. "Let's go."

The spider's back pressed upwards suddenly, and the whole body lurched sideways. The SWAT team stumbled backwards, lifting their swords again. *It can't be alive,* Fisher thought dully. *It can't be alive when Hawk is dead.* The spider's back protruded suddenly in one spot and then burst apart as a gore-streaked axehead tore through it. A bloody hand appeared after the axe, and then Hawk's head burst out beside it, gulping great lungfuls of the stinking air. The SWAT team stared at him uncomprehendingly, and then Fisher shrieked with savage joy and scrambled up on top of the spider again. She cut quickly at the torn hide with her sword, opening the hole wider. Barber and Winter climbed up beside her, and between them they hauled Hawk out of the spider's body and helped him clamber down into the water again. Fisher clung to him all the way, unable to let go, as though afraid he might vanish if she did. He was covered in blood and gore from head to toe, but none of it seemed to be his. He was still breathing harshly, but he found the strength to hug her back, and even managed a small, reassuring smile for her.

"What the hell happened?" she said finally. "We'd all given you up for dead!"

Hawk raised a sardonic eyebrow. "I demand a second opinion."

Fisher snorted with laughter. "All right, then; why didn't you drown?"

Hawk grinned. "You should have known I don't die that easily, lass. When the damned thing collapsed on top of me, the weight of its body forced me through the hole I'd made in its guts, and I ended up inside it. Turned out the thing was largely hollow, for all its size. There was just enough air in there to keep me going while I cut my way through its body and out the top. It was hard going, and the air was getting pretty foul by the end, but I made it." He took a deep lungful of the tunnel air. "You know, even this stench can smell pretty good if you have to do without it for a while."

Fisher hugged him again. "We tried to lift the spider off you, but we couldn't budge it. At least, most of us tried. MacReady had already given you up for dead. He wouldn't have helped at all if I hadn't made him."

"That right?" Hawk gave MacReady a long, thoughtful look. "I'll have to remember that."

MacReady stared back, unconcerned. Winter cleared her throat loudly. "If you're feeling quite recovered, Captain Hawk, we ought to get a move on. The hostages are still depending on us, and they're running out of time."

The atmosphere in the parlour was getting dangerously tense, and Saxon was getting worried. There'd been no word on how negotiations were going, but whatever the terrorists' deadline was, it had to be getting closer. Madigan had disappeared with his people some time back, leaving twenty mercenaries to watch the hostages. Talking wasn't allowed, and the mercenaries had taken an almost sadistic pleasure in denying the hostages food or drink while taking turns at stuffing their own faces. Time dragged on, and the mercenaries grew bored while the hostages grew restless. Sooner or later, someone on one side or the other was going to do something stupid, just to break the monotony. Which would be all the excuse the mercenaries needed to indulge in a little fun and games. . . .

Saxon smiled coldly. Whatever happened, he wasn't going to make any trouble. The terrorists could kill every man and woman in the room, and he wouldn't give a damn. These people represented all the vile and corrupt authority that had made Haven what it was. He was in no real danger himself. He had a way out, just in case things started getting really out of hand. He knew Champion House well from his earlier days, when he'd been a rising politician and much courted by those seeking patronage or influence with the Council. What he knew, and presumably the terrorists didn't, was that the House was riddled with secret doors and hidden passageways, a holdover from the House's orig-

inal owners, who'd raised the fortune needed to build
Champion House by being Haven's most successful smug-
glers. Apparently the passages, with their magically warded
walls, had come in handy more than once for concealing
goods and people from investigating customs officers who
were outraged at being denied their rightful cut.

As far as Saxon knew, the passages were still there, unless they'd been discovered and blocked off during the
years while he was away. Either way, if he remembered
correctly, there was a concealed door right there in the
parlour, not too far away. All he had to do was press a
section of the paneling in just the right place, the wall
would open, and he'd be gone before the mercenaries knew
what was happening. That was the theory, anyway. But he
didn't think he'd try it until he had no other choice. The
way his luck had been going, the secret door would probably turn out to be nailed shut and booby-trapped.

The tension was so thick on the air now, he could practically taste it. The two Kings were sitting stiffly but not
without dignity, trying to set a good example, but no one
was paying them much attention. The military types were
watching the mercenaries like hawks, waiting for someone
to make a slip. The Quality were pointedly ignoring the
mercenaries, as though hoping they might go away once
they realized how unwelcome they were. The merchants
stood close together and kept a hopeful watch on the closed
door. They'd given up on trying to bribe the mercenaries,
but they obviously still thought they could make some kind
of deal with Madigan or one of his people. Saxon knew
better. He knew fanatics when he saw them, and this bunch
worried the hell out of him. It was clear they had their own
agenda, and if they were as committed to their Cause as
they seemed, once they'd started they wouldn't turn aside
for hell or high water. You'd have to kill them all to stop
them.

Saxon glanced again at the hidden door, and his hand
tightened around the smoke bomb he'd palmed while he
was being searched. If trouble broke out, he was off, and
to hell with all of them. Whatever the terrorists were up
to, it was none of his business.

The door slammed open and everyone jumped, including
most of the mercenaries. Eleanour Todd stood in the door-

way with the young killer Glen at her side, and Saxon's heart sank. He could tell from their faces that the deadline had come and gone without being met. Todd looked calm, almost bored, but there was an air of unfocused menace about her, as though she was readying herself for some bloody but necessary task. Glen was grinning broadly. Todd looked unhurriedly about her, and the hostages stared back like so many rabbits mesmerized by a snake.

"It seems your city Council has chosen not to take us seriously," said Todd. "They have refused to meet our legitimate demands. It's time we showed them we are not to be trifled with. It's time for one of you to die."

She let her gaze drift casually over the hostages, and faces paled when her gaze lingered for a moment before passing on. People began to edge away from each other, as though afraid proximity to the one chosen might prove dangerous. No one raised a voice in protest. A few of the braver souls looked as though they might, but one look from Glen was all it took to silence them. Saxon held the smoke bomb loosely in his hand, and cast about for a good spot to lob it. He'd wait until Todd had chosen her victim, and all eyes were on them, and then he'd make his move.

Eleanour Todd finally stepped forward and smiled at a young girl in the front row, not far from where Saxon was standing. The girl couldn't have been more than fourteen or fifteen, some merchant's daughter wearing her first formal gown to an important function. She'd been vaguely pretty before, but now sheer terror made her face ugly as she tried to back away from Todd's smile. Her father stepped forward to stand before her, opening his mouth to protest, and Todd hit him with a vicious, low blow. He fell to the floor, moaning. Glen strolled forward and kicked him casually in the face a few times. The girl stared desperately around her for help, but no one would meet her eyes. She turned back to Todd and held herself erect with a pathetic attempt at dignity. She didn't know she was whimpering quietly, and that her face was so pale her few amateurish attempts at makeup stood out against her pallor like a child's daubings.

"It's nothing personal," said Todd. "We always choose a young girl for our first execution. Makes more of an impact. Don't worry; it'll all be over before you know it."

"My name is Christina Rutherford," said the girl steadily. "My family will avenge my death."

"Your name doesn't matter, girl. Only the Cause matters. Now, will you walk or would you rather be dragged?"

"I'll walk. I just want to . . . say goodbye to my family and friends."

"How touching. But we don't have time. Glen; drag her."

His grin broadened, and Christina shrank away from him. She started to cry, and tears ran down her face as Glen grabbed her by the arm and pulled her towards the door. Saxon swore tiredly, and stepped forward to block their way.

"That's enough, Glen. Let her go."

"Get out of the way, guard, or we'll take you too."

"Try it."

Glen chuckled suddenly, and thrust Christina behind him. Todd took her firmly by the arms. Glen studied Saxon thoughtfully. "So; someone here's got some guts after all. I was hoping someone had. Now I get to have some fun. How far do you think you can run, hero, with your intestines dragging down around your ankles?"

His sword was suddenly in his hand, and he lunged forward incredibly quickly. Saxon sidestepped at the last moment, and the blade's edge just caressed the chain mail over his ribs as it hissed past. Glen stumbled forward, caught off balance, and Saxon brought his knee up savagely. Glen fell to his knees, the breath rattling in his throat. Saxon kicked him in the ribs, slamming him back against the wall. He leant forward and picked up Glen's sword, ignoring the unpleasant sounds behind him as the young killer vomited painfully. He turned to face Eleanour Todd, who had a knife at Christina's throat. The young girl was looking at him with the beginnings of hope. The mercenaries standing around the room were staring at him open-mouthed. Saxon flashed them his most confident politician's smile and then looked back at Todd.

"Let the girl go. We can talk about this."

"No," said Todd. "I don't think so." She drew the knife quickly across Christina's throat, and then pushed the girl away from her. She fell onto her knees, her eyes wide in horror. She tried to scream, but only a horrid bubbling sound came out. Blood ran thickly down her neck and chest, and she put her hands to her throat as though she could hold the wound together, but the blood gushed through her fingers. She held out a bloody hand to Saxon, but she was already dead by the time he took it. He lowered her body to the floor, then looked up at Todd. There was death in his eyes, but she didn't flinch.

"You bitch," Saxon said numbly. "You didn't have to do that."

"She wasn't important," said Todd. "And at least she died in a good Cause. Now it's your time to die, hero. Can't have the sheep getting ideas, can we?"

She gestured impatiently to the watching mercenaries, and they began to close in.

"I'll kill you for this," said Saxon flatly. "I'll kill you all."

He threw the smoke bomb onto the floor before him and it cracked open, spilling out thick clouds of choking black smoke that billowed quickly through the parlour. Todd lashed out with her sword but Saxon was already gone, sprinting for the hidden door. Mercenaries loomed out of the smoke in front of him and he smashed his way through, tossing them aside like broken dolls. The hostages were shouting and screaming, and some made a dash for the door. Saxon hoped some of them made it. He found the right stretch of panelling, hit it smartly in just the right place, and a section of the wall swung open on silent counterweights. He darted forward into the gloomy passageway, and a knife came flying out of nowhere to bury itself in the panelling behind him. He hurried on without looking back, and a sourceless glow appeared around him, lighting the way ahead. It was nice to know the passage's built-in magics were still functioning. He glanced back, and swore harshly as he saw the concealed door had jammed half shut, caught on the thrown knife. Todd would be sending mercenaries into the passage after him any time now. He grinned coldly. Good. Let them come. Let them all come. There were secrets in these passageways that only he knew about, and anyone foolish enough to come after him was in for some nasty surprises. And when they were all dead, he would go out into the House and kill Madigan and Todd and all the other terrorists.

They shouldn't have killed the girl. He'd make them pay for that.

Back in the parlour, the smoke was slowly starting to clear, but terrorists and hostages alike were still coughing helplessly and wiping tears from their smarting eyes. The mercenaries had rounded up the escaping hostages without too much trouble, and the situation was more or less back under control. Todd glared into the hidden passageway, and gestured quickly to two mercenaries. "Horse, Bishop; take five men and go in there after him. You needn't bother to bring all of him back; just the head will do. After that, check the passage for other concealed exits. I don't want anyone else suddenly disappearing on me. Move it!"

The two mercenaries nodded quickly, gathered up five men with a quick series of looks and nods, and led the way into the passage. Glen started to go in after them, but Todd stopped him.

"Not you, Glen. I need you here, with me."

"I want that bastard. No one does that to me and gets away with it."

"He won't get away. Even if he gets out of the passage, there's nowhere he can go. The House is full of our people."

Glen scowled unhappily. "I don't know, Eleanour. He's fast. I've never seen anyone move like that. And anyway, I want to kill him myself."

"Glen, we've got work to do. The guard can wait. He isn't important. Not compared to our purpose here. Now, get yourself another sword, and get the girl's body out of here. Show it to the city negotiators, and tell them we'll kill another hostage every half hour until our demands are met."

Glen looked at her, puzzled. "I thought the hostages were just a cover," he said quietly.

"They are," said Todd, just as quietly, "but as long as the city's concentrating on them, they won't be getting suspicious about what we're really up to. Now, do as you're told, Ellis; there's a dear."

Glen blushed at the endearment, and turned quickly away to bark orders at the mercenaries. The hostages watched silently as the girl's body was dragged out. Todd coughed suddenly as the smoke caught in her throat again.

"Someone open those bloody windows!"

*　　　*　　　*

Horse and Bishop led their men cautiously down the narrow stone corridor of the secret passage, checking for other exits as they went. A sourceless glow had formed around them, enough to show them the way ahead, but it didn't carry far into the darkness. The rogue guard could be lurking just ahead of the light, waiting in the dark to ambush them, and they'd never know it until it was too late. Horse shook his head determinedly, pushing aside the thought. The guard had enough sense to keep running. He'd be long gone by now. But if he was dumb enough to be still hanging around, then he and Bishop would take care of him. They'd dealt with would-be heroes before, and in Horse's experience they died just as easily as anyone else. Particularly if you outnumbered them seven to one.

Horse was a large, heavily built man in his late twenties, with thick, raggedly cut black hair and a bushy beard. He'd fought in seventeen campaigns, for various masters, and had never once been on the losing side. Horse didn't believe in losing. In his experience, the trick to winning was to have all the advantages on your side, which was why he'd teamed up with Bishop. His fellow mercenary was the same age as he, a head or so taller, but almost twice Horse's size. It wasn't all muscle, but then, it didn't have to be. He wasn't the brightest of men either, but Horse was bright enough for both of them, and they both knew it. Besides, Bishop was very creative when it came to interrogating prisoners. Especially women. Horse grinned. Bishop stopped suddenly, and Horse stopped with him, glaring back at the other mercenaries when they almost ran into him.

"What is it, Bishop?" he said quietly.

"I'm not sure." The big mercenary fingered the heavy iron amulet he wore on a chain round his neck, and glowered unhappily into the gloom ahead. "Something's wrong, Horse. This place doesn't feel right."

"Have you seen something? Heard something?"

"No. It just doesn't . . . feel right."

The other mercenaries looked at each other, but Horse glared them into silence. He respected Bishop's hunches. They'd paid off before. He gestured to the two nearest men. "Check out this section. Inch by inch, if necessary."

The two men looked at each other, shrugged, and moved

warily forward, swords at the ready. The light moved with them. There was still no sign of the rogue guard. The passageway was eerily silent, the only sound the scuffing of their boots on the plain stone floor. They'd gone about ten paces before part of the floor gave slightly under one of the men's feet, and there was a soft clicking noise. They both looked down automatically, and consequently never saw the many long, pointed wooden stakes which shot out of concealed vents in both walls. The stakes slammed into the two men with brutal force, running them through in a dozen places. They hung there limply, their feet dangling, and blood pooled on the floor below them. They didn't even have time to scream. There was another soft click as the lever in the floor reset itself, and then the stakes retracted silently into the walls. The two bodies sagged slowly to the floor, the blood-slick wood making soft, sucking noises as it slid jerkily out of the dead flesh. Bishop swore slowly, his voice more awed than anything else.

"Booby trap," said Horse grimly. "And if there's one, you can bet there are more. For all we know, the whole place could be rigged with them."

"Then there's no point in going on," said one of the mercenaries behind him. "Is there?"

"Do you want to go back and tell Todd that?" said Horse, without bothering to look round. He smiled briefly at the silence that answered him. "All right, then; we're going on. I'll take the lead. Walk where I do, and don't touch anything."

He set off slowly, studying the ground before him carefully before gradually lowering his foot onto it. Bishop followed close behind him, all but treading on his heels. The other mercenaries brought up the rear, grumbling quietly among themselves. Horse glowered into the dark ahead of him. The guard they were pursuing had to have known about the booby traps and how to avoid them, which suggested he was no ordinary guard. It had been obvious from the other hostages' faces that they'd known nothing about the hidden passageway. If they had, they'd have used it.

With the guard's special knowledge, he could avoid all the traps and be anywhere in the House by now, but even so, they had to press on. They might not be able to run down the man himself, but at least they could identify the other hidden exits and block them off.

There was a soft click from somewhere close at hand, and Horse threw himself forward instinctively, Bishop at his side as a heavy crash sounded behind them and a cloud of dust puffed up, filling the passage. Horse clutched briefly at Bishop to make sure he was all right, and then looked back. A huge slab of solid stone had dropped from the passage ceiling, crushing two of the mercenaries beneath it. Blood welled out from under the stone and lapped at the toes of Horse's boots. The sole surviving mercenary on the other side of the stone block was standing very still, his face white as a sheet. Horse called out to him, but he didn't answer. Horse called again, and the man turned and ran. Some of the light went with him as he fled down the passageway, and then a section of the floor dropped out from beneath his feet and he disappeared screaming into a concealed pit. There was a flash of shining blades, and then the trapdoor swung shut, cutting off his scream, and the passage was still and silent again.

"This place is a deathtrap," said Bishop.

"Yeah," said Horse. "But the guard got through alive. Probably somewhere out there in the dark right now, watching us and laughing."

"He's no ordinary guard, Horse. Did you see the way he flattened Glen? I didn't think anyone was faster than Glen."

"He's just one man. We can take him. And then you can show him some of your nasty little tricks with a hot iron."

"You're welcome to try," said Saxon.

The two mercenaries spun round to find Saxon standing behind them, just out of sword's reach. He was smiling. Horse could feel his heart beating hard and fast in his chest, but somehow he kept the shock out of his face. He lifted his sword, and Bishop did the same a second later. Saxon's sword was still in his scabbard, and his hand was nowhere near it.

"You shouldn't have come back," said Horse. "You're a dead man now. You're walking and you're breathing, but you're dead. And we're going to make it last a long time."

Saxon just smiled back at him, his eyes cold. "I've had a really bad day. You're about to have a worse one."

Bishop growled something indistinct, and launched himself at Saxon, his sword out before him, his great bulk moving with surprising speed. Saxon casually batted the sword blade aside, and slammed a fist into Bishop's side. The big mercenary stopped as though he'd run into a wall. The sound of his ribs breaking was eerily loud on the quiet. He stood hunched over before Saxon, breathing in short, painful gasps, trying to lift his sword and failing. Saxon hit him again, burying his fist in the man's gut up to his wrist. Blood flew from Bishop's mouth, and he sank to his knees. Horse looked at him incredulously. It had all happened so *fast*. He looked back at Saxon, his sword forgotten in his hand.

"Who are you?" he whispered.

"I'm Saxon. Wulf Saxon."

Horse tried for some of his usual bravado, but the words came out flat and empty. "You say it like it's supposed to mean something, but I've never heard of you."

Saxon shrugged. "I've been away for a while. People forget. But they'll remember, once I've reminded them a few times. You shouldn't have killed the girl, mercenary."

"That wasn't me. That was Todd."

"You stood by and let it happen. You're guilty. You're all guilty, and I'm going to kill every last one of you."

"What was she to you, Saxon? Your girlfriend? Family?"

"I never saw her before in my life."

"Then why . . . ?"

"She was so young," said Saxon. "She had all her life before her. She had friends and family who cared for her. And you took all that away." He leaned forward and took Bishop's head in his hands. The big mercenary shuddered, but hadn't the strength to pull away. Saxon looked at Horse.

"I'm going to send you back to the others with a message, mercenary. Be sure to tell them who sent it. Tell them Wulf Saxon is back."

A moment later, the passage was full of someone screaming.

Eleanour Todd paced up and down, scowling angrily, and the hostages shrank back from her as she passed. She didn't bother to hide her contempt for them. Nothing but sheep, all of them, shocked and terrified because their comfortable little world had been overthrown and the wolves had finally caught the flock undefended. They deserved everything that was going to happen to them. The guard had been the only one with any backbone. And that was the problem. It had been almost a quarter of an hour since she'd sent her mercenaries into the hidden passage after him, and there'd been no word from them since. There couldn't be that many passages to search, surely? She stopped herself pacing with an effort. The guard was only one man; there was nothing he could do to upset the plan. Nothing could go wrong now. But what the hell had happened to the mercenaries? Could they have got lost in the passages? She glared out over the hostages, taking a quiet satisfaction in the way their faces paled.

"Who can tell me about the hidden passageways?" she said flatly. The hostages looked at each other, but no one said anything. Todd let her scowl deepen into a glare. "Someone here must know something about the passageways. Now, either that someone starts talking, or I'm going to have my men pick out someone at random and we'll take turns cutting him or her into little pieces until someone else starts remembering things."

"Please believe me, no one here knows anything about the passageways," said Sir Roland. He stepped forward diffidently, and the crowd shrank back to give him plenty of room. "You see, the only people who might know anything are the House's actual owners, and they're not here. The whole Family moved out so we could have the place to ourselves."

Todd nodded unhappily. It figured Madigan's pet traitor would turn out to be the one with the answers, even if they weren't the ones she wanted. "So how did that guard know about them?"

"I don't know. He was one of a number of men the Brotherhood of Steel supplied us for use as honour guards. Perhaps he'd been here before and knew the Family. After all, the Brotherhood recruits from all the social strata."

Todd grunted, and dismissed him with a wave of her hand. Sir Roland bowed politely, and stepped quickly back into the crowd. There was a murmur of praise for his courage from the other hostages, but it died quickly away as the watching mercenaries stirred menacingly. Todd beckoned to Glen, who was lounging by the door, and he hurried over to her with his usual puppyish grin.

"The mercenaries I sent into the hidden passage have been gone too long," she said quietly. "Something must have happened. Take a dozen men and search the passageways from end to end. I want to know exactly what happened to Horse and his men, and I want that guard dead. Is that clear?"

"Oh, sure. But I won't need a dozen men."

"Take them anyway. There's something about that guard. . . ."

"I can take him," said Glen confidently. "I just wasn't ready for him last time."

"Take the men. That's an order. I don't want anything to happen to you."

Glen's face brightened. "You don't?"

"Of course not. You're a valuable member of our group."

Glen's face dropped, and he nodded glumly. "Don't worry," he said, for something to say. "Horse will probably have caught him by now. He's a good man."

"Horse? He couldn't catch the clap from a Leech Street whore. I should never have sent him. Now get a move on."

Glen winced slightly at her crudeness, and turned away to pick out his men. He wished she wouldn't talk like that. It wasn't fitting in a woman. And it seemed she still didn't see him as anything more than an ally. She never would . . . as long as Madigan was around. The thought disturbed him, and he pushed it aside, but it wouldn't go away entirely. He scowled. That guard had made him look bad in front of Eleanour. He'd make the bastard bleed for that. It was amazing how long you could keep the other party in a sword fight alive before finally killing them. Sometimes they even begged him to do it.

He liked that.

He chose his men quickly, impatient to be off, and set them over to the opening in the wall to wait for him. He glanced back for one last look at Eleanour, and then stopped as he saw Bailey was talking to her urgently. From the expression on both their faces, it had to be something important, and bloody unwelcome news at that. He hurried back to join them. Bailey acknowledged his presence with a nod, but Eleanour ignored him, her gaze fixed on Bailey.

"Are you sure about this?"

"Of course I'm sure!" Bailey struggled to keep his voice low, but his eyes were angry. "Do you think I'd have come to you with something like this if I wasn't sure?"

"Keep your voice down. This isn't something we want the hostages to hear. It just seems impossible, that's all. How can we have lost twenty-seven men without anyone seeing anything?"

Bailey shrugged. "They were all found dead at their posts. No one even suspected anything was wrong until some of them didn't report in at the proper times. We did a check, and found twenty-seven of our people had been killed, all in the last twenty minutes or so."

"How did they die?" asked Glen, frowning.

"Some were stabbed, some were strangled. And two," said Bailey, his voice never wavering, "were torn literally limb from limb."

Todd and Glen looked at him for a moment, trying to take it in. Bailey shrugged, and said nothing. Todd glowered, her face flushing angrily as she tried to make sense of the situation.

"These deaths took place not long after the guard disappeared into the hidden passageways. There has to be a connection."

"One man couldn't be responsible for twenty-seven deaths," said Bailey. "Not in such a short time. And I saw the bodies that had been torn apart. Nothing human is that strong."

"All right," said Todd, "Maybe there was some kind of creature living in the passages, and he let it loose."

"If there was, then he's probably dead as well," said Glen. "Damn. Now I'll never know whether I could have taken him."

"Oh, stop whining, Glen! This is important." She didn't bother to look at Glen, her gaze turned inward as she struggled with the problem. So she didn't see the hurt in his face quickly give way to anger, and then disappear behind a cold, impassive mask. Todd glared once at the secret doorway, and then turned the glare on Glen and Bailey.

"We can't afford to have things going wrong this late in

the game. We're spread too thin as it is. So, this is what we're going to do. Bailey, pass the word back that from now on our people are to work in groups of five or six, and under no conditions are they to let their partners out of their sight, even for a moment. And they're to check in every ten minutes, regardless. As soon as you've done that, take Glen and round up a dozen men and search those hidden passages from end to end. Don't come back until you've found the guard or the creature or some kind of answer. Got it?"

Bailey started to nod, and then turned away suddenly and looked at the opening in the wall. "Did you hear that?"

Todd and Glen looked at each other. "Hear what?" said Todd.

"There's something in the passage," said Bailey, "and it's coming this way."

"It could be Horse and his men," said Glen.

"I don't think so," said Bailey.

He drew his sword and headed towards the opening, followed quickly by Glen. Todd snapped orders to the mercenaries to watch the hostages closely, and then hurried after Glen, her sword in her hand. They stood together before the opening, blocking it off from the rest of the room, and strained their eyes against the gloom in the passageway. Slow, scuffing footsteps drew steadily closer. One man's footsteps. And then a glow appeared in the passage, and Horse came walking towards them out of the dark. His face was unnaturally pale, and his eyes were wild and staring. Drool ran from the corners of his mouth. Blood had splashed across the front of his clothes, soaking them, but there was no sign of any wound. In his hands he carried Bishop's head.

He came to a stop before Todd and the others, and his eyes were as unseeing as Bishop's. The severed head wore an expression of utter horror, and the mouth gaped wide, as though in an endless, silent scream. Some of the hostages were whimpering quietly, only kept from screaming by fear of what the mercenaries might do to them if they did. A few had fainted dead away. Even some of the hardened mercenaries looked shocked. Todd glanced quickly round, and knew she had to do something to take control of the situation before it got totally out of hand. She stepped forward and slapped Horse hard across the face. His head swung loosely under the blow, but when it turned back his eyes were focused on hers.

"What happened, Horse?" said Todd. "Tell me what happened."

"Wulf Saxon sends you a message," said Horse, his calm, steady voice unsettling when set against the horror that still lurked in his eyes. "He says that all the terrorists in this House are going to die. He's going to kill us all."

"Who the hell's Wulf Saxon?" said Glen, when it became clear Horse had nothing more to say. "Is he the guard? What happened to the rest of your men?"

"They're in the passages," said Horse. "The House killed them. And then Saxon killed Bishop, and sent me back here with his message."

"Why did he cut off Bishop's head?" asked Bailey.

Horse turned slowly to look at him. "He didn't. He tore it off with his bare hands."

Glen recoiled a step, in spite of himself. Bailey frowned thoughtfully. Todd found her voice again and gestured to the two nearest mercenaries. "Take that bloody thing away from him, and get him out of here. Find an empty room and then grill him until you've got every detail of what happened. Do whatever it takes, but get me that information. Find the sorcerer Ritenour, and give him Bishop's head. Maybe he can get some answers out of that. Then get word to Madigan about what's happened, including the twenty-seven deaths. I know he gave orders he wasn't to be disturbed, but he's got to be told about this. I'll take full responsibility for disturbing him. Now move it!"

The two mercenaries nodded quickly, took Horse by the arms, and led him away. The hostages retreated quickly as he passed. Blood dripped steadily from the severed head in his hands, leaving a crimson trail on the carpet behind him. The hostages began to murmur among themselves, some of them clearly on the edge of hysteria. Todd glared at the other mercenaries. "Keep these people quiet! Do whatever it takes, but keep them in line. I'll be just outside if you need me for anything."

She nodded curtly for Bailey and Glen to follow her, and strode hurriedly out of the parlor and into the corridor. She shut the door carefully behind them, and then leaned back against it, hugging herself tightly. "What a mess. What a bloody mess! How could everything go so wrong so quickly? Everything was going exactly to plan, and now this. . . . At least now we know who killed the twenty-seven men. Wulf bloody Saxon, whoever or whatever he is."

"He used to be a city Councillor, but that was some time ago," said Bailey. "He was supposed to have died more than twenty years ago."

"Then what the hell's he doing here now, disguised as a guard?" said Todd. "And how come you know so much about him?"

"I knew him, long ago. But I don't see how it can be him. He'd be my age now, in his late forties, and the guard was only in his twenties." Bailey paused suddenly. "About the age Saxon would have been when he died . . ."

They all looked at each other. "He hasn't aged . . . he's incredibly strong . . . and he's supposed to be dead," said Todd slowly. "I think we may have a supernatural on our hands."

"Oh, great. Now we're in real trouble," said Glen. "Want me to go get the sorcerer?"

"Let's not panic just yet," said Bailey. "We don't know that it's really Wulf Saxon. He could be using the name just to throw us. The Saxon I knew was never a killer."

"A lot can happen to a man when he's been dead for more than twenty years," said Todd sharply. "You're missing the point, Bailey, as usual. What Madigan has planned for this place is very delicate. We can't afford any magical interruptions. And we definitely can't afford to lose any more men, or we won't be able to hold the House securely. Damn this Saxon! He could ruin everything!"

"From what I remember of him," said Bailey, "I think he could."

Down in the cellar, the sorcerer shaman Ritenour strode unhappily back and forth, staring about him. The single lamp on the wall behind him cast a pale silver glow across the great stone chamber and glistened on the moisture running down the wall. The cellar was a vast open space, and Ritenour's footsteps echoed loudly on the quiet. The place had been a real mess until Madigan had had his men clear it out for the ritual, but Ritenour wasn't sure he wouldn't have preferred the cellar the way it was. It was too empty now, as though waiting for something to come and fill it.

It was painfully cold, and his breath steamed on the still air, but that wasn't why his hands were trembling. Ritenour was scared, and not just at the thought of what Madigan wanted him to do down here. All his instincts, augmented by his magic, were screaming at him to get out of the cellar while he still could. The House's wards interfered with his magic and kept him from Seeing what was there too clearly, for which he was grateful. Something was bubbling beneath the surface of reality, something old and awful, pushing and pressing against the barriers of time and sorcery that held it, threatening to break through at any moment. Ritenour could smell blood on the air, and hear echoes of screams from long ago. He clasped his trembling hands together, and shook his head back and forth.

I've torn the heart from a living child and stood over dying bodies with blood up to my elbows, and never once given a damn for ghosts or retribution. I've gone my own way in search of knowledge and to hell with whatever paths it took me down. So why can't I stop my hands shaking?

Because what lay waiting in the cellar knew nothing of reason or forgiveness, but only an endless hatred and an undying need for revenge. It was a power born of countless acts of blood and suffering, held back by barriers worn thin by time and attrition. It could not be harmed or directed or appeased. And it was because of this power that Madigan had brought him to Champion House.

Ritenour scowled, and wrapped his arms around himself against the cold. He had to go through with it. He had to, because Madigan would kill him if he didn't, and because there was no way out of the House that Madigan hadn't got covered. It was at times like this that Ritenour wished he knew more about killing magics, but his research had never led him in that direction. Besides, he'd always known Madigan was protected by more than just his bodyguards.

There was a clattering on the steps behind him, and a mercenary appeared, staring down into the gloom. "Better get your arse back up here, sorcerer. We've got problems. Real problems."

He turned and ran back up the stairs without waiting for an answer. Ritenour took a deep breath to try and calm

imself. He didn't want the others to be able to tell how
uch the cellar scared him.

A quiet sound caught his attention and he looked quickly
round, but the cellar was empty again now that the merce-
ary had left. He smiled briefly. He'd been down there on
is own too long. His nerves were getting to him. The
ound came again, and his heart leaped painfully in his
hest. He glared about him, wanting to run, but determined
ot to be chased out of the cellar by his own fear. His gaze
ell up on a wide circular drain set into the floor, and the
ension gradually left his body and his mind. The drain had
learly been built into the floor back when the cellar had
een a part of the old slaughterhouse. Probably led directly
ito the sewers, and that was what he could hear, echoing
p the shaft. He strolled casually over to the drain and
ooked down it. The yard-wide opening was blocked off
ith a thick metal grille, but there was nothing to be seen
eyond it save an impenetrable blackness. As he stood
nere, he heard the quiet sound again, this time clearly from
omewhere deep in the shaft. Ritenour smiled. Just nerves.
Iothing more. He cleared his throat and spat into the
rain. He listened carefully, but didn't hear it hit anything.
Ie shrugged, and turned away. No telling how far down
ne sewers were. He supposed he'd better go back up and
ee what Madigan wanted. Maybe, if he was really lucky,
Iadigan had changed his mind about the ritual, and he
ouldn't have to come back down here again after all.

Yeah. And the tides might go out backwards.

He strode stiffly over to the stairs and made his way back
p into the House, away from the cellar. He wasn't hur-
ying. He wasn't hurrying at all.

)own in the sewers, at the bottom of the shaft that con-
ected with the drain, Hawk look at the gob of spittle that
ad landed on his shoulder, and pulled a disgusted face.
The dirty bastard . . .''

"Count your blessings," said Barber, trying to hide a grin
nd failing. "He could have been looking for a privy."

"I don't know what you're making such a fuss about,"
aid Fisher calmly. "You're already covered in blood and
uts from the spider and God knows what else from the

sewer water, so what harm's a little spittle going to d
you?"

Hawk looked down at himself, and had to admit she ha
a point. He supposed he must have looked worse sometim
in the past, but he was hard pressed to think when. "It'
the principle of the thing," he said stiffly. "Anyway, i
sounds like he's left, so we can finally get a move on.
thought he was never going to go. . . ."

He looked unenthusiastically at the opening above him
The cellar drain emptied out into the sewer through
broad circular hole in the tunnel ceiling. It was about three
feet wide, and dripping with particularly repellent blacl
slime that Hawk quickly decided he didn't want to study
too closely. He looked back at Winter. "What was this
originally?"

"Originally, it carried blood and offal and other thing
down from the old slaughterhouse," said Winter offhand
edly. "These days, Champion House uses it for dumping
garbage and slops and other things."

"Other things?" repeated Hawk suspiciously. "Wha
other things?"

"I don't think I'm going to tell you," said Winter. "Be
cause if I did you'd probably get all fastidious and refuse
to go, and we have to go up that shaft. It's the only way
in. Now get a move on; we're way behind schedule as it is
It's quite simple; you just wedge yourself into the shaft
press hard against the sides with your back and your feet
and wriggle your way up. As long as you watch out for
the slime, you'll be fine. It's not a long climb; only ten o
twelve feet."

Hawk gave her a look, and then gestured for Fisher to
make a stirrup with her hands. She did so, and then pulled
a face as he set a dripping boot into her hands. Hawk
braced himself, and jumped up into the shaft, boosted on
his way by Fisher. It was a tighter fit than he'd expected
and he had to scrunch himself up to fit into the narrow
shaft. His knees were practically up in his face as he set
his feet against the other side and began slowly inching his
way up. The others clambered in after him, one at a time
and light filled the shaft as MacReady brought up the rear
carrying his lantern. Fisher had put hers away so that she
could concentrate on her climbing. As it turned out, one

was more than enough to illuminate the narrow shaft, and emphasize how claustrophobic it was.

The slime grew thicker as they made their way up, and Hawk had to press his feet and back even harder against the sides to keep from slipping. He struggled on, inch by inch, sweat running down his face from the effort. A growing ache filled his bent back, and his shoulders were rubbed raw. Every time he shifted his weight, pain stabbed through him in a dozen places, but he couldn't stop to rest. If he relaxed the pressure, even for a moment, he'd start to slip, and he doubted he had the strength left to stop himself before he crashed into the others climbing below him. He pressed on, bit by bit—pushing out with shoulders and elbows while repositioning his feet, and then pressing down with his feet while he wriggled his back up another few precious inches. Over and over again, while his muscles groaned and his back shrieked at him.

"Not unlike being born, this, only in reverse," said Fisher from somewhere down below him, in between painful-sounding grunts.

No one had the breath to laugh, but Hawk managed to grin. The grin stretched into a grimace as muscles cramped agonizingly in his thighs, and he had to grit his teeth to keep from crying out. A pale light showed, further up, marking the end of the shaft and sparking the beginning of a second wind in Hawk. He struggled on, trying to keep the noise to a minimum just in case there was someone still in the cellar. If anyone was to take a look down the drain and spot them, they'd be helpless targets for all kinds of unpleasantness. He tried very hard not to think about boiling oil, and concentrated on maintaining an even rhythm so his muscles wouldn't cramp up again. As a result, when his head slammed into something hard and unyielding, he was taken completely by surprise and slid back a good foot or more before he could stop himself. He stayed where he was for a moment, his heart hammering, feeling very glad that he hadn't dropped onto the person below, and then he craned his neck back to get a look at what was blocking the shaft.

"Why have we stopped?" asked Winter, from somewhere below. "Is there a problem?"

"You could say that," said Hawk. "The top of the shaft's sealed off with an iron grille."

"Can you shift it?"

"I can try. But it looks pretty solid, and I don't have much room for leverage. Everyone stay put, and I'll see what I can do."

He struggled back up the shaft, braced himself just below the iron grille, and studied it carefully. There were no locks or bolts that he could see, but on the other hand there were no hinges either. Damned thing looked as though it had been simply wedged into a place, and left to rust solid. He reached up and gave it a good hard push with one hand, but it didn't budge. He tried again, using both hands, but only succeeded in pushing himself back down the shaft. He fought his way back up again, set his shoulders against the grille, and heaved upwards with all his strength. He held the position as long as he could, but his strength gave out before the grille did, and he started sliding slowly back down the shaft. He used his aching legs to bring himself to a halt again, and thought furiously. They couldn't have come all this way, just to be stopped by a stubborn iron grille. There had to be a way to shift it.

An idea came to him, and he forced his way back up the shaft until he was right beneath the grille. He drew his axe, with a certain amount of painful contorting, and jammed the edge of the blade into the fine crack between the grille and the shaft itself. He braced himself again, took several deep breaths, and then threw all his weight against the axe's haft, using the weapon as a lever. The iron grille groaned loudly, shifted a fraction, and then flew open with an echoing clang.

Hawk grabbed the edge of the hole to keep from falling, and hauled himself painfully out into the cellar. He glared quickly about him, in case anyone had heard the noise, but there was no one else in the vast stone chamber. He crawled away from the hole and tried to stand up, but his legs gave way almost immediately, the muscles trembling in reaction to everything he'd put them through. He sat up, put his axe to one side, and set about massaging his leg muscles. His back was killing him too, but that could wait. He just hoped no one would come to investigate the noise. In his present condition he'd be lucky to hold off a midget with a sharpened comb. He shook his head, and concentrated on kneading some strength back into his legs.

Fisher hauled herself out of the drain shaft next, her back dripping with slime, and pulled herself over to collapse next to Hawk. They shared exhausted grins, and then helped each other to their feet as MacReady scrambled out of the drain, still clutching his lantern. For the first time, Hawk realised that there was already a lamp burning on the far wall. Considerate of someone. He frowned suddenly. It might be a good idea to get the hell out of the cellar before whoever it was came back for their lamp. Winter pulled herself out of the drain, waving aside MacReady's offer of help, and stretched painfully as she moved away from the shaft on slightly shaking legs. Barber was the last one up, and bounded out of the drain as though he did this sort of thing every day and twice on holidays. Everyone looked at him with varying degrees of disgust, which he blithely ignored, ostentatiously studying the cellar. Hawk sniffed. He never had liked showoffs.

"This is a bad place," said MacReady suddenly. "I don't like the feel of it at all."

"Oh, I'm sorry," said Hawk. "Hang on and I'll take it back to the store and get you another one. What do you mean, you don't like the *feel* of it?"

"Ease off, Hawk," said Winter. "Mac has a sensitivity to magic. I trust his hunches. Still, this used to be part of the old slaughterhouse, remember? There's bound to be a few bad resonances left over."

"It's more than that," said MacReady, without looking at her. "Contact Storm. See what he makes of this."

Winter shrugged. *Storm? Can you hear me?*

They waited, but there was no reply in their minds.

"Damn," said Winter. "I was afraid of that. Now we're in the House proper, the defensive wards are blocking him off from us. We're on our own."

"Terrific," said Hawk. "I already figured that out when he didn't offer to levitate us up the drain shaft."

"There's more here than just old slaughterhouse memories," said MacReady slowly. "There have always been stories about Champion House. Hauntings, apparitions, strange sightings; uneasy feelings strong enough to send people screaming out into the night rather than sleep another hour in Champion House. The place has been quiet the past year or so, ever since the sorcerer Gaunt performed an exorcism here, but all the recent activity has awakened something. Something old, and powerful.

"Did any of you ever wonder why Champion House has four stories? Four stories is almost unheard of in Haven, with our storms and gales. The amount of magic built into this House to keep it secure from even the worst storms staggers the imagination. But there had to be four stories. The original owner insisted on it. According to legend, the owner said the House would need the extra weight to hold something else down."

"If you're trying to spook me," said Fisher, "you're doing a bloody good job. How come you never mentioned this before?"

"Right," said Hawk.

"I never really believed it before," said MacReady. "Not until I came here. Something's down here with us. Watching us. Waiting for its chance to break free."

"Mac," said Winter firmly, "stop it. When our mission is over, we can send a team of sorcerers down here to check things out, but in the meantime let's just concentrate on the job at hand, shall we? The sooner we're done, the sooner we can get out of here."

"You're not going anywhere," said a voice behind them.

The SWAT team spun round as one, automatically falling into defensive positions, weapons at the ready. The stairs leading from the House down into the cellars were packed with armed men, dressed in various clothing but all wearing the distinctive black iron torc of the mercenary on their left wrist. Their leader was a large, squarish figure with a barrel chest wrapped in gleaming chain mail. He grinned down at the SWAT team, raising an eyebrow at their generally filthy condition.

"One of my men came down here to collect the lamp the sorcerer left behind, and heard suspicious noises down the drain. So, being a good and conscientious lad, he came and told me, and I brought a whole bunch of my men with me, just in case. And here you are! The Gods are good to me today. I reckon Madigan will be good for a tidy little bonus once I turn you over to him. Now you can drop your weapons and walk out of here, or be dragged. Guess which

I'd prefer." He looked them over one at a time, waiting for a response, and seemed a little shaken at their calm silence. His gaze stopped on Hawk, covered from head to foot in blood and gore, and for the first time his confidence seemed to slip. "Who the hell are you people?"

Hawk grinned suddenly, and a few of the mercenaries actually flinched a little. "We're the law," said Hawk. "Scary, isn't it?"

He launched himself forward, swinging his axe with both hands, and suddenly the mercenaries realised that while they were crowded together on the stairway they had no room in which to manoeuver. They started to retreat up the stairs, pushing each other aside for room in which to draw their swords. Their leader leveled his sword at Hawk, but Hawk batted it aside easily and buried his axe in the man's chest. The heavy axehead punched clean through the chain mail, and the force of the blow drove the dead mercenary back against his men. Hawk jerked his axe free and charged into the mass of mercenaries, cutting viciously about him. Fisher and Barber were quickly there at his side, with Winter only a second or two behind them. Hawk burst through the crowd and blocked off the stairs so that none of them could break free to warn Madigan.

Winter and Fisher fought side by side, cutting down the mercenaries one by one with cold precision, while Barber spun and danced, his sword lashing out with incredible speed, spraying blood and guts across the cold stone walls. His face was casual, almost bored. Soon there were only two mercenaries left, fighting back to back halfway up the stairs. Winter ran one through, and the other immediately dropped his sword and raised his arm in surrender. The SWAT team leaned on each other, breathing hard, and looked thoughtfully at the single survivor.

"We don't have the time to look after prisoners," said Barber.

"We can't just kill him in cold blood!" said Hawk.

Barber smiled. "Sure we can. I'll do it, if you're squeamish."

He moved closer to the mercenary, and Hawk stepped forward to block his way. The prisoner looked at them both frantically.

"Barber's right," said Winter slowly. "We can't take him with us, and we can't risk him escaping to warn the others."

"He surrendered to us," said Hawk. "He surrendered to me. And that means he's under my protection. Anyone who wants him has to go through me."

"What's your problem, Hawk?" said Barber. "Got a soft spot for mercenaries, have we? It didn't stop you from carving up this young fellow's friends and colleagues, did it?"

"That was different," said Hawk flatly. "Isobel and I kill only when it's necessary, to enforce the law. And the law says a man who has surrendered cannot be killed. He has to stand trial."

"Be reasonable, Hawk," said Winter. "This scum has already killed the Gods know how many good men just to get in here, and he was ready to stand by while defenseless hostages were killed one by one! The world will be a better place without him, and you know it. Talk to him, Fisher."

"I agree with Hawk," said Fisher. "I'll fight anyone dumb enough to come at me with a sword in his hand, but I don't kill helpless hostages. And isn't that what he is? Just like the ones we've come to rescue?"

"I don't have time for this!" snapped Winter. "Barber, kill that man. Hawk, Fisher; stand back and don't interfere. That's an order."

"Come here, friend," said Barber to the sweating mercenary. "Cooperate, and I'll make it quick and easy. If you like, I'll give you back your sword."

He stopped as Hawk and Fisher stood side by side between him and the mercenary. "Back off," said Fisher flatly.

"We only kill when we have to," said Hawk to Winter, though his eyes never left Barber. "Otherwise, everything we do and everything we are would be meaningless."

"You've got soft, Hawk," said Barber, his voice openly contemptuous. "Is this the incredible Captain Hawk I've heard so much about? Sudden death on two legs, and nasty with it? One should never meet one's heroes. They're always such a disappointment in the flesh. Now get out of my way, Hawk, or I'll walk right through you."

Hawk grinned suddenly. "Try it."

At which point the mercenary took to his heels and ran up the stairs as though all the devils in Hell were after him. Hawk and Barber both charged after him, with Fisher close behind.

"Stop him!" yelled Winter. "Damn you, Hawk, he mustn't get away, or all the hostages are dead!"

Barber pulled steadily ahead of Hawk as they pounded up the stairs. Hawk fought hard to stay with him, but it had been a long, hard day. His stamina was shot to hell, and his legs were full of lead after climbing up the drain. Fisher ran at his side, struggling for breath. Somehow they managed to at least keep Barber and the mercenary in sight. There was a door at the top of the stairs, standing slightly ajar, and Hawk felt a sudden stab of fear as he realized that if the mercenary could get to it first, he could slam it in their faces and lock them in the cellar while he spread the alarm. Winter would be right. He would have thrown the hostages' lives away for nothing. His face hardened. No. Not for nothing.

The mercenary glanced back over his shoulder, saw Barber gaining on him, and found an extra spurt of speed from somewhere. He'd almost reached the door when it flew open suddenly, and Wulf Saxon stepped through to punch the mercenary out. He flew backwards into Barber, and the two of them fell sprawling in a heap on the stairs. Hawk and Fisher stumbled to a halt just in time to avoid joining the heap, and looked blankly up at Saxon. He smiled at them charmingly.

"I take it you're here to rescue the hostages. So am I. From the look of things, I'd say you needed my help as much as I need yours."

They bundled the unconscious mercenary into a convenient closet on the ground floor, and then found an empty room to talk in. MacReady stood in the doorway, keeping an eye out for Madigan's patrols, while the rest of the SWAT team sank gratefully into comfortable chairs, ignoring his visible irritation. Saxon leaned casually against the mantelpiece, and waited patiently for them to settle themselves. Barber and Hawk had exchanged some pointed looks, but had declared an unspoken truce for the time being. They listened silently with the rest of the team as Saxon brought them up to date on what had been happening in Champion House. Fisher whistled admiringly when he finally stopped.

"Twenty-seven men in twenty minutes. Not too shabby, Saxon. But the last time I saw you, you'd just escaped from Messerschmann's Portrait, stark naked and mad as a hatter, and were busily attacking everything in sight. What happened?"

Saxon smiled. "I wasn't really myself at the time. I'm a lot calmer now."

"You still haven't explained where you got that honour guard's uniform from," said Winter. "You're not telling us you came by that honestly, are you?"

"We've got about five minutes before Madigan kills the next hostage," said Saxon. "Let's save the interrogation till later, shall we? They've already killed one girl; I'm damned if I'll stand by and let them murder another. Now, I'm going to stop Madigan, with or without your help, but it seems to me the hostages' chances for survival would be a lot better if you were involved. Right?"

"Right," said Hawk, getting to his feet. "Let's do it."

"I'm the leader of this team, dammit!" Winter jumped to her feet and glared at Hawk. Then she turned to face Saxon. "If you want to work with us, you'll follow my orders. Is that clear?"

"Oh, sure," said Saxon. "But first, may I suggest you swap your clothes for those of the mercenaries you just killed? I don't know what you people have been doing, or what that stuff is you have all over you, but it's bound to raise awkward questions. Besides, you all smell quite appalling, and there's always the chance we might want to sneak up on someone. Now let's hurry, please. Some poor hostage is running out of time."

Winter nodded stiffly, and led the SWAT team back into the cellar to change their clothes. Saxon stayed at the top of the stairs and watched the corridor for Madigan's people. Typical Guards. Here he was trying to help, and they were trying to nail him for stealing an honor guard's uniform. Typical. The last he'd heard, when someone wanted to join the Guard they made him take an intelligence test—and if he failed, he was hired. Still, they had their uses. He'd use them to get the hostages clear, but then he was going after Todd and Madigan, and to hell with anyone who got in his way, mercenary or Guard.

The SWAT team came back up out of the cellar, wearing

their new clothes, and Saxon had to hide a smile. Despite a lot of swapping back and forth, their new clothes mostly fitted where they touched. They each wore their black iron torcs ostentatiously, in the hope other mercenaries would look at them first, and the clothes second. They'd cleaned themselves up with spit and handkerchiefs as best they could, but it hadn't been all that successful, especially in Hawk's case. But given the look on Hawk's face, Saxon didn't think too many people would challenge him about it.

"All right, this is the plan," said Winter finally. "We haven't time for anything complicated, so we'll make it very basic. Our mission is to rescue the hostages, so their safety comes first. We'll split into two teams. Team One will infiltrate the parlour, as mercenaries. Team Two will cause a diversion outside. When the real mercenaries go to investigate, Team One will kill those mercenaries remaining in the room and then barricade the parlour, thus sealing off the hostages from the terrorists. Team Two will then get the hell out of Champion House, and tell the army to come in and clean this place up. Anyone have any problems with that? Hawk?"

"Yeah," said Hawk evenly. "When the terrorists figure out what's happening, they're going to hit the parlour with everything they've got. How the hell is Team One supposed to keep the hostages alive until the army gets there?"

"You'll think of something," said Winter. "According to your file, you and Fisher specialise in last-minute miracles. Besides, you'll have Barber to help you."

Hawk looked at Fisher. "I just knew she was going to say that. Didn't you just know she was going to say that?"

"What's this about a file?" said Fisher. "Did you know we were in a file?"

"What kind of diversion did you have in mind?" asked Saxon. "These men are professionals. I've got them all nicely stirred up, but they wouldn't leave their posts guarding the hostages for just anything."

"They'd abandon their own families for a chance at you," said Winter. "You've scared them, and mercenaries don't like being scared. Don't worry, Saxon; you'll make excellent bait for our trap."

Never trust a bloody Guard, thought Saxon, nodding politely to Winter. "Shall we go? The deadline for the hostages must be getting dangerously close."

"Of course. If Madigan chooses the wrong hostage to kill, there could be all kinds of political repercussions. Let's go."

"You're all heart, Winter," said Saxon.

They made their way through the largely deserted House without attracting too much attention. The mercenaries were watching for attacks from outside rather than from within, and only those in the parlour knew what Saxon actually looked like. Winter hurried along, saluting officers with brisk efficiency and glaring at anyone who tried to speak to her. Saxon strolled along beside her as though he owned the place. The rest of the team did their best to look unobtrusive, while still keeping their hands near their weapons at all times. They reached the main parlour without being challenged, and Winter, Saxon, and MacReady hung back at the end of the corridor to let the others go on ahead.

Hawk looked at Barber. "I'll handle the talking. Right?"

"Sure," said Barber. "That seems to be what you're best at."

Hawk gave him a hard look, and then strolled casually up to the mercenary at the parlour door. "Any trouble inside?"

"No, they're quiet as mice. Why? You expecting trouble?"

"Could be. Madigan will be here in a minute to select the next victim. We're here to help make sure things go smoothly this time."

"Glad to have you," said the mercenary, pushing open the parlour door. "You hear what that rogue guard did to us?"

"Yeah. Better keep an eye open; he might turn up here again."

"I hope he does," said the mercenary grimly. "I hope he does."

Hawk and Fisher strolled casually into the parlour and took up positions by the buffet table. Barber leaned against the wall by the door. Hawk's stomach rumbled loudly at such proximity to food, but he ignored it, trying to take in as much of the situation as he could without being too obvious about it. There were sixteen mercenaries, scattered round the room in twos and threes, and fifty-one hostages, including the two Kings. Most of the hostages looked scared and thoroughly cowed, but there were a few military types here and there who looked as though they might be useful when the action started.

Hawk frowned slightly. Once the mercenaries in the parlour realized they were under attack, the odds were they'd try and grab the most important hostages to use as bargaining points; and that meant the two Kings. They had to be protected at all costs. Winter had been very specific about that. According to her orders, all the other hostages were expendable, as long as the two Kings came out of it safe and sound. Hawk had nodded politely to that at the time, but as far as he was concerned the Kings could take their chances with everyone else. They knew the job was risky when they took it. Still, it might be a good idea to get a message to them, so that their own people could protect them once the fighting started.

He nodded for Fisher to stay where she was, and headed casually towards the two Kings at the back of the room. Team One was now pretty much in position: Barber by the door, ready to slam and barricade it, Fisher covering the middle of the room, and Hawk by the Kings. Everything was going according to plan, which made Hawk feel distinctly nervous. In his experience, it was always when a scheme seemed to be going especially smoothly that Lady Fate liked to step in and really mess things up. Still, he had to admit he couldn't see what could go wrong this time. They'd covered every eventuality. He stopped before the two Kings, and gave them his best reassuring smile. Both monarchs ostentatiously ignored him, while the nearby Quality glared at him with undisguised loathing. Hawk coughed politely, and leaned forward as though studying the Kings' finery.

"Don't get too excited," he murmured, his voice little more than a breath of air, "but help has arrived. When the excitement starts, don't panic. It's just part of a diversion to lure away the mercenaries. My associates and I will take care of those who remain, and then barricade the room and hold it until help arrives from outside. Got it?"

"Got it," said King Gregor, his lips barely moving. "Who are you?"

"Captain Hawk, Haven SWAT."

"How many of you are there?" said King Louis of Outremer quietly.

"Only three here in the room, but there are more outside, ready to start the commotion."

"No offense, Captain Hawk," said King Gregor, "but it's going to take a lot more than three men to hold this room against a concerted attack."

Hawk smiled. "I was hoping you might be able to suggest a few good men we could depend on when things start getting rough."

King Gregor nodded slowly. "I think I might be able to help you there, Captain."

He gestured surreptitiously for a young noble to approach him. The noble looked casually around to see if any of the mercenaries were watching, and then wandered unhurriedly over to stand beside King Gregor. He glanced at Hawk, and then looked again, more closely. King Gregor smiled.

"Exactly, my young friend. It seems we're about to be rescued, and this gentleman is one of our rescuers. But he could use a little help. Alert those with the stomach for a little action, would you, and tell them to stand by."

"Of course, Your Majesty. We've been waiting for something like this to happen." Sir Roland bowed slightly to the two Kings, looked hard at Hawk, and moved back into the crowd. Hawk looked carefully around, but the mercenaries didn't seem to have noticed the brief, muttered conversations. Very slack, but mercenaries functioned best as fighting men, not prison guards. He checked that Fisher and Barber were still in position, and let his hand rest impatiently on the axe at his side. Surely something should have happened by now. What were they waiting for outside? He looked around him to see how the young noble was getting on with his search for support, and then froze as he saw the man talking openly with a group of mercenaries by the double windows. The mercenaries looked straight at Hawk, and the noble gave him a smile and a mocking bow. Hawk swore, and drew his axe.

"Isobel, Barber; we've been betrayed! Get Team Two in here, and then barricade the door and hold it. Move it!"

He charged at the two nearest mercenaries, and cut them down with swift, vicious blows while they were still trying to work out what was going on. The hostages screamed, and scattered this way and that as mercenaries ploughed through them to get to Hawk. He grinned broadly, and went to meet them with his axe dripping blood. Barber yelled out the door to Team Two, and then had to turn and defend himself against a concerted attack by three mercenaries. His sword flashed brightly as he spun and thrust and parried with impossible grace and speed, holding off all three men at once and making it look effortless. Fisher tried to get to him, to keep the door open for Team Two, but was quickly stopped and surrounded by more mercenaries. She put her back against the nearest wall and cut viciously about her with her sword, manoeuvering constantly so that the mercenaries got in each other's way as often as not.

The parlour was full of the din of battle, punctuated by screams and shouts from the hostages, but the noise grew even louder as Team Two finally burst in through the open door. Winter and Saxon tore into the scattered mercenaries like an axe through rotten wood, and for a moment it seemed as though the reunited SWAT team might have the advantage, but only a few seconds later a crowd of mercenaries streamed through the open door, led by Glen and Bailey. The room quickly filled to its limit, and the sheer press of numbers made fighting difficult, but the terrorists didn't shrink from cutting a way through the defenseless hostages to get at their opponents. Some of the hostages tried to help their rescuers, grappling barehanded with the mercenaries, but others worked openly with Sir Roland to help the soldiers. Screams filled the air, and the rich carpets were soaked with blood and gore.

Glen launched himself at Barber as he cut down the last of his three assailants, and the two swordsmen stood toe to toe, ignoring everything else, caught up in their own private battle of skill and speed and tactics. Hawk made his way slowly through the chaos to fight at Fisher's side, and they ended up together with their backs to the double windows. Hawk fought furiously, trying to open up some space around him so that he could use his axe to better advantage, but there were just too many mercenaries, and more were pouring through the door every minute.

Winter ducked and weaved and almost made it out the door a dozen times, but always at the last moment there was someone there to block the way. She fought on, desperate to break away. She had to get word out of the House that the SWAT team's mission was a failure. Saxon ploughed through the soldiers, dodging their blows easily and breaking skulls with his fists. He snatched up one opponent, and tried to use him as a living club with which to beat the others, but there wasn't enough room. He threw the unconscious body aside, and flailed about him with his fists and feet, grinning widely as blood flew on the air, and well-armed mercenaries fell back rather than face him. But for all his efforts, he was still outnumbered and surrounded, and it was all he could do to hold his ground. MacReady stood alone in a corner, unable to escape or intervene, but protected by his magic from any personal danger. Mercenaries kept trying to seize him, only to end up dead or injured as MacReady's charm turned their attacks back against them. Even the hostages were afraid to go near him, though their numbers kept him blocked off from the only exit.

Glen and Barber cut and stamped and thrust, grinning humourlessly as they panted and grunted with every moment. Sweat ran down their faces as they both tried every trick they knew, only to see their moves blocked or countered by the other's skill or speed. Finally a mercenary bumped into Barber from behind, throwing him off balance for a fraction of a second, and that was all Glen needed. He lunged forward with all his weight behind it, and his sword slammed between Barber's ribs and punched bloodily out of his back. Barber sank to his knees, fighting for breath as blood filled his lungs, and tried to lift his sword. Glen put his foot against Barber's chest and pushed him backwards, jerking out his sword as he did so. Barber fell on his back, blood filling his mouth. There was no pain yet, held off for the moment by shock, and his mind seemed strangely clear and alert. He rolled awkwardly onto his side and channeled all his will into his sole remaining talent: the ability to move unseen and unheard. He crawled towards the door, where Winter was fighting fiercely, leaving a trail of his own blood behind him on the thick pile carpet, and neither the mercenaries nor the hostages paid him any attention. He grinned crazily, feeling blood roll down his chin. He'd get out of there and hole up somewhere till the army stormed the place. He'd done all that could be expected of him. As far as he was concerned, the fight was over. And then a shadow fell across his path, and he sensed someone leaning over him. A quiet voice spoke right next to his ear.

"Nice try. But I know that trick too."

Glen thrust his sword through the back of Barber's neck, skewering him to the floor. Blood gushed out of Barber's mouth in a seemingly endless flow.

Winter hit Glen from behind, slamming him against the wall and knocking the breath out of him. She drew back her sword for a killing thrust but then had to turn and run as mercenaries burst out of the milling crowd after her. She glanced briefly at Barber's unmoving body, and then sprinted out the door and down the empty corridor, not daring to look back at her pursuers. All thoughts of plans and revenge were forgotten for the moment, her mind filled only with the need to survive. She ran on, from corridor to corridor, never slowing, long after her pursuers had given up and turned back.

Hawk and Fisher were backed right up against the double windows, facing a solid block of mercenaries. None of them seemed particularly anxious to get within sword's range and risk their lives unnecessarily. There were more than enough of them to block off any hope of escape, and they were happy to settle for that. Hawk and Fisher stood side by side, weapons at the ready, using the opportunity to get their breath back. They had a strong feeling there might not be another.

Bailey ploughed through the crowd towards Saxon, using his great size to open up a path before him. Hostages and mercenaries alike hurried to get out of his way, reacting as much to the grim determination in his face as his imposing size. Saxon spun round to face the new threat, not even breathing hard. There was blood on his hands and his clothing, and none of it was his. Bailey bore down on Saxon, swinging his great sword with both hands. Saxon waited till the last minute, and then ducked easily under the blow and sank his fist into Bailey's gut. The fist drove clean through Bailey's chain mail and brought him to a sudden halt, as though he'd run into a wall. He convulsed as the fist plunged on, burying itself in his gut, and the heavy sword slipped from his numb hands. Bailey felt the strength go out of his legs and deliberately slumped forward, trying to bring Saxon down with the sheer weight of his huge frame. Saxon stopped Bailey's fall and picked him up easily, as though the huge mercenary weighed practically nothing, and threw him against the nearest wall.

Bailey hit the wall hard, the impact driving all the breath out of him. Ribs cracked audibly, driving spikes of pain into his side, and his eyesight faded out for a moment, but somehow he got his feet under him again, and his hands curled into fists before him. Saxon stepped forward and drove his fist into Bailey's stomach, crushing it between his fist and the wall. Blood flew from Bailey's mouth, and he collapsed as the last of his strength went out of him. He sat with his back against the wall, looking unflinchingly up at Saxon as he raised his fist for the final blow that would crush Bailey's skull. And then Saxon hesitated, and lowered his fist. He crouched down before the huge man and looked at him thoughtfully. The watching hostages and mercenaries made no move to intervene. Bailey stared back at Saxon, breathing slowly and painfully.

"Finish it. I'm dying anyway. Feels like you broke something important inside."

"Who are you?" said Saxon. "I feel like I ought to know you."

Bailey smiled, and blood ran from the corners of his mouth. "It's been a long time, Wulf. Twenty-three years, since you ran out on us."

Saxon looked at him for a long moment, and then his blood ran cold as he saw the ghost of familiar features in Bailey's battered and weather-worn face. "No . . . Curt? Is that you, Curt?"

"Took you long enough, Wulf. Or had you forgotten all about your baby brother?"

"They told me you were dead!"

Bailey smiled again. "They said the same about you. But

I recognized you the first moment I saw you, pretending to be a guard. You haven't changed at all, Wulf.''

"You have. Look at the size of you. Dammit, Curt, you were always such a scrawny kid. . . . Why the hell did you fight me? We're family.''

"No," said Bailey flatly. "You stopped being family when you ran out on us. These people are my family now. I would have killed you if I could. But you always were a better fighter than me. Finish it, Wulf. Don't let me die slow, if there's a spark of honor left within you.''

"Curt, don't make me do this. I can't let you go, not after finding you again. Don't leave me here alone.''

"Selfish as ever, Wulf. Do it, damn you! Put me out of my misery! You owe me that much.''

Bailey coughed harshly, spraying blood across Saxon's face. Saxon brushed it away with his sleeve, and then reached out tenderly and took Bailey's head in his hands. "Rest easy, brother.''

He snapped Bailey's head round sharply, and there was a loud crack as the neck broke. Saxon released him, and Bailey slumped back against the wall and was still. Saxon looked at him for a long moment, and then reached out and closed his brother's eyes. He rose clumsily to his feet, and looked around him, and the mercenaries shrank back from the rage and despair in his eyes. He strode over to the hidden door in the wall, still wedged half-open, and disappeared into the concealed passageway. No one made any move to stop him, or follow after him.

By the time Madigan and Ritenour appeared on the scene, shortly afterwards, the fighting was over. The hostages had been rounded up and put under guard again. Hawk and Fisher stood at bay before the windows, and MacReady watched calmly from his corner. Madigan looked at the dead and injured lying scattered across the room, and beckoned to Glen, who hurried over to join him, grinning broadly.

"What happened?" said Madigan.

"Local SWAT team tried for a rescue," said Glen. "One's dead, two ran away, including that bastard Saxon, and we've got the other three boxed in. They're not going anywhere. I thought you'd want to talk to them before we killed them.''

"Quite right," said Madigan, smiling at him briefly. "You've done well, Glen. Now have the bodies removed, and see to the wounded."

Glen frowned. "Does that include the hostages?"

"Of course. They'll die when I decide, not before." He nodded for Ritenour to accompany him, and strode unhurriedly over to MacReady. "And who might you be?"

"John MacReady, negotiator for the Haven SWAT team. I assure you there's no need for any further violence. If we could just sit down somewhere and talk, I'm sure we could find a way out of this situation."

"That's very kind of you," said Madigan. "But I really have no need for a negotiator. I like the situation the way it is." He looked across at Glen. "Kill this one."

"You can't," said MacReady quickly. "I cannot be harmed."

Madigan looked at Ritenour. "Is that right?"

"Normally, yes." Ritenour looked at MacReady, and smiled. "But, unfortunately for him, there's so much magic built into these walls it's quite simple for me to put aside the charm that protects him. He's all yours, Madigan. But I should cut off the head, just to be sure."

"An excellent suggestion." Madigan nodded to Glen. "Cut off his head."

Glen gestured to two mercenaries, who grabbed MacReady by the arms and dragged him out of his corner. At first it seemed he couldn't believe it, but then he began to struggle and shout as they forced him onto his knees in front of Glen. They held him easily. Glen raised his sword, took careful aim, and brought it down in a long, sweeping stroke. The blade bit deeply into the back of MacReady's neck, and blood spurted over a wide area. He heaved against the mercenaries' hands, and almost got his feet under him before they forced him down again. Glen struck again and again, hacking at MacReady's neck like a woodsman with a stubborn tree trunk. Many of the hostages cried out, or turned their faces away as MacReady's screams gave way to horrid sounds. Glen's sword cut through at last, and MacReady's head rolled away across the carpet, the mouth still working though the eyes were glazed. The two mercenaries dropped the twitching body, stepped back, and tried to wipe some of the blood from their clothes. Glen wiped the sweat from his forehead, and grinned at Madigan.

"Never actually beheaded a man before. Hard work, that. Executioners always make it look so easy."

"Imagine the wooden block makes a lot of difference," said Madigan. "Remove the head and the body. Burn the body, but give the head to the city negotiators, so they can see what happens to those foolish enough to try and stage a rescue." He turned away and looked at Hawk and Fisher, staring grimly at him from their place before the double windows. "And now, finally, we come to you. The infamous Captains Hawk and Fisher. I always thought you'd be taller. No matter. I think we'll make your deaths last a little longer, as an example to those who would dare defy me. I wish I had more time, to allow for some real inventiveness, but even so, I promise you you'll beg for death before I'm done." He turned to the nearest mercenary. "Heat some irons in the fire." He smiled at Hawk and Fisher. "I've always been a traditionalist in such things." He gestured for his men to come forward. "Disarm them, and then strip them."

Hawk glanced over his shoulder, out the windows. Madigan smiled. "Don't even think about it, Captain. We're on the top floor, remember? It's four stories, straight down. The fall would undoubtedly kill you both."

Hawk put away his axe, and gestured for Fisher to do the same. He grinned back at Madigan, his single eye burning coldly. "Better a quick death than a slow one. Right, Isobel?"

"Right, Hawk. Burn in hell, Madigan."

Hawk turned and kicked the windows open. The mercenaries surged forward. Hawk took Fisher's hand in his, and together they jumped out of the windows, and disappeared from sight.

5

At Play in the Fields of the Lord

Madigan looked at the open windows for a moment, and then shrugged and turned away. "A pity. Now I'll never know whether or not I could have broken them. Still, that's life. Or in their case, death."

"Shall I take the irons out of the fire, sir?" asked the mercenary by the fireplace.

Madigan considered the matter briefly, and then shook his head. "No, leave them there. You never know; someone else might annoy me. In the meantime, send someone down to recover Hawk and Fisher's bodies, and then deliver them to the city negotiators. When they ask how their famous Captains died, you can tell them that the illustrious Hawk and Fisher leapt to their deaths rather than face me."

Madigan dismissed the mercenary and the subject with a wave of his hand, and moved away to stare thoughtfully down at Bailey's body. The big man looked somehow even larger in death, despite the blood and the limply lolling head. Glen was crouching beside him, staring into Bailey's empty face as though waiting for him to explain what had gone wrong. A lock of Bailey's hair had fallen across his eyes, and Glen tucked it back out of the way with an almost gentle touch. He realized Madigan was standing over him, and looked up quickly, expecting some scathing comment at such a show of weakness. Instead, to his surprise, Madigan crouched down beside him.

"It's not wrong to grieve, boy. We've all lost friends and loved ones. That's what brought most of us into the Cause in the first place. You'll get your chance to avenge him."

"He always looked out for me," said Glen. "Taught me how to work as part of a team. I wish I'd listened to him more now."

"I wonder what they talked about," said Madigan.

Glen looked at him, puzzled. "Who?"

"Bailey and the man who killed him, Wulf Saxon. They talked for a moment, before Saxon broke Bailey's neck. If I can find the time, I think I'll have Ritenour call up Bailey's spirit, and ask him. It might be important. Saxon is becoming dangerously meddlesome." He realized Glen was staring at him, shocked. "Is something wrong, Ellis?"

"Bailey's dead. He died for us! It isn't right to disturb his rest."

Madigan put his hand on Glen's shoulder. "He died for the Cause, because he knew nothing was more important than what we plan to do here tonight. He'd understand that sometimes you have to do unpleasant things because they're necessary. We took an oath, Ellis, remember? All of us. *Anything for the Cause.*"

"Yes," said Glen. "Anything for the Cause." He got to his feet and sat on the edge of the buffet table while he cleaned the blood from his sword with a piece of cloth. He didn't look at Madigan or Bailey.

Madigan sighed quietly, and moved to the other end of the table, where the sorcerer Ritenour was dubiously sampling some of the more exotic side dishes. He picked up a wine bottle to study the label, and Madigan produced a silver hip flask and offered it to him. "Try some of mine. I think you'll find it a far superior vintage to anything you're likely to find here. Whoever stocked this House's cellar had a distinctly pedestrian palate."

Ritenour took the flask, opened it, and sniffed the bouquet cautiously. His eyebrows rose, and he studied Madigan with a new respect. "You continue to surprise me, Daniel. It's hard to picture you sampling vintages in between the kidnappings and assassinations."

Madigan shrugged easily. "Every man should have a hobby."

Ritenour poured a healthy measure into a glass, and then stopped and looked at Madigan suspiciously. "Aren't you joining me, Daniel?"

"Of course," said Madigan. He took back the flask, found himself a glass, and filled it almost to the brim. He rolled the wine in the glass to release the bouquet, savored it for a moment, and then drank deeply. He sighed appreciatively, and then lowered the glass and looked coldly at the sorcerer. "Really, Ritenour, you don't think I'd poison my own wine, do you? Particularly a fine vintage like this."

Ritenour bowed slightly. "My apologies, Daniel. Old habits die hard."

"A toast, then. I think we're ready to begin the final phase. To success!"

They both drank deeply, and Madigan took the opportunity to look around the room. Most of the hostages were still in shock from the sudden death and violence, and the dashing of their hopes of rescue, but some were clearly seething with anger at being betrayed by those they'd thought they could trust. Violence was bubbling just below the surface, and several of the mercenaries were watching the situation carefully, swords at the ready. Sir Roland and his fellow conspirators had been herded off to one side by the mercenaries, at their own request, and now stood close together, their faces wearing an uneasy blend of self-righteousness and apprehension. Some of them looked to Madigan for support, but he just looked back impassively. The traitors had done as he'd expected, but their usefulness had passed. They were expendable now. Just like everyone else.

As he watched, the crowd of hostages suddenly parted as the two Kings strode forward together to glare at the traitors. A thin line of mercenaries kept the two groups apart with raised swords. King Gregor of the Low Kingdoms ignored them, fixing Sir Roland with a burning gaze. The traitor stared back unflinchingly, with mocking self-assurance.

"Why?" said King Gregor finally. "Why did you betray us? I trusted you, Roland. I gave you wealth and position and favor. What more could you want?"

"Power," said Sir Roland easily. "And a great deal more wealth. I'll have both, once Outremer and the Low Kingdoms are at war. My associates and I had been planning for some time on how best to take advantage of a small, carefully controlled war on our outer borders, and we weren't about to abandon all our plans just because both Parliaments suddenly got cold feet. War is too important to the right sort of people to be left to politicians."

"You won't get away with this," said King Louis of Outremer, his voice calm and quiet and very dangerous.

"There's nowhere you can go, nowhere you can hide, that my people won't find you. I'll see you dragged through the streets by your heels for this."

Sir Roland smiled arrogantly. "You're in no position to threaten anyone, old man. You see, you don't really understand what's going on here. To begin with, you can forget about being ransomed. Madigan doesn't give a damn about the money. Like us, he's in favor of war, so he's planned an atrocity so shocking that war will be inevitable, once carefully planted rumors have convinced both sides that the other is really to blame."

"What . . . kind of atrocity?" said King Gregor.

"You're going to be executed, Your Majesty," said Sir Roland. "You, and King Louis, and all the other hostages, save for those few like myself, who can be trusted to tell the story in the right way. Isn't that right, Madigan?"

"In a way," said the terrorist. He looked at Ritenour, ignoring Sir Roland's angry, puzzled gaze. "It's time, sorcerer. Have you absorbed enough magic from the House?"

"Yes," said Ritenour, putting down his empty glass and patting his mouth delicately with a folded napkin. "It's been a slow process. I couldn't risk hurrying it, or the build-up of power would have been noticed by those monitoring the situation from outside. But your hostage negotiations brought me the time I needed. I'm ready now. We can begin."

"Begin?" snapped Sir Roland. "Begin what?" He started toward Madigan, and then stopped as the mercenaries raised their swords threateningly. "What is this, Madigan? What is he talking about?"

Madigan looked at him calmly. "You didn't really think I'd settle for just the Kings and a handful of hostages, did you? That wouldn't have had nearly enough impact. No, traitor, my hatred for the Low Kingdoms and Outremer Parliaments requires a more extravagant gesture than killing two political figureheads and a crowd of toadying hangers-on. I'm going to destroy your whole city. Starting with everyone in this House. Do it, sorcerer."

Ritenour grinned, and gestured sharply. An oppressive weight fell across the room, crushing everyone to their knees, except for Madigan, Glen, and Ritenour. Hostages and mercenaries alike screamed and cursed and moaned in horror as the life drained slowly out of them. A few tried to crawl to the door, dragging themselves painfully across the rich pile carpet, but Glen moved quickly to block their way, grinning broadly. The victims clawed and clutched at each other, but one by one their eyes glazed and their breathing slowed, and the sorcerer Ritenour glowed like the sun. Stolen lives boiled within him, the mounting energy pressing against his controlling wards, and he laughed aloud as his new power beat within him like a giant heart. The glow faded away as his control firmed, and he looked slowly around him. Lifeless bodies covered the floor from wall to wall. Mercenaries in their chain mail, hostages in their finery, and the two Kings, staring up at the ceiling with empty eyes. Ritenour wanted to shout and dance and shriek with glee. He looked triumphantly at Madigan, who bowed formally. Over by the doorway, Glen was giggling. They all looked round sharply as they heard hurried footsteps approaching down the corridor outside, and then relaxed as Horn and Eleanour Todd appeared in the doorway. Horn and Todd looked briefly at the bodies on the floor, and then nodded to Madigan.

"Everyone inside Champion House's walls is now dead, Daniel," said Todd briskly. "Everyone but us, of course."

Horn laughed. "You should have seen the mercenaries' faces when the spell hit them! Dropped like flies, they did."

"We'll have to move fast," said Todd, ignoring Horn. "The mercenaries out in the grounds are unaffected, but it won't be long before the city sorcerers watching this place realize something's happened. They'll hold off for a while out of caution, but once they realise there's no longer any contact with anyone inside the House, they'll come charging in here like a brigade of cavalry to the rescue."

"They'll be too late," said Madigan calmly. "By the time they've worked up their courage, the ritual will have taken place. And then it will be too late for many things."

Horn chuckled quietly, brimming with good humor as he stirred a dead body with his foot. "You know, in a few minutes we're going to do what no army's been able to do for centuries. We're going to destroy the city of Haven, and grind it into the dust. They'll write our names in the history books."

"If we don't get a move on, they'll write it on our tomb-stones," growled Todd.

Madigan raised a hand, and they fell silent. "It's time, my friends. Let's do it."

Down below the parlour's double windows, Hawk was clinging grimly to the thick, matted ivy that covered the ancient stone wall. Fisher was clinging equally grimly to his waist and trying to dig her boots into the greenery. Hawk clenched his hands around the ivy, and dug his feet deeper into the thick, spongy mass. For the moment it was holding his weight and Fisher's, but already he could hear soft tear-ing sounds as parts of the ivy pulled away from the wall. Fisher tested the mass of leaves under her feet with some of her weight, and when it held she cautiously transferred her hands to the vines, one at a time, taking care not to throw Hawk off balance as she did so. They both froze where they were for a moment, and struggled to get their harsh breathing back under control.

"Tell me something," said Fisher. "Did you know this ivy was here when you jumped out the window?"

"Oh, sure," said Hawk. "I saw it when I looked out the windows that first time. Mind you, I was only guessing it would hold our weight. But it looked pretty thick. Besides, under the circumstances we didn't have much choice. Didn't you know about the ivy?"

"No. I just assumed you had something in mind. You usually do."

"I'm touched. You want your head examined, but I'm touched."

They grinned at each other, and then looked carefully about them.

"All right, clever dick, what do we do now?" said Fisher.

"There's a window directly below us. We climb down, break the glass with as little noise as possible, and climb in. And we'd better do it quickly, before some bright spark up above thinks to look out the window to see where we landed."

They slowly clambered down the thick carpet of green leaves, which creaked and tore under their weight, but still clung stubbornly to the wall. Hawk wondered vaguely if perhaps the magic in the House's walls had somehow affected the vines as well, but didn't have time to dwell on the matter. He was pretty sure they couldn't be seen against the ivy in the evening gloom, but once someone discovered their bodies weren't where they were supposed to be, all hell would break loose. He pushed the pace as much as he dared, but while it was only a few more feet down to the third-floor window, it seemed like miles.

He grabbed at another strand of ivy as he lowered himself toward the window, and it came away in his hand. He swung out away from the wall, holding desperately on with his other hand, suddenly all too aware of the long drop beneath him. He tried to pull himself back towards the wall, and the vine creaked threateningly. Fisher saw what was happening and reached out a hand to grab him. She couldn't reach him, and pushed herself further out from the wall. The whole mass of ivy beneath her ripped away from the wall, and she fell like a stone. Hawk snatched at her as she fell past him, and grasped her hand in his. She jerked to a halt and swung back towards the wall. Her feet thudded to a halt beside the third-floor window, but there was no ivy within reach of her free hand or her feet, which she could use to stabilize herself. She hung beneath Hawk, twisting and turning, and his mouth gaped soundlessly in agony as her weight pulled at his arm, threatening to tear it from its socket. The vine he clung to jerked and gave under his other hand as their combined weight pulled it from the old stone wall bit by bit.

"Drop me," said Fisher.

"Shut up," said Hawk quickly. "I've got you. You're safe."

"You've got to let me go, Hawk," said Fisher, her voice calm and steady. "If you don't, our weight is going to rip the ivy right off that wall, and we're both going to die."

"I won't let you go. I can't."

"If you die, who's going to avenge me? Do you want those bastards to get away with it? Do it, Hawk. While there's still time. Just tell me you love me, and let go. Please."

"No! There's another way! There has to be another way." Hawk thought furiously as the ivy jerked and trembled beneath his hand. "Isobel, use your feet to push yourself away from the wall. Get yourself swinging, work up a good momentum, and then crash right through the bloody window!"

"Hawk," said Fisher, "that is the dumbest plan you've ever come up with."

"Have you got a better idea?"

"Good point. Brace yourself, love."

Hawk set his teeth against the awful pain in his shoulder, and clutched desperately at the ivy as though he could hold it to the wall by sheer willpower. Sweat ran down his face, and his breathing grew fast and ragged. Fisher pushed herself away from the wall, swinging out over the long drop, back and forth, back and forth. It seemed to take forever to build up any speed, like a child trying to get a swing moving on its own. She could hear Hawk panting and groaning above her, and she could tell both their hands were getting dangerously sweaty. She pushed hard against the wall, swinging out and away, and then twisted her arm slightly so that she was flying back towards the window. The heavy glass loomed up before her, and she tucked her knees up to her chest. Her heels hit the glass together, and the window shattered. She flew into the room beyond, and fell clumsily to the floor as Hawk's hand was jerked out of hers by the impact. She scrambled to her feet and was there at the window to catch him as he half climbed, half fell through the window. They clung to each other, shaking and trembling and gasping for breath.

"Drop you?" said Hawk, eventually. "Did you really think I'd do a dumb thing like that?"

Fisher shrugged. "It seemed a good idea at the time. But your idea was better. For a change."

"I will rise above that remark. Go and take a look out the door. The amount of noise we made crashing in here, someone must have heard us."

Fisher nodded, and padded over to the door, sword in hand. She eased it open a crack, looked out into the corridor, and then looked back at Hawk and shook her head. He nodded, and collapsed gratefully into the nearest chair.

"I hate heights."

"You needn't think you're going to sit there and rest," said Fisher mercilessly. "We haven't got the time. We've got to figure out what the hell we're going to do next. Our original plan was based on us having the element of surprise, and we've blown that. So what do we do? Get the hell out of here, tell the Council we failed, and they'd better start getting the ransom money together? Or do we stick around, and see if maybe we can pick off the terrorists one by one?"

"No," said Hawk reluctantly. "We can't risk that. They'd just start executing the hostages, in reprisal. Standard terrorist tactic, But, on the other hand, we can't afford to leave just yet. We need more information about what's going on here." He frowned suddenly, and looked intently at Fisher. "You know, we could be all that's left of the SWAT team. Barber and MacReady are dead, Winter's hiding somewhere in a panic, and Storm's trapped outside, unable to reach us. Whatever happens now, it's down to us."

Fisher smiled and shrugged. "As usual. Mind you, Saxon's still around here somewhere. At least, I suppose he is. He disappeared during the fighting."

Hawk sniffed. "Yeah, well, Saxon didn't exactly strike me as being too stable, even at the best of times. Hardly surprising, I suppose, after spending all those years trapped in the Portrait. I just hope he hasn't had a relapse, ripped all his clothes off, and reverted back to the way he was when we first met him. That's all we need."

"I don't know," said Fisher. "If nothing else, a naked, bloodthirsty madman stalking the corridors would make one hell of a distraction." Hawk gave her a hard look, and she laughed. "I know; don't tempt Fate. Come on, get up out of that chair. We've got work to do."

Hawk hauled himself out of the chair, stretched painfully, and together they moved silently over to the door and slipped out into the corridor, weapons at the ready. It was completely deserted, and deathly quiet. They moved cautiously down the corridor, and up the stairs to the next floor, but there was no trace of movement anywhere. Hawk scowled unhappily. They ought to have run across some kind of patrol by now. Madigan hadn't struck him as the type to overlook basic security measures. He and Fisher hurried down the empty corridors, impelled by a strange inner sense of urgency, the only sound the quiet scuffling of their feet. They rounded a corner and then stopped abruptly as they discovered the first bodies. Two mercenar-

…es lay sprawled on the floor, their bulging eyes fixed and sightless. Hawk and Fisher looked quickly about them, but there was no sign of any attackers. Hawk moved quickly forward, and knelt by the bodies to examine them while Fisher stood guard.

"Could it have been Saxon?" said Fisher quietly. "After all, he killed twenty-seven mercenaries before he joined up with us."

"I don't think so," said Hawk. "I can't find any wound, any cause of death. This stinks of magic."

"Maybe Storm finally broke through the House's wards and decided to help."

"No. He'd have contacted us by now, if he could. And the only other sorcerer in this place belongs to Madigan."

They looked at each other. "Double cross?" said Fisher finally. "Maybe they had a falling out."

"Could be," said Hawk. He got to his feet again, and hefted his axe thoughtfully. "I think we'd better head back to the main parlour and see if we can get a look at what's happening there. I'm starting to get a really bad feeling about this."

They padded quickly down the corridor. As they made their way through the fourth floor they came across more and more bodies, and by the time they reached the corridor that led to the main parlour they were running flat out, no longer caring if anyone saw or heard them. They slowed down as they approached the parlour, stepping carefully around the dead mercenaries lying scattered the length of the hall. The parlour door stood open, and the air was still and silent as a tomb. Hawk and Fisher moved forward warily, weapons held out before them, and peered in through the doorway. The dead lay piled together, hostage and mercenary, so that it was almost impossible to tell them apart. Hawk and Fisher checked the room with a few quick, cursory glances, but it was obvious the killers were long gone. They examined some of the bodies for signs of life, just in case, but there were no survivors, and nothing to show how they died. There was no trace of Madigan or any of his people among the bodies, but they'd expected that. And then they found the two Kings, and the heart went out of them.

"So it will be war, after all," said Fisher dully. "We

failed, Hawk. Everything we've done has been for nothing
Why did they do it? Why did they kill them all?"

"I don't know," said Hawk. "But one thing's clear now
the situation isn't what we thought it was. Madigan neve
had any interest in the ransom money, or any of his othe
demands. He had his own secret agenda, and the hostage
were just window dressing. A distraction, to keep us from
guessing what he was really up to."

"But why kill his own men, too?" said Fisher. "He's lef
the House practically undefended. It doesn't make sense!"

"It has to, somehow! Madigan's not stupid or insane. H(
always has a reason, for what ever he's doing."

Hawk! Fisher! Storm's voice crashed into their minds lik(
thunder, and they both winced. *Listen to me! You must ge
down to the cellar immediately! Something's happening
down there. Something bad.*

What kind of something? snapped Hawk. *We've got ou*
own problems. The Kings and the hostages are all dead.

*Forget them! Ritenour's getting ready to perform a forbid
den ritual. No wonder Madigan chose him; he's a shamar
as well as a sorcerer.*

Fisher looked at Hawk. "What's a shaman?"

"Some kind of specialized sorcerer, I think. Deals with
spirits of the dead, stuff like that." *Storm! Talk to us; what'(
happening down in the cellar? Is it part of Madigan's plan*

Yes. They're going to open the Unknown Door.

What?

Run, damn you! Get to the cellar while there's still time
*A storm is building in the Fields of the Lord, and the beasts
are howling, howling. . . .*

Down in the cellar, Ritenour was on his knees, painstak-
ingly drawing a blue chalk pentacle on the floor. Glen anc
Eleanour Todd watched with interest, while Madigan stood
a little apart, his gaze turned inward. Horn padded up and
down at the base of the stairs, scowling impatiently. He
didn't trust Ritenour, and deep down he didn't trust the
spell to do what it was supposed to. Madigan had explained
the plan to him many times, and he still didn't really understand it. He had no head for magic, and never had. His
scowl deepened. It was bad enough they were depending
on untried magic to destroy Haven, but they were also de-

endent on Ritenour, and Horn didn't trust that shifty-eyed id-killer any further than he could throw him.

It had all seemed different, up in the main parlour. He'd een happy and confident and full of enthusiasm for the lan, then. But now he was down in the gloom of the cellar, e only illumination a single lamp on the wall, and his ood had changed, darkened. He didn't like the cellar. he place felt bad; spoiled, on some elemental level. He huddered suddenly, and made a determined effort to row off the pessimistic mood. Everything was going to be ne. Madigan had said so, and he understood these things. lorn trusted Madigan. He had to, or nothing in his life ad meaning anymore.

He deliberately turned his back on the sorcerer, and cowled nervously up the stairs. He kept thinking he heard ovement somewhere up above, just beyond the point here the light gave way to an impenetrable darkness. It as just nerves. There couldn't be anyone there. The sorerer had killed them all. For a moment his imagination howed him dead bodies rising to their feet and stumbling lowly through the House, making their way down to the ellar to take a hideous revenge on those who had killed hem. Horn shook his head, dismissing the thought. He'd illed many men in his time, and none of them had ever ome back for revenge. It took a lot of magic to resurrect he dead, and the only sorcerer in Champion House was Ritenour. Horn breathed deeply, calming himself. Not long ow, and then the ritual would be under way. Once started, othing could stop it. And his long-awaited vengeance on Outremer would finally begin. He looked round sharply as Ritenour rose awkwardly to his feet, his knees making loud racking sounds in the quiet.

"Is that it?" said Horn quickly. "Can we start now?"

"We're almost ready," said Madigan, smiling pleasantly. How long have you been my man, Horn?"

Horn frowned, thrown for a moment by the unexpected uestion. "Six years. Why?"

"You've always obeyed my orders and followed my wishes. ou swore the oath to me. Anything for the Cause. emember?"

"Sure I remember." Horn looked at Madigan warily.

This was leading up to something, and he didn't like th feel of it. "You want me to do something now? Is that it?

"Yes, Horn. That's it. I want you to die. Right here an now. It's an important part of the ritual."

Horn gaped at him, and then his mouth snapped shu and set in a cold, straight line. "Wait just a minute. . . ."

"Anything for the Cause, Horn. Remember?"

"Yeah, but this is different! I joined up with you t avenge my family. How can I do that if I'm dead? If yo need a sacrifice, take that weird kid, Glen. You don't nee him anyway, as long as you've got me."

Madigan just stared at him calmly. Horn began to bac away, a step at a time. He looked to Eleanour Todd fo support, but she just stared at him, her face cold and dis tant. Glen looked confused. Horn raised his sword, th lamplight shining on the blade.

"Why me, Madigan? I'm loyal. I've always been loya I've followed you into combat a hundred times. I woul have died for you!"

"Then die for me now," said Madigan. "Trust me. It' necessary for the ritual, and for the Cause."

"Stuff the Cause!"

Horn turned and ran for the stairs. Madigan looked a the sorcerer. Ritenour smiled, and gestured briefly with hi left hand. Horn crashed to the floor as something snatche his feet out from under him. The impact knocked th breath out of him, and his sword went flying from hi numbed hand. He tried to get his feet under him, but some thing took him firmly by the ankles and began to drag hir back towards the sorcerer waiting in his pentacle. He sav again the mercenaries dying slowly as Ritenour drained th life out of them, and he panicked, thrashing wildly an doubling up to beat at his own ankles with his fists. Non of it made any difference. He tried to grab at the floor t slow himself down, but his fingernails just skidded acros the worn stone. He snarled soundlessly, wriggled over ont his back, pulled a knife from a hidden sheath, and threw i at Ritenour. The sorcerer stepped to one side at just th right moment, and the knife flew harmlessly past his heac Horn was almost at the edge of the pentacle when h opened his mouth to scream. Ritenour gestured sharply and life rushed out of Horn and into the sorcerer. Wha would have been a scream came out as a long, shuddering sigh as Horn's lungs emptied for the last time.

Glen looked at Horn's body, and then at Madigan. "I don't understand. Why did he have to die? Did he betray us?"

"No," said Madigan patiently. "Weren't you listening, Ellis? His death was a necessary part of the ritual. Just as yours is, and Eleanour's."

"No!" said Glen immediately. "Leave Eleanour out of this! I don't know what's going on here, but you never mentioned any of this before. And you can bet I wouldn't have come anywhere near you if you had. You're crazy, Madigan! Come over here, Eleanour; we're getting out of this madhouse. Damn you, Madigan! I believed in you! I thought you believed in me."

"Do be quiet, Ellis. Eleanour's not going anywhere, and neither are you."

He turned to Eleanour Todd, and Glen threw himself at Madigan, his sword reaching for the terrorist's heart. Madigan went for his sword, but it was already too late. Ritenour raised his hand, knowing even as he did so, that the spell wouldn't work fast enough to save Madigan. But even as Glen made his move, Eleanour Todd's blade swept out to deflect his, and then swept back to cut Glen's throat. He dropped his sword and fell to his knees. His hands went to his throat, as though trying to hold shut the wound, and blood poured between his fingers. He looked up at Eleanour, standing before him with his blood dripping from her sword, and mouthed the word *Why*?

"Anything for the Cause, Ellis," said Eleanour Todd.

Glen fell forward as the sorcerer's spell sucked out what was left of his life. Todd looked down at the still figure and shook her head.

"I was hoping it wouldn't come to that, Eleanour," said Madigan, sheathing his sword. "He liked you, you know."

"Yes. I know." Todd returned her sword to its scabbard and smiled at Madigan. "My turn now, my love."

"Are you ready?"

"Oh yes. I've been waiting for this ever since we first discussed it." She took a long, shuddering breath, and let it out again. "After all this time, my parents will finally be avenged. Do it, sorcerer." She smiled widely at Madigan.

"No regrets, Daniel. And . . . it's all right that you never loved me. I understand."

Ritenour gestured, and the life went out of her. Madigan caught her as she fell forward, and lowered her gently to the floor.

"So you did know, after all. I'm sorry, Eleanour. But there was never room in my life for you." He looked at Ritenour. "Two willing sacrifices. That was the last ingredient of the ritual, wasn't it?"

"That's right," said Ritenour carefully. "She'll count as one, but you'll have to be the other. Or everything we've done so far will have been for nothing."

"Take it easy, sorcerer. I've no intention of backing out. I just want to see the ritual begin. I've waited a long time for this moment, and I want to savor it. You start the ball rolling, and I'll tell you when I'm ready."

Ritenour shrugged, and turned away. He took up a position in the exact center of the pentacle and began a low, strangely cadenced chant accompanied by quick, carefully timed gestures. A vicious headache was pounding in his left temple, and he was feeling uncomfortably hot and sweaty. Probably the close air in the cellar. He'd never liked confined spaces. He made himself concentrate on what he was doing, but after all the work he'd put into memorizing the spell he could have practically done it in his sleep.

The blue chalk lines of his pentacle began to glow with an eerie blue light, and the air outside the lines seemed to ripple as though in a heat haze. A sudden rush of excitement swept through him, leaving him giddy. He could feel the forces building around the pentacle. He'd known of this spell for years, but had never dreamed that one day he'd be able to use it. Of course, it could still go wrong. If Madigan was getting cold feet . . .

He shot a quick glance at the man, but Madigan was just sitting quietly not far away, with his back to the wall, watching the ritual. Madigan would come through eventually. He wasn't the type to back down, once he'd set his mind to something. Everyone said so. Ritenour smiled. It'd be his name they'd remember now, not Madigan's. When this was all over and he was safely away from the ruins of what had once been Haven, he'd be both rich and famous, as the sorcerer who dared to open the Unknown Door.

Madigan blinked as sweat ran down his forehead and into his eyes. He was feeling very weak now, and he'd had to sit down before his legs betrayed him. The poison was taking hold of him. It was quicker than he'd expected, but hardly surprising. The wine in his hip flask had held enough poison to kill a dozen men. Which was, of course, why he'd insisted Ritenour share it with him. There was no way he was going to let the sorcerer run free after this was all over, boasting about his part in it. This was going to be remembered as Madigan's greatest triumph. No one else's.

Madigan had given his life to the Cause, to the destruction of Outremer, but he wasn't the man he used to be, and he knew it. He'd been a legend in his time, but the best days of his legend were gone, lost in the past, and other, newer names had appeared to replace his. No one doubted his loyalty to the Cause, but among those who mattered it was whispered more and more that he was getting old and cautious, slowing down. So the money went to younger men, and he had to find support for his plans where he could. But after this night, his legend would be secure. He'd already planted rumors in all the right places, so that when the investigators finally came to sift through the rubble of the city, word would already be going round that he was the one responsible. The rumours would blame both sides for hiring him, of course, and as the outrage mounted, the right people would quietly fan the flames until war was inevitable.

Madigan smiled as the sorcerer shot another quick glance at him. Probably thought he had cold feet, or second thoughts. Fool. He wasn't afraid to die. Better to die at the height of his fame, at his greatest moment, than to grow old and bitter watching his schemes collapse for lack of funding, or lack of skill. The Cause would go on without him, and that was all that really mattered. Poor Eleanour had never understood. The Cause had been friend and lover and religion to him, and he had never wanted anyone or anything else in his life.

He watched the sorcerer work, smiling slightly. Madigan knew he wouldn't live to see the opening of the Unknown Door, but it was enough to know that his own willing death would open it. The sorcerer would live a little longer, since he'd drunk less of the wine, but when he finally saw the horror he'd helped to unleash, he'd probably be glad of an easy death. Because once the Door had been opened, no one in this world could shut it again. No one.

Madigan smiled and closed his eyes.

Hawk and Fisher ran through the fourth floor, heading for the stairs. The bodies of the fallen mercenaries seemed to watch them pass with horrified, unmoving eyes. Hawk started counting the bodies, but had to give up. There were too many. He scowled furiously as he pounded down the stairs to the third floor, pushing his pace a little to keep up with Fisher. Why the hell had Madigan killed his own people, as well as the hostages? Hawk knew better than to expect honor or loyalty among terrorists, but even so, to wipe out his own people on such a scale suggested a coldness on Madigan's part that was more frightening than any number of dead bodies. And even apart from that, didn't the man feel the need for any protection anymore? Whatever he and his pet sorcerer were involved with down in the cellar, surely he still needed some protection, if only to keep them from being interrupted at the wrong moment. Unless whatever they were planning was so powerful that nothing could stop it once it had been started . . .

Hawk didn't like the turn his thoughts were taking. It was becoming clearer all the time that this whole business had been very carefully planned, right from the beginning. Which suggested the deaths had also been planned. But why? What could Madigan have hoped to gain from such a massacre? Power. That had to be the answer. Some sorcerers could use stolen life energy to power spells that couldn't otherwise be controlled. But what kind of ritual could Madigan and Ritenour be contemplating, that needed so many lives to make it possible?

Something's happening down there. Something bad.

He and Fisher had just reached the bottom of the second flight of stairs when Fisher stopped suddenly and leaned against the banisters, breathing hard. Hawk stopped with her, and looked at her worriedly. He was usually the first to run out of breath, as Isobel never tired of reminding him. On the other hand, she hated to be coddled.

"You all right, lass?" he said carefully.

"Of course I'm all right," she muttered. "Don't be too

obvious about it, but take a look around. I thought I saw something moving, down the corridor to your right. Could be someone Madigan left here to guard his back."

"Good," said Hawk. "I'm in the mood to hit someone."

"I'd be hard pressed to remember a time when you weren't, Captain Hawk," said Winter, as she stepped out of the shadows of the corridor. She looked angrily at both Captains. "What kept you? I've been waiting here for ages. I take it Storm has contacted you? Good; then you know as much about the situation as I do. Which is, essentially, damn all, except that it's bloody urgent we get to the cellars. Let's go."

She set off down the stairs to the next floor, without looking back to see if they were following. Hawk and Fisher exchanged a brief look, shrugged more or less in unison, and went after her. Hawk felt he ought to say something, but was damned if he knew what. The last he'd seen of the SWAT team's leader, she'd been running from the parlour in a blind panic with half a dozen mercenaries right behind her. Hawk couldn't honestly say he blamed her. The odds against her had been overwhelming, and she'd just seen her strongest team member cut down as though he was nothing. Hawk would have run too, if he and Isobel hadn't been trapped by the windows.

But she'd panicked, and she knew that they'd seen it. Which could lead to all sorts of problems. Panic was hard for some people to acknowledge, never mind deal with. Winter was the sort who prided herself on her courage and self-control, and that pride would make dealing with her problem that much harder. Hawk had seen this kind of thing before. She'd come up with all kinds of rationalizations that would let her believe she hadn't really panicked, and that way she wouldn't have to think about it. But put her under real stress again, and there was no telling what she might do. Given the situation they were heading into, Winter could be a disaster waiting to happen. As though she could feel his gaze on her back, Winter suddenly began talking, though she was still careful not to look back at Hawk or Fisher.

"I thought I was the only one left and the rest of the team were dead. I shook off my pursuers easily enough, and went to ground till they gave up looking for me. I used the time to put together a plan that would get me safely out of the House. It was imperative that I get word to the Council that our mission was a failure, and they couldn't count on us to save the Kings. Then . . . something happened. After our narrow escape from the creatures of power in Hell Wing, I'd taken the precaution of removing a suppressor stone from Headquarters' Storeroom. I thought we might need protection against magic at some point on this case, and the stone has always worked well for me in the past, even if it has fallen out of favor at the moment. Anyway, the stone suddenly started glowing brightly, and the House seemed to shake. I braced myself, but the stone protected me from whatever magic it was. The glow soon faded away, but I thought it best to lie low until I had some idea of what had happened. Then Storm contacted me, told me that Mac was dead and you were still alive, and that our mission wasn't over yet."

"Did Storm tell you what was happening down in the cellar?" said Fisher, when Winter paused for a moment.

"Not really. Just that the sorcerer Ritenour was up to something nasty. It doesn't matter. We'll stop him. The Kings may be dead, but we can still avenge them."

"It may not be as simple as that," said Hawk carefully. "According to Storm, the whole city may be in danger from what Madigan has planned."

"Storm worries too much," said Winter. "There are any number of powerful sorcerers in the city, not to mention all the Beings on the Street of Gods. You're not telling me that between them they couldn't handle anything Ritenour can come up with. After all, what could one shaman sorcerer call up that all the Powers and Dominations in Haven couldn't put down?"

"Good question," said Fisher. "And if we don't get to the cellar in time, I have an awful suspicion we're going to find out the hard way."

Winter sniffed, but increased her pace. Hawk and Fisher hurried after her. Winter was careful always to keep just a little ahead of them, so they wouldn't see her face. She'd managed to stop herself trembling, but she knew that if they got a good look at her face, they couldn't help but see the fear that was still there. She'd been afraid before, but never like this. She'd never run from anything in her life before, but she'd run from the parlour. It wasn't just the number of mercenaries, though that had been part of it. No; it had been the speed, the almost casual way in which Barber had been killed. He'd always been so much better than her, and Madigan's man had swept him aside as though he were nothing. And then Saxon was gone, and Mac and Hawk and Fisher had been cornered, and all she could think of was that she had to get out of there, *out of there*!

She'd hidden from her pursuers in the back of a dusty little cupboard, underneath a pile of old clothing she'd pulled over herself. She'd concentrated on the thought that it was vital she didn't get caught, that she had a responsibility to stay free so she could get a message out to the Council. But when she finally heard the mercenaries depart, and it was time to leave, she couldn't bring herself to leave the safety of the cupboard. She stayed there, in the dark, curled into a ball and trembling violently, clutching the suppressor stone in her fist like a child's lucky charm. After a while, a long while, Storm's voice came to her, telling her that Hawk and Fisher were still alive, and that the mercenaries were dead, and she was finally able to leave her hiding place. She wasn't alone after all, and she had a chance for revenge. It didn't matter what Madigan and Ritenour were doing down in the cellar; she was going to kill them both. they would pay for the murders of the two Kings, and for the theft of her courage and conviction.

She strode along, looking neither left nor right, and bit at the inside of her cheeks until they ached, to keep her teeth from chattering. She couldn't afford to let Hawk and Fisher see how badly Madigan had got to her. She was the leader of the SWAT team. She had to lead.

Winter led the way down the steps into the cellar, moving quietly and confidently, her sword held out before her. Hawk and Fisher followed close behind, keeping a wary eye on her. If Winter had a plan of attack, she hadn't seen fit to confide in them. Hawk found that worrying; normally Winter was full of herself over that kind of thing, and couldn't wait to impress everyone with her latest plans and strategies. Perhaps this time she didn't have a plan, and was just playing it by ear. If she was, Hawk for one didn't

blame her. He hadn't got a clue what to do for the best.
On the other hand, the only actual fighter in the cellar was
Madigan, according to Storm, and they outnumbered him
three to one. But on the other hand, Madigan was a first-
class swordsman and had with him a sorcerer who was
probably brimming over with stolen power and just looking
for a target to use it on. Which would seem to argue against
a frontal attack. Personally, Hawk favoured sneaking up on
them from behind, and taking out both of them with his
axe before they even knew what was happening. Hawk was
a great believer in keeping things simple and to the point.

Winter eased to a stop at the point where the stairway
curved round a long corner before leading down into the
cellar itself. Hawk and Fisher stopped too, and listened to
the silence. There wasn't a sound to be heard, but a strange,
eerie blue light flickered across the wall below them. Hawk
looked at Fisher, who shrugged. Winter stared at the flickering light for a long moment, and then moved slowly forward, keeping her shoulder pressed against the inner wall
so as to stay hidden in the shadows. Hawk and Fisher
moved silently after her. As they eased around the corner,
the vast stone chamber swung gradually into view, and
Hawk swore to himself as he saw the sorcerer Ritenour,
standing in the middle of a glowing pentacle. They were
too late. Whatever the ritual was, it had already started.
The eerie blue light that blazed from the lines of the pentacle filled the cellar, and gave the sorcerer's skin the look
of something that had been dead for a week. In between
the stairway and the pentacle lay Glen and Todd, both
dead. Madigan was sitting on the floor with his back against
the wall, his eyes closed. Hawk thought for a moment he
might be dead too, but his hopes were quickly dashed as
he realized the terrorist's chest was still rising and falling.
Pity, thought Hawk. *It would have simplified things no end.*
Fisher leaned in beside him, looked at Madigan, and raised
an eyebrow. Hawk shrugged. Maybe the man was asleep.
He'd had a busy day.

The air in the cellar had a tense, brittle feel, as though
any loud noise or sudden movement might shatter it like
glass and reveal what lay behind it. The blue light clung to
the wall like lichen, and the solid stone seemed to stir and
seethe with slow, viscous movements. Shadows flickered

here and there, come and gone in an eye blink, though
there was nothing in the cellar to cast them. Ritenour began
chanting in an unfamiliar tongue, but his voice seemed
strangely quiet, as though it had crossed some great distance to reach them. He turned slowly in a circle, widder-
shins, slowly against the course of the sun's path right to
left, light to darkness. Hawk could see his eyes were tightly
shut. Possibly to help him concentrate, or possibly because
he was afraid of what he might see if he opened them.
Hawk moved down a step for a better look, and then
stopped abruptly. His stomach muscles tensed, and sweat
broke out on his forehead. He felt as though he were looking out over some vast, unimaginable gulf. The cellar
seemed to be stretching, with Madigan and Ritenour moving slowly away from the stairs, until the gap between them
seemed horribly great and impossible to cross. Fisher
grabbed Hawk by the arm, and he all but jumped out of
his skin. She gestured that she and Winter were moving
back up the stairs round the curve of the wall, and Hawk
nodded quickly. He looked back at the cellar, and then
away again, and followed Fisher and Winter back up into
the concealing shadows. He realised he was breathing too
quickly, and made himself take several deep breaths to
calm himself down.

They stopped just beyond the curve, and Hawk leaned
in close to Winter, keeping his voice little more than a
murmur. "We've got to do something while we still can.
Things down there are getting out of hand fast."

"I'm open to suggestions, Captain," said Winter sharply.
"In order to stop the ritual we have to get to Ritenour, but
as long as he stays within the pentacle we can't touch him.
It'll knock us out if we even get too close to it."

"What about your suppressor stone?" said Hawk.

"Burned out by whatever happened earlier."

"No problem," said Fisher. "Hawk can throw an axe like
you wouldn't believe. He can cut the wings off a fly at
twenty paces, and if flies had other things he could cut
them off too. Right, Hawk?"

"More or less," said Hawk. "My axe is rather special,
and it should cut through any magical protection, but I've
still got to get within throwing range. An axe is too heavy
to throw accurately over any distance. And you can bet

once any of us step out into plain sight, Madigan is going to come up off that floor like a cat with a thorn up its arse and carve whoever's there into bite-sized chunks. I saw him fight in the parlour. He's good, Winter. Very good."

"We can handle him," said Winter confidently. "You get into a position where you can throw your axe, and Fisher and I will keep Madigan occupied."

"Right," said Fisher. "We kill Madigan, you kill the sorcerer, and then we all get the hell out of here. Simple as that."

"I'm afraid not," said Madigan calmly. "It's a good plan, and it might even work, though I hate to think what might happen to your precious city if the forces Ritenour is working with were to break free. But it's all immaterial. To get to him you have to get past me. And you're not that good. Any of you."

He was standing at the foot of the stairs, looking up at them, and his smile was a death's-head grin. He looked pale and drawn and ill, but his back was straight and the sword in his hand was quite steady.

Hawk and Fisher ran down the stairs and circled around him, weapons at the ready. He moved easily to follow them, never letting either of them entirely out of his sight. He laughed softly, charged with energy, as though all the strength he'd ever had was his again, gathered for just this moment. He laughed at them, and in that harsh, mocking sound there was no trace of weakness, or thought of failure. His eyes burned in his gaunt face, and every move he made was calm, calculated, and very deadly.

It's like he knows we can't win, thought Hawk. *That whatever happens, he's already won.*

He pushed the thought aside, and moved warily forward. Madigan was all that stood between him and Ritenour, and no matter how good he was, Madigan was only one man. Hawk had faced a hell of a lot worse in his time. He swung his axe in a vicious arc, and Madigan's sword was in just the right place to deflect it. The return thrust had Hawk jumping desperately back, and Fisher darted in quickly to draw Madigan's attention. Their swords clashed again and again in a flurry of spark, but Fisher was the one who was forced to retreat. Hawk tried to circle round behind Madigan, but the terrorist drove him back with a flurry of blows that took all of Hawk's skill to counter.

Hawk and Fisher threw themselves at Madigan, but neither of them could touch him. He moved as though inspired, parrying and striking back with a tireless energy. His strength was incredible, his speed bordering on inhuman. He thrust and cut and parried with a simple economy of movement that was too brutal to be truly graceful, but somehow he was always in just the right place to block a blow or strike at his opponent's weakness. Hawk was hard put to save himself a dozen times over, and blood ran thickly down his side from a blow he hadn't seen coming till it was almost too late. If he or Fisher had been fighting alone they would have been dead by now, and all of them knew it. Madigan was never where he should be, and their weapons swept harmlessly past him again and again while his sword crept gradually closer with every attack. Madigan had been a legend in his day, and there in the cellars under Champion House, it was his day again, for a while. Hawk and Fisher fought on determinedly, grunting with the effort of their blows and fighting for breath, but Madigan just smiled at them, his eyes wild and fey, his time come round again in the last minutes of his life.

Ritenour's chant grew louder as he shuffled round and round in his pentacle, eyes squeezed shut as though against a blinding light. The air in the cellar grew steadily more tense, and an alien presence slowly permeated the stone chamber, pressing relentlessly against the barriers that held it back from reality and the waking world.

Winter watched the fighting from the foot of the stairs, unable to move. There was no point in trying to help. Hawk and Fisher were much better fighters than she, and Madigan was making them look like fools. If she even raised a sword against him, he'd kill her. She thought about trying to sneak past him to try and get to Ritenour, but she'd seen what happened when Hawk tried to circle round Madigan. The terrorist had blocked him off without even trying. There was nothing she could do. Nothing.

Think, dammit, think! You're supposed to be the tactician, the one with plans and strategies for every contingency. There's always something you can do!

And of course there was. The answer came to her in

a flash of inspiration, and she knew she had to act on it immediately, while she still had the courage. Because if she stopped and thought about it, she'd come up with all kinds of reasons not to do it. She ran forward, her sword held high above her head, and threw herself at Madigan. He spun round impossibly quickly, and his sword plunged into her stomach and out her back. Winter dropped her sword and forced herself along the blade until she could grab his sword arm with both hands. He tried to break her grip, but her hands had closed like vises. She smiled at him. There was blood in her mouth, and it rolled down her chin as she spoke.

"Did you think you were the only one prepared to die for what they believe in?"

Madigan snarled at her and backed desperately away, dragging her with him, but Hawk's axe came swinging round in a wide arc out of nowhere and smashed into his rib cage. Bones broke and splintered, and the force of the blow drove him to his knees, crying out in pain and shock. Winter sank down with him, still smiling. Their eyes met for a moment, sharing hatred, and then the light went out of Winter's eyes and she slumped forward.

Hawk jerked his axe free in a gusher of blood, and Madigan cried out again as the pain cleared his head. He clung somehow to his sword as he lurched to his feet, avoiding Fisher's sword with desperate speed. Blood was pouring from the gaping wound in his side, but he ignored it. He was dying anyway, and the knowledge gave him strength. He bolted for the stairs, blood spilling onto the ground as he ran. A slow numbness crept through his body as the poison began to win out over his need and desperation. He could no longer feel his hands or his feet, and the strength was draining out of his legs. He forced himself on, concentrating on the flaring pain in his side to keep his head clear. He coughed painfully, and blood filled his mouth. He spat it out, and glanced back over his shoulder. Hawk and Fisher were pounding up the stairs after him.

He laughed giddily. Let the fools chase him. While they were preoccupied with him, Ritenour was completing the ritual. All he had to do was buy the sorcerer a little more time, and he'd spite Hawk and Fisher yet. He was glad he hadn't killed them, after all. He wanted them alive when the Unknown Door opened, so that they could see what he'd let loose on their precious city. He wanted them to know they'd failed before they died screaming, in agony and despair. He laughed breathily, ignoring the pain and the blood, and then Wulf Saxon appeared on the steps before him. Madigan snarled at him and lunged forward, his sword still steady in his numb hand. Saxon slapped the blade aside and hit Madigan in the face with all his strength. The blow picked Madigan up and threw him back down the stairs, almost crashing into Hawk and Fisher. They pressed back against the wall, and Madigan slid and tumbled the rest of the way down the steps and back into the cellar. He lay still at the bottom of the stairs, his head at an unnatural angle, his neck broken.

Hawk and Fisher ran back down the stairs, and stood staring down at Madigan's body. Hawk stirred it with his boot, and the head lolled limply from side to side. And then Madigan's eyes snapped open, and Hawk fell back a step, his heart jumping painfully. Fisher raised her sword and stood ready to strike. Madigan stared up at them, and his mouth stretched slowly in a ghastly grin.

"You've achieved nothing. Won nothing. I was dying anyway. I've beaten you. Beaten you all. Your precious city's going to burn, and everyone and everything you ever cared for is going down into Hell. You lose, heroes! You lose!"

Hawk lifted his axe and brought it sweeping down with all his strength behind it. The razor edge sliced through Madigan's neck and bit deeply into the stone floor beneath. The terrorist's head rolled away across the floor, still smiling. Hawk glared down at the twitching body, and jerked his axe out of the floor as though he meant to strike at the body again. Fisher grabbed him by the arm.

"Forget about him, Hawk! We still have to stop the sorcerer. He made us forget the bloody sorcerer!"

They spun round to stare at Ritenour, standing fixed and frozen in his pentacle. His eye sockets were empty, and bloody trails down his face showed where the eyes had melted and run. *He must have finally opened his eyes and looked,* thought Hawk numbly.

Saxon appeared out of the shadows of the stairway and came to stand beside Hawk and Fisher. He started to ask what was going on, but his voice dried up as he stared at the sorcerer. Power beat on the still air like the wings of an enormous bird, and the gathering presence swept through their minds like an icy wind. It was very close now. Countless, unblinking eyes watched hungrily from the borderlands of reality, driven by an ancient hatred and an unwavering purpose.

Hawk shook his head violently, and looked across at the sorcerer, who had fallen to his knees inside his pentacle. The light from the chalk lines was almost blinding now. On some basic level beyond his understanding, Hawk could sense the stolen life energy pouring out of the sorcerer and passing beyond reality, to where the presence was waiting. He tried to lift his axe, but his arm seemed far away, and the sounds in his head roared and screamed, drowning out his thoughts.

Saxon stepped forward, and the air seemed to press against him as though he were wading through deep water. Hawk and Fisher were as still as statues, though sweat ran down their empty faces, and sudden tremors ran through them as they fought to lift their weapons. Saxon concentrated on the sorcerer in his pentacle. There was no one to help him; he was on his own, as he had been ever since he left the Portrait. He pressed on, putting everything out of his mind except the pentacle, as it drew nearer step by step. Something was screaming. Something was howling. The air stank of blood and death. The blazing blue lines of the pentacle flared up before him as he lashed out with his fist. The cellar shuddered like a drumhead, but the pentacle held. Saxon struck at it again and again, calling up every last vestige of his unnatural strength, but though the blazing light shuddered and trembled beneath his blows, it would not fall.

And then something bright and shining flashed past him, and Ritenour lurched suddenly forward, Hawk's axe buried between his shoulder blades. His hands came back to paw feebly at the axe's haft, and then he fell, face down, and lay still, one outflung hand crossing a line of the pentacle. The blinding blue light snapped off in an instant, and Saxon lurched forward to kneel at the sorcerer's side. Ritenour turned his head and looked up at him with his bloody eye sockets.

"Listen. Can you hear them? The beasts are here. . . ."

The breath went out of him. He was dead, and the last part of the ritual was complete. The Unknown Door swung open a crack, and the presence slammed through into reality, throwing aside the barriers of time and space, life and death. And what had waited for so long for revenge was finally loose in the world.

From out of the shadows of the slaughterhouse, from the time of blood and pain and horror, the beasts returned. Thousands upon thousands of animals, butchered and torn apart in the bloody cellar by men who laughed and joked as they killed. And from every scream and every death, and all the long years of suffering, came a legacy of hatred that drew upon the strange magics in that place, derived in turn from the unnatural building that had been replaced by the slaughterhouse. The small souls gathered together into something larger and more powerful that would not rest, but waited at the borders of the spirit lands, determined to return and take vengeance for what had been done to them. And finally, after all the many years, the willing and unwilling sacrifices of the forbidden ritual had opened the Unknown Door, and the beasts surged forward using Ritenour's stolen life energies to manifest themselves once again in the lands of the living. The beasts had returned, and they would have their revenge.

Champion House trembled on its foundations, and jagged cracks split open the massive stone walls. The restraining magics built into the stone were ripped apart and scattered in a moment, and all the souls of all the many animals went rushing out into the city, a spiral of raging energy that swept outward from the House, leaving madness and devastation in its wake. Herds of scarlet-eyed cattle thundered through the narrow streets, trampling fleeing crowds underfoot. Blood soaked their hooves and legs, but it was never enough. Weapons tore and cut at them, but they felt no pain and took no hurt. They were dead, beyond fear or suffering anymore, and nothing could stop them now. They crushed men and women against walls, and tossed the broken bodies effortlessly on their splintered horns. Blood ran down the curving horns and disappeared into gaping holes in the cattle's skulls, made by sledgehammers long ago. The herd thundered on, and behind them their lesser cousins tore and worried at the bodies of the fallen, as even the mildest of creatures gloried in the taste of human flesh and blood. Sheep and lambs buried their faces in ripped-open guts, and blood stained their woollen muzzles as they bolted down the warm meat.

The soulstorm of raging spirits roared through the city, driving people insane with its endless cry of blood and pain and horror. Centuries of accumulated suffering and abuse were turned back upon their ancient tormentors, and men and women ran wild in the streets, screaming and howling with the voices of animals. Many killed themselves to escape the agony, or killed each other, driven by a fury not their own. There were islands of sanity in the madness, as isolated sorcerers and Beings from the Street of Gods struggled to hold back the soulstorm, but they were few and far between.

In the great prison of Damnation Row, cell doors burst from their hinges and blood ran down the walls. Shadows prowled the narrow corridors with glowing eyes, ignoring locks and bars, and prisoners and prison staff alike fell to cruel fangs and claws. Inmates grew hysterical in their cells and turned on their cellmates, tearing at them viciously, like creatures that had been penned together too long in battery cages, and had never forgotten or forgiven.

At Guard Headquarters the doors were locked and the shutters closed, but still beasts rampaged through the building, and no one could stand against them. Guards fought running battles where they could, gathering together in groups to protect each other, and Guard sorcerers roared and chanted and raised their wards, but the beasts were everywhere and would not be denied.

The Council chambers rang to the sound of a hundred hoofbeats as wild-eyed horses thundered back and forth through the corridors and meeting rooms. Desks and chairs were overturned, and the great round ceremonial table was split from end to end. People ran before the raging herd until their breath gave out or their hearts burst in their chests and it was not enough, never enough.

Down in the Docks the waters boiled as things came crawling up out onto the harbourside, clacking claws and waving antennae a dozen times the size they were in life. Death changes all things, and rarely for the better. They had grown as their hatred grew, and people ran screaming before them as they clattered across the Docks on their huge, segmented legs.

Around the great houses and mansions of the Quality dark shadows gathered, pressing against hastily erected wards with remorseless strength, and both those inside and outside knew it was only a matter of time before the wards fell.

Prayers went up on the Street of Gods, to all the many Beings and creatures of Power that resided there, but none of them answered. The beasts could not enter the Street of Gods, and that was all that mattered. The Gods had turned their faces away, for a time. They would not interfere. They understood about hatred and revenge.

Restaurants became abattoirs, and kitchens ran with blood. Death filled the streets, and buildings shook and shattered at the voice of the soulstorm. Fires broke out all over Haven, and there was no one to stop them. And from every street and every house and every room, came the howling of the beasts.

In the cellar under Champion House, Hawk and Fisher and Saxon huddled together inside the pentacle, and watched dark formless shapes drifting around the perimeter, never quite crossing the palely-glowing blue chalk lines. Storm's voice has told them to shelter inside the pentacle, and had raised its glowing wards around them, but that had been a long time ago, and they hadn't heard from him since. At least it seemed a long time. It was hard to be sure of anything anymore. Screams of dying animals echoed back from the blood-spattered walls. There was a quiet clattering from steel hooks and chains that hung on the air, reaching up into an unseen past. Torsos and heads hung on the chains and hooks, long dead but still suffering. Blood fell from the ceiling in sudden spurts and streams, steaming on the cold air.

Hawk would have closed his eye against the grisly sights, but when he did he saw visions of what was happening in Haven, and that was worse. He saw the buildings fall and the fires mount, and watched helplessly as the people he had sworn to protect died screaming in pain and anguish and horror. He clutched his axe until his hands ached, but he didn't leave the pentacle. He didn't need a vision to show him what would happen if he did. He looked at Fisher, kneeling beside him. Her face was drawn and gaunt, but her mouth was set and her gaze was steady. She saw he was looking at her worriedly, and squeezed his arm briefly. Saxon sat with his back to them, ignoring everything, lost in his private world of regrets and self-recriminations. He didn't answer when Hawk or Fisher spoke to him, and eventually they gave up. They sat up a little straighter as Storm's voice crashed into their minds again.

Can you hear me? Are you still all right?

Depends on how you define all right, said Hawk roughly. *We're still trapped in this pentacle, we're still surrounded by blood and madness, and Saxon's still out to lunch. That sound all right to you?*

Trust me, Captain; it's worse out here. The city's being torn apart, and the people massacred. Some of us are fighting back, but it's all we can do to hold our ground. There are centuries of accumulated hatred running loose in the streets. I've never seen such concentrated malevolent power. . . .

Are you saying there's nothing we can do? said Fisher. *That it's hopeless?*

No. There is something. If you're willing.

Of course we're willing! snapped Hawk. *We can't just sit here and watch Haven being destroyed! Tell us what to do, sorcerer. And you'd better make it fast. The pentacle's lines aren't burning anywhere near as brightly as they were.*

There's only one solution, Captain. The beasts must be comforted, and the Unknown Door must be closed. Two people died willingly to open the Door; it will take two more willing sacrifices to close it.

Hawk and Fisher looked at each other. *Let me get this straight,* said Hawk. *You want us to kill ourselves?*

Yes. Your souls will pass through the Unknown Door into the Fields of the Lord, the spirit land of the animals. Once there, you must make peace with the unquiet spirits of the beasts. Maybe then they will return to their rest, and the Door will close behind them.

Maybe? said Fisher. *Did I just hear you say* maybe? *You want us to kill ourselves, and you're not even sure it will work?*

It's the only hope we've got.

Then why don't you do it?

I can't get to Champion House, and the ritual must take place where the Unknown Door was opened.

Great, said Hawk. *It's all down to us, again. What are these spirit lands like, anyway? And are we going to end up trapped there, or do we go on to our own . . . spirit lands?*

I don't know. To my knowledge, no one has ever passed beyond the Unknown Door and returned to tell of it.

"This gets better by the minute," growled Fisher. *All right, Storm, you've said your piece. Now shut up and let us think for a minute.*

Hawk and Fisher sat for a while in silence, looking at each other. Dark shadows pressed close against the lines of the pentacle, and the air was thick with the stench of blood and offal.

"I never thought we'd die like this," said Hawk finally. "I never really expected to die in my own bed, but I always hoped it would be a lot further down the line than this. At the very least, I wanted it to be on my feet, fighting for something I believed in."

"You believe in the city," said Fisher. "And its people. Just like me. You said it yourself; we can't sit back and do nothing. And at least this way, we get to die together. I wouldn't have wanted to go on without you, Hawk."

"Or me, without you." Hawk sighed, and put his axe down on the floor beside him. He patted it once, like an old dog that had served well in its time, and smiled at Fisher. "A short life, but an interesting one. Right, lass?"

"You got that right. We squeezed a lifetime's love and adventure into our few years together. We can't really complain. We came close to dying many times in the Forest Kingdom, during the long night. Everything since then has been borrowed time anyway."

"Yeah. Maybe. I'm not ready to die, lass."

"No one ever is."

"There's so much I wanted to do. So many things I wanted to tell you, and never did."

Fisher put her fingertips against his lips to hush him. "I knew them anyway."

"Love you, Isobel."

"Love you, Hawk."

They clasped each other's hands and smiled tenderly. A

kind of peace came over them, not unlike the relief one feels after finally putting down a heavy burden.

"How shall we do it?" said Hawk. His mouth was dry, but his voice was more or less steady. "I couldn't stand to see you suffer. I could . . . kill you quickly, and then throw myself on your sword."

"I couldn't ask you to do that," said Fisher, her eyes gleaming with tears she wouldn't let go. "Let the sorcerer do it. He probably knows all kinds of ways to kill from a distance."

"Yeah. He strikes me as that type." They shared a small smile. Hawk looked out into the darkness. "Spirit land of the animals . . . Never occurred to me that all animals would have souls."

"Makes sense, when you think about it. I had a dog once, when I was a kid. Died in an accident, when I was twelve. He was never what you'd call bright, but I was always convinced I'd meet him again, after I died. He had too much personality to just disappear."

Hawk nodded slowly. "So; one last adventure together, then."

They both jumped as Saxon turned suddenly and glared at them. "You were just going to go and leave me behind, I suppose?"

"What the hell are you talking about?" said Hawk. "You don't have to die. Storm said it only needed two willing sacrifices. And that's us."

"He also said the beasts have to be comforted, and from the way they've been acting, they're going to take a hell of a lot of persuading. Which is where I come in. No offense, but you two aren't exactly known for your diplomatic skills. I, on the other hand, have years of experience as a politician and con man. I could persuade a blue whale it could fly, and teach it to loop the loop while it was up there. I'm coming too. You need me."

"Think about what you're saying," said Fisher. "It's one thing for us to die; we're not leaving anyone behind. But what about you? Don't you have any friends, family?"

"My family are all dead," said Saxon. "And I don't know my friends anymore. There's no one and nothing I'll regret leaving behind. This city isn't the one I remember. Haven was always a cesspit, but it was never this bad."

"It's still worth saving," said Hawk. "There are villains and bastards beyond counting, but most of the people in Haven are good people, just trying to get through their lives as best they can, protecting their family and friends, and looking for what love and comfort they can find along the way."

"I know," said Saxon. "That's why I'm coming with you."

"You don't have to do this," said Fisher. "Hawk and I . . . It's our job. Our duty."

"This is my city," said Saxon. "My home. Much as I loathe it sometimes, it's still my home, and I couldn't bear to see it destroyed. I'm really not afraid of dying. I was dead for twenty-three years anyway. At least this time, I'll have died for something that mattered. Now let's get on with it. While our nerve still holds out."

"Sure," said Hawk. *Have you been listening, sorcerer?*

Yes. I'm here.

Then do it.

Goodbye, my friends. You will not be forgotten.

Elsewhere in the city the sorcerer Storm spoke a Word of Power, and Hawk and Fisher and Saxon slumped forward. They sprawled limply on the cold stone floor, and their breathing slowed and then stopped as the life went out of them. They died together, and the blue lights of the pentacle flickered and collapsed, until there was only darkness in the cellar.

There were fields and meadows that stretched away into an endless horizon. A forest stood to one side, full of sunlit glades and dark, comforting shadows. A river ran, bright and sparkling, and the riverbanks were honeycombed with holes and warrens. The summer sky was soft and blue, with gray-tinged clouds that promised soothing rain for the evening. The sun was fat and warm, and the air lay heavily upon the earth like the height of summer, when the heat warms your bones and makes all thoughts calm and drowsy, and winter seems so far away it may never come again. Insects murmured on the quiet, and butterflies fluttered by like animated scraps of color. A gentle breeze stirred the long grass, rich with the scent of earth and grass and living things. And everywhere, the beasts at play, running and hiding, jumping and tumbling, chasing and being chased with never a care or worry for predators or the fall of night. The land was theirs, and nothing could hurt them ever again.

Hawk and Fisher and Saxon stood together on the bank of the river, and felt no need to move. They were where they were, and for a long time in that timeless summer morning, that was enough. Hawk's face bore no scars, and he had both his eyes again. Fisher's scars were gone too, and they both stood a little taller, as though no longer bowed down by the weight of years and memories. Saxon looked like a different man, his face at peace for the first time since they'd met.

"It's like coming home," said Hawk finally. "Everyone's home."

"It reminds me of Hillsdown, and the Forest Kingdom," said Fisher. "Only more so. This is where we began, in the days before cities, when we all lived in the woods."

"I'd never pictured the afterlife as being so rural," said Saxon. "But then, I'm a city boy at heart."

"This is the animals' heaven," said Hawk. "It's shaped by their needs and natures, not ours."

"Heaven," said Fisher slowly. "Are we really dead? I don't feel dead. . . ."

"I remember dying," said Hawk, and for a long moment no one said anything.

"All right," said Saxon. "We're in animal heaven. What do we do now?"

Hawk smiled and shrugged. "Talk to the animals, I suppose. That's why we came here. All we have to do is find some that look as though they might listen."

He broke off as a lion walked slowly out of the wood towards them. Even at a distance it looked huge and majestic, the father of every lion that ever was. It walked unhurriedly among the gamboling animals and they gave way before it, but none of them seemed to fear the lion, or be alarmed by its presence. Hawk and Fisher and Saxon watched it approach, but felt no need to run or fight. It finally came to a halt before them, and the warm, sharp smell of cat washed over them. It stood a good five feet tall at the shoulder, its broad, massive head on a level with theirs. It sheer presence was almost overwhelming. Its eyes were a tawny gold, and full of all the understanding in the world. When it spoke, its breath was warm and sweet.

You can't stay here, growled a voice in their minds, low and soft like the wind that has within it the promise of a storm. *This is not your place. You don't belong here.*

"Where is here?" said Hawk tentatively. "Is this . . . the animals' spirit lands? The Fields of the Lord?"

No, said the lion, and there was amusement in the deep, calm voice. *You have not traveled that far. This is the place the slaughtered beasts made for themselves. Dying in pain and horror, they drew on the power in the place they came from, the magic that had been invested in that place long before the slaughterhouse was built over it. As more and more blood was spilled, so the many deaths awakened the ancient magic and made it strong again, and the beasts used it to build this place. Their bodies died in the slaughterhouse, but their spirits lived on, here. And here they stayed, down all the many years, nursing their fears and hatreds and planning their revenge, until finally the Unknown Door was opened in the only way it could be; from the other side.*

The lion paused, and looked briefly around him before returning his ancient, discomforting gaze to the humans before him. *Not all the animals have gone, despite the opening of the Door. The small and the timid have stayed, happy in their rest from the cares of the world. And some beasts with greater hearts would not go, having put aside thoughts of vengeance. Hatred has never come easily to the animal kind. It is not in their nature, though some have learned it from humans.*

"The ones who did go are killing people," said Hawk, his voice seeming small and insignificant after the restrained thunder of the lion. "We came here to try and put a stop to the hatred. If we can."

Why should they stop? They are only doing what you did to them.

"That doesn't make it right," said Saxon. "You can't put right a wrong by doing wrong yourself. I found that out. Vengeance feels really good while you're planning it, but in the end you've achieved nothing, and all you feel is empty."

"The soulstorm must stop," said Fisher. "They're killing

the good along with the bad, the innocent along with the guilty, the caring along with the uncaring.''

"And if they don't stop," said Hawk, "they'll become exactly what they've hated all these years, and then they'll never know peace."

The lion nodded its great head slowly. *You're right. The soulstorm has stopped.*

The three humans looked at each other. "Just like that?" said Fisher.

Just like that. Through me the beasts have heard your words and seen the colors of your hearts, and they have listened. You have shown them the darkness in their own hearts, and they are ashamed. The soulstorm is over, and the beasts are returning. They wanted blood and vengeance for so long, but having tasted its cold cruelty, they found it sickened them. Beasts may kill and even torture in the heat of their blood, but vengeance is a human trait, and they have turned their back on it.

"So, what happens now?" said Hawk.

The beasts will leave this place. It has served its purpose, and they are now free to go on to what awaits them. And you must go back to your own world.

"We can't," said Fisher. "We gave up our lives to get here."

And the beasts give them back to you, and all the other lives they took. Goodbye, my children. Until we meet again.

The lion turned, and walked back towards the woods. Hawk stumbled a step or two after it. He felt deep within him that he was saying goodbye to something great and wonderful, and part of him didn't want to go.

"Wait! Who are you?"

The lion looked back over its shoulder and smiled. *Don't you know?*

The spirit lands faded away and were gone.

Back in the cellar under Champion House, Hawk sat up slowly and looked around him. Fisher and Saxon lay beside him in a scuffed chalk pentacle, and as he watched, they began to stir and sit up. Hawk rose awkwardly to his feet and stretched slowly, feeling the muscles reluctantly unkink. The blood and the chains and the dark presences were gone, and the cellar was just an old stone chamber again.

Fisher and Saxon got to their feet and looked around them. Hawk chuckled. They looked just as bewildered as he felt. He grabbed Fisher and hugged her to him, and she hugged back with a strength that threatened to force all the breath out of him.

"We're alive!" yelled Hawk. "We're alive again!"

Hawk and Fisher whooped and shrieked and staggered round in circles, still clinging tightly to each other, as though afraid that one might vanish if the other let go. Saxon moved quietly away, and crouched down beside Horn's body, still lying on the floor. He examined it carefully, and then moved over to Eleanour Todd's body. Hawk and Fisher finally broke apart, and went to see what he was doing. Saxon rose to his feet again, and there was a knife in his hand, dripping blood. Hawk looked quickly at the bodies. Both Horn and Todd had had their throats cut. Saxon met Hawk and Fisher's gaze calmly.

"I just wanted to make sure they stayed dead. Unlike Madigan and Ritenour and Glen, they didn't have a mark on them, and since the beasts are supposed to be returning all the life forces Ritenour stole . . ."

Fisher suddenly froze, and clutched at Hawk's arm. "Listen . . . can you hear movement up above?"

Hawk looked at Fisher, and then they both bolted for the stairs, with Saxon close behind. They ran through the House with broad, disbelieving grins on their faces, passing bewildered mercenaries who'd also apparently just risen from the dead. Hawk and Fisher knocked them unconscious again, just to be on the safe side, and then pounded up the stairs to the fourth floor, with Saxon right there at their side. They heard the clamour of voices from the main parlour long before they got there. Finally they stood in the doorway and watched as the two Kings and their fellow hostages milled round the room, talking excitedly and trying to figure out what the hell had happened. Apparently some of the hostages had shaken off their daze faster than the mercenaries, and had taken advantage of their captors' dazed state to get in the first blow. As result of which, the hostages were now in charge of a rather battered-looking group of disarmed mercenaries.

Take it easy, said Storm's voice in their heads suddenly. *I've alerted the Council as to what's happened, and they're sending men in to secure the House. And maybe then you'd care to explain exactly what the bloody hell has been going on, and how come you've all come back from the dead!*

Hawk grinned. *You'd never believe me. . . .*

6

Goodbyes

The council sent a small army of men-at-arms into Champion House to mop things up, and the Guard sent in an equally small army of Captains and Constables, just to make sure they weren't left out of anything. Even in the aftermath of a disaster, there were still politics to be played. Also present were a hell of a lot of honour guards from the Brotherhood of Steel, watching the entrances and exits. They weren't really needed, but nobody wanted to be the one to tell them that. Their pride was still hurting from how easily they'd been brushed aside by Madigan's people. The Council carefully assigned them lots of busywork to keep them out of everybody's hair.

The two Kings and their fellow hostages were still in the main parlour, trying to get their wits together long enough to work out whether they should postpone the Treaty-signing for a more auspicious occasion, or sign the bloody thing now before anything else could go wrong. The raised voices could be heard on the floor below, but luckily most of those arguing were still feeling too poorly after their narrow escape from death to get really out of hand. Everyone else stayed well out of their way and let them get on with it.

The cellar was full of mercenaries, tied hand, foot, and throat, waiting to be carted off to gaol as soon as enough cells could be found to hold them all. Being a mercenary wasn't illegal in Haven. Neither was planning assassinations or a *coup d'état*. But taking part in one and losing was. Particularly when the intended royal targets survive, and are known for holding grudges. The rest of the hostages weren't too keen on the mercenaries either. At the moment they were taking turns using the cellar for a latrine. Some made several trips.

Sir Roland and his fellow traitors had already been escorted to Damnation Row, where special cells had been reserved for them. They were mostly Quality, after all.

With so many people in Champion House, the place was packed from wall to wall, and it was fairly easy for Hawk, Fisher, and Saxon to blend into the crowd and disappear. They finally ended up in the kitchens, where Hawk eyed a joint of beef uneasily.

"You thinking about turning vegetarian?" asked Fisher.

Hawk shrugged. "I don't know. Maybe. But I don't think that was what they were really mad about. Animals eat other animals on a regular basis, after all. I think it was more to do with the way they were treated. Maybe if the abattoirs were more humanely run . . ."

"You mean kill them in a nice way?" said Saxon.

"I'm going to have to think about this," said Hawk.

"While he's busy doing that, I think you'd better make yourself scarce," said Fisher to Saxon. "With everything that's going on at the moment, it's probably going to be some time before they get around to taking an interest in you, but . . ."

"Quite," said Saxon. "I think I've pretty much outworn my welcome here."

"I've got a question for you," said Hawk. "Why didn't Ritenour's spell affect you? It drained the life right out of everyone else. Isobel and I survived only because we were outside the House at the time clinging to some ivy. But you . . ."

"But I," said Saxon, "was back in the hidden passages again, and they're shielded against all offensive magics, by spells built into the walls themselves long ago. Simple as that."

"What will you do now?" said Fisher.

"Beats me. But I'll think of something. Maybe I'll start a society for the prevention of cruelty to animals."

"In Haven?" said Fisher.

Saxon grinned. "There are soft hearts everywhere, if you just know the right ways to approach them. You know, it wouldn't surprise me if there was a tasty amount of money to be made out of such a society. See you around."

He nodded quickly to them both, slipped out the back door, and was gone. Hawk carefully shut the door after him, and then he and Fisher sat down together on a bench before the open kitchen fire, leaning against each other companionably, and staring at nothing much in particular.

"As with most of our cases, we won some and we lost some," said Fisher. "Most of the SWAT team are dead, rest their souls, but at least we saved the Kings."

"Not just the Kings," said Hawk. "We put the beasts to rest, saved most of Haven from destruction, and prevented a war between Outremer and the Low Kingdoms. Not bad for one day's work."

"I just hope we're getting overtime," said Fisher.

"I've a strong feeling that will depend on whether we can come up with a story our superiors can believe. I don't even want to try and explain about the beasts' spirits and the Fields of the Lord. Never mind our part in it."

"Right," said Fisher. "Hawk, how much do you remember about the spirit lands? It seems to me the more I try to remember, the hazier things get."

Hawk nodded. "Same here. It's all fading away. Probably just as well. I've a feeling we got a little too close to things the living aren't supposed to know about."

"So, in the meantime, we just make up some comforting lies for our superiors?"

"Got it in one."

They both jumped guiltily as the kitchen door opened, but it was only the sorcerer Storm. He nodded to them both.

"It's all right, there's no need for you to get up."

"That's good," said Fisher. "Because we weren't going to. Anything we can do for you, sir sorcerer?"

"Just a few questions. I was most impressed by your fortitude in all this. Most people would have been driven insane by all you've endured, but you survived with all your wits intact. How is that?"

Hawk and Fisher looked at each other, and Hawk smiled at the sorcerer. "We've seen worse, in our time."

"You got that right," said Fisher.

Coming Next Month From Roc

A special tenth anniversary trade edition...

from Guy Gavriel Kay

Tigana

William R. Forstchen

The Lost Regiment #8: Men of War

Anne Lesley Groell
Cauldron of Iniquity